Grindin'

ALSO BY DANIELLE SANTIAGO

Little Ghetto Girl

Cream

Grindin'

A Novel

DANIELLE SANTIAGO

ATRIA BOOKS

New York • London • Sydney • Toronto

ATRIA BOOKS

1230 Avenue of the Americas
New York, NY 10020

This book is a work of fiction. Names, characters, places and incidents are products of the author's imagination or are used fictitiously. Any resemblance to actual events or locales or persons, living or dead, is entirely coincidental.

Library of Congress Cataloging-in-Publication Data is available.

ISBN-13: 978-0-7432-7760-0
ISBN-10:   0-7432-7760-0

First Atria Books hardcover edition April 2006

10 9 8 7 6 5 4 3 2 1

ATRIA BOOKS is a trademark of Simon & Schuster, Inc.

Manufactured in the United States of America

For information about special discounts for bulk purchases, please contact Simon & Schuster Special Sales:
1-800-456-6798 or business@simonandschuster.com.

For Kurtrina D. Williams: you were my biggest fan,
and not just because you were my cousin

Grindin'

Vegas Nights

Damn, Nina, how much of that shit did you put in his drink?"

"Same amount as usual. Why?"

" 'Cause his ass looks dead."

Nina glanced at the middle-aged white man lying across the bed. He was in a deep sleep from the mickey she'd slipped him less than thirty minutes ago. "Kennedy, ain't nothing wrong with that man. He looks like that 'cause he drank everything the bar had to offer! Just hurry and finish wiping everything down. We can't afford to get sloppy now."

"I'm through wiping. You hurry up and crack that safe so we can get that shit and be out."

Nina tried but couldn't crack the code to the hotel-room safe.

Kennedy was becoming impatient. "Look, Nina, fuck whatever is in that safe. We got his Rolex and four thousand cash. We need to go ship this shit and catch our flight!"

"Ken, I've always told you patience is a virtue," Nina said calmly, never taking her eyes from the safe.

"Haven't you noticed I'm not big on virtues?"

"Besides, I know this old bastard got way more paper in this safe. You should have seen how much he was spending on chips—about ten Gs a table. His bar tab was a G and he paid everything in cash."

Nina continued to give her full attention to the safe. She looked like a high-fashion runway model, not a hustler and part-time scam artist. All five feet ten inches of her was slim but curvy in the right places. Her 36D cups were perfect for the knee-length red Valentino tube dress that she was wearing. Her legs were especially beautiful in the Manolo Blahnik stilettos. The rich white Vegas gamblers couldn't keep their eyes off her smooth chocolate skin and her shoulder-length jet-black hair.

Once she had worked her way into their rooms, Nina would slip them a mickey while her cousin robbed the gamblers blind.

Kennedy was the mastermind behind the scheme. At twenty-two, she was a genius at crime. If it had been a major in college, she would have graduated summa cum laude.

She'd come up with this particular scheme after the ATF and DEA had raided them. The only thing that had kept Kennedy and Nina from going to state or federal prison was that thirty minutes before the raid, they had been robbed. Nina's boys' father and his brother had hit them for four kilos and all of their firearms. After everything was over, Kennedy considered the robbery to have been a blessing.

Kennedy looked on, aggravated, as Nina continued to try to crack the safe's code.

Nina exhaled. "There, I did it. Told you, ma, just be easy." As she pulled the safe's door open she could not believe what she was seeing. She covered her mouth with a gloved hand to keep from screaming.

Kennedy slid off the bar stool and walked toward her cousin to see what the excitement was about. "Nina, what is it?"

"Yo, it must be fifty Gs in here! And, Ken, look at this black bag. It looks like diamonds, ma."

"Nigga, let me see! Damn, it's like thirty loose stones in here. This nigga must be a criminal himself. Come on, bag all this up. Let's be out."

• • •

Kennedy drove back to their hotel on the outskirts of Las Vegas. She was tired and weary; they had checked in four days earlier. That meant four days of not much sleep and no play.

The night before, she had worked three different casino hotels, getting four different men for their loot. She had cleared forty-five thousand dollars in cash and jewelry. She'd worn a black Gucci minidress. Now she was wearing a white tee and cut-up jean shorts with a crispy white pair of uptowns to replace the Jimmy Choo stilettos. Her beautiful makeup job was gone. Her long reddish-brown hair was pulled back into a neat ponytail. Her lips were covered only by a hint of MAC Lip Glass.

Kennedy had to take No-Doz to stay awake while driving. Nina had already fallen into a deep sleep. Kennedy thought about playing a prank to get her up but decided to let her cousin sleep for the remaining thirty minutes of the ride. Kennedy thought, *Nina did a wonderful job tonight. She was determined to get that safe open.*

After what felt like an eternal thirty minutes, they arrived at the hotel.

"Yo, Nina, get up. We're here. Come on, it's six-fifteen already."

Without opening her eyes, Nina groggily responded, "Just let me sleep twenty more minutes."

"No. Get up! We have to pack all this shit up, ship it, and get to the airport by nine forty-five. In case you forgot, our plane leaves at ten-fifty."

Nina rose up from the reclined seat with an attitude and fresh drool on her face.

"All right, all right, damn! You get on my nerves. Everybody ain't like you! I can't stay up for forty-eight hours with no sleep."

"Nina, I don't want to hear that shit. You can sleep as long as you want when we get home."

"Stop bugging, chick, I'm up."

Inside the room, they got right to the job at hand. Kennedy lined souvenir vases with cash and jewelry. Nina carefully wrapped each one in tissue paper and plastic bubble before placing them in the box.

After they finished, Kennedy stood up and scanned the room to make sure nothing had been left behind. "Is that everything, Nina?"

"Yeah, ma, that's everything."

"All right, then, we only have forty-five minutes to get ready. I'll go ahead and get in the shower! I already have my clothes out."

They finished dressing, packed the rented Suburban, and headed for UPS. Kennedy was glad to see the same black man who had been there each day, working the counter.

He had openly flirted with her, even though he was old enough to be her grandfather. He had even given her a discount on shipping. He began to smile now, revealing a gold crown, at the sight of Kennedy in a pair of tight Chloé jeans, a black halter top, and spike sandals. Her tanned red skin and her beautiful smile entranced him. With his husky voice, he greeted her. "Hey, young lady, I see you came back to see me."

Showing her pearly whites, she responded, "And how are you this morning, sir?"

"I'm a lot better now that I've seen your pretty face. Now tell me, did you come back to take me up on my offer of marriage?" The greasy old man and his gold crown literally made Kennedy sick. But she played along with him, licking her lips and smiling as she answered. "Not this time, baby, but I will let you know next week."

"Girl, you can have all my money."

Kennedy thought to herself, *I'd rather be broke.*

She was tired of playing, so she got to the point. "I have to catch a flight to Louisiana, and I need to overnight these to my sisters in New York. I need to insure both boxes for ten thousand dollars apiece."

"Damn, girl, what you got in the boxes, gold? You wanted the same amount on all those other boxes."

"Only thing in those boxes is antique vases. Only reason I insure them for so much is because I know they won't get messed up or stolen. If anything happens to them, someone will lose their job when United Parcel Service has to kick out ten Gs or more."

"Well, look here, baby girl, just pay for the insurance. I won't charge you for the shipping and handling."

"Okay, that's what's up."

She paid him and turned toward the door. As she walked away his eyes were fixed on her ass. He thought to himself, *I'm going to have some of that sweet young thing.*

When Kennedy approached the truck she saw Nina bending down in the seat. As she looked closer, she saw three white lines on Nina's compact mirror and a rolled-up fifty-dollar bill up her nose. Her nostrils vacuumed the powder trails clean. Kennedy yanked the door open, jumped in.

"What the fuck are you doing?" she barked at Nina.

"Come on, Ken-Ken, with that self-righteous shit—"

Kennedy cut her off. "No, Nina! I don't want to hear that shit. One, how can you even ride around with that shit knowing what we are out here doing? Come on, B, how fucking stupid is jeopardizing everything we came out here for over some fucking blow? Damn, bitch, are you twenty-nine or nineteen?"

Nina couldn't believe how her baby cousin had just blown up at her. "Kennedy, it's not that serious. I always have to toot a little powder before I get on the plane. You know I get nervous about flying."

"That's no excuse. You can get a doctor to prescribe you something for that. How long you been back on that shit? I thought you was clean."

Tears welled up in Nina's eyes as she thought back to a time when crack and heroin had ruled her every move. At the time, Kennedy was only eighteen, but she had helped Nina overcome her addiction after their entire family had given up on her. At twenty-two, she'd been strung-out with two kids. After nearly killing herself and her younger son, she checked into a twenty-eight-day program at a clinic.

No one had expected it to work; she had been there and done that so many times before. While Nina was away for that particular stretch of sobriety, Kennedy had gotten tired of hearing family members talking about Nina like she was some stranger in the street. They were the same people who had kept their hands open for a handout when Nina's money was long.

Furthermore, she was just sick of seeing her older cousin, whom she admired so much, fading away. All of her life she had looked up to Nina: she liked the way Nina got her own paper. While most girls were begging boys for sneaker, doobie, and nail money, Nina was getting her hustle on. Kennedy had always thought that her cousin was the flyest chick in Harlem. Plus, Nina's beautiful dark skin enhanced her beauty.

The heroin addict that Nina had turned into was someone whom Kennedy did not know. At the time, her once-meticulous cousin was wearing the same clothes for days on end. Her smooth chocolate skin had become blotchy and dry. Her long, thick hair became simply long and stringy.

At the end of the twenty-eight days, Kennedy had been there to pick her up. She moved into Nina's house, cooked good meals for her, and took care of her sons. A year later, Nina was back on her feet and clean. She was even more beautiful and healthier than she'd been before the drugs.

She could not deny that Kennedy was one of the few people who loved her unconditionally. Now, as she sat in the Suburban, she knew her cousin was only barking on her out of true love. It had been three years since Nina had closed the book on that chapter of her life.

Nina snapped back to reality. "Ken-Ken, I swear I only toot every now and then. Only when I'm completely stressed or I'm about to fly. And I promise you I'm not fucking with that heroin."

"Look, Nina, I love you no matter what, but I never want to see you go through that shit again. I'm not eighteen anymore. I don't have the energy to go through that shit with you again. And what about your kids? Niko and Taylor are old enough to know now. And Madeline is only two. She needs you to be there for her."

"Kennedy, I promise I'll never go back to that again."

"Aight, ma, whatever you say. But check this: whatever you got left, you need to toss it. I be damned if I get knocked for some petty blow shit."

Home to Harlem

The ride to the airport and the flight home were silent: Kennedy was still upset about the blow. They picked up their luggage and caught the shuttle to the parking deck to pick up her X5.

Once they were on the highway, Nina broke the silence. "Kennedy, I said I was sorry, so can you kill the cold-shoulder act already?"

"Nina, I'm past that already. I'm quiet because I'm exhausted."

"Well, what are you going to do tonight?"

"First, I'm going home and I'm going to sleep, and sleep, and sleep."

"When are you going to Aunt Karen's house to pick up the boxes?"

"Nina, I thought you were going to pick up everything."

"I can't. Once I pick up the truck, I have to drive all the way to Central Islip and pick up the kids from my stepmother's."

Kennedy was too tired to negotiate, so she gave in. "Well, I'll just wait until tomorrow so that the packages we sent this morning will be there, too. Besides, I already have plans for tonight," she said with a sneaky smile on her face.

Nina was curious about that smile. Everyone knew that Kennedy had not had a steady companion since she'd given birth to her son, Jordan, a year ago. "Ken-Ken, who do you have plans with?" Nina asked, still studying the expression on her cousin's face.

"It ain't nothing special. Hassan is coming over to hang with me."

"Hassan who? The rapper from Lincoln Projects?"

"Yes, Nina, the same Hassan."

"You still fucking him? Don't he still go with that same girl he been with forever?"

Kennedy looked at Nina from the corner of her eye. "Yeah, why? You gonna call her or something?"

Nina rolled her eyes. "No, bitch, don't play yourself. I'm just saying, you got mad niggas chasing you from everywhere, with crazy paper, trying to wife you. And you still fucking with this rapping nigga who got a bitch at home? Come on, what part of the game is that, ma?"

Kennedy felt her face turning red. She kept her eyes on the road. "Are you through?"

"What?"

"Are you through expressing your opinion on my life?"

"What are you talking about, Kennedy?"

"Look, ma. I like my relationship with Hassan. The rules are clear and defined. I know he got a girl. We don't lie to each other about the obvious. You heard what Hova said: *'Our time together is our time together.'* And as far as all these niggas out here chasing me, they don't want to do nothing but play with my mind. I've been through all the games before, and I ain't for it now. Plus, I'm not trying to have no frivolous niggas around my son. I've been through too much. What you think I should do? Be like you and Cream? Well, that's not the type of nigga I want in my cipher."

Nina folded her arms across her chest and began moving her neck as she started speaking. "And what the fuck is that suppose to mean, Kennedy?"

"Oh *please,* don't play coy with me, ma. So what, you got a nigga at home! Are you happy with him? Tell me, are you? How can you be happy with a man who punches you in the face whenever you say something he doesn't like? Or better yet, a nigga you caught fucking your best friend!"

An annoyed Nina finally interrupted Kennedy before she could go any further. "Please stop with all that bullshit you kicking! You making it sound worse than what it is. And so what he fucked that bitch? You see who he's with. And don't act like he just be hitting me for no reason because I do provoke him most of the time."

Kennedy nearly crashed the truck from laughing so hard at Nina's last comment. Nina was frozen, holding on to the dashboard. "Bitch, what is wrong with you?"

Kennedy, still laughing, replied, "I don't want you to say anything else to me, just for saying that bullshit!"

"What bullshit?" Nina asked, looking bewildered.

"That stupid shit you just said about you be provoking him. Ma, you really sound like you suffering from battered women's syndrome. That's exactly why I don't want you to call me no more when he choking your simple ass out."

"Oh, so you wouldn't help me if you saw that nigga beating me?"

"Fam, come on, don't even play me like that. Every time I jump in a fight between you two, you go right back to him. And let's not forget that night in Club NV when he was fucking your face up and I hit him over the head with that Hypnotiq bottle. You had the nerve to buck up to me, screaming on me and shit, in front of all those people. I should have duffed your ass. So hell yeah, the answer is no."

"Damn, Ken, I didn't know the shit was that serious."

"Yeah, it's that serious, 'cause I can't understand how a bitch of your caliber be fucking with these bum-ass niggas. And no, I'm not talking 'bout their financial status. I'm talking about their mental capacity."

Nina didn't want to discuss it anymore, so she just let the remark go with no response.

Kennedy was beginning to hate the way the day was going. She and Nina had never argued that much. She really hated it when people tried to analyze her life, especially when they didn't have their own in check.

As Kennedy pulled into the garage Nina began going off. "Damn Cream's ass! Nobody told him to come get my truck and leave this fucked-up shit here." She pulled out her cell phone and made a call, with no luck.

Kennedy asked, "What's wrong with the Lex? Don't you have keys to it?"

"Yeah, I got keys to it, but don't you see all those key scratches all over it?"

"Oh shit, yo, I didn't even peep that."

Nina hopped out of the truck and began tossing her bags into the back of the Lexus. Still heated, she walked over to Kennedy's side of the truck. "I know one of his bitches done keyed his car. I hate him so much. Anyway, what time do you want to hook up tomorrow?"

"Early! The rest of the boxes are supposed to be there by nine. We have to do everything early, Nina, 'cause I'm going down south to get Jordan."

"You driving all the way to NC by yourself?"

"Nah, Kneaka is going to ride with me. Yesterday was the last day of summer school at Fordham."

"I might ride with you, too. I need to go see my mother."

"Well, let me know. I have to go. I'm about to pass out. Holla back."

"One."

Kennedy drove down the hill to her apartment; she did not

even bother to go to the garage to park. She was too tired to walk or catch a cab. She parked on the street down the block from her building.

Kennedy walked into her apartment and dropped everything by the door, including the mail she had picked up from the mailbox, not even bothering to look at it. She fell onto her bed, kicked off her shoes, and within seconds was in a deep sleep.

As Nina pulled up to her building, she saw her Benz truck parked on the opposite side of the street. Cream and about twenty other guys were standing by the truck playing C-Lo.

When Cream spotted Nina, he walked across the street, smiling from ear to ear. "Hey, Nee, baby, when did you get back? Give me a hug, ma." He grabbed her with his six-foot-five, well-built body and hugged her tight.

She squirmed until she broke free of his firm grasp. "Cream, get the hell away from me before I smack fire out your trifling ass. And take this keyed-up shit so I can go get my kids."

"Ma, what the fuck is wrong with you? Why you breaking? Damn, ain't you happy to see your man?"

"I might be happy to see your ass if, when I came home, drama didn't hit me dead in the face."

"What are you talking about, Nina?"

"What am I talking about? Don't play stupid: you know what I'm talking about. That bitch keying your car up like this."

"No, I don't know what you're talking about, 'cause some little punks did that shit."

Nina was becoming furious. She hated when someone tried to play on her intelligence.

"Look, Cream, stop while you are ahead. If your lazy ass ever bothered to check the voice mail, you would know she left me a long message concerning your relationship with her. Oh, you don't believe me? Her name is Tasha Eaton and she said she is pregnant by you. And before she became pregnant, you was all in love with her, spending money, taking her on trips with you and your boys. And the two of you even have a little love nest over in Lenox Terrace. But as soon as she said she was pregnant by you, that is the first time you ever mentioned Mattie or me to her. And you told her she better get an abortion."

Nina gave him the business from the top of her lungs, so everyone in the street was staring. It was already a hot July day. Nina's confrontation had made Cream sweat even more than he was already sweating. His crisp white tee and baggy jean shorts were soaked in perspiration. He looked over his shoulder only to see his boys laughing at him. He turned back to Nina. "Oh, so you don't think we could have discussed this shit in private rather than putting all my business out in the street?"

Nina began laughing like a madwoman.

"You already put your business out in the street when you were flaunting your little whore in front of all your niggas. And furthermore, there ain't shit for us to discuss. I want you to get your shit and get the fuck out of my house." Nina pushed past him, walking toward her truck. All of his boys were staring at her, which really ticked her off. Because they all knew what was going on and yet they came into her house every day, eating her food and smiling in her face. "And what the fuck are y'all looking at?"

They all turned their heads and looked the other way.

Nina got in her truck and merked off, leaving Cream in the middle of the street, looking like an ass next to his keyed-up car.

"Get your shit and get out!" one of his boys jokingly yelled out to him. Laughter roared on the block.

Cream walked back to the corner, trying to laugh it all off. "You know I ain't going nowhere, nigga. All I have to do is buy that big baby a gift and she will be okay."

• • •

The loud ringing awakened Kennedy. Just as she reached for the phone the ringing stopped. She rolled over, and as soon as she closed her eyes her cell phone began to ring. She fumbled around the bed until she found it. "Hello!" she called out, irritation in her voice.

"Dang, girl, where you at?" Nina asked on the other end.

"I was in the state of sleep—a good sleep, too. What time is it?"

"It is a quarter to ten."

"Damn, I been asleep for six hours?"

"You was taking all them No-Doz. When you come down off them things, you come down hard."

"Tell me about it. What up, though?"

"Ain't nothing, packing up Cream's shit."

"Say word."

"Word, my nigga."

"Why?"

"Come to find out he been messing with some young girl from Jefferson the last six months. He moved her into Lenox Terrace. And now she pregnant. So you know she keyed the Lex because he wants her to have an abortion."

Kennedy sat listening in silence. She had known about Cream and Tasha's relationship but had not bothered to tell Nina. Kennedy had learned her lesson about telling Nina things she heard in the street. Nina would go back and tell Cream what she had heard from Kennedy, and then take Cream's word over Kennedy's.

Kennedy's line beeped. "Hold on, Nina, I got another call." She clicked over. "Hello?"

"What up, ma? Where you at?"

"Hi, Has. I'm home. Hold on right quick. Let me get off the other line."

She clicked back over to Nina.

"Yo, Nina, I have to go. That's Hassan."

"Oh, so you just gonna hang up with me like that? For that nigga?"

"Come on, Nee, you know it's not like that."

"Go on, Kennedy, you know I'm just messing with you. Handle your BI and hit me later."

"Aight, Nina, be careful, and don't let that nigga buy his way back in. I love you, ma. Be easy."

"I love you, too, Kennedy. Holla back."

Kennedy clicked back over. "What up, Has?"

"You know I was about to hang up."

"My bad. You still coming over?"

"Yeah, I'm still coming over, but can you come get me off my block? I already put my truck in the garage for the night."

"That's cool. I'll be there in about thirty minutes. I need to take a shower first."

"Aight, ma. One."

Kennedy got up and slipped off her sweaty clothes then turned up the air conditioner to counter the muggy and humid air outside. She took a ten-minute steamy shower, washing away the sticky sweat with peppermint soap.

She felt like a new person after her long nap and refreshing shower. She rubbed her body down with lotion then put on a pair of gray cotton short shorts and a gray fitted tee. She stood in the mirror brushing her hair, thinking, *I need a fresh doobie and maybe a relaxer, too.* Then she was out the door.

When Kennedy pulled up to Hassan's block, everyone turned around and tried to figure out who was in the gray X5 with the gray tints. She rolled down her window and called out to Hassan. "Yo, you going with me?"

"Yo, Ken, what up? I didn't know that was you. Hold up, I'm coming."

Hassan's cousin EB began questioning him. "Yo, who that pretty young thing pushing that X?"

"You remember Kennedy from a Hundred Forty-first and Eighth."

EB squinted to get a closer look. "Li'l thick Kennedy, who used to rap? That's her?"

"Yeah, man, that's her."

"Damn, I didn't know y'all still kept in contact."

"I hadn't seen her in almost two years. I bumped into her last week at the Gucci store, but she was on her way out of town or something."

"You know I could hit that, right?" EB told Hassan with a sly smile on his face.

Hassan just laughed. "Nigga, you couldn't hit that with a bat. Anyway, I'm out. Get at me tomorrow."

Hassan exchanged pounds with everyone on the block before going to the truck.

EB walked over to speak to Kennedy. "What up, girl? How you been?"

"I been okay. What about you, EB?"

"I'm straight, you know, doing my thug thizzle."

"Aight, then, be easy, my nigga."

Hassan got in the truck and gave Kennedy a hug. "What's poppin', Ken? I didn't know who you were pulling up on me like that. I thought you still had the Acura."

"I got rid of that after I had my son."

"Yeah? How's your baby doing?"

"He straight. He down south with my mother. I'm going to get him tomorrow."

"That's what's up. What was you doing out in Vegas, vacationing?"

"Something like that."

"Ma, what you out here doing in the world? And don't lie, 'cause I heard you was doing your thing-thing."

"Come on, you know me, Has. And now I got my son, so I have to grind harder."

"I feel you. Just be careful. You know these streets is ugly."

"Trust me, I know," she replied, her voice full of emotion, then shook it off. "You hungry, Has?"

"A little. Why?"

"Cause I'm going to get something from the Jamaican spot on Forty-fifth and Eighth. I haven't went food shopping, so ain't shit to eat at my house."

"That's straight. Get me whatever you getting, as long as it's not pork."

"Boy, you know I don't hardly eat no pork. I'm getting curry chicken, rice and peas, and plantains."

"Get me that and some half-and-half. Here, is twenty enough?"

"Keep that; it's my treat. You're a guest in my home tonight." She got out of the truck and walked toward the store.

As she walked away his eyes were fixed on her thick thighs. He just sat and reminisced about how good she was in bed, especially that thing she did with her tongue. It had been more than two years since they'd slept together and just thinking about it made his dick hard.

The sound of Kennedy opening the door brought him back to reality.

"Damn, Has, what was you thinking about? You didn't even see me standing here with the bags in my hand."

"I was just thinking about hitting that," he said, slipping his hand between her legs.

At Kennedy's, they ate, drank Heinekens, and talked about

life. Hassan pulled out a sandwich bag filled with weed. "Ken, you ever smoke purple haze?"

"I tried that shit before; it's strong as hell. I just stick to dro and a little Branson from time to time."

"Well, you 'bout to smoke some of this haze with me."

He pulled out an Optimo cigar, cracked it, emptied the contents, and filled it with the haze. Before they had finished smoking the first blunt, he had already rolled another. Kennedy was able to take only two hits of the second blunt.

"That is enough for me. I'm stuck," she said. She got up and attempted to cross over Hassan. He grabbed her by the hips and pulled her in front of him, caressing her thighs with his hands. He slid his hands under her shorts and massaged her throbbing, moist, warm middle.

"Let me take these shorts off, ma."

She could only nod her head up and down as he removed the shorts. The haze had her gone, and it had been so long since she had slept with anyone. The touch of his hands alone simply made her melt. He stood up; his six-foot two-inch frame towered over her five-foot seven-inch body.

He removed his T-shirt and dropped his shorts and boxers. He pulled her tee over her head, revealing her bare breasts. He bent down and began giving her ears and neck wet tongue kisses. Hassan sat back on the couch. He grabbed Kennedy by the thighs and pulled her down on top of him.

She held her breath as she slowly slid onto him, letting out a slight whimper when he was all the way in. She was extra tight after about a year of no sex. Hassan moaned from the tightness and wetness of her walls. The quicker she began to move, the better it felt to both of them.

He stood up, never pulling out, and carried her to the bedroom. He laid her on the bed, placing both legs on his shoulders.

He pulled halfway out and dropped all the way down, causing her to moan.

As he began to stroke her faster, she bit down on her lip to keep from screaming. She was getting wetter and wetter, and he could feel it.

"Ma, you coming?"

Still unable to speak, she just nodded.

"Wait, don't come yet."

He flipped her onto her stomach and entered from the back. He stroked her faster and faster until her body trembled in ecstasy.

"Oh my God, baby," she moaned over and over as she came all over his dick. He pulled out and let off all over her back. Out of energy, he collapsed on her back, gasping for air, heart racing. Once he caught his breath, he got up and went to the bathroom. A few minutes later he returned with a warm rag. Kennedy was laying in the same position, unable to move. Hassan cleaned off her back and in between her legs.

"Ken, you okay?"

"I'm aight."

"Get up and get under the covers."

She lifted her body as much as she could and crawled under the covers. Hassan got under as well and wrapped his arms around her.

"Ma, that shit was bananas!"

Already half-asleep, she responded, "Am I suppose to say thank you?"

"You ain't got to say shit. Just don't get ghost on a nigga again."

"That you don't have to worry about."

Kennedy fell into a deep sleep, still fatigued from the past week. Hassan wasn't tired, but he knew she could not go another round. He rolled another blunt and watched television until he fell into his own nod.

Nina sat on the couch watching episodes she had missed of *Sex and the City* on TiVo. Hours ago she had bathed the kids and put them to bed. She had also finished packing all of Cream's belongings and had set them by the front door. It was 2 A.M. and he wasn't home yet.

Two forty-five, she heard his keys in the door. He saw all his bags packed. Moments later she heard him say, "She can't be serious."

He walked into the living room holding two dozen roses and bags from Chanel. Nina never took her eyes from the screen, even when he tried to start a conversation.

"So you gonna act like you don't see me standing here, huh? Look what I bought you. I got the Chanel sandals and the matching bag that you was looking at."

Nina looked at him, then at the bags, and turned up her nose. "I don't want that shit."

"This shit cost three Gs."

"So what? Give it to that young bitch. And while you at it, get your shit and take it to her house. My bad—I meant *y'all* house."

"Nina, come off it. It wasn't that serious. That bitch didn't mean nothing to me. I love only you, and I am so sorry I hurt you. Now come over here and give me a hug."

Nina was becoming irritated that he wasn't taking her serious.

"Cream, are you listening to me? Do you understand what I am saying to you? I want you to get your things and get the *fuck* out of my house."

"Bitch, I'm not going anywhere! This is my house. I take care of Mattie and them damn boys that ain't even mine! Bitch, you tripping if you think I'm going somewhere!"

"No, nigga, you bugging, 'cause I have never asked you for anything. I got my own paper. And as for Niko and Taylor, I never asked you to support my kids. And everything you do for Madeline, you're supposed to. You're her father. You know what? You are just as pathetic and trifling as Kennedy said you were."

"Kennedy! Oh, so now you listening to that bitch again? Is that who put it in your head to put me out? Since you want to listen to her, see if she's willing to take this ass whipping."

He smacked Nina, causing her to fall backward over the top of the couch. She landed on the floor with a loud thump that woke up the boys. They ran into the living room and saw Cream picking her up by her shirt and punching her repeatedly in her face.

"Mommy!" Taylor screamed out.

Between punches and efforts to fight back, she answered her older son's cry. "Tay, take your brother, go in the room, and lock the door."

Taylor grabbed the phone off the hall table and ran into the room with Niko. His hands shook as he dialed Kennedy's phone number.

Kennedy's phone rang five times before she woke up; she looked at the caller ID before answering.

"Nina, why are you calling me at three in the morning?"

"Ken, this is Tay," a tearful Taylor answered.

"Baby, what's wrong?" Kennedy slid from underneath Hassan's arm and sat straight up.

"It's Mommy. Cream is beating her bad."

Kennedy jumped out of bed, waking up Hassan. "Okay, baby, where are you now?"

"I'm locked in the room with Niko."

"Where is Mattie?"

"She's in her room."

"Listen, Tay, stay in your room. Don't come out until I get there. I will be there in five minutes, okay, baby?"

"Okay, Ken."

"See you in five minutes, bye."

She threw on the first T-shirt and jeans in sight.

"Where you going, ma?" Hassan asked her.

"Cream is beating Nina's ass again. The kids just called, terrified. You can stay here as long as want, the slam lock is on the door."

Kennedy rumbled through her drawer until she found the spare keys to Nina's apartment. She pulled out a 9mm semiautomatic handgun from under her mattress. She checked the magazine to make sure it was loaded.

Hassan saw the gun. "Kennedy, what are you taking that for? Are you sure you don't need me to go?"

"Nah, Has, that's okay. I'll call you tomorrow. I'm out."

Meanwhile, at Nina's, Taylor cracked the door and looked out of the bedroom, despite Niko's protests. He saw Nina and Cream still going at it. Cream was hitting her with hard blows all over her body, but she wasn't taking them lying down. She fought back as much she could, scratching, kicking, and swinging her arms. She reached onto the coffee table, grabbed an iron candlestick holder, and hit him in the eye, causing him to lose his balance. As he fell backward she stood up, dazed, and tried to make it to the bedroom to get her gun. She wasn't quick enough. In one swift movement he was up and right behind her.

He grabbed a handful of her hair, yanking her through the air toward him. He spun her around and began choking her. She wanted to fight back but couldn't. She could only try to remove his hands from her neck.

He released his right hand, pulled back, and hit her with a strong punch, right between the eyes. The punch packed so much power he could not even hold on to her with his left hand. She fell backward, hitting her head on the steel bar that was affixed to the glass dining table.

Glass shattered everywhere, and blood flowed from Nina's mouth and nose. She was unconscious. Cream was frozen with fear. In all of their earlier fights, nothing like this had ever happened. Blood was flowing out so fast. He knew that she had suffered more than a busted lip or nose.

He didn't know what to do. He started to panic and ran to Madeline's room and grabbed her out of the bed. He picked up one of the duffel bags that Nina had packed and ran down the stairs to the car. He laid Madeline down in the backseat, hopped in the car, and pulled off.

As Kennedy drove up to Nina's building, she saw Cream driving away. She thought to herself, *Good, the drama is over.*

She used her key to get into the building then ran up the stairs. The door to Nina's apartment was ajar. She stepped in and called out, "Nina, baby, are you okay? Taylor called me. Where are you?"

From the corner of her eye, she saw Nina lying on the floor. She ran over to her, knelt down beside her, and lifted her head. "Oh God, Nina, wake up. Taylor," she called out, "you can come out now. I'm here, baby. Hurry."

Taylor came out of the bedroom and got a surreal view of his mother.

"Tay, baby, I need you to dial 911. Tell them we need help. Tell them your mommy has been hurt very bad, and she is not moving."

Niko stood over Kennedy and Nina, his face covered in tears and mucus. "Ken, he took Mattie."

"He did? I didn't see her in the car. Well, we'll get her back. Niko, baby, I need you to go get me a glass of water and a wet rag."

Nina started coughing and gagging and more blood came out of her mouth. She looked up at Kennedy. "Ken-Ken, take care of my kids, please. Don't let nobody take them."

"Nina, stop talking like that. You're gonna be okay. The ambulance is on the way."

"I can't, Ken. The pain is too bad in my head. I want you to take my kids. Please promise me."

"I promise. But you're going to be okay. You can't leave me yet. I won't let you get off the hook that easy."

"Tell my kids I love them so much. And I hope I didn't upset you."

Kennedy had tears streaming down her face.

"Ma, I'm not upset with you."

" 'Cause you were always right about me. You were the only one who kept it gully with me. I love you."

"I love you, too. Now stop talking. Save your breath."

"Ken, please don't be mad, but I . . . I can't make it." Nina's eyes closed as she took her last breath.

A cool breeze ran through the room, causing the hair to stand up on the back of Kennedy's neck. She shook Nina's lifeless body. "Nina, wake up. No, Nina, you are not leaving me now. Come on, ma, we have too much to do."

Kennedy wiped the blood from Nina's mouth and tried CPR to no avail. Niko and Taylor looked on, crying, as Kennedy continued to talk to Nina. She rocked back and forth with Nina in her arms. "Nina, why, why, sweetie, why didn't you call me? Why didn't you call me? I would have come. I was only playing when I said don't call me."

Moments later, the paramedics and police rushed through the door. The police took Kennedy aside for questioning. She answered their questions to the best of her knowledge. She continued to watch as the paramedics worked on Nina with no success.

Kennedy looked over and saw Niko and Taylor on the couch. Niko had his head buried in Taylor's chest; Taylor was trying to console his younger brother. He was crying just as hard as Niko.

Grindin' | 25

Kennedy attempted to wrap up the conversation with the police. "Can we finish this later? The boys—they need me."

The short, round lady officer who happened to be a mother empathized with Kennedy. "That is perfectly fine. We'll be here for a while, but I need you to give me a recent picture of Madeline. And we need to speak to the boys once they settle down a little. Is there anyone I can call for you?"

"No, my aunt is on her way here now."

Kennedy went and sat down between the boys, pulled them close, and wrapped both arms around them. They sat still while the EMTs bagged Nina's body and took her away. Kennedy stared straight ahead as she spoke to the boys. "This is why you never put your hands on a woman. Always honor your mother's memory, and never hit a woman. Promise me and your mother right now you will never hit a woman."

Tearfully they answered, "I promise."

Later that morning, everyone gathered at Karen's house. Of Kennedy's seven aunts on her mother's side of the family, Karen was the strongest. Whenever something went wrong, she was the one the family called. Kennedy was her favorite niece and everyone knew it. She had favored her ever since Kennedy was a child because Kennedy reminded her of herself.

Karen could see from the other side of the living room that Kennedy looked run-down and tired. She saw others attempt to talk with Kennedy and not receive a response. She knew that Nina's passing was going to tear Kennedy to pieces sooner or later. Karen decided that it was time for her to get away from the crowd. "Kennedy, baby, come on, you need to go lay down."

"I'm aight, Auntie. I just wish she would have called me."

"Sweetie, you can't carry on like this. You can't blame yourself."

Kennedy laid her head on Karen's shoulder and broke into tearful sobs. "Auntie, you don't understand. We had an argument about Cream when we came back from Vegas. I told her not to call me the next time he was beating her. I didn't mean it; I just said it in the heat of the moment."

"Baby, I know you didn't mean it, and Nina knew you didn't mean it. You were always there for her, even when the family gave up on her."

"I know, Auntie, but we were more than cousins. She was my sister."

"I know, baby, I know. Have you talked to your mother again?"

"She called me from Auntie Klarice's house. She said Auntie Klarice was in denial."

"I can only imagine what she is going through, losing her oldest child at the hands of that low-life nigga."

"My mommy said they will be here sometime tonight. She was going home to book plane tickets for them and Grandma."

Karen fought back the tears as she looked down at Kennedy, lying in her lap like a child. For the first time, she noticed that Kennedy's dark jeans and hot-pink T-shirt were covered in blood.

"Kennedy, let me take you to your house so you can take these clothes off. You need to get away from all these people for a little while."

As they got up to leave, Cream's mother, Vivian, walked through the door, holding Madeline. Kennedy took Madeline out of her arms and hugged her, glad to have her back safely. She sat back on the couch and placed Madeline on her lap.

Vivian was very humble. She apologized many times for Cream's actions and explained that Cream had dropped Madeline off around 5 A.M. Vivian honestly felt bad and humiliated, so she didn't hang around any longer than necessary. "Mattie, honey, come give Grandma a big hug. I'm getting ready to leave now."

Madeline attempted to get up, but Kennedy wouldn't let her go. For the first time, Kennedy looked directly at Vivian. "Miss Vivian, please don't take this the wrong way or don't think I'm trying to disrespect you when I say this. But the next time you talk to your son, you need to tell him his best bet is to turn his self in to the police. Because if me or any of my cousins see him, you'll know exactly what my aunt Klarice is going through right now. But then again, he won't be safe on Rikers, or any jail in the state of New York, will he?" Kennedy smiled coldly and let Madeline go. "Go give your granny a hug so she can go."

Vivian hugged Madeline quickly and walked so fast to the door she almost ran.

Kara, Kennedy's mother's snooty rich know-it-all sister whom no one got along with, especially Kennedy, looked at Kennedy and shook her head. "Kennedy, you ought to be ashamed, talking to that nice lady like that, after she came over here so humble. I swear you have no couth."

Kennedy got right in Kara's face. "Kara, take that snooty, I-got-my-master's-degree shit back to Queens and shove it up your tight ass! I'm not for it today, not when my cousin, my sister, my best friend, just died in my arms."

Kara was scared to even breathe.

Karen placed her hand on Kennedy's shoulders and gently pulled her away. "Come on, Kennedy, sweetie, don't do it. She is not even worth it."

Kara was fuming. "Karen, why are you taking her side? She was rude and disrespectful to Vivian, and now me."

Karen stepped up to Kara's face. "I want you to leave her alone. She may have been crass in her approach, but she was right. We're glad Mattie is back, but Vivian knows where her son is, and I didn't appreciate her coming in here with all her self-serving apologies either. Come on, Kennedy, let's go."

"That's okay, Auntie, I'll drive myself. I'll take Mattie with me and get her cleaned up, too." Kennedy picked up Madeline and walked out of the door, slamming it behind her.

Kennedy placed Madeline in the backseat of the car and strapped her in. She got into the car, put on her seat belt, but could not move. After a minute or so, she took a deep breath and started the engine. She drove down Lenox in a daze, feeling like the world was moving though *she* wasn't.

She sat at the red light on 139th and Lenox, looking at all the kids in the park playing with not a care in the world. Their innocent faces were so beautiful, so full of hope. She continued to watch them play, wondering what they would be when they grew up. Her thoughts were interrupted by Madeline's tiny voice.

"Ken-Ken."

"Yes, baby?"

"Can I have an icy?"

Kennedy looked at Madeline, who was watching the kids outside, lined up at the icy cart. "Yeah, li'l mama, I'll get you one by my house after you eat some food. Okay?"

"Okay."

Kennedy turned around in time to catch the light turning green, but Madeline wasn't finished talking.

"Ken-Ken, are you taking me home?"

"We're going to my house right now. Why?"

"I want my mommy."

Kennedy had not given any thought to how she was going to explain Nina's death to Madeline. *How do you tell a two-year-old she will never see her mother again?* With tears streaming down her face, she gave the only response she could. "Baby, I want your mommy, too."

I Wish, I Wish, I Wish

Big Ma was nothing to play with. She was a God-fearing, strong black woman. Big Ma knew the Bible like the back of her hand. She could quote the Scripture verbatim. In the next breath she could curse like a sailor on leave. Big Ma's husband, Daddy James, had moved their family to New York in the forties. They traded in living under Jim Crow laws and the KKK for the equally racist NYPD.

At age seventy-five, Big Ma had seen everything—lynching in the South, rioting in the North, and the eighties crack epidemic. After Daddy James's death in 1992, she'd decided she had seen enough. Big Ma moved back to Charlotte, North Carolina. A year later Kennedy's mother, Kora, and Nina's mother, Klarice, followed, taking their children with them.

Kennedy and Nina had hated the idea of leaving New York. When they moved to Charlotte they rebelled in every way possible, until Kora and Klarice gave in and sent the girls back to New York to live with Karen.

Now, as they sat on the plane, Kora was regretting the decision she and Klarice had made. *We should have put our foot down and made those girls stay in Charlotte. They would not have gotten in so much trouble over the years. And poor Nina wouldn't be dead.*

Big Ma sat between her daughters with an ache in her heart.

Before today, she could not have fathomed what it would mean to lose another grandchild. Nina was the fourth grandchild she'd lost to violence in twelve years, the first granddaughter. Big Ma's grand girls, as she called them, were special to her. She had only five granddaughters, compared to eleven grandsons, and three of the surviving eight were in prison.

The first time Big Ma had lost a grandson, it had nearly torn her apart. By the time she lost her third grandson, she'd learned to accept death as God's will, and this she never questioned.

Losing her oldest granddaughter was an altogether different hurt. The pain she felt for Klarice was intense. She'd cried only once, when she first learned of Nina's death. *I have to be strong for Klarice. Lord, I have to be really strong for Kennedy. This may take her sanity.*

Big Ma had already witnessed Kennedy nearly go insane after the death of her boyfriend Pretty Boy.

Kennedy was fifteen when she'd met Pretty Boy. He was eighteen, and already a gangster's gangster. They had fallen hard for each other. Pretty Boy had been her first boyfriend. Kennedy was the only thing he loved. He was the product of a prostitute and a pimp. He had been in and out of foster homes the first ten years of his life. The streets had literally raised him.

Kennedy and Pretty Boy had met at the rink in Jersey. Kennedy knew who he was, but she wasn't checking for him. Every young girl uptown was sweating him, and even some older women. He had beautiful brown skin, gorgeous full lips, and pearly-white teeth. He wore his curly, jet-black hair in a very neat small Afro. The fact that Pretty Boy was getting money only made him all the more attractive to women.

Pretty Boy had watched Kennedy as she danced while skating round and round. She looked like candy to him. Kennedy was only fifteen, but her body was twenty-five. Pretty Boy had seen her around uptown in her parochial-school uniform. Usually he would see her when she came through the block to visit her cousin Alex. Pretty Boy had always admired her from afar.

That night Kennedy had on her favorite pair of red stretch Parasuco jeans. They made her voluptuous behind look even bigger. Her microbraids were pulled up in a ponytail, showing off her cute baby face. Her huge doorknocker earrings were the perfect accent. As Kennedy skated by him, Pretty Boy reached out and grabbed her. "What up, shorty?"

"Nothing. You looking for Alex? He should be here in a little while."

"I'm not looking for Alex, I'm looking for you."

"For what?"

"I want to take you out tomorrow."

This cannot be happening. The hottest nigga uptown wants to take me out. Okay, answer him, stupid! "Where do you want take me?"

"I was thinking we could go to the movies and out to eat."

"That's straight. What time?"

"Tomorrow, around six-thirty. Meet me by the train on a Hundred Forty-fifth and St. Nick. Wear something like that. Don't wear that Catholic-school uniform."

Oh my God. He has been watching me! "Okay, it's a date. I'll see you tomorrow."

The next day Kennedy and Pretty Boy had gone out. They clicked immediately; it was as if it were meant to be. From that day forward they were inseparable. Pretty Boy would come to her house and walk her to school in the morning. Kennedy would meet him on his block every day after she got out of school. It was truly young ghetto love.

After a year of dating, things began to run smoother and faster for Pretty Boy. He started to control a few more blocks. With his added responsibilities, he didn't get to spend as much time with Kennedy as he'd done before. Some mornings she would come out the house and Pretty Boy wouldn't be there to walk her to school. One morning Kennedy came out of the building and he was sitting in a brand-new Chevy Tahoe.

"Pretty, whose car are you driving? I hope it ain't some crack-head that owe you money."

"Hush, girl, and get in."

"No. Not until you tell me who it belongs to."

"It's mine. I bought it. Now get in."

Kennedy was a little apprehensive, and then she finally got in. "I'm glad you showed up this morning."

"Come on, ma. Please don't start with the time thing again. You already know what time it is. Niggas is grindin' right now."

"So what am I suppose to do now—come second to your paper chase?"

The hurt spread across Pretty Boy's face. "That ain't even fair, Ken-Ken. You know how I feel about you."

"No, I don't know! I never see you anymore."

"I know a way we can fix this. Do you feel like skipping school today?"

Kennedy thought about it. "For what?"

"I have a surprise for you; I was going to show you after school. Since I see you need some attention, we can go get it now."

Pretty Boy drove Kennedy to the Delanor Apartments. He pulled into the back parking area. "Get those keys out the glove compartment."

Kennedy followed Pretty Boy into the building. *Where in the hell is he taking me? I should've gone to school.*

Pretty Boy led her to an apartment on the fifth floor. "Unlock the bottom lock with that red key."

"Hell no! Pretty, whose apartment is this?"

"Kennedy, what the fuck is wrong with you today? Why are you so paranoid? Never mind, give me the damn keys." Pretty Boy opened the door and stepped inside. Kennedy hesitated before walking into the empty apartment. Pretty Boy grabbed her arm and pulled her inside. "Welcome home, mama!"

"What?"

"This is our home."

"Our?"

"Yes, *our*! I just thought with the way things are going lately, we should live together. That way we can see each other at night and wake up to one another every morning."

"Damn, Pretty, I didn't know you felt like that."

"That's 'cause you think you know everything." Pretty Boy playfully tugged at her plaid skirt. "Do you wanna christen the place right now or wait until the furniture gets here in two days?"

"Boy, you are so nasty. We will have to wait. I have to go to school today. I forgot I have an English test fifth period."

"Here, drive yourself," Pretty Boy said, handing her a Honda key.

"Damn, you doin' it! You bought two cars and a new apartment?"

"Stop clowning and come downstairs so you can see it."

The car was a hunter-green, '96 Honda Accord coupe. The interior was beige. Kennedy was grateful for it. "Thank you, Malik."

Pretty Boy blushed; he loved it when Kennedy called him by

his government name. "You welcome. It's only a year old. It has like twenty thousand miles on it. Don't worry, give me a couple of months. I'll get you something nicer for your graduation."

"Why? I like this. I mean, I know women in their thirties and forties who've never owned a car."

"That's why I love you, 'cause you appreciate a nigga."

Six months later, Kennedy graduated. True to his word, Pretty Boy bought her a BMW M3. Business was booming for Pretty Boy. The crew he ran with had locked a few spots in Maryland, Virginia, and South Carolina. Pretty Boy went from making two thousand dollars a day to making between ten and fifteen.

With the success of his come-up came the jealousy, the haters, and the grime, even within the crew. They were a tight crew, with the exception of one loose screw, Tony. Tony, Pretty Boy, and a few other young heads were led by Sazaar. Sazaar treated Pretty Boy and Tony like they were his sons. Pretty Boy was committed to Sazaar and the dynasty they were trying to build. That's why he went to bed late and got up early, sometimes never sleeping. Pretty Boy's commitment made Sazaar respect him and show him favor. That made Tony jealous. Tony wanted all the rewards with no sacrifice. The crew noticed Tony's jealousy and began to call him Cain and Pretty Boy, Abel.

One blazing hot August morning, Pretty Boy came back from South Carolina and instead of going home had gone straight to the block. Kennedy could not believe it when she saw him on the block holding court with his crew. She double-parked and hopped out the car. "Yo, Pretty, can I holla at you?"

Pretty Boy turned to walk toward her. *Damn, look at her face. I know she is pissed off.* When he got in front of her, he wrapped his arms around her. Instead of returning the hug, she shoved him away.

"What up, baby girl?"

"What's up with you, playboy? How long you been back?"

"I got here like, um, two hours ago."

"And this is where you came to first?"

"I had some important business to take care of."

"I can't wait until the day I become as important as your business. Why do we even live together?"

His constant absence was driving Kennedy nuts. When Pretty Boy was in New York he had to take care of the blocks he ran. Most nights consisted of him coming home around 3 A.M. and getting up at 7 A.M. Kennedy was sick of it.

Pretty Boy could tell by the look in her eyes that she was fed up. "Kennedy, you know there is nothing in the world more important than you to me. I have to take care of my business so we can maintain."

"Malik, I don't think *we* are maintaining right now."

"What are you trying to say?"

"I think I should move out. You know, get my own place." *Damn, did I just say that? Maybe he will see shit is real and give me the attention I deserve!*

"Come on, Kennedy, not today with this bullshit, aight. What the fuck do you want to move out for? Don't I provide well for you? Give me a valid reason why you want to leave. Are you fucking wit' another nigga?"

Yeah, nigga, grovel, see how I feel. "Don't play yourself; you know I would never cheat on you. Yeah, you give me more than what I need materialistically. I need you more than I need any of that shit. I want to move out because I saw you more when we didn't live together!"

Pretty Boy saw straight through her charade. He didn't like putting their business on front street by debating on the block.

He put his arm around her and walked her over to the driver's side of her car. "Kennedy, right now is not a good time for this. You are talking from emotions. Go do what you have to do. Let me wrap up all my shit on the block. Meet me at the crib at five-thirty so we can go out and talk about all of this."

"You cannot be serious." Kennedy was laughing uncontrollably. "Wow, this is unbelievable. Mr. Pretty Boy himself wants to take the train."

"I thought it would be a good idea so we can spend some time together. Since you think it's such a joke, fuck it!"

"No, baby, that's straight. Let's go."

Pretty Boy addressed the issues that Kennedy had presented to him earlier that day as they walked down Lenox toward the 2 and 3 train. They continued to talk during the ride downtown. By the end of the ride, they seemed to have resolved everything. Pretty Boy even sealed it with a promise to take Kennedy to Jamaica in a month.

The two enjoyed a movie, dinner, and a long walk through Central Park. They returned home around 1 A.M. and made love before falling into a deep sleep.

One hour later Kennedy was awakened by unfamiliar voices. She tried to open her eyes, but they were covered with duct tape; so was her mouth. Her wrists were taped together, as were her ankles. She panicked when she heard, "Shoot him now, nigga."

Kennedy wanted to cry or scream, but she could do nothing. The two loud blasts in her left ear deafened her. She felt warm, thick liquid on her skin. *Oh God, did they shoot me?* She placed her bound hands on Malik's chest, where she felt even more blood. *Oh, no, Malik, please no!*

Kennedy just laid her head on his shoulder and prayed that someone had heard the shots and would call the police. Uptown, gunshots were so normal that sometimes no one even bothered to dial 911.

Another gruesome scene unfolded that night at Sazaar's home in Queens. As Sazaar approached the house he heard his wife moaning in pain. He switched his direction. Instead of using the front door, he crept through the side door with his gun drawn. Sazaar watched as one guy paced around his wife, who sat in the middle of the family room tied to a kitchen chair. Her face was badly beaten and smeared with blood. Her nightgown was ripped open, exposing her bare chest. Sazaar felt a little comfort knowing his two young sons were away for the night. The second intruder sat next to Sazaar's daughter. She had the body of a eighteen-year-old, but she was only thirteen. Her face was battered. Tears came to his eyes, just knowing they had touched his little girl.

Sazaar let off two shots. He hit the boys in places he knew would take them down but not kill them. Other than his brothers, no one knew he had once been a trained assassin for the Panamanian government. Sazaar moved in quickly, disarming both boys and tying them together. He then freed his wife and daughter, securing them in the master bedroom. He went back downstairs and snatched the masks from the heads of the two intruders. Sazaar was utterly shocked to see two of his youngest soldiers.

Benji and Deon worked under Tony. Sazaar took a seat in front of them. He lit a cigarette and took a long drag. "Who sent you?"

Knowing death was imminent regardless of his answers, Deon said, "Fuck you, nigga, we sent ourselves."

"Why did you come for me?"

"We want your food."

"I still don't follow. I've been generous with all my workers."

"How the fuck are you generous? You living out here in this big-ass house and we in the hood *starvin'*."

"*Mijo,* you make a couple of Gs a week. You call that starvin'? I'm tired of talking to you. It's useless." Sazaar shot Deon once in the head. Benji emptied his bowels in his pants as he made eye contact with Sazaar. Sazaar put it to him simply: "I'm not going through the twenty fucking questions with you. Who sent you?" He already knew the answer; he just needed confirmation.

With a nervous voice Benji answered, "You already know it was the modern-day Cain. Only Tony thought he could take out his brother and God in the same night."

Sazaar raised his gun once more, pulled the lever back, and silenced Benji forever. Then picked up his cell phone and called his two older brothers, Meza and Salazar. They rushed over to help him secure his family and dispose of the bodies.

Salazar drove Sazaar's family to a safe location while Sazaar and Meza dismembered the bodies in the basement and tossed them into the furnace. Benji's statement kept running through Sazaar's head. Suddenly he realized. "Oh my God, he put a hit out on Pretty Boy, too!"

Meza looked up at him. "What?"

Sazaar explained everything to Meza as he repeatedly tried to call Pretty Boy. As soon as Salazar returned they headed toward Harlem.

As Meza drove, Sazaar sat slumped in the back of his brother's black Impala. They crept through the blocks, looking for any sign of Pretty Boy. The fifth time they rode down Pretty Boy's street, Sazaar spotted Nina walking away from Pretty Boy's building. Salazar cut her off as she crossed the street. Meza jumped out and grabbed her.

Nina was shaken until she saw Sazaar. "What the fuck, Zaar?"

"I'm looking for Pretty Boy."

"Damn, you didn't have to go all postal and have niggas snatch me up and shit! Hell, I been looking for Kennedy all morning."

"When was the last time you heard from Kennedy?"

"Last night."

"Wasn't you just leaving the apartment?"

"I came through and rang the bell after Kennedy didn't meet me at the hair salon this morning. What in the hell is going on, Zaar?"

"Nina, someone tried to pull a hit on me last night, in my own home. I think Pretty Boy and Kennedy may be in trouble."

Nina's head and heart dropped. "I have keys to the apartment. We can go upstairs and check on them."

Nina entered the apartment, followed by Sazaar, Meza, and Salazar. The living room was in perfect order. Nina heard the bedroom television blaring. She pushed the bedroom door open; the sight made her fall to her knees. She crawled over to the bed. Sazaar ran in.

Pretty Boy and Kennedy's naked bodies were covered in blood. Nina lay down on top of Kennedy and wept. Her crying woke Kennedy up. She jerked and moaned. Nina jumped back. "Zaar, she is still alive!" She slowly pulled the tape from Kennedy's eyes and mouth.

It took Kennedy a few minutes to open her eyes. Once she did, everything was blurry. She shook nervously as she tried to figure out who was releasing her. She desperately clung to Pretty Boy's body and grew so hysterical that Nina had to slap her. "Kennedy, it's me! What happened?"

Sazaar pulled the sheet from the floor and covered her naked body. "Kennedy, sweetheart, it's me—Sazaar. Who did this to you?"

After eighteen hours of lying in the bed with a dead body, Kennedy was in shock, confused, and restless. She sobbed loudly and shrugged her shoulders.

Nina thought it might be better if she asked the questions. "Ken, are you sure you don't know anything? Can you just tell us what happened?"

"I . . . I don't know . . . we went to bed and then I heard voices, but I couldn't see anything . . . Malik, baby, get up," she wailed, falling on top of his body.

Sazaar looked over at Nina. "I have to go now. Call 911 in about half an hour. Call me later on today and keep me posted. Tell no one that you saw me or that I'm alive. Kennedy, anything you ever need, call me." He kissed Kennedy on the top of her head, then left.

Two days later Kennedy stopped talking altogether. She didn't like talking anymore, because every time she opened her mouth she cried. After Pretty Boy's funeral, Big Ma took her to Charlotte. She stayed secluded in a back room for six months. During those six months, she barely ate, and she didn't speak a word to anyone. Kennedy just sat in the room and wrote in her journal.

As their plane landed in New York, Big Ma, Kora, and Klarice were all thinking the same thing. They never wanted to see Kennedy go through anything like that again. Big Ma had one goal: to keep Kennedy from going back into that deep, dark hole again.

When the trio of women walked off the plane, Karen and Janice, Big Ma's second-oldest daughter, were waiting for them. The lost look on Klarice's face made Janice extend her arm to her first. "How you holding up, Klarry?"

The sisters embraced and Klarice answered, "I'm . . . I'm okay, I guess. I really need to know how do I go on living after today. I mean, how did you go on after you lost Alex?"

The question made Janice's heart so heavy her eyes filled up with tears. She cleared her throat. "I had all of you, and a whole lot of prayer. And we're going to do the same for you, sweetie."

Kennedy sat on the love seat watching everyone in disgust. *Look at all the nosy motherfuckers. I swear to God, if they don't stop asking me questions, somebody is going to get cursed the fuck out!*

A lady with a plate in her hand who was eating a chicken leg, and smacking real loud, walked over to Kennedy, sat down, and started talking. "Now, Kennedy girl, tell me what happened?"

Kennedy looked at her like she was crazy. "Don't you think you should mind your fucking business, you nosy-ass bitch." She got up and walked toward the front door. She opened it and immediately became happy. "Big Ma!" She threw her arms around her grandmother.

"How you, sugar?"

"I'm better, now that you're here."

"Is that the only person you see?" Kora asked.

"Sorry. Hi, Mommy. Hi, Jordan." Kennedy hugged her mother and took Jordan out of her arms. "Hey, big boy, did you miss Mommy?"

"Yeah." He answered with the softest little voice.

"Mommy missed you so much." Kennedy passed Jordan back to Kora when she saw Klarice coming up the hall. She embraced her aunt. They held each other for a few moments.

Klarice whispered in Kennedy's ear. "Baby girl, I know you're not okay, 'cause I'm not either. I want you to be strong. I've been thinking about you ever since I found out this morning."

"Auntie, y'all don't have to tiptoe around me. I'm not going to crack up again. Yes, I feel like I lost a part of me, but I'm older now."

"Kennedy, get up and get dressed. You are being so ridiculous right now."

"Mommy, you and Kneaka can take my truck and go on. I will catch a cab over to Auntie's after the wake."

"Kennedy, just explain to me why you don't want to go to Nina's wake."

"Look, Mommy, I don't think I'm being disrespectful. One, I can't do it two days in a row. Two, you know how Harlem wakes are. Everybody walking around, talking, and laughing. Niggas showing up to see what chickens they can pick up. I can't do it. I might flip out and spaz on someone."

Just then Kneaka walked into the room and handed Kennedy the cordless phone. "Big Ma wants you."

Kennedy rolled her eyes as she put the phone to her ear. "Hi, Big Ma."

"What's this I hear about you not going to Nina's wake?"

"Big Ma, I'm not feeling it today."

"Baby, I was just calling to see if you was all right. Everybody over here making it seem like something's wrong with you. No, baby, you don't have to come today. If you don't think you can handle it, that's right, stay at home."

"Thanks, Big Ma."

Big Ma hung up the phone and everyone in the house waited anxiously to hear her report Kennedy's decision. "Kennedy has her own reason for not going to the wake. It ain't nobody's damn business. So when she get here later don't ask why she wasn't there."

That night Kennedy did not sleep. She lay in the bed and observed Jordan as he slept. He looked so angelic. As she watched him she pledged to keep out of the streets.

Around six-thirty, she finally dozed off. When the clock struck eight, Jordan was up and hungry. She dragged herself out of bed and picked him up. "Good morning, booby," Kennedy cooed, placing kisses all over his face and neck. "How did Mommy's boy sleep? I bet you slept better than Mommy." She tried to place Jordan in his high chair. He arched his back and kicked, out of protest. "Come on, J, not right now."

Once Jordan had settled down, Kennedy handed him his favorite breakfast—dry Cheerios and fresh strawberries. Kora entered the kitchen yawning and stretching. She saw Kennedy's face and gasped. "You look terrible."

"Good morning to you, too, Mommy. I know I look bad. I didn't get any rest."

"I can take care of Jordan. Go get you some rest."

"It's no use in going back to sleep now. I'm going to go get a doobie, then to Ninety-sixth Street to get a facial. 'Cause makeup can't do nothing for these bags."

After showering, Kennedy looked in the mirror. *Damn, Mommy was right. I look a hot-ass mess with these red eyes and dark circles.*

Six hours later, the Abyssinian Baptist Church was filled to capacity and Kennedy looked dynamic. She wore a sleeveless, black linen dress by Theory that stopped midknee. On her feet were the prettiest Casadei black stiletto pumps and she carried a black Chanel bag. Her black, wide-brim hat was tilted to the side so that it covered the right side of her face, and she sported silver Dior shades. Her jewels were a diamond tennis necklace and matching bracelet; both had been gifts from Nina.

She stood over Nina's coffin. Everyone looked on with sympathy as Kennedy smoothed Nina's hair with her hand. She arranged it the way Nina had always worn it. Kennedy still wasn't satisfied. "Look at you, Nina. You don't look like you're resting or in peace. Even in death you're still a fly bitch. You looking good in that cream Donna Karan linen. How ironic is it that cream was always your favorite color."

Kennedy felt someone come up behind her. "Well, Nina, I guess I have to take my seat now. Other people want to see you. I brought you some things to take home with you." She pulled a few items from her black Chanel bag and began placing them in the coffin—a gold hugs-and-kisses set; three teddy bears, one for each of Nina's kids; childhood and recent family photos; a letter she wrote to Nina the night she died; and one white long-stem rose.

Finally, Kennedy bent over and kissed Nina's cheek. She let her fingers glide along the cherrywood coffin as she turned to walk away. Kennedy stood frozen in her steps when she saw the woman in front of her.

The woman was dressed similar to Kennedy, in a black linen dress. It was easy to tell that she was prissier than Kennedy, by her black three-quarter-length gloves, pillbox hat with hair pulled back in a neat bun, and pearl necklace. Her bare arm displayed the same tattoo as Kennedy's and Nina's—the name Sanchez, a pair of praying hands, and the words *Death Before Dishonor.*

Kennedy thought, *My mind must be playing tricks on me. No, that's her. After all these years, the prodigal child has returned home.* Before Kennedy stood her sister Kenyatta. They had not spoken in more than five years. Standing with Kenyatta were

Kenyatta's three daughters: Jazz, thirteen; Jada, eleven; and Jalyn, three.

Yatta had severed all ties with Kennedy and Nina after a vicious argument with Nina. She'd been more enraged with Kennedy for taking Nina's side in the disagreement than with Nina herself.

The two women stared at each other for about forty-five seconds. It seemed more like five to ten minutes. *I've already lost Nina. I'm not about to let some dispute from five years ago keep me from cherishing every moment I have left with Yatta.* Kennedy slowly stepped toward Yatta and embraced her. "I am so glad you came."

"I should have come sooner."

Kora was sitting on the front pew. No longer shedding tears of grief; now her tears came from the joy of seeing her two girls finally speaking again. *I wish Yatta and Nina could have straightened things out before Nina passed.*

Kennedy barely cried during the church service. Even though seeing Nina in her coffin made everything real for her. The graveside service was another story. Hearing the words *Ashes to ashes and dust to dust* caused Kennedy to pass out momentarily. When she came to, she didn't want to leave Nina's grave. It was a heart-wrenching scene. Not Kora, Klarice, Janice, or Karen could get her to walk away from the casket. Kennedy did not leave until she was ready. That was forty-five minutes after the graveside service was over.

Yatta's return took most of the unwanted attention away from Kennedy. The family and mourners went to Karen's house for the postfuneral dinner. Everyone was excited to see Yatta. She had been living a secluded life in a wealthy Boston suburb. Kennedy walked past as everyone surrounded Yatta and bombarded her with questions.

"Kennedy, come in here for a minute, baby."

Big Ma was in the kitchen, along with Kora, Klarice, Janice, Kara, and Karen. "What's up, Big Ma?"

"We're in here talking 'bout what we're going to do with the kids. Your mother says she can help Klarice with Niko and Mattie. We want to know if Taylor could stay up here with you."

"No, Big Ma, we can't separate them like that. I can keep all three of them up here. Anyway, I made a promise to Nina that I would take care of them."

Klarice walked over to Kennedy. "Baby, I cannot let you burden yourself down like that. They're my grandkids. Once I retire next year, I will be able to handle them by myself."

"Auntie, it's not a burden. It's what Nina wanted."

After the custody discussion, Kennedy excused herself from the room. She grabbed a Heineken and stepped onto the balcony. Yatta was already sitting out there drinking a glass of wine. This was their first time alone since their reconciliation.

Yatta looked at Kennedy. After a long pause she said, "What's good, little sister?"

"You know, same movie, different script."

"That little boy of yours is off the meat rack and he is so handsome."

"Girl, please, my nieces are gorgeous. What are you going to do when little niggas start knocking at the door?"

"Show them my P89!"

They both laughed as they looked for the right words to say. Kennedy stopped laughing and got serious. "So, Yatta, how come you never called me? If only to let me know that you were okay. Didn't you at least want to know how I was doing? Did you really hate me that much for voicing my own opinion?"

"For the same reasons you ain't picked up your phone and called me in five years. We're both stubborn. Now, you know I kept up with you through Mommy and Kneaka. I really thought you would at least have called me when you had your *first child*. Plus, the real story is longer than that."

"Well, we have all night!"

"Kennedy, don't act like Mommy hasn't already told you some of the story, if not all."

"Yatta, don't take this the wrong way. I told Mommy a long time ago, I didn't want to hear shit about you unless it pertained to my nieces. So go ahead and spill the beans."

Yatta poured a glass full of wine and took a few sips before she began to speak. "I wasn't still holding that grudge against you and Nina. The last five years with Petey have been hell. He has been so mentally abusive toward me. He put his bitches before me. He humiliated me in every way possible. I could not have any friends. All he wanted me to do was take care of the girls."

"Are you serious?"

"Yes, girl. So for the last year I have been secretly stashing money in a bank account. I bought new furniture and hid it in storage. I moved most of the girls' and my clothes out and he didn't even notice."

"Damn, I didn't know Petey had changed like that. So you were leaving him?"

"Hell yeah, I just wanted to make one clean move back to New York. I knew once I was back here with *my* family, I would be safe. 'Cause all he used to tell me is if I ever left he would kill me." Yatta swallowed the remaining wine in her glass. "And one morning, like a blessing in disguise, Bernice called me. She was the one friend I was allowed to have 'cause she was his partner's wife. I was dropping the girls off at day camp when she called. Bernice said she turned on my street and saw the feds raiding my house."

"Say *word*."

"Word. She met me around the corner, I got in her car and we watched the entire thing from down the street. I don't wish that shit on nobody, but when I saw them bringing Petey out, I was smiling on the inside. Them feds ain't no joke. They got his ass for everything in the book! They got him for conspiracy, murder, kidnapping, extortion, and interstate trafficking."

Kennedy was blown away. "So the feds took everything from y'all?"

"Not really. I mean they got like a million and a half out of the house. After I saw them taking Petey away, I emptied out all of our joint bank accounts. I emptied out all the accounts with just my name on it. I took money to his lawyer. I took some to his mother and put the rest in safe-deposit boxes. Later that night Bernice and I snuck in the house and removed as many clothes as we could fit into her Suburban."

"So what are you going to do now?"

"What I had already planned to do. I bought a remodeled brownstone."

"That's good. You know *I am glad you're back.*"

"I'm glad to be back. I just wish I could have made things right with Nina."

Tears clouded Kennedy's eyes. Yatta reached over and hugged her. "I love you, little sis."

"Don't ever leave me again, big sis."

"Never, sister. I will die before I dishonor this name."

"You and the girls are more than welcome to stay at my house tonight."

"Thanks, but I already moved into my place. I'll be over to your house, since Mommy thinks she can't leave your side."

"Yeah, everybody thinks I'm going to crack up or some shit like when Pretty Boy died. I really can't take much more of all these people here. I'm going home to lie down. I know Mommy not ready to go, so can you bring her?"

"Now, you know you didn't even have to ask me *that*. Go on and get out of here, girl."

Kennedy moved quickly and quietly through the crowded apartment so no one would get in the way of her early exit. She waved good-bye to a few guests who were standing outside on the stoop smoking. She slid into her truck and started the ignition. The sound of R. Kelly's *TP-2.com* CD came blasting from the speakers. *Kneaka must have driven last, 'cause I know Mommy ain't listening to R. Kelly.* She listened to the CD as she drove up Eighth Avenue.

As the song played, she unconsciously sang along. Once she realized the words she was singing, tears began flowing down her face, but she continued to sing. *"I wish that I could hold you now. I wish that I could touch you now. Wish that I could talk with you. Wish that I could walk with you, be with you somehow."*

Is It Too Soon to Love You?

Two months after Nina's passing, Kennedy had finally wrapped up all of her cousin's personal business. She set up educational and mutual funds for Nina's kids with Nina's half of the money from Las Vegas. Nina had left over $2 million to her kids in insurance money. Kennedy found close to $100,000 in a safe-deposit box. She gave Klarice all of it, every last dime.

Kennedy moved into a four-bedroom brownstone in order to accommodate the kids. Her new home was next door to Yatta's. Having Yatta back in her life felt like old times, but it also reminded her too often that Nina was gone forever.

Cleaning out Nina's apartment was something Kennedy was not looking forward to. She knew she needed to get it done before the kids returned from North Carolina for school. Kennedy and Yatta agreed to let the kids miss the first week of school.

While they were packing Nina's things, Yatta came across an old photo album. "Look, Ken-Ken, here are the pictures from the last time we went to the bike rally in '96."

"Wow, look at us looking like some chickens."

"No, Kennedy, look at you and that crazy-ass Guyanese nigga! What's his name?"

"Dwight. That was my first boyfriend after Pretty Boy died. I was loving him, too."

"Loving? Y'all was two simple muthafuckas. Remember when he caught you on that nigga bike from Baltimore? That shit was too funny when Dwight chased you down the strip and snatched you off the bike. Your crazy ass was really buggin' when you tried to knock him and that girl off his bike with a bat."

"That was my baby. He was the first nigga to break my heart. It was for the best, though. 'Cause at the rate we was going, we would have ended up like Nina and Cream. Most likely he would be the one in the body bag."

Yatta noticed the sad look growing on Kennedy's face, so she changed the subject. "Where are these pictures from?"

"These are from Memorial Day weekend 2000. That week was crazy. Nina wanted to go to Cancún and I wanted to go to Miami. So we did both. Yo, we was buggin', doing some extra shit as usual. That was Nina and me." Kennedy turned and walked away so Yatta wouldn't see her cry.

Kennedy and Yatta arrived in Charlotte around 5:30 A.M. that Tuesday. Everyone in the house was asleep. Exhausted from the ten-hour drive, the two sisters fell asleep in the den. A few hours later, Kora came into the room screaming, "Turn on the television . . . turn on the television!"

Kora's screaming scared Kennedy out of her sleep. "Mommy, what is it? What's wrong?"

"A plane just hit the one of the Twin Towers."

"What?" Kennedy and Yatta asked in unison.

Once Kora got the digital box on, she turned to MSNBC. The sisters saw the answer to their question for themselves. "What in the hell was that plane doing flying so low?" Yatta asked, talking to no one in particular.

Kennedy saw something creeping onto the left side of the television screen. "Oh my God. Look y'all—it's another plane."

They couldn't believe their eyes as they witnessed the second plane slam into the north tower. Yatta stood up. "Hell no, this shit ain't no accident."

Kora thought about her youngest daughter as they watched the terror unfold. "Somebody please call Kneaka. Call and make sure my baby is all right. Call my sisters and check on them, too."

Kennedy pulled out her cell phone. "I'll call, Mommy. Don't worry, Mommy, everybody is going to be all right." *Lord, please let everybody in my family be okay. I don't think we can take another tragedy.*

Their fear and anguish grew when they could not reach their loved ones in the New York. The attacks didn't stop in New York; two more planes were hijacked. One of those planes crashed into the Pentagon. The fourth plane mysteriously crashed in a field in Pennsylvania.

Kennedy could not bear to continue to watch the repeated images of those planes slamming into the towers. She took a break and went outside to get some fresh air with Jordan. The town was entirely too quiet. Charlotte is the nation's second-largest banking center, so the city was under tight patrol.

Jordan was sleeping in Kennedy's arms as she slowly rocked him back and forth. She looked down at his innocent face. Jordan had the prettiest pecan-tan complexion. He had the biggest, brightest eyes and they lit up like lightbulbs when he smiled.

The first thing Kennedy had ever said to Jordan the day he was born was: "You are so beautiful. I will give my life before I let anyone harm a hair on your head." Tears streamed down her face now as she wondered, *What type of world did I bring my child into? How do I protect him from terrorists?* Kennedy felt vulnerable and naked; that is the loneliest, most hopeless feeling anyone can experience.

Yatta had been standing in the doorway watching Kennedy. She stepped out onto the porch and sat next to her on the steps. "Are you okay?"

Kennedy quickly dried her tears with the back of her hand. "No, I'm not. First Nina, now this. I just don't know what to do."

"I don't know either, Ken-Ken. All we can do is turn to God."

"I never turned away."

"At one time I did . . . Anyway, it looks like we couldn't go home if we wanted to."

"Why?"

"They closed all bridges and tunnels into the city until further notice."

"This shit is really bugged out. Did Mommy get in touch with Kneaka yet?"

"Yeah, she talked to her. Kneaka said everyone is okay."

"Thank God for that."

After a month Kennedy settled into her new role as a mother of four. It was demanding, but that was the good part. The kids took her mind off Nina and terrorism. Kennedy tried to put all her time and thoughts into the children, especially Taylor. She tried to instill in him life lessons, since he was the oldest.

Kennedy sat him down often and told him things that she one day planned on telling Jordan. "Rule one: treat girls and women the way you want men to treat the women in our family. Rule two: there is nothing feminine about dressing neat and cleaning a house. No woman wants a lazy, messy-ass man."

Kennedy even began training Taylor and Niko in financial matters. "Taylor, I'll give you twenty dollars a week. Niko, I'll give you fifteen dollars a week. That will be your allowance. You can spend half of it on whatever you want. The other half goes into a savings account. At the end of the year, you can take the money out of savings and buy something big."

Taylor's face lit up. "Can I get an electric scooter?"

"I want one, too," Niko chimed in.

"Wait, boys, let me finish . . . Or you can take that money and invest it. That means you put it into another account, which will make you even more money."

"I want to make more money," Taylor said.

Kennedy smiled at him. "You are definitely Nina's son."

Hassan was standing in front of Dr. Jays on 125th Street exchanging jokes with his entourage when he turned and saw three girls coming out of the store. One of the females looked familiar.

When the girl got closer, Hassan realized that it was Kennedy. "Yo, Ken-Ken, what up, ma?" He grabbed her and pulled her in for a tight hug.

Kennedy smiled because she was happy to see him. "What's good, Has?"

"I don't know. You tell me. You act like you can't hit a nigga back. Don't tell me you back on that bullshit."

"Not at all. I've had some difficult days lately."

"I'm sorry about Nina. I know how close the two of you were."

"Thanks for the beautiful flowers and the cards you sent. That was really nice of you."

"That was nothing, ma. But what's up with you wearing these big-ass clothes and dark shades. This not even you, Kennedy."

"Come on; not you, too. I have four kids now; I don't have time to be cute every day."

"I didn't say you wasn't cute."

"Why, thanks," Kennedy responded sarcastically. "I have to be going now. I'll give you a call later."

Hassan grabbed her hand before she could walk away. "Do me one better. I want you to come hang out with me, at the 9/11 fund-raiser. T.O.N.Y. Records is throwing it this Sunday."

Kennedy thought about it for a couple of seconds. "Nah, that's okay."

Kneaka, who had been with Kennedy in the store, jumped into the conversation. "Ken-Ken, stop acting like that. You know you want to go. Besides, I want to go, too."

Damn, her li'l nosy ass is always in my conversations. Kennedy shot Kneaka an evil look. Hassan smirked at Kennedy. "See, your girl wants to go."

"Excuse me for being rude. These are not my girls. These are my sisters, Kneaka and Yatta. I thought you had met them before."

Yatta shook his hand. "It's nice to finally meet you and I'll make sure she gets to that party. It will do her ass some serious good to get out the house."

"Damn, I'm starting to believe this is a conspiracy," Kennedy responded. "Well, I guess you win, Has. If big sister say I'm coming, I'll be there."

As soon as they walked away, Kneaka tore into Kennedy. "I know you're going through a lot right now. But do you *have* to look like that? And what happened to going out on dates?"

"Kneaka, mind your young-ass neck."

"No." Yatta broke into the conversation. "Don't tell her to mind her business. She is concerned about you just like I am. I know life seems pretty fucked up right now. But you have to pick yourself up and keep it moving."

"And I am fine with that, but everybody keeps acting like a part of that is getting or having a man."

"Kennedy, companionship is only natural and you shun it every chance you get."

"Look, Yatta, and Kneaka, I shun men because I can't deal

with the heartache of having another one die on me, fill my head with lies, and break my heart. I will never love hard again."

The 9/11 fund-raiser was filled with A-list celebrities. It was a world that Kennedy had once dreamed of being a part of. She once dreamed of being a rap star. Kennedy was sixteen when Foxy Brown and Lil' Kim came on the scene. She'd loved their style; they were fly, and they spit like dudes. Before them her favorite rapper had been Roxanne Shanté.

Over the years, Kennedy had honed her rap skills. She'd even appeared on several mix tapes. An excellent writer, she would have made a great female rapper. She was the total package: she was pretty, she could flow, and she had a presence that commanded attention.

Those dreams now seemed like a lifetime ago. Watching her sisters mingle brought her back to reality. The two glasses of champagne Kennedy had drunk were making her feel a little light-headed. She laughed at herself. *I'm up in here drinking like I ain't on crazy meds.*

Kennedy looked gorgeous. Yatta had picked out her clothes when she caught her trying to wear all black, digging in Kennedy's closet until she found some color. She outfitted Kennedy in a burgundy leather button-up blouse, a crisp blue-jean micro miniskirt, and a pair of matching burgundy knee-high stiletto boots. Kennedy's hair was braided straight back in cornrows that hung down to the middle of her back. Her makeup was immaculate. Still afraid to show her eyes, she wore a pair of tinted brown-and-gold Chanel frames.

All sorts of famous men had been hitting on Kennedy all night—actors, rappers, CEOs, singers, and athletes. To her sisters' dismay, she didn't give any of them the time of day. There was one guy, though, who caught her eye.

For another minute or so, Kennedy tried to figure out what it was about him that made her want him. There was nothing special about the guy's gear. He had on the regular rapper/block-boy gear. That is, an oversize white T-shirt, baggy blue Evisu jeans, and an iced-out platinum chain. Maybe it was the way he was watching her from under the brim of the two-tone, red-and-white Philadelphia 76ers hat he wore.

Kennedy knew that he was watching and whispering about her to his man. This made her move in a more delicate and sexy way. What she didn't know was that he was trying to gather his strength to walk over and talk to her. All night he'd watched her turning away famous men. He figured, *What chance do I have?*

He finally stepped away from his crew, whom he'd been holding up the wall with, and stepped to Kennedy. "Can I get you another drink?"

Although nervous inside, Kennedy kept it short, with an attitude, and answered, "No."

"Can I talk to you for a minute?"

"Can you?"

"Yo, shorty, what's up with all the hostility. I just wanted to holla at you. You look real nice and shit, I guess you don't have the personality to match," he said, turning to walk away.

Kennedy reached out and grabbed his arm. "Look, I'm sorry. Right now all this isn't for me. I'm Kennedy, and you are?"

"I'm Chaz, but some people call me Schiz."

"Well, I like Chaz; that's my son's middle name."

"That's a good thing. Where you from?"

"Uptown. Where are you from, *Chaz*?"

"I'm from BK."

"Oh, what part?"

"Bed-Stuy, Lafayette Gardens."

There was an awkward moment of silence, and then Chaz

asked her, "What brings you here tonight? Do you work for one of the labels?"

"Nah, my sisters and I are guest of Hassan's."

"Oh, is that your man or something?"

"Not hardly. We're friends from the same hood."

The guy Chaz had been talking to earlier walked over to him. "Yo, come on, man. Strick is calling for you."

"Aight, Rob, tell him I'm coming. Let me finish up here." He turned his attention back to Kennedy. "Ma, can we exchange numbers?"

Kennedy hesitated, but there was something about him. "Sure." They both pulled out their two-way pagers. Chaz smiled at her. "I love a woman up on her technology. Beam me your information."

Rob interrupted them again. "Come on, man, we have to go now!"

"Chill, I'm coming right now. Kennedy, I'll call you tomorrow. Maybe we can go out for lunch or something." Chaz was whisked away immediately, followed by ten guys.

Kneaka and Yatta walked over to Kennedy. "Who was that?" Yatta asked.

"I don't know him. He said his name is Chaz."

"He looks real familiar. Chaz must be pretty special to get Miss Thang's number," Kneaka teased.

Kennedy rolled her eyes at Kneaka. "Look, Has is about to perform."

"I'm sure you've seen him perform a million times," Yatta said, with enough humor to make even Kennedy laugh.

"Look, we can talk about all this later, because after this, I'm leaving."

After Hassan left the stage, Kennedy walked over to him and waited patiently. Every time he turned to talk to her, someone else vying for his attention would grab him. Finally she grabbed him and hugged him. "Thanks so much for inviting us. I have to get home now."

"I wanted you to come home with me."

"Not on a school night. I have to get the kids ready in the morning."

"Can I come to your crib?"

"I don't care. How long are you going to be?"

"I'm leaving here in twenty minutes. I just want to see this next kid perform."

As Kennedy and her sisters headed for the exit, Derrick "Strick" Strickland, the CEO of T.O.N.Y records, was onstage giving a speech about his new protégé. "After a vicious bidding war with other great labels, we finally got this talented young man over at Top Of New York Records. He brings a very refreshing flavor to the label. And following in the path of other great Harlem and Brooklyn relationships, such as Puff and Big, Dame and Jay, I can comfortably say this will be another great one. So without further ado, give it up for Schiz."

Kennedy almost tripped going out the door. Kneaka smiled from ear to ear. "I told y'all he looked familiar. I saw him in *The Source*."

Kennedy took one look back at the stage. *Boy, I sure do know how to pick 'em. Always the ones running game.*

Every morning after dropping the kids at school, Kennedy and Yatta would retreat to one of their homes and share their morning routine. That routine included drinking coffee, reading the papers, and talking. On this Monday morning they were ironing out Thanksgiving plans; the holiday was only a week away.

Kennedy had been pondering what her next move in the game would be. Before hooking up with Petey, Yatta had been a hustler's dream. She could move any product given to her. Drug dealers who wanted to hustle upstate or outside of New York would send Yatta to get in good with the locals. Once she found out how the town ran, they would come in and lock it down.

Naturally, Kennedy sought out her advice. Yatta was reading the *New York Post,* sipping coffee from a small blue-and-white paper cup, from the corner bodega. Kennedy was reading an article in the *Daily News* that had captivated her. The article was about students from New York attending college out of state. They were getting money by buying wholesale guns down south and in the Midwest, then defacing the serial numbers. They would sell them in New York at half the retail price and still make a good profit. The only flaw in their plan was that defacing the gun no longer concealed the serial numbers. New technology allowed the police to raise and look at the numbers.

"Yatta, did you read this article about these college kids running the guns?"

"Yeah, I read about they dumb asses."

"They only dumb 'cause they bought the guns in their own names."

Yatta could look in Kennedy's eyes and tell she was scheming on something. "Kennedy, what are you thinking?"

"I'm thinking I need a new hustle. My expense money is getting low. I refuse to start dipping in my stash—my stocks and bonds or my mutual funds."

"How bad is it? Do you need me to front you some dough?"

"Nah, it's not that bad. I'm sitting decent. I was thinking about getting back into the dope game. All that shit is on fire right now after Bin Laden's ass came through. I bumped into Noodles the other day and he had the nerve to ask me to start running bricks for him again."

"What did you say?"

"I told him, if I did, I need five thousand per brick and it's a five-brick minimum. And I need five thousand for any off weeks."

"Why don't you take some of your money and go back to college? If you get out the game now, you'll come out on top."

"Don't start with that school shit, Mommy number two."

"Why not?"

" 'Cause school just ain't for me, man."

"Go for something you like. How come you don't get back into your writing? You could even start writing music again. There's a lot of money in that shit. You could even start rapping again; get Hassan to put you on."

The conversation was cut short by the ringing of Kennedy's cell phone. "Hello?"

"Can I speak to Kennedy?"

"Who is this?"

"This is Chaz. Is she available?"

With a hint of sarcasm in her voice, she answered, "This is she."

"What's good, ma?"

"What brings this call a week later?"

"Let me tell you, ma. As if my life is not complicated enough right now, my two-way froze up on me. I had to send it off to the company to be fixed. I just got it back today."

"Is that so?"

"Yes, *that* is so. I'm sneaking into the city in a minute. I wanted to go get something to eat."

"Is that an invitation for me to join you?"

"That was kind of the point."

Kennedy debated on it in her head for a few seconds. "Yeah, we can have lunch. Where do you want me to meet you at?"

"I can pick you up."

"How do you know I want you to know where I live?"

"Aight, ma, I'm feeling that. Meet me in an hour at Carmine's."

"See you in an hour."

Kennedy, usually not one to let her feelings show, closed the phone with a smile on her face. Yatta could not help but notice her sister's instant mood change. "What are you smiling so hard for?"

"What? Ain't nobody smiling hard. That was that boy Chaz from the party. I'm going to meet him for lunch."

"You? Going out? This sounds promising. And please don't wear black."

"This sounds promising for what? I'm not trying to turn this into anything else. I'm never loving another nigga hard, *true story.*"

She is prettier than I remember, Chaz thought as the hostess directed Kennedy to his table. Kennedy had chosen a hunter-green sweater, butterscotch leather pants, and boots. She wore her hair hanging, the front pulled back by a clip in the top middle of her head.

Chaz stood up and embraced her. "How you feeling? You look real nice today."

"Thank you. I'm doing okay. And how are you?"

"I'm good. I can't complain."

After ordering the food, Chaz started with the twenty questions. "So, mystery lady, I tried to do a background search on you and came up empty."

"That's what you get for being *nosy.*"

"So what do you *do*?"

"I'm a businesswoman."

"What type of business?"

"*Business.*"

Chaz laughed, showing off his immaculate teeth.

"What are you laughing at?" Kennedy asked, becoming annoyed.

"That's the same answer I used to give when I hustled."

Kennedy blushed. "So when were you going to tell me who you were?"

"Why? Would you have given me more play, instead of attitude?"

"No, I would have given you more attitude."

"Why?"

" 'Cause, I already did your type."

"*My type?*"

"Yes, *your type.*"

"And what is that?"

"Street niggas, athletes, rappers . . . et cetera, et cetera. They're all the same."

"That's kind of harsh, ma. I'm not even going to touch that one."

Kennedy, knowing how to pose questions without stating the obvious, asked him, "So, do you have any kids?" She thought to herself, *What I really mean is, do you have an overdramatic baby mother or mothers?*

It wasn't that easy to get over on Chaz. He already knew what she was trying to ask. "Yes, I have two daughters. They're eight and six years old. And no, I'm not with their mother.

"What's the story with you and your baby's daddy?"

"Ain't no story. He's in prison doing a five-to-ten."

"Are you bidding it out with 'im?"

"Hell no, *see him when they free him.*"

"Damn, baby girl, that's ugly."

"We were not together when I got pregnant. He treated me

like shit while I was pregnant, and after I birthed his son, he denied him without ever seeing him. If he'd done right by his son, he wouldn't be locked up now."

"How do you figure?" Chaz asked with a confused expression on his face.

"It's very simple. If he had done right by his child, bad things would not have happened to him."

The waitress set their drinks in front of them. Chaz took a sip of his tea before speaking. "Damn, that's deep. So it's just you and your son?"

"No, I have three other kids."

Chaz's face looked like he was searching for the nearest exit.

Kennedy took a long swig of her strawberry lemonade before speaking again. "I didn't mean to alarm you." She laughed. "I can tell by the look on your face what you're thinking. Don't stress yourself. I adopted my little cousins after their mother passed away."

When the words escaped her lips, Chaz breathed a sigh of relief. "I'm sorry to hear that. Was she sick?"

Kennedy opened her mouth, but nothing came out. Suddenly tears were rolling down her face. She found herself still unable to speak about Nina's death without crying.

"Kennedy, are you okay?" Chaz asked.

After taking five deep breaths, she was able to speak. "Yeah, I'm fine. I guess I'm still not over losing Nina. We were really close and it has been so hard the last few months."

Chaz and Kennedy sat and conversed for two hours after eating. Kennedy told him everything about her and Nina's relationship up until the day Nina died. He shared his feelings about how his life had changed since he got his record deal. "Ma, everything is so crazy right now. I mean, I'm not complaining. I just thought once I was getting that legal paper, shit would be gravy."

He looked at her and shook his head. Just talking about it frustrated him. "When I was in the streets, I broke day almost every day. Now there are days I don't even see my house. My baby mother act like I wasn't getting money before. Now every time she call, it's about money. And niggas that I could have sworn were thorough be on my dick like a bitch."

The conversation would have carried on for hours if Chaz's producer had not called and reminded him that he was two hours late for his session. He walked Kennedy to her truck and was impressed by her choice of wheels. They hugged and promised to see each other the next day.

Later that night, around 1 A.M., Chaz dialed Kennedy's number.

She answered on the third ring. "Hello?"

"Ma, I can't wait until tomorrow. I need to see you now."

"Come on over."

Upon entering Kennedy's home a short time later, Chaz was further impressed. He liked the vintage white chaise, chairs, and oversize beige upholstered sofa that sat in the living room. He fell in love with the black-and-white poster-size picture of Kennedy and Jordan. In the picture, Kennedy was nude from the waist up. Jordan was completely nude and Kennedy held him so that his tiny body covered her breasts. The picture was tastefully done. "You have a nice home, Kennedy. I might have to hire you to decorate my new crib in Jerz."

Kennedy liked conversing with Chaz as much as he liked conversing with her. It felt like they had known each other for years. She even found it easy to talk about Pretty Boy's death, something she rarely discussed with anyone except Big Ma.

Chaz even shared his feelings about growing up without his mother. "She was always in and out of rehab. Then one day she killed a white executive. She said he was trying to rape her.

What's a black junkie's word against a rich white man? My mother was sentenced to fifteen years. She came home last year." He took in a deep breath, like it was too heavy to even talk about. "She came home last year," he repeated. "I looked out for her. I put her in a nice apartment out in Canarsie and bought her a Honda Accord. I never want to see her turn into that junkie from my childhood memories. I keep money in her pockets and food in her fridge. I don't want her to have any reason to run back to the streets. I'm trying to build a relationship with her. That's something we never had."

Kennedy listened intently, thinking, *I could never live without my mother.* They were still talking as the sun was coming up. Kennedy never brought any men around Jordan, but she knew Chaz was tired. "You can lie on my bed. I'll sleep on the couch in my room. You have to stay in the room. I have to wake the kids up in two hours and I don't want them to see you."

"Are you coming to my house?" Yatta asked Kennedy when they were returning from taking the kids to school.

"Not this morning, sister. I have company."

"Who?"

"Chaz, nosy."

"Say word." Yatta was shocked. She had expected Kennedy to say Hassan.

"He came over to talk to last night. We didn't go to sleep until this morning."

"I bet y'all didn't."

"Now, you know it wasn't like that. Anyway, I'll be over when he leaves."

Kennedy returned home to find Chaz already awake. He was in the bathroom washing his face. She walked up behind him. "You leaving me already?"

"Yeah. Do you have any extra toothbrushes?"

"Look in the medicine cabinet."

"I'm sorry, ma, but I have an important session this morning. You can come to the studio with me if you want."

"Nah, I don't want to come through and take your shine," Kennedy said jokingly.

"Take my shine. How?"

"When I get on the mike."

"Quit playing, girl, you can't spit."

"Yes I can!"

"Let me hear something."

Kennedy smiled and began rhyming. "These chicks are quarter water I'm Cristal's daughter/I'm coppin' bricks they coppin' quarters/That's ounces, OT when I bounces/In the six with my One Forty-first cuties/And I meant OC we out the country/New York chicks in Atl actin' country?/They fuckin' dummies!/Unlimited accounts in Prada/Cash we got a lotta/Mischievous fam fifty mil or more you're just a low-price whore/And don't come to me with dick on your breath/I rocks it to death/Jacob on my wrist glistening, turns your eyes to slits/I burn like Al Green and grits/Hard nipples firm tits/Your man wanted to lick my clit/Feel some type of way?/Then see me bitch/One Forty-first and Eighth find me and big Sanchez/Every nigga we date get cash or move that weight!"

Chaz stood there, stunned. "I knew it was more to you than you were telling. That's why you were at the party. What label are you signed to?"

"I'm not signed to anyone, true story. I gave all that up after Pretty Boy died."

"You shouldn't have. You sound like you have skills from that little bit I heard."

"All of that was a lifetime ago. I have three new priorities now."

"I'm trying to make you my new priority," Chaz said with a sneaky smile.

Kennedy walked him to the door. He turned to her. "Seriously, ma, I'm very particular when it comes to chicks. But you I'm interested in. I want to see you a lot more."

Blushing, she answered, "I definitely think we can arrange that. Now go on and get to the studio. I don't want to be the reason you're late."

"Believe me, it would be a good reason," he said, kissing her on the cheek and wrapping her in a tight hug.

"Bye, Chaz. Call me later." She watched as he walked up the street and got into his car. Kennedy was impressed with his black CL600. It was beautiful, with sheer black tints on the window, black leather interior, and eighteen-inch Mercedes rims.

Chaz couldn't get Kennedy off his mind as he sat in traffic on the FDR. He sang along with the new Faith Evans CD. *"Is it too soon to love you? When I just met you the other day. Why do I believe it's perfect?"*

Kennedy was blasting the same song from her stereo. She was in the shower thinking of Chaz and singing along. *"Could it be I'm scared to take a chance? Thinking we are moving fast and I don't know where we stand. I don't know where we stand."*

Dreams Do Come True

A month had passed since Kennedy's first date with Chaz. Their relationship blossomed. Just when they'd gotten into a comfortable routine of seeing each other on a daily basis, Chaz had to go to work in California for three weeks. Kennedy hated that he would be gone for the holidays.

The night before Chaz was to leave for California, he and Kennedy went through their normal ritual: Chaz came over after the kids went to bed. He ate his plate that Kennedy set aside for him every night. They watched a few television shows, the news, and a DVD. Afterward they talked until they fell asleep. Usually Kennedy got up in the morning and took the kids to school while Chaz slept.

This morning, when the alarm clock woke Kennedy, she sat up and did not see Chaz. *I know this nigga did not leave without waking me up and we're not going to see each other for three whole weeks.* She was so busy fussing in her head she almost missed the small red box sitting on the pillow.

Kennedy reached over and picked up the box. A small piece of paper was attached to it. It read simply: *Merry Christmas, Chaz.* Kennedy cracked the box like a little girl and peeked in. Inside were a pair of two-carat solitaire diamond earrings. *Oh my, these are beautiful. He is too sweet; he might just fuck around and make me love him.*

Kennedy picked up the house phone and dialed Chaz's number. When his voice mail picked up, she looked at her diamond Chopard watch. *He must be on the plane already.* As she waited for the beep, she looked down at the earrings and began to smile again. "Hi, Chaz; it's Kennedy. I got the earrings you left me. Thank you so much, they are so beautiful. Call me when you touch down."

The relationship was new and Kennedy didn't know quite what she should buy him for Christmas. She decided that some nice clothing would make a great gift. She told herself, *I'll buy him some things that are not too significant but not too insignificant.* So she went to Philadelphia and purchased him three Mitchell & Ness throwback jerseys and fitted baseball caps to match.

To Kennedy, the jerseys and hats were not significant enough. She wanted to buy him more. She went to Gucci and purchased Chaz a belt, a wallet, and a pair of sneakers. *I still need to get him one more thing,* she thought. Kennedy found him a beautiful blue Lacoste sweater. She bought him a pair of blue-and-green alligator sneakers to match. *Now, that is significant.*

Chaz was getting some of the best rest he had gotten since he'd arrived in L.A. when the loud banging on the front door of the three-story rental condo interrupted his peaceful sleep. He continued to lie in bed, hoping one of the other ten guys would answer the door. The knocking started all over again. "Damn, I know them muthafuckas hear the door."

Chaz opened the door just in time to see a FedEx deliveryman returning to his truck. He yelled out to him, "Yo, my man, you got something for this address?"

"Yes, I'm looking for Chaz Harris."

"That's me."

"I need your signature here." He handed Chaz the electronic clipboard. "I would have left it by the door, but it was signature release only."

"Thanks, my man, good lookin' out."

"Merry Christmas, Mr. Harris."

"Same to you."

Chaz retrieved the box from the man and walked back into the house. *Who in the hell sent me something way out here?* he wondered as he went to the kitchen to get a knife to open the box.

Chaz smiled when he saw the note sitting on top. *Merry Christmas! I hope we can bring the New Year in together. With much love, Kennedy!*

Chaz took each item out of the box, one at a time, getting more and more excited about each one. He grabbed his cell phone, scrolled down to Kennedy's name, and pressed talk. She picked up on the third ring. "What up?"

"You, ma! Thanks for my gifts. That was so nice of you. No other girl, not even my baby mother, ever did anything nice like this."

"You're welcome. I'm glad you like everything."

"I would fly to NC from here, but I have to get back to New York to record the last four songs by the fourth of January."

"I'll be back in New York on New Year's Eve. I'm letting the kids spend the rest of their vacation down here. So we can have some time alone."

"That sounds like a winner, ma." Chaz looked up to see his road manager and childhood friend, Rob, coming down the stairs.

"You know you have to be at the studio in thirty minutes."

"Nigga, I know that." Chaz rolled his eyes, turning his attention back to his conversation with Kennedy. "Aight, ma-ma, I have to go take a quick shower so I can get to the studio. But again, good looking out on the gifts."

"You got that, baby boy. Call me when you have time."

Rob was busy rummaging through Chaz's gifts. "Ol' girl spent some serious dough on your ass. You must have blew her back the fuck out!"

"Come on, man, it ain't even like that."

Rob studied Chaz's face for a few moments. "Hold the fuck up. You bought those expensive-ass earrings for a bitch you not even fucking?"

Chaz became tight in a matter of seconds. He stood up, coming face-to-face with Rob. "Don't ever disrespect her again. And don't worry about what I buy with my money."

"My bad. I didn't know it was like that. I thought she was some groupie."

"No, my man, she ain't nobody groupie. She got her own shit, and if she didn't, I would still fuck with her off of GP."

January fourth had come and gone. It was the fifth and Chaz's CD was lacking its last track, a duet with a female rapper named Lady Heroin. Chaz, Strick, Rob, and Shy, the producer, sat around the mixing board. Chaz was mad because Lady Heroin's label would not give her clearance to do the record. "Can't we get somebody else? Who the fuck they think that bitch is anyway, Foxy or Kim? If anything, I would be helping *her* career."

"Calm down, man," Shy told Chaz. "I'm going to see if we can get Eve or Remy. But I think both of them are on the road and we need to get this done today. I don't care if we have to get a nobody and write her lyrics for her."

"Who else do you have in mind, Shy?" Strick asked.

"I need a real fly chick with that attitude to match. I mean, I want her to be able to stand up to Chaz on the track. And this shit is going to be the first single, so she has to be a little hot to make jump off."

Everyone quietly thought of other female rappers who could be called on. "Oh shit! I know who we could get," Chaz blurted out.

"Who?" everybody else asked at the same time.

"My girl. I can get her to do the track. She can spit."

"Oh boy, here he goes again about his imaginary girlfriend that nobody else has seen." Rob chuckled.

"Fuck you, fat boy. Anyway," he said, ignoring Rob and focusing his attention on Strick and Shy, "ma spit like a nigga and she a little fly uptown chick."

Strick thought about it. "Who is she signed to?"

"Nobody. She not even trying to get on. She used to rap when she was younger. She did a few mix tapes throughout the city."

"Call her. 'Cause this shit needed to be done yesterday."

Rob smiled at Chaz. "Yeah, call her, man, so we can see if she really exists."

After convincing Kennedy that he had an emergency at the studio, Chaz went downstairs to meet her. When she pulled up he immediately went into begging mode. "Ma, please do me this one favor. I need you to get on track with me. This CD is starting to stress me. I just want it to be over with. I would rather be spending time with you and be able to hang out with my daughters before I go on this promo tour."

Kennedy stared at him with a serious expression on her face. Then she broke a smile. "I'll do it for you, booby."

Chaz reached over and hugged her. "That's what's up, ma. Good looking out."

• • •

When Chaz entered the studio with Kennedy, it was plain to see why he'd kept her hidden. The way her Seven jeans hugged her ass made the men drool in her face. Strick could tell she had a style all her own. Kennedy was rocking a white fitted tee, a blue mink baseball jacket and cap, and a pair of blue Dolce & Gabbana lace-up stiletto boots.

"She is perfect," Shy said. "Now, if she can rap like you say she can, we can pull this shit off." He played the beat for Kennedy and explained the concept of the song to her. "It's basically a ghetto breakup song. Chaz has been caught cheating on the girl who has been down with him for years and helped him accumulate his wealth."

"I think I can put something together for that."

Kennedy listened to the beat a few more times before writing her verse. She wrote several different verses before she came up with one that she felt fit the beat. "Aight, Shy, I'm ready."

"Get in the booth and get this shit poppin'." Shy called everyone into the recording room as Kennedy was stepping into the recording booth.

Being inside the booth felt natural to Kennedy. *This feels so right.* She placed the headphones on her head, then looked out through the glass and locked eyes with Chaz. He smiled at her and winked. She blushed and winked back.

Kennedy said a quick Hail Mary while Shy cued up the instrumentals. She closed her eyes so she couldn't see the eyes watching her. Her heart was racing as she began to rap, but it all came out cool and confident. "When I met you, you had nada, zip, zilch, zero/Not a dollar on a fuckin' hero/You was huggin' the block servin' rocks/Lettin' every other crackhead suck your cock/That shit had to stop/Started rollin' wit' me/Took you from pushin' OZs of trees to powder-white Ks/Niggas never saw the likes of me/The way I left 'em duct tape in they Vs/On the strength of me you rock that platinum shit/Fuck Nikes, nigga, I put you in Prada kicks/Off of all my trips cocaine numbing my clit/Now you OT fuckin' with some next bitch/Now you suck my dick you leaving all my shit/Plus my name still on the title to that hot-ass Six."

Strick was feeling Kennedy's flow. He wanted to hear more. When she stepped out of the booth he told her, "I want to hear you spit some more. Shy, throw on some different beats."

Kennedy rapped different songs off the top of her head for the next thirty-five minutes, songs that she'd written over the last ten years. Strick fell in love with her flow, too. As she continued to rap he saw a star in the making. When the tenth beat finished and she stopped rapping, Strick told her, "I think you're a perfect package, ma. I want to sign you to a deal. I can turn you into an overnight celebrity."

"I don't know if I have time for a music career now. I'm raising four kids."

"Look at it this way: you'll never have to worry about being unemployed."

"No offense, but I'm not worried about that now."

"I guarantee you that I can make you see more money than any other female rapper out right now."

Before she could come back with a quick response, she heard Nina's voice in her head. *Ken-Ken, this is your dream, ma. This is your chance to leave the streets behind.* Kennedy snapped out of her trance, "Aight, Strick, I'm game," she said as she walked back into the booth to redo her verses.

Strick told Chaz and Shy, "That girl has all the qualities of a star. I'm going to make her one. That's my word."

Two weeks later, Kennedy was quietly celebrating her birthday with Chaz. He had taken her to a posh little resort in upstate New York. Chaz was falling harder for Kennedy every day. She was so laid-back—she didn't take herself too seriously. Chaz loved those things about her, but he especially loved her sense of humor. Earlier in the day, she had dragged him up to the ski slopes, even though she couldn't ski herself. Every time she fell down, she would fall out laughing.

The night of her birthday, they dined at the resort's four-star restaurant. For the first time Chaz was nervous about giving a female a gift. From his point of view, Kennedy was independent and could purchase anything she desired herself. After they finished eating, he handed her a card. "Baby girl, I didn't know what to get you. I know you like to shop so . . . I thought this would be a bangin'-ass gift."

Kennedy opened the card; it contained three gift certificates of one thousand dollars each for Barneys. The card read: *Baby girl, I have never met anyone like you. You are so beautiful inside and out. Happy birthday, li'l mama, I pray that we will share many more.*

The lyrics to an old Etta James song came to her. *"At last, my love has come along. My lonely days are over."* A single tear ran down the right side of her face. "Thank you so much, Chaz. I love the gift, but I love the card more."

"Why are you crying?"

"You make me so happy—something I haven't been in a long time. I think you gonna fuck around and make me fall in love with you."

"Ma, you know you got my heart."

The wait staff came toward the table singing "Happy Birthday." The first waiter was carrying a cake with twenty-three burning candles. When they finished singing, Kennedy was blushing red with embarrassment. She took a deep breath and blew out her candles. Chaz asked her, "What did you wish for?"

High off the four martinis she had drunk, she answered, with sex in her eyes, *"You."*

Just then Chaz's two-way went off; he opened it and read it.

"I'll be right back. I need to go up to the room and use the phone." He looked up and noticed the "negro, please" look Kennedy was giving him. "Ken-Ken, you know, don't neither one of our cell phones work good out here."

Kennedy eased up a little. Chaz slid her his platinum American Express. "Go ahead and pay the bill. I don't want these assholes thinking I'm running out on it."

After twenty-five minutes and two more martinis, she was growing impatient and returned to the room. Standing by the door, she heard Chaz yelling. Kennedy unlocked the door and cracked it open so she could hear what he was saying.

"Fuck you, too. Yo, you are the most simplest *bitch* I know. Next time anybody in my family come to get my daughters, you better let them go. You are so petty! All the fucking money I give you, B. You better learn the rules to this shit. 'Cause in a minute I'm gonna file for custody of my daughters and your ass won't see another piece of my paper."

He slammed the phone down, sat down on the couch, and dropped his head into the palms of his hands. Kennedy walked over and stood next to him. "Chaz, what was that about?"

He was a little startled. He hadn't heard her come in. "Nothing, man, my dumb-ass baby mother. She wouldn't let my sister and mother pick up the girls today all because I left her five Gs instead of eight. She pissed because that delayed her in getting her furniture."

Kennedy didn't press him for any more information. She had never seen him this mad before. *I hope it's really over between you and her,* she thought. She sat down next to him and wrapped her arms around him. "Let me take your mind off of that. Here, I brought you a bottle of Grey Goose from the bar." She fixed him a vodka straight and poured a cranberry juice and vodka for herself.

"Here, have a drink. Get your mind off that bullshit, baby."

Kennedy pressed play on the CD player. Mary J. Blige's *No More Drama* CD began playing. She sat down on the couch next to Chaz and raised her glass to him. "Here's to no more drama."

He sat his drink down and laid his head in her lap. Kennedy could feel how tense he was; she massaged his temples as they talked and listened to the music. *I like this song,* Chaz thought. "What track is this?"

"I think it's number three."

"I'm feeling Mary on this one. Let's just steal away."

"No, I'm feeling Mary on *this* one," Kennedy said, picking up the remote and skipping over to track thirteen, "Never Been." By no means was Kennedy a singer, but she leaned over and playfully sang into his ear: *"Pardon me, excuse me, I can't help it. But I see the energy between you and me and I'm selfish. Don't want no other girls calling you never ever. 'Cause I want us to stay together forever."* She kissed the top of his ear and licked his lobe with the tip of her tongue. Chaz's dick shot straight up.

Finally—the moment they had been waiting for. Kennedy had been craving him sexually, but she hadn't wanted to seem too forward. From their conversations, he could tell that she had been hurt in the past. He didn't want to rush her into anything or make her feel obligated to have sex with him.

Chaz grabbed her hand and stood up, pulling her up with him. He led her over to the bed, then pulled her in close and began kissing her as he unzipped her suede tube dress and let it fall to her feet. Kennedy reached down and unbuckled his pants. He stepped out of them and moved back to pull off his shirt. Kennedy bent over and unzipped her boots.

"No, leave them on," Chaz told her, removing her strapless bra while kissing her neck and shoulders. He laid her flat on the bed and pulled her thong off. "I just want to touch you." He ran his hands over her entire body, massaging every curve and taking in the tender feel of her skin. Chaz rubbed her inner thigh, running his hand upward until he found what he wanted. He parted her vagina lips with his middle finger and gently pushed it inside of her. The wetness and tightness of her inner walls aroused him further.

His hands alone felt so good that Kennedy thought, *He can skip the foreplay and just slide it inside of me. God, please don't let him have a little dick.* She slipped her hands inside of his boxers. *Oh shit, he's packing. Maybe a little too much for me.*

Chaz continued to bring her pleasure with his hand as he planted wet tongue kisses on her neck. He worked his way down to her nipples, sucking and gently biting them. He knew exactly what he was doing, circling his finger around inside her and gently stroking her clit with his thumb. The way she was grinding on his finger, he knew he was bringing her to ecstasy.

I am about to cream all over his hands. "Oh, Chaz," she shrieked while coming all over his hand. In one swift motion he removed his boxers and slid his large dick inside of her. Kennedy winced a little as he went deeper. "You okay, baby girl?" he whispered.

"Yes, please don't stop." The feeling of him going inside her while she was coming was like nothing that she had ever felt before. Chaz wrapped his hands around her three-inch heels and pushed her legs back until she was spread-eagled. He stroked her insides, dipping up and down so smoothly it looked like he was dancing. Chaz rolled her onto her stomach without pulling out. Kennedy let out a giggle, thinking, *Wow, that's one move I never experienced before.*

He pulled her body to the edge of the bed until she was standing. The stilettos made her ass sit up perfectly as she bent over on the bed with chest lying flat against the sheets. The visual alone almost caused Chaz to cum early. He squeezed each cheek as his strokes picked up more and more pace. The more comfortable Kennedy became with the size of his dick, the more she got into the rhythm of his strokes and began to throw it back at him.

Letting her know that he was still in control, using his body, Chaz laid her flat onto the bed and continued to pump all his strength into her. He licked the back of her neck, causing her to cum all over again. The liquid exploding onto him from her was so warm there was no way he could continue to hold on. "Ma, your pussy feels so good."

"So does your dick. Are you ready to *cum*?" she asked, tightening her muscles.

"I am now." He rolled her onto her side, pulling her leg up to her chest. His strokes became faster and longer. Kennedy grabbed his free hand and put her mouth around his middle finger and began sucking it. Chaz's entire body shut down as he bust a long hard nut inside of her. Kennedy gently slid her body from beneath him and turned to face him. She kissed him on the cheek.

"Ma, that was so beautiful," Chaz told her.

"Was it worth the wait?"

"Of course it was. Shit. Was I worth the wait?"

"You were worth every single minute. Now, are you ready for round two?"

Kennedy had never imagined that recording that song would change the course of her life. Funk Flex introduced the song to New York City and he showed it so much love. Strick called Kennedy, excited. "Yo, Ken-Ken, Flex is dropping crazy bombs on the song. Mad A 'n' Rs are two-waying me wanting to know who you are and if you have a deal yet. Didn't I tell you I was going to make you a star?"

Strick wanted to get the visuals out to the public immediately while the song was new and hot. He knew that a video would catapult the song to the top of the charts. He scheduled the filming of the video for three weeks after the single was released to radio.

Kennedy arrived at the video set at 5 A.M. It was her first taste of what the music industry was really like. After her hair had been flat-ironed and her makeup was done, the stylist Strick had hired for the shoot arrived. On sight, Kennedy was not feeling her. The biggest problem she had with the girl was the way she was hanging all over Chaz when they came through the door and laughing extra hard at his jokes.

Strick walked the stylist over to Kennedy. "Ken-Ken, this is your stylist, Tameeka."

"Hi, Tameeka."

"It's nice to finally meet you. I brought you some great things to wear today. I'm going to lay them out on the table so we can go through them." She yelled over her shoulder, "Chaz, can you bring those bags over here, sweetie?"

Kennedy rolled her eyes, thinking, *Sweetie? This bitch must be trying to test my fuckin' patience.* Chaz walked over, sipping on a large morir soñando. He stopped in front of Kennedy. "What's up, baby girl?" He bent over to kiss her on the cheek.

Kennedy moved her face so that he wouldn't make contact. "So you just now making your way over here to speak? I didn't sleep with you last night."

"Come on, Ken-Ken, I know you saw everybody stopping me to talk."

"Yeah, but you sure made your way over here when your little friend called you. Go on over there and help her with her bags, *sweetie.*"

Chaz walked away mumbling, "Here she go with the bull-shit."

Once Kennedy's hair was finished, she walked over to the wardrobe area. She looked at Strick and frowned. "I'm not wearing none of this wack-ass shit."

"What?" Tameeka squawked.

Kennedy leaned back and placed her right hand on her hip, using her left to punctuate her words. "You heard me the first time; I'm not wearing none of this cheap shit. Strick, how much money did you give her to work with? It couldn't have been a lot 'cause this shit look like it came off of Fordham Road."

Tameeka rolled her eyes and said, "Well, I never."

"And you never will . . . dress me, that is. Strick, you couldn't get Misa, June, or whoever dresses Charlie Baltimore? I got shoes that cost more than all this shit put together. You could've told me to bring something out of my closet. She can dress them other chicks," Kennedy said, pointing to the extras, "but she not dressing me."

Tameeka, growing tired of the insults, told Strick, "I'm good at what I do. I don't have to take this shit from some wannabe diva."

"Chill. Y'all just be easy," Strick pleaded, standing between the two women.

I'm not trying to hear this shit Strick kicking. Kennedy opened her cell phone and began dialing. "I'm not even entertaining her last remark. I'm calling my sister. Trust, she can style circles around this bird." She waited for Yatta to answer. When she did, Kennedy could tell she'd been sleeping.

"Kennedy, it is early on a Saturday. What do you want?"

"I need you to get up and go to the Village to get me some clothes. 'Cause this shit this broad brought up in here is hideous."

Kennedy closed the phone. As she walked past Tameeka she told her, "Stick around. You could get an education in styling. And, Strick, I suggest you get a refund." She walked out into the cold winter air smiling.

She didn't know Chaz was walking behind her. "Kennedy, what the fuck is up with that jealous shit you just did?"

"That wasn't no jealous shit. I didn't like the clothes and now I don't like the bitch."

"I know what it might've looked like when we walked in, but she didn't know you was wifey."

"And why is that, Chaz? What am I, your dirty little secret?"

Chaz didn't say anything.

Kennedy stared at him, waiting for some type of answer. For the first time she let her insecurities show. "I knew this shit was going to happen if I started fucking with you."

"What shit, Kennedy? What the fuck are you talking about?"

"Chaz, I'm going to my trailer to lie down. Please show Yatta where I'm at when she gets here."

Kennedy turned and walked away. Chaz called out to her, but she kept walking, scared that if she turned around she would break down and cry.

Yatta showed up at Kennedy's trailer door with eight oversize bags from Limpas', Petit Peton, Versailles, and Shoe Fetish. Kennedy was so relieved. "Thank you so much for coming."

"It's nothing, li'l sis. Here, take some of the bags."

Strick walked in behind Yatta. "Is this little cutie your sister?"

"Yeah, this is Yatta, and Yatta, this Strick."

"It's nice to meet you, ma," Strick said, looking at Yatta like he wanted to eat her up.

Yatta returned an equally lustful look, which didn't go unnoticed by Kennedy. Strick loved the clothes that Yatta had purchased. He thought to himself, *I've found myself a new stylist and maybe a new shorty.*

All eyes were on Kennedy when she walked onto the video set. She was wearing a navy-blue leather hooded halter top. The matching skirt looked like a piece of loincloth. But her boots sent the outfit over the top; they were baby-blue-and-navy thigh-high stilettos.

Tameeka rolled her eyes at Kennedy and Yatta caught it. "What's her problem, Kennedy?" Yatta asked, pointing at Tameeka.

"That's the fake-ass stylist bitch I was telling you about."

"She *is* hideous and who the fuck she thought she was styling with that horrible dry wet-and-wavy weave?"

The two sisters fell out laughing. The director yelled out from his chair, "Everyone take your places."

Chaz walked onto the set followed by his usual entourage. He had a fresh haircut and his goatee was trimmed to perfection. His well-kept physique looked terrific in the Evisu sweater and jeans he wore. Even though she was still pissed, Kennedy couldn't help thinking, *My booby is fly as hell.* She wouldn't dare let him know that and rolled her eyes as he approached her.

"You feeling better?"

"I'm straight," she answered, with her nose in the air, as she walked away to take her place on the set.

Chaz looked over at Yatta. "What's good, ma?"

"My sister, and if you hurt her I'm going to fuck you up!"

The tension between Kennedy and Chaz made for a good video, given the point of the song. Kennedy was a natural in front of the camera. By midnight, she was tired and filming wasn't close to being over. She continued to put forth her best effort, even though her head was throbbing and her feet ached like hell.

Around 5 A.M. the director yelled, "It's a wrap."

I never knew I would be so happy to hear those three words, Kennedy thought as she washed the makeup off her face inside her trailer. She was so ready to get home to her bed. She threw on her clothes. The comfort of her Nike Air Max felt like good sex.

She gathered all of her things and rushed out the door to find Strick and Chaz standing outside.

Strick grabbed her and gave her a huge hug. "You did your thing today, ma, especially for your first video." He handed her a card. "This is a gift certificate for you to the Bella Spa. Take the next three days off and pamper yourself, 'cause next week we're kicking this shit into high gear. I'm talking 'bout performances, promo tours, and a whole lot of studio time."

"Thank you, Strick. This is so nice of you. Is the car service here yet?"

Chaz interrupted. "I told Strick to cancel your car. You can ride home with me, if that's okay with you."

"I don't care. I'm just ready to lie down."

Kennedy took off her coat and jeans, dropping both in the middle of Chaz's bedroom floor. She wasted no time getting into his king-size bed. She was drifting off as soon as her head hit the pillow. Chaz got into the bed and began rubbing on her thighs and kissing her neck. Kennedy groaned at him. "Not now, Chaz. I'm too tired."

"Turn around and look at me."

"What?"

"Look, I'm not those other niggas. I'm not cheating, I'm not lying, and I'm not going to leave you."

"You know, Chaz, it all sounds good. But I heard it all before."

So Emotional

"Auntie, Auntie, your video is number one on *106 and Park*."
Jazz ran into Kennedy's room, waking her up from some much-needed rest.

"It is! Okay, wake me up and let me know what number it is on *Direct Effect*." Kennedy rolled over and went back to her pill-induced sleep. Since the single had made it onto the *Billboard* Top Ten, her life was no longer her own and the road had become her new home.

Traveling, at first, was cool. Then came the stress. Chaz had his entire crew and she didn't have anyone. Kennedy missed her kids dearly, especially Jordan. Even more, she missed the quality time she and Yatta had begun spending together.

The worst part of being on the road was watching the groupies all over Chaz at the after-parties. After a while Kennedy started showing up at them and staying for one hour, which she was required to do by contract. Chaz told her, "You're being petty about the after-parties. If the groupies bother you that much, why don't you stay next to me during the parties?"

"Them hos don't give a fuck. If I'm standing next to you, they'll still try to suck your dick and tell me to hold it for them."

• • •

The after-party at Club Dream in Washington was the best so far, and Kennedy had consumed numerous alcoholic beverages. She found solace on the dance floor away from the VIP, Chaz, and his groupies. She'd even found a great dance partner, Drico.

Drico was from the Bronx. Kennedy had seen him a few times around New York at different events and parties. The familiarity and the liquor made her dance a little sexier and closer than usual. They were even whispering and laughing in each other's ears.

What the fuck? Chaz thought as he looked down from the VIP and saw Kennedy on the dance floor. *She done lost her fucking mind.* "Yo, I'm ready to go," he told his entourage. On the way out he yanked Kennedy from the dance floor.

Kennedy protested all the way to the parking lot. "Who said I was ready to go?"

"I said you was ready to go. You was being a little too cute dancing all close with that nigga. What was you doing dancing with another nigga anyway? As a matter of fact, don't dance with no more niggas."

"Chaz, who the fuck you think you talking to? I'm not your child and I don't say shit when these hos be grinding up against your dick night after night."

"Kennedy, don't start with that groupie shit again. Get your ass on the bus."

"Oh, you getting real offensive. Did I strike a guilty chord? You think I don't know you fucking them groupie-ass hos?"

"Damn, is it time for your period or something? Lately all you do is nag the hell out of me. You'll make a nigga cheat."

Kennedy knew Chaz was drunk, but she still took his comment to heart. "Oh well, if that's how you feel, baby boy, beat ya fuckin' feet, my man, 'cause I'll never beg a nigga to stay where he don't want to be."

"I didn't mean it that way, Kennedy."

"Whatever." Kennedy got onto the tour bus and didn't say a word to anyone on the ride to the hotel.

Once she was back in her room, she got all her bags together and called a cab. Kennedy hurried downstairs to the lobby, avoiding anyone from the tour. She had the cabdriver take her to the bus station, where bought a ticket for the 6 A.M. bus to New York.

When Kennedy arrived in front of her brownstone that morning, she instantly spotted the cream Bentley sitting out front. *Who the hell is this?* she wondered. She paid the cabdriver, retrieved her bags, and rushed inside. When she opened the door Strick and Yatta were sitting next to each other on the couch.

Yatta jumped up. "Ken, where have you been? Why didn't you let anyone on the tour know you were leaving? And why haven't you been answering your phone? Everyone's calling, worried about you."

"Damn, Yatta, slow down. I left my phone charger in the hotel room. My battery been dead since last night." Kennedy ignored Yatta's other questions and turned her attention to Strick. "What up? What you doing here?"

"I'm trying to figure out why my artists are pulling disappearing acts on the road."

Kennedy plopped down on her chaise and began to explain the previous night's events to Strick and Yatta. She went on to share how lonely and stressed she felt while out on the road.

Strick took everything Kennedy said into consideration before he began to speak. "Look, Ken, if it's one thing I know about you, I know you understand business. You have to apply the same rules to this industry that you apply to the streets. One of the most important rules is never let your emotions get in the way."

Kennedy knew that he was right, and that was the exact reason she had vowed to never fall in love. Her train of thought was *being all soft over a nigga is never good for business. If you're worried about where he at and what he's doing, you can't concentrate on what's most important—your money.* Now here she was so emotional over Chaz, totally disregarding her own number one rule.

Strick continued giving her his speech. "Ma, I'm not mad at you. I understand what you're going through. The next time you go out on the road, take a few of your girls with you so it's more comfortable for you. Is that straight with you?"

"That's what's up!"

"Aight, go get dressed. I want you to take a ride with me."

Kennedy sat down on the extra-soft leather inside the Bentley. She looked around the car and was thoroughly impressed. Strick noticed. "You like this?"

"Actually, now that I'm inside, I do. I mean, I always thought they were overrated; still do a little."

"I could see you in an Aston Martin."

"What's that?"

"The meanest luxury sports car. You would stop the show in that, ma. I can call up my car dealer and see if he can get you one."

"Nah, I'm cool. I can tell by the way you talking about it that it cost an arm and a leg."

"Did I say anything about you paying for it?"

Strick pulled his car into a garage on East Twenty-eighth Street. He still had not told Kennedy where they were going. Once the attendant took the car, he led her inside the office building next door.

"Strick, I trust you, but where are we going?"

"Fall back, Mama, it's a surprise."

"What kind of surprise? How do you know I even like surprises?"

"All women like surprises. And don't worry, it ain't nothing bad. Someone wants to do a song with you."

"Who?"

"Didn't I say it was a surprise?" He pushed the up button for the elevator; he gave her a taunting smile all the way to the tenth floor. When the doors opened they stepped off the elevator into the Hip Rock Studio. The receptionist buzzed them through the glass door and then through the steel door, which led to the recording rooms.

Kennedy smiled at the sight of Hassan bent over, enthralled in a game of C-Lo. She walked over and tapped him on his shoulder.

"Give me five minutes and I'll be ready to record my verse. I'm on a roll right now," Hassan responded, thinking it was the pesky studio engineer.

"You ain't winning no real money."

Hassan turned around, and when he saw Kennedy, he grabbed her and hugged her tight. "What's good, ma?"

"Ain't shit, playboy. You know me, just trying to maintain."

"You making big moves and not even hollering at your boy."

"Stop it, Hassan. You doing ten-million-dollar deals. I'm small potatoes to you."

"Well, you ready to jump on this track with us?"

"Who is us?"

"Me, S.C., Joaquin, and Kicks. Have you ever met them?"

"No."

"Let me introduce you to them."

Hassan led Kennedy into a mixing room where the three rappers were sharing a blunt. Hassan took care of all introductions.

Grindin' | 91

The three guys gave Kennedy a warm reception. They all told her they had her on various mix tapes and how they thought she had a bright career ahead of her. She was so happy to hear these things coming from three of her favorite veteran rappers.

Eight hours later, Kennedy had finally finished recording her verse and ad-libs. She stepped out of the booth and sat on the couch between Strick and the CEO of Vegas Records, Caz. "I'm done, finally!"

Caz looked at her and smiled. "I like you, ma; you a fly little bitch. Come holla at me if this nigga Strick not paying you your worth," he said with his overcocky demeanor.

Hassan and Strick laughed at the look on Kennedy's face. She had to admit she was a little amused by his cockiness, but too tired to indulge it. "I would love to stay and kick it with y'all, but I'm tired."

"Give me thirty minutes and I'll be ready," Strick told her.

"No, Strick, you stay. Can you give me thirty cash so I can get a cab uptown? I left my wallet in my other bag."

Before Strick could answer, Hassan grabbed Kennedy by the arm. "That's aight, Strick, I got her."

Strick watched them closely as they exited the room. Chaz was more than an artist to him; they had become close friends. He could tell from the way Hassan was acting that there was more to him and Kennedy than she had let on. Strick had no plans on running to tell Chaz anything, but he wasn't going to stand by and let his boy get played either. Kennedy wasn't flirting with Hassan. But Strick couldn't tell if that was because he was there or because whatever they might have had was really over.

In the elevator Hassan leaned up against Kennedy and wrapped his arms around her waist. "What's good wit' you? You not fucking wit' a nigga no more?"

"Come on, Has, you know I'm with Chaz."

Hassan backed away from her. "No, I didn't know."

"Now you do, and you know when I'm messing with someone that's the only one."

"I thought it was gonna be you and me."

"You can't be serious. How is it going to be you and me and you have a girl? I'm not into playing second to another bitch for the rest of my life."

"I'm not even wit' my baby's mom no more."

"Oh, so now she just your baby's mom."

The elevator door opened and Chaz was standing there. He observed the serious expressions on Kennedy and Hassan's faces. "What's up?"

"What are *you* doing here?" Kennedy asked.

"I came to meet Strick. Where were you on your way to?"

"Hassan was just walking me out to catch a cab."

Chaz reached out and gave Hassan a pound. "Good looking out, my man. I got it from here."

"It's nothing. Kennedy is my homegirl. We go way back," Hassan said with a sly smirk.

Chaz tried to talk to Kennedy about small things on the ride up-town, but she wasn't having it. He rubbed the top of her hand. "What's wrong? You still mad about that D.C. shit?"

"Ain't nothing wrong with me. I'm just tired and don't feel like talking."

"You always tired when it's convenient for your ass. But you revved up when it's time to get in my shit with your false accusations! I'm the one who should be pissed after your bullshit in D.C."

"Well, that's your business."

"I'm getting real sick of your smart-ass mouth, too."

"Why you still here, then, Chaz?"

"Maybe I'm still here 'cause I love you."

Hearing those three words made Kennedy's heart melt. She loved Chaz, too, but she wasn't about to let him know it. She had already let her guard down too much. "That's real *nice,* if you mean it."

Chaz pulled the car over in front of Kennedy's brownstone. She hopped out and turned to him. "You not coming up?"

"I don't have a reason, do I?"

"I *know* you're not going to drive to BK or all the way to Jersey tonight."

"Who said I have to do either?"

"Well, do whatever the fuck you want to do."

Chaz pulled away from the curb, not even waiting to see if she got in the building okay.

He drove downtown and checked into the W Hotel. Any other night he would have fallen asleep as soon his body hit a comfortable mattress. But tonight was different. Thoughts of Kennedy filled his head. *Why am I loving this chick like this? I think I'm going to fall back for a while. That's exactly what I need to do, just fall the fuck back.*

The sound of his cell phone woke him early the next morning. Without opening his eyes, he patted around the bed until he found the phone. He flipped it open and put it to his ear. "Speak on it."

"What up, dun-dun?"

"Jay?"

"Yeah, nigga, it's me."

"Jay! My nigga, what's poppin'? You hit the bricks yet?"

"Yeah, nigga, I'm free! Chaz, I ain't going soft on you or nothing. But good looking out on all the shit you did for me the last two years while I was on lock."

"That's nothing, Jay, you got that. Real recognize real. I already know when the heat is on you'll be one of the very few holding me down." Chaz's line beeped; he looked at the caller ID. "Yo, Jay, I'ma come through and scoop you in like an hour. I need to take this call. This nigga been ducking me about my paper for a minute."

"Handle your BI. I'll be at my baby mom's crib. One hundred."

"One hundred." Chaz switched lines and his attitude. "What is it?"

"Yo, this Macon."

"I know who this is, nigga! I hope you calling about my paper."

"I'll have all that for you in two weeks."

"Have my fuckin' paper in five days or your ass is gonna have problems." Chaz terminated the call.

Chaz cruised through downtown Brooklyn and his old stomping grounds. He pulled up to the place that had raised him— Lafayette Gardens—to pick up Jay. The police were everywhere. They had a blood-soaked area taped off. In the middle of the tape was a pink-and-white bike identical to the one he had bought one of his own daughters for Christmas. He stepped out of the car and watched the crime lab work the scene.

"Yo, what up, baby?" Jay asked, walking up on him. They exchanged a quick hug and a pound.

Chaz turned his attention back to the crime scene. "Yo, what happened here?"

"You remember old-ass crazy Bill from when we was little?"

"The one who used to beat his wife and kids all the time?"

"Yeah, him! You know all his kids bounced as soon as they were old enough. His wife finally decided she'd had enough; her oldest daughter came to move her out this morning. Bill came out the building and started blasting at them while they were getting in the car. He completely missed them and hit Lanae's little girl instead."

"*Word.*"

"*Word,* my nigga."

A paramedic walked out of the building carrying a small body covered by a small white sheet in his arms. Two long thick ponytails with a purple ribbon were hanging from beneath the sheet. It was a horrific sight for any parent to watch. As he watched, Chaz's heart broke. "Come in, Jay, I can't take this shit."

"I thought we were going to Manhattan," Jay commented, noticing the direction they were traveling in.

"We are, but after seeing that shit, I have to swing by and check my daughters."

"I feel you, dawg. When I saw that baby laid out on the curb like that, I had to run back upstairs and hug my little shorties up."

Chaz parked his car in front of his baby mother's building in the Clinton Hill section of Brooklyn. His two daughters were outside playing hopscotch. Eight-year-old Tiki and six-year-old Chasity ran over to him and jumped in his arms. "Daddy!" they screamed in unison.

"What's up with daddy's girls?"

"Can we go to your house today?" Chasity asked.

"Not today, baby. Daddy has work to do."

"But we miss you, Daddy. Only time we get to see you is on TV," Tiki whined.

"I promise you next weekend we'll do something special. Whatever you girls wanna do."

Chasity started jumping up and down. "Ooh-ooh, Daddy, can we go to Disney World and see Mickey Mouse?"

Chaz couldn't say no to the pound-puppy face she was giving him. "Sure, li'l mama, if that's what y'all want."

"Thank you, Daddy!" they cheered in unison.

"Where's your mommy?"

"Upstairs cleaning."

"Come on, let's go upstairs and get her."

Chaz entered the aging building holding on to each of his daughters' hands. The walls along the hallways could have used a couple of fresh coats of paint. The older ladies in the building did their best to keep it looking neat by sweeping and mopping three times a week. Chaz's daughters' mother, Ria, was standing in the doorway when they got to the second floor.

She was wearing the usual cleaning gear, a T-shirt and cutoff sweatpants. Short and slim, Ria was nice and curvy in all the right places. Her beautiful pecan-tan complexion was set off by beautiful brown slanted eyes that made her look exotic. Her short hair was always immaculately done.

"What's up, Ria?" Chaz asked, walking by her into the apartment.

"Nothing. What brings you by?"

"I wanted to see my daughters. You know, it's not safe to let them be out there playing by themselves."

"I was watching them from the window. How do you think I saw you? And why you bringing that frontin'-ass Jay around here?"

Chaz rolled his eyes at her. "Tiki, take your sister in the room to watch cartoons." Feeling she was about to ask for money, he beat her to the punch and offered. "What you need for the girls?"

Pleasantly surprised, Ria answered, "I need money for their spring and summer clothes. Its getting warm and they only have a few pieces from last year."

Chaz pulled out a knot containing two thousand dollars or more. "Here, that should be a G for each of them."

"Thank you."

"No need to thank me; those are my daughters." He paused and said, "Ria, I still want you to move out to Jersey."

"I told you before; I really don't want to leave Brooklyn. All my peoples are here."

Chaz looked at her like she was crazy. "Your peoples? Fuck your peoples! I'm talking about my daughters' safety. We didn't have a choice but to grow up in this zoo. I just saw a little girl Chasity's age being carried away covered by a white sheet. If you really want to stay in Brooklyn, I'll buy you a house in Canarsie near my mother or somewhere way out."

"I thought you wanted us to move to Manhattan so you could see the girls when you left the studio. You must don't want your bitch from Harlem to know about us."

"Your simple ass will never change. My girl don't have nothing to do with this situation. The reason I'm telling you to move to Jersey is because I have a house there now. I no longer have an apartment in Manhattan." He pulled out another knot of cash. "This should be enough to get you started. Call and let me know if you need some more."

"Can you bring me some cash so I can trade the car in and not owe anything?"

"Trade it in for what? I just bought you that truck last year."

"I want the new Lexus 430."

"Yeah, whatever. I'll bring it next week when I pick up the girls to take them to Disney World. Kiss them good-bye for me. I don't want them out here crying."

Chaz walked back to the car feeling good about seeing his girls. But he was frustrated by Ria. The little girl's death was still weighing heavy on his heart. Growing up in Brooklyn, he had seen plenty of tragedies, even caused a few. But having kids put things in a new perspective.

• • •

Yatta walked into Kennedy's living room eating a bowl of farina. Jay-Z's latest CD, *Blueprint,* was blaring from the speakers while Kennedy ran top speed on the treadmill. Perspiration caused her clothes to stick to her body and her hair to stick to her face.

Yatta knew her sister's extra-hard workout ethic was due to Chaz's absence in her life. She also knew if Kennedy was hurting she would never show it. Yatta picked up the remote and turned the stereo down. She stood in front of the treadmill. "Have you called Chaz yet?"

"Has he called me? Fuck him, I'm not sweating him."

"Didn't nobody say nothing about you sweating him. You hard on a nigga. He tells you he loves you and you go cold. But I know you love him. If you didn't you wouldn't react the way you do."

Kennedy slowed the treadmill down, bringing it to a complete stop. She grabbed the towel hanging on the rail and wiped the sweat from her face. "I'm done talking about Chaz. If he wants to talk to me, he knows where to find me."

Kennedy and Yatta were sitting under the hair dryers flipping through fashion magazines at their favorite Dominican hair salon, Marisol's. When Kennedy received a call on her cell phone, Yatta could tell from the pissed expression on her face that it was serious.

"What happened?" Yatta asked once Kennedy hung up.

"That was Taylor's teacher. She's having a problem with him. She wants me to come over and meet with her right now."

"I wonder what's going on. Taylor never gives anyone trouble."

"I don't know. He's been real cranky with me lately. I figured it was because I'm gone all the time."

Kennedy tapped lightly on Mrs. Shooda's door. The petite lady rose from her desk. She was around forty-five and gorgeous. Her sun-bleached blond dreadlocks went perfectly with her beautiful smooth chocolate skin. Mrs. Shooda's proud West Indian heritage shined through in her attitude. She opened the door, and before she stepped into the hallway, she turned to the class. "Class, continue reading until page 201, and no talking. Good morning, Ms. Sanchez. How are you doing?"

"I'm fine, and you?"

"Ms. Sanchez, Taylor threatened to cut a student. This is my second year teaching Taylor and he has been one of my best students in the twenty years I've been teaching. That is one of the reasons I didn't turn this matter over to the monsignor. The other reason is, I know this has been a very traumatic year for him."

"He *what*?"

"He threatened to cut a student and he planned to make good on his threats today with this." Mrs. Shooda pulled a lime-green box cutter from her pocket.

The box cutter belonged to Kennedy. "Mrs. Shooda, I am so sorry. I had no idea."

"I truly believe the boy is still grieving the loss of his mother. He needs attention. Maybe other children have teased him about his mother. Maybe that's why he brought the blade to school. Whatever the case, Ms. Sanchez, I have zero tolerance for thuggish behavior. I want you to keep him home for three days. I put all of his assignments in his bag. I also included Teresa Weston's phone number. She is a highly recommended child therapist and a great friend of mine."

Kennedy was overwhelmed with guilt. *How did I miss all the signs? I've been too wrapped up in my new career to pay attention to the kids' needs.* "Thank you, Mrs. Shooda," she said in a barely audible voice.

"No need to thank me. I just wanted to give you a chance to rectify the problem before it gets out of control." Mrs. Shooda opened the classroom door. "Taylor, gather your things and come out, please."

Taylor slowly walked out the door. He could tell by Kennedy's glare that she was fuming. Mrs. Shooda stopped him, placing her hands upon his shoulders. "Remember our little talk. You are a special young man. Do not mess up now." Taylor nodded in agreement, too afraid to speak. Mrs. Shooda embraced him tightly before turning him over to Kennedy.

She didn't say a word to him as they walked to the car. Kennedy yanked the back door open and nearly pushed Taylor in before she climbed into the front passenger side.

"What happened?" Yatta asked, sensing her sister's anger.

Kennedy dropped the box cutter in Yatta's lap. "Billy badass here threatened to cut another little boy." She turned around and stared at Taylor. "Yo, what's wrong with you? Are you trying to get kicked out of school forever? What would've happened if Mrs. Shooda didn't confiscate that blade from you? Would you really have cut that little boy?"

"Maybe," he replied, unable to look up at Kennedy.

"Then what? You go to Spofford and start a life of endless trips to jail?"

Yatta interrupted. "Calm down, Kennedy. Let me talk to him. You're too upset. Tay, what did this boy do to you that was so bad you wanted to cut him?" She handed him a tissue. "Here, clean your face and talk to me like a big boy."

Taylor composed himself. "Li'l man was telling everybody that my mother was a crack whore. And he said my own grand-mother don't want us, that why we live with Kennedy."

Yatta made eye contact with Kennedy. Kennedy dropped her head. *Damn,* she thought, *why did I go so hard on him before hearing his side?* "Taylor, he only said those things to hurt you. You know as well as I do that none of those things are true. No one loves you more than your grandmother. So don't ever let lies hurt you. Your mother was a wonderful woman and you have every right to defend her honor, but not with violence. Now, next time you have a problem, bring it to my attention or Yatta's attention. Okay?"

"Okay."

"Give me a hug. I love you."

"I love you, too, Kennedy."

Kennedy's stress level was about to go from bad to worse as she sat in an image-and-marketing meeting with Yatta, Strick, the label's staff, and her nemesis, Brooke Colbert. Brooke, the presi-dent of marketing for T.O.N.Y. Records, was the epitome of the black yuppie. She even had a degree from Yale University to go along with her attitude that she was better than most black women.

The hatred between Brooke and Kennedy was mutual. Ken-nedy believed Brooke was intentionally trying to ruin her career. "I think you should tone it down a bit with all the *gangsta* rhymes," Brooke suggested.

"Ma, stop while you're ahead. Everything I rhyme about I'm qualified to rhyme about, because I lived it. Your skin may be black, but you don't know shit about being *black*. And you don't know shit about hip-hop."

"I know marketing!"

"And that's your fucking business, *bitch*!"

"Okay, okay." Strick interrupted. "Brooke, let Shy and myself handle the music. You just get the product pushed once we get it out."

"Okay, but what about her image?" Brooke asked.

Kennedy interjected before Strick could answer. "What about it?"

"Well, it's my job to give you a style that's marketable."

Everyone in the room knew Kennedy was ready to flip out. "Let me explain something to you, *ma*. You can't even join a conversation with me on style. This chick sitting next to me is my stylist, and not because she's my sister, but because she is the fly-est bitch I know. There is nothing you can tell either of us about style. We been fly since the cradle, courtesy of Kora Sanchez. You can't even dress yourself with those go-to-hell acid-wash jeans on. This meeting is adjourned for me."

"Kennedy, in my office *now*!" Strick demanded.

Brooke and her assistant gave Kennedy dirty looks as she and Yatta left the conference room. She shot them back an even dirtier look.

Kennedy followed Strick into his office. He put on his baseball cap and grabbed a few small items from his desk. As she watched him Kennedy said, "Strick, I thought you wanted to talk to me?"

"I just wanted to get out of that meeting, too. You know I had to front on you, though. I can't let you spaz on my staff like that and have them thinking I don't get on you about that shit. Seriously, can you ease up on Brooke a little?"

"Nope. She hates me and I hate her more. I'm going to dig into her ass every time her and her little pissy-ass assistant try to get slick!"

"Kennedy, your ass might really need anger management. Come on, I got something that will make you feel better."

• • •

"This shit is bangin', Strick," Kennedy said, examining a beautiful gray sport coupé. The burnt-orange-and-gray interior fascinated her; she had never seen such an exquisite car. "This shit is
nuts. What kind of car is this?"

"This is the Aston Martin DB7 Vantage."

"Damn, I see what you was talking about now. This is the most
luxurious car I've seen. You gotta let me push this sometime."

"You can push it all the time. It's yours."

What did he just say? "Huh?"

"It's yours, Kennedy. It's a gift from the label."

Kennedy hugged Strick and rocked him side to side. "Thank
you, thank you." She stepped back and stared at the car for a moment. Then a solemn expression fell upon her face.

Strick noticed the mood change. "Ken-Ken, what's wrong?"

"I was just thinking about Pretty Boy. He surprised me with
my first car, a Honda Accord. He was a beautiful person just like
you."

"Thanks. Come on, let's be out before you get all mushy
on me."

Kennedy zoomed through the streets of downtown Manhattan.
She dipped in and out of traffic, nearly giving Strick a heart attack. "Kennedy, you drive like a nigga. You're going to kill the
clutch."

"I love this car and I usually don't like selfish cars."

Chaz, Jay, Shy, and Rob were standing in front of the building
where the studio was located when Kennedy and Strick pulled
up. It was the first time Kennedy and Chaz had seen each other in
a week, since they had argued. "Strick, you done copped another
hot whip?" Shy said, checking out the car.

"Nah, homey, that's Ken-Ken's."

"Say word! Ma, this is a real good look for you."

Kennedy couldn't even respond to Shy's comment. She was too occupied in a staring match with Chaz. Jay asked Chaz, "What's up wit' homegirl? Strick hittin' that?"

"Fall back, that's *wifey.*"

"Oh, that's Kennedy. She's even prettier in person."

When Strick got out of the car, Chaz jumped in and just stared at Kennedy. *Here he go with his bullshit,* Kennedy thought. "What?"

"You ate?"

"No."

"Let's go get something."

Kennedy pulled away from the curb and drove in silence. Chaz continued to stare at her. "What's up with you, Red?"

Kennedy couldn't help but to blush; she loved when he called her Red. "Nothin' much. How've you been?"

"I've been aight. You could've called a nigga."

"Did you call me?"

"So now you on some ol' tit-for-tat shit."

"I have to protect my feelings."

"Protect them from what?"

"From getting hurt."

I know I said I was going to fall back. But fuck that, you only live once, he thought. "Kennedy, how many times do I have to tell you I'm not them other niggas? I'm not out here chasing skirts. I did that already; I don't want those headaches anymore. I just want to come home to you and for you to trust me the way I trust you."

Emotional conversations always overwhelmed Kennedy. She pulled the car over. "Chaz, I know you're different. That's why I love you." *There, I said it,* she thought. "I know I act like a bitch, but I'm so afraid of being hurt again."

"Ma, please believe me when I say you are like no one I've ever met before. You got me and I'm not going anywhere." He sealed his words with a long deep kiss. "What do you think about Disney World?"

"Huh?" she asked, laughing.

"I'm taking my daughters to Disney World tomorrow. I want you to come."

"I can't."

"Why?"

" 'Cause Yatta and I have been promising our kids that we would take them to Disney. How would that look if I go with you and your kids?"

"You can bring Yatta and the kids. My sister and her son are coming, too."

"I still can't go and not bring Jordan and Mattie. They're still in Charlotte with my mother."

"Here." He handed her a black American Express card. "Call your mother. She can meet us down there and just pay for whoever is going."

Kennedy looked at the card, shocked. "You have one of these now? You have to spend a lot of moola just to get invited to have one of these."

By the next morning, Kennedy's house had been turned into *Romper Room*. Seven kids high off of syrup were running through the house. Kennedy was just about to lose her mind. "Chaz, I can't wait on the car service any longer. We're just going to have to take two cars and leave them at the airport."

"You read my mind."

Kennedy felt a little hand tugging on her shirt from behind. "What is it now, Niko? Oh, I'm sorry—Chasity. What do you need, baby?"

"Can I call my mommy? She didn't give me my inhaler."

"Sure, baby, the phone is right over there."

In Brooklyn, Ria rolled over and read the caller ID on her ringing phone: *Kennedy Sanchez.* She answered, "Hello?"

"Mommy, you forgot to give me my inhaler."

"No, I didn't. I gave it to your daddy."

"Oh! Okay, bye, Mommy."

"Chasity, don't hang up. Where are you at?"

It was too late. Chasity had already hung up. Ria looked at the caller ID again. *Kennedy, Kennedy. Oh hell, no! I know he don't have my daughters around his bitch.* Ria picked up the phone to dial his number. Then she thought about it. She had big plans this weekend. There was no way she was going to get into it with Chaz and give him a reason to bring the girls home. She copied the number down from the caller ID and saved it for future use.

Jealous One's Envy

Who the hell is calling me at six-thirty in the morning? Kennedy reached over and grabbed the phone off of the nightstand. "Hello?"

"Put Chaz on the phone!" an angry female voice demanded.

Kennedy sat up. "Who is this?"

"Bitch, this his baby mother! Now put his ass on the phone."

Chaz rolled over. "Kennedy, what's wrong? Who is that?"

Kennedy held up the palm of her hand toward him and continued to speak into the phone. "First off, this is not Chaz's house. If you wish to speak to him, address me the correct way, you disrespectful slut. And since you called here being cute, you damn sure ain't talking to him. And keep playing with me, I'll stomp a hole in your ass."

Ria let out a loud laugh, "Bitch, *please,* you better ask Chaz how I get down. I'll bring it uptown."

"Well bring it, ma, 'cause I guarantee you won't leave the same way you came. Hey!"

Chaz snatched the phone from Kennedy. "Yo, why the fuck is you calling here? I'ma see you about this dumb shit. That's my word." He slammed the phone down. He didn't even want to look over at Kennedy.

As she went to the bathroom she told him, "You better check that bitch 'cause I don't do baby mothers."

• • •

It was just one of those days that started out bad and was destined to end worse. Kennedy was at a photography studio in SoHo, getting her makeup done for a photo shoot. Yatta was laying Kennedy's clothes out. Meanwhile Yatta's phone kept ringing. Kennedy tried to ignored it, but couldn't. "Dang, Yatta, answer that shit! Put it on vibrate or something. It's irking my nerves."

"I'm not answering it. That ain't nobody but Petey calling, making empty threats."

"For what?"

"He mad 'cause I sent the girls with his mother. He wants me to come visit him."

The phone started ring again. "Hand me the phone," Kennedy told Yatta. "What's the problem, Petey?"

"Who is this? Oh shit, I know this not little tough-ass Kennedy. Now don't go filling Yatta's head up with all those ideas like you did Nina. I heard you might be the reason she dead. Telling her to leave her man."

Kennedy waved her makeup artist away. "You 'bout a ignorant motherfucker. I don't know why you so worried about what Yatta doing out here. I hear all the bodies they trying to stick to you, you got one foot in the electric chair."

"Ha ha, that's real cute. Bet y'all evil-ass bitches won't be laughing for long." Petey slammed the phone down.

Chaz filled Jay and Rob in on the morning's events as they drove through midtown on the way to the studio. Rob was jealous of the relationship Chaz had with Kennedy, and jealous of Chaz in general. "What you flip on Ria for? That's your daughters' mother. She can call you anytime she get ready," he said to Chaz.

"She sure can call me anytime. On any of my phones, but not Kennedy's."

"I'm tired of everybody actin' like Kennedy don't do dirt."

"Shut up, nigga," Jay said, cutting his eyes at Rob.

"Nah, Jay, I want to know what the fuck he talking about," Chaz said.

"He ain't talking about nothing," Jay pleaded, trying to squash the conversation.

Against Jay's wishes, Rob continued talking. "Man, the way I hear it is, it's more to her and Hassan than she telling. That nigga cousin, EB, told me Hassan been hitting that since that nigga Pretty Boy died. They was still fucking when y'all met at that party."

Chaz got heated on the inside. He made a drastic U-turn in the middle of the street. "Yo, where you going?" Jay asked.

Chaz didn't answer as he drove in the direction of SoHo.

Jay turned and looked at Rob in the backseat. "That why I don't fuck with you now. You been li'l pussy-ass nigga since we was young. Always got your name in the middle of some gossip, just like a bitch."

Chaz stormed into the studio and snatched Kennedy off the set. He shoved her through her dressing-room door. His glare scared and nearly silenced her. "Baby . . . baby, what's wrong?"

"You're a fucking liar, that's what's wrong!"

"What? I never lied to you."

"Yes you did! You lied about you and Hassan. You said he was just your homeboy. Do you fuck all your homeboys?"

Kennedy dropped her head.

"Look at me, damn it!" Chaz yelled at her. "Why did you lie?"

"I didn't lie. You never asked me if I was jaying him."

"Yeah, this shit is becoming real clear to me now. That night when y'all was on the elevator, you was on the way to fuck him. Wasn't you?"

"Yo, you are unbelievable B. Wasn't shit going on between him and me that night. And I haven't fucked Hassan or anybody since we been together."

"If you not fucking him, why didn't you keep it gully with me from the door?"

"Do I have to tell you every nigga I've fucked before you? Shit. Do you name every groupie you've fucked? Instead they write me letters."

Chaz backed Kennedy into the corner. "I swear to God, if you fucking that nigga, I'm going to choke the shit out of you. I ought to knock the shit out of you for playing games with me anyway."

"Who do you think you're talking to? I don't have to explain shit to you. And you're dead wrong if you think you're ever going to put your hands on me. Just get the fuck out! I don't care if I ever see your petty ass again!"

"I'm not going anywhere!"

Kennedy picked up a pair of cutting shears. "Get out or I will stab you."

"Fuck you, Kennedy. You dirty bitch."

"If I'm such a dirty bitch, Chaz, why you here?"

Yatta entered. "What is wrong with y'all?"

Chaz turned to leave. "Ask your sister. She might not tell you, though. She real good at keeping secrets." Chaz backed away, never taking his eyes off of Kennedy as he left the room.

"Kennedy, what is he talking about?"

"He found out about me and Hassan."

"What do you mean he found out? I thought he knew."

"He knew we were friends. I didn't volunteer any extra information." Kennedy reached in her purse, pulled out a prescription bottle, and took one pill. Yatta picked up the pill bottle and read the label aloud. "Effexor XR, one hundred and fifty milligrams! Kennedy, you're going hard with the pills lately."

"Whatever it takes to get me through the day."

"Well, an addict is an addict, no matter the drug of choice."

That night Kennedy lay naked under her warm duvet listening to the humming sound of the central air unit. The house was empty and the quietest it had been in a long time. Yet she was unable to fall asleep or to get Chaz off of her mind.

Kennedy got up and went into the kitchen. She poured a glass of wine before rummaging through the kitchen drawers. "Got it." She smiled once she located her emergency stash of sleeping pills. She popped one in her mouth and chased it down with the wine. Within ten minutes she was down like a baby.

"Ain't that your baby's daddy?" Nee asked Ria.

"Where?"

"Over there."

"Yeah, that's that motherfucker. I wonder if his little rapping bitch in here."

Nee suddenly became excited. "Ooh, girl, I knew I had somethin' to tell you."

"About what?"

"Girl, you know Kisha's sister was doing hair at that picture studio. She said Chaz busted in there and drug that bitch off the set. She said you could hear him screaming on her throughout the building. Something about her fucking Hassan."

"The rapper?"

"Exactly!"

"I told him about messing with them bourgeois uptown hos. Them scandalous, gold-diggin' bitches."

• • •

The club Slate was filled to capacity with industry insiders for Triad Records' annual party. Strick, Chaz, and Jay were talking to S.C., Kicks, and a few other guys when Hassan and a few of his boys walked up. Hassan exchanged pounds with S.C. and Kicks. When he got to Chaz with his hand raised in the air, Chaz looked at him like he was crazy. *I should knock him out on some real live Brooklyn shit. Just leave it alone for now, don't fuck up this man's party,* Chaz told himself as he turned to walk away.

"Damn, Has, what was that shit all about?"

Never the one to let someone play him, Hassan addressed the problem immediately. "That nigga must be mad 'cause I'm fucking his bitch."

As Chaz moved through the crowd he felt a small hand grab him from behind. He knew it was the touch of a female and hoped that it was Kennedy. He was surprised and disappointed to see Ria. "What are you doing here?" he asked, frowning.

"The same thing you're doing here."

"I doubt that, and where are my daughters at?"

"Why? You're not watching them."

"Ria, don't play with me! I haven't forgot about that bullshit you did this morning."

"My aunt Sheryl got them. Enough of all that, I heard your little girlfriend is fucking all the rappers."

"Mind your fucking business, Ria."

"Why don't you just come home to your family? I heard that bitch already got like five kids anyway, and this the bitch you abandoning us for?"

"Are you serious? Do you know how stupid you sound? We're not together 'cause you're a fucking whore and you burnt me. We'll never be together!" Chaz walked away.

Upset, Ria was ready to go. Since she'd driven, that meant her friends were going to have to be ready, too. After dropping her friends off at their homes, Ria arrived at her own and retreated to her bedroom. She grabbed her cordless phone and pressed *67 before dialing Chaz's cell-phone number. When he answered she didn't say anything; she just listened to his surroundings. Judging by the loud music, she knew he was still in the club. *Perfect,* she thought, hanging up the phone to dial another number.

The shrill ringing of the phone scared Kennedy out of a deep sleep. She was mad at herself for not turning the ringer off. "Hello?"

"It must be real lonely in that bed tonight, since my children's father is home where he belongs."

"Ria?"

"Yeah, ho, it's me."

"I don't give a fuck if he is there with you. You can have his bum ass, 'cause you need him. I made myself, so I'll never need a nigga. Since he's there with you, he can never come here again. Now lose my number, bitch, and die slow." Kennedy slammed the phone down. Her feelings were hurt. *I bet he been messing with that bitch all along. I should've gone with Hassan that night.*

A few seconds later the phone rang again. *I can't believe this heifer.* "What now, bitch?"

Instead of Ria's aggravating voice, she heard a man's deep dull voice. The voice sounded like it was devoid of all emotion. "I'm going to destroy your world the same way you destroyed mine." The phone line went dead. The man's voice sent chills up Kennedy's back. It took a few minutes to shake them. *Great, now some deranged fan has my number. Guess I'll have to get that changed, too.*

$$\bullet \quad \bullet \quad \bullet$$

"Kennedy, wake up," Yatta said, shaking Kennedy.

"What is it?" Kennedy said, pulling the covers over her head.

Yatta pulled the covers off of her. "The white party is tonight and we still have to find you something to wear. We've been calling here for hours. Why aren't you answering the phone?"

"The ringer is off."

"Why?"

"Unwanted phone calls." Kennedy got out of the bed. "I really don't feel like going to this party."

"You better start feeling it; you're performing tonight. It's your introduction to the industry."

"You know, your ass is starting to sound a lot like Strick."

"Shut up. Hurry, we still have to find two outfits for you."

Running around with Yatta looking for something to wear had taken all of Kennedy's energy. After receiving her glamour makeover, she lay down on the couch in her dressing room. She slept with her hands propped under her chin, being cautious not to mess up her hair or makeup. A firm knock on the door startled her out of her sleep. "Who?"

"It's Strick. Are you decent?"

"Yeah, come on in." Kennedy sat up and closed her robe.

Strick entered the room looking quite dapper in a custom-made white linen suit. Kennedy smiled at him; he was so fly and sophisticated. Everything about Strick was smooth. It didn't matter if he was in a two-thousand-dollar Ralph Lauren suit or sneakers and jeans; he gave off the same persona.

Strick pulled up a chair and sat directly across from Kennedy. He looked her square in the face, trying to study her. "You aight, Mama?"

"I'm straight."

"I just wanted to make sure. You know, I want you to shine

tonight. Chaz is going on first. At the end of his performance he will call you onstage to perform your duet. After you perform your two singles, Hassan, S.C., and Joaquin will come on with you."

"Does Chaz know that Hassan is going to be here?"

"Yeah, he knows. Chaz is professional; he not gonna start no bullshit up in here."

"If you say so." Kennedy sighed. "You heard what happened yesterday."

"Chaz ain't dwelling on that shit. Him and Hassan saw each other last night at Slate and didn't nothing happen."

"Who told you that?"

"Didn't nobody have to tell me. I was there. Chaz and I went to a couple of parties last night before we went to the studio."

Kennedy rolled her eyes. "Yeah right. What you trying to do—clean his shit up?"

"Whoa, whoa," Strick said, shaking his head. "Kennedy, what are you talking about?"

"Ria called me last night and told me that he was there with her."

"Ken, baby, you cannot let her get to you. Ria is miserable and she has no plans on letting Chaz be happy with another woman. Don't worry about her, Ken—"

"Oh, trust me. I'm not worried about her at all. She can have her baby daddy back. As far as I'm concerned, Chaz and I are only label mates from here on out."

Strick leaned forward. "Ken, what you're dealing with is a man's pride. I know Chaz kirked out on you yesterday, but look at the way Rob brought it to him."

"Rob? I knew his hatin' ass had something to do with all this." Kennedy shook her head.

"Put that on top of all the grief Ria caused him. Chaz was no angel. He did his share of dirt, but he took care of her. I mean, I don't know what he's told you about that relationship, but ol' girl did a lot of foul shit to him."

"Like what?"

"That bitch was fucking wild niggas, even the ones she knew Chaz had beef with. The worst thing of all was when she burnt him."

"Are you serious? He never told me that."

"And through all that, he still respects her as his daughters' mother and never throws dirt on her."

The door opened and Yatta walked in, carrying Kennedy's freshly pressed outfits. "What up?"

"How you doing, Yatta?" Strick asked, blushing.

"I'm doing great, Strick," Yatta said, displaying a flirtatious smile.

"That's what's up," Strick said, admiring Yatta's beauty as he stood up. He bent over and kissed Kennedy on her cheek. "Tonight is yours, li'l mama. You exude a confidence like no other woman I know. I want you to rock this shit, and afterward we're going to party until the sun comes up."

T.O.N.Y.'s annual White Linen and Diamonds party was huge, to say the least. It was also the venue where Strick showcased his up-and-coming artists before the industry. Kennedy had just stepped off the stage after giving a dynamic performance. She looked stunning in a white off-the-shoulder minidress. As she moved through the crowd people were congratulating and complimenting her, making it hard for her to accomplish her mission of finding her sisters and cousin.

Strick grabbed Kennedy and whisked her into the VIP, where all the execs were located. The room was filled with the real big dogs of the industry. A good portion of the room was filled with Jewish men, European men, and Asian men, some of them over the age of fifty, with young model chicks hanging on to their arms. Strick took her around, introducing her to all of the important people. Kennedy was in awe, and not because of the power around her. She was in awe of the open drug use that was going down. Candy dishes of Xstasy pills were being passed around. Lines of cocaine were being snorted.

It wasn't like Kennedy had never seen people partying with drugs before. She just never thought that she would witness it here. These were some of the wealthiest and most respected people in America. She was even more taken aback by the way that they were offering her drugs as if they were drinks. But she was really disgusted. She remained polite, professional, and decided to keep it moving. On her way out she stopped to talk to Perri, the label's premier R&B singer and its only other female artist. She had been signed right after Kennedy. They were featured on each other's upcoming CDs and the pair had quickly bonded.

Perri stood up and embraced Kennedy. "Hey, mama, you did so good."

"So did you, Perri."

"Come sit with me," Perri said, handing Kennedy a mimosa.

Kennedy put the glass up to her mouth then suddenly placed it back on the table. "No offense to you, but, um, I don't trust no drinks that have been sitting around in here. I'll pour my own."

"No offense taken. I understand with all the dope being passed around in here."

Perri and Kennedy made small talk for a few minutes. Chaz was standing on the other side of the room staring at Kennedy, which was making her uneasy. Rob was also staring, with a sneaky smile plastered all over his face. Kennedy's hatred for Rob was growing every time she looked at him.

Time seemed to suddenly stand still when Hassan and Caz walked through the entrance. Kennedy and Perri were sitting directly to the right of the door. Hassan made a beeline to their table. "Hey, ladies." He kissed each of them on the cheek. "Y'all both did ya thing tonight."

"Thanks," they said in unison. Kennedy's eyes darted over to the corner where Chaz was standing. Instead of staring at her, he now glared.

Sensing the tension, Hassan decided to keep it moving. Kennedy could still feel Chaz watching her. "Perri, I'ma go out and mingle. I'm not feeling this shit in here and Chaz keep giving me greasy-ass looks."

Perri glanced over at Chaz. "He still tripping?"

"I guess, girl. I haven't even talked to him."

"I'm leaving out with you. I have to piss like a Russian race-horse."

As Kennedy and Perri made their way through the crowd, a girl with a familiar face stopped Kennedy. Perri continued on to the restroom. The pressure in her bladder was too intense for her to stop.

The girl smiled at Kennedy. "You did your thing tonight, homegirl."

"Thanks, ma. Do I know you? Your face looks familiar."

"We've met over the phone a few times but never in person. We should have, though, since you took my girls to Disney World."

I don't believe this. No wonder her face looks familiar. Chasity and Tiki look just like her. "Ria?"

"Yes, it's me in the flesh."

Chaz, Strick, Jay, Rob, and Yatta were walking out of the VIP area when Chaz saw Kennedy and Ria. "Oh shit."

"What?" everybody asked him in unison.

"Ria is over there talking to Kennedy."

"Your baby mother?" Yatta asked.

"Yes, I don't even know what she's doing here."

"You and Kennedy may not be speaking right now, but you have to go stop whatever is going on. 'Cause if she say the wrong shit, Kennedy will duff her ass and this is not the time or the place."

Meanwhile Ria, figuring she had Kennedy intimidated, began talking much shit. "Yeah, just like I thought, you uptown hos ain't nothing but some phone gangstas."

Kennedy finally interrupted her. "You're one pathetic, miserable skank. And phone gangsta, ma, I *highly* doubt that. I'm two steps from knocking you the fuck out."

"Try your luck, bitch, and my girls"—Ria pointed to three girls behind her—"will mop the floor with your ass."

"I'm not worried about you or them funky-ass hos. My entire family up in here, so the question is: Do you feel lucky, bitch? Keep poppin' shit and I'm going to drop your ass like you hot."

Just in the nick of time Chaz slipped his arm around Kennedy's waist. He finessed the situation like only he could. "I see you met wifey." Placing a huge kiss on Kennedy's lips.

Ria's friends couldn't believe how he was playing Ria. Usually Ria could make him dis another chick on the strength of being his babies' mother. Ria became heated. "So now you disrespecting me for this bitch?"

Chaz stepped up, pushing Kennedy behind him. "You disrespecting yourself trying to show out for the dizzy-ass broads. You just can't stand the thought of me being happy with someone else, can you?"

Ria threw her drink in Chaz's face. As he struggled to get the stinging alcohol out of his eyes, Kennedy reached around him and mugged Ria in the head, knocking her to the ground. Strick's security team stepped up and expeditiously resolved the situation. While being taken away by security, Ria yelled out to Kennedy, "I'ma see you in the streets, bitch."

Outside, while they waited for the valet to bring the car around, Kennedy was flipped on Chaz. "I don't know what kind of games you play with that bitch, but I'm not for it. How the fuck she just rolling up on me at my own shit? You better put that bitch in her place or your daughters will be motherless! That's word to everything I love!"

Noticing the stares they were getting, Chaz didn't want her to go on anymore. "Kennedy, that's enough. We can finish this in the car."

"In what car? Motherfucker, you can't be *serious*. I'm not going anywhere with you."

Just as the valet pulled the car around, Hassan and his crew walked out of the party. Hassan stopped to check on Kennedy. "You aight, Ma?"

Chaz answered for her. "She straight, my man."

"I asked *her*, fam." Both of their respective crews put their guards up in case something popped off. Not wanting the situation to escalate, Kennedy spoke up. "I'm fine, that shit in there was nothing. You know my family got me," she said, pointing to Yatta and a few of her cousins and friends.

"Aight, ma, if you say so. I'll check you later." Hassan and Chaz continued to stare each other down.

Still trying to smooth the situation over, Kennedy told Chaz, "Come on, baby, get in the car. I'm ready to go."

Chaz reluctantly agreed. They argued all the way to his home in Jersey. Kennedy made the situation worse by holding a phone conversation with Yatta the entire ride. She continued to talk to Yatta once she and Chaz got to the house. Already pissed off at her refusal to hang up the phone, Chaz snatched the phone from her, opened the patio door, and tossed it into the black night.

Kennedy screamed, "You bastard!"

"I guess I have your attention now, don't I?"

"I can't believe you did that. You're going to buy me a new phone! Give me the keys to your car so I can go home. Now! Before I smack the shit out of you."

"You ain't going nowhere and you ain't smacking nobody. So stop it."

Kennedy shook her head, sitting down on the couch. "Chaz, I don't want to be here, just take me home."

"I want you here."

"Yesterday you were ready to beat me about some shit from my past."

"I apologize for overreacting yesterday. I know I could have handled that a lot better. You know I'll never put my hands on you." He sat down next to her.

Kennedy looked over at him. "You are the only man I've truly loved since Pretty Boy died. And as good as that feels, I can't deal with this relationship. I can't deal with the press, the industry, your baby mother, and your boys being in our business. I know in the end I'll be the one who gets hurt."

Chaz removed his baseball cap and ran his fingers over his head. "You can end it now if that's the way you feel. But then I would be the one hurting. If you love me the way you say you do, can't nobody tear down what we build. Not the industry, my baby mother, your people, or my people. Nobody, Kennedy."

Kennedy nodded in agreement. Chaz leaned over and kissed her softly. Gently biting down on her bottom lip, parting her lips with his tongue, he kissed her slowly and intensely. They kissed for the next five minutes. Kennedy had been kissed by the best, but she had never experienced anything like this. The kiss was like something out of the movies.

Chaz pulled back and asked her, "You still mad at me, li'l mama?"

She shook her head. "No. For some strange reason, I can never stay mad at you for long." Chaz pulled her in close and lay across the couch with her in his arms. They fell asleep and slept that way until the next afternoon.

Takin' It to the Streets

New York's most notorious gossip DJ broke the exclusive story about Kennedy and Ria's confrontation at the party live from her morning show. She even touched on the rumors that suggested there was a beef between Chaz and Hassan.

Adding fuel to the fire, Hassan recorded a freestyle rap that was filled with thinly veiled subliminal messages towards Chaz. Chaz retaliated with a no-holds-barred rap of his own. And voilà, a new hip-hop beef was born.

Kennedy was sick of it all. She wanted to run to that back room in Big Ma's house and hide. But this was the profession she'd chosen and she was slowly beginning to learn to handle it. When reporters posed questions about the escalating beef between Chaz and Hassan, or about her and Chaz's relationship, she respectfully refused to comment.

At the end of the week Kennedy needed a stress reliever. This time her remedy of choice was shopping, and she took her niece Jazz and Jazz's best friend, Candace, with her. Jazz was used to her aunt splurging on her, but it was new to Candace.

Kennedy knew that Candace's mother was single and that she worked two jobs to support the child. Candace didn't get a lot of extra clothes and trinkets. Kennedy was more than happy to spoil her because she was a good kid, respectful and not too grown for her age. She even bought a special gift for Candace's mother.

Kennedy spent five thousand dollars on the girls that day. They capped off the evening with dinner at the Hard Rock Cafe.

Day was turning to night when Kennedy parked in front of her building. She told the girls, "Y'all can spend the night with me. We can order some movies or something."

"Okay, Auntie, I'll go see if my mother wants to come over," Jazz said enthusiastically.

After several trips from the car to the stoop, the girls emptied it of their shopping bags, and went into the house. Kennedy was retrieving one last bag from the trunk when she heard someone call her name. She closed the trunk and turned to see who it was. She saw Ria coming toward her screaming, "Talk that shit now, bitch."

Noticing the two girls walking a few steps behind Ria, Kennedy was sure that they were there to jump her. Aware as she was of the rules of street fighting, she knew she had to grab just one of them. She dropped her bags and swung her heavy purse forcefully with her right hand, knocking Ria to the ground. Kennedy jumped on top of Ria. She used her left hand to pin her down by her neck, then pounded her face with hard punches from her right fist. Ria couldn't swing back because she was too busy trying to get Kennedy's hand off her neck. Ria's two friends, Nee and Chula, were delivering hard blows to Kennedy's body, trying to get her off of Ria.

Jazz and Candace came out of Kennedy's house to see where she was only to witness the action unfolding. "AUNTIE!" Jazz screamed out.

"Y'ALL STAY ON THE STOOP, JAZZ! DON'T COME DOWN HERE."

Jazz jumped off the stoop and ran over to her mother's brownstone; she began ringing the bell hysterically. Candace picked up a metal pipe that was lying next to the garbage can. She ran up behind Nee, swinging the pipe like her name was Barry Bonds. Nee fell to the side from the first strike. Candace continued to beat Nee with the pipe the entire length of her body.

Inside, Yatta was stepping out of the shower when she heard the back-to-back ringing of the bell. *Who the hell?* She walked over to the intercom and in a very disgruntled voice asked, "Who is it?"

"Mommy, it's Jazz. Come down quick. Some girls are jumping Auntie."

Yatta ran to her room, searching frantically for something to throw on. She grabbed a T-shirt and a pair of gray sweatpants and stuck her feet down in a pair of old Timberlands. She reached behind the headboard and retrieved the Glock that she kept taped there.

Outside, Chula, one of Ria's sidekicks, spit a straight razor blade out of her mouth and into her hand. She grabbed a handful of Kennedy's hair and pulled her head back. In one swift move she had sliced open the right side of Kennedy's face. Kennedy howled in pain, falling flat on top of Ria. Ria pushed Kennedy off of her. With Chula's help, Ria stood to her feet. She was woozy from all the blows her head had sustained.

Ria began kicking and stomping Kennedy's body. "That's what you get for fucking with me, bitch! I told you Chaz is mine. You see that Lexus. Bitch, he bought that and my new house! Bitch, he don't want your stankin' ass." Ria hawked and spit in Kennedy's hair.

Chula freed Nee from Candace's fierce swings by hitting the girl in the head. She and Ria helped Nee to the car just as Yatta came running out of the house with her gun cocked. Yatta aimed and took a shot at them. The gunshot scared Chula so bad she ran the car up on the curb, almost hitting a pole as she drove away.

Yatta was about to let off another shot when she caught sight of Kennedy lying in the street. Her hair and clothes were soaked in blood. She was going into shock from the pain. Yatta ran to her little sister's side and dropped to her knees. Kennedy's face was stained with blood and her hair was sticking to the open wound. Yatta pushed Kennedy's hair back. "Jazzy, get Kennedy's phone out her bag and dial 911 now. Kennedy, baby, hang on."

Yatta sat in St. Luke's emergency room next to Kennedy's bed. Her pain was being treated with a high dosage of Vicodin. She had also received nearly two hundred stitches in her face. Yatta was ready to call her cousins, who were laying low in North Carolina, and take the beef with Ria to the street. The real bloodshed was about to begin. "Kennedy, I'm calling Kane and E. We going to get that bitch. I'ma stomp a hole in Ria's ass. And that bitch that cut you, I'ma cut from ass to appetite."

"No, Yatta." Kennedy spoke slowly. "You not fighting Ria. Nor am I. This shit is all because of Chaz, so he is going to fight her. I'm not going to keep fighting this bitch over my man. He's going to put her in her place once and for all or we're through!"

At that moment Strick walked into the room followed by a tall, dark, good-looking white man. Strick kissed Kennedy on her cheek. "Chaz will be here in a minute. Let me introduce you to a good friend of mine. This is Dr. Rodstat, one of, if not the best plastic surgeon in the world."

Dr. Rodstat stepped forward and lifted Kennedy's hand. He kissed it softly. "Did we . . . did we meet at the white party?" she asked, thinking he looked familiar.

"We sure did, beautiful." He flashed a smile, showing off a mouth full of sparkling white porcelain veneers.

"Please don't patronize me, Dr. Rodstat. I'm scarred for life."

"Call me Phil. Here, let me get at look at your face." He gently removed the bloody bandage from Kennedy's face and examined it. "Kennedy, I will have your face more beautiful than before this terrible incident. When I'm finished with you, the scar will merely be a memory."

Kennedy blushed, forgetting about the scar already. "How long do I have to wait before the surgery?"

"We can start as early as the beginning of next week. The sooner the better."

"How much is this going to run me?"

Strick, who had been sitting back tripping off of Phil's pimp juice, spoke up. "Don't worry about that, Kennedy. This one's on Chaz."

"Thanks, Phil."

"You're very welcome. I hate to rush out, but I have a very early flight. Take care, get plenty of rest, and I'll see you next week."

Chaz entered the room as Phil was leaving. The two men greeted each other like they were old friends and held a brief conversation. After exchanging a pound and a hug with Chaz, Phil left the room.

Dreading the moment, but greatly concerned, Chaz sat down on the bed next to Kennedy. He leaned over and pulled her into a tight embrace. "Baby, I'm so sorry. I'll do whatever it takes to make it up to you."

"That you will," she stated. Her voice was so cold and empty that Chaz pulled out of the embrace.

"Why did you say it like that? What do you mean?"

"That means you're going to beat that bitch ass and check her once and for all."

"Kennedy, you know I'm going to check her about this. But she is still my baby mother."

Yatta and Kennedy looked at each other. Kennedy looked back at Chaz. "Get the fuck out! NOW!"

"What's wrong with you?"

"What's wrong with me? This is what's wrong with me." Kennedy ripped the bandage off of her face and pointed to the nasty, swollen laceration that was oozing with yellowish pus and congealed blood.

Chaz couldn't form his next sentence. Seeing the damage to her face took the wind out of his body.

"Yeah, nigga, look at it long and hard. It hurts like hell. It hurts worse than it looks, if you can imagine that. Now, what I can't imagine is how you were ready to beat my ass over some shit from my past. But you won't get at this bitch about fucking up my face. Fuck you! You don't love me. I'm not going to keep fighting your baby mother over you. If I have to get at that bitch again, it's going to be a lot of slow singing and flower bringing."

Chaz's blood was boiling now. "Get dressed."

Chaz made two phone calls on the way out of the hospital. The first call was to Jay. As soon as he answered Chaz got straight to the point. "I need you to meet me at the block party."

"I'll be there."

The second call was to his sister. "Shorty, you still got my daughters?"

"Yeah. Why?"

"Don't let Ria take them tonight at all."

"What's going on, Chaz?"

"I gotta get at Ria. Her and some other bitches jumped Kennedy. One of them cut Kennedy's face."

"WHAT? Where is Kennedy?"

"She's right here; we're leaving the emergency room now."

"Let me speak to her."

Chaz handed his cell phone to Kennedy. "What's up, Shorty?"

"Are you okay, ma?"

"I'm okay now 'cause I know my face is going to be fixed. I'm drugged up so it doesn't hurt as bad."

"Ma, you know I will fuck that ho up for messing with you."

"Shorty, there's no need for you to get involved. Your brother has to handle this one."

"I know that's right, girl, make him fuck that bitch up. I don't condone a man hitting a woman, but she is one them hos a man have to beat. I told him a long time ago to punch that bitch in her face. That's the problem now. She knows he won't fuck her up. That's why she keeps on disrespecting him."

Pulling up to the annual block party, Chaz knew Ria was there. Not only because she had never missed the event since they were kids, but because he spotted the Lexus he had bought her months earlier parked a few cars ahead.

Jay walked over to Chaz's car as Chaz, Kennedy, and Yatta were getting out. He didn't have a clue about why Chaz had called him. That is, until he saw the big-ass bandage on Kennedy's face. "What the fuck happen to her face?" he asked Chaz as they exchanged pounds.

"Ria and her dumb-ass friends went uptown and jumped her. Man, one of them hos gave her a buck-fifty. I thought that shit was going to be a little-ass nick. Man, that shit is long and nasty as hell."

People were breaking their necks to speak to Chaz and Jay as they maneuvered through the crowd. The bandage on Kennedy's face attracted a lot of stares and whispers. One girl didn't even lower her voice as she pointed at the bandage and boldly said, "Damn, Chaz, what happened to your girl's face?"

Standing in the middle of seven girls, Ria was giving a play-by-play of her altercation with Kennedy. All of the girls were laughing at her animated account. Oversize Gucci shades covered Ria's eyes, hiding the bruises left by the pounding Kennedy had given her head.

BAM! Ria's shades suddenly flew off her face and shattered all over the concrete. She didn't know what had hit her. But before she hit the ground, Chaz grabbed her by her neck and held her in the air. All the girls who had been laughing at her story stood frozen.

Chaz tightened his grip on her neck and spoke sternly, gritting his teeth. "The games stop now, you deranged bitch. Don't fuck with Kennedy no more! Don't call her house. If you see her don't speak. Don't even frown your face up. If you do, I swear I'll body your little ass." He released her neck. Her body fell onto the black street.

Yatta pulled her leg back as far as she could and swung it forward with great force, kicking Ria square in her left cheek. Then she stood back and pulled all the phlegm and saliva she could lock up from her throat and then unleashed her personal fluids from her mouth onto Ria's face. "I told you not to fuck with my sister, you trifling slut."

Jay pulled Yatta away. "Come on, Yatta, that's enough."

As they approached the car Ria ran up on their heels screaming, "Fuck you, Chaz. You and that bitch ain't gonna make it. When that snooty ho dump your ass, don't come back round here. I hate you, you fucking bastard. How could you do this to me? I loved you when you ain't have shit. I'm your baby's mother! I'm supposed to be number one, motherfucker! I should've sliced that bitch's *throat*."

Stopping in her tracks, Kennedy turned to Yatta and pulled a gun from Yatta's purse. Ria froze, fearing she was about to be shot. Instead, Kennedy walked over to Ria's beautiful six-month-old Lexus and riddled it with bullet holes, emptying the entire clip. She looked at Ria, smiling. "That should have been you. I hope your insurance is up-to-date. 'Cause Chaz ain't replacing this one."

"You crazy bitch," Ria cried, running over to her car, her baby.

Kennedy giggled as she held the gun to up to her lips and blew the smoke off the muzzle like her name was Annie Oakley. Jay took the gun from her. "Go get in the car, girl. The Jakes is coming!"

But Kennedy had to taunt Ria once more before she left. "When you tell the police I shot your car up, be sure to tell them about the scar I received courtesy of you and your homegirls."

I wonder if I did the right thing, Chaz thought as he lay next to Kennedy in bed. *Knowing Ria's psycho ass, I made it worse. I hate I had to embarrass her, but she had that shit coming. Look at what she did to my baby's face. I can't believe I ever thought about marrying her.*

Full of herself, Kennedy was lying with her body tucked under Chaz's, thinking. *I bet that bitch will respect my gangsta now. How ill is that? I made her own baby daddy handle her. I told these hos, I'm not the baddest bitch or the queen bitch. I'm that bitch! Hmm, I think I'll write a song about it in the morning.*

"Jay, you think that nigga lived?" Chaz asked as he handed his clothes to him to be put in the garbage bag.

"Man, if that nigga survived all that firepower I put in him, God was with him."

"I just want to know what the deal is so I can know what I'm up against."

"Don't you mean what *we're* up against? If he lived he can be finished off. Chill, I'm going to get rid of these clothes and the burner. I got some gear at this chick crib in Laurelton. I'll bring you back something to wear so we can keep it movin'." Jay opened the door, stuck his head out, and looked both ways before stepping outside.

Chaz sat down on the bed and lay back. He looked at the ceiling, constantly running the previous night's events through his head, wondering how they had gone awry. All he had wanted to do was hang out with Jay and Tony, maybe have a few drinks and smoke some weed to ease his stress.

He had been in the studio all day working on a sound track for the label. After the session he and Jay drove Kennedy home. She had been feeling uneasy all day. She was worried about the feeling that was weighing on her heart; she knew it all too well. It was the feeling that always preceded a tragic event. When her body became idle, the feeling took over from head to toe.

"Chaz, why do you have to go out tonight?"

"I'm only going out for a minute. Ma, I'll be back around two."

Kennedy wondered for a moment if he was going out in search of sex. In the seven weeks since her surgery, she hadn't had the urge to have intercourse. All the bandages, followed by the swelling, had been a turnoff even to her. Her face was almost healed, and just as Phil had promised, she was more beautiful than before. Kennedy told herself she was ready to be intimate with her man again and if she wasn't she'd damn sure fake it. "Baby, we can have sex tonight. I know it's been hard for you."

Chaz could see the insecurities showing through in her eyes. "No, ma, stop. Don't do that. I'm not going out to chase hos. But I'm definitely not going to rush you back into having sex."

"You're not rushing me. I want to."

"Okay, I'm going to have a few drinks and build on some things with Jay. When I get home we can do that—if *you're* ready."

Cruising down Flatbush Avenue, Jay had gone ballistic seeing all the ballers' cars in front of the secret gambling spot. "It's some money in there, kid! You wanna go take some?" he asked Chaz.

"You know I'm game, nigga, but what about Tony?"

"That nigga can wait."

Chaz and Jay had entered the spot, ready to get their gamble on. Chaz's enthusiasm was shattered by the sight of Macon actively engaged in a game of C-Lo. He was betting three Gs at a time. *Can you believe this?* he said to himself. Chaz walked over to him and snatched his betting money out of his hands. "Run them fucking pockets, nigga."

"What the fuck is you doing?" Macon turned around and was facing Chaz. He was shocked. This was the last place he had expected to run into him. Macon knew he was in heavy debt to this nigga. Fuck all that. He couldn't come up in the spot and embarrass him in front of all the major players. "Nigga, I ain't running shit. Business hours is from eight to five."

Chaz threw a mean left upper cut, hitting Macon right under his chin. The sixty-five-year-old man who owned the illegal establishment loved Chaz like a grandson. But the shit couldn't go down in his spot. He had pleaded with Chaz: "Not in here. Please not in here."

Chaz scooped Macon's body up and threw him out the door. He hit the concrete ass first. Macon quickly jumped to his feet and snatched his white tee off. He put his fist up and stood in a fighter's stance. All the gamblers had run outside to watch the action. Some were even placing bets.

Macon took a swing at Chaz, throwing a sloppy right. Chaz ducked quick, narrowly missing contact with Macon's fist, then delivered a crucial blow to Macon's stomach. Then hit him with a mean two-piece to each side of his face. Macon's feet were not planted, so they slipped from under him, sending him to the ground once more.

A little dazed and tired, Macon was ready for the fight to end. He pulled up his pant leg in an attempt to retrieve the small gun that he kept in his boot. Jay saw him going for the gun, but Chaz didn't. Pushing Chaz of the way, Jay pulled out his gun and let off a shot. Hitting Macon inches from his groin, the bullet ripped through his pelvic bone. He let off four more shots. All four bullets landed in his abdomen area.

All the spectators had made a beeline for their cars. The sounds of screeching wheels speeding away could be heard for blocks. Jay and Chaz jumped in their own ride and sped away. They'd driven until they reached the hotel where Chaz now lay. His head began to throb just from the thought of what had taken place the night before.

His head was going to be hurting a lot worse if he didn't hurry up and talk to Kennedy. He opened his cell phone, forgetting that his battery was dead. Closing the phone, he picked up the room phone and dialed her number. She answered on the first ring. "Hello!"

"What's up, li'l mama?"

"You can't be serious, nigga! Where the fuck you been all night that you couldn't call me? Since that bitch pussy that good that you couldn't answer my calls, call her." Kennedy slammed down the phone.

He called right back, deciding he would get straight to the point once she answered. And she answered with her attitude in full swing. "What?"

"Kennedy, some real live shit jumped off last night. I need you to pack me some clothes and come to Queens. Once you get off the Triboro take the Grand Central. Call me when you get on the Grand Central so I can tell how to get here."

Less than an hour later Kennedy felt her skin crawl at the sight of the cruddy hotel. It looked worse than the Bates Motel. It hadn't seen fresh paint in years. Half of the rooms were no longer safe to enter and had been boarded up. Just the sight of it made her want to make a U-turn.

Chaz grabbed and hugged her tight as soon as she crossed the threshold. "Thanks for coming, baby."

Kennedy pulled her head back so she could see his face. "Chaz, I hope some bitch ain't rob you and leave you up in here without your shit. I know the game very well. I used to play it."

"Hell no, ain't no bitch leave me up in here. For the thousandth time, I'm not fucking nobody else. And if I was, I sure as fuck wouldn't bring 'em here. Sit down and let me fill you in."

He spent the next thirty minutes explaining everything to her, minus a few important details, like the fact that dope money was the real reason that he and Macon had been beefing. He had yet to reveal to her that he was still dealing heroin. When he finished telling her the story, her response was, "Sweetie, what do you want to do? We can go wherever you want until this shit blows over."

Her response warmed his heart. The fact that she'd said "we" let him know that she was his rider and that made him love her all the much more.

Hopeful Retribution

A luxurious resort in Mexico was the perfect place for Chaz and Kennedy to lay low. For two weeks they bonded and refreshed their relationship before Chaz received word that it was okay to return to New York. Macon had survived his gunshot wounds, and he didn't snitch to the police. Chaz wasn't sure if his silence was a blessing or a curse, though. Either Macon was scared or he was out for revenge.

Kennedy sat in the chair attempting to get her emotions in check. Her first CD, *Married to the Streets,* was due to be released the next day.

She had a million things on her mind. Like the deranged fan who had gotten her address and was sending her dead white roses almost every other week. The person sent letters filled with threats and vulgar drawings, always signing them *Your Watcher.* Weekly, Yatta would beg her to report the incidences to the authorities or at least hire full-time security, but Kennedy refused. "I'm not letting no fucking coward turn my life upside down. For all we know, it could be Ria's crazy ass."

"Kennedy, explain to me how this person knew that you put white roses on Nina's grave every week?"

"I don't know. Maybe they read the article in *Vibe*—you know, when the reporter visited the grave with me."

"No. The dead roses were coming weeks before that article ran."

"Like I said, I'm not going through *no* changes."

"I still think you should tell Chaz or Strick."

"I'm not telling anyone and neither are *you*."

As Kennedy's makeup artist, Chichi, finished up her lips, the butterflies flipped harder in Kennedy's stomach. She continued to tell herself, *Breathe deep, li'l mama. You got everything under control. Remember, you're that bitch!*

Next thing Kennedy knew she was stepping out of the limo and walking into Float, where her album-release party was being held. By the time she made it upstairs to the VIP, a hundred pictures had already been taken of her. Chaz grabbed her and hugged her tight. She was glad to see him. Their conflicting schedules had kept them apart for the last few days. He stepped back and looked her over. She was sexier than ever in a beige Roberto Cavali halter cat suit and beige-and-green snakeskin stiletto boots. The cat suit hugged every curve on her body. Chaz was ready to take her home and get rid of his erection. "I gotta start going with Yatta to pick out your clothes. She dressing you a little too sexy."

"If you don't like it, take it off of me."

"Don't worry, I have every intention of doing that."

Yatta and Strick came in at the same time. They'd been doing that a lot lately. The VIP area was overflowing with celebrities from various industries. Ty Boogie was on the ones-and-twos, spinning the hottest songs, keeping the dance floor packed. Everyone was already having an excellent time. But the club went bonkers when Kennedy got on the mike and performed from the VIP section overlooking the dance floor. She gave it her all.

Sitting on the couch between Chaz and Strick after her performance, Kennedy had her first drink of the night. She swayed to the music as Ty Boogie continued to play hit after hit. A steady stream of people came through to congratulate her, make small talk, and network.

A half hour later, there was a loud commotion in the area leading to the VIP. It sounded as if an army was marching up the stairs. Club security along with Strick's personal security team secured the VIP's entrance.

Unfortunately, the people causing the commotion outranked them. Instantly the music came to a halt. Within seconds, the VIP was filled with FBI agents.

Kennedy wondered. A slim, plain-Jane-looking white lady in the navy-blue nylon FBI jacket took control. "Good evening, ladies and gentlemen. I am Agent Sorcosky. I have an arrest warrant for Kennedy Sanchez and Kenyatta Sanchez."

Obviously knowing who Kennedy was, two of the agents grabbed her off the couch and attempted to cuff her. She put up a light struggle, "What the fuck is going on?"

Agent Sorcosky walked over to her and explained. "You are now under federal arrest."

"On what *charges*?"

"Conspiracy and interstate trafficking. Be still and let Agent Rivers cuff you or I will *add* resisting a federal officer. Now, which one of the lucky ladies is your sister? And don't lie, I can get her mug shot sent up."

Without flinching, Kennedy returned Sorcosky's stare. "Fuck you."

"Get this stupid bitch out of my face," Sorcosky ordered the agents.

Yatta stood up and extended her arms so that she could be cuffed.

Facing the stares and whispers of the crowd, Kennedy told herself as she was led through the sea of people, *Hold it together, ma. Never let them see you break. No tears. No tears. You are that bitch.*

She and Yatta were transported downtown in separate cars. Once inside the Metropolitan Correctional Center, the sisters were placed in different interrogation rooms. Agent Sorcosky sat across the table from Kennedy. She gave Kennedy a stare that was meant to intimidate. Sorcosky looked over some notes that she had taken. Then she looked back at Kennedy. "Do you know Peter Jameson?"

"Do you know my lawyer, *Agent Sorcosky*? Can you spell *lawyer? L-a-w-y-e-r.* I'm choosing to remain silent until she arrives. You know that little Miranda thing you read to me. Do you comprehend it or just recite it?"

The agent was growing tired of the little charade both sisters were playing. Fuck it. She would have the last laugh once their stupid young asses were put away. "Once the judge hands you thirty to forty years, you'll be running and begging me to let you cooperate." She called out to the guard, "Muñez, get this stupid cunt out of here."

In four days, Kennedy had been allowed only two phone calls. She had not seen Yatta since the night they were booked. The food was grotesque. She refused to eat it and it showed. She felt as if the walls were closing in on her.

Yatta was built for jail. She had been there before. But she worried about her sister.

Kennedy's lawyer, Ms. Bovani, visited her on the evening of the fourth day. She showed Kennedy the motion of discovery, which their arrest had been based on. Kennedy couldn't believe the lies Petey had told about her and Yatta. "Ms. Bovani, we both know I'm no saint. But all this shit is a *lie*. I never introduced him to anybody in Norfolk, Charlotte, or Greensboro. And I sure as hell did not traffic any of his drugs. And these witnesses . . . I've never even heard of these people."

Ms. Bovani could see the hysteria in Kennedy's face. She attempted to calm her. "Kennedy, don't worry. This is the way the sneaky feds work. Paul Mazetti is representing your sister. He and I worked together on your cousin Kisa's case." She looked down at her notes. "He is going to be the lead attorney on this case. He has a very good record in federal court. As we speak, his office is in the process of getting you girls a bail hearing for tomorrow. And Mazetti is writing a motion for dismissal."

"At this moment I just want to get out of here. They're treating me like I blew up the Twin Towers. I've only been allowed two monitored calls . . . And no visitors . . . If I'm not out of here by tomorrow . . . I'm going to spaz."

The next day the sisters were granted a bail hearing. The judge set their bail at $1 million each. Strick and Chaz put the money up, reassuring Kora and Big Ma that they had nothing to worry about.

The girls were released six hours after their hearing, and Strick and Chaz were waiting to pick them up in white stretch limo. When Kennedy and Yatta emerged from the courthouse, their weight loss was more apparent than it had been in the courtroom earlier. Chaz joked as he approached them. "We got to hurry up and get y'all uptown so Big Ma can feed y'all. Y'all looking real slim. People might start talking."

"Boy, shut up and give me a hug," Kennedy said, grabbing him, pulling him close.

"Ma, I'm glad you're home. I was fucked up."

"Me, too, baby . . . Me, too. Let's get out of here. I'm ready for a hot plate of food and my mattress."

Chaz smiled, putting his nose in the air. "I hope you're for a bath, too."

"Fuck you."

"I know you want to."

The smell of Big Ma's cooking welcomed them into Kennedy's brownstone. She had prepared endless dishes for them, which Kennedy was ready to devour. Kennedy ripped the foil from each pan, almost missing the note her mom had left. Yatta walked in while she was reading it. "Who's that from, Ken-Ken?"

"Um . . . um, this is from Mommy. It says she and Big Ma took all the kids to Auntie Karen's house so we can eat and get some rest." Kennedy grabbed a plate and loaded it with fried chicken, barbecued chicken, catfish, collard greens, creamed corn, and macaroni and cheese, all made from scratch.

When she came out of the kitchen Chaz looked at her plate, then back at her. "Kennedy, you know as well as I know you not gonna eat all that."

"I was not playing when I said I didn't eat. All I did was drink water. And I didn't trust that."

Chaz placed a sloppy kiss on her cheek. "I'ma lay down for a minute."

Savagely, Kennedy and Yatta ate all the food in almost ten minutes. Strick laughed at them. "Damn, y'all ate that shit like two wild beasts."

They all fell out in laughter. Kennedy chased her food down with her favorite drink, homemade strawberry lemonade with fresh strawberries and lemon slices. Her lighthearted mood then became serious. "This some fucked-up shit Petey doing to us. And that fucking Agent Sorcosky . . . That bitch got a real hard-on for us. She could have come for me at any time. Why the fuck she have to come to my party and embarrass me?"

"That embarrassment boosted your record sales," Strick told her. "You were on the cover of the *Daily News* and the *Post*. They were talking about it on MTV, BET, and even CNN. You sold almost two hundred and fifty thousand copies in two days! That is unheard of for a new female rap artist. People are even saying we did it just to boost your sales."

"Get the fuck out of here." Kennedy laughed. "That's nuts! I go to jail and my sales go crazy."

Kennedy talked to Yatta and Strick for another hour. After they left, she walked into the kitchen and looked around. *I'm not cleaning all this tonight.* She turned and went to her bedroom. Chaz was lying diagonally across her bed. She hit the power button on her stereo. "Love and Happiness" by Al Green came blaring through the speakers. Chaz jumped up. Kennedy hurriedly turned the stereo down. "I'm so sorry, baby. I didn't know it was up that loud."

"That's aight, ma, I needed to get up anyway. Strick still here?"

"Nah, he left when Yatta did. He said call him later," Kennedy said, peeling out of her clothes. Chaz's dick became rock hard as he watched her move around the room ass naked. Kennedy went into the bathroom and turned on the water, allowing it to steam up the room. She stuck her head out the door into the bedroom. "I thought you were going to take a shower with me. Are you still asleep?"

When he didn't answer she stepped into the shower. She

stood under the hot water, letting it drench her from head to toe. It felt so good. Little things like this she would never take for granted again. She jumped when she suddenly felt a cool trickle run down her back. When she turned around Chaz was holding a bottle of peppermint soap and a bath sponge. She hadn't heard him come in. "I see you decided to join me."

"Why wouldn't I? Turn around so I can wash you."

Kennedy followed his instructions, turning toward the water. Chaz poured shampoo in the palm of his hand. He lathered her hair and began to massage the shampoo into her scalp. "Hold your head under the water." He ran his hand through her hair, helping to rinse off the excess shampoo. He picked the sponge up and covered it in peppermint soap. He washed her back slowly and firmly, making his way down to her ample ass. "Turn around," he whispered. Gently he washed her face, shoulders, underarms, and breasts, working his way across her abs. Squatting down, he washed her smooth thick thighs. Standing back up, he began rubbing her between her legs and kissing her neck. Nudging her under the water, he rinsed the soap off her body while planting kisses all over her chest. He sucked and licked her swollen nipples.

"Oh, Pa-pa," she moaned.

Chaz planted kisses all the way down to her stomach, circling the outline of her navel with his tongue. He traced her pelvic bone with wet tongue kisses, then ran his cool tongue over her hot pulsating pussy. He tickled her clit with the tip of his tongue, causing her whole body to shudder. *Don't come yet . . . Don't come yet,* she told herself. She couldn't hold back as her walls became flooded. He stood up, pressing his body against hers. His dick was at full attention. Grabbing her by both sides of her thighs, he lifted her body up, spreading her wide. He rubbed his dick around her inner folds, teasing her.

"Stop teasing me," she panted.

"You want it?"

"Lo necesito ahora."

"You telling me you need it now?"

"Sí, Pa-pa."

He laughed as he eased inside her, causing her to growl. Gyrating his hips, he rolled around inside of her, stroking at a nice medium-paced rhythm. Kennedy licked his neck, flicking her tongue up and down. His strokes became faster and she became wetter. *"Muy bueno."*

"Oh, it's very good, Ma-ma?"

"Sí. Sí."

"You ready to come?"

"Un momento."

Chaz fought vigorously to hold the oncoming nut off. He tried to think of other places and things. Kennedy was making his work difficult. The faster he stroked, the louder she moaned. *"Ah, sí. Ah, sí."*

"Like that, baby?"

"Sí . . . Pa-pa . . . sí." Kennedy screamed, exploding all over him. Her warm cream was kryptonite to his hard dick. He busted an explosive strength-draining nut. Still holding her thighs in midair, he collapsed his head into her chest. Trying to catch their breath, they stayed in that position for almost two minutes, letting the water continue to drench their bodies.

Out of the blue Kennedy let out a deep laugh. Chaz lifted his head and looked at her. "What are you laughing at?"

"I was just thinking . . . I need to go to jail and come home again if it's going to be that *good!*"

After trying repeatedly to reach Yatta on the phone the next morning, Kennedy walked over to her place and let herself in. She walked through the house calling for her. "Yatta, are you okay? Where are you?" The house was completely silent. Kennedy opened Yatta's bedroom door. "What the . . . I knew it—I knew it." She jumped around laughing like a kid at the sight of Strick and Yatta scrambling to put on their clothes. "I knew y'all was creeping around here. I been peeped the way y'all be looking at each other. No wonder you wasn't answering the phone, *Yatta*. My bad for busting in on y'all. I didn't know you had *company*." With that, Kennedy left, not giving them a chance to explain.

She literally skipped back to her house. Once inside, she ran into her bedroom. "Chaz, get up!"

"What?" he asked, still half-asleep.

"You will never guess who I just caught in the bed."

"Who?"

"Yatta and Strick."

Chaz woke all the way up. "Get the fuck out of here."

"I put that on everything I love," Kennedy said with a wide grin on her face. "The funny shit was seeing them trying to throw their clothes on." She doubled over in laughter as she got up from the bed. "Let me get dressed."

"Come here," he told her lustfully.

"No, Chaz, I don't have time. Ms. Bovani said our appointment is ten sharp."

He got out of the bed and wrapped his arms around her. "You sure you don't want me to go with you?"

On the inside she was screaming, *Yes, please go with me. I need you to hold my hand. I don't think I can go through this without you.* On the outside she sang a different song. "No, sweetie, I can handle this one. You've done enough."

"Aight, baby girl, Call me as soon as you finish."

• • •

During the ride downtown, Kennedy teased Yatta to no end about catching her and Strick. But once they arrived at the U.S. attorney's office, all jokes stopped.

The sisters sat side by side with their lawyers beside them. Kennedy's stomach turned as they waited for the assistant U.S. attorney to join them. Mazetti noticed the perspiration on Yatta's face. And he could feel the vibration on the floor from the shaking of her leg. He gave her leg a firm pat to calm her down. "Kenyatta, stop worrying yourself. I can assure you this bullshit will be so far behind you in a matter of minutes."

Ten minutes later, the assistant U.S. attorney, John O'Malley, strolled in, followed by Agent Sorcosky. He looked to be in his thirties, Irish, with classic American white-boy good looks. He was confident that he had the case in the bag. That was before Mazetti tore into him like a pit bull. He didn't even give the pair time to make acquaintances or have a seat.

"No need to sit and converse." Mazetti handed O'Malley a blue legal document. "Here is my motion to dismiss all charges. Your CI should have informed you that he is using you as a tactic to seek revenge against my clients. We do have recorded phone calls of him threatening retribution toward my clients." Mazetti gave Sorcosky a devilish smile. "And if the case does go to trial, you know I'll destroy your lying-ass witnesses on cross. As far as the dates that Mr. Jameson is saying Kennedy Sanchez transported his narcotics . . ." He reached into his briefcase and pulled out a small stack of papers. "We have notarized attendance records from Norfolk State University that indicate she was in all of her classes on those dates. So you can take you fairytale case and shove it up your tight ass. And, Agent Sorcosky, if you come after my clients again with a half-cocked case, I will sue you personally and the entire U.S. attorney's office for malicious prosecution. Come on, ladies, let's leave."

Ms. Bovani was the first to rise from her chair. She always loved to see the great Mazetti in action. Kennedy and Yatta were too shocked to move. Neither could believe how he had just spoken to an FBI agent and an assistant U.S. attorney. Even more, they couldn't believe the bitch, Sorcosky, or O'Malley weren't saying anything. Slowly Kennedy and Yatta rose from their chairs and followed their lawyers. Mazetti stopped in front of Agent Sorcosky. "After 9/11, shouldn't you be out chasing terrorists instead of harassing the innocent?"

"Fuck you, Mazetti!" she hissed, and shoved past him out of the office.

Mazetti was worth the outrageous fees he charged. Two weeks later, all of the charges were officially dismissed. The family gathered and threw a huge feast to celebrate. The day after the dismissal, Kennedy was back on the grind. Along with Yatta and her personal beauty team, she was off on a ten-week promotional tour. The tour proved to be more challenging, stressful, and exhausting than any of the previous ones.

Reporters and DJs would ask her only a few questions about her album and her career. The rest of the questions pertained to her public arrest, her relationship with Chaz, and the growing beef between him and Hassan. This time around, her professional "no comment" reply was no longer working. So it was a challenge for her to handle herself. She came close to telling a few of the reporters who didn't understand the meaning of her reply to fuck off.

Having to maintain a professional face regardless of the circumstances was driving Kennedy nuts. She started depending on prescription drugs to get her though each day.

Imaginary Friends

Lord, protect me from my friends . . .
I can handle my enemies.

"**D**amn it! I missed six calls," Kennedy told Kneaka. "And all of them were from Chaz." She pressed talk on her cell, calling him back. "Hey, baby, what's up?"

"Yo, where the fuck you at? I been calling you all day!"

"Hold up. First of all, I don't know *who* you think you're talking to, but you can come better than that!" She pressed the end button.

"Did you hang up on him?" Kneaka asked, laughing.

"Hell yeah!" Kennedy proclaimed proudly.

Chaz called right back. "I know you didn't hang up on me."

"I sure did!"

"Why?"

" 'Cause, you need to check yourself before you start feeling like you can talk to me any kind of way."

"Come on with that bullshit, man. I'm at your house right now. You not here, Yatta ain't seen you since y'all got back, and you not answering none of my calls. If that was you looking for me, you would've been breaking."

She smiled at his jealousy. "To answer your question, I'm in the Village eating with Kneaka and her roommates. Since you were *too busy*. And I wasn't answering my phone 'cause it was on vibrate in my purse. I'll be home in about forty-five minutes."

"Nah, don't rush now. I'm going out."

"How you going to go out and I just got off the road? You haven't even seen me! Whatever, Chaz, do *you*." Kennedy hung up the phone. This time he didn't call back.

After dropping Kneaka and her friends off at a club in midtown, Kennedy was focused on getting home and into her bed. Kay Slay's latest drama CD was blasting from the speakers. Kennedy was bobbing her head to the freestyles. Suddenly she felt like her ears were playing tricks on her when Hassan's latest dis song to Chaz came on the air.

"It's senseless to tell Schiz to suck my dick/He already did it when he kissed his bitch."

Kennedy almost hit the car in the next lane as she tried to get off the FDR. She sped over to Sure Gold Studios, parked illegally, and ran upstairs.

Her instincts were correct. Hassan was up there with Caz, his entourage, and some groupies. He stood up smiling when he saw her come through the door. "Ken, what up, ma?"

"No! What the fuck is up with you?"

The room fell completely silent. Judging by her expression, Hassan knew she meant business. "Come on, Ken. Let's talk back in the office."

"Fuck no! So you can have some more shit to say about me on one of your petty-ass songs. We can talk outside." She turned and walked out. Hassan followed.

Kennedy paced around the concrete until she got her words together. "Damn, Has, not for nothing I thought we were better than this bullshit. I know you and Chaz is beefing. And I may be at the center of your beef. But you know it's so fucked up for you to put me on Broadway like that. I mean, before anything, we were friends first. Maybe I'm wrong about that, and you. You've turned into a fake, shysty motherfucker just like the rest of these industry assholes."

Her comments hurt Hassan because he really cared about her. For the first time he saw how his and Chaz's beef was affecting her. "Ken, I know you don't want to hear I'm sorry, but I am. I just went crazy after that shit at the party. Then the way he dissed me on the last song. You have to know I never meant to put you out there like that. I knew it was only a matter of time before you got at me about it."

Shaking her head, Kennedy let out an insane little laugh. "You know, once I got this opportunity, I *thought* that everything was finally going to be okay. Now it seems like everything is more fucked up than it was before. I've lost several good friends, including you. A man hates my sister so much that he sent the feds after us." She laughed again. "At first I was grindin' to keep up my lifestyle. Then I found myself grindin' harder for the sake of my son. Now . . . now I just feel like I'm grindin' to keep my sanity."

Looking her directly in the eye, Hassan told her, "Believe it or not, I know exactly how you feel. I'm sorry that I added to the bullshit. I'll even apologize to you publicly for what I said on that song."

"That's peace. I just hate it all had to end like this." Kennedy got into her 745i and sped away, leaving Hassan on the curb.

Chaz's attention was fully captured by the sexy chocolate grinding her perfectly round ass against his crotch. This shorty was gorgeous and her body was mean. The red leather microminiskirt she was wearing was so short that her ass cheeks were hanging out. She was driving Chaz crazy as he partied it up at Mars 2112 along with Jay and Rob. He was ready to slide her home. *Damn, it's been four months since I fucked a chick besides Ken . . . and shorty right here, she could get it tonight!*

Suddenly an image of Kennedy flipping out popped into his head. He heard her voice saying, "All you trifling niggas is just alike. You claim to be different, but you're all the same." Chaz was determined to prove that he was different. A feeling of disgust came over him. *Why the fuck am I even contemplating sliding with this groupie bitch?*

Chaz looked over at Jay. "Man, I'm going to home to wifey."

"Yeah, you need to go home before you get fucked up," Jay said, eyeing the chick's unbelievable shape.

The crowded dance floor emptied as four guys started fighting, throwing wild blows. The rumble was headed right in their direction. Rob turned and pushed Chaz and Jay toward the back exit, out of the way of the oncoming brawl. Rob ushered them through the door and right into the hands of four masked men. Three of the men grabbed Chaz and pinned him to the concrete wall. It all happened so quickly that he didn't have time to react.

Jay was grabbed from behind by the biggest masked man and placed in a choke hold. He was utterly shocked when he saw Rob go back inside the club and pull the door shut. That would be the last thing he saw. The masked assailant placed a razor-sharp nine-inch blade against his neck. With precision, he sliced Jay's neck open like a piping-hot baked potato. Blood poured profusely from his gaping wound. The killer then released him and stepped back, allowing Jay's lifeless body to hit the pavement. A single tear escaped Jay's right eye.

In horror, Chaz screamed out, "JAY!"

"Shut the fuck up, *nigga*!" Macon said, removing his mask. "Your punk ass ain't shit now that your muscle laying there with his shit sliced open!"

"Suck my dick, *bitch*!" Chaz hawked and spit right in Macon's face, infuriating him. He was supposed to be begging for his life, not rebelling. Macon swung hard and landed a bone-crushing punch to the left side of Chaz's face. His body fell onto the man on his left.

"Straighten that fucker up!" Macon barked. "Now gut him," he instructed the killer who had just taken Jay's life.

The killer moved his five-ten, two-hundred-and-eighty-pound frame closer to Chaz. Through the hole in the mask, his mouth displayed a chilling, evil grin. He drew his blade and rammed it into the side of Chaz's stomach. The squishing sound of the knife splitting Chaz's skin was disgusting. He pulled it out and stabbed it into the middle of Chaz's abdomen below his navel. As if he was gutting an animal, he ran the knife upward. Intense pain ran through Chaz's body, causing him to black out. Macon danced around laughing like a kid, so happy to see his biggest foe being taken out.

Just then, three bouncers, who had removed the fighters from the club moments earlier, were coming in through the back. The first bouncer to turn the corner and see the attack screamed out, "Yo! What the fuck is going on up there?" The other two followed his lead and ran up the alley behind him.

Macon pulled his mask down. "Let's go. Now, nigga, let's go."

The assassin pulled the knife from Chaz's body. The two men who were holding him released him from their grasp. His body fell forward. He hit the pavement face-first, breaking his nose. The first bouncer stopped and turned his body over. "Oh shit, it's Chaz." On his cell phone he called for help. The other bouncers gave chase to the four attackers, but they fled in a waiting car.

Kennedy stopped at the bodega to pick up some snacks to absorb some of the liquor and stress. She parked her car in the garage and walked the five blocks to her building. From the corner she could see Yatta's new Jaguar. *I can't believe she has her baby parked on the street.* As she walked past Yatta's car the darkly tinted passenger window rolled down. "Ken-Ken," her aunt Karen called out to her.

"Damn, Auntie, don't scare me like that. What the hell y'all doing sitting out here?" Kennedy asked, looking over at Yatta in the driver's seat. When she noticed the tears in Yatta's eyes, her heart dropped. "What's wrong? Are the kids okay?"

"The kids are fine," Yatta answered. "Get in."

"No, not until you tell me what wrong!"

Karen looked at Yatta. "Tell her."

Yatta inhaled deeply. "Strick called me from Cali an hour ago. He's on his way back here now." Yatta stopped talking.

Kennedy looked at her, waiting for her to finish. "Why is he coming back, *Yatta*?"

"He got a call . . . Chaz and Jay were stabbed at Mars 2112 two hours ago."

Did she just tell me Chaz was stabbed? I just talked to him. Kennedy's head began to throb. Her stomach bubbled. Saliva filled her mouth. She dropped her purse and bags. Feeling the rush coming from the pit of her stomach, she doubled over. Vomit exploded from her mouth onto the sidewalk.

Karen and Yatta leaped from the car to help her. "Get it all out, baby," Karen told her as she patted her back and massaged the nape of her neck. "Yatta, go in the house and get a cold wet rag and some Sprite or ginger ale."

Once Kennedy stopped vomiting, she sobbed heavily as she questioned Yatta. "Is he okay? Please tell me. He's not dead, is he? I can't lose him now . . . I swear to God I can't."

"Baby, I won't know his condition until we get to the hospital. Please get in so we can go see about him."

• • •

Entering the crowded family waiting area, Kennedy saw Chaz's mother, Sal; and his sister, Shorty. She could tell that they had been crying. But now it seemed as if they were more focused on consoling Jay's baby's mother, India. And she appeared to be inconsolable. Chaz's cousins, closest friends, workers from the label, people from the club, and police filled the room.

Shorty looked up and saw Kennedy standing in the waiting-room entrance. She rushed over to her, and they embraced and held on to each other. "Please tell me he's not dead," Kennedy said in a low muffle.

"No, Kennedy, he's not dead. He's holding on. But Jay didn't make it."

"No! Not Jay." Kennedy wailed, causing India to cry harder and louder.

"Come on, Ken. Let's go outside and get some air."

"I don't want to go anywhere. I want to see Chaz *now.*"

"He just came out of surgery. He's in recovery. Once he gets in his room, they said we can see him."

As the hours passed and daylight approached, the waiting room thinned out. Kennedy was staring straight ahead, looking at nothing in particular, when the nurse came in to update the family. "Mr. Harris is out of recovery. He's in room 2610. He's under heavy sedation and will probably sleep until tonight."

"Can we see him?" Shorty asked.

"Sure. It will do him good to hear familiar voices."

Shorty and Sal stood up, but Kennedy didn't. Turning around to look at her, Shorty said, "Come on, Kennedy."

"Nah, y'all go ahead. Spend some time alone with him."

Sal extended her hand to Kennedy. "Come on, baby. If he needs to hear anybody's voice, he needs to hear yours."

Kennedy stared at Sal's hand for about twenty seconds before grabbing it and standing up. Hand in hand, the three women walked down the hallway.

The sight of Chaz lying there battered and banged reminded Kennedy of Pretty Boy's death. She paused and stood by the door while Shorty and Sal went into the room. Sal stood next to the bed, looking down at her son, noticing that his face held the same sad expression it had worn when he was a young boy sitting on a courtroom bench, watching his mother being led away to prison. She'd missed the best years of Shorty and Chaz's lives, but they never judged her. Now here was her child, pulled inches away from dying. And just when she was getting know him.

God, thanks for saving my baby, she said inside her own mind. She picked up his left hand, gently rubbing it with her own. "Hi, Chaz, it's Mommy. I don't know if you can hear me. We've talked so many times since I came home. But I guess we've never had the conversation that counts. I'm so sorry that I wasn't there for you and Shorty when you needed me the most. I hated myself for so long for not being there to do the things that mothers are supposed to do." Sal's tears escaped both eyes despite her effort to hold them back. "I know you had Grandma, but you needed me. Because of my mistakes, the two of you were left to fend for yourselves out here in the world. And you had to teach yourself how to be a man. I'm so proud of the man you've become. I can only hope and pray that I've made you proud." She covered her mouth to mask her sobs as she walked from the room. Shorty followed her out.

When they were gone, Kennedy eased toward the bed. She focused on Chaz's bandaged broken nose. Her teardrops hit his hospital gown, leaving huge wet spots. She took his hand. "I hate that we argued last night. If you would've . . . I mean, I love you so much, baby. If you had died last night, I would've died with you."

Suddenly Chaz squeezed her hand and she jumped. A smile lit up her face. His eyes remained closed, but her heart warmed a little, knowing that he recognized her. Never letting go of his hand, she pulled a chair close to the bed and sat down. Resting her head against the bed rail, she said a silent prayer. *God, I know I don't need any man more than I need you. But I love him so much. Please, God . . . please heal his body. Please bring him back to me whole again. All my faith is in You. And, Lord, I know Jay did dirt, but he had a beautiful heart. God, please let him come home and rest with You. These and all blessings I ask in Your holy and righteous name. Amen.* Kennedy drifted off to sleep. Still holding Chaz's hand.

"Good morning, this is Nancy Michaels with this morning's top story. Chaz Harris, also known as Schiz, a well-known rapper from Brooklyn, was brutally stabbed while leaving a local Manhattan nightclub early this morning." A picture of Chaz flashed behind the reporter's head. "Jason Simms, who was with Harris, was fatally stabbed. Harris is listed in serious but stable condition. Police said they have several suspects who will be brought in for questioning. They are asking for anyone with information to come forward."

Rob hit the power button furiously, turning the television off. He scrolled his cell-phone contacts until he came to the name that he was looking for, then pressed the send button so hard it nearly stuck.

The phone rang four times before there was an answer. "Nigga, don't start callin' me every time a news report come on. Trust, I'm watchin' the same shit you watchin'!" Macon said.

"Don't give me that shit, muthafucka!" Rob yelled. "You promised me this would be eighty-sixed. It's my ass on the line if he lives. Even if he don't put it together, which I know he will, he's gonna think I ran like a little bitch. If your ass hadn't tried to be so fucking personal and put one in his dome, this shit would be over."

"Whoa, hold the fuck up! Who in the hell you think you talking to, nigga? Don't ever try and tell me how to handle mines, dawg. You'll fuck around and have two in your head dun. I gave you your cake, now take it and get low if that's what you feel. Fuck that nigga. He done anyway. He can't go to five-o wit'out blowin' his own spot up. And he can't get at nobody without his muscle!"

Rob couldn't believe his ears. "Macon, you're more foolish than I thought. Chaz got all kind of connections. Damn, don't you listen to the streets? You *keep* disrespecting that man's gangsta. Fuck Chaz, that nigga Strick got some straight wolves on his team. *And* he ain't afraid to let them loose."

"Why do I get the feeling you ready to sell me to those niggas to save your ass?"

"It ain't neva like that! I'm just trying to show you what you up against. I just know I'm not sticking around and waiting for it to get busy."

"I don't need your punk-ass suggestions! Macon don't run from shit. Chaz started this and I'm going to finish it. You ain't got no choice but to run 'cause you a rat! You got tired of being a little go-boy for Chaz, so you decided to sell him out to highest bidder. And that was your man since free lunch. So don't pretend like you give a fuck about me. 'Cause if that's what you'd do to your man, I'd hate to see what you'll do to me. Maybe it *is* best if you get low and lose my number, faggot!" Macon slammed the flip on the cell phone closed and threw it hard on the glass table, cracking the tabletop.

He looked over at his younger brother, Marcus, then over at his cousins Rashan and Damon. Macon lit a blunt filled with dro and laced with dust. Taking a long pull on the blunt, he held the smoke in for about thirty seconds before exhaling. Looking at his brother through slanted eyes, he told him, "Young Marc. Find that nigga before he get missing. When you find him put two in his head."

Awakened by a tap on the shoulder, Kennedy opened her eyes and saw Strick and Yatta standing there. Blinking, she tried to focus in on her surroundings, then feeling Chaz's hand in hers quickly reminded her. Looking at him sleeping brought her an instant sadness. She looked back at Strick with tear-glazed eyes. Her face was pale and she looked disheveled. "What up, Strick?" she asked as she stood up and hugged him, never letting go of Chaz's hand.

"How's my man holding up?" asked Strick.

"I think he's all right. The doctor said that he should make a full recovery. He hasn't woken up yet." She paused. "I just don't understand why . . . why he couldn't stay home and wait for me." Kennedy started to sob and leaned her head on Strick's shoulder.

Yatta was concerned because Kennedy was gripping Chaz's hand so fanatically. She stepped forward and told her sister, "Come on, ma, let's go get some air. You need some food, too. I know you haven't eaten anything since yesterday."

"No, I'm fine, I can't leave him until he wakes up. I can't leave him. I wasn't where I was supposed to be last night and look what happened."

Strick searched his mind for words of comfort to give Kennedy. Before he could utter a single one, Chaz began gasping for air. His eyes were wide open, and his grip on Kennedy's hand tightened. But it didn't matter how bad her hand hurt; all her concern was for Chaz.

Strick ran from the room in search of a doctor. Within seconds, two doctors and three nurses arrived. One of the nurses peeled Chaz's fingers from Kennedy's hand. Strick helped to take

Kennedy from the room. Sal and Shorty, who had been to the hospital cafeteria, ran toward the room to see what all the commotion was about. Yatta explained everything as they walked toward the waiting room.

Fifteen minutes later, the lead doctor walked into the waiting room and scanned it until he saw Sal. "Um, Miss Harris, Chaz is okay. He had a reaction common to a lot of patients coming out of anesthesia. His vitals are looking good and we've stabilized him. He's asking for you, his sister, and his wife."

Chaz's voice sounded like it no longer belonged to him; it was rough and raspy. Everyone stood around his bed. Sal was on his right with Shorty next to her. Yatta and Strick were at the foot of the bed and Kennedy was on his left. Through his drowsy eyes he stared back at them. No one's face stood out more than Kennedy's, marked with her pain and guilt. Her eyes kept apologizing to him over and over as tears slid down her face. She could not look directly at him.

To get her attention, he squeezed her hand. "Don't cry, Kennedy," he said, his voice very hoarse. "It's not your fault."

Kennedy bit her lip and nodded. Chaz closed his eyes to the hurt faces in front of him and drifted into a much happier place—his dreams.

Dreams were his refuge, but that didn't last for long. An hour into his sleep they turned volatile. Chaz dreamed of the night that Jay had shot Macon, but in his dream, he was the one who was shot and killed. He could see himself lying on the ground next to a throat-slit Jay. He relived that same dream for the next three days. He kept hearing the heavy steel door from the club slamming shut, and at that exact moment he would wake up, every time.

On the fourth day, he awoke from the dream with a question

to ask Kennedy. *"Where the fuck was Rob?"* It occurred to him that Rob had intentionally shut the door that night. He needed to talk to someone about the subject immediately.

For the first time in four days, Kennedy wasn't by his side when he opened his eyes, but Chaz knew she wasn't far away. He heard her voice right outside his hospital-room door. She was in a heated exchange with someone. There were three other voices. The only other recognizable one was Strick's.

"Next time you want to talk, call my attorney," Kennedy said over her back as she entered the room and sat down on the bed. "Hey, I didn't know you were awake."

Chaz knew from her reaction and the commotion that something wasn't quite right. "What's up, Ken? What was that about?"

"That was some DTs from homicide. Before I get into what they were saying, let me explain this to you." She inhaled deeply. "The night that you were stabbed, I went to see Hassan at the studio. Before you start thinking some off-the-wall shit, I swear on everything I love nothing happened. I went over there to spaz on him, which I did! 'Bout that bullshit he said on his last dis record toward you. After saying what I had to say, I was out. And of course he used me as his alibi when the jakes went to see him. And just now they right out accused me of being a part of a conspiracy with Hassan and Caz to murder you. All that noise you just heard was Strick and me telling them to fuck off."

"I know Hassan didn't have anything to do with this."

"How come you seem so sure about that?" Kennedy said, reading into his confidence.

"Quiet as kept, ma . . . I already know."

"Know *what*?"

"I know who tried to eighty-six my ass. It was Macon."

"And when were you going to tell me? And since we're on the subject, what are y'all really beefing about? 'Cause between your niggas and Strick, I've been hearing a whole lot of whispering about drug money."

Might as well set this shit straight. "Before I get into all that, have you heard anything from Rob?"

"Hell no, ain't *nobody* heard from that faggot! I heard he ran like the bitch he is."

"Nah, I think he did more than run."

"What? You think he set you up?"

"It's starting to look that way."

"Chaz, what does all this have to do with drug money and Macon?"

"I fronted the nigga some work when his spots down south got raided. That wasn't a problem. I usually fronted him whatever he wanted on top of what he copped. He always paid on time with no problem. I gave him time to get back on his feet before I stepped to him about my paper. Every time I got at him, it was a story. Then that night at the gambling spot, the nigga disrespected me when I told him to run them pockets. And well, you know the rest."

"So this beef is from when you used to move weight?"

"You just don't get it?"

"Get what?"

"I never stopped."

"Wait a minute." Kennedy got up from the bed. "What the fuck? You never *stopped*! I can't believe this shit."

"What you mean, you *can't* believe this shit?"

"Fuck it, I'm not going there with you, not while you laid up in this hospital."

"No, ma, don't ever bite your tongue. Say what you got to say *now.*"

"I mean, I don't understand you. Chaz, you received one of the biggest advances ever heard of in rap and yet you're risking your life and those around you to do the same shit you were doing before. What kinda shit *is* you on?"

"Ma, half that shit went to the fuckin' IRS! The other half I put up. This rap shit only gave me the green light to spend my real money. Do you know how long and spaced out royalty checks be? Fuck that. I'm stackin' for the future right now!"

"So you telling me you can't take that twenty Gs you get per show and stack that versus that twenty-five to thirty you get per brick?"

"Girl, you must be up out your mind. Them is coke prices. That's what you used to dealing with. I move boy. Bricks of that go for fifty to a hundred Gs or more easy."

"I feel you on that, but we've met so many of the same people—people who've shown me how to flip my money legally."

"You so fucking off."

"Fuck you, nigga!"

"No, fuck you! Them same people you braggin' about, them bourgeois niggas and millionaire-billionaire crackers, is some of my best customers. Blew your mind, huh? Here, your fresh-out-the-street ass thought these muthafuckas was so straight and narrow. And how the fuck you even actin' like you turning your nose up at me? You just stopped hustlin'."

"Yes and the key word is *stopped*!"

"And you'd probably still be hustling if I didn't put you on." Chaz paused to get the conversation under control. "Look, Kennedy, it ain't as easy for me to walk away as it was for you. You know how many people eat off the money I make? All I'm asking is . . . for you not to judge me. I didn't judge you when the feds picked your ass up."

"You can't even compare that. And nobody is judging you. The least you could've done was put me on to how shit was going down wit' you." Kennedy's face was red. "I'm not some square broad. You know me: I'm down for whatever. I just can't deal with this deceit. I already have enough to look over my shoulder for." She snatched her purse from the window seat and knocked over a get-well potted plant. The damp black soil spilled onto her beige canvas Chanel sneakers. "Fuck fuck!" she yelled.

"Are you all right?" Chaz asked, truly concerned.

"*Wow,* so now you're concerned with me."

"Yo, stop playing wit' me for real."

"Whatever. I'm out."

"Be out, then, you selfish b—" Chaz caught himself.

"Go ahead—say it! Call me a bitch. That's what you're really feelin', you fuckin' faggot," Kennedy said, jerking the door open.

Shorty walked in as Kennedy was exiting the room. "You all right, Kennedy?"

"I'm good, ma. I'll see you later."

"Damn, Chaz, what's wrong with Kennedy?"

"Man, she just buggin' *again.*"

Consequences

Rob stepped out into the early-morning darkness. Cautiously, he looked up and down the street. It had been a week since the incident at Mars 2112. If he hadn't had so many loose ends to tie up, he would've disappeared three days earlier. Instead, he hid out in Tompkins's Projects with his young girl, Yameek. This wasn't one of his better choices. She had a mouth like the hood rat that she was. Therefore, his hideout wasn't a huge secret. And he had his head so far up his own ass he couldn't see what was going on around him.

Yameek, who Rob so foolishly thought was down for him, had once shared a bed with Macon's little brother, Marcus. Finding out that Rob was laid up with Yameek was priceless information to Marcus. He knew that for a price she would set Rob's snake ass up with no problem. The girl craved money; sadly, she loved it more than she loved life. And her price for a little information about Rob was only three thousand dollars. Yameek might have been ghetto, among other things, but she wasn't anyone's fool. She knew that Rob didn't give a flying fuck about her. So possibly giving up information that could end his life didn't even cause her to flinch.

A sense of relief came down over Rob as he walked over to the Dodge Stratus rental car that his baby's mother had dropped off the night before. *I'll be straight once I make it to Baton Rouge,* he thought as he threw his duffel bag into the trunk. No one knew that he still had family in Louisiana, making it a perfect hideout. He knew that his name had been connected to Macon's. Knowing that it would only be a matter a time before Chaz sent someone after him, he had to get on the road. He hated to make the twenty-hour drive by himself. He'd begged Yameek for two days straight to ride with him, but she promised him only that she would fly down the next week. *Fuck her bum ass,* he thought. *I'ma get me one of them thick-ass, biscuit-eating Creole bitches while I'm down there.*

While the car was warming up, Rob prepared for the long ride, taking out his P89 Ruger and placing it in between the seat and the center console. Pulling out a leather CD booklet, he scanned through the pages before choosing a classic DJ Clue disc. When he heard Chaz's voice come through the speakers, dropping a hard freestyle, the voice sent chills down his spine. He immediately hit the skip button changing the track. "The Best of Both Worlds" came blasting through the speakers. From his coat pockets he pulled out four packs of Newports and various candies and tossed them on the passenger seat. Now he was ready to roll.

As Rob drove up the street, he noticed four guys on motorcycles ahead of him. They were doing all kinds of tricks, driving top speed then popping wheelies. One of the guys leaned his bike real low to the ground, pulled it back up, sped up, and stopped on his front wheel with the back of his bike suspended in the air. Rob smiled, thinking to himself, *These niggas is wildin'. They better calm that shit down before five-o bag 'em.* The bikes stopped at a four-way stop long enough for Rob to pull up behind them. He grabbed a pack of cigarettes and pulled the plastic wrapper off the package. Too busy fiddling with the pack, Rob never noticed the movements of the bikers. One lone biker remained in front of the car while the other three made U-turns, surrounding the car. The first bike pulled up, stopping on the driver's side, the second bike stopped at the rear of the car, and the third stopped on the passenger side.

From the corner of his eye, Rob noticed the bike next to him and he looked up. The biker propped his helmet on top of his head. Rob's heart stopped when he saw Marcus's face wearing an "I gotcha" smirk. Simultaneously the four bikers raised their guns. "I'm not going out like this," Rob mumbled to himself. Sliding his hand between the seat and the console, he reached for his gun. He had trouble removing it, and in a panic he yanked at the gun with his finger around the trigger, causing it to go off, shooting himself in the leg.

A wide grin spread across Marcus's face. *Look at this dumb nigga,* he thought. The feeling of power gave him an adrenaline rush. It was he who decided whether this human lived or died. Marcus squeezed the lever of his gun twice. The window shattered and the back left side of Rob's head exploded. The three other gunmen emptied their clips into the car. Just as quickly as they had appeared, they went their separate ways. Each man ditched his stolen bike in a different location and got in his waiting transportation. Marcus took a cab to Kennedy Airport, where Macon was waiting.

Judging by the murderous smile on his brother's face, Macon could tell that the job had been done. "Is everything copacetic?" he asked as he embraced Marcus.

"Everything is love, nigga. No casualties on our side. Yo, son was so shook he shot his own self in the leg."

"Say word."

"Word! That fool made it easy as hell on us. I put two right in the back of his melon."

Macon still couldn't find any kind of calm. He knew that Chaz had to be terminated and the sooner the better. That was the only way he would be able to regain his sense of security. Macon also knew that it would be impossible to touch Chaz anytime soon.

"Damn, bro, what got you zoned out like that?" Marcus asked.

"Man, I need all this shit to end. I don't know how Chaz survived anyway. And all this shit is fucking up my money, yo. Just gotta lay low and plan this shit right."

"Revenge is best served cold anyway."

Macon agreed. "Yeah, catch that nigga when and where he least expect it."

Running from Love

Chaz's home had been filled with family, friends, and security since his release from the hospital a week earlier. It was way too much for Kennedy. Her stress level had gone through the roof already, but news of Rob's murder sent it up another notch. She had hated him with a passion and felt that he had gotten what his hand called for, but his death shed light on how much more serious the situation was becoming with each succeeding episode. At this point she would've given her left arm to return to the solitude of her own home. But when she even suggested that she wanted to spend one night at her own house, Chaz would call her selfish. That would then snowball into an even bigger argument about her giving up her brownstone in Harlem.

"I'm concerned about your safety," Chaz would argue. "Don't you know them niggas know where you stay? They'll touch anybody to get at me. I told my mother, Shorty, and Ria to find new places and I'll pay for everything. Hell, I'm selling this house. You don't have to leave the city. Just find somewhere downtown."

Just to be spiteful, Kennedy argued back. "I'll move, *temporarily*. But don't tell me where to move. I'm not moving downtown. I want to stay uptown, and I mean Harlem."

"Kennedy, be the fuck reasonable, aight? You know downtown is more secure. You know what? Just fuck it, 'cause your ass is hardheaded."

"I wouldn't have to be making a decision about moving if your ass had kept it gully with me."

"Here we go again," Chaz said with a sigh. "You are so fucking unbelievable. And I'm getting tired of you walking around here saying your little slick shit. You act like I wanted this shit to happen. I shouldn't have told you nothing. This is the thanks I get for keeping it real."

"You should have kept it real from the door and we wouldn't be here now."

"What the hell does that suppose to mean? What you trying to say, Kennedy? You don't want to be with me no more?"

Rolling her eyes, Kennedy answered, "Look, before I say something I don't mean, I'm gonna leave. 'Cause all this is too much for me right now. Since Sal and Shorty are here, I'm going down south to spend some time with the kids. I don't think we should make any crucial decisions right now. We're too emotional."

"There you go," Chaz said with a sarcastic laugh.

"There I go what?"

"There you go with that selfish shit you be on."

"Don't give me that guilt-trip bullshit. I don't need it now. If I don't get away for a little while . . . we're not gonna make it. That's true story."

"Just get the fuck out, Kennedy. I thought you would always hold me down. Damn, even *Ria* wouldn't leave me at a time like this."

"Fuck you. *Fuck you!* And since you feel that way, my man, call her ass over here. She can have this bullshit job back!"

Kennedy stormed out of the den through the semicrowded living room. Without telling anyone good-bye, including Sal and Shorty, she went out the front door and slammed it behind. One of the huge security guards ran behind her. "Kennedy, do you want me to go with you?"

"No! I won't be coming back," she said, hopping into her 745i. After cutting off her cell phone and two-way pager, she headed straight to the New Jersey Turnpike south.

"You aight, baby bro?" Shorty asked, walking into the den to check on Chaz after Kennedy's big exit.

"I'm straight. Kennedy still buggin' on some real live shit. She—" The sound of the ringing doorbell stopped his tirade. "Damn, who the fuck is that *now*? I mean . . . I'm glad everybody coming through showing me love, but it's too much commotion. I see what Kennedy meant. If anybody call tomorrow, tell them the doctor said I need my rest."

Moments later, Chaz was happy to see that his latest visitors were Strick and Yatta. Maybe he could get some insight on Kennedy's irrational behavior from Yatta.

"What up, baby?" Strick asked, extending a pound to Chaz.

"For once it's a different script and movie. Yo, did you find out if that was your people that touched Rob?"

"Nah, it wasn't my team. I think your boy Macon might've got at 'im."

"The nigga got what his hand called for regardless of who gave it to him. If Macon did get at him, he was a smart nigga for that move."

"Enough of that," Yatta said, interrupting their conversation. "How you feeling today, Chaz?"

"I'm feeling a little better. What up wit' you, though?"

"Nothin' much. Where my sister?" Yatta asked, plopping her body down in the plush suede recliner next to the couch.

"I don't know. Somewhere going seven-thirty."

"Oh boy, what's wrong with y'all now?"

"Man, she want to fight about every little thing. Before I got stabbed, we was already talking about moving downtown. Now all of a sudden she's telling me she don't want to leave Harlem. Then all week she been trying to find an excuse to leave here and stay at her house, knowing I need her here."

"You know how she is. She probably just needed a moment to breathe."

"She got her moment. She left out of here a little while ago, going down south."

"What?" Yatta asked with a frown.

"She used the kids as her final excuse. I'm not complaining. I'm never trying to come between her and the kids. And I know she miss them. But at the same time she know I would've paid somebody to drive them up here or fly with them. She just been buggin' since I told her the truth."

"The truth about what?"

"Stop frontin', Yatta. I know Kennedy tell you everything."

"On everything I love, she didn't tell me nothing."

"I told her the real story about Macon and me."

"Which is what?"

"The nigga was into me for a couple of bricks of diesel."

Yatta's face wore a look of perplexity. "Okay, and . . . ? "

"Once she found out that I was still moving work, she spazzed."

"Hell, I thought she knew."

"What would make you think that?"

"*I* figured it out from being around you. Damn, she didn't know? No wonder she flipped," Yatta said, shaking her head.

"But why?"

"First of all, you kept it from her. Secondly, what did she tell you about Pretty Boy's death?"

"She told me that she was in the bed when he got killed and was left with his body for hours."

"Did she tell you what happed after that?"

"No."

Yatta leaned forward, resting her elbows on her thighs. "After his funeral, she stopped talking for about six months. She went to Big Ma's house and stayed shut up in a room the entire time. So when Nina died, we were so sure that she would shut down again. If she didn't have the kids, I think she would have. So much happened to her in the last year and a half, I don't know how much more she can take. Then, when you almost died, it was too much for her. Knowing my sister, she's so scared of hurt and loss that she's probably withdrawing."

"What do I have to do make it right?"

"Don't put her under pressure. You know how she feels about that."

"Let me show y'all something," Chaz said, reaching into the pocket of his baggy sweatpants and pulling out a small black velvet ring box. He opened it, turning it around so that Yatta and Strick could see.

"That is gorgeous," Yatta said, taking the box from his hand and examining the ring. It was a four-carat princess-cut solitaire with a wide band that was covered in two and half carats of diamonds, making it six and a half carats total. The clarity was so amazing that it sparkled in the dimmest of light.

Yatta handed the box back to him. He looked at it once more before closing the box. "I was going to ask Kennedy to marry me the day she came back from tour. We kept missing each other. Then I got mad at her and decided to go out that night. Even after she pleaded with me to stay home and wait on her. Now I wish that I had, and maybe Jay would still be alive."

Ten hours later Kennedy had arrived in North Carolina. She'd driven straight there, stopping only for gas. When she got to her mother's house it was after midnight. She tried sneaking in, but that failed. Her mother was up watching television with Jordan and Mattie. Their eyes lit up when they saw Kennedy. They jumped up simultaneously, screaming.

"Mommy!"

"Auntie!"

They both grabbed her legs and hugged them, hindering her movement. "Hi, babies! I've missed you two so much," Kennedy said, smiling so hard that she was laughing. "And what are y'all still doing up?"

"Watching Disney, Mommy," Jordan said with a giggle. He had grown so much since the last time Kennedy had seen him. Anytime she was away from him, even for a week, she could see the difference. But having been away for two months, she could really see how much he'd grown. He was a rambunctious two-year-old going on three. He was her little handsome man with his beautiful cappuccino-brown skin. Dusty brown curls crowned his head. He was the spitting image of his father. It seemed she'd given birth to him only yesterday. *Boy, where does the time go?* she wondered.

And she just couldn't get over Mattie. Her hair was getting so long and thick, so much like Nina's. For her age, Mattie was tall and slim. Kennedy could already tell that she was going to grow up to look just like Nina.

"Auntie, Auntie, look at my earrings," Mattie said, pushing her right earlobe forward with her finger.

"They're beautiful, li'l mama. Where did you get them from?" Kennedy asked, looking at the obviously expensive diamond earrings. Mattie shrugged.

Kennedy looked over at her mother. Kora shrugged, too. "They were delivered to Klarice's house a few weeks ago. We thought you sent them."

"No, I didn't. Maybe her grandmother sent them, since she *missed* her only grandchild's birthday party."

"Hell, Kennedy, did you really expect her to come, the way you stare her down and interrogate her about her son every time you see her?"

"Whatever, Mommy. Why y'all up *so* late?"

"Now, you know you had your phone off, so Yatta *and* Chaz been calling here back-to-back for the last four hours. And why you leave that boy to come down here? You know I would've brought the kids up there."

"Mommy, it too much going on up there right now for the kids to come up. Plus, I just needed a minute to myself. I just need to clear my head. I'm only staying two days. I have to go back and get in the studio before I go on the road again."

"I understand that you needed a break. But please don't shut everybody out."

Kora's last comment saddened Kennedy for a moment. She knew that her mother was referring to her breakdown after Pretty Boy's death. She looked her mother in the eye. "Don't worry, Mommy. I'll never go back there again."

Over the next two days Kennedy spent every moment attempting to make up for all the time she'd spent away from the kids. Her days were filled with trips to Chuck E. Cheese, Jeepers, and Paramount's Carowinds. Jordan, Niko, and Mattie had the time of their little lives, loving the way that anything they pointed at, Kennedy bought for them.

Kennedy gave Taylor special time in the evening. At age eleven, he was well on his way to becoming a man. Kennedy felt he needed special attention, so each night she treated him to a movie and dinner. During dinner, they discussed girls, puberty, social behavior, and finances. Kennedy enjoyed the special time with Taylor so much that she promised him that when he returned to New York in the fall, they would have a movie night once a month.

When the two days were up, Kennedy hated leaving the kids. But there was work to be done and *too* much drama going down for her to take them back with her in the middle of the summer.

Leaving her 745i with her mother, Kennedy decided to catch a flight back New York. Her short trip had really made a difference. It was so refreshing to get away from the hustle of the city and be able to do only what she wanted to do.

Kennedy promised herself that she would visit the Dominican Republic, where her little sister, Kneaka, would be staying for the summer. She planned to go a week after Chaz got back on his feet.

Kennedy talked to Chaz twice while she was in Charlotte. Both conversations went no deeper than asking and answering basic questions. "How are you?" "What did you do today?" "All right, I'll call you tomorrow."

Before going to the airport, Kennedy stopped at the ultrachic Philips Place shopping enclave and picked up a few expensive trinkets for Chaz just so he would know he'd been on her mind while she was away.

"Hey, Yatta bear!" Kennedy said, wearing a huge smile, when she spotted her sister in baggage claim. "I can't believe you're here on time." She gave Yatta a huge hug.

"I know your always-late ass ain't talking about nobody and time."

"*Whatever.* Let's rock."

"Don't we have to wait on the rest of your bags?"

"Nigga, this is all I took," Kennedy said, holding up her large Vuitton tote.

"Your ass ain't got a lick of sense, jumping on the highway like that. All jokes aside, how are you feeling?"

"I feel a whole lot better. I feel refreshed. I feel like I can deal with Chaz without having to pop a pill daily."

"That's always good to hear. Well, I have a little surprise for you. I think it'll make you feel even better."

"*What* surprise, Yatta?"

Yatta smiled, remembering how Kennedy hated being kept in the dark about surprises. She knew that her sister was going to nag her all the way to Manhattan. And that's exactly what she did—all the way to the front door.

As she opened the door to her home Kennedy's heart fluttered when she saw that her living room was filled with pink roses. Instantly, she knew that her surprise had something to do with Chaz. She turned to Yatta. "Let me guess: Chaz is here, right?"

"Nah, ma, he's not here. But you should go shower, and your outfit is on the bed."

"*Un momento, hermana . . .* What outfit?"

On Kennedy's bed lay a gorgeous pale pink Max Mara sleeveless wrap dress. Lying next to it was a Casadei shoe box. Kennedy picked up the box and opened it, revealing a pair of pale pink-and-cream open-toe stilettos. She eyed her sister suspiciously. "Okay, Yatta, what is this about?"

"I don't know. I was just given the money and told to buy you a pretty pink dress. And also, wear your hair hanging straight with the part down the middle. And wear these in your ears," Yatta said, handing her the red box containing the diamond earrings that Chaz had given Kennedy for Christmas a year earlier.

"What the hell do he want me to do? Get all spiffy to go out to his house and play nurse?"

"You know just as much as I do, Ken. When you finished getting dressed, I'll have more instructions for you."

Kennedy laughed. "Y'all two niggas is funny. So you helping him now? That's what's up. I'm in a good mood today, so I'm game."

After showering, Kennedy slipped on a pink strapless La Perla bra and matching tanga that Chaz had bought her the previous Valentine's Day. She put on some makeup. She used three different shades of pink on her eyes, creating a beautiful shimmering effect.

When she was done, Kennedy walked out into the living room, where Yatta was waiting. Yatta smiled, thinking, *She looks so beautiful.* "You look so *wonderful,* baby sister . . . It's something about you. I just can't seem to put my finger on it. Anyway, here are your final instructions." She handed her sister an envelope.

Pulling the pink embroidered invitation from the envelope, Kennedy looked up at Yatta. "Oh, I know that you had something to do with this." The invitation read: *You're invited to dine with Chaz Harris. Location: where we spent our first date. Time: 6 P.M. Please be on time.*

"Where was our first date?" Kennedy asked aloud.

"Your first date was at Carmine's dingy."

"Technically, that wasn't our first date. Whatever, can you take me to the garage so I can get a car?"

A few minutes later, Kennedy whipped her Aston Martin out of the garage and was zipping in and out of traffic all the way down Broadway.

When she entered the restaurant, a hostess directed her to the table where Chaz was sitting. Butterflies fluttered in her stomach when she saw him. A few tables behind him she spotted two of his security guards. There he sat in a white Lacoste polo-style shirt and blue-jean shorts. His eyes were covered by Dior aviator shades to hide the last traces of bruises. The swelling around his nose had yet to go all the way down, so he wore his baseball cap cocked low.

Chaz looked up in time to see Kennedy coming toward the table. She was so pretty that she looked like a baby doll to him. He stood up, greeting her with a hug, squeezing her as tight as he could without causing his stomach too much discomfort. It felt so good to hold her in his arms. And to Kennedy it felt great to be back in his arms. "Hi, baby. I missed you."

"I missed you, too, li'l mama."

Taking his seat, Chaz asked, "How was your trip?"

"It was great."

"What's up with the kids?"

"The kids are nuts! Jordan is so big and he is off the meat rack. Mattie is so grown and fresh. She is four going on twenty-four. Niko is into his sports. It's just t-ball season and he's already talking about football. And Taylor has discovered girls . . . so you know I'm recruiting all the men in the family, including *you,* to talk to him. And what did I miss here?"

"Not shit," he answered drily. "When you left I went and spent the day in the studio laying down tracks for the new CD. Then I went house shopping. I had to do something to busy myself while you were gone."

Guilt came down over Kennedy; she couldn't even look him in the eye. "My bad for bouncing on you like that. I'm sorry about that, true story. I just needed some time to clear my head so my attitude wouldn't be so hateful toward you."

Reaching across the table, he grabbed her hand. "I hate it when you run from me. Just talk to me. Can you give me that much?"

"I'll try, but what can you give me in return? I need honesty

. . . I need you to confide in me, too. I don't need to find out shit about my man from industry gossip and niggas in the street. And how long are you going to keep slanging them thangs?"

"Ma, I accept you in every way. I need you to accept everything about me—my faults, my flaws and imperfections. And I'm not trying to sell them thangs forever. Just long enough to make sure I'm sitting on enough paper to live comfortably and take care of my people with or without this rap shit. Can you live with that, Kennedy?"

"I guess I don't have a choice if I want to be with you. Do I?"

"Well then, will you marry me?"

"What did you say?"

Chaz pulled the ring box from his pocket. Taking the ring out of the box, he told her, "Let me see your hand." He placed the ring at the tip of her finger. "I said, will you marry me?"

Tears filled Kennedy's eyes. She could barely speak. She nodded. "Yes, baby, yes."

Chaz got up from his seat, and pulling Kennedy from hers, he hugged her tight. "Ma, what are you crying for?"

In between gasps she answered, "I'm . . . so . . . happy. I never thought anyone would propose to me."

"I don't know why you thought that. You're so beautiful inside and out. Everyone around you loves you."

Kennedy blushed through her tears. Her heart was thumping. She couldn't believe this was happening to her. She felt like a little basketball was bouncing inside her. She was nervous like a schoolgirl with a crush. An older, well-manicured white lady sitting at a nearby table with two friends yelled over to Chaz, "What did she say?"

Her question caught them both off guard. Chaz laughed at Kennedy. "Tell her what you said."

Kennedy giggled, with tears still streaming from her eyes. "I said yes."

"She said yes," the lady announced to the entire restaurant. Everyone applauded, turning their attention toward Kennedy and Chaz. "Come here, sweetie," the lady said, motioning for Kennedy. "Let me get a look at the ring?" Kennedy got up, walked over to the lady, and extended her hand. "Beautiful. He must really love you," she said.

"Thanks," Kennedy said, still giggling and blushing.

The lady grabbed her waiter as he walked by. "I want to be the first to congratulate this lovely couple on their engagement. Please bring them out your finest bottle of Clicquot, on me."

"You don't have to do this. Your kind words were enough," Kennedy said.

"No, darling, I insist."

After Kennedy returned to her table, the lady turned to her friends. "Did you see the clarity on that ring? It must've cost thirty thousand or more. I wonder what he does. I can't see his face with those shades and that cap on."

Once the champagne had been brought out, Kennedy insisted that the ladies—who were already tipsy—share a toast with her. Kennedy also properly introduced herself and shook each of their hands. She shook hands with the lady who'd done all the talking last. Holding Kennedy's hand firmly, the lady told her, "I'm Darcy Neal."

"Darcy Neal! Of Manhattan Power Management?"

"So you've heard of me?" she asked, smiling, so full of herself.

"Who hasn't heard of you? I've been trying to get an appointment with your firm for the last six months."

Darcy pulled a business card from her purse, "Give me a call on my personal line and tell my assistant that I said to give you the earliest appointment available. And what business are you in?"

Kennedy caught herself before she blurted out "I'm a rapper." Instead, she said, "I'm a musician."

The rest of the night was spectacular. The newly engaged couple took a horse-and-carriage ride, with security following close by. Kennedy was all smiles. No other man besides Pretty Boy had ever treated her so romantically and Chaz knew it. That's why he'd gone out of his way to make his proposal special. He promised himself that he would be more sensitive to Kennedy in every way.

His heart pounded with excitement during the carriage ride. He watched Kennedy as she looked down at her ring, smiling. The joy that he saw in her eyes made him feel guilty about hiding part of his life from her. "Baby, I really do feel bad for keeping you in the dark and I'm sorry. I know how you get down and I know without a doubt that you ride for me. I just want you to understand that what you don't know will keep you from being my co-de. I *never* wanted to tell you about Jay shooting Macon." He was tensing up so bad that he was he was squeezing her left thigh hard without realizing it.

Kennedy rubbed the top of his hand softly until he eased up on his grip. She looked him the eye. "Sweetie, there is nothing we can't share with each other. No matter what you share with me—even if I don't like it, I'll be there for you. And I'll always-always hold you down." She placed a tender kiss on his lips, sealing her words.

Reality of the Situation

Over the next few weeks, Kennedy moved through life with her head in the clouds. She didn't let anything worry or stress her. Not even the threatening and grotesque letters that she was receiving from "the fan" could spoil her mood. The letters and dead roses had started coming more frequently with each passing week. They were even becoming more consistent, arriving now on the same days. Kennedy took the letters with a grain a salt. After a while she began tossing them in the garbage without opening them.

Despite this, every morning when she awoke she felt brand-new. It showed in the way her face glowed and her eyes shined. Even her walk was different. When people questioned her about her sudden happiness, she'd answer as if she were Jay-Z himself, "I got my swagger back."

Kennedy and Chaz had even let Yatta convince them to keep their engagement a secret, even from both their mothers. Yatta planned a celebration for friends and family at which they would finally make the announcement. She even started gathering all the information needed to plan a wedding and giving it to Kennedy.

One day Chaz walked into what was soon to be his old home in New Jersey. Yatta and Kennedy, in the middle of moving boxes, were sitting looking through magazines. Shaking his head

at the sight, Chaz joked, "I thought y'all was supposed to be helping me pack, not staring at wedding dresses."

Kennedy greeted him with a big hug and a kiss. "Hey, baby,
you came just in time. Yatta's been showing me all this wedding
stuff and I was thinking we haven't even set a date yet or where
we're going to have it."

"Now, li'l mama, you already know I'm leaving all this wedding shit up to you."

"I have no problem doing all the planning. But the location
and date should be something that we both agree on."

"What date did you have in mind?"

"I was thinking a year from now. You know, a nice fall wedding?"

"A year from now? Why so long?" Chaz questioned with a
raised eyebrow.

"You mean you want to do it sooner?"

"I was thinking we'd have it in six months or so."

Kennedy gave it some thought. "I tell you what. Let's do it six
months from now, in the middle of May."

"So where do you want to have it?"

A sly smile crept across Kennedy's face. "Can we have it in
Charlotte?"

Chaz looked at her wondering why she was asking, like that
would be a problem. "Kennedy, it's your day. Wherever you want
to have it is fine with me."

Excitedly, Kennedy began jumping around the cluttered living room like a little kid on a sugar high. "We're going to have a
big outdoor wedding with lots of flowers and a huge wedding
party. The train on my dress is going to be *really long*, just like the
one I dreamed about when I was a little girl." She stopped her
rambling when she became aware of the stares she was receiving
from Yatta and Chaz.

For that moment in time, Kennedy had the most joyful, innocent look about her. Chaz saw a part of her so pure he nearly cried. Even Yatta found herself becoming watery-eyed. Growing up, Kennedy had never let on that she'd dreamed of such things. Now, seeing her so excited made Yatta even happier for her. Yet she was also sad for all the years Kennedy had spent hiding that part of herself from the outside world.

Oh, no, Kennedy thought, *they heard me, they saw me.* She'd never felt more exposed and vulnerable. The room was closing in on her. She needed air immediately. She needed to escape. Grabbing her purse and keys, she ran toward the door, saying only, "I'm going to the store. I'll be back."

After Kennedy's exit, Chaz and Yatta gave each other a look that said, *Leave it alone.* And neither of them ever spoke of the moment again.

The following day Kennedy patiently sat in the lobby of Manhattan Power Management, excited inside to have the opportunity to be represented by such a reputable entertainment agency. Sleeping pills had cured her insomnia, and she was well rested. She was also relaxed, courtesy of the one hundred and fifty milligrams of Effexor she'd popped that morning. Darcy Neal came out and greeted her instead of sending her assistant. To Kennedy's surprise, Darcy was wearing an expensive light blue Yves Saint-Laurent blouse and cream slacks. "Good morning, Kennedy. It's so nice to see you again."

"It's nice to see you again also, Darcy."

"Come on, follow me."

Kennedy's stomach flip-flopped as she followed Darcy down the corridor leading to her office. Pictures of the firm's celebrity clients lined the walls.

Just like Darcy herself, her office said money in a not flashy way. There were only a few pieces of furniture—all very contemporary—which complemented the all-glass corner office that overlooked Manhattan. Kennedy took a seat in a high-backed wood-and-white-leather chair in front of Darcy's desk. Darcy leaned against the front of her desk facing Kennedy. She gave Kennedy a once-over before getting down to business. "Darling, I took the liberty of checking you out. And from what my sources tell me, you're one of the hottest females in hip-hop, with nearly two million records sold. I hadn't even realized that you were the rapper who was arrested at her own album-release party. Then I found out that you were in the middle of some type of rap war between your boyfriend and another very famous rapper."

Kennedy was becoming uneasy. She wanted to know where Darcy was going with the conversation. Darcy got up and walked to the other side of her desk, taking a seat in a white plush chenille-upholstered oversize chair. She spun around, facing Kennedy with a huge smile showing off her beautiful dental work. She told her, "All of those things make you my kind of client. Scandal always sells! Nobody likes boring, goody-goody celebrities. Look at all the scandalous headlines I've made myself."

Darcy's change of pace put Kennedy at ease; she'd almost begun to think that Darcy wasn't going to take her on as a client. "How fast can you get your attorney to look over this contract?" Darcy asked, handing Kennedy a set of stapled papers. "Because I already have something lined up for you with Mischief Jeans. They have a shoot in two days for ads that they're running in *XXL, Vibe,* and *Honey.* The ad pays one hundred and fifty thousand dollars. Mischief is also looking for someone very hot and urban to represent their new line of jeans. That ad campaign pays two million dollars. So if everything goes according to plan, that campaign will be yours."

Kennedy was floored. She could barely process what Darcy was telling her. With a wide smile, she asked Darcy, "Are you serious?"

"Honey, when it comes to money I'm always serious. That's just the beginning. I have a few other things lined up for you, including a possible tour sponsorship. As soon as you sign these papers and get them back to me, I can confirm everything."

"If everything is in order, I will have this signed, sealed, delivered, and back to you in the morning."

Not in her wildest dreams could Kennedy have imagined that such wonderful things were to come to her in the days ahead. Her days were more exhausting yet well worth it for the humungous paycheck. The Mischief photo shoot lasted nearly twenty hours. In one day Kennedy went through five hair and makeup changes and thirty-two wardrobe changes. The following day she met with the CEO of Mischief, Malesa Corbin. Kennedy had not known that like many other fashion execs, Malesa was a black female in her twenties. She was also a huge fan of Kennedy's. She and Kennedy hit it off immediately.

Once the photos and test shots came back, Malesa offered Kennedy the $2 million ad campaign, which included the best of perks and bonuses. Darcy kept Kennedy's days booked with business meetings with companies looking for a young hip spokesperson. Between the meetings, studio time, and the Mischief campaign, Kennedy was absolutely worn out. Anytime she sat down for more than five minutes, she would nod off like a dope fiend.

One day about three and a half weeks into her new hectic schedule, Kennedy was in the studio with Strick and his close friend, superproducer, and CEO of Bricklayers Entertainment, Coco. She was laying down vocals to a track Coco was producing. For some unknown reason, the session had been terribly challenging.

Every fifteen minutes Kennedy needed a break. She complained constantly. "Yo, it's burning the fuck up in here. Can I get some A/C?" she yelled from the recording booth.

"No problem," Strick answered, sending one of his flunkies to turn up the air.

That wasn't enough for Kennedy; five minutes later she was at it again. "I can't breathe in here. I need a break. I want some food and water."

All the complaining was unlike Kennedy, and quite frankly, it was was getting on Strick's nerves. He tried his best to be patient with her. "Ken, can you please give me one more take. If you do that we'll get a two break."

Kennedy huffed as she went back into the booth and slammed the door. Strick looked at Coco. "She is really blowing mines today. I don't know what the fuck is *wrong* with her."

Kennedy placed the large headphones back on her head and Coco started the beat. She bopped her head while waiting for her cue to begin rapping. When her cue came she opened her mouth, but nothing came out. Suddenly her head felt light and she felt the need to sit down, but she couldn't get out of the booth quick enough. Everything went blurry then black as Kennedy collapsed to the floor.

Strick and Coco ran toward the booth. Strick snatched the door open and pulled her limp body out. "Kennedy, wake up. Wake up! *Please wake up!*" he said in a panic. Guilt came over him quickly; he'd pushed her too far. Strick's assistant handed him a wet towel and he wiped it over Kennedy's face a few times in a failed attempt to wake her up.

"Man, watch out, that shit ain't working," Coco said, pushing Strick to the side and dousing Kennedy's face with a bottle of water. The ice-cold water shocked her back to consciousness and her eyes popped open extra wide. Totally forgetting where she was, she jumped up, ready to swing. Strick bear-hugged her to keep her from hitting anyone. Once everything came back into focus and she recognized her surroundings, she told Strick, "You can let me go now. I'm okay."

"You sure?"

"Yeah, what happened?"

"You passed out in the booth."

"I *did*? I wonder what happened."

"I don't know. But I think you need to see a doctor."

Forty-five minutes later, Kennedy was sitting on the examination table of the label's private doctor. Strick sat in a nearby chair. She'd begged him to stay in the room with her. They were both on pins and needles waiting for the blood work and urinalysis to come back. For some unknown reason, Kennedy was fearing that the doctor would return and tell her that it was cancer. Strick was silently praying that her illness wasn't his fault. He was pissed with himself that he hadn't given her a break when she'd asked. The office door opened, and Dr. Steinbeck walked in, followed by a Japanese nurse pushing an ultrasound machine.

Strick's eyes became wide at the sight of the machine. He didn't know what it was, but Kennedy did. "Um, Dr. Steinbeck, what is that for?"

"Ms. Sanchez, your pregnancy test came back positive, and I suspect that you're more than a few months pregnant. This will let us know for sure."

Kennedy laughed. "There must be some mistake. My last period was—" Her smile suddenly faded.

"Just relax and lie back so we can see how far along you are."

Unable to relax, Kennedy lay back on the table thinking, *This cannot be happening right now.* She held her breath as the nurse applied the cold gel to her skin. Strick watched the procedure intently. Having no kids, he'd never seen anything like it before.

Sliding the transducer over Kennedy's abdomen, Dr. Steinbeck focused on the screen. As the view of the fetus became clear he gasped. *"My goodness!"*

"My *goodness* what?" Kennedy asked, stretching her neck so that she could see the monitor.

"By the size of the fetus, you appear to be about five months pregnant, which explains your high HCG levels."

"I can't be five months! I was huge when I was five months with Jordan."

"Your schedule and the stress you've been under most likely had some effect on your weight gain and loss." Dr. Steinbeck continued to stare at the monitor, noting odd movements. He noticed that every time the baby moved, he caught a glimpse of what appeared to be another set of arms and legs.

Studying his facial expression; Kennedy knew that something wasn't right. "What is it now?" she asked with a huff.

"How many surprises can you handle in one day?"

"It depends on the surprise."

Turning from the monitor, Dr. Steinbeck looked her in the eye. "Can you handle twins?"

Hours later, as she walked into Chaz's house, Kennedy still couldn't grasp the fact that she was having twins. Hell, it still hadn't sunk in that she was five months pregnant. Chaz was sitting on the couch surrounded by hundreds of moving boxes, waiting for her. He'd already heard about her fainting spell earlier in the day. By the pale drained look on her face, he could tell that she was still sick. Grabbing her up in his arms and hugging her, he asked, "You okay, li'l mama?"

She buried her face in his shoulder. "I'm pregnant."

"What'd you say, Ken? I couldn't hear you, you mumbling."

Lifting her head, she looked him in the eye. "I said I'm *pregnant*!"

Chaz's face lit up with joy. "You are, baby? That's what's up! Maybe I can finally get my boy."

"You're probably getting more than that," Kennedy said, her words dripping with sarcasm.

"So how many weeks are you?"

Kennedy looked at him, disgusted. "*Weeks?* Nigga, I'm five *months.*"

"Fuck *outta* here. You're smaller than you were when we met."

"I ain't lying, nigga. Here, look at the ultrasound pictures. Dr. Steinbeck said my schedule and stress is affecting my weight. And that ain't even the shocker."

"What's the shocker?"

"I'm having twins."

"Ain't no way," Chaz said in disbelief.

"Yes way, *my* man. One girl and one boy."

"This shit is crazy. I'ma finally get my boy. Seriously, Kennedy, you wouldn't play about this."

Rolling her eyes, Kennedy huffed, "Didn't I give you the ultrasound pictures?"

He began hugging her even tighter, rocking her side to side. "Damn, I can't wait to tell my mother and Shorty."

"No," Kennedy protested, pulling out of clutches. "I want to surprise everyone and tell them at the engagement party. The only other person who knows I'm pregnant is Strick and I've sworn him to secrecy."

Chaz couldn't tell if Kennedy was happy or sad about the pregnancy. Her facial expression was neutral. "How you feeling, li'l mama?"

"To tell you the truth. I really don't feel any kind of way. It's not even reality to me yet."

Watching

After a few days of seclusion and emotional changes, Kennedy's pregnancy finally became real to her. She happily began taking everything in stride. She and Chaz moved into a beautiful home in a gated community in northern New Jersey. She was having the time of her life decorating the sprawling twelve-thousand-square-foot home.

Kennedy stood back, admiring the wonderful work she'd put into the informal living room. She'd filled it with neutral colors that were perfect for all four seasons. The room was lined with floor-to-ceiling windows that gave a fascinating view of the swimming pool and grilling area. The bar area looked as if it belonged in a Miami nightclub. Kennedy had even stocked it with various liquors, like a real bar. Above the bar she hung martini glasses, wine goblets, and whiskey glasses. She put on the final touches with a one-thousand-dollar martini shaker on each end of the bar.

Kennedy hated that all the drama with Macon had prevented her from having their engagement party at the house. It was to be held later that evening at a posh, exclusive Italian restaurant in Manhattan. But she felt better knowing that tomorrow she would have the pleasure of hosting a cookout for both her family and Chaz's. The sound of the ringing house phone broke her reverie. When Kennedy spun around she felt light-headed. The fainting and dizzy spells were all new to her. She had never experienced any of those things when she was pregnant with Jordan. She balanced herself on the back of the couch and picked up the cordless phone. "Hello?" she answered, a little short of breath.

"What's wrong with you?" Yatta asked on the other end of the line.

"Nothing. What's up?"

"Everyone is in from the airport."

"Are you bringing Mommy and Big Ma out here?"

"They said that they want to stay at Aunt Karen's."

"Why?"

"Look, I don't know why. I'm picking up li'l sis right now and we're taking all the smaller kids to Toys 'R' Us on Thirty-fourth Street to get some toys to play with tonight so they don't give babysitter hell. Do you want to meet us down there?"

"Yeah, I'll be there."

One thing Kennedy loved about living with Chaz was the car options. When Chaz switched the cribs up, he switched up the cars, too. He bought a black Range Rover just like Kennedy's white one. He traded his CL600 for an S-class 600. He also copped a Denali. Chaz had every car including Kennedy's outfitted with stash boxes for firearms and bulletproof windows.

Today, Kennedy decided to take the Benz. It was top-of-the-line. She had only to run her fingertips under the chrome door handle, and upon recognition of her fingerprints, it unlocked and started the ignition. *This shit is crack,* she thought, and laughed to herself. After backing out of the garage, Kennedy set the house alarm with a push of a button on the remote attached to her key chain.

Kennedy sped through the hilly community, passing some of the most luxurious homes on the entire East Coast. She slowed down only to wait for the security guard to open the gates that separated the neighborhood from the outside world. Living in a gated community didn't make Kennedy feel any safer. From her rearview mirror she watched as the gates closed, thinking, *Them gates and that ol'-ass security guard ain't stopping real niggas from getting in here. It's only slowing them down!*

Seeing the kids ripping and running through the mega Toys "R" Us was a sight for sore eyes. Jordan was terrorizing the store employees. He was pulling down everything in sight that his two-and-a-half-year-old stature could reach. He so busy running and laughing that he hadn't even noticed his mother watching him from a short distance away. He was the cutest little badass she'd ever met, and not just because he was her son. Jordan was the best parts of her and Brian, his father, mixed together. Although Jordan had never met his father, the resemblance between them was undeniable. The older Jordan got, the more he looked like his father, which caused Kennedy to think of Brian quite often. She didn't even hate Brian; nor did she love him. It just hurt her to think that Jordan might never know his father. It would be a void that she would never be able to fill with any amount of money or quality time.

"Mommy!" Jordan suddenly yelled, running toward his mother.

"Hi, baby boy. You're having fun, I see."

"Yes, Mommy. Auntie Yatta has my toys."

"I bet she has a lot of them, too."

"Mm-hmm," he said, nodding. "Mommy, Mommy, he told me to give this to you." Jordan handed her a folded piece of paper.

"What man?" she asked, taking the paper from Jordan's small hands.

Jordan pointed toward an empty aisle, but no one was there.

She put Jordan down and unfolded the paper. Her heart stopped when a single dead white rose petal fell from the paper. Her vision went blurry, making it hard to read the words. She blinked a few times until the words were in focus. They were big, bold, and straight to the point:

SEE HOW CLOSE I CAN GET TO YOU,
Your Watcher

Kennedy had to force herself to breathe deeply and slowly just to keep from passing out. Frantically, her eyes searched the store for her sisters and the other kids. Holding Jordan tightly, she searched a few aisles before spotting Yatta, Jalyn, and Mattie. She ran toward them as fast as she could. Yatta looked up and saw her panic-stricken sister heading her way. "Kennedy, what's wrong?"

"Where's Kneaka? Where are the other kids?"

"Calm down. They didn't come. *What is going on?*"

"He's here!"

"Who's here?"

"The fan! The stalker!"

"You saw him?"

"No, I didn't, but he gave this to Jordan," Kennedy said, shoving the note into Yatta's hands.

Yatta scanned the note. "Oh my God, Kennedy, this is getting out of hand now. You're gonna have to call the police or get security involved. Something has got to give."

Kennedy, overcome by the thoughts of the stalker getting close to Jordan, began crying in the middle of the store. Yatta wrapped her arms around her sister, consoling her. "Don't cry, li'l mama, it's going to be okay." Still embracing her sister, she pulled out her cell and dialed Strick's number.

"Yo?" Strick answered.

"Strick, it's me. Is Chaz up at the studio with you?"

"Yeah, what's up?"

"I'll explain when we get there. I need y'all to send security downstairs to meet us in ten minutes."

"Yatta, what's the problem? Do you need us to come meet you?"

"No, Strick. Let me get Kennedy together so I can get her out of here." Yatta ended the call. Keeping her composure, she paid for the toys. Never showing her nervousness, she kept her family close together and got them the hell out of there.

Chaz, along with two burly guards from his security team, waited in front of the building for Kennedy and Yatta to arrive. When they pulled up and Kennedy got out of the car, he knew that something was wrong. Her face said it all. She couldn't even fake a smile. "Baby, what's going on?" he asked, grabbing her face.

Biting down on her lip, Kennedy began to cry. Yatta stepped up and began talking. "Chaz, can you have one the guards take the kids uptown to Aunt Karen's? 'Cause y'all need to talk."

"That's nothing; come on." Chaz sent the more experienced of the two guards to take the kids uptown, instructing him to stay with them until he called.

Upstairs in Strick's office, Kennedy took a seat on the couch. Yatta sat next to her, holding her hand, giving her full support. Kennedy didn't quite know where to begin the story. And the stares that she was receiving from Strick and Chaz weren't making it any easier. After inhaling deeply, she just let it all out. "Look, someone is stalking me. It started with phone calls, letters, and dead white roses. First it seemed like nothing, but the contacts have escalated. Today the stalker approached Jordan in the toy store and gave him this." She pulled the note from her purse and handed it to Chaz.

Strick couldn't believe that Kennedy hadn't told anyone

about this. Leaning back in his big office chair, he swiveled around and said, "Ken, this shit was serious from the first phone call you received. You should've at least come to me so that we could've provided you with security."

"I just didn't really pay it any attention at first. Before today, I thought this person was harmless—a little crazy, but harmless."

Chaz was pissed. He wasn't buying her justification. "Come on, Kennedy, you got to come better than that, *ma*. You're not naive. What if this is some psycho hit nigga Macon sent after you?"

"This doesn't have anything to do with Macon."

"How do you know that?"

"This started six months before Jay shot him."

"You mean to tell me this shit been going on for over a year and this is the first time *I'm* hearing about it? You got some nerve calling me deceitful, B."

Yatta interrupted. "Now is not the time, Chaz."

"Yes it is. What if this person had just taken Jordan today? You could've prevented all this shit if you would've opened your fucking mouth. I can't understand why you wouldn't say something. Unless it's some nigga you been fucking."

"It's not *that*!" Kennedy screamed at him, tears flowing down her face. "I'm sorry for letting it go this far. Don't you know I would literally die if anything were to happen to Jordan! If I had any clues to who this person is, I would've sent the wolves after them." She placed her head in her lap, sobbing heavily; her shoulders heaved up and down.

Yatta and Strick left the room. Chaz took a seat next to Kennedy on the couch. Rubbing her back, he told her, "I'm sorry I yelled at you like that. All this shit is getting too far out of control. It's nothing, though. We're going to get through this, too." Kennedy's face was still in her lap. "You aight, ma? Say something."

Kennedy looked up at him. Her eyes were dark and lonesome. "I just don't know how much more of this I can take before . . ." She paused, staring off into space.

"Before what?"

Oblivious to Chaz's question, Kennedy continued to stare into space.

Lightly, he squeezed her shoulder. "Kennedy, before what?"

"Oh, nothing, baby . . . nothing for you to worry about. Come on, baby, let's go home and get ready for the party. This bullshit is not going to ruin our night." Wiping the tears from her face with the back of her hand, she stood up and left the room.

Just that quick, she'd gone from sixty back to zero. Chaz stared at the open door, perplexed and wondering, *How the fuck she just switch up like that?*

All of Yatta's planning had yielded a perfect engagement party. She was wonderful at planning events. People told her all the time that she needed to make a business of it. The party was held at Trattoria Dopo Teatro in the theater district. Only family, close friends, and the label staff had been invited. Everyone in attendance received gift bags containing chocolates from Godiva, a miniature bottle of Clicquot, a fifty-dollar gift card to Dean & DeLuca, and a one-hundred-dollar gift card to either Henri Bendel, Barneys, or Bergdorf.

When Kennedy made her entrance, she looked better than ever, worry-free, showing no evidence of the problems plaguing her personal life or the frantic episode with her stalker earlier in the day. She looked fabulous in an olive-green Alexander McQueen halter dress. Keeping her shoe game tight, but slightly comfortable, for her feet were feeling the effects of her pregnancy, she had donned a pair of olive-green-and-white Ferragamo pumps with two-and-half-inch heels—as opposed to her usual four. To complement her beautiful dress, she wore a white-gold necklace with a blinding three-carat-diamond half-heart pendant. Her ears sparkled with two-carat princess-cut diamonds. Kennedy's right wrist was wrapped in a five-carat cuff of yellow diamonds accented with striking green emeralds. The only thing on her lower her left arm was her most prized piece of jewelry: her engagement ring.

Chaz was the most handsome man in the room in a black linen suit and black sling-back gators. For once he'd left his chain at home, wearing only a wide fifteen-carat platinum-and-diamond bracelet and a four-carat pinkie ring. His Caesar haircut was lined up just right and his goatee was trimmed to perfection. Kennedy thought he looked magnificent. She also thought it was a blessing that he didn't show up with his usual doo-rag and Yankee fitted.

Yatta, Big Ma, and Kora all noticed that there was a difference in Kennedy's body. She was still able to suck her stomach in so that she wouldn't show, but there was nothing she could do to hide her huge breasts, which seemed to be getting bigger with each passing day. He already wide hips were spreading like wildfire. Old people would say that she was carrying the baby in her breasts and hips.

The first chance that Yatta got, she pulled Kennedy to the side and interrogated her. "Kennedy, why in the hell is your titties looking so damn big?"

"Huh?" was the only reply that Kennedy could come back with while she got her lie together.

"Don't play with me, Kennedy. You heard what I said. And look at your hips. Come to think of it, you've been on some baggy jogging-suit shit lately."

Kennedy let out a little laugh. "Yatta, you analyzing my body a little too much. I look big because I'm coming on my period. You know how bloated I get. Having this tight-ass dress on only makes it more noticeable."

"Um-hmm," Yatta said, rolling her eyes as she turned to walk away.

Kennedy envied her sister's outfit as she strutted away. She loved the way that Yatta was working the black minidress with the plunging neckline and a pair of supersexy four-inch John Galliano sandals. Kennedy wasn't seriously envious, but she did like Yatta's dress better than her own. It would be a long time before she could again slip into anything that sexy. Kennedy scanned the room, searching for Strick. When she spotted him talking to Big Ma and Klarice, she walked over and politely snatched him from the conversation.

Kennedy pulled him to the side and spoke through her teeth, barely above a whisper. "Did you tell Yatta about me being knocked up?"

"No. Why?"

" 'Cause she just put me through the third degree about my weight gain. And when I told her it was because of my period, she acted like she didn't believe me."

"I didn't tell her shit, *true story*. She probably tripping on you 'cause she swear she been dreaming about fish."

"Oh, yeah, that will do it in my family."

Standing in the front of the crowded room, Yatta took a mike in her hand and called Kennedy up to join her. They shared a short but meaningful embrace. Under certain circumstances, Kennedy could become quite shy, and this was one of them. She grabbed Yatta's hand before she could walk away. "Could you stay? *Please?*"

"You got it, baby girl."

After flashing her dazzling white smile, Kennedy began to speak to the small crowd. It felt as if a thousand butterflies were fluttering in her stomach. "I would like to thank all of you for coming out and celebrating my success as an entertainer. I'm so happy just to be here celebrating anything, because for a long time I didn't think I would ever be able to accomplish anything that I once dreamed of. But this party isn't really to celebrate my career. The real reason for this celebration is to celebrate the growth of the love between Chaz and me. A little over five weeks ago, he proposed to me and I said yes!" Kennedy held her hand up showing off her ring to the crowd.

A wave of chatter and applause swept through the crowd. Chaz approached the stage, carrying tiny black-and-gold gift bags in each hand. He hugged his wife-to-be and gave her a kiss that made the crowd whistle and howl. When Kennedy tried to pass him the mike, he refused to take it.

From the crowd, his sister, Shorty, began to yell, "Speech, speech, speech." Following suit, the crowd joined in, forcing him to take the mike.

With a nervous smile he began to speak. "I think Kennedy and I feel the same sense of gratitude toward all of you. Once again, thanks for joining us. Like I told my mother, I love this girl. I swear I do. And I knew there was nothing else I could do but make her my wife. Physically, I think she is one of the prettiest women I've ever seen. But on the inside, she is even more beautiful. One of the first things that made me fall in love with her was seeing her with Nina's kids. She treated them no different than Jordan, as if she'd birthed them herself. I think it takes a special woman to be so giving. And that's why I love her." Hugging her once more, he told her," I love you, baby."

"I love you, too." Taking over the mike again, Kennedy started rolling her neck. "That's my man, y'all, and what." The crowd laughed at her theatrics. "Aight, aight, let me stop playing so much. I have a few special gifts to hand out. The first two are for my mother and Chaz's mother. Since you will now share children, we thought the two of you should spend some time alone. Inside your bags are gift cards to various stores throughout Manhattan and a gift card from the Bella Spa which entitles you to a full spa treatment."

Chaz passed out the bags as Kennedy continued to talk about the significance of each gift. "The second set of gifts are pretty much the same. And they are for my sisters, Kneaka and Yatta, and my new sister-in-law, Shorty. I want the three of you to spend the day together bonding, since we're all sisters now. I also have a little something for you, Darcy—just a little something to say thanks for taking my career to the next level."

Having already tossed back four martinis, Darcy simply gave Kennedy a thumbs-up from the audience as Chaz handed her her gift bag.

Knowing that the next gift was going to be difficult, Kennedy swallowed hard. "Aunt Klarry, I can say without an ounce of doubt that if Nina were here today, I would be giving her this bag. Thanks for all the late-night calls that comforted me when I should've been comforting you. I love you always."

"I love you, too," Klarice yelled from the audience, blowing Kennedy a kiss.

Kennedy moved on to avoid crying. "Aunt Karen, this only small token of my undying love and appreciation for you. You have always been in my corner, even when I'm dead wrong. And I thank you for that. Last but not least, Big Ma, you are the love of my life, my refuge, and my resting place. I really didn't know what to give you, so I gave you my heart." She walked over to Big Ma, and presented her with a white-gold necklace that held the other half of the diamond heart pendant that Kennedy was wearing.

While returning to the front of the room, Kennedy caught a glimpse of her aunt Kara giving her a pissed-off look. She knew that Kara was hurt that she hadn't gotten a special gift or any type of recognition. If she had been anyone else, Kennedy would have felt bad. But she sure didn't give a damn about Kara's feelings. For as long she could remember, Kara had always looked down on her entire family. Kennedy shot a nasty smirk at Kara before continuing. "Okay, y'all, this is my last gift. And it's for my husband-to-be." Taking the small square box from Yatta, she turned to Chaz. "I know that one of your favorite songs is 'If This World Were Mine,' a song made famous by the great Luther Vandross. I just wanted you to always know that if this world were mine, I would give you everything. So I thought that this would be a constant reminder for you." She opened the box, displaying a miniature yellow-gold globe. The phrase *If This World Were Mine* was encrusted in diamonds around its surface.

"Girl, you gon' make me cry," Chaz said, actually laughing to keep from crying. He hugged her tight, holding her close for a few seconds. "Thank you, ma. I love this."

"It's nothing, baby, you know that." Letting Chaz go, she faced the crowd once more. "I know y'all are ready to get your grub on, so I'ma say this and get out the way. Chaz and I had planned on having our wedding six months from now. But due to unforeseen circumstances, there has been a change in plans."

Yatta gave Kennedy a perplexed look. Kennedy giggled. "Yes, Yatta, this is one that even you don't know about. But you did suspect it. A week ago I went to the doctor and got the shock of my life when he told me that I'm five months pregnant." The news sent the crowd into an excited uproar. Raising her hand, Kennedy got them to calm down. "That ain't all."

"What more can there be?" a voice shouted out.

"I'm having twins." That sent the crowd into a complete frenzy.

From their seats, Sal and Kora jokingly threatened to whip Chaz and Kennedy for keeping secrets. Kennedy just smiled and laughed, loving the crowd's reaction. "I promise y'all, three to four months after I drop this load, there will be a wedding. Seriously, though, thanks again for coming out. I love all of you."

After the party all the family members gathered at Kennedy and Chaz's new home. It was a wonderful night, filled with laughter and joy. The couple's family members shared hilarious childhood stories about them. Big Ma said that she felt like Sal was one of her own daughters.

As Kennedy sat back with her feet propped up in Chaz's lap, watching her family, she thought, *Hands down, this has to be the best night of my life.*

Almost Like Déjà Vu

Over the next weeks Kennedy completed all her open projects, including her sophomore CD, which was slated for release a few months after her due date. She was all too happy after her final photo shoot for the Mischief ad campaign. Finally she could throw caution about weight gain to the wind and eat all the fatty and high-carb foods she wanted. Her appetite seemed to be endless and her weight gain was rapid. In four weeks she'd gained nearly twenty-eight pounds.

Kennedy adored the attention that she was receiving from Chaz on a daily basis. She really appreciated it because she hadn't received that kind of treatment at all when she was carrying Jordan. Chaz loved that she basked in his cooing over her and their babies. He was enjoying his experience with Kennedy's pregnancy. It was the exact opposite of what he'd experienced during both of Ria's pregnancies. Ria had been evil when she was carrying his daughters. By no means was Kennedy a pleasure every single day, especially when her hormones were raging. But living with Ria while she was pregnant had been only one level above hell. When Chaz touched her big belly, Ria cringed and cursed him out. She had done nothing but complain all day. The only time she showed any type of courtesy was when she wanted Chaz to get out of bed in the middle of the night and go out to get her something to eat. Kennedy's positive attitude was a breath of fresh air. On the nights he didn't have to travel or perform. Chaz would try to make it home before Kennedy went to bed. He would rub her belly until they fell asleep together. If she was already asleep when he arrived, he'd slide right up behind her and wrap his arms around her protruding tummy.

Knowing that Kennedy had had to do everything alone while she was pregnant with Jordan, Chaz made it his priority to help her prepare for the babies. He attended every doctor's appointment. He helped design and decorate the nursery. Every Friday afternoon he put aside time to go out with Kennedy and shop for the twins.

On one particular Friday, Kennedy's energy was down and her ankles were swelling up. Her Seven maternity jeans were irritating her stomach. Although it was a cool December day, she was burning up. After only an hour and a half of shopping, she was too tired to go on. "Chaz, baby, I'm ready to go. I'm tired. And I'm starving."

"Aight, let's walk up to Jimmy Jazz first. They got the limited-edition Jordans for babies."

"No," she whined. "Can't you come back and pick them up later?"

"Okay, li'l mama, what you wanna eat?"

"I already know it's somewhere you're not going to want to eat."

"Why, what is it?"

"I'm really craving some sticky wings from BBQ's."

"Now, you know we'll *never* be able to eat in peace in there."

"Just have House or Yak go inside before us and get us a table in the back. And when we go in, just pull your hat real low. Besides, who gonna to recognize my fat ass?"

"Aight, ma. BBQ's. You got that."

"Thanks, baby." Kennedy smiled.

To their surprise BBQ's was not crowded, unusual for the

lunchtime rush. *No crowd means faster service,* Kennedy thought. When her food arrived she demolished it. Eight huge sticky wings, a salad, a plate of fries, and two pieces of corn on the cob. "Damn, Ken," Chaz exclaimed, "you want something to go, too?"

"Ha ha ha, I sure do," she said, sticking her tongue out like a little kid.

Chaz laughed at her silliness. "But yo, seriously, we doing all this shopping, planning, decorating, and we haven't even thought of any names."

"*I've* thought about names."

"Like what?"

"For the girl, I was thinking about Carlie, Tatum, or Brooklyn. For the boy, I like Sy, Angel, Nasir, or Micah."

"You know, I'm feeling Brooklyn for the girl. I don't like any of those boy's names, though. Why can't his name be Chaz Junior?"

"I was thinking about that, too, but you know Chaz is Jordan's middle name."

"Yeah, that is right. We gotta sit down together and come up with some better boy names."

"Maybe if you come home early enough tonight, we can go through some name books."

"We gonna do more than look at name books," Chaz said with a sexually charged smile. "Why don't you just wait til I finish my session and we can ride home together."

"Baby, I'm too tired."

"You can lay down at the studio."

"Nah, I want to go home, eat Almond Kisses, and fall asleep in our bed."

On the short ride to the building that housed the studio and garage, Kennedy fell asleep on Chaz's shoulder in the backseat.

When they arrived inside the garage, he gently squeezed her thigh. "Wake up, baby."

"I dozed off that quick? Damn, I don't have *no* energy today."

"You sure you don't want House to drive you home?"

"No, he can just follow me as usual. Give me a kiss. I'm out."

Chaz pulled her close, giving her deep kiss. "I love you, girl."

"I love you, too, baby. See you later."

Kennedy pulled up to the gate and waited for the security guard to open it. House waited patiently as she entered through the gate. He didn't drive off until the gate was closed and her car was out of sight.

Sitting in the driveway, Kennedy waited for the garage door to open. Suddenly she had an urge to urinate. Once the door was high enough, she zoomed into the garage. Pressing the remote on her key chain, she shut off the house alarm. Leaning over, she picked up her purse and a few of its contents that had fallen to the floor on the passenger side. Sitting up, Kennedy pushed the garage remote, shutting the door, never noticing the two intruders who had slipped in.

A chill ran down Kennedy's spine as she stuck the key in the lock. Shaking it off, she proceeded to open the door. When she'd gotten the door only halfway open, she felt a hard shove from behind. *Oh God,* she thought, bracing herself so that she would fall onto her knees and not her stomach. Her purse and keys fell from her hands and slid across the kitchen floor. Crawling, Kennedy desperately tried to reach her key chain. "Stop trying to be slick, bitch," one of the assailants said, viciously kicking her in the butt, causing her to fall flat on her stomach.

Excruciating pain shot through her abdomen. Suddenly Kennedy was yanked up by her hair and spun around to face a man who was unfamiliar to her. She could only wonder if this was the man who had been stalking her.

"Where the fuck that nigga at?" the man asked aggressively. Never answering his question, Kennedy stared blankly at his face at the same time as she tried to ignore her pain. With the back of his free hand, the man smacked her across her face. Blood gushed from her nose. "Answer me, slut!" he yelled.

"I don't know," she answered through clenched teeth, trying not to cry.

"You're lying!" he screamed, punching her between the eyes. Kennedy nearly blacked out from the blow. Releasing her hair, the man let her body fall to the ground. "Yo, Zee, give me that duct tape." The second man walked over, handing the tape to the assailant, who bound Kennedy's wrists together, telling her, "I don't got nothing but time. We can sit here all day. Shit, I don't care if that nigga don't come home till tomorrow or next week." After taping Kennedy's ankles together, he covered her eyes and mouth.

Pull it together. Think—think. Pull it together now, Kennedy told herself, but she couldn't. Her mind and heart were racing at an unbelievable speed. With the tape covering her mouth, she had to concentrate on catching her breath and breathing through her nose. The entire scene felt way too familiar to her, felt like she was living the night of Pretty Boy's death all over again. Judging by the man's question, she had pretty much figured out that he wasn't her stalker, but that he was there for Chaz. Kennedy found herself concentrating on staying conscious as she started to feel dizzy. Her face, buttocks, and stomach were all aching. *Why didn't I wait to turn off the alarm once I got inside?* she questioned. *My stupidity will probably cost me my life, my babies—oh God, my babies. And Chaz is going to walk right into a trap. God, please let House and Yak come home with him.* She drifted away, slowly passing out.

Yeah, this is how you get shit done, Marcus told himself, sitting back watching Kennedy. *Macon should've let me take care of this shit from jump street. I told him get a nigga's bitch first, then you guaranteed to get the nigga.* He watched Zee rubbing Kennedy's thigh and looking at her lustfully. "Yo, Zee, what the fuck is you doin'?"

"Man, I want some of this," he said, crouching over Kennedy with his short stocky body. "You know what they say about pregnant pussy."

If one needed a good, efficient hit man, Zee was the one to hire. But he had an immaturity about him. Marcus found him childish and highly annoying. He could never fathom how Macon hung around him as a partner. Laying his gun down beside him, Marcus jumped off the counter and walked over to Zee. He yanked Zee's arm, pulling him to his feet. "I don't give a fuck what *they* say about a pregnant bitch! We came here for one thing and that's to merk that nigga and anybody who gets in the way. So you not fucking nothing. That's how niggas get caught slipping."

Having to scold your partner can be a deadly distraction, and neither Marcus nor Zee had noticed that another person had quietly slid into the room. Suddenly the sound of rapid gunfire filled the kitchen. Two bullets ripped through Marcus's back. The first bullet exited through his throat and the second one lodged in the middle of his spinal cord, almost severing it. Catching a glimpse of the man still aiming a gun in his direction, Zee reached for the gun in his waistband as Marcus's body hit the floor. For his effort, he received a bullet in his hand, which went straight through, hitting him in the pelvis. His body fell across Kennedy's legs. Howling in pain, Zee made a second attempt to retrieve his gun.

With his gun aimed at Zee's head, the man stood over him. Then he squeezed the lever, firing three shots into Zee's head. Kennedy sat frozen. She'd been awakened by the initial gunshots. She silently prayed that the body lying across her legs was

not that of Chaz. The silence was deafening. She could only wonder why she wasn't hearing any voices or noises. *This can't be happening again,* she thought.

"Ouch!" Kennedy yelled from the pain of the duct tape being
snatched from her mouth. Gasping for air, she asked, "Who's
there?" There was no answer, just silence, but she could feel the
presence of another person. Kennedy let out a shrill scream as the
tape was snatched from her eyes, ripping out chunks of her eyelashes and eyebrows. She couldn't open her eyes, but she could
feel the tape being cut from her wrists and her ankles. She rubbed
her eyes, trying to ease the stinging. Blinking vigorously, she tried
to bring her blurry vision back into focus. Looking down, she
was relieved to see that it wasn't Chaz lying dead on her. A few
moments later, she could see the silhouette of a man standing by
the kitchen sink with his back to her. He had the hood of his blue
Akademics sweatshirt over his head.

"Who are you?" Still standing with his back to her, the man
maintained his silence. Who was this man who had saved her
life? Why wouldn't he face her or answer? Kennedy slowly rolled
the dead body off of her lap. She tried to stand up, but the pain
was overwhelming. She looked down at her pants and realized
they were drenched in amniotic fluid, urine, and blood. "Oh
God!" Kennedy screamed. "Can you help me, please, I'm bleeding. I need to go to the hospital."

The strange man let out an evil laugh, one that Kennedy knew
too well.

It can't be, she thought.

"I'm not the mu-fucking cavalry, bitch. I'm *tha Watcher.* I
didn't come here to save yo' ho ass. I didn't plan on comin' for
you so soon, but I couldn't let them niggas kill you and have all
the fun." Pulling his hood back, he turned to face her. His face
was grossly unshaven, his hair was wild, and he was extremely
frail. But it was him, just as Kennedy had thought when she'd

heard him laugh. It was *Cream.* No doubt about it. He'd never even crossed Kennedy's mind when she was trying to figure out who her stalker might be. Suddenly she felt like a fool for putting him to the back of her mind. She should've hunted him down instead of figuring that she would catch him slipping. Her fear turned to extreme anger.

Cream smiled at her. "Yeah, it's me, you arrogant bitch! Bet you didn't expect to see me, huh?"

"Fuck you, *faggot.*"

"Damn, baby, no 'thank you, Cream, for saving my life'?"

"Die slow, you *bastard*!" Kennedy said, rising to her feet.

"That's so cute and original coming from a bitch that stole my life."

"How did I steal your life? You killed Nina! You killed the mother of your child, faggot-ass nigga!" Looking down at the bodies, then back at him, she said, "I'm glad you finally graduated to killing men."

Cream ran toward her, socking her in the mouth. Kennedy gathered what little strength she had and swung back, landing a hard right to his left eye. The punch did indeed hurt, but he laughed it off. "That's all you got? You big-mouth *bitch*!" Cream violently palmed the side of her head, forcing her body to the floor. He then battered her face and body with blow after blow. He taunted her the entire time, blaming her for the last fight he'd had with Nina. "My girl wouldn't be dead if your nosy ass minded your own damn business!"

Kennedy was slipping in and out of consciousness. She didn't have the strength or energy to combat him seriously. She could barely move to avoid his punches.

In Cream's sadistic mind, fighting Kennedy was turning out to be a major disappointment. "All that shit you popped and you ain't shit but a punk-ass slut. At least Nina could roll with the punches. Damn, I thought you would make this a little fun for me." He unzipped his pants and pulled out his penis then urinated all over Kennedy's face. "Wake up, bitch! Ain't no sleeping."

Wiping the burning urine from her eyes, Kennedy tried to spit the salty liquid from her mouth. From the corner of her swollen eyes, she could see her keys and they were not that far out of her reach. Cream looked down at her, then throwing his head back, he laughed hysterically like a madman. Mustering what little strength she had, Kennedy lifted her leg and kicked him forcefully in the groin. Cream doubled over from the intense pain and fell onto Kennedy's legs. Kennedy struggled desperately to free her legs, and once she got from beneath him, she crawled as fast as she could to her key chain. Pressing the remote, she tripped the silent alarm.

Kennedy slid the keys across the room so that Cream wouldn't catch on to what she'd done. With the pain passing, he rose to his feet. "Whew! That's what I'm talking about. It's on and poppin' *now*! And you not the only one who can kick." Bringing his leg all the way back, he kicked Kennedy in her side. Her amniotic sac exploded on contact and it was very audible. The ringing of the house phone stopped him from delivering the second kick. Cream snatched the phone from the wall and slammed it into the side of Kennedy's head, knocking her out completely.

Pushing his Denali down Route 4 with House riding shotgun, Chaz bopped his head in time to one of his new singles that featured Kennedy. The song was blazing hot. He couldn't wait to get home so that she could hear the final mix. Chaz felt his phone vibrating in his pocket, *This bet' not be another unknown number.* His last four incoming calls had been unknown. He never answered those. Looking down at his phone, he saw that he had a text message.

The message read: *Please call Safe Zone Security concerning an urgent matter immediately. Give code 3117. Thank you.*

Chaz's heart dropped to the bottom of his stomach. "Oh shit!"

"What is it, man?" House asked.

"That was the fucking alarm company."

Wasting no to time, Chaz called Safe Zone. "Good evening, Safe Zone Security, this is Steven."

"Yes, uh . . . code 3117," Chaz said nervously.

"Is this Mr. Harris?"

"Yes."

"Are you at home, Mr. Harris?"

"No."

"Your panic alarm has been set off. The police are en route to your residence. Are we correct by not assuming that this is a false alarm?"

"You are correct. My pregnant fiancée is home alone."

"I'll send an ambulance to your residence also."

After terminating the call, Chaz pressed down on the gas pedal and picked up speed. He couldn't seem to gather his thoughts as he tried calling Kennedy's cell phone again and again with no success. He could only hope and pray that Kennedy had hit the alarm because she was going into labor. *Something must've happened. That's why she never called. It can't be that nigga Macon. I know it can't be.* The more he thought about it, the faster he drove.

Cream took the extra set of car keys from the kitchen wall. Grabbing Kennedy by her hair, he dragged her out to the garage and threw her into the trunk of her 745i. Then he jumped into the driver's seat and pressed the remote on the visor to open the garage door. As he backed out he found himself blocked in the driveway by three police cruisers. Five uniformed Bergen County police officers were walking up the driveway. Two of the officers quickly drew their guns, yelling. "POLICE! TURN THE IGNITION OFF AND STEP OUT OF THE CAR."

Banging his head on the steering wheel, Cream began talking to his self. "You didn't come this far to fuck up now. The bitch has got to die right now." Following the orders he'd been given, he opened the door and stepped out. He thought, *If I could get off a couple of shots into the trunk, I could still kill her . . . or die trying.* He hated Kennedy just that much that he was willing to end his own life in order to stop hers. In one swift motion, he went for his gun and attempted to fire at the trunk.

"HE GOT A GUN!" a young black rookie officer yelled. All of the officers wasted no time firing their guns. The rookie emptied half of his magazine before he stopped shooting. The gun slipped from Cream's hand as his body fell backward onto the concrete. Blood trickled from the corner of his evil grin. "I got her back" were his last words.

The sound of screeching tires coming to a halt took the cops' attention away from Cream's lifeless body. Putting the truck in park, Chaz jumped out, followed by House. The cops pointed their weapons toward them. An older white cop said, "Hold it right there!"

Growing up in the hood, both Chaz and House knew not to act irrational. Not to mention there was already one dead black body on the ground. Chaz calmly spoke to the cop. "Officer, this is my house. The alarm company notified me that there was a disturbance."

The cop gave him a "yeah, right" look. It was a blessing that that the black rookie cop was a fan of Chaz and he stepped up, saying, "Richards, he's telling the truth. He's a famous musician."

The officers lowered their guns. Officer Richards gave Chaz an apologetic look. "Sorry, I didn't know."

"Sure you didn't," Chaz responded sarcastically. The sound of the approaching ambulance sirens brought his mind back to the real situation. He asked the officers, "Where is my fiancée?"

The rookie took over the job of talking to him, "Mr. Harris, I'm Officer Sanders. We haven't been inside yet. We're about to go in now and canvass the house to make sure it's safe. What's your fiancée's name?"

"Her name is Kennedy."

The cops had entered the house and were calling out to Kennedy when they stumbled onto the bodies of Marcus and Zee. They knew the scene could only get worse. The only sign of Kennedy was her purse, its contents scattered across the floor. Looking at Zee, they knew without doubt that he was dead. "Get the medics in here. This one is still breathing," Richards said, looking at Marcus. "And bring Mr. Harris in here so we can find out who's supposed to be here and who's not."

Chaz stepped inside. As he took in the scene a terrible feeling came over him. "Are these men supposed to be here?" Richards asked.

"Fuck no."

"Do you know them?"

Chaz's eyes said yes, but his mouth said, "No."

"What about the man outside?" Sanders asked.

"I really *don't know* him."

The other officers continued calling out to Kennedy and doing a complete search of the house. Chaz watched Officer Richards studying a wide trail of blood and liquid that ran across the kitchen floor to the garage entry. Richards yelled over his shoulder to Sanders, "I think I know where she is."

He followed the trail out to the garage. Figuring it out, Chaz ran past him. Reaching into the BMW, he popped the trunk. His heart stopped when he got to the back of the car and saw Kennedy lying in there. Her eyes were swollen shut. Huge purple-

and-black bruises ran rampant across her face and neck. Chaz pulled her unconscious body from the trunk. He was completely floored by how badly beaten she was. He couldn't even tell if she was alive. He zoned out, oblivious to everyone around him. Holding her close, he rocked back and forth slowly, tears steadily streaming down his face.

Reasons and Seasons

Kennedy continued living in Charlotte with Big Ma, although she had been healed for about a year. She was still not ready to return to New York or the music industry. She and Strick had remained close. They really didn't have a choice about the matter since they were now in-laws, Strick and Yatta having married in Bermuda earlier that year. They were now expecting their first child together and Yatta's fourth daughter.

Chaz had gone on to record his third and most critically acclaimed CD, which sold more than ten million copies worldwide. The CD was filled with songs about his personal struggles, like the pain of growing up without his mother and losing his best friend, Jay. He had also recorded three songs inspired by his relationship with Kennedy. Each song displayed a different emotion toward her; one showed anger, one showed love, and the third showed confusion. The authenticity of the emotions behind the songwriting was what made the CD such a success, proving the old saying that "in order to be a great writer you must first experience pain."

Not a day went by that he didn't think of Kennedy. At every performance, his eyes would scan the audience in the hope that she was there. Sex didn't even feel right anymore, and he had it coming from groupies, executives, female athletes, models, actresses, and singers. But no one could ever fill Kennedy's place in his heart.

Big Ma sat in her rocking chair watching Kennedy looking at Chaz as he was being interviewed on the red carpet at the MTV video awards the night before. Kennedy's eyes could never lie. Big Ma could tell that she still loved Chaz. Kennedy was so engrossed with Chaz that she didn't notice Big Ma get up and walk out of the room.

Closing the bedroom door behind her, Big Ma sat on the edge of her bed. She rummaged through her nightstand drawer until she found the paper she was looking for. She picked up the cordless and dialed the number off the paper. The phone rang a few times before the person answered, "Hey, Big Ma!"

"Hi, baby. Big Ma not calling to trouble you, but I think it's time for you to come down south and get baby girl."

Three days later, on a hot Saturday afternoon, Big Ma was sitting on the porch watching her great-grandkids and a few neighborhood kids playing out in the yard. A black Lincoln Town Car with black-tinted windows pulled up in front of the yard. All the kids paused to see who was inside. The driver got out first, walking to the rear of the car, where he removed two duffel bags from the trunk and placed them on the sidewalk. He then walked to the back passenger door and opened it. A big smile spread across Jordan's face when he saw Chaz stepping out of the car. *"Chaz!"* Jordan, Mattie, and Niko yelled as they ran toward him and hugged his legs.

It made Chaz feel so good that the kids were excited to see him. "What's up, y'all?"

The sound of an approaching ice-cream truck quickly diverted the three kids' attention from Chaz. Niko ran to stop the truck while all the other kids ran toward Big Ma, yelling, "Can we have some money for ice cream, Big Ma?"

"Wait, wait," Chaz told the kids. "Leave Big Ma alone. Here, take this and pay for everybody's ice cream." He handed Mattie three ten-dollar bills. "That should be enough to get all of you whatever you want." All of the kids ran past Chaz, almost knocking him down. Chaz picked up his duffel bags and walked up onto the porch. Tossing his bags to the side, he gave Big Ma a huge hug. "Hey, Big Ma, how've you been?"

"I'm fine, baby, and you?"

"I'm okay."

"It's so good to see you. Stand back and let me look at you. You look good, but you done lost a good bit of weight."

"I don't get those good home-cooked meals anymore."

"How're your girls doing?"

"They doing real good. Getting big. Wanting everything they see in the store."

"What 'bout your mama and your sister?"

"They doing fine, too."

The group of kids floated back into the yard. In unison, they all said, "Thank you, Chaz" as they headed into the backyard. Chaz took a seat next to Big Ma. "So where is your baby girl?"

"She and my grandnieces went for a ride. They should be back at any time now."

Chaz dropped his head and stared down at his feet. "Big Ma, you think she'll come back to me?"

"I know she will."

"How do you know that?"

"Her face lights up when she sees you on the television or in one of those magazines." Big Ma let out a little chuckle. "Then she gets this little sad look about her. That's how I know her heart is still with you."

"I can't thank you enough for staying in touch with me through all of this."

"Y'all babies just needed some time apart. And she needed time to heal. But this time, together you will be stronger. Chaz, you must never forget that there are reasons and seasons and everything on this earth has a reason."

Big Ma's words stuck in Chaz's mind. The events that had led up to the termination of his and Kennedy's relationship were still fresh in his memory. Although he'd gotten through it all, he had never gotten over it.

"My babies didn't make it, did they?" Kennedy had asked, lying in her hospital bed the day after the brutal assault. It was the first time she had fully regained consciousness since being admitted.

Smoothing her hair with his hand, Chaz answered the question that no one else wanted to answer. "No, baby . . . they—they didn't make it."

Kennedy squeezed her eyes tight, trying hard to fight off the feeling of loss. The tears rushed from her eyes as she moaned and hollered loudly. Calling out to her mother, she asked in tearful sobs, *"Mommy, why? Why is it always me?"*

At a complete loss for words, Kora simply got into the bed with her daughter. Kora held on to her girl while Kennedy poured her soul out in tears and mournful screams. Kora didn't let her go until she fell asleep.

Since the twins were stillborn, the hospital had offered to bury them free of charge. Chaz wasn't having that. He had them properly buried in the same tiny white casket. He bought a beautiful headstone for their grave. Engraved on it was a girl and boy on each side, and it read: *Mommy and Daddy's Little Angels, Brooklyn and Micah.*

Chaz also had the funeral home take pictures of the babies in case Kennedy ever wanted to see them. Every time he thought about the twins or looked at their little bodies lying in the casket, he saw red. He saw Macon's blood. It had been on before, but the war was really on now. He'd searched high and low for Macon, but was unsuccessful in locating him. It hadn't been hard for him to find Marcus, who, due to his gunshot wounds, had been recovering at Holy Name, under twenty-four-hour police supervision. And it hadn't been hard at all for Chaz to get Marcus hit. Fifteen thousand to the beat cop who guarded the door to take a five-minute break. And sixty thousand to a beautiful hit woman named Mish to replace his IV bag with highly concentrated pure liquid cocaine.

Chaz had sent the message to Macon loud and clear. *Fuck with mines and I will annihilate yours.*

After a week-and-a-half stay in the hospital, Kennedy was released. Chaz knew there was no way that she could ever return to the house in Jersey. So he rented a five-bedroom condo in midtown just three and a half blocks from T.O.N.Y.'s new offices and studio. He tried to make the place as comfortable as possible for her. He hired someone to come in and cook for her. He even had fresh flowers delivered daily.

A little over a month after the attack, Kennedy seemed to doing fine, at least to judge by her appearance. But it was a front that was becoming increasingly hard for her to keep up when she was actually dying on the inside. She had barely made it through a weekend visit from the kids without breaking all the way down. Watching them laugh and play had only made her wonder what the twins would have been like.

Sunday-morning breakfast with the kids became especially hard for Kennedy often Jordan asked, "Mommy, where-where my sister and brother?"

Then Mattie chimed in. "Yeah, Ken, where *are* my new cousins?"

Chaz, Niko, and Taylor looked nervously at Kennedy.

Smiling, Kennedy explained to them: "Micah and Brooklyn are in heaven now."

"With my mommy?" Mattie asked.

"Yes, baby, they're with your mommy. Excuse me, ya'll," Kennedy then said, getting up from the table. She walked briskly down the hall straight to the bathroom. Shutting the door, she balled over from the hurt in the pit of her stomach. She covered her mouth to keep from crying aloud. After a good long cry, she left the bathroom only to go into her bedroom and fall into a deep sleep. She woke up just in time to get the kids ready for Yatta to pick them up for their flight back to Charlotte.

When Yatta arrived and saw her sister, the first thing she noticed was the drastic amount of weight that Kennedy had lost. When Kennedy greeted her with a warm smile and a hug, Yatta held on to her, wanting to cry. She could see through Kennedy's smile and she saw nothing but pain. Yatta didn't want to leave her sister, but she had to chaperone the kids on the flight. With her styling and party-planning businesses both thriving, Yatta had not had much time to spend with Kennedy. She promised herself that when she returned the next day, she would spend the entire day with her.

That night Kennedy was sleeping peacefully when she was awakened by the sound of crying babies. She sat straight up in the bed and looked around. Chaz was next to her snoring, deep in his sleep. Suddenly the noise stopped. Shaking it off, Kennedy lay back down. As soon as her head hit the pillow the crying started all over again. For two hours Kennedy tossed and turned, unable to fall asleep, still hearing the sound of the crying babies.

Finally she got up, grabbed her purse, and went into the bathroom. Sitting on the edge of the tub, Kennedy rambled through her purse until she found her old bottle of prescription sleeping pills. Although the instructions said *Take one pill before going to bed,* Kennedy poured three pills into the palm of her hand and popped them into her mouth. And when her head hit the pillow that time, she fell into a coma-like sleep instantly.

The following morning she was still feeling drugged up from the sleeping pills. She was so incoherent that she could barely return Chaz's kiss before he headed to the studio around noon. Kennedy crawled out of bed around one-thirty that afternoon. Not five minutes after she woke up, she was sitting on the toilet urinating when she began to hear the crying again.

Kennedy turned the radio and television on full blast, attempting to drown out the cries of the babies. When that didn't work, she sat in the middle of the living-room floor for two hours with her knees close to her chest. Rocking back and forth, she covered her ears with her hands. Huge tears slid down her face as she chanted over and over, "Stop crying. Please . . . please stop crying." Suddenly, as if something had clicked in her head, she jumped up and ran from room to room searching for the twins.

When she was unsuccessful in finding them, she burst from the apartment still wearing her green silk nightgown and matching robe, her hair very disheveled. People stopped and stared as a barefoot Kennedy ran three and a half blocks to the studio.

The security guard of the building where the studio was housed recognized her when she ran through the door. Allowing her to pass, he picked up the phone and called upstairs to the studio to warn them about her appearance.

Chaz was already in front of the elevator when the doors

opened and Kennedy stepped off. She fell into his arms scream-ing, "I can't find the babies! They won't stop crying. Can you *please* come home and make them stop?"

Wrapping a blanket around her, Chaz held her tightly. He didn't know what to say. He couldn't lie and tell her that every-thing was going to be okay. He himself didn't know if *anything* was going to be okay ever again. With his arm around her, ignor-ing the stares from people in the hall, he led her back to Strick's private office. He took a seat behind the desk with Kennedy in his arms. The room was completely silent as Chaz rocked her slowly, like an infant, until she fell asleep.

Beaten down by jet lag, Yatta had been enjoying a wonderful af-ternoon nap. The constant ringing of her house phone and cell phone brought an end to her peaceful slumber. Never opening her eyes, she reached out to her nightstand and grabbed her cell phone. "Hello?"

"Yatta, this Chaz."

"What's up?"

"Yo, that thing we talked about the other day. I think it's hap-pening."

Yatta's heart sank. She sat up in the bed. "Oh God. What hap-pened?"

After Chaz explained to Yatta what Kennedy had done, the only words she said were: "Yeah, we have to take her to get some help before it's too late."

The thought of putting Kennedy in any kind of mental institu-tion killed Chaz. He closed his eyes to fight off the oncoming tears. "Damn, Yatta, but I don't even know if can take her to one of those places. I want and I do need for her to get better. I mean I want *my* Kennedy back. She's here physically, but she not my li'l mama. When I look into her eyes they're just blank."

"I understand what you're going through. She's my sister and I love her more than anybody else. But we can't be in denial. For two years she's been self-medicating with pills and alcohol. She needs to get help now."

"You right. Can you bring her some clothes, a brush, and one of those things to put her hair in a ponytail?"

"That's nothing. I'll see you in a half."

A deafening silence filled Strick's truck as he drove to the facility in Eastchester. Yatta sat in the passenger seat staring out the window. Chaz sat in the back holding on to Kennedy, who was still sleeping. None of the passengers were up for conversation. All their minds were focused on one thing: getting Kennedy the help that she needed.

Kennedy finally awakened once Strick had stopped the car at the facility. She sat up stretching and looking around. "Where are we?"

None of the three knew how to tell her. Feeling that Kennedy was her responsibility, Yatta turned around and grabbed her little sister's hand. Looking Kennedy in the eye, she told her, "Baby, everyone who loves you feels that you're very tired and you need a little help resting. There are people here who can help you with that."

Like a helpless child, Kennedy whined, "But why can't I go to Big Ma's house?"

"No, Kennedy. This time you need professional help." The sad look on Kennedy's face crushed Yatta's heart. She began having second thoughts. *Maybe I should take her to Big Ma's house.* "I would much rather take you to Big Ma's house any day than to leave you here. But that wouldn't be getting you the help that you need."

"How long do I have to stay?"

"Until you feel better."

"Will I get to see y'all?"

"Yes, sweetie. They have visitation days and I'll be here for every one of them."

Kennedy lowered her head, sniffling like a child. "Will you bring Big Ma and Mommy to see me?"

"I'll do whatever you ask me to."

From the outside, the Better Days Therapeutic Center looked like a resort spa. The center had been the temporary home to some of the top celebrities and wealthiest mental patients and recovering addicts in the Northeast. A young, beautiful, dark-skinned female greeted them at the door. "Welcome to Better Days. I'm Dr. Kisha Webster. Here, we're all on a first-name basis, so feel free to call me Kisha."

"Hi, Kisha. I'm Kenyatta Sanchez. We spoke on the phone earlier. And this is my sister Kennedy Sanchez."

"Yes, I remember our conversation. How are you, Kennedy? I hear that you're exhausted."

"I'm okay . . . I guess."

"We're going to help you get the rest you need. I'll give you a few minutes to say your good-byes."

"That's okay, I've already said them," Kennedy responded, coldly cutting her eyes at Yatta, Chaz, and Strick. She walked into the building, never looking back.

Her sudden coldness was a hard blow, especially to Yatta and Chaz. Chaz wasn't feeling it. "Yatta, let's just take her to Big Ma's."

"Chaz, we can't turn back now. One day she'll thank us for this."

Kennedy spent her first two days at the facility sleeping, only waking up to eat and shower. On her third day, she had her first meeting with one of the resident psychiatrists. Kennedy walked into the office and plopped down on a brown suede chaise. She sat up straight on purpose, thinking, *It'll be a cold day in hell before I lay down on this shit and pour out my life story to this bitch.* The ultrapetite therapist had golden blond hair and piercing ocean-blue eyes. From the outset, the perkiness of her voice irked Kennedy. "Hi, I'm Dr. Irena Kapolski. You already know that you can call me Irena. And you are Kennedy?"

"I am," Kennedy answered with a slight attitude.

"In reading your file, I saw that you've had a breakdown before."

"If that's what you wanna call it," Kennedy said snidely.

"It appears that a lot of the issues in your life begin with the men in your life."

"You're the shrink. You tell me."

"According to your file, your first breakdown came right after the death of your boyfriend Malik when you were just a teenager." Kennedy tensed up as Irena continued to talk. "Being a single mother with no help from the child's father can be a great source of stress—"

Kennedy cut her off immediately. "Raising my son without his father has never been and will never be a source of stress, so that's where you're wrong."

Irena continued on as if Kennedy had never stopped her. "And the latest traumatic event in your life was your miscarriage. It happened because you were attacked by the man who killed your cousin."

Tears burned the back of Kennedy's eyes as thoughts of the twins and Nina danced through her head. "So, Doc, it is your opinion that the men in my life are the problem?"

"I do believe that maybe your choice in men does play a major role. But let's focus on why you pick these men. Tell me . . . what kind of men did your mother date when you were growing up?"

"Despite what you think, Marcia *fucking* Brady, all black and Hispanic women are not single mothers raising a bunch of crumb snatchers."

"I never said that."

"You didn't have to *say* it. I can see it in your eyes . . . the way they judge me. My mother didn't have to date any men while I was growing up. She'd been married to my father since before her children were born, you perky *bitch*. You know what, I don't need this shit. I'm out of here."

"Kennedy, please sit back down."

"Fuck you," Kennedy said, yanking the door open. She ran down the hallway, straight to the pay phones.

Humming "Precious Lord," Big Ma placed the lid on top of the collard greens she was cooking. Opening the oven door, she checked on her squash casserole, but quickly closed the door when her house phone began ringing. She made her way to the phone hanging on the wall as quick as aching knees would allow. "Hello?"

"This is AT&T with a collect call from Kennedy. Will you accept the charges? If yes, please press one now."

Anxious to find out why Kennedy was calling her collect, Big Ma hurriedly pressed one.

"Thanks for using AT&T. Caller, go ahead." Barely giving the automated voice a chance to finish, Big Ma began talking. "Kennedy, baby, where you at?"

"Don't you know, Big Ma?"

"Nah, I wouldn't have asked if I knew!"

"I'm at a mental facility upstate."

"No, grandgirl, I didn't know anything about you being there. How did you get there?"

"Yatta arranged it, but that ain't important right now. I want to leave here now. I want to come stay with you, Big Ma."

"You know you can come here, chile."

"I don't have any cash or credit cards on me here. Can you charge my flight on your card?"

"Sure, baby."

"Thank you, Big Ma. And whatever you do, don't tell Yatta I'm leaving. And don't tell my mother because she'll tell Yatta. As a matter of fact, don't tell anyone."

Three days after Kennedy's call to Big Ma, Yatta and Chaz arrived for Kennedy's first visitation day. Chaz brought with him two dozen multicolored roses, Kennedy's favorite. Carrying a Vuitton duffel bag full of new clothes for Kennedy, Yatta anxiously approached the reception desk. "Good afternoon. We're here to see Kennedy Sanchez."

"One second, let me pull up her room number and I'll call her." After keying in Kennedy's information, the receptionist looked at the screen, then nervously at Yatta. "Let me get Dr. Webster for you."

"Is there a problem?" Chaz asked.

"No, Dr. Webster has requested that all phone calls and visitors for Kennedy be directed to her first."

As Dr. Webster approached, the serious look on her face spoke volumes. "Good afternoon. Please follow me into my office." The warm smile and kindness that she had greeted them with days earlier was now gone. Yatta and Chaz sat down in the two chairs directly in front of her desk. Getting right to the point, Yatta asked, "Is everything okay with my sister?"

"Your sister left the program."

"What do you mean she left?" Chaz demanded.

"She checked out yesterday."

Yatta shook her head in disbelief. "This is fucking un-believable! Why didn't you call me? And why did you let her leave?"

"Ms. Sanchez, you know that she signed herself in voluntarily. So therefore she could check herself out. She also requested that we not inform you. If I'd called you, it would've violated doctor-client privilege."

"I don't care about that privilege shit. My sister is unstable. She could be somewhere DEAD!"

"I can assure you that your sister is very safe." Reaching into her desk drawer, Dr. Webster pulled out two envelopes. "Kennedy left these for the two of you."

Sitting in the parking lot of Better Days, Chaz and Yatta both stared at the envelopes in their hands. Opening his first, Chaz pulled the paper out. Pain literally shot through his heart when he unfolded the paper and Kennedy's engagement ring fell out. He held it tightly in his left hand while he read the letter.

Chaz,
I need space to clear my mind. For some reason, I can't get past the recent events. Maybe it's because I still haven't gotten over some of the painful events in my past. Please don't pursue me. I need time to heal my mind and my soul. I cannot do that and build with you at the same time. In the meantime, if you find an-other woman, that's okay. I have too many issues to expect you not to find someone else better. Whatever happens with me, please know that I will always love you and will never forget you.

Sincerely, Kennedy

Seeing the single tear fall from Chaz's eye had Yatta afraid to open her letter. Putting her fear to the side, she opened it and began reading.

Yatta,
I know you probably think I'm mad at you for bringing me here. Well, I'm not. I know that your intentions were good. Better Days just was not the place for me to heal. I'm going back to that same old room I had to go to eight years ago. If you really care about my healing process, do not lead Chaz to me. Please reassure him that I never blamed him.

See you soon, Kennedy

Neither spoke a word on the drive back to the city until they pulled in front of Yatta's brownstone. Yatta looked over at Chaz in the driver's seat. He was staring straight ahead, lost in a trance. Reaching over, she touched his shoulder gently, getting his attention. "Chaz, she loves you very much. She just needs time."

"I know," Chaz said, turning his head and looking out the window so that Yatta wouldn't see the tears forming in his eyes.

Feeling his pain, Yatta told him, "Come in and hang out with me and Strick for a while. We can watch a few movies and I'll cook you something good. You look like you ain't ate since Kennedy's breakdown."

"Nah, that's okay, Shorty's gonna bring the girls by the house later on."

Yatta could tell that he was lying, but she decided not to press the issue. She planted a sisterly kiss on his cheek. "Be safe, okay? See you later."

"Aight, Yatta, I'll hit you tomorrow."

Chaz watched Yatta until she got into the house. After she closed the door, he looked over at the town house where Kennedy used to reside. It was now rented out to a young white couple. He sat there for a minute staring at the house, thinking, *I remember the first night I ever came over. All those late nights after the studio . . . Kennedy would hide me from the kids. She always had a hot plate waiting for a nigga. It was all love back then. I miss those days . . . I miss her.* Banging his fist on the steering wheel, he yelled out, "WHAT THE FUCK, MAN? On everything I love, I'ma kill that nigga." Speeding away from the curb, he drove recklessly all the way to his midtown apartment.

Even in his apartment Chaz was still unable to find solace. Everything inside of those walls reminded him of Kennedy. Pictures of her, him, and their kids lined the foyer. Her clothes, shoes, and handbags were spread throughout the house. Walking into the den, he snatched an unopened liter bottle of Hennessy from the bar. After cracking the top, he chugged half the bottle down in one swig. He removed the bottle from his lips and let out a loud deep cough. The burning sensation moved from his throat down to his chest before warming his entire body.

Chaz fell back on the couch as the liquor slowly crept over him. He picked up the CD-player remote that was lying next to him and pressed play. The sounds of Anthony Hamilton's "I'm a Mess" poured through the speakers like thick molasses. "I'm a Mess" just happened to be one of Kennedy's favorite songs. It was also very ironic how the song mirrored his exact feelings at the moment. *"I'm a mess right now. Can't believe I lost you, my soul mate, my best friend. We invested in a set of twins."* Listening to the words, he stared at a beautiful poster-size picture of him and Kennedy on the red carpet at the *Vibe* awards. It was displayed proudly between his first platinum plaque and Kennedy's.

Out of nowhere, Chaz hurled the Hennessy bottle right at the picture. Glass shattered everywhere and the brown liquor splashed against the wall. The wooden frame slid down the wall, breaking into huge pieces when it crashed against the hardwood floor. Enraged, Chaz ran over to the wall and began snatching all the plaques and pictures, throwing them all across the room. He knocked over everything in sight. Angrily, he put his fist through the wall with one punch. He pushed over the huge entertainment unit, completely smashing it, the plasma television, and the home-theater system.

Chaz dropped to his knees in the middle of the destruction; looking toward the sky, he moaned loudly from a broken heart, "Why now? *God, why now?*"

His answer would come soon enough. He had to learn that God moves in mysterious ways. And all His ways are not meant to be understood by the human mind.

Now, more than a year later, three loud motorcycle engines roaring up the street brought Chaz back from his trip down memory lane.

"Here they come," Big Ma said, "riding them bikes like damn fools."

"Who is *they*?" Chaz asked.

"Kennedy and my crazy grandnieces. They been down here since they got into some problems back in New York."

"Since when Kennedy been riding motorcycles?"

"She's been riding them things. Reckon she didn't mention it because she didn't ride for a long time after Nina died. Nina's purple bike is still back there in the garage. Kennedy don't let *nobody* touch it."

The three girls pulled into the driveway all wearing helmets, which made it hard for Chaz to tell which one was Kennedy. The two other girls had the same Sanchez tattoo on their right arm as Yatta, Kennedy, and Nina. Chaz spotted Kennedy by the black panther tattooed on her left leg.

From the driveway, Kennedy couldn't see Chaz where he was

sitting on the porch, but he had a perfect view of her. Kennedy pulled off her helmet and shook out her hair. Chaz could see that she had dyed it burgundy. He thought that she looked more beautiful than before. Her new hair color complemented the red tones in her skin. When the two other girls removed their helmets, they looked, at first glance, like twins. "Are they twins, Big Ma?"

"Nah, they first cousins—just been together like sisters since the cradle."

"Man, E, I dusted y'all bum asses," Kennedy taunted her cousins as they walked toward the porch.

"You should have! The way you got that bitch kitted out," E replied. They continued laughing and joking as they stepped onto the porch. Seeing Chaz stopped Kennedy right in her tracks, causing her cousins to bump into her and making her fall down on the steps. Chaz jumped up and ran over to help her. "Are you all right?"

"Yeah, I'm fine. What are you doin' here?" Kennedy said, getting to her feet.

"Damn, what happened to hello? How are you?"

"Hi, *Chaz,* how are you? Now, what are you doing in Charlotte, North Carolina?"

"A little birdy told me that it was time I came down."

Kennedy glared at Big Ma. Smiling, Big Ma turned her head and looked the other way.

"Now, Kennedy, I know Kora taught your high-yella ass some manners."

Kennedy gave her cousin the evil eye. "Sorry, didn't know your red ass was so big on manners. Chaz, these are my cousins Kisa and Eisani. Y'all, this is Chaz."

"Nice to finally meet the two of you," Chaz said, extending his hand toward them. "I was starting to think that you were figments of her imagination."

"We're real," Kisa replied.

"Yes, flesh and blood," Eisani added.

Jumping back in, Kisa told him, "And your baby mother better be glad that we *wasn't* around when she decided to play Edward Scissorhands."

Eisani jumped right back in, too. " 'Cause it would've been a lot of slow singing and flower bringing."

Big Ma stood up. "Come on in the house, you two trouble-makers. Stop starting shit."

"We just messing with him, Auntie," Kisa said, winking at Chaz.

"I know you two very well and you're not joking," Big Ma replied.

"Did Sincere pick up the kids?" Kisa asked Big Ma as the girls followed her into the house.

Eisani went through the door last, leaving Kennedy and Chaz alone on the porch. There was an awkward moment of silence. "I want to see more of Charlotte," Chaz said.

"Well, my mother has my truck right now."

"I was thinking we could take the bikes."

"Can you ride or would like for me to pull you?" Kennedy teased with a smirk.

"Pull me? You can't be serious, homegirl. And can *I* ride? I could beat you on a moped."

Kennedy laughed. "Now, don't write a check your ass can't cash."

It turned out that Chaz was a very skillful rider and Kennedy barely beat him. She knew that he had wanted to visit the Bank of America Stadium, home of the Carolina Panthers. Slowing down in front of the two giant panthers on Mint Street, Kennedy parked in front of the stadium. Chaz pulled up, parking behind her, gloating even though he'd lost the race. "Baby girl, you gotta get your skills up if you want to beat me."

"I did beat you, punk!"

"Only 'cause you got a little something extra in that engine, plus I don't know my way around."

"Whatever. Don't be a sore loser. Take it like a man."

Chaz focused his attention on the stadium. "This is real nice on the outside. I can't wait to see the inside. Maybe we can go to a game when the season starts."

"Yeah, maybe." They stood silent for a few seconds, making it another awkward moment.

Chaz reached into his pocket. "Here, you forgot this," he said, extending his closed hand toward her.

"What is it?"

He opened his hand, revealing its contents to Kennedy. A nervous smile lit up her face. "My ring. I can't believe you still have it."

"I kept it hoping that you would wear it again one day."

Kennedy's heart melted as she became overwhelmed with guilt. "Chaz, I'm sorry that I hurt you. But I had to do what was best for me so that I could get better. I need you to understand that I wouldn't have been any good to you as long as I was messed up in the head. Most of all, I need you to forgive me."

"I forgave you a long time ago. I just wish you would've let me decide if you would've been any good to me."

"Chaz, you yourself knew that I was a heavy burden. I would've only stagnated you. And at that time you needed to focus on your career and all that shit that was going on in the streets."

"Kennedy, do me a favor. Stop always trying to think for everybody. You don't know what I could've handled." He placed the ring in the palm of her hand. "I'm not trying to pressure you, but I would like for you to wear this again."

Shaking her head, Kennedy placed the ring back in his hand. Chaz felt his heart breaking all over again. "It's like that? You couldn't even think about it?"

"No, it's not like that at all. I just wanted *you* to put it on for me."

Smiling hard, Chaz quickly slipped the ring onto her finger. He pulled Kennedy into him, embracing her tightly. "I love you so much, girl, you just don't know."

"I love you too, baby."

"Let's go so I can get you out of those little-ass shorts."

"I suggest that you go around the corner to the Westin 'cause ain't no sleeping together up in Big Ma's house unless you're married."

"You know that's nothing."

Kennedy stood on her tiptoes and gave Chaz a soft peck on the lips. Looking her in the eye, he told her, "Don't ever leave me like that again."

"I won't. Just don't ever give me a reason."

They both climbed back onto the bikes. Chaz called out to Kennedy as she was putting her helmet on, "Baby girl, a little birdy told me that you weren't ready to return to the city yet."

"I'm going to hurt Big Ma."

"It's okay if you're not. I think I'm going to like Charlotte. Might even buy a house out here."

"I've been looking at town houses and condos. I do plan on moving back to New York one day."

"Let's get a big house so we can fill it up with five or six more kids."

"You had some more kids?" Kennedy asked, laughing.

"I'm talking about the ones that you're going to give me."

"Nigga, you good if you get one baby out of me. You see my body? I wear size six now. I'm in the best shape of my life. That's courtesy of Dr. Atkins and Peak Fitness."

238 | *Danielle Santiago*

"You're so vain."

"And you love it."

As Kennedy pulled away from the curb she thought, *Mommy always said if a lost love is meant to be, it will find its way back.* Looking up, she spotted a beautiful rainbow spread across the sky. She thought about Nina. *I wish you could've met this one, Nina. He's a keeper. And I know he loves me for me, even with all my flaws. Guess I can move on now. It's back to grinding . . . grinding for keeps.*

Acknowledgments

Thank you, Heavenly Father, for saving me through your most wonderful grace and mercy. I'm so grateful for all the many blessings you've given me, especially the blood of your son, and your divine favor.

Kaden, you are still my greatest creation and my best inspiration. Mommy loves you always.

Carlos, I'm here and I will always be here. You are my best friend, and I'm so happy I'm yours. I love you.

Mommy and Daddy, quite often I thank God for blessing me with you. Yeah, we fuss and disagree, but at the end of the day we're smiling and joking again. I'm most thankful for the loyalty, pride, morals, and love that you've instilled in me.

Aundi, I could not have asked for a more perfect little sister. There is nothing in the world I would not do for you. You were my first and biggest supporter. Thanks for always holding your big sister down.

Darion, baby boy, keep following your dreams. No matter where they lead you, your big sis will be there.

Mont, over the years, due to our hectic lives, we've grown somewhat distant and a lot of that is because of me. I promise that soon we're going to get together and take a long family vacation. I want you to know you're an excellent big brother, a wonderful man, and I think the world of you.

TT, I'm grown now! Stop being so overprotective and let ya li'l sis live! Trust me—I know you got my back.

Teon and Shani, you are the most wonderful godparents to my Kaden. You love him just as if he were yours, and I thank you for that.

Special thanks to my loving grandparents. Many hugs and kisses to my all my aunts, uncles, and cousins for all of your love and support.

I would like to acknowledge a few special ladies who are helping me develop spiritually: Nikki Long (my beautiful stylist), Doris Mumtaz, Prophetess Brittany Woods, and Ms. Betty.

Thank you, D. Adams, for being my emergency hairstylist and one of my best friends for more than ten years. To all my true friends, you know who you are, and just because I didn't name you individually doesn't mean I don't cherish our friendship.

Thanks to a few of my favorite authors who happen to be my friends: Tu-Shonda Whitaker, K. Elliot, TN Baker, Kiesha Ervin, Tonya Blount, and Kwan Foye.

Thank you, James Muhammad and Two of a Kind Publishing, for every single thing you did to help me take my career to the next level.

A special thanks to Miss Nakia Murray and As the Page Turns Literary.

Malaika Adero, thank you so much for taking a chance on a li'l ghetto chick like me (lol). I promise I won't let you down. Krishan, I know I can be a pain in the ass when you're trying to catch up with me, but I don't mean to be. Thanks for all your hard work. Thanks to the entire staff at Atria and Simon & Schuster who worked hard to make *Grindin'* happen.

Vickie Stinger, I've told you before, you are more than my agent. I can't thank you enough for going above and beyond your duty of looking out for me as an agent and a friend.

I would like to extend a heartfelt thanks to Charlotte, the

"Queen City," for welcoming me home, supporting *Little Ghetto Girl,* and all the love. Shouts out to the Chop Shop, Dynasty Books, *Power 98* morning show, Imaginations, and Salon Retro.

They say home is where the heart is, and mine is still in Harlem. Thank you, uptown, for all the love. I've been around the world and back, and I still haven't been anywhere like Harlem, USA. Somehow I even believe the air is different in Harlem.

And last but not least, to my fans: I love you all. It makes me feel so good when I meet you and you tell me you enjoy my works. Your support makes me work harder on my next story, because I want to make sure I give you something you enjoy every time you purchase a Danielle Santiago novel. Thank you so much for all the love and support.

God bless all of you.

THE OXFORD AUTHORS

General Editor: Frank Kermode

OSCAR WILDE was born in Dublin in 1854. Self-advertised, he became the most notorious of late nineteenth-century aesthetes, renowned for his conversation and wit. He published early poetry, followed by short stories, fairy-tales, and the sensational novel *The Picture of Dorian Gray*. He wrote two sparkling critical dialogues, and achieved public success as a comic playwright, crowned by *The Importance of Being Earnest* in 1895. But in that year the flamboyance of his lifestyle and his friendship with Lord Alfred Douglas led at last to his trial and imprisonment for two years' hard labour, for homosexual offences. After his imprisonment he wrote his most famous poem, *The Ballad of Reading Gaol*. He died in Paris in 1900.

ISOBEL MURRAY, Senior Lecturer in English at Aberdeen University, edited *The Picture of Dorian Gray* in the Oxford English Novels series in 1974, and Wilde's *Complete Shorter Fiction* for Oxford University Press in 1979.

THE OXFORD AUTHORS

OSCAR WILDE

EDITED BY
ISOBEL MURRAY

Oxford   New York
OXFORD UNIVERSITY PRESS
1989

Oxford University Press, Walton Street, Oxford OX2 6DP

Oxford New York Toronto
Delhi Bombay Calcutta Madras Karachi
Petaling Jaya Singapore Hong Kong Tokyo
Nairobi Dar es Salaam Cape Town
Melbourne Auckland

and associated companies in
Berlin Ibadan

Oxford is a trade mark of Oxford University Press

Introduction, edited text, and editorial matter
© Isobel Murray 1989

British Library Cataloguing in Publication Data
Wilde, Oscar, 1854–1900
Oscar Wilde.—(The Oxford authors).
I. Title   II. Murray, Isobel
828'.809
ISBN 0–19–254195–1
ISBN 0–19–281978–X

Library of Congress Cataloging in Publication Data
Wilde, Oscar, 1854–1900.
[Selections. 1989]
Oscar Wilde/edited by Isobel Murray.
p. cm.—(The Oxford authors)
Bibliography: p.   Includes index.
I. Title.
828'.809—dc19   PR5812.M87 1989
ISBN 0–19–254195–1
ISBN 0–19–281978–X (pbk.)

Typeset by Wyvern Typesetting Ltd.
Printed in Great Britain by
Richard Clay Ltd.
Bungay, Suffolk

CONTENTS

INTRODUCTION

Art is the only serious thing in the world. And the artist is the only person who is never serious.

PERHAPS the most unfortunate of Oscar Wilde's memorable remarks is one he made to André Gide—that he had put his genius into his life, and only his talent into his work. Ideal ammunition, that, for critics and commentators only too ready to belittle that work, or to say, as Gide did, that at its best it was only a faint echo of his conversation or his story-telling. The original remark was made in January 1895, just before that public catastrophe with which Wilde has been inescapably linked ever since. Interest in Wilde's private life—in his offences, his trials, and his imprisonment—has not diminished. The interest has sometimes been sympathetic, and often prurient. But the drama of Wilde's life has certainly overshadowed his work, and has often led even literary critics to concentrate too narrowly on themes in his work of guilty secrets, or suppressed confession, or to search in the writings for material suggested by knowledge of the life, material that is most certainly to be found there. So two outstanding imbalances have been perpetuated, Wilde the wonderful talker, too lazy to write down his best work, and Wilde the scandalous pervert, or the sacrificial scapegoat—or even the unjustly accused, though modern biographical evidence has surely disposed of that argument.

The popular perception of Wilde has thus been of the notorious homosexual whose fall was the major scandal of the close of the nineteenth century. And in the popular imagination he has only otherwise survived as a writer of witty stage comedies and the coiner of some memorable and quotable witticisms—'Work is the curse of the drinking classes', 'Nothing succeeds like excess', 'Divorces are made in Heaven'.

I suggest it is time to redress these major imbalances. And we have at last reached a state of things where it should be able to be done. The most important contributor to Wilde scholarship is without a doubt Rupert Hart-Davis, who edited Wilde's *Letters* in 1962, and issued a (generously) *Selected Letters* in 1979, which is readily available. He followed it in 1985 with *More Letters of Oscar Wilde*, containing all the notable letters he had been assembling since 1962. And in 1987 the long-awaited definitive biography, *Oscar Wilde*, by the late Richard

Ellmann was published. It is written not just by a fine biographer, but by a literary critic and scholar of high distinction. Now it can be said that justice has been done to the life, but other issues still need elucidation. The problem of Wilde's wit remains. His Irish contemporaries were sure from the outset that the English would misunderstand it. Wilde's younger contemporary and friend W. B. Yeats reviewed *Lord Arthur Savile's Crime* in 1891 for *United Ireland*—that is, as an Irishman of his time speaking to his countrymen of a fellow countryman. This is part of his notice:

> 'Beer, bible and the seven deadly virtues have made England what she is,' wrote Mr Wilde once; and a part of the Nemesis that has fallen upon her is a complete inability to understand anything he says. We should not find him so unintelligible—for much about him is Irish of the Irish. I see in his life and works an extravagant Celtic crusade against Anglo-Saxon stupidity.[1]

Joyce, again with a shared Irish background, thought the comedies 'brilliant', and placed Wilde along with Irish writers of comedy from Sheridan and Goldsmith to Bernard Shaw as 'like them, court jester to the English'.[2] And Shaw himself, whose own wit is perhaps the nearest to Wilde's that we have seen, teased out more of the implications of what Yeats said above, when he reviewed *An Ideal Husband* in 1895.

First, there were the epigrams, which seemed to evoke almost resentful laughter:

> They laugh angrily at his epigrams, like a child who is coaxed into being amused in the very act of setting up a yell of rage and agony. They protest that the trick is obvious, and that such epigrams can be turned out by the score by any one lightminded enough to condescend to such frivolity. As far as I can ascertain, I am the only person in London who cannot sit down and write an Oscar Wilde play at will. (Beckson 176)

Much more remains to be said about the epigrams, of course, about their techniques of interference with unthinking cliché, and about Wilde's major objects of attack: hypocrisy, cant, moral rules raised to absolutes, moral rules debased to mindless conventions, uniformity, Philistinism, and generally life distorted or limited by preconceptions. But Shaw comes back to the question of Wilde's Irishness, and what Yeats called

---

[1] This reference and many others in the Introduction can be found in Karl Beckson's *Oscar Wilde: The Critical Heritage* (1970), 110–11. Other references will be given in the text as (Beckson 000).
[2] Richard Ellmann (ed.), *Oscar Wilde: A Collection of Critical Essays* (Englewood Cliffs, NJ, 1969), 57–8.

his 'crusade against Anglo-Saxon stupidity': he understands why so much of Wilde's work is about the importance of not being earnest:

> Ireland is of all countries the most foreign to England, and . . . to the Irishman . . . there is nothing in the world quite so exquisitely comic as an Englishman's seriousness. It becomes tragic, perhaps, when the Englishman acts on it; but that occurs too seldom to be taken into account, a fact which intensifies the humour of the situation, the total result being the Englishman utterly unconscious of his real self, Mr Wilde keenly observant of it and playing on the self-unconsciousness with irresistible humour, and finally, of course, the Englishman annoyed with himself for being amused at his own expense, and for being unable to convict Mr Wilde of what seems an obvious misunderstanding of human nature. He is shocked, too, at the danger to the foundations of society when seriousness is publicly laughed at. (Beckson 177)

This whole passage bears thoughtful analysis, on more than one level, and has new resonance, of course, in hindsight.

Shaw's last point is important: as Orwell knew, 'whatever is funny is subversive'. But Shaw's point about Wilde being observant of his subject's self-unconsciousness is crucial. Wilde's work is again and again directed to show the need for self-awareness: a man so intent on his case or his beliefs that he cannot see himself in relation to that case or those beliefs is not seeing the whole story, and is likely to be, not persuasive, but a bore. Lord Illingworth, the ageing dandy in *A Woman of No Importance*, is so aware of the problem that he says taking sides at all in any matter is a mistake:

> One should never take sides in anything, Mr Kelvil. Taking sides is the beginning of sincerity, and earnestness follows shortly afterwards, and the human being becomes a bore.[3]

'Sincere' and 'earnest' are two of the words most often debunked by Wilde's wit, and in his fiction and plays. The two most sincere and earnest characters in his fairy-tales, for example, are the 'devoted friend' Hans, who foolishly ends by giving his life for his selfish and hypocritical 'friend', Hugh the Miller (pp. 36–45), and the heroic nightingale who immolates herself on a thorn, with big words like Love and Death, to produce a marvellous red rose, which shallow and self-centred humans will quite fail to appreciate.[4] There are only two important exceptions to Wilde's open debunking of such sincerity and earnestness. In the short story 'Lord Arthur Savile's Crime' the ironic success of the piece depends on the narrator gravely seeming to accept the protagonist's own

---

[3] Edited by Ian Small in *Two Society Comedies* (1983), 26.
[4] 'The Nightingale and the Rose' in *Complete Shorter Fiction* (1979), 104–9.

earnest view of his duty to his high mission, to commit the murder and the marriage only in the right order. And similarly in *The Importance of Being Earnest*, the ironic success depends on group earnestness and gravity. In this Through-the-Looking-Glass world, the two girls both share a solemn and absolute ideal, to marry a man called Ernest, and both young men respond courageously, by undertaking the ordeal of a second christening. Group earnestness about patently absurd ideals is infinitely comic; especially when both the absurd ideals and the high seriousness with which they are professed are a partial reflection of the world on this side of the looking-glass.

For of course Wilde was writing in a very earnest world, in an age when politicians and writers alike too readily fell into pulpit oratory. Many great Victorian writers, from Carlyle to Matthew Arnold, from Ruskin to George Eliot, raised their voices against the abuses of their age, against an infinity of affronts to human dignity. They showed up the abuses of the Industrial Revolution and of rampant capitalism; they variously attacked economic, political, social, and cultural ills, and castigated shoddy moral attitudes prevalent in Victorian England (the same so-called Victorian values we hear much about in the 1980s). Wilde was not essentially in disagreement with their goals, or out of sympathy with their protests, for all the apparent irresponsibility of the young dandies in his dialogues and plays. Indeed, his own opinions were in some ways very 'advanced' for his time—his sympathy with feminism, for instance, or his espousal of an individual political attitude mixing an *avant-garde* version of socialism with anarchism. He was of his time and altogether with the great Victorians in being moved by dramatic inequalities, by poverty, oppression, and hunger. Tennyson most schematically outlined the artist's unhappy awareness of these inequalities in 'The Palace of Art' (1832), but Wilde's own mother denounced the ills of Ireland and the potato famines in her *Poems*, published when he was 10, and dedicated to Wilde and his elder brother. He admitted to being moved by these same inequalities in his 1877 review of the Grosvenor Gallery exhibition,[5] and his early fairy-tales; and his last published prose works were letters about ill treatment, especially of children and the insane, in English prisons. But he did not set out to tackle such problems seriously in his writings.

He was intensely suspicious of the means by which even the great writers sometimes made their protests, the rhetoric, the preaching, the moral imperatives, and these weapons in the hands of lesser writers he found terrible indeed. Too much moral passion, too little light and

[5] *Miscellanies* (1908), 5–23.

lucidity; too little reason, too little examination of unthinking habits of mind and language: Oscar Wilde sets out to right some of these imbalances. If your mental picture remains that of an idle dandy with a cigarette drawling clever epigrams at a society audience, the verdict 'A Writer of No Importance' is possible. If you examine more closely the paradox and irony of an Irishman commended by his great Irish contemporaries for ruthless undercutting of (English) complacency, convention and hypocrisy, another verdict is more likely. Arthur Symons (English, certainly, but a Cornishman!) sums it up thus, as early as 1891:

> Mr Wilde, with a most reasonable hatred of the *bourgeois* seriousness of dull people, has always taken refuge from the commonplace in irony. Intentionally or not—scarcely without intention—he has gained a reputation for frivolity which does injustice to a writer who has at least always been serious in the reality of his devotion to art. (Beckson 94)

Irony is a key term in Modernist approaches to literature: perhaps Wilde has more in common with some of the 'Great Modernists' than has hitherto been allowed.

Certainly his general critical stature is still uneasy: his presence is tolerated; he tends to be given fairish marks for witty (but wooden) comedies, and a doubtful mention for *Dorian Gray*. But if we look back, beyond the myth of the outstanding but lazy conversationalist, and the myth of his scandalous fall, and if we suspend the label of clever coiner of phrases, we find among his contemporaries some sharply different attitudes to Wilde. On the one hand he deliberately provoked the publicity he experienced in his early days in London, the aesthetic young writer-about-town who blatantly advertised himself and was regularly lampooned in *Punch* and mocked by the mass of the media. And his only real popular success before his fall was in the theatre, with his social comedies. But on the other hand, the most perspicacious of his contemporaries, like Arthur Symons above, had different things to say, and judged him from perspectives that have not been available to our century.

Walter Pater, for example, began his review of the enlarged *Dorian Gray* with an introductory generalization which included the critical dialogues:

> There is always something of an excellent talker about the writing of Mr Oscar Wilde; and in his hands, as happens so rarely with those who practise it, the form of dialogue is justified by its being really alive. His genial, laughter-loving sense of life and its enjoyable intercourse, goes far to obviate any crudity there may be in the paradox, with which, as with the bright and shining truth which often underlies it, Mr Wilde, startling his 'countrymen', carries on, more perhaps than

any other writer, the brilliant critical work of Matthew Arnold. *The Decay of Lying*, for instance, is all but unique in its half-humorous, yet wholly convinced, presentment of certain valuable truths of criticism. (Beckson 83)

This is merely the preliminary to his review: he does not feel impelled to back up his suggestion that Wilde carries on 'the brilliant critical work of Matthew Arnold' by any hint that the claim may be regarded as extravagant: it must have seemed a more reasonable thing to say then than some would have it now. In a similar aside to his review of *Lord Arthur Savile's Crime* Yeats wrote:

Dorian Gray with all its faults of method, is a wonderful book. *The Happy Prince* is a volume of as pretty fairy tales as our generation has seen; and *Intentions* hides within its immense paradox some of the most subtle literary criticism we are likely to see for many a long day. (Beckson 111).

What was it, then, that was available to Pater and Yeats and has not been available to us? I suggest that Wilde's range, in every sense, was clearer to them. Without our dubious benefit of the tag 'playwright' for Wilde, they saw him in turn as teller of modern short story and fairy-tale, as author of a sensational and resonant novel, as reviver of the humorous critical dialogue, and so on, attempting all the genres in-dicated on the contents page of the present volume, and more ('The Portrait of Mr W. H.',[6] for example, is literary criticism and long short story combined). His variousness was obvious to them. And to no one more than to Wilde himself. He made some fairly startling claims for his own achievements in *De Profundis*, the long letter to Lord Alfred Douglas that he composed in Reading Gaol. 'I was a man', he says, 'who stood in symbolic relations to the art and culture of my age.' Of his published work he goes on:

I made art a philosophy, and philosophy an art: I altered the minds of men and the colours of things: there was nothing I said or did that did not make people wonder: I took the drama, the most objective form known to art, and made it as personal a mode of expression as the lyric or the sonnet, at the same time that I widened its range and enriched its characterization: drama, novel, poem in rhyme, poem in prose, subtle or fantastic dialogue, whatever I touched I made beautiful in a new mode of beauty: to truth itself I gave what is false no less than what is true as its rightful province, and showed that the false and the true are merely forms of intellectual existence. I treated Art as the supreme reality, and life as a mere mode of fiction: I awoke the imagination of my century so that it created myth and legend around me: I summed up all systems in a phrase, and all existence in an epigram.[7]

[6] *Complete Shorter Fiction*, 139–69.   [7] *Selected Letters of Oscar Wilde* (1979), 194.

It is possible to take these claims soberly, and to give verdicts and pass sentence on each count, as if Wilde were yet again in the dock. It is clear that he seeks no pardon here, and indicates no saving modesty. But of course it is important to remember the peculiar circumstances in which these lines were written. Out of context they seem over-weening indeed, out of proportion with reality, lacking in self-criticism. But even in the letter we see that one point of these high claims is the self-criticism which immediately follows: he admits in the next paragraph how he neglected his work for 'long spells of senseless and sensual ease', and amused himself with being 'a *flâneur* [a lounger], a dandy, a man of fashion', and 'the spendthrift of my own genius'.

His contemporaries had immediate advantages over us. Without our misleading hindsights, and with something perhaps even more important, they watched his development, with admiration or jealousy according to their natures. Their great advantage was that they shared so much of Wilde's culture, the medium in which he self-consciously existed, with reference to which he made every utterance in his art. Here I am not merely offering the obvious truth that contemporaries tend to have a special appreciation of the particular flavour of any writer, sharing much of his or her reading and general knowledge, and the cultural experience and world situation of the time: I suggest that in this regard Wilde is a very special case. His culture, the medium in which he might be said to float, is a very rich and varied culture, and he is always aware of it, as he is aware of himself and his reader, constantly making open or covert reference to the tradition in which he exercises his individual talent, and treating all the great writers he knows as in some sense his living contemporaries, to whom he can bow in appreciation, or with whom he can continue to debate. Until now anything like an educated contemporary appreciation of all this has been virtually irrecoverable.

This is the first large-scale edition of Wilde which begins to make available to the modern reader the Wilde who was recognized by his sensitive and educated contemporaries like Pater, Yeats, and Symons. It is the first to attempt to render as much as possible of that distinctive culture, and of Wilde's always self-conscious interaction with it. Unlike the majority of modern readers, Wilde's literary contemporaries for the most part shared at least some part of his classical education. Wilde was exceptional here in that he not only studied Greek and Latin at school, but went on to pursue his studies at not one but two universities, winning the Berkeley Gold Medal for Greek at Trinity College, Dublin, and taking First Class Honours in Greats at Oxford. He was exceptional also in his devotion, grasp, and memory (with odd and generally unimportant lapses). Today's reader tends to need something like the explanatory notes supplied at the end of this volume to get the full flavour of his literary and mythological references.

Wilde also knew English literature very thoroughly, with considerable love, and the same encyclopaedic memory: how else, we might unkindly ask, could he have written his early poems? *Poems* (1881) has the distinction of being a gift requested and then uniquely refused by the library of the Oxford Union. Young Oliver Elton—later a professor of English—famously accused Wilde of plagiarism here, the first of many such accusations:

> They are for the most part not by their putative father at all, but by a number of better-known and more deservedly reputed authors. They are in fact by William Shakespeare, by Philip Sidney, by John Donne, by Lord Byron, by William Morris, by Algernon Swinburne, and by sixty more, whose works have furnished the list of passages which I hold in my hand at this moment. The Union Library already contains better and fuller editions of all these poets: the volume which we are offered is theirs, not Mr Wilde's: and I move that it be not accepted.[8]

It is true that there was more of graceful compliment to acknowledged masters than stunning originality and individuality in *Poems*, and none of them are included here as part of his mature work. But as Wilde's work develops, accusations of plagiarism seem increasingly beside the point. The many source-searching articles in which critics (myself very much included) have engaged miss the point if they think to establish stolen echoes from single sources with any neatness: they begin to get the point if they recognize that they are helping to define the resonant traditions inside which Wilde was creating his own contributions. Such sources are virtually never single ones: Wilde is always aware of how the genre or motif has been exploited to date, and draws on these traditions wherever appropriate in the fashioning of his new work of art. So, for example, I summed up one of many studies of sources for *Dorian Gray* in 1972 by suggesting that whatever individual echoes we might find, Wilde was essentially combining two well-known traditions, the Gothic horror novel and the novel of aesthetic sensibility.[9]

Wilde also had expert and catholic knowledge of French literature. He devoured French novels and plays by the dozen, as can be seen for example in the many parcels of French books listed in the sadly imperfect

---

[8] Quoted in Richard Ellmann, *Oscar Wilde* (1987), 140.
[9] 'Some Elements in the Composition of *The Picture of Dorian Gray*', *Durham University Journal*, xxxiii, 3 (June 1972), 220–31.

catalogue of his library for the bankruptcy sale. He was particularly devoted to Flaubert, Baudelaire, and Balzac, as the notes here indicate, and I was especially struck, re-surveying the field for this volume, by the extent of his indebtedness to Gautier. Indeed, it is too simple to talk simply of *his* debt to Gautier. That was something he was aware of, and he signalled his devotion, quoting, and reflecting on the poems of *Emaux et Camées* in *Dorian Gray* and elsewhere, and adding to his novel a Preface, to echo the celebrated Preface to *Mademoiselle de Maupin*. Gautier's influence was wider. In the long-running battle of wits with Whistler, which began when Whistler accused Wilde of plagiarism of ideas, and which is traced to some extent in the notes to *The Decay of Lying* and *The Critic as Artist*, we notice that material calculated to enrage Whistler is carefully added to the revised form of *The Decay of Lying* (p. 232n). But the attack in *The Critic as Artist* is particularly subtle. There Gilbert is told by Ernest (whose name indicates he is a born loser) that 'in the best days of art there were no art-critics'. Gilbert replies:

> I seem to have heard that observation before, Ernest. It has all the vitality of error and all the tediousness of an old friend. (p. 245.)

Informed contemporaries aware of the friction between Wilde and Whistler would have identified the 'old friend' as Whistler at once: Whistler had been loudly saying just this sort of thing. But Ernest's peroration is a very close echoing *not* of Whistler, but of Gautier (p. 247n), and its effect is to indicate to the really 'tuned-in' reader that Whistler rather than Wilde was the plagiarist, stealing without acknowledgment of any kind. As Ellmann says, Wilde 'knew, as Whistler had perhaps forgotten, that many of Whistler's attitudes had been formed by Gautier's Preface to *Mademoiselle de Maupin*.'[10]

One other example which cropped up almost by accident makes me think a full-scale study of Gautier's influence on Wilde and the Nineties (at least) would be interesting. I suspect Lord Alfred Douglas knew his *Mademoiselle de Maupin* too. 'Two Loves', the infamous Douglas sonnet which was used against Wilde at his trial, ends: 'I am the Love that dare not speak its name.' I suspect the line may have its origin in chapter v of Gautier's novel, where D'Albert writes sulkily, as his love for Rosette dwindles, and needs extra stimulation. He wishes she were false or fickle, or that he had a new love: 'When it is a new friendship that takes you away from the old it is easier to get free.' As it is, he hankers after emotion that would impel him toward 'all the obscurity and isolation sought by the love which dares not show itself'.

[10] Ellmann, *Oscar Wilde*, 225.

Pater or Symons might share Wilde's close knowledge of the ancient world and its literatures, and of French and English literature. Not even they, it seems, shared also his considerable knowledge of American literature, again in part reflected in the notes to this volume. He attends not only to Poe, who had been 'adopted' by Baudelaire and made famous in France, but to Longfellow, Hawthorne, and Whitman. Today's unsuspecting British reader is particularly unlikely to detect Wilde's frequent tributes to and developments of Emerson: 'the Sage of Concord' is nowadays little known on the eastern side of the Atlantic. A fair number of Emerson's essays are quoted by Wilde, but it is 'Self-Reliance', with its call for inconsistency and nonconformity in the interests of self-realization, that is outstandingly influential: it is echoed in many places, including of course *The Critic as Artist*, and I would argue is a major inspiration for Wilde's essay 'The Soul of Man Under Socialism'. The 'Individualism' Wilde puts forward there has considerable similarities to Emerson's notion of Self-Reliance.

And above all, Emerson is free of the 'earnestness' so prevalent in English Victorian essayists and prose-writers—and he writes with clarity, individuality, and style, coining epigrammatic phrases that Wilde relishes. 'I wish I had said that,' Wilde is reputed to have said to Whistler, who is reputed to have replied, 'You will, Oscar, you will.' But he never echoed Whistler's phrasing—rarely in itself outstanding—with the zest with which he repeated Emerson's phrase, 'to be great is to be misunderstood' (p. 248n).

Wilde's artistic interests were by no means confined to literature. Baudelaire and Gautier had been accepted in France as expert commentators on painting, and Pater and Ruskin were accepted in England. Wilde modelled himself on these men in many ways. Pater's most celebrated work, and the one which most pervasively influenced Wilde, was *The Renaissance*, which dealt far more with painting than with literature. Apart from the notorious Conclusion of 1873, which influenced Wilde so profoundly and pervasively that decisions as to how often to mention echoes of it in the Notes had to be haphazard, the most famous passage in *The Renaissance* is Pater's description of Leonardo's *Mona Lisa*. This is the passage that the young men of *The Critic as Artist* recite to each other as they stand before the painting, and the passage Yeats arranged as verse and made the first 'poem' in *The Oxford Book of Modern Verse*. Wilde similarly paid tribute to Ruskin's imaginative renderings of Turner into prose.

It was only natural that he should try to emulate these men. His first serious publication of any length was a review of the first exhibition at the newly opened Grosvenor Gallery in 1877, which he contributed to the *Dublin University Magazine*. He was an eager advocate of the Pre-Raphaelites, and, especially during the years before their friendship came to an end, of Whistler. In France he seems to have developed a particular taste for Corot, and he generally welcomes the pictures of the Impressionists, which he repeatedly discusses in the dialogues. In the second part of *The Critic as Artist* he characteristically reveals a desire to be very up to date, and considerably qualifies his appreciation of the Impressionists in favour of a newer group, the *Archaicistes*, who worked on different principles, as their chosen name indicates. He was a particular admirer of Gustave Moreau, who so often and so memorably painted Salome, and Ellmann's biography gives a fascinating account of his insatiable appetite for paintings on this subject, by all manner of painters.[11]

Thus for once we can perhaps see further than the well-read and sensitive contemporaries I have been envying. Contemporary reviewers of *Salome* responded with accusatory lists of literary sources only. One anonymous—and very unenthusiastic—reviewer of the (French) *Salome* points out that 'Mr Wilde has many masters', and points knowledgeably to an impressive number; Gautier, Maeterlinck, Anatole France, Marcel Schwob, and above all Flaubert (Beckson 135–6). William Archer, drama critic and champion of Ibsen's new mode of drama, suggests intriguingly that 'Salome is an oriental Hedda Gabler' (Beckson 142). And of course the outstanding literary influence on the play is the Authorized Version of the Bible. But the accepted modern wisdom adds one other literary influence as central, and sees behind it another inspiration, a visual one from painting. Huysmans' *A Rebours* is rightly seen as important for *Salome*, as indeed for *Dorian Gray*. And it is a very plausible suggestion that *Salome* is at least in part the outcome of Wilde's reading the musings of Huysmans' hero Des Esseintes over two paintings of Salome by Gustave Moreau. Ellmann's account of his interest in other Salome paintings fits in beautifully here. *Salome* can then be seen as a pre-eminent example of what Wilde called 'the art-literature of the nineteenth century', what he admired in Ruskin, Pater, and Browning and emulated himself in the dialogues, where he also investigated its nature. In 'Pen, Pencil, and Poison' he declared: 'In a very ugly and sensible age, the arts borrow, not from life, but from each other.'[12]

The accepted relationship of illustration to text is an older one, to which we are more accustomed. But the relationship of Beardsley's bizarre and memorable illustrations for the English *Salome* to Wilde's

[11] Ibid. 322–6.   [12] *Intentions* (1891), 75.

text is unusual. His drawings often bear no recognizable relationship to the text of the play, and he goes so far as to caricature the play's author in several cases. Rodney Shewan has added a new twist to this relationship by suggesting that Beardsley's illustrations are inspired directly by Moreau.[13] Between them, Beardsley and Wilde succeed in disturbing accepted ideas of the relation of art to literature, and literature to art. Both would be pleased, although their alliance was always uneasy. When Wilde was first dissatisfied with Lord Alfred Douglas's translation of *Salome* into English, Beardsley wanted to translate the play himself, but his offer was not accepted: thus perhaps the animus that inspired the caricatures. But details remain unclear. Ellmann says that it was a Beardsley drawing of Salome in *The Studio* for April 1893 that caused Wilde to engage Beardsley as illustrator, but this would not explain the inscription Wilde made for Beardsley in a copy of the French edition: 'March '93. For Aubrey: for the only artist who, besides myself, knows what the dance of the seven veils is, and can see that invisible dance. Oscar.' We must conclude that Wilde had seen the drawing he admired earlier, at an exhibition at the New English Arts Club in March 1893.

So we are wise to consider the visual inspiration of paintings for Wilde, and especially Moreau's watercolour *L'Apparition*, described by Huysmans in his novel. But we must not regard anything as solved, or final. I now suggest that Moreau's influence on Wilde was not primarily through Huysmans, and that the whole elaborate chain of connections has to be revised, when we learn that the Moreau watercolour was actually exhibited at the first exhibition at the Grosvenor Gallery in 1877, the same exhibition Wilde reviewed at length and with care. It remains a pity that he prudently confined his notice to the British painters he already knew!

But even if we concentrate on literary sources and verbal echoes, the tracing of Wilde's indebtedness to one author is always liable to be upset because of the many instances of multiple and overlapping influences. Take the case of Chuang Tzŭ, Taoist philosopher, and his influence on *The Critic as Artist*. In 1890 Wilde reviewed H. A. Giles's *Chuang Tzŭ: Mystic, Moralist and Social Reformer* at length and with great enthusiasm (*Rev* 528–38), and he incorporated echoes of and references to Chuang Tzŭ in his prose writings thereafter, still echoing him even in *De Profundis*, when he certainly had no text to hand, and relied only on his amazing memory.[14] Chuang Tzŭ wittily and pithily preached inaction,

---

[13] Rodney Shewan, *Oscar Wilde: Art and Egotism* (1977), 143.

[14] See I. Murray, 'Oscar Wilde's Absorption of "Influences": The Case History of Chuang Tzŭ', *Durham University Journal*, xxxiii, 1 (Dec. 1971), 1–13.

the fundamental uselessness of everything useful, contemplation, self-culture, and spontaneity. As Wilde wrote *The Critic as Artist*, echoes of Chuang Tzŭ were combined with echoes from Pater's *Appreciations*, which he reviewed a few weeks later, quoting with approval Pater's account of Wordsworth: 'the end of life is not action but contemplation—*being* as distinct from *doing*.' Chuang Tzŭ said: a man 'should *be* rather than *do*'. When Gilbert says (p. 277) that the critical spirit can give us the contemplative life, 'the life that has for its aim not *doing* but *being*, and not *being* merely, but *becoming*', it is only tunnel vision that seeks to point to a single source, and cannot recognize the confluence of three minds here—or four, if we include Wordsworth. And behind these are the ancient Greeks who recommended contemplation—and inevitably Gautier, whose famous Preface, like Chuang Tzŭ, and like Wilde's subtitle, recommended idleness: 'The most fitting occupation for a civilized man is to do nothing, or smoke analytically his pipe or cigar.' Chuang Tzŭ's aim of self-culture and Emerson's central self-reliance again have so much in common that it is often impossible to pinpoint Wilde's phrases as indebted to single sources: both warn against conformity as a serious danger to the individual self—an attitude intrinsically attractive to Wilde—and both repeatedly attack phil-anthropy, as so many Wilde characters and passages do. In the dialogues, above all, Wilde reacts allusively and creatively to the writers who appeal to him, from any period and any cultural context.

The choice of texts for this volume was sometimes easy. Some texts select themselves, and on the other hand I think on the whole Wilde reads better without his early and his unfinished plays, and without the early poems. It was relatively easy to select from the short fiction, because the *Complete Shorter Fiction* is available in The World's Classics series, and it was similarly relatively easy to omit *De Profundis*, because the *Selected Letters* are also easily available. It cost a wrench to leave out *A Woman of No Importance*, although I agree with Ellmann that it is the weakest of Wilde's comedies. The hardest decisions were about the other essays, especially 'The Soul of Man Under Socialism'. I am currently preparing a World's Classics edition of mainly 'Prison Writings', which will highlight that essay as it deserves, and juxtapose it with *De Profundis*.

ACKNOWLEDGEMENTS

I AM indebted to Wilde's grandson, Merlin Holland, and to the William Andrews Clark Memorial Library, University of California, Los Angeles, first for permission to consult and then to quote from unpublished Wilde manuscripts. I am grateful to the British Library which allowed me to consult the manuscript of the 'final draft' of *The Sphinx* in my attempts to approximate to Wilde's original punctuation. I have had patient assistance from the House of Commons Library, the Reference Library of the Bank of England, and the Library of the Institute of Bankers. Most of all I am indebted to Aberdeen University's Queen Mother Library and its staff, with particular mention of the Inter-Library Loan personnel, and of Jennifer Beavan, who thrives on the kind of questions that turn other people's hair white.

My debts to other writers on Wilde are many: I am gratefully conscious of particular indebtedness to Sir Rupert Hart-Davis's editions of the letters, and the New Mermaid editions of Wilde's comedies by Russell Jackson and Ian Small.

Among colleagues at Aberdeen University who helped out in tracing Wilde's encyclopaedic range of references are J. H. Alexander, Wendy Craik, James Forsyth, John Gash, J. Derrick McClure, David Mannings, Thomas Pearce, John Roach, Alasdair Stewart. Other valuable assistance was rendered by Nicholas Savage, Horst Schroeder, Alison Smith, and Grant Wilson.

Frank Kermode's advice was most helpful, and I particularly appreciate his encouraging me to let the volume get bigger! I am endlessly in the debt of Hilary Feldman and Judith Luna at Oxford University Press, who fielded my puzzled questions and tackled the thankless task of editing my manuscript. And Bob Tait made his mark on the typescript, very many times.

CHRONOLOGY

1854   Oscar Wilde born in Dublin, second son of distinguished parents, both authors, Dr (later Sir) William Wilde, leading oculist and ear-surgeon, and Jane Francesca Elgee, poet and translator, who wrote for the Young Ireland movement of the 1840s, under the name Speranza.

1857   First edition of Baudelaire's *Les Fleurs du mal*: Baudelaire is fined for offences against public morals.

1864–71   At Portora Royal School, Enniskillen.

1864   Matthew Arnold delivers from the Chair of Poetry at Oxford the first version of his essay 'The Function of Criticism at the Present Time', which Wilde would answer in *The Critic as Artist*.

1867   Death of Wilde's younger sister Isola, aged 8.

1871–4   At Trinity College, Dublin, reading Classics.

1873   Publication of the first edition of Pater's *Renaissance*, with its notorious and far-reaching 'Conclusion'.

1874   Berkeley Gold Medal for Greek at Trinity: matriculates, with a scholarship, at Magdalen College, Oxford. Flaubert's *Temptation of St Antony* published. First Impressionist exhibition in Paris.

1875   Summer: visits Italy with Dublin professor J. P. Mahaffy.

1876   Death of Sir William Wilde. Wilde takes a First Class in Classical Moderations.

1877   Visits Greece with Mahaffy, returns via Rome. Grosvenor Gallery opens in London: Wilde covers the first exhibition for *Dublin University Magazine*. Whistler prepares to sue Ruskin over his review of the Whistler paintings in the Grosvenor Gallery.

1878   Wins the Newdigate Prize for his poem *Ravenna*. Takes a First Class in *Literae Humaniores*.

1879   Settles in London, as 'professor' of aesthetics: regularly lampooned in *Punch* from now on.

1881   *Poems* published. Gilbert and Sullivan's *Patience* produced, satirizing the aesthetes.

1882   Spends year lecturing in United States and Canada, on such subjects as 'The English Renaissance of Art' and 'The House Beautiful'.

1883   Three months in Paris: lectures in Britain: the early play *Vera* rather unsuccessfully produced in New York.

1884   Marries Constance Lloyd; settles in Chelsea. Begins regular book-reviewing, which continues until 1890. J.-K. Huysmans publishes *A Rebours*.

1885   Son Cyril born. Whistler's 'Ten O'Clock' Lecture. Pater publishes

Marius the Epicurean. Passing of the Criminal Law Amendment Act 1885, which for the first time prohibited indecent relations between consenting males, the offence for which Wilde would serve his years in prison.

1886 Wilde meets Robert Ross. Son Vyvyan born.

1887–9 Edits *The Woman's World*.

1888 *The Happy Prince and Other Tales* published.

1889 'The Portrait of Mr W. H.' published in *Blackwood's*.

1890 The first version of *Dorian Gray* published in *Lippincott's Monthly Magazine*.

1891 Meets Lord Alfred Douglas. *The Duchess of Padua* produced in New York as *Guido Ferranti*. Publishes the revised *Dorian Gray*, *Intentions*, *Lord Arthur Savile's Crime and Other Stories*, *A House of Pomegranates*. 'The Soul of Man under Socialism' published in the *Fortnightly Review*. Irish political leader Parnell, having been vindicated on charges of political murder, is publicly ruined because of his involvement in a divorce suit.

1892 *Lady Windermere's Fan* produced. *Salome* is refused a licence for production in London by Sarah Bernhardt.

1893 *Salome* (original French version) published in Paris. *A Woman of No Importance* is produced in London and *Lady Windermere's Fan* is published.

1894 *Salome* is published in English translation, with illustrations by Aubrey Beardsley. *The Sphinx* and *A Woman of No Importance* published.

1895 *An Ideal Husband* and *The Importance of Being Earnest* produced in London. Wilde charges Lord Alfred Douglas's father, the Marquess of Queensberry, with criminal libel. On Queensberry's acquittal, Wilde is arrested for 'acts of gross indecency with other male persons'. The first trial jury fails to agree a verdict: at the second trial Wilde is found guilty and given the maximum sentence, two years hard labour, and sent to Pentonville. He is moved to Wandsworth, and finally to Reading Gaol. He is declared bankrupt.

1896 Death of Lady Wilde. *Salome* produced in Paris.

1897 Writes *De Profundis* (a long letter to Lord Alfred Douglas) in prison. On his release Wilde writes to the *Daily Chronicle* about the treatment of children in prison. He settles first at Berneval, near Dieppe: later he joins Lord Alfred Douglas in Italy, causing a new rift with his family.

1898 Moves to Paris. Publishes *The Ballad of Reading Gaol*, and writes another long letter about prison conditions to the *Daily Chronicle*. Death of Constance Wilde.

1899 *The Importance of Being Earnest* and *An Ideal Husband* published. Travels in Europe.

1900 Visits Rome, returns to Paris. During serious illness is baptized a Roman Catholic. Dies 30 November.

NOTE ON THE TEXT

THE general principle of this edition is to use the last printed text which was overseen or accepted by Wilde: in practice, this often also means the first volume edition. In the case of works which appeared first as contributions to periodicals, the earlier printed versions have been compared, and major changes only are signalled. In all doubtful cases, the texts given by Wilde's friend and literary executor Robert Ross in his massive fourteen-volume edition of Wilde's work (1908) have also been compared. The huge task of comparing different manuscript versions and drafts has not been attempted. I have used texts previously established by my own Oxford English Novels edition of *The Picture of Dorian Gray* (1974) and by my edition of Wilde's *Complete Shorter Fiction* (1979). Clear minor errors in the base texts have been silently corrected.

There are special problems in following the first edition of the long poem *The Sphinx*, because the designer Ricketts presented it in block capitals throughout, with larger capitals at beginnings of lines and sections. Wilde's own punctuation is often lacking in consistency, but for the punctuation here, uniquely, I have referred to manuscript versions of the poem and have followed the capitalization of the last draft throughout. That draft does not have lines 75 to 88, so I have attempted parallel uses of capitals there. Interestingly, all the manuscripts before that final draft present the poem in four-line stanzas, the so-called In Memoriam stanza.

Wilde's works were mostly composed in a few crowded years, and a rigidly chronological presentation of them here would be both messy and confusing: order of first publication often fails to reflect order of composition, and periodical and volume publications overlap endlessly. I have chosen therefore to present them as a series of ventures in different genres. The order in fact remains generally chronological also. See the Chronology for volume dates, and Stuart Mason's *Bibliography of Oscar Wilde* (1914) for dates of all the periodical publications.

The degree sign (°) indicates a note at the end of the book. More general notes and headnotes are not cued.

LORD ARTHUR SAVILE'S CRIME

A Study of Duty°

I

It was Lady Windermere's last reception before Easter, and Bentinck House was even more crowded than usual. Six Cabinet Ministers had come on from the Speaker's Levée° in their stars and ribands, all the pretty women wore their smartest dresses, and at the end of the picture-gallery stood the Princess Sophia of Carlsrühe, a heavy Tartar-looking lady, with tiny black eyes and wonderful emeralds, talking bad French at the top of her voice, and laughing immoderately at everything that was said to her. It was certainly a wonderful medley of people. Gorgeous peeresses chatted affably to violent Radicals, popular preachers brushed coat-tails with eminent sceptics, a perfect bevy of bishops kept following a stout prima-donna from room to room, on the staircase stood several Royal Academicians, disguised as artists,° and it was said that at one time the supper-room was absolutely crammed with geniuses. In fact, it was one of Lady Windermere's best nights, and the Princess stayed till nearly half-past eleven.

As soon as she had gone, Lady Windermere returned to the picture-gallery, where a celebrated political economist was solemnly explaining the scientific theory of music to an indignant virtuoso from Hungary, and began to talk to the Duchess of Paisley. She looked wonderfully beautiful with her grand ivory throat, her large blue forget-me-not eyes, and her heavy coils of golden hair. *Or pur* they were—not that pale straw colour that nowadays usurps the gracious name of gold, but such gold as is woven into sunbeams or hidden in strange amber; and they gave to her face something of the frame of a saint, with not a little of the fascination of a sinner. She was a curious psychological study. Early in life she had discovered the important truth that nothing looks so like innocence as an indiscretion; and by a series of reckless escapades, half of them quite harmless, she had acquired all the privileges of a personality. She had more than once changed her husband; indeed, Debrett° credits her with three marriages; but as she had never changed her lover, the world had long ago ceased to talk scandal about her. She was now forty years of age, childless, and with that inordinate passion for pleasure which is the secret of remaining young.

Suddenly she looked eagerly round the room, and said, in her clear contralto voice, 'Where is my cheiromantist?'.

'Your what, Gladys?' exclaimed the Duchess, giving an involuntary start.

'My cheiromantist, Duchess; I can't live without him at present.'

'Dear Gladys! you are always so original,' murmured the Duchess, trying to remember what a cheiromantist really was, and hoping it was not the same as a cheiropodist.

'He comes to see my hand twice a week regularly,' continued Lady Windermere, 'and is most interesting about it.'

'Good heavens!' said the Duchess to herself, 'he is a sort of cheiropodist after all. How very dreadful. I hope he is a foreigner at any rate. It wouldn't be quite so bad then.'

'I must certainly introduce him to you.'

'Introduce him!' cried the Duchess; 'you don't mean to say he is here?' and she began looking about for a small tortoise-shell fan and a very tattered lace shawl, so as to be ready to go at a moment's notice.

'Of course he is here, I would not dream of giving a party without him. He tells me I have a pure psychic hand, and that if my thumb had been the least little bit shorter, I should have been a confirmed pessimist, and gone into a convent.'

'Oh, I see!' said the Duchess, feeling very much relieved; 'he tells fortunes, I suppose?'

'And misfortunes, too,' answered Lady Windermere, 'any amount of them. Next year, for instance, I am in great danger, both by land and sea, so I am going to live in a balloon, and draw up my dinner in a basket every evening. It is all written down on my little finger, or on the palm of my hand, I forget which.'

'But surely that is tempting Providence, Gladys.'

'My dear Duchess, surely Providence can resist temptation by this time. I think every one should have their hands told once a month, so as to know what not to do. Of course, one does it all the same, but it is so pleasant to be warned. Now, if some one doesn't go and fetch Mr Podgers at once, I shall have to go myself.'

'Let me go, Lady Windermere,' said a tall handsome young man, who was standing by, listening to the conversation with an amused smile.

'Thanks so much, Lord Arthur; but I am afraid you wouldn't recognize him.'

'If he is as wonderful as you say, Lady Windermere, I couldn't well miss him. Tell me what he is like, and I'll bring him to you at once.'

'Well, he is not a bit like a cheiromantist. I mean he is not mysterious, or esoteric, or romantic-looking. He is a little, stout man, with a funny, bald head, and great gold-rimmed spectacles; something between a family doctor and a country attorney. I'm really very sorry, but it is not my fault. People are so annoying. All my pianists look exactly like poets, and all my poets look exactly like pianists; and I remember last season asking a most dreadful conspirator to dinner, a man who had blown up ever so many people, and always wore a coat of mail, and carried a dagger up his shirt-sleeve; and do you know that when he came he looked just like a nice old clergyman, and cracked jokes all the evening? Of course, he was very amusing, and all that, but I was awfully disappointed; and when I asked him about the coat of mail, he only laughed, and said it was far too cold to wear in England. Ah, here is Mr Podgers! Now, Mr Podgers, I want you to tell the Duchess of Paisley's hand. Duchess, you must take your glove off. No, not the left hand, the other.'

'Dear Gladys, I really don't think it is quite right,' said the Duchess, feebly unbuttoning a rather soiled kid glove.

'Nothing interesting ever is,' said Lady Windermere: '*on a fait le monde ainsi.*° But I must introduce you. Duchess, this is Mr Podgers, my pet cheiromantist. Mr Podgers, this is the Duchess of Paisley, and if you say that she has a larger mountain of the moon than I have, I will never believe in you again.'

'I am sure, Gladys, there is nothing of the kind in my hand,' said the Duchess gravely.

'Your Grace is quite right,' said Mr Podgers, glancing at the little fat hand with its short square fingers, 'the mountain of the moon is not developed. The line of life, however, is excellent. Kindly bend the wrist. Thank you. Three distinct lines on the *rascette*!° You will live to a great age, Duchess, and be extremely happy. Ambition—very moderate, line of intellect not exaggerated, line of heart——'

'Now, do be indiscreet, Mr Podgers,' cried Lady Windermere.

'Nothing would give me greater pleasure,' said Mr Podgers, bowing, 'if the Duchess ever had been, but I am sorry to say that I see great permanence of affection, combined with a strong sense of duty.'

'Pray go on, Mr Podgers,' said the Duchess, looking quite pleased.

'Economy is not the least of your Grace's virtues,' continued Mr Podgers, and Lady Windermere went off into fits of laughter.

'Economy is a very good thing,' remarked the Duchess complacently; 'when I married Paisley he had eleven castles, and not a single house fit to live in.'

'And now he has twelve houses, and not a single castle,' cried Lady Windermere.

'Well, my dear,' said the Duchess, 'I like——'

'Comfort,' said Mr Podgers, 'and modern improvements, and hot water laid on in every bedroom. Your Grace is quite right. Comfort is the only thing our civilization can give us.'

'You have told the Duchess's character admirably, Mr Podgers, and now you must tell Lady Flora's;' and in answer to a nod from the smiling hostess, a tall girl, with sandy Scotch hair, and high shoulder-blades, stepped awkwardly from behind the sofa, and held out a long, bony hand with spatulate fingers.

'Ah, a pianist! I see,' said Mr Podgers, 'an excellent pianist, but perhaps hardly a musician. Very reserved, very honest, and with a great love of animals.'

'Quite true!' exclaimed the Duchess, turning to Lady Windermere, 'absolutely true! Flora keeps two dozen collie dogs at Macloskie, and would turn our town house into a menagerie if her father would let her.'

'Well, that is just what I do with my house every Thursday evening,' cried Lady Windermere, laughing, 'only I like lions better than collie dogs.'

'Your one mistake, Lady Windermere,' said Mr Podgers, with a pompous bow.

'If a woman can't make her mistakes charming, she is only a female,' was the answer. 'But you must read some more hands for us. Come, Sir Thomas, show Mr Podgers yours;' and a genial-looking old gentleman, in a white waistcoat, came forward, and held out a thick rugged hand, with a very long third finger.

'An adventurous nature; four long voyages in the past, and one to come. Been shipwrecked three times. No, only twice, but in danger of a shipwreck your next journey. A strong Conservative, very punctual, and with a passion for collecting curiosities. Had a severe illness between the ages of sixteen and eighteen. Was left a fortune when about thirty. Great aversion to cats and Radicals.'

'Extraordinary!' exclaimed Sir Thomas; 'you must really tell my wife's hand, too.'

'Your second wife's,' said Mr Podgers quietly, still keeping Sir Thomas's hand in his. 'Your second wife's. I shall be charmed;' but Lady Marvel, a melancholy-looking woman, with brown hair and sentimental eyelashes, entirely declined to have her past or her future exposed; and nothing that Lady Windermere could do would induce Monsieur de Koloff, the Russian Ambassador, even to take his gloves off. In fact, many people seemed afraid to face the odd little man with his stereotyped smile, his gold spectacles, and his bright, beady eyes; and when he told poor Lady Fermor, right out before every one, that she did not care a bit for music, but was extremely fond of musicians, it was generally felt that cheiromancy was a most dangerous science, and one that ought not to be encouraged, except in a *tête-à-tête*.

Lord Arthur Savile, however, who did not know anything about Lady Fermor's unfortunate story, and who had been watching Mr Podgers with a great deal of interest, was filled with an immense curiosity to have his own hand read, and feeling somewhat shy about putting himself forward, crossed over the room to where Lady Windermere was sitting, and, with a charming blush, asked her if she thought Mr Podgers would mind.

'Of course, he won't mind,' said Lady Windermere, 'that is what he is here for. All my lions, Lord Arthur, are performing lions, and jump through hoops whenever I ask them. But I must warn you beforehand that I shall tell Sybil everything. She is coming to lunch with me to-morrow, to talk about bonnets, and if Mr Podgers finds out that you have a bad temper, or a tendency to gout, or a wife living in Bayswater, I shall certainly let her know all about it.'

Lord Arthur smiled, and shook his head. 'I am not afraid,' he answered. 'Sybil knows me as well as I know her.'

'Ah! I am a little sorry to hear you say that. The proper basis for marriage is a mutual misunderstanding.° No, I am not at all cynical, I have merely got experience, which, however, is very much the same thing. Mr Podgers, Lord Arthur Savile is dying to have his hand read. Don't tell him that he is engaged to one of the most beautiful girls in London, because that appeared in the *Morning Post* a month ago.'

'Dear Lady Windermere,' cried the Marchioness of Jedburgh, 'do let Mr Podgers stay here a little longer. He has just told me I should go on the stage, and I am so interested.'

'If he has told you that, Lady Jedburgh, I shall certainly take him away. Come over at once, Mr Podgers, and read Lord Arthur's hand.'

'Well,' said Lady Jedburgh, making a little *moue* as she rose from the sofa, 'if I am not to be allowed to go on the stage, I must be allowed to be part of the audience at any rate.'

'Of course; we are all going to be part of the audience,' said Lady Windermere; 'and now, Mr Podgers, be sure and tell us something nice. Lord Arthur is one of my special favourites.'

But when Mr Podgers saw Lord Arthur's hand he grew curiously pale, and said nothing. A shudder seemed to pass through him, and his great bushy eyebrows twitched convulsively, in an odd, irritating way they had when he was puzzled. Then some huge beads of perspiration broke out on his yellow forehead, like a poisonous dew, and his fat fingers grew cold and clammy.

Lord Arthur did not fail to notice these strange signs of agitation, and, for the first time in his life, he himself felt fear. His impulse was to rush from the room, but he restrained himself. It was better to know the worst, whatever it was, than to be left in this hideous uncertainty.

'I am waiting, Mr Podgers,' he said.

'We are all waiting,' cried Lady Windermere, in her quick, impatient manner, but the cheiromantist made no reply.

'I believe Arthur is going on the stage,' said Lady Jedburgh, 'and that, after your scolding, Mr Podgers is afraid to tell him so.'

Suddenly Mr Podgers dropped Lord Arthur's right hand, and seized hold of his left, bending down so low to examine it that the gold rims of his spectacles seemed almost to touch the palm. For a moment his face became a white mask of horror, but he soon recovered his *sang-froid*, and looking up at Lady Windermere, said with a forced smile, 'It is the hand of a charming young man.'

'Of course it is!' answered Lady Windermere, 'but will he be a charming husband? That is what I want to know.'

'All charming young men are,' said Mr Podgers.

'I don't think a husband should be too fascinating,' murmured Lady Jedburgh pensively, 'it is so dangerous.'

'My dear child, they never are too fascinating,' cried Lady Windermere. 'But what I want are details. Details are the only things that interest. What is going to happen to Lord Arthur?'

'Well, within the next few months Lord Arthur will go a voyage——'

'Oh yes, his honeymoon, of course!'

'And lose a relative.'

'Not his sister, I hope?' said Lady Jedburgh, in a piteous tone of voice.

'Certainly not his sister,' answered Mr Podgers, with a deprecating wave of the hand, 'a distant relative merely.'

'Well, I am dreadfully disappointed,' said Lady Windermere. 'I have absolutely nothing to tell Sybil tomorrow. No one cares about distant relatives nowadays. They went out of fashion years ago. However, I suppose she had better have a black silk by her; it always does for church, you know. And now let us go to supper. They are sure to have eaten everything up, but we may find some hot soup. François used to make excellent soup once, but he is so agitated about politics at present, that I never feel quite certain about him. I do wish General Boulanger° would keep quiet. Duchess, I am sure you are tired?'

'Not at all, dear Gladys,' answered the Duchess, waddling towards the door. 'I have enjoyed myself immensely, and the cheiropodist, I mean the cheiromantist, is most interesting. Flora, where can my tortoise-shell fan be? Oh, thank you, Sir Thomas, so much. And my lace shawl, Flora? Oh, thank you, Sir Thomas, very kind, I'm sure;' and the worthy creature finally managed to get downstairs without dropping her scent-bottle more than twice.

All this time Lord Arthur Savile had remained standing by the fireplace, with the same feeling of dread over him, the same sickening sense of coming evil. He smiled sadly at his sister, as she swept past him on Lord Plymdale's arm, looking lovely in her pink brocade and pearls, and he hardly heard Lady Windermere when she called to him to follow her. He thought of Sybil Merton, and the idea that anything could come between them made his eyes dim with tears.

Looking at him, one would have said that Nemesis had stolen the shield of Pallas, and shown him the Gorgon's head.° He seemed turned to stone, and his face was like marble in its melancholy. He had lived the delicate and luxurious life of a young man of birth and fortune, a life exquisite in its freedom from sordid care, its beautiful boyish insouciance; and now for the first time he became conscious of the terrible mystery of Destiny, of the awful meaning of Doom.

How mad and monstrous it all seemed! Could it be that written on his hand, in characters that he could not read himself, but that another could decipher, was some fearful secret of sin, some blood-red sign of crime? Was there no escape possible? Were we no better than chessmen, moved by an unseen power, vessels the potter fashions at his fancy, for honour or for shame? His reason revolted against it, and yet he felt that some tragedy was hanging over him, and that he had been suddenly called upon to bear an intolerable burden. Actors are so fortunate. They can choose whether they will appear in tragedy or in comedy, whether they will suffer or make merry, laugh or shed tears. But in real life it is different. Most men and women are forced to perform parts for which they have no qualifications. Our Guildensterns play Hamlet for us, and our Hamlets have to jest like Prince Hal. The world is a stage, but the play is badly cast.

Suddenly Mr Podgers entered the room. When he saw Lord Arthur he started, and his coarse, fat face became a sort of greenish-yellow colour. The two men's eyes met, and for a moment there was silence.

'The Duchess has left one of her gloves here, Lord Arthur, and has asked me to bring it to her,' said Mr Podgers finally. 'Ah, I see it on the sofa! Good evening.'

'Mr Podgers, I must insist on your giving me a straightforward answer to a question I am going to put to you.'

'Another time, Lord Arthur, but the Duchess is anxious. I am afraid I must go.'

'You shall not go. The Duchess is in no hurry.'

'Ladies should not be kept waiting, Lord Arthur,' said Mr Podgers, with his sickly smile. 'The fair sex is apt to be impatient.'

Lord Arthur's finely-chiselled lips curled in petulant disdain. The poor Duchess seemed to him of very little importance at that moment. He walked across the room to where Mr Podgers was standing, and held his hand out.

'Tell me what you saw there,' he said. 'Tell me the truth. I must know it. I am not a child.'

Mr Podgers's eyes blinked behind his gold-rimmed spectacles, and he moved uneasily from one foot to the other, while his fingers played nervously with a flash watch-chain.

'What makes you think that I saw anything in your hand, Lord Arthur, more than I told you?'

'I know you did, and I insist on your telling me what it was. I will pay you. I will give you a cheque for a hundred pounds.'

The green eyes flashed for a moment, and then became dull again.

'Guineas?' said Mr Podgers at last, in a low voice.

'Certainly. I will send you a cheque tomorrow. What is your club?'°

'I have no club. That is to say, not just at present. My address is——, but allow me to give you my card;' and producing a bit of gilt-edged pasteboard from his waistcoat pocket, Mr Podgers handed it, with a low bow, to Lord Arthur, who read on it,

> MR SEPTIMUS R. PODGERS
> *Professional Cheiromantist*
> 103a West Moon Street

'My hours are from ten to four,' murmured Mr Podgers mechanically, 'and I make a reduction for families.'

'Be quick,' cried Lord Arthur, looking very pale, and holding his hand out.

Mr Podgers glanced nervously round, and drew the heavy *portière*° across the door.

'It will take a little time, Lord Arthur, you had better sit down.'

'Be quick, sir,' cried Lord Arthur again, stamping his foot angrily on the polished floor.

Mr Podgers smiled, drew from his breast-pocket a small magnifying glass, and wiped it carefully with his handkerchief.

'I am quite ready,' he said.

II

Ten minutes later, with face blanched by terror, and eyes wild with grief, Lord Arthur Savile rushed from Bentinck House, crushing his way through the crowd of fur-coated footmen that stood round the large striped awning, and seeming not to see or hear anything. The night was bitter cold, and the gas-lamps round the square flared and flickered in the keen wind; but his hands were hot with fever, and his forehead burned like fire. On and on he went, almost with the gait of a drunken man. A policeman looked curiously at him as he passed, and a beggar, who slouched from an archway to ask for alms, grew frightened, seeing misery greater than his own. Once he stopped under a lamp, and looked at his hands. He thought he could detect the stain of blood already upon them, and a faint cry broke from his trembling lips.

Murder! that is what the cheiromantist had seen there. Murder! The very night seemed to know it, and the desolate wind to howl it in his ear. The dark corners of the streets were full of it. It grinned at him from the roofs of the houses.

First he came to the Park, whose sombre woodland seemed to fascinate him. He leaned wearily up against the railings, cooling his brow against the wet metal, and listening to the tremulous silence of the trees. 'Murder! murder!' he kept repeating, as though iteration could dim the horror of the word. The sound of his own voice made him shudder, yet he almost hoped that Echo might hear him, and wake the slumbering city from its dreams. He felt a mad desire to stop the casual passer-by, and tell him everything.

Then he wandered across Oxford Street into narrow, shameful alleys. Two women with painted faces mocked at him as he went by. From a dark courtyard came a sound of oaths and blows, followed by shrill screams, and, huddled upon a damp doorstep, he saw the crook-backed forms of poverty and eld. A strange pity came over him. Were these children of sin and misery predestined to their end, as he to his? Were they, like him, merely the puppets of a monstrous show?

And yet it was not the mystery, but the comedy of suffering that struck him; its absolute uselessness, its grotesque want of meaning. How incoherent everything seemed! How lacking in all harmony! He was amazed at the discord between the shallow optimism of the day, and the real facts of existence. He was still very young.

After a time he found himself in front of Marylebone Church. The silent roadway looked like a long riband of polished silver, flecked here and there by the dark arabesques of waving shadows. Far into the distance curved the line of flickering gas-lamps, and outside a little walled-in house stood a solitary hansom, the driver asleep inside. He walked hastily in the direction of Portland Place, now and then looking round, as though he feared that he was being followed. At the corner of Rich Street stood two men, reading a small bill upon a hoarding. An odd feeling of curiosity stirred him, and he crossed over. As he came near, the word 'Murder', printed in black letters, met his eye. He started, and a deep flush came into his cheek. It was an advertisement offering a reward for any information leading to the arrest of a man of medium height, between thirty and forty years of age, wearing a billy-cock hat, a black coat, and check trousers, and with a scar upon his right cheek. He read it over and over again, and wondered if the wretched man would be caught, and how he had been scarred. Perhaps, some day, his own name might be placarded on the walls of London. Some day, perhaps, a price would be set on his head also.

The thought made him sick with horror. He turned on his heel, and hurried on into the night.

Where he went he hardly knew. He had a dim memory of wandering through a labyrinth of sordid houses, of being lost in a giant web of sombre streets, and it was bright dawn when he found himself at last in Piccadilly Circus. As he strolled home towards Belgrave Square, he met the great waggons on their way to Covent Garden. The white-smocked carters, with their pleasant sunburnt faces and coarse curly hair, strode sturdily on, cracking their whips, and calling out now and then to each other; on the back of a huge grey horse, the leader of a jangling team, sat a chubby boy, with a bunch of primroses in his battered hat, keeping tight hold of the mane with his little hands, and laughing; and the great piles of vegetables looked like masses of jade against the morning sky, like masses of green jade against the pink petals of some marvellous rose. Lord Arthur felt curiously affected, he could not tell why. There was something in the dawn's delicate loveliness that seemed to him inexpressibly pathetic, and he thought of all the days that break in beauty, and that set in storm. These rustics, too, with their rough, good-humoured voices, and their nonchalant ways, what a strange London they saw! A London free from the sin of night and the smoke of day, a pallid, ghostlike city, a desolate town of tombs! He wondered what they thought of it, and whether they knew anything of its splendour and its shame, of its fierce, fiery-coloured joys, and its horrible hunger, of all it makes and mars from morn to eve. Probably it was to them merely a mart where they brought their fruits to sell, and where they tarried for a few hours at most, leaving the streets still silent, the houses still asleep. It gave him pleasure to watch them as they went by. Rude as they were, with their heavy, hobnailed shoes, and their awkward gait, they brought a little of Arcady° with them. He felt that they had lived with Nature, and that she had taught them peace. He envied them all that they did not know.

By the time he had reached Belgrave Square the sky was a faint blue, and the birds were beginning to twitter in the gardens.

III

When Lord Arthur woke it was twelve o'clock, and the midday sun was streaming through the ivory-silk curtains of his room. He got up and looked out of the window. A dim haze of heat was hanging over the great city, and the roofs of the houses were like dull silver. In the flickering green of the square below some children were flitting about like white butterflies, and the pavement was crowded with people on their way to the Park. Never had life seemed lovelier to him, never had the things of evil seemed more remote.

Then his valet brought him a cup of chocolate on a tray. After he had drunk it, he drew aside a heavy *portière* of peach-coloured plush, and passed into the bathroom. The light stole softly from above, through thin slabs of transparent onyx, and the water in the marble tank glimmered like a moonstone. He plunged hastily in, till the cool ripples touched throat and hair, and then dipped his head right under, as though he would have wiped away the stain of some shameful memory. When he stepped out he felt almost at peace. The exquisite physical conditions of the moment had dominated him, as indeed often happens in the case of very finely-wrought natures, for the senses, like fire, can purify as well as destroy.

After breakfast, he flung himself down on a divan, and lit a cigarette. On the mantel-shelf, framed in dainty old brocade, stood a large photograph of Sybil Merton, as he had seen her first at Lady Noel's ball. The small, exquisitely-shaped head drooped slightly to one side, as though the thin, reed-like throat could hardly bear the burden of so much beauty; the lips were slightly parted, and seemed made for sweet music; and all the tender purity of girlhood looked out in wonder from the dreaming eyes. With her soft, clinging dress of *crêpe-de-chine*, and her large leaf-shaped fan, she looked like one of those delicate little figures men find in the olive-woods near Tanagra;° and there was a touch of Greek grace in her pose and attitude. Yet she was not *petite*. She was simply perfectly proportioned—a rare thing in an age when so many women are either over life-size or insignificant.

Now as Lord Arthur looked at her, he was filled with the terrible pity that is born of love. He felt that to marry her, with the doom of murder hanging over his head, would be a betrayal like that of Judas, a sin worse than any the Borgia had ever dreamed of. What happiness could there be for them, when at any moment he might be called upon to carry out the awful prophecy written in his hand? What manner of life would be theirs while Fate still held this fearful fortune in the scales? The marriage must be postponed, at all costs. Of this he was quite resolved. Ardently though he loved the girl, and the mere touch of her fingers, when they sat together, made each nerve of his body thrill with exquisite joy, he recognized none the less clearly where his duty lay, and was fully conscious of the fact that he had no right to marry until he had committed the murder. This done, he could stand before the altar with Sybil Merton, and give his life into her hands without terror of wrongdoing. This done, he could take her to his arms, knowing that she would never have to blush for him, never have to hang her head in shame. But done it must be first; and the sooner the better for both.

Many men in his position would have preferred the primrose path of dalliance to the steep heights of duty; but Lord Arthur was too conscientious to set pleasure above principle. There was more than mere passion in his love; and Sybil was to him a symbol of all that is good and noble. For a moment he had a natural repugnance against what he was asked to do, but it soon passed away. His heart told him that it was not a sin, but a sacrifice; his reason reminded him that there was no other course open. He had to choose between living for himself and living for others, and terrible though the task laid upon him undoubtedly was, yet he knew that he must not suffer selfishness to triumph over love. Sooner or later we are all called upon to decide on the same issue—of us all, the same question is asked. To Lord Arthur it came early in life—before his nature had been spoiled by the calculating cynicism of middle-age, or his heart corroded by the shallow, fashionable egotism of our day, and he felt no hesitation about doing his duty. Fortunately also, for him, he was no mere dreamer, or idle dilettante. Had he been so, he would have hesitated, like Hamlet, and let irresolution mar his purpose. But he was essentially practical. Life to him meant action, rather than thought. He had that rarest of all things, common sense.

The wild, turbid feelings of the previous night had by this time completely passed away, and it was almost with a sense of shame that he looked back upon his mad wanderings from street to street, his fierce emotional agony. The very sincerity of his sufferings made them seem unreal to him now. He wondered how he could have been so foolish as to rant and rave about the inevitable. The only question that seemed to trouble him was, whom to make away with; for he was not blind to the fact that murder, like the religions of the Pagan world, requires a victim as well as a priest. Not being a genius, he had no enemies, and indeed he felt that this was not the time for the gratification of any personal pique or dislike, the mission in which he was engaged being one of great and grave solemnity. He accordingly made out a list of his friends and relatives on a sheet of notepaper, and after careful consideration, decided in favour of Lady Clementina Beauchamp, a dear old lady who lived in Curzon Street, and was his own second cousin by his mother's side. He had always been very fond of Lady Clem, as every one called her, and as he was very wealthy himself, having come into all Lord Rugby's property when he came of age, there was no possibility of his deriving any vulgar monetary advantage by her death. In fact, the more he thought over the matter, the more she seemed to him to be just the right person, and, feeling that any delay would be unfair to Sybil, he determined to make his arrangements at once.

The first thing to be done was, of course, to settle with the cheiromantist; so he sat down at a small Sheraton writing-table that stood near the window, drew a cheque for £105, payable to the order of Mr Septimus Podgers, and, enclosing it in an envelope, told his valet to take it to West Moon Street. He then telephoned to the stables for his hansom, and dressed to go out. As he was leaving the room, he looked back at Sybil Merton's photograph, and swore that, come what may, he would never let her know what he was doing for her sake, but would keep the secret of his self-sacrifice hidden always in his heart.

On his way to the Buckingham, he stopped at a florist's, and sent Sybil a beautiful basket of narcissi, with lovely white petals and staring pheasants' eyes, and on arriving at the club, went straight to the library, rang the bell, and ordered the waiter to bring him a lemon-and-soda, and a book on Toxicology. He had fully decided that poison was the best means to adopt in this troublesome business. Anything like personal violence was extremely distasteful to him, and besides, he was very anxious not to murder Lady Clementina in any way that might attract public attention, as he hated the idea of being lionized at Lady Windermere's, or seeing his name figuring in the paragraphs of vulgar society-newspapers. He had also to think of Sybil's father and mother, who were rather old-fashioned people, and might possibly object to the marriage if there was anything like a scandal, though he felt certain that if he told them the whole facts of the case they would be the very first to appreciate the motives that had actuated him. He had every reason, then, to decide in favour of poison. It was safe, sure, and quiet, and did away with any necessity for painful scenes, to which, like most Englishmen, he had a rooted objection.

Of the science of poisons, however, he knew absolutely nothing, and as the waiter seemed quite unable to find anything in the library but Ruff's *Guide* and Bailey's *Magazine*,° he examined the bookshelves himself, and finally came across a handsomely-bound edition of the *Pharmacopœia*, and a copy of Erskine's *Toxicology*, edited by Sir Mathew Reid, the President of the Royal College of Physicians, and one of the oldest members of the Buckingham,° having been elected in mistake for somebody else; a *contretemps* that so enraged the Committee, that when the real man came up they black-balled him unanimously. Lord Arthur was a good deal puzzled at the technical terms used in both books, and had begun to regret that he had not paid more attention to his classics at Oxford, when in the second volume of Erskine, he found a very complete account of the properties of aconitine, written in fairly clear English. It seemed to him to be exactly the poison he wanted. It was swift—indeed, almost immediate, in its effect—perfectly painless, and when taken in the form of a gelatine capsule, the mode recommended by Sir Mathew, not by any means unpalatable. He accordingly made a note, upon his shirt-cuff, of the amount necessary for a fatal dose, put the books back in their places, and strolled up St James's Street, to Pestle and Humbey's, the great chemists. Mr Pestle, who always attended personally on the aristocracy, was a good deal surprised at the order, and in a very deferential manner murmured something about a medical certificate being necessary. However, as soon as Lord Arthur explained to him that it was for a large Norwegian mastiff that he was obliged to get rid of, as it showed signs of incipient rabies, and had already bitten the coachman twice in the calf of the leg, he expressed himself as being perfectly satisfied, complimented Lord Arthur on his wonderful knowledge of Toxicology, and had the prescription made up immediately.

Lord Arthur put the capsule into a pretty little silver *bonbonnière* that he saw in a shop-window in Bond Street, threw away Pestle and Humbey's ugly pill-box, and drove off at once to Lady Clementina's.

'Well, *monsieur le mauvais sujet*,'° cried the old lady as he entered the room, 'why haven't you been to see me all this time?'

'My dear Lady Clem, I never have a moment to myself,' said Lord Arthur, smiling.

'I suppose you mean that you go about all day long with Miss Sybil Merton, buying *chiffons* and talking nonsense? I cannot understand why people make such a fuss about being married. In my day we never dreamed of billing and cooing in public, or in private for that matter.'

'I assure you I have not seen Sybil for twenty-four hours, Lady Clem. As far as I can make out, she belongs entirely to her milliners.'

'Of course; that is the only reason you come to see an ugly old woman like myself. I wonder you men don't take warning. *On a fait des folies pour moi,*° and here I am, a poor, rheumatic creature, with a false front and a bad temper. Why, if it were not for dear Lady Jansen, who sends me all the worst French novels she can find, I don't think I could get through the day. Doctors are no use at all, except to get fees out of one. They can't even cure my heartburn.'

'I have brought you a cure for that, Lady Clem,' said Lord Arthur gravely. 'It is a wonderful thing, invented by an American.'

'I don't think I like American inventions, Arthur. I am quite sure I don't. I read some American novels lately, and they were quite nonsensical.'

'Oh, but there is no nonsense at all about this, Lady Clem! I assure you it is a perfect cure. You must promise to try it;' and Lord Arthur brought the little box out of his pocket, and handed it to her.

'Well, the box is charming, Arthur. Is it really a present? That is very sweet of you. And is this the wonderful medicine? It looks like a *bonbon.* I'll take it at once.'

'Good heavens! Lady Clem,' cried Lord Arthur, catching hold of her hand, 'you mustn't do anything of the kind. It is a homœopathic medicine, and if you take it without having heartburn, it might do you no end of harm. Wait till you have an attack, and take it then. You will be astonished at the result.'

'I should like to take it now,' said Lady Clementina, holding up to the light the little transparent capsule, with its floating bubble of liquid aconitine. 'I am sure it is delicious. The fact is that, though I hate doctors, I love medicines. However, I'll keep it till my next attack.'

'And when will that be?' asked Lord Arthur eagerly. 'Will it be soon?'

'I hope not for a week. I had a very bad time yesterday morning with it. But one never knows.'

'You are sure to have one before the end of the month then, Lady Clem?'

'I am afraid so. But how sympathetic you are today, Arthur! Really,

Sybil has done you a great deal of good. And now you must run away, for I am dining with some very dull people, who won't talk scandal, and I know that if I don't get my sleep now I shall never be able to keep awake during dinner. Goodbye, Arthur, give my love to Sybil, and thank you so much for the American medicine.'

'You won't forget to take it, Lady Clem, will you?' said Lord Arthur, rising from his seat.

'Of course I won't, you silly boy. I think it is most kind of you to think of me, and I shall write and tell you if I want any more.'

Lord Arthur left the house in high spirits, and with a feeling of immense relief.

That night he had an interview with Sybil Merton. He told her how he had been suddenly placed in a position of terrible difficulty, from which neither honour nor duty would allow him to recede. He told her that the marriage must be put off for the present, as until he had got rid of his fearful entanglements, he was not a free man. He implored her to trust him, and not to have any doubts about the future. Everything would come right, but patience was necessary.

The scene took place in the conservatory of Mr Merton's house, in Park Lane, where Lord Arthur had dined as usual. Sybil had never seemed more happy, and for a moment Lord Arthur had been tempted to play the coward's part, to write to Lady Clementina for the pill, and to let the marriage go on as if there was no such person as Mr Podgers in the world. His better nature, however, soon asserted itself, and even when Sybil flung herself weeping into his arms, he did not falter. The beauty that stirred his senses had touched his conscience also. He felt that to wreck so fair a life for the sake of a few months' pleasure would be a wrong thing to do.

He stayed with Sybil till nearly midnight, comforting her and being comforted in turn, and early the next morning he left for Venice, after writing a manly, firm letter to Mr Merton about the necessary postponement of the marriage.

IV

In Venice° he met his brother, Lord Surbiton, who happened to have come over from Corfu in his yacht. The two young men spent a delightful fortnight together. In the morning they rode on the Lido, or glided up and down the green canals in their long black gondola; in the afternoon they usually entertained visitors on the yacht; and in the evening they dined at Florian's, and smoked innumerable cigarettes on the Piazza. Yet somehow Lord Arthur was not happy. Every day he studied the obituary column in the *Times*, expecting to see a notice of Lady Clementina's death, but every day he was disappointed. He began to be afraid that some accident had happened to her, and often regretted that he had prevented her taking the aconitine when she had been so anxious to try its effect. Sybil's letters, too, though full of love, and trust, and tenderness, were often very sad in their tone, and sometimes he used to think that he was parted from her for ever.

After a fortnight Lord Surbiton got bored with Venice, and determined to run down the coast to Ravenna, as he heard that there was some capital cock-shooting in the Pinetum.° Lord Arthur, at first, refused absolutely to come, but Surbiton, of whom he was extremely fond, finally persuaded him that if he stayed at Danielli's by himself he would be moped to death, and on the morning of the 15th they started, with a strong nor'-east wind blowing, and a rather sloppy sea. The sport was excellent, and the free, open-air life brought the colour back to Lord Arthur's cheeks, but about the 22nd he became anxious about Lady Clementina, and, in spite of Surbiton's remonstrances, came back to Venice by train.

As he stepped out of his gondola on to the hotel steps, the proprietor came forward to meet him with a sheaf of telegrams. Lord Arthur snatched them out of his hand, and tore them open. Everything had been successful. Lady Clementina had died quite suddenly on the night of the 17th!

His first thought was for Sybil, and he sent her off a telegram announcing his immediate return to London. He then ordered his valet to pack his things for the night mail, sent his gondoliers about five times their proper fare, and ran up to his sitting-room with a light step and a buoyant heart. There he found three letters waiting for him. One was from Sybil herself, full of sympathy and condolence. The others were from his mother, and from Lady Clementina's solicitor. It seemed that the old lady had dined with the Duchess that very night, had delighted every one by her wit and *esprit*, but had gone home somewhat early, complaining of heartburn. In the morning she was found dead in her bed, having apparently suffered no pain. Sir Mathew Reid had been sent for at once, but, of course, there was nothing to be done, and she was to be buried on the 22nd at Beauchamp Chalcote. A few days before she died she had made her will, and left Lord Arthur her little house in Curzon Street, and all her furniture, personal effects, and pictures, with the exception of her collection of miniatures, which was to go to her sister, Lady Margaret Rufford, and her amethyst necklace, which Sybil

Merton was to have. The property was not of much value; but Mr Mansfield the solicitor was extremely anxious for Lord Arthur to return at once, if possible, as there were a great many bills to be paid, and Lady Clementina had never kept any regular accounts.

Lord Arthur was very much touched by Lady Clementina's kind remembrance of him, and felt that Mr Podgers had a great deal to answer for. His love of Sybil, however, dominated every other emotion, and the consciousness that he had done his duty gave him peace and comfort. When he arrived at Charing Cross, he felt perfectly happy.

The Mertons received him very kindly, Sybil made him promise that he would never again allow anything to come between them, and the marriage was fixed for the 7th June. Life seemed to him once more bright and beautiful, and all his old gladness came back to him again.

One day, however, as he was going over the house in Curzon Street, in company with Lady Clementina's solicitor and Sybil herself, burning packages of faded letters, and turning out drawers of odd rubbish, the young girl suddenly gave a little cry of delight.

'What have you found, Sybil?' said Lord Arthur, looking up from his work, and smiling.

'This lovely little silver *bonbonnière*, Arthur. Isn't it quaint and Dutch? Do give it to me! I know amethysts won't become me till I am over eighty.'

It was the box that had held the aconitine.

Lord Arthur started, and a faint blush came into his cheek. He had almost entirely forgotten what he had done, and it seemed to him a curious coincidence that Sybil, for whose sake he had gone through all that terrible anxiety, should have been the first to remind him of it.

'Of course you can have it, Sybil. I gave it to poor Lady Clem myself.'

'Oh! thank you, Arthur; and may I have the *bonbon* too? I had no notion that Lady Clementina liked sweets. I thought she was far too intellectual.'

Lord Arthur grew deadly pale, and a horrible idea crossed his mind.

'*Bonbon*, Sybil? What do you mean?' he said in a slow, hoarse voice.

'There is one in it, that is all. It looks quite old and dusty, and I have not the slightest intention of eating it. What is the matter, Arthur? How white you look!'

Lord Arthur rushed across the room, and seized the box. Inside it was the amber-coloured capsule, with its poison-bubble. Lady Clementina had died a natural death after all!

The shock of the discovery was almost too much for him. He flung the capsule into the fire, and sank on the sofa with a cry of despair.

V

Mr Merton was a good deal distressed at the second postponement of the marriage, and Lady Julia, who had already ordered her dress for the wedding, did all in her power to make Sybil break off the match. Dearly, however, as Sybil loved her mother, she had given her whole life into Lord Arthur's hands, and nothing that Lady Julia could say could make her waver in her faith. As for Lord Arthur himself, it took him days to get over his terrible disappointment, and for a time his nerves were completely unstrung. His excellent common sense, however, soon asserted itself and his sound, practical mind did not leave him long in doubt about what to do. Poison having proved a complete failure, dynamite, or some other form of explosive, was obviously the proper thing to try.

He accordingly looked again over the list of his friends and relatives, and, after careful consideration, determined to blow up his uncle, the Dean of Chichester. The Dean, who was a man of great culture and learning, was extremely fond of clocks, and had a wonderful collection of timepieces, ranging from the fifteenth century to the present day, and it seemed to Lord Arthur that this hobby of the good Dean's offered him an excellent opportunity for carrying out his scheme. Where to procure an explosive machine was, of course, quite another matter. The London Directory gave him no information on the point, and he felt that there was very little use in going to Scotland Yard about it, as they never seemed to know anything about the movements of the dynamite faction till after an explosion had taken place, and not much even then.

Suddenly he thought of his friend Rouvaloff, a young Russian of very revolutionary tendencies,° whom he had met at Lady Windermere's in the winter. Count Rouvaloff was supposed to be writing a life of Peter the Great, and to have come over to England for the purpose of studying the documents relating to that Tsar's residence in this country as a ship carpenter; but it was generally suspected that he was a Nihilist agent, and there was no doubt that the Russian Embassy did not look with any favour upon his presence in London. Lord Arthur felt that he was just the man for his purpose, and drove down one morning to his lodgings in Bloomsbury, to ask his advice and assistance.

'So you are taking up politics seriously?' said Count Rouvaloff, when Lord Arthur had told him the object of his mission; but Lord Arthur, who hated swagger of any kind, felt bound to admit to him that he had not the slightest interest in social questions, and simply wanted the explosive machine for a purely family matter, in which no one was concerned but himself.

Count Rouvaloff looked at him for some moments in amazement, and then seeing that he was quite serious, wrote an address on a piece of paper, initialled it, and handed it to him across the table.

'Scotland Yard would give a good deal to know this address, my dear fellow.'

'They shan't have it,' cried Lord Arthur, laughing; and after shaking the young Russian warmly by the hand he ran downstairs, examined the paper, and told the coachman to drive to Soho Square.

There he dismissed him, and strolled down Greek Street, till he came to a place called Bayle's Court. He passed under the archway, and found himself in a curious *cul-de-sac*, that was apparently occupied by a French Laundry, as a perfect network of clothes-lines was stretched across from house to house, and there was a flutter of white linen in the morning air. He walked to the end, and knocked at a little green house. After some delay, during which every window in the court became a blurred mass of peering faces, the door was opened by a rather rough-looking foreigner, who asked him in very bad English what his business was. Lord Arthur handed him the paper Count Rouvaloff had given him. When the man saw it he bowed, and invited Lord Arthur into a very shabby front parlour on the ground-floor, and in a few moments Herr Winckelkopf, as he was called in England, bustled into the room, with a very wine-stained napkin round his neck, and a fork in his left hand.

'Count Rouvaloff has given me an introduction to you,' said Lord Arthur, bowing, 'and I am anxious to have a short interview with you on a matter of business. My name is Smith, Mr Robert Smith, and I want you to supply me with an explosive clock.'

'Charmed to meet you, Lord Arthur,' said the genial little German laughing. 'Don't look so alarmed, it is my duty to know everybody, and I remember seeing you one evening at Lady Windermere's. I hope her ladyship is quite well. Do you mind sitting with me while I finish my breakfast? There is an excellent *pâté*, and my friends are kind enough to say that my Rhine wine is better than any they get at the German Embassy,' and before Lord Arthur had got over his surprise at being recognised, he found himself seated in the back-room, sipping the most delicious Marcobrünner out of a pale yellow hock-glass marked with the Imperial monogram, and chatting in the friendliest manner possible to the famous conspirator.

'Explosive clocks,' said Herr Winckelkopf, 'are not very good things for foreign exportation, as, even if they succeed in passing the Custom

House, the train service is so irregular, that they usually go off before they have reached their proper destination. If, however, you want one for home use, I can supply you with an excellent article, and guarantee that you will be satisfied with the result. May I ask for whom it is intended? If it is for the police, or for any one connected with Scotland Yard, I am afraid I cannot do anything for you. The English detectives are really our best friends, and I have always found that by relying on their stupidity, we can do exactly what we like. I could not spare one of them.'

'I assure you,' said Lord Arthur, 'that it has nothing to do with the police at all. In fact, the clock is intended for the Dean of Chichester.'

'Dear me! I had no idea that you felt so strongly about religion, Lord Arthur. Few young men do nowadays.'

'I am afraid you overrate me, Herr Winckelkopf,' said Lord Arthur, blushing. 'The fact is, I really know nothing about theology.'

'It is a purely private matter then?'

'Purely private.'

Herr Winckelkopf shrugged his shoulders, and left the room, returning in a few minutes with a round cake of dynamite about the size of a penny, and a pretty little French clock, surmounted by an ormolu figure of Liberty trampling on the hydra of Despotism.

Lord Arthur's face brightened up when he saw it. 'That is just what I want,' he cried, 'and now tell me how it goes off.'

'Ah! there is my secret,' answered Herr Winckelkopf, contemplating his invention with a justifiable look of pride; 'let me know when you wish it to explode, and I will set the machine to the moment.'

'Well, today is Tuesday, and if you could send it off at once——'

'That is impossible; I have a great deal of important work on hand for some friends of mine in Moscow. Still, I might send it off tomorrow.'

'Oh, it will be quite time enough!' said Lord Arthur politely, 'if it is delivered tomorrow night or Thursday morning. For the moment of the explosion, say Friday at noon exactly. The Dean is always at home at that hour.'

'Friday, at noon,' repeated Herr Winckelkopf, and he made a note to that effect in a large ledger that was lying on a bureau near the fireplace.

'And now,' said Lord Arthur, rising from his seat, 'pray let me know how much I am in your debt.'

'It is such a small matter, Lord Arthur, that I do not care to make any charge. The dynamite comes to seven and sixpence, the clock will be three pounds ten, and the carriage about five shillings. I am only too pleased to oblige any friend of Count Rouvaloff's.'

'But your trouble, Herr Winckelkopf?'

'Oh, that is nothing! It is a pleasure to me. I do not work for money; I live entirely for my art.'

Lord Arthur laid down £4:2:6 on the table, thanked the little German for his kindness, and, having succeeded in declining an invitation to meet some Anarchists at a meat-tea on the following Saturday, left the house and went off to the Park.

For the next two days he was in a state of the greatest excitement, and on Friday at twelve o'clock he drove down to the Buckingham to wait for news. All the afternoon the stolid hall-porter kept posting up telegrams from various parts of the country giving the results of horse-races, the verdicts in divorce suits, the state of the weather, and the like, while the tape ticked out wearisome details about an all-night sitting in the House of Commons, and a small panic on the Stock Exchange. At four o'clock the evening papers came in, and Lord Arthur disappeared into the library with the *Pall Mall*, the *St James's*, the *Globe*, and the *Echo*, to the immense indignation of Colonel Goodchild, who wanted to read the reports of a speech he had delivered that morning at the Mansion House, on the subject of South African Missions, and the advisability of having black Bishops in every province, and for some reason or other had a strong prejudice against the *Evening News*. None of the papers, however, contained even the slightest allusion to Chichester, and Lord Arthur felt that the attempt must have failed. It was a terrible blow to him, and for a time he was quite unnerved. Herr Winckelkopf, whom he went to see the next day, was full of elaborate apologies, and offered to supply him with another clock free of charge, or with a case of nitro-glycerine bombs at cost price. But he had lost all faith in explosives, and Herr Winckelkopf himself acknowledged that everything is so adulterated nowadays, that even dynamite can hardly be got in a pure condition. The little German, however, while admitting that something must have gone wrong with the machinery, was not without hope that the clock might still go off, and instanced the case of a barometer that he had once sent to the military Governor at Odessa, which, though timed to explode in ten days, had not done so for something like three months. It was quite true that when it did go off, it merely succeeded in blowing a housemaid to atoms, the Governor having gone out of town six weeks before, but at least it showed that dynamite, as a destructive force, was, when under the control of machinery, a powerful, though a somewhat unpunctual agent. Lord Arthur was a little consoled by this reflection, but even here he was destined to disappointment, for two days afterwards, as he was going upstairs, the Duchess called him into her boudoir, and showed him a letter she had just received from the Deanery.

'Jane writes charming letters,' said the Duchess; 'you must really read her last. It is quite as good as the novels Mudie° sends us.'

Lord Arthur seized the letter from her hand. It ran as follows:–

THE DEANERY, CHICHESTER,

27th May.

My Dearest Aunt,

Thank you so much for the flannel for the Dorcas Society,° and also for the gingham. I quite agree with you that it is nonsense their wanting to wear pretty things, but everybody is so Radical and irreligious nowadays, that it is difficult to make them see that they should not try and dress like the upper classes. I am sure I don't know what we are coming to. As papa has often said in his sermons, we live in an age of unbelief.

We have had great fun over a clock that an unknown admirer sent papa last Thursday. It arrived in a wooden box from London, carriage paid; and papa feels it must have been sent by some one who had read his remarkable sermon, 'Is License Liberty?' for on the top of the clock was a figure of a woman, with what papa said was the cap of Liberty° on her head. I didn't think it very becoming myself, but papa said it was historical, so I suppose it is all right. Parker unpacked it, and papa put it on the mantelpiece in the library, and we were all sitting there on Friday morning, when just as the clock struck twelve, we heard a whirring noise, a little puff of smoke came from the pedestal of the figure, and the goddess of Liberty fell off, and broke her nose on the fender! Maria was quite alarmed, but it looked so ridiculous, that James and I went off into fits of laughter, and even papa was amused. When we examined it, we found it was a sort of alarum clock, and that, if you set it to a particular hour, and put some gunpowder and a cap under a little hammer, it went off whenever you wanted. Papa said it must not remain in the library, as it made a noise, so Reggie carried it away to the schoolroom, and does nothing but have small explosions all day long. Do you think Arthur would like one for a wedding present? I suppose they are quite fashionable in London. Papa says they should do a great deal of good, as they show that Liberty can't last, but must fall down. Papa says Liberty was invented at the time of the French Revolution. How awful it seems!

I have now to go to the Dorcas, where I will read them your most instructive letter. How true, dear aunt, your idea is, that in their rank of life they should wear what is unbecoming. I must say it is absurd, their anxiety about dress, when there are so many more important things in this world, and in the next. I am so glad your flowered poplin turned out so well, and that your lace was not torn. I am wearing my yellow satin, that you so kindly gave me, at the Bishop's on Wednesday, and think it will look all right. Would you have bows or not? Jennings says that every one wears bows now, and that the underskirt should be frilled. Reggie has just had another explosion, and papa has ordered the clock to be sent to the stables. I don't think papa likes it so much as he did at first, though he is very flattered at being sent such a pretty and ingenious toy. It shows that people read his sermons, and profit by them.

Papa sends his love, in which James, and Reggie, and Maria all unite, and, hoping that Uncle Cecil's gout is better, believe me, dear aunt, ever your affectionate niece,

JANE PERCY.

P.S.—Do tell me about the bows. Jennings insists they are the fashion.

Lord Arthur looked so serious and unhappy over the letter, that the Duchess went into fits of laughter.

'My dear Arthur,' she cried, 'I shall never show you a young lady's letter again! But what shall I say about the clock? I think it is a capital invention, and I should like to have one myself.'

'I don't think much of them,' said Lord Arthur, with a sad smile, and, after kissing his mother, he left the room.

When he got upstairs, he flung himself on a sofa, and his eyes filled with tears. He had done his best to commit this murder, but on both occasions he had failed, and through no fault of his own. He had tried to do his duty, but it seemed as if Destiny herself had turned traitor. He was oppressed with the sense of the barrenness of good intentions, of the futility of trying to be fine. Perhaps, it would be better to break off the marriage altogether. Sybil would suffer, it is true, but suffering could not really mar a nature so noble as hers. As for himself, what did it matter? There is always some war in which a man can die, some cause to which a man can give his life, and as life had no pleasure for him, so death had no terror. Let Destiny work out his doom. He would not stir to help her.

At half-past seven he dressed, and went down to the club. Surbiton was there with a party of young men, and he was obliged to dine with them. Their trivial conversation and idle jests did not interest him, and as soon as coffee was brought he left them, inventing some engagement in order to get away. As he was going out of the club, the hall-porter handed him a letter. It was from Herr Winckelkopf, asking him to call down the next evening, and look at an explosive umbrella, that went off as soon as it was opened. It was the very latest invention, and had just arrived from Geneva. He tore the letter up into fragments. He had made up his mind not to try any more experiments. Then he wandered down to the Thames Embankment, and sat for hours by the river. The moon peered through a mane of tawny clouds, as if it were a lion's eye, and innumerable stars spangled the hollow vault, like gold dust powdered on a purple dome. Now and then a barge swung out into the turbid stream, and floated away with the tide, and the railway signals changed from green to scarlet as the trains ran shrieking across the bridge. After some time, twelve o'clock boomed from the tall tower at Westminster, and at each stroke of the sonorous bell the night seemed to tremble. Then the railway lights went out, one solitary lamp left gleaming like a large ruby on a giant mast, and the roar of the city became fainter.

At two o'clock he got up, and strolled towards Blackfriars. How unreal everything looked! How like a strange dream! The houses on the other side of the river seemed built out of darkness. One would have said that silver and shadow had fashioned the world anew. The huge dome of St Paul's looked like a bubble through the dusky air.°

As he approached Cleopatra's Needle he saw a man leaning over the parapet, and as he came nearer the man looked up, the gas-light falling full upon his face.

It was Mr Podgers, the cheiromantist! No one could mistake the fat, flabby face, the gold-rimmed spectacles, the sickly feeble smile, the sensual mouth.

Lord Arthur stopped. A brilliant idea flashed across him, and he stole softly up behind. In a moment he had seized Mr Podgers by the legs, and flung him into the Thames. There was a coarse oath, a heavy splash, and all was still. Lord Arthur looked anxiously over, but could see nothing of the cheiromantist but a tall hat, pirouetting in an eddy of moonlit water. After a time it also sank, and no trace of Mr Podgers was visible. Once he thought that he caught sight of the bulky misshapen figure striking out for the staircase by the bridge, and a horrible feeling of failure came over him, but it turned out to be merely a reflection, and when the moon shone out from behind a cloud it passed away. At last he seemed to have realized the decree of destiny. He heaved a deep sigh of relief, and Sybil's name came to his lips.

'Have you dropped anything, sir?' said a voice behind him suddenly.

He turned round, and saw a policeman with a bull's-eye lantern.

'Nothing of importance, sergeant,' he answered, smiling, and hailing a passing hansom, he jumped in, and told the man to drive to Belgrave Square.

For the next few days he alternated between hope and fear. There were moments when he almost expected Mr Podgers to walk into the room, and yet at other times he felt that Fate could not be so unjust to him. Twice he went to the cheiromantist's address in West Moon Street, but he could not bring himself to ring the bell. He longed for certainty, and was afraid of it.

Finally it came. He was sitting in the smoking-room of the club having tea, and listening rather wearily to Surbiton's account of the last comic song at the Gaiety, when the waiter came in with the evening papers. He took up the *St James's*, and was listlessly turning over its pages, when this strange heading caught his eye:

SUICIDE OF A CHEIROMANTIST.

He turned pale with excitement, and began to read. The paragraph ran as follows:–

Yesterday morning, at seven o'clock, the body of Mr Septimus R. Podgers, the eminent cheiromantist, was washed on shore at Greenwich, just in front of the Ship Hotel. The unfortunate gentleman had been missing for some days, and considerable anxiety for his safety had been felt in cheiromantic circles. It is supposed that he committed suicide under the influence of a temporary mental derangement, caused by overwork, and a verdict to that effect was returned this afternoon by the coroner's jury. Mr Podgers had just completed an elaborate treatise on the subject of the Human Hand, that will shortly be published, when it will no doubt attract much attention. The deceased was sixty-five years of age, and does not seem to have left any relations.

Lord Arthur rushed out of the club with the paper still in his hand, to the immense amazement of the hall-porter, who tried in vain to stop him, and drove at once to Park Lane. Sybil saw him from the window, and something told her that he was the bearer of good news. She ran down to meet him, and, when she saw his face, she knew that all was well.

'My dear Sybil,' cried Lord Arthur, 'let us be married tomorrow!'

'You foolish boy! Why the cake is not even ordered!' said Sybil, laughing through her tears.

VI

When the wedding took place, some three weeks later, St Peter's was crowded with a perfect mob of smart people. The service was read in a most impressive manner by the Dean of Chichester, and everybody agreed that they had never seen a handsomer couple than the bride and bridegroom. They were more than handsome, however—they were happy. Never for a single moment did Lord Arthur regret all that he had suffered for Sybil's sake, while she, on her side, gave him the best things a woman can give to any man—worship, tenderness, and love. For them romance was not killed by reality. They always felt young.

Some years afterwards, when two beautiful children had been born to them, Lady Windermere came down on a visit to Alton Priory, a lovely old place, that had been the Duke's wedding present to his son; and one afternoon as she was sitting with Lady Arthur under a lime-tree in the garden, watching the little boy and girl as they played up and down the rose-walk, like fitful sunbeams, she suddenly took her hostess's hand in hers, and said, 'Are you happy, Sybil?'

'Dear Lady Windermere, of course I am happy. Aren't you?'

'I have no time to be happy, Sybil. I always like the last person who is introduced to me; but, as a rule, as soon as I know people I get tired of them.'

'Don't your lions satisfy you, Lady Windermere?'

'Oh dear, no! lions are only good for one season. As soon as their manes are cut, they are the dullest creatures going. Besides, they behave very badly, if you are really nice to them. Do you remember that horrid Mr Podgers? He was a dreadful impostor. Of course, I didn't mind that at all, and even when he wanted to borrow money I forgave him, but I could not stand his making love to me. He has really made me hate cheiromancy. I go in for telepathy now. It is much more amusing.'

'You mustn't say anything against cheiromancy here, Lady Windermere; it is the only subject that Arthur does not like people to chaff about. I assure you he is quite serious over it.'

'You don't mean to say that he believes in it, Sybil?'

'Ask him, Lady Windermere, here he is;' and Lord Arthur came up the garden with a large bunch of yellow roses in his hand, and his two children dancing round him.

'Lord Arthur?'

'Yes, Lady Windermere.'

'You don't mean to say that you believe in cheiromancy?'

'Of course I do,' said the young man, smiling.

'But why?'

'Because I owe to it all the happiness of my life,' he murmured, throwing himself into a wicker chair.

'My dear Lord Arthur, what do you owe to it?'

'Sybil,' he answered, handing his wife the roses, and looking into her violet eyes.

'What nonsense!' cried Lady Windermere. 'I never heard such nonsense in all my life.'

THE HAPPY PRINCE

HIGH above the city, on a tall column, stood the statue of the Happy Prince. He was gilded all over with thin leaves of fine gold, for eyes he had two bright sapphires, and a large red ruby glowed on his sword-hilt.

He was very much admired indeed. 'He is as beautiful as a weathercock,' remarked one of the Town Councillors who wished to gain a reputation for having artistic tastes; 'only not quite so useful,' he added, fearing lest people should think him unpractical, which he really was not.

'Why can't you be like the Happy Prince?' asked a sensible mother of her little boy who was crying for the moon. 'The Happy Prince never dreams of crying for anything.'

'I am glad there is some one in the world who is quite happy,' muttered a disappointed man as he gazed at the wonderful statue.

'He looks just like an angel,' said the Charity Children° as they came out of the cathedral in their bright scarlet cloaks, and their clean white pinafores.

'How do you know?' said the Mathematical Master, 'you have never seen one.'

'Ah! but we have, in our dreams,' answered the children; and the Mathematical Master frowned and looked very severe, for he did not approve of children dreaming.

One night there flew over the city a little Swallow. His friends had gone away to Egypt six weeks before, but he had stayed behind, for he was in love with the most beautiful Reed. He had met her early in the spring as he was flying down the river after a big yellow moth, and had been so attracted by her slender waist that he had stopped to talk to her.

'Shall I love you?' said the Swallow, who liked to come to the point at once, and the Reed made him a low bow. So he flew round and round her, touching the water with his wings, and making silver ripples. This was his courtship, and it lasted all through the summer.

'It is a ridiculous attachment,' twittered the other Swallows, 'she has no money, and far too many relations;' and indeed the river was quite full of Reeds. Then, when the autumn came, they all flew away.

After they had gone he felt lonely, and began to tire of his lady-love. 'She has no conversation,' he said, 'and I am afraid that she is a coquette, for she is always flirting with the wind.' And certainly, whenever the wind blew, the Reed made the most graceful curtsies. 'I admit that she is domestic,' he continued, 'but I love travelling, and my wife, consequently, should love travelling also.'

'Will you come away with me?' he said finally to her; but the Reed shook her head, she was so attached to her home.

'You have been trifling with me,' he cried, 'I am off to the Pyramids. Goodbye!' and he flew away.

All day long he flew, and at night-time he arrived at the city. 'Where shall I put up?' he said; 'I hope the town has made preparations.'

Then he saw the statue on the tall column. 'I will put up there,' he cried; 'it is a fine position with plenty of fresh air.' So he alighted just between the feet of the Happy Prince.

'I have a golden bedroom,' he said softly to himself as he looked round, and he prepared to go to sleep; but just as he was putting his head under his wing a large drop of water fell on him. 'What a curious thing!' he cried, 'there is not a single cloud in the sky, the stars are quite clear and bright, and yet it is raining. The climate in the north of Europe is really dreadful. The Reed used to like the rain, but that was merely her selfishness.'

Then another drop fell.

'What is the use of a statue if it cannot keep the rain off?' he said; 'I must look for a good chimney-pot,' and he determined to fly away.

But before he had opened his wings, a third drop fell, and he looked up, and saw—Ah! what did he see?

The eyes of the Happy Prince were filled with tears, and tears were running down his golden cheeks. His face was so beautiful in the moonlight that the little Swallow was filled with pity.

'Who are you?' he said.

'I am the Happy Prince.'

'Why are you weeping then?' asked the Swallow; 'you have quite drenched me.'

'When I was alive and had a human heart,' answered the statue, 'I did not know what tears were, for I lived in the Palace of Sans-Souci,° where sorrow is not allowed to enter. In the daytime I played with my companions in the garden, and in the evening I led the dance in the Great Hall. Round the garden ran a very lofty wall, but I never cared to ask what lay beyond it, everything about me was so beautiful. My courtiers called me the Happy Prince, and happy indeed I was, if pleasure be happiness. So I lived, and so I died. And now that I am dead they have set me up here so high that I can see all the ugliness and all the misery of my city, and though my heart is made of lead yet I cannot choose but weep.'

'What, is he not solid gold?' said the Swallow to himself. He was too polite to make any personal remarks out loud.

'Far away,' continued the statue in a low musical voice, 'far away in a little street there is a poor house. One of the windows is open, and through it I can see a woman seated at a table. Her face is thin and worn, and she has coarse, red hands, all pricked by the needle, for she is a seamstress. She is embroidering passion-flowers on a satin gown for the loveliest of the Queen's maids-of-honour to wear at the next Court-ball. In a bed in the corner of the room her little boy is lying ill. He has a fever, and is asking for oranges. His mother has nothing to give him but river water, so he is crying. Swallow, Swallow, little Swallow, will you not bring her the ruby out of my sword-hilt? My feet are fastened to this pedestal and I cannot move.'

'I am waited for in Egypt,'° said the Swallow. 'My friends are flying up and down the Nile, and talking to the large lotus-flowers. Soon they will go to sleep in the tomb of the great King. The King is there himself in his painted coffin. He is wrapped in yellow linen, and embalmed with spices. Round his neck is a chain of pale green jade, and his hands are like withered leaves.'

'Swallow, Swallow, little Swallow,' said the Prince, 'will you not stay with me for one night, and be my messenger? The boy is so thirsty, and the mother so sad.'

'I don't think I like boys,' answered the Swallow. 'Last summer, when I was staying on the river, there were two rude boys, the miller's sons, who were always throwing stones at me. They never hit me, of course; we swallows fly far too well for that, and besides, I come of a family famous for its agility; but still, it was a mark of disrespect.'

But the Happy Prince looked so sad that the little Swallow was sorry. 'It is very cold here,' he said; 'but I will stay with you for one night, and be your messenger.'

'Thank you, little Swallow,' said the Prince.

So the Swallow picked out the great ruby from the Prince's sword, and flew away with it in his beak over the roofs of the town.

He passed by the cathedral tower, where the white marble angels were sculptured. He passed by the palace and heard the sound of dancing. A beautiful girl came out on the balcony with her lover. 'How wonderful the stars are,' he said to her, 'and how wonderful is the power of love!' 'I hope my dress will be ready in time for the State-ball,' she answered; 'I have ordered passion-flowers to be embroidered on it; but the seamstresses are so lazy.'

He passed over the river, and saw the lanterns hanging to the masts of the ships. He passed over the Ghetto,° and saw the old Jews bargaining with each other, and weighing out money in copper scales. At last he came to the poor house and looked in. The boy was tossing feverishly on his bed, and the mother had fallen asleep, she was so tired. In he hopped, and laid the great ruby on the table beside the woman's thimble. Then he flew gently round the bed, fanning the boy's forehead with his wings. 'How cool I feel,' said the boy, 'I must be getting better;' and he sank into a delicious slumber.

Then the Swallow flew back to the Happy Prince, and told him what he had done. 'It is curious,' he remarked, 'but I feel quite warm now, although it is so cold.'

'That is because you have done a good action,' said the Prince. And the little Swallow began to think, and then he fell asleep. Thinking always made him sleepy.

When day broke he flew down to the river and had a bath. 'What a remarkable phenomenon,' said the Professor of Ornithology as he was passing over the bridge. 'A swallow in winter!' And he wrote a long letter about it to the local newspaper. Every one quoted it, it was full of so many words that they could not understand.

'Tonight I go to Egypt,' said the Swallow, and he was in high spirits at the prospect. He visited all the public monuments, and sat a long time on top of the church steeple. Wherever he went the Sparrows chirruped, and said to each other, 'What a distinguished stranger!' so he enjoyed himself very much.

When the moon rose he flew back to the Happy Prince. 'Have you any commissions for Egypt?' he cried; 'I am just starting.'

'Swallow, Swallow, little Swallow,' said the Prince, 'will you not stay with me one night longer?'

'I am waited for in Egypt,' answered the Swallow. 'Tomorrow my friends will fly up to the Second Cataract. The river-horse couches there among the bulrushes, and on a great granite throne sits the God Memnon.° All night long he watches the stars, and when the morning star shines he utters one cry of joy, and then he is silent. At noon the yellow lions come down to the water's edge to drink. They have eyes like green beryls, and their roar is louder than the roar of the cataract.'

'Swallow, Swallow, little Swallow,' said the Prince, 'far away across the city I see a young man in a garret. He is leaning over a desk covered with papers, and in a tumbler by his side there is a bunch of withered violets. His hair is brown and crisp, and his lips are red as a pomegranate, and he has large and dreamy eyes. He is trying to finish a play for the

Director of the Theatre, but he is too cold to write any more. There is no fire in the grate, and hunger has made him faint.'

'I will wait with you one night longer,' said the Swallow, who really had a good heart. 'Shall I take him another ruby?'

'Alas! I have no ruby now,' said the Prince; 'my eyes are all that I have left. They are made of rare sapphires, which were brought out of India a thousand years ago. Pluck out one of them and take it to him. He will sell it to the jeweller, and buy food and firewood, and finish his play.'

'Dear Prince,' said the Swallow, 'I cannot do that;' and he began to weep.

'Swallow, Swallow, little Swallow,' said the Prince, 'do as I command you.'

So the Swallow plucked out the Prince's eye, and flew away to the student's garret. It was easy enough to get in, as there was a hole in the roof. Through this he darted, and came into the room. The young man had his head buried in his hands, so he did not hear the flutter of the bird's wings, and when he looked up he found the beautiful sapphire lying on the withered violets.

'I am beginning to be appreciated,' he cried; 'this is from some great admirer. Now I can finish my play,' and he looked quite happy.

The next day the Swallow flew down to the harbour. He sat on the mast of a large vessel and watched the sailors hauling big chests out of the hold with ropes. 'Heave a-hoy!' they shouted as each chest came up. 'I am going to Egypt!' cried the Swallow, but nobody minded, and when the moon rose he flew back to the Happy Prince.

'I am come to bid you goodbye,' he cried.

'Swallow, Swallow, little Swallow,' said the Prince, 'will you not stay with me one night longer?'

'It is winter,' answered the swallow, 'and the chill snow will soon be here. In Egypt the sun is warm on the green palm-trees, and the crocodiles lie in the mud and look lazily about them. My companions are building a nest in the Temple of Baalbec, and the pink and white doves are watching them, and cooing to each other. Dear Prince, I must leave you, but I will never forget you, and next spring I will bring you back two beautiful jewels in place of those you have given away. The ruby shall be redder than a red rose, and the sapphire shall be as blue as the great sea.'

'In the square below,' said the Happy Prince, 'there stands a little match-girl. She has let her matches fall in the gutter, and they are all spoiled. Her father will beat her if she does not bring home some money, and she is crying. She has no shoes or stockings, and her little head is bare. Pluck out my other eye, and give it to her, and her father will not beat her.'

'I will stay with you one night longer,' said the Swallow, 'but I cannot pluck out your eye. You would be quite blind then.'

'Swallow, Swallow, little Swallow,' said the Prince, 'do as I command you.'

So he plucked out the Prince's other eye, and darted down with it. He swooped past the match-girl, and slipped the jewel into the palm of her hand. 'What a lovely bit of glass,' cried the little girl; and she ran home, laughing.

Then the Swallow came back to the Prince. 'You are blind now,' he said, 'so I will stay with you always.'

'No, little Swallow,' said the poor Prince, 'you must go away to Egypt.'

'I will stay with you always,' said the Swallow, and he slept at the Prince's feet.

All the next day he sat on the Prince's shoulder, and told him stories of what he had seen in strange lands. He told him of the red ibises,° who stand in long rows on the banks of the Nile, and catch gold fish in their beaks; of the Sphinx, who is as old as the world itself, and lives in the desert, and knows everything; of the merchants, who walk slowly by the side of their camels, and carry amber beads in their hands; of the King of the Mountains of the Moon, who is as black as ebony, and worships a large crystal; of the great green snake that sleeps in a palm-tree, and has twenty priests to feed it with honey-cakes; and of the pygmies who sail over a big lake on large flat leaves, and are always at war with the butterflies.

'Dear little Swallow,' said the Prince, 'you tell me of marvellous things, but more marvellous than anything is the suffering of men and of women. There is no Mystery so great as Misery. Fly over my city, little Swallow, and tell me what you see there.'

So the Swallow flew over the great city, and saw the rich making merry in their beautiful houses, while the beggars were sitting at the gates. He flew into dark lanes, and saw the white faces of starving children looking out listlessly at the black streets. Under the archway of a bridge two little boys were lying in one another's arms to try and keep themselves warm. 'How hungry we are!' they said. 'You must not lie here,' shouted the Watchman, and they wandered out into the rain.

Then he flew back and told the Prince what he had seen.

'I am covered with fine gold,' said the Prince, 'you must take it off, leaf by leaf, and give it to my poor; the living always think that gold can make them happy.'

Leaf after leaf of the fine gold the Swallow picked off, till the Happy Prince looked quite dull and grey. Leaf after leaf of the fine gold he brought to the poor, and the children's faces grew rosier, and they laughed and played games in the street. 'We have bread now!' they cried.

Then the snow came, and after the snow came the frost. The streets looked as if they were made of silver, they were so bright and glistening; long icicles like crystal daggers hung down from the eaves of the houses, everybody went about in furs, and the little boys wore scarlet caps and skated on the ice.

The poor little Swallow grew colder and colder, but he would not leave the Prince, he loved him too well. He picked up crumbs outside the baker's door when the baker was not looking, and tried to keep himself warm by flapping his wings.

But at last he knew that he was going to die. He had just strength to fly up to the Prince's shoulder once more. 'Goodbye, dear Prince!' he murmured, 'will you let me kiss your hand?'

'I am glad that you are going to Egypt at last, little Swallow,' said the Prince, 'you have stayed too long here; but you must kiss me on the lips, for I love you.'

'It is not to Egypt that I am going,' said the Swallow. 'I am going to the House of Death. Death is the brother of Sleep, is he not?'

And he kissed the Happy Prince on the lips, and fell down dead at his feet.

At that moment a curious crack sounded inside the statue, as if something had broken. The fact is that the leaden heart had snapped right in two. It certainly was a dreadfully hard frost.

Early the next morning the Mayor was walking in the square below in company with the Town Councillors. As they passed the column he looked up at the statue: 'Dear me! how shabby the Happy Prince looks!' he said.

'How shabby indeed!' cried the Town Councillors, who always agreed with the Mayor, and they went up to look at it.

'The ruby has fallen out of his sword, his eyes are gone, and he is golden no longer,' said the Mayor; 'in fact, he is little better than a beggar!'

'Little better than a beggar,' said the Town Councillors.

'And here is actually a dead bird at his feet!' continued the Mayor. 'We must really issue a proclamation that birds are not to be allowed to die here.' And the Town Clerk made a note of the suggestion.

So they pulled down the statue of the Happy Prince. 'As he is no longer beautiful he is no longer useful,' said the Art Professor at the University.

Then they melted the statue in a furnace, and the Mayor held a meeting of the Corporation to decide what was to be done with the metal. 'We must have another statue, of course,' he said, 'and it shall be a statue of myself.'

'Of myself,' said each of the Town Councillors, and they quarrelled. When I last heard of them they were quarrelling still.

'What a strange thing!' said the overseer of the workmen at the foundry. 'This broken lead heart will not melt in the furnace. We must throw it away.' So they threw it on a dustheap where the dead Swallow was also lying.

'Bring me the two most precious things in the city,' said God to one of His Angels;° and the Angel brought Him the leaden heart and the dead bird.

'You have rightly chosen,' said God, 'for in my garden of Paradise this little bird shall sing for evermore, and in my city of gold the Happy Prince shall praise me.'

THE DEVOTED FRIEND

ONE morning the old Water-rat put his head out of his hole. He had bright beady eyes and stiff grey whiskers, and his tail was like a long bit of black india-rubber. The little ducks were swimming about in the pond, looking just like a lot of yellow canaries, and their mother, who was pure white with real red legs, was trying to teach them how to stand on their heads in the water.

'You will never be in the best society unless you can stand on your heads,' she kept saying to them; and every now and then she showed them how it was done. But the little ducks paid no attention to her. They were so young that they did not know what an advantage it is to be in society at all.

'What disobedient children!' cried the old Water-rat; 'they really deserve to be drowned.'

'Nothing of the kind,' answered the Duck, 'every one must make a beginning, and parents cannot be too patient.'

'Ah! I know nothing about the feelings of parents,' said the Water-rat; 'I am not a family man. In fact, I have never been married, and I never intend to be. Love is all very well in its way, but friendship is much higher. Indeed, I know of nothing in the world that is either nobler or rarer than a devoted friendship.'

'And what, pray, is your idea of the duties of a devoted friend?' asked a Green Linnet,° who was sitting in a willow-tree hard by, and had overheard the conversation.

'Yes, that is just what I want to know,' said the Duck, and she swam away to the end of the pond, and stood upon her head, in order to give her children a good example.

'What a silly question!' cried the Water-rat. 'I should expect my devoted friend to be devoted to me, of course.'

'And what would you do in return?' said the little bird, swinging upon a silver spray, and flapping his tiny wings.

'I don't understand you,' answered the Water-rat.

'Let me tell you a story on the subject,' said the Linnet.

'Is the story about me?' asked the Water-rat. 'If so, I will listen to it, for I am extremely fond of fiction.'

'It is applicable to you,' answered the Linnet; and he flew down, and alighting upon the bank, he told the story of The Devoted Friend.

'Once upon a time,' said the Linnet, 'there was an honest little fellow named Hans.'°

'Was he very distinguished?' asked the Water-rat.

'No,' answered the Linnet, 'I don't think he was distinguished at all, except for his kind heart, and his funny round good-humoured face. He lived in a tiny cottage all by himself, and every day he worked in his garden. In all the country-side there was no garden so lovely as his. Sweet-william grew there, and Gilly-flowers, and Shepherds'-purses, and Fair-maids of France. There were damask Roses, and yellow Roses, lilac Crocuses, and gold, purple Violets and white. Columbine and Ladysmock, Marjoram and Wild Basil, the Cowslip and the Flower-de-luce, the Daffodil and the Clove-Pink bloomed or blossomed in their proper order as the months went by, one flower taking another flower's place, so that there were always beautiful things to look at, and pleasant odours to smell.

'Little Hans had a great many friends, but the most devoted friend of all was big Hugh the Miller. Indeed, so devoted was the rich Miller to little Hans, that he would never go by his garden without leaning over the wall and plucking a large nosegay, or a handful of sweet herbs, or filling his pockets with plums and cherries if it was the fruit season.

'"Real friends should have everything in common," the Miller used to say, and little Hans nodded and smiled, and felt very proud of having a friend with such noble ideas.

'Sometimes, indeed, the neighbours thought it strange that the rich Miller never gave little Hans anything in return, though he had a hundred sacks of flour stored away in his mill, and six milch cows, and a large flock of woolly sheep; but Hans never troubled his head about these things, and nothing gave him greater pleasure than to listen to all the wonderful things the Miller used to say about the unselfishness of true friendship.

'So little Hans worked away in his garden. During the spring, the summer, and the autumn he was very happy, but when the winter came, and he had no fruit or flowers to bring to the market, he suffered a good deal from cold and hunger, and often had to go to bed without any supper but a few dried pears or some hard nuts. In the winter, also, he was extremely lonely, as the Miller never came to see him then.

'"There is no good in my going to see little Hans as long as the snow lasts," the Miller used to say to his wife, "for when people are in trouble they should be left alone, and not be bothered by visitors. That at least is my idea about friendship, and I am sure I am right. So I shall wait till the spring comes, and then I shall pay him a visit, and he will be able to give me a large basket of primroses, and that will make him so happy."

'"You are certainly very thoughtful about others," answered the Wife, as she sat in her comfortable armchair by the big pinewood fire; "very thoughtful indeed. It is quite a treat to hear you talk about friendship. I am sure the clergyman himself could not say such beautiful things as you do, though he does live in a three-storied house, and wear a gold ring on his little finger."

'"But could we not ask little Hans up here?" said the Miller's youngest son. "If poor Hans is in trouble I will give him half my porridge, and show him my white rabbits."

'"What a silly boy you are!" cried the Miller; "I really don't know what is the use of sending you to school. You seem not to learn anything. Why, if little Hans came up here, and saw our warm fire, and our good supper, and our great cask of red wine, he might get envious, and envy is a most terrible thing, and would spoil anybody's nature. I certainly will not allow Hans's nature to be spoiled. I am his best friend, and I will always watch over him, and see that he is not led into any temptations. Besides, if Hans came here, he might ask me to let him have some flour on credit, and that I could not do. Flour is one thing, and friendship is another, and they should not be confused. Why, the words are spelt differently, and mean quite different things. Everybody can see that."

'"How well you talk!" said the Miller's Wife, pouring herself out a large glass of warm ale; "really I feel quite drowsy. It is just like being in church."

'"Lots of people act well," answered the Miller; "but very few people talk well, which shows that talking is much the more difficult thing of the two, and much the finer thing also;"° and he looked sternly across the table at his little son, who felt so ashamed of himself that he hung his head down, and grew quite scarlet, and began to cry into his tea. However, he was so young that you must excuse him.'

'Is that the end of the story?' asked the Water-rat.

'Certainly not,' answered the Linnet, 'that is the beginning.'

'Then you are quite behind the age,' said the Water-rat. 'Every good story-teller nowadays starts with the end, and then goes on to the beginning, and concludes with the middle. That is the new method. I heard all about it the other day from a critic who was walking round the pond with a young man. He spoke of the matter at great length, and I am sure he must have been right, for he had blue spectacles° and a bald head, and whenever the young man made any remark, he always answered "Pooh!" But pray go on with your story. I like the Miller immensely. I have all kinds of beautiful sentiments myself, so there is a great sympathy between us.'

'Well,' said the Linnet, hopping now on one leg and now on the other, 'as soon as the winter was over, and the primroses began to open their pale yellow stars, the miller said to his wife that he would go down and see little Hans.

'"Why, what a good heart you have!" cried his Wife; "you are always thinking of others. And mind you take the big basket with you for the flowers."

'So the Miller tied the sails of the windmill together with a strong iron chain, and went down the hill with the basket on his arm.

'"Good morning, little Hans," said the Miller.

'"Good morning," said Hans, leaning on his spade, and smiling from ear to ear.

'"And how have you been all the winter?" said the Miller.

'"Well, really," cried Hans, "it is very good of you to ask, very good indeed. I am afraid I had rather a hard time of it, but now the spring has come, and I am quite happy, and all my flowers are doing well."

'"We often talked of you during the winter, Hans," said the Miller, "and wondered how you were getting on."

'"That was kind of you," said Hans; "I was half afraid you had forgotten me."

'"Hans, I am surprised at you," said the Miller; "friendship never forgets. That is the wonderful thing about it, but I am afraid you don't understand the poetry of life. How lovely your primroses are looking, by-the-bye!"

'"They are certainly very lovely," said Hans, "and it is a most lucky thing for me that I have so many. I am going to bring them into the market and sell them to the Burgomaster's° daughter, and buy back my wheelbarrow with the money."

'"Buy back your wheelbarrow? You don't mean to say you have sold it? What a very stupid thing to do!"

'"Well, the fact is," said Hans, "that I was obliged to. You see the winter was a very bad time for me, and I really had no money at all to buy bread with. So I first sold the silver buttons off my Sunday coat, and then I sold my silver chain, and then I sold my big pipe, and at last I sold my wheelbarrow. But I am going to buy them all back again now."

'"Hans," said the Miller, "I will give you my wheelbarrow. It is not in very good repair; indeed, one side is gone, and there is something wrong with the wheel-spokes; but in spite of that I will give it to you. I know it is very generous of me, and a great many people would think me extremely foolish for parting with it, but I am not like the rest of the world. I think that generosity is the essence of friendship, and, besides, I have got a new wheelbarrow for myself. Yes, you may set your mind at ease, I will give you my wheelbarrow."

'"Well, really, that is generous of you," said little Hans, and his funny round face glowed all over with pleasure. "I can easily put it in repair, as I have a plank of wood in the house."

'"A plank of wood!" said the Miller; "why, that is just what I want for the roof of my barn. There is a very large hole in it, and the corn will all get damp if I don't stop it up. How lucky you mentioned it! It is quite remarkable how one good action always breeds another. I have given you my wheelbarrow, and now you are going to give me your plank. Of course, the wheelbarrow is worth far more than the plank, but true friendship never notices things like that. Pray get it at once, and I will set to work at my barn this very day."

'"Certainly," cried little Hans, and he ran into the shed and dragged the plank out.

'"It is not a very big plank," said the Miller, looking at it, "and I am afraid that after I have mended my barn-roof there won't be any left for you to mend the wheelbarrow with; but, of course, that is not my fault. And now, as I have given you my wheelbarrow, I am sure you would like to give me some flowers in return. Here is the basket, and mind you fill it quite full."

'"Quite full?" said little Hans, rather sorrowfully, for it was really a very big basket, and he knew that if he filled it he would have no flowers left for the market, and he was very anxious to get his silver buttons back.

'"Well, really," answered the Miller, "as I have given you my wheelbarrow, I don't think that it is much to ask you for a few flowers. I may be wrong, but I should have thought that friendship, true friendship, was quite free from selfishness of any kind."

'"My dear friend, my best friend," cried little Hans, "you are welcome to all the flowers in my garden. I would much sooner have your good opinion than my silver buttons, any day;" and he ran and plucked all his pretty primroses, and filled the Miller's basket.

'"Goodbye, little Hans," said the Miller, as he went up the hill with the plank on his shoulder, and the big basket in his hand.

'"Goodbye," said little Hans, and he began to dig away quite merrily, he was so pleased about the wheelbarrow.

'The next day he was nailing up some honeysuckle against the porch, when he heard the Miller's voice calling to him from the road. So he jumped off the ladder, and ran down the garden, and looked over the wall.

'There was the Miller with a large sack of flour on his back.

'"Dear little Hans," said the Miller, "would you mind carrying this sack of flour for me to market?"

'"Oh, I am so sorry," said Hans, "but I am really very busy today. I have got all my creepers to nail up, and all my flowers to water, and all my grass to roll."

'"Well, really," said the Miller, "I think that, considering that I am going to give you my wheelbarrow, it is rather unfriendly of you to refuse."

'"Oh, don't say that," cried little Hans, "I wouldn't be unfriendly for the whole world;" and he ran in for his cap, and trudged off with the big sack on his shoulders.

'It was a very hot day, and the road was terribly dusty, and before Hans had reached the sixth milestone he was so tired that he had to sit down and rest. However, he went on bravely, and at last he reached the market. After he had waited there some time, he sold the sack of flour for a very good price, and then he returned home at once, for he was afraid that if he stopped too late he might meet some robbers on the way.

'"It has certainly been a hard day," said little Hans to himself as he was going to bed, "but I am glad I did not refuse the Miller, for he is my best friend, and, besides, he is going to give me his wheelbarrow."

'Early the next morning the Miller came down to get the money for his sack of flour, but little Hans was so tired that he was still in bed.

'"Upon my word," said the Miller, "you are very lazy. Really, considering that I am going to give you my wheelbarrow, I think you might work harder. Idleness is a great sin, and I certainly don't like any of my friends to be idle or sluggish. You must not mind my speaking quite plainly to you. Of course I should not dream of doing so if I were not your friend. But what is the good of friendship if one cannot say exactly what one means? Anybody can say charming things and try to please and to flatter, but a true friend always says unpleasant things, and does not mind giving pain. Indeed, if he is a really true friend he prefers it, for he knows that then he is doing good."

'"I am very sorry," said little Hans, rubbing his eyes and pulling off his night-cap, "but I was so tired that I thought I would lie in bed for a little time, and listen to the birds singing. Do you know that I always work better after hearing the birds sing?"

'"Well, I am glad of that," said the Miller, clapping little Hans on the back, "for I want you to come up to the mill as soon as you are dressed, and mend my barn-roof for me."

'Poor little Hans was very anxious to go and work in his garden, for his flowers had not been watered for two days, but he did not like to refuse the Miller, as he was such a good friend to him.

'"Do you think it would be unfriendly of me if I said I was busy?" he inquired in a shy and timid voice.

'"Well, really," answered the Miller, "I do not think it is much to ask of you, considering that I am going to give you my wheelbarrow; but of course if you refuse I will go and do it myself."

'"Oh! on no account," cried little Hans; and he jumped out of bed, and dressed himself, and went up to the barn.

'He worked there all day long, till sunset, and at sunset the Miller came to see how he was getting on.

'"Have you mended the hole in the roof yet, little Hans?" cried the Miller in a cheery voice.

'"It is quite mended," answered little Hans, coming down the ladder.

'"Ah!" said the Miller, "there is no work so delightful as the work one does for others."

'"It is certainly a great privilege to hear you talk," answered little Hans, sitting down and wiping his forehead, "a very great privilege. But I am afraid I shall never have such beautiful ideas as you have."

'"Oh! they will come to you," said the Miller, "but you must take more pains. At present you have only the practice of friendship; some day you will have the theory also."

'"Do you really think I shall?" asked little Hans.

'"I have no doubt of it," answered the Miller; "but now that you have mended the roof, you had better go home and rest, for I want you to drive my sheep to the mountain tomorrow."

'Poor little Hans was afraid to say anything to this, and early the next morning the Miller brought his sheep round to the cottage, and Hans started off with them to the mountain. It took him the whole day to get there and back; and when he returned he was so tired that he went off to sleep in his chair, and did not wake up till it was broad daylight.

'"What a delightful time I shall have in my garden," he said, and he went to work at once.

'But somehow he was never able to look after his flowers at all, for his friend the Miller was always coming round and sending him off on long errands, or getting him to help at the mill. Little Hans was very much distressed at times, as he was afraid his flowers would think he had forgotten them, but he consoled himself by the reflection that the Miller was his best friend. "Besides," he used to say, "he is going to give me his wheelbarrow, and that is an act of pure generosity."

'So little Hans worked away for the Miller, and the Miller said all kinds of beautiful things about friendship, which Hans took down in a note-book, and used to read over at night, for he was a very good scholar.

'Now it happened that one evening little Hans was sitting by his fireside when a loud rap came at the door. It was a very wild night, and the wind was blowing and roaring round the house so terribly that at first he thought it was merely the storm. But a second rap came, and then a third, louder than either of the others.

'"It is some poor traveller," said little Hans to himself, and he ran to the door.

'There stood the Miller with a lantern in one hand and a big stick in the other.

'"Dear little Hans," cried the Miller, "I am in great trouble. My little boy has fallen off a ladder and hurt himself, and I am going for the Doctor. But he lives so far away, and it is such a bad night, that it has just occurred to me that it would be much better if you went instead of me. You know I am going to give you my wheelbarrow, and so it is only fair that you should do something for me in return."

'"Certainly," cried little Hans, "I take it quite as a compliment your coming to me, and I will start off at once. But you must lend me your lantern, as the night is so dark that I am afraid I might fall into the ditch."

'"I am very sorry," answered the Miller, "but it is my new lantern, and it would be a great loss to me if anything happened to it."

'"Well, never mind, I will do without it," cried little Hans, and he took down his great fur coat, and his warm scarlet cap, and tied a muffler round his throat, and started off.

'What a dreadful storm it was! The night was so black that little Hans could hardly see, and the wind was so strong that he could scarcely stand. However, he was very courageous, and after he had been walking about three hours, he arrived at the Doctor's house, and knocked at the door.

'"Who is there?" cried the Doctor, putting his head out of his bedroom window.

'"Little Hans, Doctor."

'"What do you want, little Hans?"

'"The Miller's son has fallen from a ladder, and has hurt himself, and the Miller wants you to come at once."

'"All right!" said the Doctor; and he ordered his horse, and his big boots, and his lantern, and came downstairs, and rode off in the direction of the Miller's house, little Hans trudging behind him.

'But the storm grew worse and worse, and the rain fell in torrents, and little Hans could not see where he was going, or keep up with the horse. At last he lost his way, and wandered off on the moor, which was a very dangerous place, as it was full of deep holes, and there poor little Hans was drowned. His body was found the next day by some goatherds, floating in a great pool of water, and was brought back by them to the cottage.

'Everybody went to little Hans's funeral, as he was so popular, and the Miller was the chief mourner.

'"As I was his best friend," said the Miller, "it is only fair that I should have the best place;" so he walked at the head of the procession in a long black cloak, and every now and then he wiped his eyes with a big pocket-handkerchief.

'"Little Hans is certainly a great loss to every one," said the Black-smith, when the funeral was over, and they were all seated comfortably in the inn, drinking spiced wine and eating sweet cakes.

'"A great loss to me at any rate," answered the Miller; "why, I had as good as given him my wheelbarrow, and now I really don't know what to do with it. It is very much in my way at home, and it is in such bad repair that I could not get anything for it if I sold it. I will certainly take care not to give away anything again. One always suffers for being generous."'

'Well?' said the Water-rat, after a long pause.

'Well, that is the end,' said the Linnet.

'But what became of the Miller?' asked the Water-rat.

'Oh! I really don't know,' replied the Linnet; 'and I am sure that I don't care.'

'It is quite evident then that you have no sympathy in your nature,' said the Water-rat.

'I am afraid you don't quite see the moral of the story,' remarked the Linnet.

'The what?' screamed the Water-rat.

'The moral.'

'Do you mean to say that the story has a moral?'

'Certainly,' said the Linnet.

'Well, really,' said the Water-rat, in a very angry manner, 'I think you should have told me that before you began. If you had done so, I certainly would not have listened to you; in fact, I should have said "Pooh," like the critic. However, I can say it now;' so he shouted out 'Pooh' at the top of his voice, gave a whisk with his tail, and went back into his hole.

'And how do you like the Water-rat?' asked the Duck, who came paddling up some minutes afterwards. 'He has a great many good points, but for my own part I have a mother's feelings, and I can never look at a confirmed bachelor without the tears coming into my eyes.'

'I am rather afraid that I have annoyed him,' answered the Linnet. 'The fact is, that I told him a story with a moral.'

'Ah! that is always a very dangerous thing to do,' said the Duck.

And I quite agree with her.

THE PICTURE OF DORIAN GRAY

THE PREFACE°

THE *artist is the creator of beautiful things.*

To reveal art and conceal the artist is art's aim.

The critic is he who can translate into another manner or a new material his impression of beautiful things.

The highest as the lowest form of criticism is a mode of autobiography.

Those who find ugly meanings in beautiful things are corrupt without being charming. This is a fault.

Those who find beautiful meanings in beautiful things are the cultivated. For these there is hope.

They are the elect to whom beautiful things mean only Beauty.

There is no such thing as a moral or an immoral book.

Books are well written, or badly written. That is all.

The nineteenth century dislike of Realism is the rage of Caliban seeing his own face in a glass.

The nineteenth century dislike of Romanticism is the rage of Caliban not seeing his own face in a glass.

The moral life of man forms part of the subject-matter of the artist, but the morality of art consists in the perfect use of an imperfect medium.

No artist desires to prove anything. Even things that are true can be proved.

No artist has ethical sympathies. An ethical sympathy in an artist is an unpardonable mannerism of style.

No artist is ever morbid. The artist can express everything.°

Thought and language are to the artist instruments of an art.

Vice and virtue are to the artist materials for an art.

From the point of view of form, the type of all the arts is the art of the musician. From the point of view of feeling, the actor's craft is the type.

All art is at once surface and symbol.

Those who go beneath the surface do so at their peril.

Those who read the symbol do so at their peril.

It is the spectator, and not life, that art really mirrors.

Diversity of opinion about a work of art shows that the work is new, complex, and vital.

When critics disagree the artist is in accord with himself.

We can forgive a man for making a useful thing as long as he does not admire it. The only excuse for making a useless thing is that one admires it intensely.

All art is quite useless.

OSCAR WILDE

THE PICTURE OF DORIAN GRAY

CHAPTER I

THE studio was filled with the rich odour of roses, and when the light summer wind stirred amidst the trees of the garden there came through the open door the heavy scent of the lilac, or the more delicate perfume of the pink-flowering thorn.

From the corner of the divan of Persian saddlebags on which he was lying, smoking, as was his custom, innumerable cigarettes, Lord Henry Wotton could just catch the gleam of the honey-sweet and honey-coloured blossoms of a laburnum, whose tremulous branches seemed hardly able to bear the burden of a beauty so flame-like as theirs; and now and then the fantastic shadows of birds in flight flitted across the long tussore-silk curtains that were stretched in front of the huge window, producing a kind of momentary Japanese effect, and making him think of those pallid jade-faced painters of Tokio who, through the medium of an art that is necessarily immobile, seek to convey the sense of swiftness and motion. The sullen murmur of the bees shouldering their way through the long unmown grass, or circling with monotonous insistence round the dusty gilt horns of the straggling woodbine, seemed to make the stillness more oppressive. The dim roar of London was like the bourdon note of a distant organ.

In the centre of the room, clamped to an upright easel, stood the full-length portrait of a young man of extraordinary personal beauty, and in front of it, some little distance away, was sitting the artist himself, Basil Hallward, whose sudden disappearance some years ago caused, at the time, such public excitement, and gave rise to so many strange conjectures.

As the painter looked at the gracious and comely form he had so skilfully mirrored in his art, a smile of pleasure passed across his face, and seemed about to linger there. But he suddenly started up, and, closing his eyes, placed his fingers upon the lids, as though he sought to imprison within his brain some curious dream from which he feared he might awake.

'It is your best work, Basil, the best thing you have ever done,' said Lord Henry, languidly. 'You must certainly send it next year to the Grosvenor. The Academy is too large and too vulgar. Whenever I have gone there, there have been either so many people that I have not been able to see the pictures, which was dreadful, or so many pictures that I have not been able to see the people, which was worse. The Grosvenor is really the only place.'°

'I don't think I shall send it anywhere,' he answered, tossing his head back in that odd way that used to make his friends laugh at him at Oxford. 'No: I won't send it anywhere.'

Lord Henry elevated his eyebrows, and looked at him in amazement through the thin blue wreaths of smoke that curled up in such fanciful whorls from his heavy opium-tainted cigarette. 'Not send it anywhere? My dear fellow, why? Have you any reason? What odd chaps you painters are! You do anything in the world to gain a reputation. As soon as you have one, you seem to want to throw it away. It is silly of you, for there is only one thing in the world worse than being talked about, and that is not being talked about. A portrait like this would set you far above all the young men in England, and make the old men quite jealous, if old men are ever capable of any emotion.'

'I know you will laugh at me,' he replied, 'but I really can't exhibit it. I have put too much of myself into it.'

Lord Henry stretched himself out on the divan and laughed.

'Yes, I knew you would; but it is quite true, all the same.'

'Too much of yourself in it! Upon my word, Basil, I didn't know you were so vain; and I really can't see any resemblance between you, with your rugged strong face and your coal-black hair, and this young Adonis, who looks as if he was made out of ivory and rose-leaves. Why, my dear Basil, he is a Narcissus,° and you—well, of course you have an intellectual expression, and all that. But beauty, real beauty, ends where an intellectual expression begins. Intellect is in itself a mode of exaggeration, and destroys the harmony of any face. The moment one sits down to think, one becomes all nose, or all forehead, or something horrid. Look at the successful men in any of the learned professions. How perfectly hideous they are! Except, of course, in the Church. But then in the Church they don't think. A bishop keeps on saying at the age of eighty what he was told to say when he was a boy of eighteen, and as a natural consequence he always looks absolutely delightful. Your mysterious young friend, whose name you have never told me, but whose picture really fascinates me, never thinks. I feel quite sure of that. He is some brainless, beautiful creature, who should be always here in winter when we have no flowers to look at, and always here in summer when we want something to chill our intelligence. Don't flatter yourself, Basil: you are not in the least like him.'

'You don't understand me, Harry,' answered the artist. 'Of course I

am not like him. I know that perfectly well. Indeed, I should be sorry to
look like him. You shrug your shoulders? I am telling you the truth.
There is a fatality about all physical and intellectual distinction, the sort
of fatality that seems to dog through history the faltering steps of kings. It
is better not to be different from one's fellows. The ugly and the stupid
have the best of it in this world. They can sit at their ease and gape at the
play. If they know nothing of victory, they are at least spared the
knowledge of defeat. They live as we all should live, undisturbed,
indifferent, and without disquiet. They neither bring ruin upon others,
nor ever receive it from alien hands. Your rank and wealth, Harry; my
brains, such as they are—my art, whatever it may be worth; Dorian
Gray's good looks—we shall all suffer for what the gods have given us,
suffer terribly.'

'Dorian Gray? Is that his name?' asked Lord Henry, walking across the
studio towards Basil Hallward.

'Yes, that is his name. I didn't intend to tell it to you.'

'But why not?'

'Oh, I can't explain. When I like people immensely I never tell their
names to any one. It is like surrendering a part of them. I have grown to
love secrecy. It seems to be the one thing that can make modern life
mysterious or marvellous to us. The commonest thing is delightful if one
only hides it. When I leave town now I never tell my people where I am
going. If I did, I would lose all my pleasure. It is a silly habit, I dare say,
but somehow it seems to bring a great deal of romance into one's life. I
suppose you think me awfully foolish about it?'

'Not at all,' answered Lord Henry, 'not at all, my dear Basil. You seem
to forget that I am married, and the one charm of marriage is that it
makes a life of deception absolutely necessary for both parties. I never
know where my wife is, and my wife never knows what I am doing. When
we meet—we do meet occasionally, when we dine out together, or go
down to the Duke's—we tell each other the most absurd stories with the
most serious faces. My wife is very good at it—much better, in fact, than I
am. She never gets confused over her dates, and I always do. But when
she does find me out, she makes no row at all. I sometimes wish she
would; but she merely laughs at me.'

'I hate the way you talk about your married life, Harry,' said Basil
Hallward, strolling towards the door that led into the garden. 'I believe
that you are really a very good husband, but that you are thoroughly
ashamed of your own virtues. You are an extraordinary fellow. You never
say a moral thing, and you never do a wrong thing.° Your cynicism is
simply a pose.'

'Being natural is simply a pose, and the most irritating pose I know,' cried Lord Henry, laughing; and the two young men went out into the garden together, and ensconced themselves on a long bamboo seat that stood in the shade of a tall laurel bush. The sunlight slipped over the polished leaves. In the grass, white daisies were tremulous.

After a pause, Lord Henry pulled out his watch. 'I am afraid I must be going, Basil,' he murmured, 'and before I go, I insist on your answering a question I put to you some time ago.'

'What is that?' said the painter, keeping his eyes fixed on the ground.

'You know quite well.'

'I do not, Harry.'

'Well, I will tell you what it is. I want you to explain to me why you won't exhibit Dorian Gray's picture. I want the real reason.'

'I told you the real reason.'

'No, you did not. You said it was because there was too much of yourself in it. Now, that is childish.'

'Harry,' said Basil Hallward, looking him straight in the face, 'every portrait that is painted with feeling is a portrait of the artist, not of the sitter. The sitter is merely the accident, the occasion. It is not he who is revealed by the painter; it is rather the painter who, on the coloured canvas, reveals himself. The reason I will not exhibit this picture is that I am afraid that I have shown in it the secret of my own soul.'

Lord Henry laughed. 'And what is that?' he asked.

'I will tell you,' said Hallward; but an expression of perplexity came over his face.

'I am all expectation, Basil,' continued his companion, glancing at him.

'Oh, there is really very little to tell, Harry,' answered the painter; 'and I am afraid you will hardly understand it. Perhaps you will hardly believe it.'

Lord Henry smiled, and, leaning down, plucked a pink-petalled daisy from the grass, and examined it. 'I am quite sure I shall understand it,' he replied, gazing intently at the little golden white-feathered disk, 'and as for believing things, I can believe anything, provided that it is quite incredible.'

The wind shook some blossoms from the trees, and the heavy lilac-blooms, with their clustering stars, moved to and fro in the languid air. A grasshopper began to chirrup by the wall, and like a blue thread a long thin dragon-fly floated past on its brown gauze wings. Lord Henry felt as if he could hear Basil Hallward's heart beating, and wondered what was coming.

'The story is simply this,' said the painter after some time. 'Two months ago I went to a crush° at Lady Brandon's. You know we poor artists have to show ourselves in society from time to time, just to remind the public that we are not savages. With an evening coat and a white-tie, as you told me once, anybody, even a stock-broker, can gain a reputation for being civilized. Well, after I had been in the room about ten minutes, talking to huge overdressed dowagers and tedious Academicians, I suddenly became conscious that some one was looking at me. I turned half-way round, and saw Dorian Gray for the first time. When our eyes met, I felt that I was growing pale. A curious sensation of terror came over me. I knew that I had come face to face with some one whose mere personality was so fascinating that, if I allowed it to do so, it would absorb my whole nature, my whole soul, my very art itself. I did not want any external influence in my life. You know yourself, Harry, how independent I am by nature. I have always been my own master; had at least always been so, till I met Dorian Gray. Then——but I don't know how to explain it to you. Something seemed to tell me that I was on the verge of a terrible crisis in my life. I had a strange feeling that Fate had in store for me exquisite joys and exquisite sorrows. I grew afraid, and turned to quit the room. It was not conscience that made me do so: it was a sort of cowardice. I take no credit to myself for trying to escape.'

'Conscience and cowardice are really the same things, Basil. Conscience is the trade-name of the firm.° That is all.'

'I don't believe that, Harry, and I don't believe you do either. However, whatever was my motive—and it may have been pride, for I used to be very proud—I certainly struggled to the door. There, of course, I stumbled against Lady Brandon. "You are not going to run away so soon, Mr Hallward?" she screamed out. You know her curiously shrill voice?'

'Yes; she is a peacock in everything but beauty,' said Lord Henry, pulling the daisy to bits with his long, nervous fingers.

'I could not get rid of her. She brought me up to Royalties, and people with Stars and Garters,° and elderly ladies with gigantic tiaras and parrot noses. She spoke of me as her dearest friend. I had only met her once before, but she took it into her head to lionize me. I believe some picture of mine had made a great success at the time, at least had been chattered about in the penny newspapers, which is the nineteenth-century standard of immortality. Suddenly I found myself face to face with the young man whose personality had so strangely stirred me. We were quite close, almost touching. Our eyes met again. It was reckless of me, but I asked Lady Brandon to introduce me to him. Perhaps it was not so reckless, after all. It was simply inevitable. We would have spoken to each other without any introduction. I am sure of that. Dorian told me so afterwards. He, too, felt that we were destined to know each other.'

'And how did Lady Brandon describe this wonderful young man?' asked his companion. 'I know she goes in for giving a rapid *précis* of all her guests. I remember her bringing me up to a truculent and red-faced old gentleman covered all over with orders and ribbons, and hissing into my ear, in a tragic whisper which must have been perfectly audible to everybody in the room, the most astounding details. I simply fled. I like to find out people for myself. But Lady Brandon treats her guests exactly as an auctioneer treats his goods. She either explains them entirely away, or tells one everything about them except what one wants to know.'

'Poor Lady Brandon! You are hard on her, Harry!' said Hallward, listlessly.

'My dear fellow, she tried to found a *salon*, and only succeeded in opening a restaurant.° How could I admire her? But tell me, what did she say about Mr Dorian Gray?'

'Oh, something like, "Charming boy—poor dear mother and I absolutely inseparable. Quite forget what he does—afraid he—doesn't do anything—oh, yes, plays the piano—or is it the violin, dear Mr Gray?" Neither of us could help laughing, and we became friends at once.'

'Laughter is not at all a bad beginning for a friendship, and it is far the best ending for one,' said the young lord, plucking another daisy.

Hallward shook his head. 'You don't understand what friendship is, Harry,' he murmured—'or what enmity is, for that matter. You like every one; that is to say, you are indifferent to every one.'

'How horribly unjust of you!' cried Lord Henry, tilting his hat back, and looking up at the little clouds that, like ravelled skeins of glossy white silk, were drifting across the hollowed turquoise of the summer sky. 'Yes; horribly unjust of you. I make a great difference between people. I choose my friends for their good looks, my acquaintances for their good characters, and my enemies for their good intellects. A man cannot be too careful in the choice of his enemies. I have not got one who is a fool. They are all men of some intellectual power, and consequently they all appreciate me. Is that very vain of me? I think it is rather vain.'

'I should think it was, Harry. But according to your category I must be merely an acquaintance.'

'My dear old Basil, you are much more than an acquaintance.'

'And much less than a friend. A sort of brother, I suppose?'

'Oh, brothers! I don't care for brothers. My elder brother won't die, and my younger brothers seem never to do anything else.'

'Harry!' exclaimed Hallward, frowning.

'My dear fellow, I am not quite serious. But I can't help detesting my relations. I suppose it comes from the fact that none of us can stand other people having the same faults as ourselves. I quite sympathize with the rage of the English democracy against what they call the vices of the upper orders. The masses feel that drunkenness, stupidity, and immorality should be their own special property, and that if any one of us makes an ass of himself he is poaching on their preserves. When poor Southwark got into the Divorce Court, their indignation was quite magnificent. And yet I don't suppose that ten per cent of the proletariat live correctly.'

'I don't agree with a single word that you have said, and, what is more, Harry, I feel sure you don't either.'

Lord Henry stroked his pointed brown beard, and tapped the toe of his patent-leather boot with a tasselled ebony cane. 'How English you are, Basil! That is the second time you have made that observation. If one puts forward an idea to a true Englishman—always a rash thing to do— he never dreams of considering whether the idea is right or wrong. The only thing he considers of any importance is whether one believes it oneself. Now, the value of an idea has nothing whatsoever to do with the sincerity of the man who expresses it. Indeed, the probabilities are that the more insincere the man is, the more purely intellectual will the idea be, as in that case it will not be coloured by either his wants, his desires, or his prejudices. However, I don't propose to discuss politics, sociology, or metaphysics with you. I like persons better than principles, and I like persons with no principles better than anything else in the world. Tell me more about Mr Dorian Gray. How often do you see him?'

'Every day. I couldn't be happy if I didn't see him every day. He is absolutely necessary to me.'

'How extraordinary! I thought you would never care for anything but your art.'

'He is all my art to me now,' said the painter, gravely. 'I sometimes think, Harry, that there are only two eras of any importance in the world's history. The first is the appearance of a new medium for art, and the second is the appearance of a new personality for art also. What the invention of oil-painting was to the Venetians, the face of Antinoüs° was to late Greek sculpture, and the face of Dorian Gray will some day be to me. It is not merely that I paint from him, draw from him, sketch from him. Of course I have done all that. But he is much more to me than a model or a sitter. I won't tell you that I am dissatisfied with what I have done of him, or that his beauty is such that Art cannot express it. There is nothing that Art cannot express, and I know that the work I have done, since I met Dorian Gray, is good work, is the best work of my life. But in some curious way—I wonder will you understand me?—his personality has suggested to me an entirely new manner in art, an entirely new mode of style. I see things differently, I think of them differently. I can now recreate life in a way that was hidden from me before. "A dream of form in days of thought":—who is it who says that? I forget; but it is what Dorian Gray has been to me. The merely visible presence of this lad— for he seems to me little more than a lad, though he is really over twenty—his merely visible presence—ah! I wonder can you realize all that that means? Unconsciously he defines for me the lines of a fresh school, a school that is to have in it all the passion of the romantic spirit, all the perfection of the spirit that is Greek. The harmony of soul and body—how much that is! We in our madness have separated the two, and have invented a realism that is vulgar, an ideality that is void. Harry! if you only knew what Dorian Gray is to me! You remember that landscape of mine, for which Agnew° offered me such a huge price, but which I would not part with? It is one of the best things I have ever done. And why is it so? Because, while I was painting it, Dorian Gray sat beside me. Some subtle influence passed from him to me, and for the first time in my life I saw in the plain woodland the wonder I had always looked for, and always missed.'

'Basil, this is extraordinary! I must see Dorian Gray.'

Hallward got up from the seat, and walked up and down the garden. After some time he came back. 'Harry,' he said, 'Dorian Gray is to me simply a motive in art. You might see nothing in him. I see everything in him. He is never more present in my work than when no image of him is there. He is a suggestion, as I have said, of a new manner. I find him in the curves of certain lines, in the loveliness and subtleties of certain colours. That is all.'

'Then why won't you exhibit his portrait?' asked Lord Henry.

'Because, without intending it, I have put into it some expression of all this curious artistic idolatry, of which, of course, I have never cared to speak to him. He knows nothing about it. He shall never know anything about it. But the world might guess it; and I will not bare my soul to their shallow, prying eyes. My heart shall never be put under their microscope. There is too much of myself in the thing, Harry—too much of myself!'

'Poets are not so scrupulous as you are. They know how useful passion is for publication. Nowadays a broken heart will run to many editions.'

'I hate them for it,' cried Hallward. 'An artist should create beautiful things, but should put nothing of his own life into them. We live in an age when men treat art as if it were meant to be a form of autobiography. We have lost the abstract sense of beauty. Some day I will show the world what it is; and for that reason the world shall never see my portrait of Dorian Gray.'

'I think you are wrong, Basil, but I won't argue with you. It is only the intellectually lost who ever argue. Tell me, is Dorian Gray very fond of you?'

The painter considered for a few moments. 'He likes me,' he answered, after a pause; 'I know he likes me. Of course I flatter him dreadfully. I find a strange pleasure in saying things to him that I know I shall be sorry for having said. As a rule, he is charming to me, and we sit in the studio and talk of a thousand things. Now and then, however, he is horribly thoughtless, and seems to take a real delight in giving me pain. Then I feel, Harry, that I have given away my whole soul to some one who treats it as if it were a flower to put in his coat, a bit of decoration to charm his vanity, an ornament for a summer's day.'

'Days in summer, Basil, are apt to linger,' murmured Lord Henry. 'Perhaps you will tire sooner than he will. It is a sad thing to think of, but there is no doubt that Genius lasts longer than Beauty. That accounts for the fact that we all take such pains to over-educate ourselves. In the wild struggle for existence, we want to have something that endures, and so we fill our minds with rubbish and facts, in the silly hope of keeping our place. The thoroughly well-informed man—that is the modern ideal. And the mind of the thoroughly well-informed man is a dreadful thing. It is like a bric-à-brac shop, all monsters and dust, with everything priced above its proper value. I think you will tire first, all the same. Some day you will look at your friend, and he will seem to you to be a little out of drawing, or you won't like his tone of colour, or something. You will bitterly reproach him in your own heart, and seriously think that he has behaved very badly to you. The next time he calls, you will be perfectly cold and indifferent. It will be a great pity, for it will alter you. What you have told me is quite a romance, a romance of art one might call it, and the worst of having a romance of any kind is that it leaves one so unromantic.'

'Harry, don't talk like that. As long as I live, the personality of Dorian Gray will dominate me. You can't feel what I feel. You change too often.'

'Ah, my dear Basil, that is exactly why I can feel it. Those who are faithful know only the trivial side of love: it is the faithless who know love's tragedies.' And Lord Henry struck a light on a dainty silver case, and began to smoke a cigarette with a self-conscious and satisfied air, as if he had summed up the world in a phrase.° There was a rustle of chirruping sparrows in the green lacquer leaves of the ivy, and the blue cloud-shadows chased themselves across the grass like swallows. How pleasant it was in the garden! And how delightful other people's emotions were!—much more delightful than their ideas, it seemed to him. One's own soul, and the passions of one's friends—those were the fascinating things in life. He pictured to himself with silent amusement the tedious luncheon that he had missed by staying so long with Basil Hallward. Had he gone to his aunt's, he would have been sure to have met Lord Goodbody there, and the whole conversation would have been about the feeding of the poor, and the necessity for model lodging-houses.° Each class would have preached the importance of those virtues, for whose exercise there was no necessity in their own lives. The rich would have spoken on the value of thrift, and the idle grown eloquent over the dignity of labour. It was charming to have escaped all that! As he thought of his aunt, an idea seemed to strike him. He turned to Hallward, and said, 'My dear fellow, I have just remembered.'

'Remembered what, Harry?'

'Where I heard the name of Dorian Gray.'

'Where was it?' asked Hallward, with a slight frown.

'Don't look so angry, Basil. It was at my aunt, Lady Agatha's. She told me she had discovered a wonderful young man, who was going to help her in the East End,° and that his name was Dorian Gray. I am bound to state that she never told me he was good-looking. Women have no appreciation of good looks; at least, good women have not. She said that he was very earnest, and had a beautiful nature. I at once pictured to myself a creature with spectacles and lank hair, horribly freckled, and tramping about on huge feet. I wish I had known it was your friend.'

'I am very glad you didn't, Harry.'

'Why?'

'I don't want you to meet him.'

'You don't want me to meet him?'

'No.'

'Mr Dorian Gray is in the studio, sir,' said the butler, coming into the garden.

'You must introduce me now,' cried Lord Henry, laughing.

The painter turned to his servant, who stood blinking in the sunlight. 'Ask Mr Gray to wait, Parker: I shall be in in a few moments.' The man bowed, and went up the walk.

Then he looked at Lord Henry. 'Dorian Gray is my dearest friend,' he said. 'He has a simple and a beautiful nature. Your aunt was quite right in what she said of him. Don't spoil him. Don't try to influence him. Your influence would be bad. The world is wide, and has many marvellous people in it. Don't take away from me the one person who gives to my art whatever charm it possesses: my life as an artist depends on him. Mind, Harry, I trust you.' He spoke very slowly, and the words seemed wrung out of him almost against his will.

'What nonsense you talk!' said Lord Henry, smiling, and, taking Hallward by the arm, he almost led him into the house.

CHAPTER II

As they entered they saw Dorian Gray. He was seated at the piano, with his back to them, turning over the pages of a volume of Schumann's 'Forest Scenes'. 'You must lend me these, Basil,' he cried. 'I want to learn them. They are perfectly charming.'

'That entirely depends on how you sit today, Dorian.'

'Oh, I am tired of sitting, and I don't want a life-sized portrait of myself,' answered the lad, swinging round on the music-stool, in a wilful, petulant manner. When he caught sight of Lord Henry, a faint blush coloured his cheeks for a moment, and he started up. 'I beg your pardon, Basil, but I didn't know you had any one with you.'

'This is Lord Henry Wotton, Dorian, an old Oxford friend of mine. I have just been telling him what a capital sitter you were, and now you have spoiled everything.'

'You have not spoiled my pleasure in meeting you, Mr Gray,' said Lord Henry, stepping forward and extending his hand. 'My aunt has often spoken to me about you. You are one of her favourites, and, I am afraid, one of her victims also.'

'I am in Lady Agatha's black books at present,' answered Dorian, with a funny look of penitence. 'I promised to go to a club in Whitechapel with her last Tuesday, and I really forgot all about it. We were to have played a duet together—three duets, I believe. I don't know what she will say to me. I am far too frightened to call.'

'Oh, I will make your peace with my aunt. She is quite devoted to you. And I don't think it really matters about your not being there. The audience probably thought it was a duet. When Aunt Agatha sits down to the piano she makes quite enough noise for two people.'

'That is very horrid to her, and not very nice to me,' answered Dorian, laughing.

Lord Henry looked at him. Yes, he was certainly wonderfully hand-some, with his finely-curved scarlet lips, his frank blue eyes, his crisp gold hair. There was something in his face that made one trust him at once. All the candour of youth was there, as well as all youth's passionate purity. One felt that he had kept himself unspotted from the world.° No wonder Basil Hallward worshipped him.

'You are too charming to go in for philanthropy, Mr Gray—far too charming.' And Lord Henry flung himself down on the divan, and opened his cigarette-case.

The painter had been busy mixing his colours and getting his brushes ready. He was looking worried, and when he heard Lord Henry's last remark he glanced at him, hesitated for a moment, and then said, 'Harry, I want to finish this picture today. Would you think it awfully rude of me if I asked you to go away?'

Lord Henry smiled, and looked at Dorian Gray. 'Am I to go, Mr Gray?' he asked.

'Oh, please don't, Lord Henry. I see that Basil is in one of his sulky moods; and I can't bear him when he sulks. Besides, I want you to tell me why I should not go in for philanthropy.'

'I don't know that I shall tell you that, Mr Gray. It is so tedious a subject that one would have to talk seriously about it. But I certainly shall not run away, now that you have asked me to stop. You don't really mind, Basil, do you? You have often told me that you liked your sitters to have some one to chat to.'

Hallward bit his lip. 'If Dorian wishes it, of course you must stay. Dorian's whims are laws to everybody, except himself.'

Lord Henry took up his hat and gloves. 'You are very pressing, Basil, but I am afraid I must go. I have promised to meet a man at the Orleans. Goodbye, Mr Gray. Come and see me some afternoon in Curzon Street. I am nearly always at home at five o'clock. Write to me when you are coming. I should be sorry to miss you.'

'Basil,' cried Dorian Gray, 'if Lord Henry Wotton goes I shall go too. You never open your lips while you are painting, and it is horribly dull standing on a platform and trying to look pleasant. Ask him to stay. I insist upon it.'

'Stay, Harry, to oblige Dorian, and to oblige me,' said Hallward, gazing intently at his picture. 'It is quite true, I never talk when I am working, and never listen either, and it must be dreadfully tedious for my unfortunate sitters. I beg you to stay.'

'But what about my man at the Orleans?'

The painter laughed. 'I don't think there will be any difficulty about that. Sit down again, Harry. And now, Dorian, get up on the platform, and don't move about too much, or pay any attention to what Lord Henry says. He has a very bad influence over all his friends, with the single exception of myself.'

Dorian Gray stepped up on the dais, with the air of a young Greek martyr, and made a little *moue* of discontent to Lord Henry, to whom he had rather taken a fancy. He was so unlike Basil. They made a delightful contrast. And he had such a beautiful voice. After a few moments he said to him, 'Have you really a very bad influence, Lord Henry? As bad as Basil says?'

'There is no such thing as a good influence, Mr Gray. All influence is immoral—immoral from the scientific point of view.'

'Why?'

'Because to influence a person is to give him one's own soul. He does not think his natural thoughts, or burn with his natural passions. His virtues are not real to him. His sins, if there are such things as sins, are borrowed. He becomes an echo of some one else's music, an actor of a part that has not been written for him. The aim of life is self-development. To realize one's nature perfectly—that is what each of us is here for. People are afraid of themselves, nowadays. They have forgotten the highest of all duties, the duty that one owes to one's self. Of course they are charitable. They feed the hungry, and clothe the beggar. But their own souls starve, and are naked. Courage has gone out of our race. Perhaps we never really had it. The terror of society, which is the basis of morals, the terror of God, which is the secret of religion—these are the two things that govern us. And yet—'

'Just turn your head a little more to the right, Dorian, like a good boy,' said the painter, deep in his work, and conscious only that a look had come into the lad's face that he had never seen there before.

'And yet,' continued Lord Henry, in his low, musical voice, and with that graceful wave of the hand that was always so characteristic of him, and that he had even in his Eton days, 'I believe that if one man were to live out his life fully and completely, were to give form to every feeling, expression to every thought, reality to every dream—I believe that the world would gain such a fresh impulse of joy that we would forget all the maladies of mediævalism, and return to the Hellenic ideal—to something finer, richer, than the Hellenic ideal, it may be. But the bravest man amongst us is afraid of himself. The mutilation of the savage has its tragic survival in the self-denial that mars our lives. We are punished for our refusals. Every impulse that we strive to strangle broods in the mind, and poisons us. The body sins once, and has done with its sin, for action is a mode of purification. Nothing remains then but the recollection of a pleasure, or the luxury of a regret. The only way to get rid of a temptation is to yield to it.° Resist it, and your soul grows sick with longing for the things it has forbidden to itself, with desire for what its monstrous laws have made monstrous and unlawful. It has been said that the great events of the world take place in the brain.° It is in the brain, and the brain only, that the great sins of the world take place also. You, Mr Gray, you yourself, with your rose-red youth and your rose-white boyhood, you have had passions that have made you afraid, thoughts that have filled you with terror, day-dreams and sleeping dreams whose mere memory might stain your cheek with shame—'

'Stop!' faltered Dorian Gray, 'stop! you bewilder me. I don't know what to say. There is some answer to you, but I cannot find it. Don't speak. Let me think. Or, rather, let me try not to think.'

For nearly ten minutes° he stood there, motionless, with parted lips, and eyes strangely bright. He was dimly conscious that entirely fresh influences were at work within him. Yet they seemed to him to have come really from himself. The few words that Basil's friend had said to him—words spoken by chance, no doubt, and with wilful paradox in them—had touched some secret chord that had never been touched before, but that he felt was now vibrating and throbbing to curious pulses.

Music had stirred him like that. Music had troubled him many times. But music was not articulate. It was not a new world, but rather another chaos, that it created in us. Words! Mere words! How terrible they were! How clear, and vivid, and cruel! One could not escape from them. And yet what a subtle magic there was in them! They seemed to be able to give a plastic form to formless things, and to have a music of their own as sweet as that of viol or of lute. Mere words! Was there anything so real as words?

Yes; there had been things in his boyhood that he had not understood. He understood them now. Life suddenly became fiery-coloured to him. It seemed to him that he had been walking in fire. Why had he not known it?

With his subtle smile, Lord Henry watched him. He knew the precise psychological moment when to say nothing. He felt intensely interested. He was amazed at the sudden impression that his words had produced, and, remembering a book that he had read when he was sixteen, a book which had revealed to him much that he had not known before, he wondered whether Dorian Gray was passing through a similar experience. He had merely shot an arrow into the air.° Had it hit the mark? How fascinating the lad was!

Hallward painted away with that marvellous bold touch of his, that had the true refinement and perfect delicacy that in art, at any rate, comes only from strength. He was unconscious of the silence.

'Basil, I am tired of standing,' cried Dorian Gray, suddenly. 'I must go out and sit in the garden. The air is stifling here.'

'My dear fellow, I am so sorry. When I am painting, I can't think of anything else. But you never sat better. You were perfectly still. And I have caught the effect I wanted—the half-parted lips, and the bright look in the eyes. I don't know what Harry has been saying to you, but he has certainly made you have the most wonderful expression. I suppose he has been paying you compliments. You mustn't believe a word that he says.'

'He has certainly not been paying me compliments. Perhaps that is the reason that I don't believe anything he has told me.'

'You know you believe it all,' said Lord Henry, looking at him with his dreamy, languorous eyes. 'I will go out to the garden with you. It is horribly hot in the studio. Basil, let us have something iced to drink, something with strawberries in it.'

'Certainly, Harry. Just touch the bell, and when Parker comes I will tell him what you want. I have got to work up this background, so I will join you later on. Don't keep Dorian too long. I have never been in better form for painting than I am today. This is going to be my masterpiece. It is my masterpiece as it stands.'

Lord Henry went out to the garden, and found Dorian Gray burying his face in the great cool lilac-blossoms, feverishly drinking in their perfume as if it had been wine.° He came close to him, and put his hand upon his shoulder. 'You are quite right to do that,' he murmured. 'Nothing can cure the soul but the senses,° just as nothing can cure the senses but the soul.'

The lad started and drew back. He was bare-headed, and the leaves had tossed his rebellious curls and tangled all their gilded threads. There was a look of fear in his eyes, such as people have when they are suddenly awakened. His finely-chiselled nostrils quivered, and some hidden nerve shook the scarlet of his lips and left them trembling.

'Yes,' continued Lord Henry, 'that is one of the great secrets of life— to cure the soul by means of the senses, and the senses by means of the soul. You are a wonderful creation. You know more than you think you know, just as you know less than you want to know.'

Dorian Gray frowned and turned his head away. He could not help liking the tall, graceful young man who was standing by him. His romantic olive-coloured face and worn expression interested him. There was something in his low, languid voice that was absolutely fascinating. His cool, white, flower-like hands, even, had a curious charm. They moved, as he spoke, like music, and seemed to have a language of their own. But he felt afraid of him, and ashamed of being afraid. Why had it been left for a stranger to reveal him to himself? He had known Basil Hallward for months, but the friendship between them had never altered him. Suddenly there had come some one across his life who seemed to have disclosed to him life's mystery. And, yet, what was there to be afraid of? He was not a schoolboy or a girl. It was absurd to be frightened.

'Let us go and sit in the shade,' said Lord Henry. 'Parker has brought out the drinks, and if you stay any longer in this glare you will be quite spoiled, and Basil will never paint you again. You really must not allow yourself to become sunburnt. It would be unbecoming.'

'What can it matter?' cried Dorian Gray, laughing, as he sat down on the seat at the end of the garden.

'It should matter everything to you, Mr Gray.'

'Why?'

'Because you have the most marvellous youth, and youth is the one thing worth having.'

'I don't feel that, Lord Henry.'

'No, you don't feel it now. Some day, when you are old and wrinkled and ugly, when thought has seared your forehead with its lines, and passion branded your lips with its hideous fires, you will feel it, you will feel it terribly. Now, wherever you go, you charm the world. Will it always be so? . . . You have a wonderfully beautiful face, Mr Gray. Don't frown. You have. And Beauty is a form of Genius—is higher, indeed, than Genius, as it needs no explanation. It is one of the great facts of the world, like sunlight, or spring-time, or the reflection in dark waters of that silver shell we call the moon. It cannot be questioned. It has its divine right of sovereignty. It makes princes of those who have it. You smile? Ah! when you have lost it you won't smile. . . . People say sometimes that Beauty is only superficial. That may be so. But at least it is not so superficial as Thought is. To me, Beauty is the wonder of wonders. It is only shallow people who do not judge by appearances. The true mystery of the world is the visible, not the invisible. . . . Yes, Mr Gray, the gods have been good to you. But what the gods give they quickly take away. You have only a few years in which to live really, perfectly, and fully. When your youth goes, your beauty will go with it, and then you will suddenly discover that there are no triumphs left for you, or have to content yourself with those mean triumphs that the memory of your past will make more bitter than defeats. Every month as it wanes brings you nearer to something dreadful. Time is jealous of you, and wars against your lilies and your roses. You will become sallow, and hollow-cheeked, and dull-eyed. You will suffer horribly. . . . Ah! realize your youth while you have it. Don't squander the gold of your days, listening to the tedious, trying to improve the hopeless failure, or giving away your life to the ignorant, the common, and the vulgar. These are the sickly aims, the false ideals, of our age. Live! Live the wonderful life that is in you! Let nothing be lost upon you. Be always searching for new sensations.° Be afraid of nothing. . . . A new Hedonism°—that is what our century wants. You might be its visible symbol. With your personality there is nothing you could not do. The world belongs to you for a season. . . . The moment I met you I saw that you were quite unconscious of what you really are, of what you really might be. There was so much in you that charmed me that I felt I must tell you something about yourself. I thought how tragic it would be if you were wasted. For there is such a little time that your youth will last—such a little time. The common hill-flowers wither, but they blossom again. The laburnum will be as yellow next June as it is now. In a month there will be purple stars on the clematis, and year after year the green night of its leaves will hold its purple stars. But we never get back our youth. The pulse of joy that beats in us at twenty, becomes sluggish. Our limbs fail, our senses rot. We degenerate into hideous puppets, haunted by the memory of the passions of which we were too much afraid, and the exquisite temptations that we had not the courage to yield to. Youth! Youth! There is absolutely nothing in the world but youth!'

Dorian Gray listened, open-eyed and wondering. The spray of lilac fell from his hand upon the gravel. A furry bee came and buzzed round it for a moment. Then it began to scramble all over the oval stellated globe of the tiny blossoms. He watched it with that strange interest in trivial things that we try to develop when things of high import make us afraid, or when we are stirred by some new emotion for which we cannot find expression, or when some thought that terrifies us lays sudden siege to the brain and calls on us to yield. After a time the bee flew away. He saw it creeping into the stained trumpet of a Tyrian convolvulus. The flower seemed to quiver, and then swayed gently to and fro.

Suddenly the painter appeared at the door of the studio, and made staccato signs for them to come in. They turned to each other, and smiled.

'I am waiting,' he cried. 'Do come in. The light is quite perfect, and you can bring your drinks.'

They rose up, and sauntered down the walk together. Two green-and-white butterflies fluttered past them, and in the pear-tree at the corner of the garden a thrush began to sing.

'You are glad you have met me, Mr Gray,' said Lord Henry, looking at him.

'Yes, I am glad now. I wonder shall I always be glad?'

'Always! That is a dreadful word. It makes me shudder when I hear it. Women are so fond of using it. They spoil every romance by trying to make it last for ever. It is a meaningless word, too. The only difference between a caprice and a life-long passion is that the caprice lasts a little longer.'

As they entered the studio, Dorian Gray put his hand upon Lord Henry's arm. 'In that case, let our friendship be a caprice,' he murmured, flushing at his own boldness, then stepped up on the platform and resumed his pose.

Lord Henry flung himself into a large wicker arm-chair, and watched him. The sweep and dash of the brush on the canvas made the only sound that broke the stillness, except when, now and then, Hallward stepped back to look at his work from a distance. In the slanting beams that streamed through the open doorway the dust danced and was golden. The heavy scent of the roses seemed to brood over everything.

After about a quarter of an hour Hallward stopped painting, looked for a long time at Dorian Gray, and then for a long time at the picture, biting the end of one of his huge brushes, and frowning. 'It is quite finished,' he cried at last, and stooping down he wrote his name in long vermilion letters on the left-hand corner of the canvas.

Lord Henry came over and examined the picture. It was certainly a wonderful work of art, and a wonderful likeness as well.

'My dear fellow, I congratulate you most warmly,' he said. 'It is the finest portrait of modern times. Mr Gray, come over and look at yourself.'

The lad started, as if awakened from some dream. 'Is it really finished?' he murmured, stepping down from the platform.

'Quite finished,' said the painter. 'And you have sat splendidly today. I am awfully obliged to you.'

'That is entirely due to me,' broke in Lord Henry. 'Isn't it, Mr Gray?'

Dorian made no answer, but passed listlessly in front of his picture and turned towards it. When he saw it he drew back, and his cheeks flushed for a moment with pleasure. A look of joy came into his eyes, as if he had recognized himself for the first time. He stood there motionless and in wonder, dimly conscious that Hallward was speaking to him, but not catching the meaning of his words. The sense of his own beauty came on him like a revelation. He had never felt it before. Basil Hallward's compliments had seemed to him to be merely the charming exaggerations of friendship. He had listened to them, laughed at them, forgotten them. They had not influenced his nature. Then had come Lord Henry Wotton with his strange panegyric on youth, his terrible warning of its brevity. That had stirred him at the time, and now, as he stood gazing at the shadow of his own loveliness, the full reality of the description flashed across him. Yes, there would be a day when his face would be wrinkled and wizen, his eyes dim and colourless, the grace of his figure broken and deformed. The scarlet would pass away from his lips, and the gold steal from his hair. The life that was to make his soul would mar his body. He would become dreadful, hideous, and uncouth.

As he thought of it, a sharp pang of pain struck through him like a knife, and made each delicate fibre of his nature quiver. His eyes deepened into amethyst, and across them came a mist of tears. He felt as if a hand of ice had been laid upon his heart.

'Don't you like it?' cried Hallward at last, stung a little by the lad's silence, not understanding what it meant.

'Of course he likes it,' said Lord Henry. 'Who wouldn't like it? It is one of the greatest things in modern art. I will give you anything you like to ask for it. I must have it.'

'It is not my property, Harry.'

'Whose property is it?'

'Dorian's, of course,' answered the painter.

'He is a very lucky fellow.'

'How sad it is!' murmured Dorian Gray, with his eyes still fixed upon his own portrait. 'How sad it is! I shall grow old, and horrible, and dreadful. But this picture will remain always young. It will never be older than this particular day of June. . . . If it were only the other way! If it were I who was to be always young, and the picture that was to grow old! For that—for that—I would give everything! Yes, there is nothing in the whole world I would not give! I would give my soul for that!'

'You would hardly care for such an arrangement, Basil,' cried Lord Henry, laughing. 'It would be rather hard lines on your work.'

'I should object very strongly, Harry,' said Hallward.

Dorian Gray turned and looked at him. 'I believe you would, Basil. You like your art better than your friends. I am no more to you than a green bronze figure. Hardly as much, I dare say.'

The painter stared in amazement. It was so unlike Dorian to speak like that. What had happened? He seemed quite angry. His face was flushed and his cheeks burning.

'Yes,' he continued, 'I am less to you than your ivory Hermes or your silver Faun. You will like them always. How long will you like me? Till I have my first wrinkle, I suppose. I know, now, that when one loses one's good looks, whatever they may be, one loses everything. Your picture has taught me that. Lord Henry Wotton is perfectly right. Youth is the only thing worth having. When I find that I am growing old, I shall kill myself.'

Hallward turned pale, and caught his hand. 'Dorian! Dorian!' he cried, 'don't talk like that. I have never had such a friend as you, and I shall never have such another. You are not jealous of material things, are you?—you who are finer than any of them!'

'I am jealous of everything whose beauty does not die. I am jealous of the portrait you have painted of me.° Why should it keep what I must lose? Every moment that passes takes something from me, and gives something to it. Oh, if it were only the other way! If the picture could change, and I could be always what I am now! Why did you paint it? It will mock me some day—mock me horribly!' The hot tears welled into his eyes; he tore his hand away, and, flinging himself on the divan, he buried his face in the cushions, as though he was praying.

'This is your doing, Harry,' said the painter, bitterly.

Lord Henry shrugged his shoulders. 'It is the real Dorian Gray—that is all.'

'It is not.'

'If it is not, what have I to do with it?'

'You should have gone away when I asked you,' he muttered.

'I stayed when you asked me,' was Lord Henry's answer.

'Harry, I can't quarrel with my two best friends at once, but between you both you have made me hate the finest piece of work I have ever done, and I will destroy it. What is it but canvas and colour? I will not let it come across our three lives and mar them.'

Dorian Gray lifted his golden head from the pillow, and with pallid face and tear-stained eyes looked at him, as he walked over to the deal painting-table that was set beneath the high curtained window. What was he doing there? His fingers were straying about among the litter of tin tubes and dry brushes, seeking for something. Yes, it was for the long palette-knife, with its thin blade of lithe steel. He had found it at last. He was going to rip up the canvas.

With a stifled sob the lad leaped from the couch, and, rushing over to Hallward, tore the knife out of his hand, and flung it to the end of the studio. 'Don't, Basil, don't!' he cried. 'It would be murder!'

'I am glad you appreciate my work at last, Dorian,' said the painter, coldly, when he had recovered from his surprise. 'I never thought you would.'

'Appreciate it? I am in love with it, Basil. It is part of myself. I feel that.'

'Well, as soon as you are dry, you shall be varnished, and framed, and sent home. Then you can do what you like with yourself.' And he walked across the room and rang the bell for tea. 'You will have tea, of course, Dorian? And so will you, Harry? Or do you object to such simple pleasures?'

'I adore simple pleasures,' said Lord Henry. 'They are the last refuge of the complex. But I don't like scenes, except on the stage. What absurd fellows you are, both of you! I wonder who it was defined man as a rational animal.° It was the most premature definition ever given. Man is many things, but he is not rational. I am glad he is not, after all: though I wish you chaps would not squabble over the picture. You had much better let me have it, Basil. This silly boy doesn't really want it, and I really do.'

'If you let any one have it but me, Basil, I shall never forgive you!' cried Dorian Gray; 'and I don't allow people to call me a silly boy.'

'You know the picture is yours, Dorian. I gave it to you before it existed.'

'And you know you have been a little silly, Mr Gray, and that you don't really object to being reminded that you are extremely young.'

'I should have objected very strongly this morning, Lord Henry.'

'Ah! this morning! You have lived since then.'

There came a knock at the door, and the butler entered with a laden tea-tray and set it down upon a small Japanese table. There was a rattle of cups and saucers and the hissing of a fluted Georgian urn. Two globe-shaped china dishes were brought in by a page. Dorian Gray went over and poured out the tea. The two men sauntered languidly to the table, and examined what was under the covers.

'Let us go to the theatre tonight,' said Lord Henry. 'There is sure to be something on, somewhere. I have promised to dine at White's, but it is only with an old friend, so I can send him a wire to say that I am ill, or that I am prevented from coming in consequence of a subsequent engagement. I think that would be a rather nice excuse: it would have all the surprise of candour.'

'It is such a bore putting on one's dress-clothes,' muttered Hallward. 'And, when one has them on, they are so horrid.'

'Yes,' answered Lord Henry, dreamily, 'the costume of the nineteenth century is detestable. It is so sombre, so depressing. Sin is the only real colour-element left in modern life.'

'You really must not say things like that before Dorian, Harry.'

'Before which Dorian? The one who is pouring out tea for us, or the one in the picture?'

'Before either.'

'I should like to come to the theatre with you, Lord Henry,' said the lad.

'Then you shall come; and you will come too, Basil, won't you?'

'I can't, really. I would sooner not. I have a lot of work to do.'

'Well, then, you and I will go alone, Mr Gray.'

'I should like that awfully.'

The painter bit his lip and walked over, cup in hand, to the picture. 'I shall stay with the real Dorian,' he said, sadly.

'Is it the real Dorian?' cried the original of the portrait, strolling across to him. 'Am I really like that?'

'Yes; you are just like that.'

'How wonderful, Basil!'

'At least you are like it in appearance. But it will never alter,' sighed Hallward. 'That is something.'

'What a fuss people make about fidelity!' exclaimed Lord Henry. 'Why, even in love it is purely a question for physiology. It has nothing to do with our own will. Young men want to be faithful, and are not; old men want to be faithless, and cannot: that is all one can say.'

'Don't go to the theatre tonight, Dorian,' said Hallward. 'Stop and dine with me.'

'I can't, Basil.'

'Why?'

'Because I have promised Lord Henry Wotton to go with him.'

'He won't like you the better for keeping your promises. He always breaks his own. I beg you not to go.'

Dorian Gray laughed and shook his head.

'I entreat you.'

The lad hesitated, and looked over at Lord Henry, who was watching them from the tea-table with an amused smile.

'I must go, Basil,' he answered.

'Very well,' said Hallward; and he went over and laid down his cup on the tray. 'It is rather late, and, as you have to dress, you had better lose no time. Goodbye, Harry. Goodbye, Dorian. Come and see me soon. Come tomorrow.'

'Certainly.'

'You won't forget?'

'No, of course not,' cried Dorian.

'And . . . Harry!'

'Yes, Basil?'

'Remember what I asked you, when we were in the garden this morning.'

'I have forgotten it.'

'I trust you.'

'I wish I could trust myself,' said Lord Henry, laughing. 'Come, Mr Gray, my hansom is outside, and I can drop you at your own place. Goodbye, Basil. It has been a most interesting afternoon.'

As the door closed behind them, the painter flung himself down on a sofa, and a look of pain came into his face.

CHAPTER III

At half-past twelve next day Lord Henry Wotton strolled from Curzon Street over to the Albany to call on his uncle, Lord Fermor, a genial if somewhat rough-mannered old bachelor, whom the outside world called selfish because it derived no particular benefit from him, but who was considered generous by Society as he fed the people who amused him. His father had been our ambassador at Madrid when Isabella was young, and Prim° unthought of, but had retired from the Diplomatic Service in a capricious moment of annoyance on not being offered the Embassy at Paris, a post to which he considered that he was fully entitled by reason of his birth, his indolence, the good English of his despatches, and his inordinate passion for pleasure. The son, who had been his father's secretary, had resigned along with his chief, somewhat foolishly as was thought at the time, and on succeeding some months later to the title, had set himself to the serious study of the great aristocratic art of doing absolutely nothing. He had two large town houses, but preferred to live in chambers as it was less trouble, and took most of his meals at his club. He paid some attention to the management of his collieries in the Midland counties, excusing himself for this taint of industry on the ground that the one advantage of having coal was that it enabled a gentleman to afford the decency of burning wood on his own hearth. In politics he was a Tory, except when the Tories were in office, during which period he roundly abused them for being a pack of Radicals. He was a hero to his valet,° who bullied him, and a terror to most of his relations, whom he bullied in turn. Only England could have produced him, and he always said that the country was going to the dogs. His principles were out of date, but there was a good deal to be said for his prejudices.

When Lord Henry entered the room, he found his uncle sitting in a rough shooting coat, smoking a cheroot and grumbling over *The Times*.

'Well, Harry,' said the old gentleman, 'what brings you out so early? I thought you dandies never got up till two, and were not visible till five.'

'Pure family affection, I assure you, Uncle George. I want to get something out of you.'

'Money, I suppose,' said Lord Fermor, making a wry face. 'Well, sit down and tell me all about it. Young people, nowadays, imagine that money is everything.'

'Yes,' murmured Lord Henry, settling his buttonhole in his coat; 'and when they grow older they know it. But I don't want money. It is only people who pay their bills who want that, Uncle George, and I never pay mine. Credit is the capital of a younger son, and one lives charmingly upon it. Besides, I always deal with Dartmoor's tradesmen, and consequently they never bother me. What I want is information: not useful information, of course; useless information.'

'Well, I can tell you anything that is in an English Blue-book,° Harry, although those fellows nowadays write a lot of nonsense. When I was in the Diplomatic, things were much better. But I hear they let them in now by examination. What can you expect? Examinations, sir, are pure humbug from beginning to end. If a man is a gentleman, he knows quite enough, and if he is not a gentleman, whatever he knows is bad for him.'

'Mr Dorian Gray does not belong to Blue-books, Uncle George,' said Lord Henry, languidly.

'Mr Dorian Gray? Who is he?' asked Lord Fermor, knitting his bushy white eyebrows.

'That is what I have come to learn, Uncle George. Or rather, I know who he is. He is the last Lord Kelso's grandson. His mother was a Devereux, Lady Margaret Devereux. I want you to tell me about his mother. What was she like? Whom did she marry? You have known nearly everybody in your time, so you might have known her. I am very much interested in Mr Gray at present. I have only just met him.'

'Kelso's grandson!' echoed the old gentleman—'Kelso's grandson! . . . Of course. . . . I knew his mother intimately. I believe I was at her christening. She was an extraordinarily beautiful girl, Margaret Devereux, and made all the men frantic by running away with a penniless young fellow, a mere nobody, sir, a subaltern in a foot regiment, or something of that kind. Certainly. I remember the whole thing as if it happened yesterday. The poor chap was killed in a duel at Spa a few months after the marriage. There was an ugly story about it. They said Kelso got some rascally adventurer, some Belgian brute, to insult his son-in-law in public, paid him, sir, to do it, paid him, and that the fellow spitted his man as if he had been a pigeon. The thing was hushed up, but, egad, Kelso ate his chop alone at the club for some time afterwards. He brought his daughter back with him, I was told, and she never spoke to him again. Oh, yes; it was a bad business. The girl died too, died within a year. So she left a son, did she? I had forgotten that. What sort of boy is he? If he is like his mother he must be a good-looking chap.'°

'He is very good-looking,' assented Lord Henry.

'I hope he will fall into proper hands,' continued the old man. 'He should have a pot of money waiting for him if Kelso did the right thing by him. His mother had money too. All the Selby property came to her, through her grandfather. Her grandfather hated Kelso, thought him a mean dog. He was, too. Came to Madrid once when I was there. Egad, I was ashamed of him. The Queen used to ask me about the English noble who was always quarrelling with the cabmen about their fares. They made quite a story of it. I didn't dare show my face at Court for a month. I hope he treated his grandson better than he did the jarvies.'°

'I don't know,' answered Lord Henry. 'I fancy that the boy will be well off. He is not of age yet. He has Selby, I know. He told me so. And . . . his mother was very beautiful?'

'Margaret Devereux was one of the loveliest creatures I ever saw, Harry. What on earth induced her to behave as she did, I never could understand. She could have married anybody she chose. Carlington was mad after her. She was romantic, though. All the women of that family were. The men were a poor lot, but, egad! the women were wonderful. Carlington went on his knees to her. Told me so himself. She laughed at him, and there wasn't a girl in London at the time who wasn't after him. And by the way, Harry, talking about silly marriages, what is this humbug your father tells me about Dartmoor wanting to marry an American? Ain't English girls good enough for him?'

'It is rather fashionable to marry Americans just now,° Uncle George.'

'I'll back English women against the world, Harry,' said Lord Fermor, striking the table with his fist.

'The betting is on the Americans.'

'They don't last, I am told,' muttered his uncle.

'A long engagement exhausts them, but they are capital at a steeplechase. They take things flying. I don't think Dartmoor has a chance.'

'Who are her people?' grumbled the old gentleman. 'Has she got any?'

Lord Henry shook his head. 'American girls are as clever at concealing their parents, as English women are at concealing their past,' he said, rising to go.

'They are pork-packers, I suppose?'

'I hope so, Uncle George, for Dartmoor's sake. I am told that pork-packing is the most lucrative profession in America, after politics.'

'Is she pretty?'

'She behaves as if she was beautiful. Most American women do. It is the secret of their charm.'

'Why can't these American women stay in their own country? They are always telling us that it is the Paradise for women.'

'It is. That is the reason why, like Eve, they are so excessively anxious to get out of it,' said Lord Henry. 'Goodbye, Uncle George. I shall be late for lunch, if I stop any longer. Thanks for giving me the information I wanted. I always like to know everything about my new friends, and nothing about my old ones.'

'Where are you lunching, Harry?'

'At Aunt Agatha's. I have asked myself and Mr Gray. He is her latest *protégé*.'

'Humph! tell your Aunt Agatha, Harry, not to bother me any more with her charity appeals. I am sick of them. Why, the good woman thinks that I have nothing to do but to write cheques for her silly fads.'

'All right, Uncle George, I'll tell her, but it won't have any effect. Philanthropic people lose all sense of humanity. It is their distinguishing characteristic.'

The old gentleman growled approvingly, and rang the bell for his servant. Lord Henry passed up the low arcade into Burlington Street, and turned his steps in the direction of Berkeley Square.

So that was the story of Dorian Gray's parentage. Crudely as it had been told to him, it had yet stirred him by its suggestion of a strange, almost modern romance. A beautiful woman risking everything for a mad passion. A few wild weeks of happiness cut short by a hideous, treacherous crime. Months of voiceless agony, and then a child born in pain. The mother snatched away by death, the boy left to solitude and the tyranny of an old and loveless man. Yes; it was an interesting background. It posed the lad, made him more perfect as it were. Behind every exquisite thing that existed, there was something tragic. Worlds had to be in travail, that the meanest flower might blow.° . . . And how charming he had been at dinner the night before, as with startled eyes and lips parted in frightened pleasure he had sat opposite to him at the club, the red candleshades staining to a richer rose the wakening wonder of his face. Talking to him was like playing upon an exquisite violin. He answered to every touch and thrill of the bow. . . . There was something terribly enthralling in the exercise of influence. No other activity was like it. To project one's soul into some gracious form, and let it tarry there for a moment; to hear one's own intellectual views echoed back to one with all the added music of passion and youth; to convey one's temperament into another as though it were a subtle fluid or a strange perfume: there was a real joy in that—perhaps the most satisfying joy left to us in an age so limited and vulgar as our own, an age grossly carnal in its pleasures, and grossly common in its aims. . . . He was a marvellous type, too, this lad, whom by so curious a chance he had met in Basil's studio, or could be fashioned into a marvellous type, at any rate. Grace was his, and the white purity of boyhood, and beauty such as old Greek marbles kept for us. There was nothing that one could not do with him. He could be made a Titan or a toy. What a pity it was that such beauty was destined to fade! . . . And Basil? From a psychological point of view, how interesting he was! The new manner in art, the fresh mode of looking at life, suggested so strangely by the merely visible presence of one who was unconscious of it all; the silent spirit that dwelt in dim woodland, and walked unseen in open field, suddenly showing herself, Dryad-like and not afraid, because in his soul who sought for her there had been wakened that wonderful vision to which alone are wonderful things revealed; the mere shapes and patterns of things becoming, as it were, refined, and gaining a kind of symbolical value, as though they were themselves patterns of some other and more perfect form whose shadow they made real: how strange it all was! He remembered something like it in history. Was it not Plato, that artist in thought, who had first analysed it? Was it not Buonarotti° who had carved it in the coloured marbles of a sonnet-sequence? But in our own century it was strange. . . . Yes; he would try to be to Dorian Gray what, without knowing it, the lad was to the painter who had fashioned the wonderful portrait. He would seek to dominate him—had already, indeed, half done so. He would make that wonderful spirit his own. There was something fascinating in this son of Love and Death.

Suddenly he stopped, and glanced up at the houses. He found that he had passed his aunt's some distance, and, smiling to himself, turned back. When he entered the somewhat sombre hall, the butler told him that they had gone in to lunch. He gave one of the footmen his hat and stick, and passed into the dining-room.

'Late as usual, Harry,' cried his aunt, shaking her head at him.

He invented a facile excuse, and having taken the vacant seat next to her, looked round to see who was there. Dorian bowed to him shyly from the end of the table, a flush of pleasure stealing into his cheek. Opposite was the Duchess of Harley, a lady of admirable good-nature and good temper, much liked by every one who knew her, and of those ample architectural proportions that in women who are not Duchesses are described by contemporary historians as stoutness. Next to her sat, on her right, Sir Thomas Burdon, a Radical member of Parliament, who followed his leader in public life, and in private followed the best cooks, dining with the Tories, and thinking with the Liberals, in accordance with a wise and well-known rule. The post on her left was occupied by Mr Erskine of Treadley, an old gentleman of considerable charm and culture, who had fallen, however, into bad habits of silence, having, as he explained once to Lady Agatha, said everything that he had to say before he was thirty. His own neighbour was Mrs Vandeleur, one of his aunt's oldest friends, a perfect saint amongst women, but so dreadfully dowdy that she reminded one of a badly bound hymn-book. Fortunately for him she had on the other side Lord Faudel, a most intelligent middle-aged mediocrity, as bald as a Ministerial statement in the House of Commons, with whom she was conversing in that intensely earnest manner which is the one unpardonable error, as he remarked once himself, that all really good people fall into, and from which none of them ever quite escape.

'We are talking about poor Dartmoor, Lord Henry,' cried the Duchess, nodding pleasantly to him across the table. 'Do you think he will really marry this fascinating young person?'

'I believe she has made up her mind to propose to him, Duchess.'

'How dreadful!' exclaimed Lady Agatha. 'Really, some one should interfere.'

'I am told, on excellent authority, that her father keeps an American dry-goods store,' said Sir Thomas Burdon, looking supercilious.

'My uncle has already suggested pork-packing, Sir Thomas.'

'Dry-goods! What are American dry-goods?' asked the Duchess, raising her large hands in wonder, and accentuating the verb.

'American novels,' answered Lord Henry, helping himself to some quail.

The Duchess looked puzzled.

'Don't mind him, my dear,' whispered Lady Agatha. 'He never means anything that he says.'

'When America was discovered,' said the Radical member, and he began to give some wearisome facts. Like all people who try to exhaust a subject, he exhausted his listeners. The Duchess sighed, and exercised her privilege of interruption. 'I wish to goodness it never had been discovered at all!' she exclaimed. 'Really, our girls have no chance nowadays. It is most unfair.'

'Perhaps, after all, America never has been discovered,' said Mr Erskine; 'I myself would say that it had merely been detected.'

'Oh! but I have seen specimens of the inhabitants,' answered the Duchess, vaguely. 'I must confess that most of them are extremely pretty. And they dress well, too. They get all their dresses in Paris. I wish I could afford to do the same.'

'They say that when good Americans die they go to Paris,' chuckled Sir Thomas, who had a large wardrobe of Humour's cast-off clothes.°

'Really! And where do bad Americans go to when they die?' inquired the Duchess.

'They go to America,' murmured Lord Henry.

Sir Thomas frowned. 'I am afraid that your nephew is prejudiced against that great country,' he said to Lady Agatha. 'I have travelled all over it, in cars provided by the directors, who, in such matters, are extremely civil. I assure you that it is an education to visit it.'

'But must we really see Chicago in order to be educated?' asked Mr Erskine, plaintively. 'I don't feel up to the journey.'

Sir Thomas waved his hand. 'Mr Erskine of Treadley has the world on his shelves. We practical men like to see things, not to read about them. The Americans are an extremely interesting people. They are absolutely reasonable. I think that is their distinguishing characteristic. Yes, Mr Erskine, an absolutely reasonable people. I assure you there is no nonsense about the Americans.'

'How dreadful!' cried Lord Henry. 'I can stand brute force, but brute reason is quite unbearable. There is something unfair about its use. It is hitting below the intellect.'

'I do not understand you,' said Sir Thomas, growing rather red.

'I do, Lord Henry,' murmured Mr Erskine, with a smile.

'Paradoxes are all very well in their way . . .' rejoined the Baronet.

'Was that a paradox?' asked Mr Erskine. 'I did not think so. Perhaps it was. Well, the way of paradoxes is the way of truth. To test Reality we must see it on the tight-rope. When the Verities become acrobats we can judge them.'

'Dear me!' said Lady Agatha, 'how you men argue! I am sure I never can make out what you are talking about. Oh! Harry, I am quite vexed with you. Why do you try to persuade our nice Mr Dorian Gray to give up the East End? I assure you he would be quite invaluable. They would love his playing.'

'I want him to play to me,' cried Lord Henry, smiling, and he looked down the table and caught a bright answering glance.

'But they are so unhappy in Whitechapel,' continued Lady Agatha.

'I can sympathize with everything, except suffering,' said Lord Henry, shrugging his shoulders. 'I cannot sympathize with that. It is too ugly, too horrible, too distressing. There is something terribly morbid in the modern sympathy with pain. One should sympathize with the colour, the beauty, the joy of life. The less said about life's sores the better.'

'Still, the East End is a very important problem,' remarked Sir Thomas, with a grave shake of the head.

'Quite so,' answered the young lord. 'It is the problem of slavery, and we try to solve it by amusing the slaves.'

The politician looked at him keenly. 'What change do you propose, then?' he asked.

Lord Henry laughed. 'I don't desire to change anything in England except the weather,' he answered. 'I am quite content with philosophic contemplation. But, as the nineteenth century has gone bankrupt through an over-expenditure of sympathy, I would suggest that we should appeal to Science to put us straight. The advantage of the emotions is that they lead us astray, and the advantage of Science is that it is not emotional.'

'But we have such grave responsibilities,' ventured Mrs Vandeleur, timidly.

'Terribly grave,' echoed Lady Agatha.

Lord Henry looked over at Mr Erskine. 'Humanity takes itself too seriously. It is the world's original sin. If the cave-man had known how to laugh, History would have been different.'

'You are really very comforting,' warbled the Duchess. 'I have always felt rather guilty when I came to see your dear aunt, for I take no interest at all in the East End. For the future I shall be able to look her in the face without a blush.'

'A blush is very becoming, Duchess,' remarked Lord Henry.

'Only when one is young,' she answered. 'When an old woman like myself blushes, it is a very bad sign. Ah! Lord Henry, I wish you would tell me how to become young again.'

He thought for a moment. 'Can you remember any great error that you committed in your early days, Duchess?' he asked, looking at her across the table.

'A great many, I fear,' she cried.

'Then commit them over again,' he said, gravely. 'To get back one's youth, one has merely to repeat one's follies.'

'A delightful theory!' she exclaimed. 'I must put it into practice.'

'A dangerous theory!' came from Sir Thomas's tight lips. Lady Agatha shook her head, but could not help being amused. Mr Erskine listened.

'Yes,' he continued, 'that is one of the great secrets of life. Nowadays most people die of a sort of creeping common sense, and discover when it is too late that the only things one never regrets are one's mistakes.'

A laugh ran round the table.

He played with the idea, and grew wilful; tossed it into the air and transformed it; let it escape and recaptured it; made it iridescent with fancy, and winged it with paradox. The praise of folly, as he went on, soared into a philosophy, and Philosophy herself became young, and catching the mad music of Pleasure, wearing, one might fancy, her wine-stained robe and wreath of ivy, danced like a Bacchante over the hills of life, and mocked the slow Silenus° for being sober. Facts fled before her like frightened forest things. Her white feet trod the huge press at which wise Omar° sits, till the seething grape-juice rose round her bare limbs in waves of purple bubbles, or crawled in red foam over the vat's black, dripping, sloping sides. It was an extraordinary improvisation. He felt that the eyes of Dorian Gray were fixed on him, and the consciousness that amongst his audience there was one whose temperament he wished to fascinate, seemed to give his wit keenness, and to lend colour to his imagination. He was brilliant, fantastic, irresponsible. He charmed his listeners out of themselves, and they followed his pipe laughing.° Dorian Gray never took his gaze off him, but sat like one under a spell, smiles chasing each other over his lips, and wonder growing grave in his darkening eyes.

At last, liveried in the costume of the age, Reality entered the room in the shape of a servant to tell the Duchess that her carriage was waiting. She wrung her hands in mock despair. 'How annoying!' she cried. 'I must go. I have to call for my husband at the club, to take him to some absurd meeting at Willis's Rooms, where he is going to be in the chair. If I am late he is sure to be furious, and I couldn't have a scene in this bonnet. It is far too fragile. A harsh word would ruin it. No, I must go, dear Agatha. Goodbye, Lord Henry, you are quite delightful, and dreadfully demoralizing. I am sure I don't know what to say about your views. You must come and dine with us some night. Tuesday? Are you disengaged Tuesday?'

'For you I would throw over anybody, Duchess,' said Lord Henry, with a bow.

'Ah! that is very nice, and very wrong of you,' she cried; 'so mind you come;' and she swept out of the room, followed by Lady Agatha and the other ladies.

When Lord Henry had sat down again, Mr Erskine moved round, and taking a chair close to him, placed his hand upon his arm.

'You talk books away,' he said; 'why don't you write one?'

'I am too fond of reading books to care to write them, Mr Erskine. I should like to write a novel certainly, a novel that would be as lovely as a Persian carpet and as unreal. But there is no literary public in England for anything except newspapers, primers, and encyclopædias. Of all people in the world the English have the least sense of the beauty of literature.'

'I fear you are right,' answered Mr Erskine. 'I myself used to have literary ambitions, but I gave them up long ago. And now, my dear young friend, if you will allow me to call you so, may I ask if you really meant all that you said to us at lunch?'

'I quite forgot what I said,' smiled Lord Henry. 'Was it all very bad?'

'Very bad indeed. In fact I consider you extremely dangerous, and if anything happens to our good Duchess we shall all look on you as being primarily responsible. But I should like to talk to you about life. The generation into which I was born was tedious. Some day, when you are tired of London, come down to Treadley, and expound to me your philosophy of pleasure over some admirable Burgundy I am fortunate enough to possess.'

'I shall be charmed. A visit to Treadley would be a great privilege. It has a perfect host, and a perfect library.'

'You will complete it,' answered the old gentleman, with a courteous bow. 'And now I must bid goodbye to your excellent aunt. I am due at the Athenæum. It is the hour when we sleep there.'

'All of you, Mr Erskine?'

'Forty of us, in forty arm-chairs. We are practising for an English Academy of Letters.'°

Lord Henry laughed, and rose. 'I am going to the Park,' he cried.

As he was passing out of the door Dorian Gray touched him on the arm. 'Let me come with you,' he murmured.

'But I thought you had promised Basil Hallward to go and see him,' answered Lord Henry.

'I would sooner come with you; yes, I feel I must come with you. Do let me. And you will promise to talk to me all the time? No one talks so wonderfully as you do.'

'Ah! I have talked quite enough for today,' said Lord Henry, smiling. 'All I want now is to look at life. You may come and look at it with me, if you care to.'

CHAPTER IV

ONE afternoon, a month later, Dorian Gray was reclining in a luxurious arm-chair, in the little library of Lord Henry's house in Mayfair. It was, in its way, a very charming room, with its high panelled wainscoting of olive-stained oak, its cream-coloured frieze and ceiling of raised plaster-work, and its brickdust felt carpet strewn with silk long-fringed Persian rugs. On a tiny satin-wood table stood a statuette by Clodion,° and beside it lay a copy of 'Les Cent Nouvelles',° bound for Margaret of Valois° by Clovis Eve,° and powdered with the gilt daisies that Queen had selected for her device. Some large blue china jars and parrot-tulips were ranged on the mantel-shelf, and through the small leaded panes of the window streamed the apricot-coloured light of a summer day in London.

Lord Henry had not yet come in. He was always late on principle, his principle being that punctuality is the thief of time.° So the lad was looking rather sulky, as with listless fingers he turned over the pages of an elaborately-illustrated edition of 'Manon Lescaut'° that he had found in one of the bookcases. The formal monotonous ticking of the Louis Quatorze clock annoyed him. Once or twice he thought of going away.

At last he heard a step outside, and the door opened. 'How late you are, Harry!' he murmured.

'I am afraid it is not Harry, Mr Gray,' answered a shrill voice.

He glanced quickly round, and rose to his feet. 'I beg your pardon. I thought—'

'You thought it was my husband. It is only his wife. You must let me introduce myself. I know you quite well by your photographs. I think my husband has got seventeen of them.'

'Not seventeen, Lady Henry?'

'Well, eighteen, then. And I saw you with him the other night at the Opera.' She laughed nervously as she spoke, and watched him with her vague forget-me-not eyes. She was a curious woman, whose dresses always looked as if they had been designed in a rage and put on in a tempest. She was usually in love with somebody, and, as her passion was never returned, she had kept all her illusions. She tried to look picturesque, but only succeeded in being untidy. Her name was Victoria, and she had a perfect mania for going to church.

'That was at "Lohengrin", Lady Henry, I think?'

'Yes; it was at dear "Lohengrin". I like Wagner's music better than anybody's. It is so loud that one can talk the whole time without other people hearing what one says. That is a great advantage: don't you think so, Mr Gray?'

The same nervous staccato laugh broke from her thin lips, and her fingers began to play with a long tortoise-shell paper-knife.

Dorian smiled, and shook his head: 'I am afraid I don't think so, Lady Henry. I never talk during music—at least, during good music. If one hears bad music, it is one's duty to drown it in conversation.'

'Ah! that is one of Harry's views, isn't it, Mr Gray? I always hear Harry's views from his friends. It is the only way I get to know of them. But you must not think I don't like good music. I adore it, but I am afraid of it. It makes me too romantic. I have simply worshipped pianists—two at a time, sometimes, Harry tells me. I don't know what it is about them. Perhaps it is that they are foreigners. They all are, ain't they? Even those that are born in England become foreigners after a time, don't they? It is so clever of them, and such a compliment to art. Makes it quite cosmopolitan, doesn't it? You have never been to any of my parties, have you, Mr Gray? You must come. I can't afford orchids, but I spare no expense in foreigners. They make one's rooms look so picturesque. But here is Harry!—Harry, I came in to look for you, to ask you something—I forget what it was—and I found Mr Gray here. We have had such a pleasant chat about music. We have quite the same ideas. No; I think our ideas are quite different. But he has been most pleasant. I am so glad I've seen him.'

'I am charmed, my love, quite charmed,' said Lord Henry, elevating his dark crescent-shaped eyebrows and looking at them both with an amused smile. 'So sorry I am late, Dorian. I went to look after a piece of old brocade in Wardour Street,° and had to bargain for hours for it. Nowadays people know the price of everything, and the value of nothing.'°

'I am afraid I must be going,' exclaimed Lady Henry, breaking an awkward silence with her silly sudden laugh. 'I have promised to drive with the Duchess. Goodbye, Mr Gray. Goodbye, Harry. You are dining out, I suppose? So am I. Perhaps I shall see you at Lady Thornbury's.'

'I dare say, my dear,' said Lord Henry, shutting the door behind her, as, looking like a bird of paradise that had been out all night in the rain, she flitted out of the room, leaving a faint odour of frangipanni.° Then he lit a cigarette, and flung himself down on the sofa.

'Never marry a woman with straw-coloured hair, Dorian,' he said, after a few puffs.

'Why, Harry?'

'Because they are so sentimental.'

'But I like sentimental people.'

'Never marry at all, Dorian. Men marry because they are tired; women, because they are curious: both are disappointed.'

'I don't think I am likely to marry, Harry. I am too much in love. That is one of your aphorisms. I am putting it into practice, as I do everything that you say.'

'Who are you in love with?' asked Lord Henry, after a pause.

'With an actress,' said Dorian Gray, blushing.

Lord Henry shrugged his shoulders. 'That is a rather commonplace *début*.'

'You would not say so if you saw her, Harry.'

'Who is she?'

'Her name is Sibyl Vane.'

'Never heard of her.'

'No one has. People will some day, however. She is a genius.'

'My dear boy, no woman is a genius. Women are a decorative sex. They never have anything to say, but they say it charmingly. Women represent the triumph of matter over mind, just as men represent the triumph of mind over morals.'

'Harry, how can you?'

'My dear Dorian, it is quite true. I am analysing women at present, so I ought to know. The subject is not so abstruse as I thought it was. I find that, ultimately, there are only two kinds of women, the plain and the coloured. The plain women are very useful. If you want to gain a reputation for respectability, you have merely to take them down to supper. The other women are very charming. They commit one mistake, however. They paint in order to try and look young. Our grandmothers painted in order to try and talk brilliantly. *Rouge* and *esprit* used to go together. That is all over now. As long as a woman can look ten years younger than her own daughter, she is perfectly satisfied. As for conversation, there are only five women in London worth talking to, and two of these can't be admitted into decent society. However, tell me about your genius. How long have you known her?'

'Ah! Harry, your views terrify me.'

'Never mind that. How long have you known her?'

'About three weeks.'

'And where did you come across her?'

'I will tell you, Henry; but you mustn't be unsympathetic about it. After all, it never would have happened if I had not met you. You filled me with a wild desire to know everything about life. For days after I met you, something seemed to throb in my veins. As I lounged in the Park, or strolled down Piccadilly, I used to look at every one who passed me, and wonder, with a mad curiosity, what sort of lives they led. Some of them fascinated me. Others filled me with terror. There was an exquisite poison in the air. I had a passion for sensations. . . . Well, one evening about seven o'clock, I determined to go out in search of some adventure. I felt that this grey, monstrous London of ours, with its myriads of people, its sordid sinners, and its splendid sins, as you once phrased it, must have something in store for me. I fancied a thousand things. The mere danger gave me a sense of delight. I remembered what you had said to me on that wonderful evening when we first dined together, about the search for beauty being the real secret of life. I don't know what I expected, but I went out and wandered eastward, soon losing my way in a labyrinth of grimy streets and black, grassless squares. About half-past eight I passed by an absurd little theatre, with great flaring gas-jets and gaudy play-bills. A hideous Jew, in the most amazing waistcoat I ever beheld in my life, was standing at the entrance, smoking a vile cigar. He had greasy ringlets, and an enormous diamond blazed in the centre of a soiled shirt. "Have a box, my Lord?" he said, when he saw me, and he took off his hat with an air of gorgeous servility. There was something about him, Harry, that amused me. He was such a monster. You will laugh at me, I know, but I really went in and paid a whole guinea for the stage-box. To the present day I can't make out why I did so; and yet if I hadn't—my dear Harry, if I hadn't, I should have missed the greatest romance of my life. I see you are laughing. It is horrid of you!'

'I am not laughing, Dorian; at least I am not laughing at you. But you should not say the greatest romance of your life. You should say the first romance of your life. You will always be loved, and you will always be in love with love. A *grande passion* is the privilege of people who have nothing to do. That is the one use of the idle classes of a country. Don't be afraid. There are exquisite things in store for you. This is merely the beginning.'

'Do you think my nature so shallow?' cried Dorian Gray, angrily.

'No; I think your nature so deep.'

'How do you mean?'

'My dear boy, the people who love only once in their lives are really the shallow people. What they call their loyalty, and their fidelity, I call either the lethargy of custom or their lack of imagination. Faithfulness is to the emotional life what consistency is to the life of the intellect—simply a confession of failure. Faithfulness! I must analyse it some day. The passion for property is in it. There are many things that we would throw away if we were not afraid that others might pick them up. But I don't want to interrupt you. Go on with your story.'

THE PICTURE OF DORIAN GRAY

'Well, I found myself seated in a horrid little private box, with a vulgar drop-scene staring me in the face. I looked out from behind the curtain, and surveyed the house. It was a tawdry affair, all Cupids and cornucopias, like a third-rate wedding-cake. The gallery and pit were fairly full, but the two rows of dingy stalls were quite empty, and there was hardly a person in what I suppose they called the dress-circle. Women went about with oranges and ginger-beer, and there was a terrible consumption of nuts going on.'

'It must have been just like the palmy days of the British Drama.'

'Just like, I should fancy, and very depressing. I began to wonder what on earth I should do, when I caught sight of the play-bill. What do you think the play was, Harry?'

'I should think "The Idiot Boy, or Dumb but Innocent".° Our fathers used to like that sort of piece, I believe. The longer I live, Dorian, the more keenly I feel that whatever was good enough for our fathers is not good enough for us. In art, as in politics, *les grandpères ont toujours tort*.'°

'This play was good enough for us, Harry. It was "Romeo and Juliet". I must admit that I was rather annoyed at the idea of seeing Shakespeare done in such a wretched hole of a place. Still, I felt interested, in a sort of way. At any rate, I determined to wait for the first act. There was a dreadful orchestra, presided over by a young Hebrew who sat at a cracked piano, that nearly drove me away, but at last the drop-scene was drawn up, and the play began. Romeo was a stout elderly gentleman, with corked eyebrows, a husky tragedy voice, and a figure like a beer-barrel. Mercutio was almost as bad. He was played by the low-comedian, who had introduced gags of his own and was on most friendly terms with the pit. They were both as grotesque as the scenery, and that looked as if it had come out of a country-booth. But Juliet! Harry, imagine a girl,° hardly seventeen years of age, with a little flower-like face, a small Greek head with plaited coils of dark-brown hair, eyes that were violet wells of passion, lips that were like the petals of a rose. She was the loveliest thing I had ever seen in my life. You said to me once that pathos left you unmoved, but that beauty, mere beauty, could fill your eyes with tears. I tell you, Harry, I could hardly see this girl for the mist of tears that came across me. And her voice—I never heard such a voice. It was very low at first, with deep mellow notes, that seemed to fall singly upon one's ear. Then it became a little louder, and sounded like a flute or a distant hautbois.° In the garden-scene it had all the tremulous ecstasy that one hears just before dawn when nightingales are singing. There were moments, later on, when it had the wild passion of violins. You know how a voice can stir one. Your voice and the voice of Sibyl Vane are two things that I shall never forget. When I close my eyes, I hear them, and each of them says something different. I don't know which to follow. Why should I not love her? Harry, I do love her. She is everything to me in life. Night after night I go to see her play. One evening she is Rosalind, and the next evening she is Imogen. I have seen her die in the gloom of an Italian tomb, sucking the poison from her lover's lips. I have watched her wandering through the forest of Arden, disguised as a pretty boy in hose and doublet and dainty cap. She has been mad, and has come into the presence of a guilty king, and given him rue to wear, and bitter herbs to taste of. She has been innocent, and the black hands of jealousy have crushed her reed-like throat. I have seen her in every age and in every costume. Ordinary women never appeal to one's imagination. They are limited to their century. No glamour ever transfigures them. One knows their minds as easily as one knows their bonnets. One can always find them. There is no mystery in any of them. They ride in the Park in the morning, and chatter at tea-parties in the afternoon. They have their stereotyped smile, and their fashionable manner. They are quite obvious. But an actress! How different an actress is! Harry! why didn't you tell me that the only thing worth loving is an actress?'

'Because I have loved so many of them, Dorian.'

'Oh, yes, horrid people with dyed hair and painted faces.'

'Don't run down dyed hair and painted faces. There is an extraordinary charm in them, sometimes,' said Lord Henry.

'I wish now I had not told you about Sibyl Vane.'

'You could not have helped telling me, Dorian. All through your life you will tell me everything you do.'

'Yes, Harry, I believe that is true. I cannot help telling you things. You have a curious influence over me. If I ever did a crime, I would come and confess it to you. You would understand me.'

'People like you—the wilful sunbeams of life—don't commit crimes, Dorian. But I am much obliged for the compliment, all the same. And now tell me—reach me the matches, like a good boy: thanks—what are your actual relations with Sibyl Vane?'

Dorian Gray leaped to his feet, with flushed cheeks and burning eyes. 'Harry! Sibyl Vane is sacred!'

'It is only the sacred things that are worth touching, Dorian,' said Lord Henry, with a strange touch of pathos in his voice. 'But why should you be annoyed? I suppose she will belong to you some day. When one is in love, one always begins by deceiving one's self, and one always ends by deceiving others. That is what the world calls a romance. You know her, at any rate, I suppose?'

'Of course I know her. On the first night I was at the theatre, the horrid old Jew came round to the box after the performance was over, and offered to take me behind the scenes and introduce me to her. I was furious with him, and told him that Juliet had been dead for hundreds of years, and that her body was lying in a marble tomb in Verona. I think, from his blank look of amazement, that he was under the impression that I had taken too much champagne, or something.'

'I am not surprised.'

'Then he asked me if I wrote for any of the newspapers. I told him I never even read them. He seemed terribly disappointed at that, and confided to me that all the dramatic critics were in a conspiracy against him, and that they were every one of them to be bought.'

'I should not wonder if he was quite right there. But, on the other hand, judging from their appearance, most of them cannot be at all expensive.'

'Well, he seemed to think they were beyond his means,' laughed Dorian. 'By this time, however, the lights were being put out in the theatre, and I had to go. He wanted me to try some cigars that he strongly recommended. I declined. The next night, of course, I arrived at the place again. When he saw me he made me a low bow, and assured me that I was a munificent patron of art. He was a most offensive brute, though he had an extraordinary passion for Shakespeare. He told me once, with an air of pride, that his five bankruptcies were entirely due to "The Bard", as he insisted on calling him. He seemed to think it a distinction.'

'It was a distinction, my dear Dorian—a great distinction. Most people become bankrupt through having invested too heavily in the prose of life. To have ruined one's self over poetry is an honour. But when did you first speak to Miss Sibyl Vane?'

'The third night. She had been playing Rosalind. I could not help going round. I had thrown her some flowers, and she had looked at me; at least I fancied that she had. The old Jew was persistent. He seemed determined to take me behind, so I consented. It was curious my not wanting to know her, wasn't it?'

'No, I don't think so.'

'My dear Harry; why?'

'I will tell you some other time. Now I want to know about the girl.'

'Sibyl? Oh, she was so shy, and so gentle. There is something of a child about her. Her eyes opened wide in exquisite wonder when I told her what I thought of her performance, and she seemed quite unconscious of her power. I think we were both rather nervous. The old Jew stood grinning at the doorway of the dusty greenroom, making elaborate speeches about us both, while we stood looking at each other like children. He would insist on calling me "My Lord", so I had to assure Sibyl that I was not anything of the kind. She said quite simply to me, "You look more like a prince. I must call you Prince Charming."'

'Upon my word, Dorian, Miss Sibyl knows how to pay compliments.'

'You don't understand her, Harry. She regarded me merely as a person in a play. She knows nothing of life. She lives with her mother, a faded tired woman who played Lady Capulet in a sort of magenta dressing-wrapper on the first night, and looks as if she had seen better days.'

'I know that look. It depresses me,' murmured Lord Henry, examining his rings.

'The Jew wanted to tell me her history, but I said it did not interest me.'

'You were quite right. There is always something infinitely mean about other people's tragedies.'

'Sibyl is the only thing I care about. What is it to me where she came from? From her little head to her little feet, she is absolutely and entirely divine. Every night of my life I go to see her act, and every night she is more marvellous.'

'That is the reason, I suppose, that you never dine with me now. I thought you must have some curious romance on hand. You have; but it is not quite what I expected.'

'My dear Harry, we either lunch or sup together every day, and I have been to the Opera with you several times,' said Dorian, opening his blue eyes in wonder.

'You always come dreadfully late.'

'Well, I can't help going to see Sibyl play,' he cried, 'even if it is only for a single act. I get hungry for her presence; and when I think of the wonderful soul that is hidden away in that little ivory body, I am filled with awe.'

'You can dine with me tonight, Dorian, can't you?'

He shook his head. 'Tonight she is Imogen,' he answered, 'and tomorrow night she will be Juliet.'

'When is she Sibyl Vane?'

'Never.'

'I congratulate you.'

'How horrid you are! She is all the great heroines of the world in one. She is more than an individual. You laugh, but I tell you she has genius. I love her, and I must make her love me. You, who know all the secrets of life, tell me how to charm Sibyl Vane to love me! I want to make Romeo jealous. I want the dead lovers of the world to hear our laughter, and grow sad. I want a breath of our passion to stir their dust into consciousness, to wake their ashes into pain. My God, Harry, how I worship her!' He was walking up and down the room as he spoke. Hectic spots of red burned on his cheeks. He was terribly excited.

Lord Henry watched him with a subtle sense of pleasure. How different he was now from the shy, frightened boy he had met in Basil Hallward's studio! His nature had developed like a flower, had borne blossoms of scarlet flame. Out of its secret hiding-place had crept his Soul, and Desire had come to meet it on the way.

'And what do you propose to do?' said Lord Henry, at last.

'I want you and Basil to come with me some night and see her act. I have not the slightest fear of the result. You are certain to acknowledge her genius. Then we must get her out of the Jew's hands. She is bound to him for three years—at least for two years and eight months—from the present time. I shall have to pay him something, of course. When all that is settled, I shall take a West End theatre and bring her out properly. She will make the world as mad as she has made me.'

'That would be impossible, my dear boy!'

'Yes, she will. She has not merely art, consummate art-instinct, in her, but she has personality also; and you have often told me that it is personalities, not principles, that move the age.'

'Well, what night shall we go?'

'Let me see. Today is Tuesday. Let us fix tomorrow. She plays Juliet tomorrow.'

'All right. The Bristol at eight o'clock; and I will get Basil.'

'Not eight, Harry, please. Half-past six. We must be there before the curtain rises. You must see her in the first act, where she meets Romeo.'

'Half-past six! What an hour! It will be like having a meat-tea, or reading an English novel. It must be seven. No gentleman dines before seven. Shall you see Basil between this and then? Or shall I write to him?'

'Dear Basil! I have not laid eyes on him for a week. It is rather horrid of me, as he has sent me my portrait in the most wonderful frame, specially designed by himself, and, though I am a little jealous of the picture for being a whole month younger than I am, I must admit that I delight in it. Perhaps you had better write to him. I don't want to see him alone. He says things that annoy me. He gives me good advice.'

Lord Henry smiled. 'People are very fond of giving away what they need most themselves. It is what I call the depth of generosity.'

'Oh, Basil is the best of fellows, but he seems to me to be just a bit of a Philistine. Since I have known you, Harry, I have discovered that.'

'Basil, my dear boy, puts everything that is charming in himself into his work. The consequence is that he has nothing left for life but his prejudices, his principles, and his common sense. The only artists I have ever known, who are personally delightful, are bad artists. Good artists exist simply in what they make, and consequently are perfectly uninteresting in what they are. A great poet, a really great poet, is the most unpoetical of all creatures. But inferior poets are absolutely fascinating. The worse their rhymes are, the more picturesque they look. The mere fact of having published a book of second-rate sonnets makes a man quite irresistible. He lives the poetry that he cannot write. The others write the poetry that they dare not realize.'

'I wonder is that really so, Harry?' said Dorian Gray, putting some perfume on his handkerchief out of a large gold-topped bottle that stood on the table. 'It must be, if you say it. And now I am off. Imogen is waiting for me. Don't forget about tomorrow. Goodbye.'

As he left the room, Lord Henry's heavy eyelids drooped, and he began to think. Certainly few people had ever interested him so much as Dorian Gray, and yet the lad's mad adoration of some one else caused him not the slightest pang of annoyance or jealousy. He was pleased by it. It made him a more interesting study. He had been always enthralled by the methods of natural science, but the ordinary subject-matter of that science had seemed to him trivial and of no import. And so he had begun by vivisecting himself, as he had ended by vivisecting others. Human life—that appeared to him the one thing worth investigating. Compared to it there was nothing else of any value. It was true that as one watched life in its curious crucible of pain and pleasure, one could not wear over one's face a mask of glass, nor keep the sulphurous fumes from troubling the brain and making the imagination turbid with monstrous fancies and misshapen dreams. There were poisons so subtle that to know their properties one had to sicken of them. There were maladies so strange that one had to pass through them if one sought to understand their nature. And, yet, what a great reward one received! How wonderful the whole world became to one! To note the curious hard logic of passion, and the emotional coloured life of the intellect—to observe where they met, and where they separated, at what point they were in unison, and at what point they were at discord—there was a delight in that! What matter what the cost was? One could never pay too high a price for any sensation.

He was conscious—and the thought brought a gleam of pleasure into his brown agate eyes—that it was through certain words of his, musical words said with musical utterance, that Dorian Gray's soul had turned to this white girl and bowed in worship before her. To a large extent the lad was his own creation. He had made him premature. That was something. Ordinary people waited till life disclosed to them its secrets, but to the few, to the elect, the mysteries of life were revealed before the veil was drawn away. Sometimes this was the effect of art, and chiefly of the art of literature, which dealt immediately with the passions and the intellect. But now and then a complex personality took the place and assumed the office of art, was indeed, in its way, a real work of art, Life having its elaborate masterpieces, just as poetry has, or sculpture, or painting.

Yes, the lad was premature. He was gathering his harvest while it was yet spring. The pulse and passion of youth were in him, but he was becoming self-conscious. It was delightful to watch him. With his beautiful face, and his beautiful soul, he was a thing to wonder at. It was no matter how it all ended, or was destined to end. He was like one of those gracious figures in a pageant or a play, whose joys seem to be remote from one, but whose sorrows stir one's sense of beauty, and whose wounds are like red roses.

Soul and body, body and soul—how mysterious they were! There was animalism in the soul, and the body had its moments of spirituality. The senses could refine, and the intellect could degrade. Who could say where the fleshly impulse ceased, or the psychical impulse began? How shallow were the arbitrary definitions of ordinary psychologists! And yet how difficult to decide between the claims of the various schools! Was the soul a shadow seated in the house of sin? Or was the body really in the soul, as Giordano Bruno thought?° The separation of spirit from matter was a mystery, and the union of spirit with matter was a mystery also.

He began to wonder whether we could ever make psychology so absolute a science that each little spring of life would be revealed to us. As it was, we always misunderstood ourselves, and rarely understood others. Experience was of no ethical value. It was merely the name men gave to their mistakes. Moralists had, as a rule, regarded it as a mode of warning, had claimed for it a certain ethical efficacy in the formation of character, had praised it as something that taught us what to follow and showed us what to avoid. But there was no motive power in experience. It was as little of an active cause as conscience itself. All that it really demonstrated was that our future would be the same as our past, and that the sin we had done once, and with loathing, we would do many times, and with joy.

It was clear to him that the experimental method was the only method by which one could arrive at any scientific analysis of the passions; and certainly Dorian Gray was a subject made to his hand, and seemed to promise rich and fruitful results. His sudden mad love for Sibyl Vane was a psychological phenomenon of no small interest. There was no doubt that curiosity had much to do with it, curiosity and the desire for new experiences; yet it was not a simple but rather a very complex passion. What there was in it of the purely sensuous instinct of boyhood had been transformed by the workings of the imagination, changed into something that seemed to the lad himself to be remote from sense, and was for that very reason all the more dangerous. It was the passions about whose origin we deceived ourselves that tyrannized most strongly over us. Our weakest motives were those of whose nature we were conscious. It often happened that when we thought we were experimenting on others we were really experimenting on ourselves.

While Lord Henry sat dreaming on these things, a knock came to the door, and his valet entered, and reminded him it was time to dress for dinner. He got up and looked out into the street. The sunset had smitten into scarlet gold the upper windows of the houses opposite. The panes glowed like plates of heated metal. The sky above was like a faded rose. He thought of his friend's young fiery-coloured life, and wondered how it was all going to end.

When he arrived home, about half-past twelve o'clock, he saw a telegram lying on the hall table. He opened it, and found it was from Dorian Gray. It was to tell him that he was engaged to be married to Sibyl Vane.

CHAPTER V

'MOTHER, mother, I am so happy!' whispered the girl, burying her face in the lap of the faded, tired-looking woman who, with back turned to the shrill intrusive light, was sitting in the one arm-chair that their dingy sitting-room contained. 'I am so happy!' she repeated, 'and you must be happy too!'

Mrs Vane winced, and put her thin bismuth-whitened hands° on her daughter's head. 'Happy!' she echoed, 'I am only happy, Sibyl, when I see you act. You must not think of anything but your acting. Mr Isaacs has been very good to us, and we owe him money.'

The girl looked up and pouted. 'Money, mother?' she cried, 'what does money matter? Love is more than money.'

'Mr Isaacs has advanced us fifty pounds to pay off our debts, and to get a proper outfit for James. You must not forget that, Sibyl. Fifty pounds is a very large sum. Mr Isaacs has been most considerate.'

'He is not a gentleman, mother, and I hate the way he talks to me,' said the girl, rising to her feet, and going over to the window.

'I don't know how we could manage without him,' answered the elder woman, querulously.

Sibyl Vane tossed her head and laughed. 'We don't want him any more, mother. Prince Charming° rules life for us now.' Then she paused. A rose shook in her blood, and shadowed her cheeks. Quick breath parted the petals of her lips. They trembled. Some southern wind of passion swept over her, and stirred the dainty folds of her dress. 'I love him,' she said, simply.

'Foolish child! foolish child!' was the parrot-phrase flung in answer. The waving of crooked, false-jewelled fingers gave grotesqueness to the words.

The girl laughed again. The joy of a caged bird was in her voice. Her eyes caught the melody, and echoed it in radiance: then closed for a moment, as though to hide their secret. When they opened, the mist of a dream had passed across them.

Thin-lipped wisdom spoke at her from the worn chair, hinted at prudence, quoted from that book of cowardice whose author apes the name of common sense. She did not listen. She was free in her prison of passion. Her prince, Prince Charming, was with her. She had called on Memory to remake him. She had sent her soul to search for him, and it had brought him back. His kiss burned again upon her mouth. Her eyelids were warm with his breath.

Then Wisdom altered its method and spoke of espial and discovery. This young man might be rich. If so, marriage should be thought of. Against the shell of her ear broke the waves of worldly cunning. The arrows of craft shot by her. She saw the thin lips moving, and smiled.

Suddenly she felt the need to speak. The wordy silence troubled her. 'Mother, mother,' she cried, 'why does he love me so much? I know why I love him. I love him because he is like what Love himself should be. But what does he see in me? I am not worthy of him. And yet—why, I cannot tell—though I feel so much beneath him, I don't feel humble. I feel proud, terribly proud. Mother, did you love my father as I love Prince Charming?'

The elder woman grew pale beneath the coarse powder that daubed her cheeks, and her dry lips twitched with a spasm of pain. Sibyl rushed to her, flung her arms round her neck, and kissed her. 'Forgive me, mother. I know it pains you to talk about our father. But it only pains you because you loved him so much. Don't look so sad. I am as happy today as you were twenty years ago. Ah! let me be happy for ever!'

'My child, you are far too young to think of falling in love. Besides, what do you know of this young man? You don't even know his name. The whole thing is most inconvenient, and really, when James is going away to Australia, and I have so much to think of, I must say that you should have shown more consideration. However, as I said before, if he is rich . . .'

'Ah! mother, mother, let me be happy!'

Mrs Vane glanced at her, and with one of those false theatrical gestures that so often become a mode of second nature to a stage-player, clasped her in her arms. At this moment the door opened, and a young lad with rough brown hair came into the room. He was thick-set of figure, and his hands and feet were large, and somewhat clumsy in movement. He was not so finely bred as his sister. One would hardly have guessed the close relationship that existed between them. Mrs Vane fixed her eyes on him, and intensified her smile. She mentally elevated her son to the dignity of an audience. She felt sure that the *tableau* was interesting.

'You might keep some of your kisses for me, Sibyl, I think,' said the lad, with a good-natured grumble.

'Ah! but you don't like being kissed, Jim,' she cried. 'You are a dreadful old bear.' And she ran across the room and hugged him.

James Vane looked into his sister's face with tenderness. 'I want you to come out with me for a walk, Sibyl. I don't suppose I shall ever see this horrid London again. I am sure I don't want to.'

'My son, don't say such dreadful things,' murmured Mrs Vane, taking up a tawdry theatrical dress, with a sigh, and beginning to patch it. She felt a little disappointed that he had not joined the group. It would have increased the theatrical picturesqueness of the situation.

'Why not, mother? I mean it.'

'You pain me, my son. I trust you will return from Australia in a position of affluence. I believe there is no society of any kind in the Colonies, nothing that I would call society; so when you have made your fortune you must come back and assert yourself in London.'

'Society!' muttered the lad. 'I don't want to know anything about that. I should like to make some money to take you and Sibyl off the stage. I hate it.'

'Oh, Jim!' said Sibyl, laughing, 'how unkind of you! But are you really going for a walk with me? That will be nice! I was afraid you were going to say goodbye to some of your friends—to Tom Hardy, who gave you that hideous pipe, or Ned Langton, who makes fun of you for smoking it. It is very sweet of you to let me have your last afternoon. Where shall we go? Let us go to the Park.'

'I am too shabby,' he answered, frowning. 'Only swell people go to the Park.'

'Nonsense, Jim,' she whispered, stroking the sleeve of his coat.

He hesitated for a moment. 'Very well,' he said at last, 'but don't be too long dressing.' She danced out of the door. One could hear her singing as she ran upstairs. Her little feet pattered overhead.

He walked up and down the room two or three times. Then he turned to the still figure in the chair. 'Mother, are my things ready?' he asked.

'Quite ready, James,' she answered, keeping her eyes on her work. For some months past she had felt ill at ease when she was alone with this rough, stern son of hers. Her shallow secret nature was troubled when their eyes met. She used to wonder if he suspected anything. The silence, for he made no other observation, became intolerable to her. She began to complain. Women defend themselves by attacking, just as they attack by sudden and strange surrenders. 'I hope you will be contented, James, with your sea-faring life,' she said. 'You must remember that it is your own choice. You might have entered a solicitor's office. Solicitors are a very respectable class, and in the country often dine with the best families.'

'I hate offices, and I hate clerks,' he replied. 'But you are quite right. I have chosen my own life. All I say is, watch over Sibyl. Don't let her come to any harm. Mother, you must watch over her.'

'James, you really talk very strangely. Of course I watch over Sibyl.'

'I hear a gentleman comes every night to the theatre, and goes behind to talk to her. Is that right? What about that?'

'You are speaking about things you don't understand, James. In the profession we are accustomed to receive a great deal of most gratifying attention. I myself used to receive many bouquets at one time. That was when acting was really understood. As for Sibyl, I do not know at present whether her attachment is serious or not. But there is no doubt that the young man in question is a perfect gentleman. He is always most polite to me. Besides, he has the appearance of being rich, and the flowers he sends are lovely.'

'You don't know his name, though,' said the lad, harshly.

'No,' answered his mother, with a placid expression in her face. 'He has not yet revealed his real name. I think it is quite romantic of him. He is probably a member of the aristocracy.'

James Vane bit his lip. 'Watch over Sibyl, mother,' he cried, 'watch over her.'

'My son, you distress me very much. Sibyl is always under my special care. Of course, if this gentleman is wealthy, there is no reason why she should not contract an alliance with him. I trust he is one of the aristocracy. He has all the appearance of it, I must say. It might be a most brilliant marriage for Sibyl. They would make a charming couple. His good looks are really quite remarkable; everybody notices them.'

The lad muttered something to himself, and drummed on the window-pane with his coarse fingers. He had just turned round to say something, when the door opened, and Sibyl ran in.

'How serious you both are!' she cried. 'What is the matter?'

'Nothing,' he answered. 'I suppose one must be serious sometimes. Goodbye, mother; I will have my dinner at five o'clock. Everything is packed, except my shirts, so you need not trouble.'

'Goodbye, my son,' she answered, with a bow of strained stateliness.

She was extremely annoyed at the tone he had adopted with her, and there was something in his look that had made her feel afraid.

'Kiss me, mother,' said the girl. Her flower-like lips touched the withered cheek, and warmed its frost.

'My child! my child!' cried Mrs Vane, looking up to the ceiling in search of an imaginary gallery.

'Come, Sibyl,' said her brother, impatiently. He hated his mother's affectations.

They went out into the flickering wind-blown sunlight, and strolled down the dreary Euston Road. The passers-by glanced in wonder at the sullen, heavy youth, who, in coarse, ill-fitting clothes, was in the company of such a graceful, refined-looking girl. He was like a common gardener walking with a rose.

Jim frowned from time to time when he caught the inquisitive glance of some stranger. He had that dislike of being stared at which comes on geniuses late in life, and never leaves the commonplace. Sibyl, however, was quite unconscious of the effect she was producing. Her love was trembling in laughter on her lips. She was thinking of Prince Charming, and, that she might think of him all the more, she did not talk of him, but prattled on about the ship in which Jim was going to sail, about the gold he was certain to find, about the wonderful heiress whose life he was to save from the wicked, red-shirted bushrangers. For he was not to remain a sailor, or a super-cargo, or whatever he was going to be. Oh, no! A sailor's existence was dreadful. Fancy being cooped up in a horrid ship, with the hoarse, hump-backed waves trying to get in, and a black wind blowing the masts down, and tearing the sails into long screaming ribands! He was to leave the vessel at Melbourne, bid a polite goodbye to the captain, and go off at once to the gold-fields.° Before a week was over he was to come across a large nugget of pure gold, the largest nugget that had ever been discovered, and bring it down to the coast in a waggon guarded by six mounted policemen. The bushrangers were to attack them three times, and be defeated with immense slaughter. Or, no. He was not to go to the gold-fields at all. They were horrid places, where men got intoxicated, and shot each other in bar-rooms, and used bad language. He was to be a nice sheep-farmer, and one evening, as he was riding home, he was to see the beautiful heiress being carried off by a robber on a black horse, and give chase, and rescue her. Of course she would fall in love with him, and he with her, and they would get married, and come home, and live in an immense house in London. Yes, there were delightful things in store for him. But he must be very good, and not lose his temper, or spend his money foolishly. She was only a year older than he was, but she knew so much more of life. He must be sure, also, to write to her by every mail, and to say his prayers each night before he went to sleep. God was very good, and would watch over him. She would pray for him too, and in a few years he would come back quite rich and happy.

The lad listened sulkily to her, and made no answer. He was heart-sick at leaving home.

Yet it was not this alone that made him gloomy and morose. Inexperienced though he was, he had still a strong sense of the danger of Sibyl's position. This young dandy who was making love to her could mean her no good. He was a gentleman, and he hated him for that, hated him through some curious race-instinct for which he could not account, and which for that reason was all the more dominant within him. He was conscious also of the shallowness and vanity of his mother's nature, and in that saw infinite peril for Sibyl and Sibyl's happiness. Children begin by loving their parents; as they grow older they judge them; sometimes they forgive them.

His mother! He had something on his mind to ask of her, something that he had brooded on for many months of silence. A chance phrase that he had heard at the theatre, a whispered sneer that had reached his ears one night as he waited at the stage-door, had set loose a train of horrible thoughts. He remembered it as if it had been the lash of a hunting-crop across his face. His brows knit together into a wedge-like furrow, and with a twitch of pain he bit his under-lip.

'You are not listening to a word I am saying, Jim,' cried Sibyl, 'and I am making the most delightful plans for your future. Do say something.'

'What do you want me to say?'

'Oh! that you will be a good boy, and not forget us,' she answered, smiling at him.

He shrugged his shoulders. 'You are more likely to forget me, than I am to forget you, Sibyl.'

She flushed. 'What do you mean, Jim?' she asked.

'You have a new friend, I hear. Who is he? Why have you not told me about him? He means you no good.'

'Stop, Jim!' she exclaimed. 'You must not say anything against him. I love him.'

'Why, you don't even know his name,' answered the lad. 'Who is he? I have a right to know.'

'He is called Prince Charming. Don't you like the name. Oh! you silly boy! you should never forget it. If you only saw him, you would think him the most wonderful person in the world. Some day you will meet him: when you come back from Australia. You will like him so much. Everybody likes him, and I . . . love him. I wish you could come to the theatre tonight. He is going to be there, and I am to play Juliet. Oh! how I shall play it! Fancy, Jim, to be in love and play Juliet! To have him sitting there! To play for his delight! I am afraid I may frighten the company, frighten or enthrall them. To be in love is to surpass one's self. Poor dreadful Mr Isaacs will be shouting "genius" to his loafers at the bar. He has preached me as a dogma; tonight he will announce me as a revelation. I feel it. And it is all his, his only, Prince Charming, my wonderful lover, my god of graces. But I am poor beside him. Poor? What does that matter? When poverty creeps in at the door, love flies in through the window.° Our proverbs want re-writing. They were made in winter, and it is summer now; spring-time for me, I think, a very dance of blossoms in blue skies.'

'He is a gentleman,' said the lad, sullenly.

'A Prince!' she cried, musically. 'What more do you want?'

'He wants to enslave you.'

'I shudder at the thought of being free.'

'I want you to beware of him.'

'To see him is to worship him, to know him is to trust him.'

'Sibyl, you are mad about him.'

She laughed, and took his arm. 'You dear old Jim, you talk as if you were a hundred. Some day you will be in love yourself. Then you will know what it is. Don't look so sulky. Surely you should be glad to think that, though you are going away, you leave me happier than I have ever been before. Life has been hard for us both, terribly hard and difficult. But it will be different now. You are going to a new world, and I have found one. Here are two chairs; let us sit down and see the smart people go by.'

They took their seats amidst a crowd of watchers. The tulip-beds across the road flamed like throbbing rings of fire. A white dust, tremulous cloud of orris-root° it seemed, hung in the panting air. The brightly-coloured parasols danced and dipped like monstrous butterflies.

She made her brother talk of himself, his hopes, his prospects. He spoke slowly and with effort. They passed words to each other as players at a game pass counters. Sibyl felt oppressed. She could not communicate her joy. A faint smile curving that sullen mouth was all the echo she could win. After some time she became silent. Suddenly she caught a glimpse of golden hair and laughing lips, and in an open carriage with two ladies Dorian Gray drove past.

She started to her feet. 'There he is!' she cried.

'Who?' said Jim Vane.

'Prince Charming,' she answered, looking after the victoria.

He jumped up, and seized her roughly by the arm, 'Show him to me. Which is he? Point him out. I must see him!' he exclaimed; but at that moment the Duke of Berwick's four-in-hand came between, and when it had left the space clear, the carriage had swept out of the Park.

'He is gone,' murmured Sibyl, sadly. 'I wish you had seen him.'

'I wish I had, for as sure as there is a God in heaven, if he ever does you any wrong, I shall kill him.'

She looked at him in horror. He repeated his words. They cut the air like a dagger. The people round began to gape. A lady standing close to her tittered.

'Come away, Jim; come away,' she whispered. He followed her doggedly, as she passed through the crowd. He felt glad at what he had said.

When they reached the Achilles Statue° she turned round. There was pity in her eyes that became laughter on her lips. She shook her head at him. 'You are foolish, Jim, utterly foolish; a bad-tempered boy, that is all. How can you say such horrible things? You don't know what you are talking about. You are simply jealous and unkind. Ah! I wish you would fall in love. Love makes people good, and what you said was wicked.'

'I am sixteen,' he answered, 'and I know what I am about. Mother is no help to you. She doesn't understand how to look after you. I wish now that I was not going to Australia at all. I have a great mind to chuck the whole thing up. I would, if my articles hadn't been signed.'

'Oh, don't be so serious, Jim. You are like one of the heroes of those silly melodramas mother used to be so fond of acting in. I am not going to quarrel with you. I have seen him, and oh! to see him is perfect happiness. We won't quarrel. I know you would never harm any one I love, would you?'

'Not as long as you love him, I suppose,' was the sullen answer.

'I shall love him for ever!' she cried.

'And he?'

'For ever, too!'

'He had better.'

She shrank from him. Then she laughed and put her hand on his arm. He was merely a boy.

At the Marble Arch they hailed an omnibus, which left them close to their shabby home in the Euston Road. It was after five o'clock, and Sibyl had to lie down for a couple of hours before acting. Jim insisted that she should do so. He said that he would sooner part with her when their mother was not present. She would be sure to make a scene, and he detested scenes of every kind.

In Sybil's own room they parted. There was jealousy in the lad's heart, and a fierce, murderous hatred of the stranger who, as it seemed to him, had come between them. Yet, when her arms were flung round his neck, and her fingers strayed through his hair, he softened, and kissed her with real affection. There were tears in his eyes as he went downstairs.

His mother was waiting for him below. She grumbled at his unpunctuality, as he entered. He made no answer, but sat down to his meagre meal. The flies buzzed round the table, and crawled over the stained cloth. Through the rumble of omnibuses, and the clatter of street-cabs, he could hear the droning voice devouring each minute that was left to him.

After some time, he thrust away his plate, and put his head in his hands. He felt that he had a right to know. It should have been told to him before, if it was as he suspected. Leaden with fear, his mother watched him. Words dropped mechanically from her lips. A tattered lace handkerchief twitched in her fingers. When the clock struck six, he got up, and went to the door. Then he turned back, and looked at her. Their eyes met. In hers he saw a wild appeal for mercy. It enraged him.

'Mother, I have something to ask you,' he said. Her eyes wandered vaguely about the room. She made no answer. 'Tell me the truth. I have a right to know. Were you married to my father?'

She heaved a deep sigh. It was a sigh of relief. The terrible moment, the moment that night and day, for weeks and months, she had dreaded, had come at last, and yet she felt no terror. Indeed in some measure it was a disappointment to her. The vulgar directness of the question called for a direct answer. The situation had not been gradually led up to. It was crude. It reminded her of a bad rehearsal.

'No,' she answered, wondering at the harsh simplicity of life.

'My father was a scoundrel then!' cried the lad, clenching his fists.

She shook her head. 'I knew he was not free. We loved each other very much. If he had lived, he would have made provision for us. Don't speak against him, my son. He was your father, and a gentleman. Indeed he was highly connected.'

An oath broke from his lips. 'I don't care for myself,' he exclaimed, 'but don't let Sibyl . . . It is a gentleman, isn't it, who is in love with her, or says he is? Highly connected, too, I suppose.'

For a moment a hideous sense of humiliation came over the woman. Her head drooped. She wiped her eyes with shaking hands. 'Sibyl has a mother,' she murmured; 'I had none.'

The lad was touched. He went towards her, and stooping down he kissed her. 'I am sorry if I have pained you by asking about my father,' he said, 'but I could not help it. I must go now. Goodbye. Don't forget that you will have only one child now to look after, and believe me that if this man wrongs my sister, I will find out who he is, track him down, and kill him like a dog. I swear it.'

The exaggerated folly of the threat, the passionate gesture that accompanied it, the mad melodramatic words, made life seem more vivid to her. She was familiar with the atmosphere. She breathed more freely, and for the first time for many months she really admired her son. She would have liked to have continued the scene on the same emotional scale, but he cut her short. Trunks had to be carried down, and mufflers looked for. The lodging-house drudge bustled in and out. There was the bargaining with the cabman. The moment was lost in vulgar details. It was with a renewed feeling of disappointment that she waved the tattered lace handkerchief from the window, as her son drove away. She was conscious that a great opportunity had been wasted. She consoled herself by telling Sibyl how desolate she felt her life would be, now that she had only one child to look after. She remembered the phrase. It had pleased her. Of the threat she said nothing. It was vividly and dramatic-ally expressed. She felt that they would all laugh at it some day.

CHAPTER VI

'I SUPPOSE you have heard the news, Basil?' said Lord Henry that evening, as Hallward was shown into a little private room at the Bristol where dinner had been laid for three.

'No, Harry,' answered the artist, giving his hat and coat to the bowing waiter. 'What is it? Nothing about politics, I hope? They don't interest me. There is hardly a single person in the House of Commons worth painting; though many of them would be the better for a little whitewashing.'

'Dorian Gray is engaged to be married,' said Lord Henry, watching him as he spoke.

Hallward started, and then frowned. 'Dorian engaged to be married!' he cried. 'Impossible!'

'It is perfectly true.'

'To whom?'

'To some little actress or other.'

'I can't believe it. Dorian is far too sensible.'

'Dorian is far too wise not to do foolish things now and then, my dear Basil.'

'Marriage is hardly a thing that one can do now and then, Harry.'

'Except in America,' rejoined Lord Henry, languidly. 'But I didn't say he was married. I said he was engaged to be married. There is a great difference. I have a distinct remembrance of being married, but I have no recollection at all of being engaged. I am inclined to think that I never was engaged.'

'But think of Dorian's birth, and position, and wealth. It would be absurd for him to marry so much beneath him.'

'If you want to make him marry this girl tell him that, Basil. He is sure to do it, then. Whenever a man does a thoroughly stupid thing, it is always from the noblest motives.'

'I hope the girl is good, Harry. I don't want to see Dorian tied to some vile creature, who might degrade his nature and ruin his intellect.'

'Oh, she is better than good—she is beautiful,' murmured Lord Henry, sipping a glass of vermouth and orange-bitters. 'Dorian says she is beautiful; and he is not often wrong about things of that kind. Your portrait of him has quickened his appreciation of the personal appearance of other people. It has had that excellent effect, amongst others. We are to see her tonight, if that boy doesn't forget his appointment.'

'Are you serious?'

'Quite serious, Basil. I should be miserable if I thought I should ever be more serious than I am at the present moment.'

'But do you approve of it, Harry?' asked the painter, walking up and down the room, and biting his lip. 'You can't approve of it, possibly. It is some silly infatuation.'

'I never approve, or disapprove, of anything now. It is an absurd attitude to take towards life. We are not sent into the world to air our moral prejudices. I never take any notice of what common people say, and I never interfere with what charming people do. If a personality fascinates me, whatever mode of expression that personality selects is absolutely delightful to me. Dorian Gray falls in love with a beautiful girl who acts Juliet, and proposes to marry her. Why not? If he wedded Messalina° he would be none the less interesting. You know I am not a champion of marriage. The real drawback to marriage is that it makes one unselfish. And unselfish people are colourless. They lack individuality. Still, there are certain temperaments that marriage makes more complex. They retain their egotism, and add to it many other egos. They are forced to have more than one life. They become more highly organized, and to be highly organized is, I should fancy, the object of man's existence. Besides, every experience is of value, and, whatever one may say against marriage, it is certainly an experience. I hope that Dorian Gray will make this girl his wife, passionately adore her for six months, and then suddenly become fascinated by some one else. He would be a wonderful study.'

'You don't mean a single word of all that, Harry; you know you don't. If Dorian Gray's life were spoiled, no one would be sorrier than yourself. You are much better than you pretend to be.'

Lord Henry laughed. 'The reason we all like to think so well of others is that we are all afraid for ourselves. The basis of optimism is sheer terror. We think that we are generous because we credit our neighbour with the possession of those virtues that are likely to be a benefit to us. We praise the banker that we may overdraw our account, and find good qualities in the highwayman in the hope that he may spare our pockets. I mean everything that I have said. I have the greatest contempt for optimism. As for a spoiled life, no life is spoiled but one whose growth is arrested. If you want to mar a nature, you have merely to reform it. As for marriage, of course that would be silly, but there are other and more interesting bonds between men and women. I will certainly encourage them. They have the charm of being fashionable. But here is Dorian himself. He will tell you more than I can.'

'My dear Harry, my dear Basil, you must both congratulate me!' said the lad, throwing off his evening cape with its satin-lined wings, and shaking each of his friends by the hand in turn. 'I have never been so happy. Of course it is sudden: all really delightful things are. And yet it seems to me to be the one thing I have been looking for all my life.' He was flushed with excitement and pleasure, and looked extraordinarily handsome.

'I hope you will always be very happy, Dorian,' said Hallward, 'but I don't quite forgive you for not having let me know of your engagement. You let Harry know.'

'And I don't forgive you for being late for dinner,' broke in Lord Henry, putting his hand on the lad's shoulder, and smiling as he spoke. 'Come, let us sit down and try what the new *chef* here is like, and then you will tell us how it all came about.'

'There is really not much to tell,' cried Dorian, as they took their seats at the small round table. 'What happened was simply this. After I left you yesterday evening, Harry, I dressed, had some dinner at that little Italian restaurant in Rupert Street, you introduced me to, and went down at eight o'clock to the theatre. Sibyl was playing Rosalind.° Of course the scenery was dreadful, and the Orlando absurd. But Sibyl! You should have seen her! When she came on in her boy's clothes she was perfectly wonderful. She wore a moss-coloured velvet jerkin with cinnamon sleeves, slim brown cross-gartered hose, a dainty little green cap with a hawk's feather caught in a jewel, and a hooded cloak lined with dull red. She had never seemed to me more exquisite. She had all the delicate grace of that Tanagra figurine° that you have in your studio, Basil. Her hair clustered round her face like dark leaves round a pale rose. As for her acting—well, you shall see her tonight. She is simply a born artist. I sat in the dingy box absolutely enthralled. I forgot that I was in London and in the nineteenth century. I was away with my love in a forest that no man had ever seen. After the performance was over I went behind, and spoke to her. As we were sitting together, suddenly there came into her eyes a look that I had never seen there before. My lips moved towards hers. We kissed each other. I can't describe to you what I felt at that moment. It seemed to me that all my life had been narrowed to one perfect point of rose-coloured joy. She trembled all over, and shook like a white narcissus. Then she flung herself on her knees and kissed my hands. I feel that I should not tell you all this, but I can't help it. Of course our engagement is a dead secret. She has not even told her own mother. I don't know what my guardians will say. Lord Radley is sure to be furious. I don't care. I shall be of age in less than a year, and then I can do what I like. I have been right, Basil, haven't I, to take my love out of poetry, and to find my wife in Shakespeare's plays? Lips that Shakespeare taught to speak have whispered their secret in my ear. I have had the arms of Rosalind around me, and kissed Juliet on the mouth.'

'Yes, Dorian, I suppose you were right,' said Hallward, slowly.

'Have you seen her today?' asked Lord Henry.

Dorian Gray shook his head. 'I left her in the forest of Arden, I shall find her in an orchard in Verona.'

Lord Henry sipped his champagne in a meditative manner. 'At what particular point did you mention the word marriage, Dorian? And what did she say in answer? Perhaps you forgot all about it.'

'My dear Harry, I did not treat it as a business transaction, and I did not make any formal proposal. I told her that I loved her, and she said she was not worthy to be my wife. Not worthy! Why, the whole world is nothing to me compared with her.'

'Women are wonderfully practical,' murmured Lord Henry,—'much more practical than we are. In situations of that kind, we often forget to say anything about marriage, and they always remind us.'

Hallward laid his hand upon his arm. 'Don't Harry. You have annoyed Dorian. He is not like other men. He would never bring misery upon any one. His nature is too fine for that.'

Lord Henry looked across the table. 'Dorian is never annoyed with me,' he answered. 'I asked the question for the best reason possible, for the only reason, indeed, that excuses one for asking any question— simple curiosity. I have a theory that it is always the women who propose to us, and not we who propose to the women. Except, of course, in middle-class life. But then the middle classes are not modern.'

Dorian Gray laughed, and tossed his head. 'You are quite incorrigible, Harry; but I don't mind. It is impossible to be angry with you. When you see Sybil Vane you will feel that the man who could wrong her would be a beast, a beast without a heart. I cannot understand how any one can wish to shame the thing he loves.° I love Sibyl Vane. I want to place her on a pedestal of gold, and to see the world worship the woman who is mine. What is marriage? An irrevocable vow. You mock at it for that. Ah! don't mock. It is an irrevocable vow that I want to take. Her trust makes me faithful, her belief makes me good. When I am with her, I regret all that you have taught me. I become different from what you have known me to be. I am changed, and the mere touch of Sibyl Vane's hand makes me forget you and all your wrong, fascinating, poisonous, delightful theories.'

'And those are . . .?' asked Lord Henry, helping himself to some salad.

'Oh, your theories about life, your theories about love, your theories about pleasure. All your theories, in fact, Harry.'

'Pleasure is the only thing worth having a theory about,' he answered, in his slow, melodious voice. 'But I am afraid I cannot claim my theory as my own. It belongs to Nature, not to me. Pleasure is Nature's test, her sign of approval. When we are happy we are always good, but when we are good we are not always happy.'

'Ah, but what do you mean by good?' cried Basil Hallward.

'Yes,' echoed Dorian, leaning back in his chair, and looking at Lord Henry over the heavy clusters of purple-lipped irises that stood in the centre of the table, 'what do you mean by good, Harry?'

'To be good is to be in harmony with one's self,' he replied, touching the thin stem of his glass with his pale, fine-pointed fingers. 'Discord is to be forced to be in harmony with others. One's own life—that is the important thing. As for the lives of one's neighbours, if one wishes to be a prig or a Puritan, one can flaunt one's moral views about them, but they are not one's concern. Besides, Individualism has really the higher aim. Modern morality consists in accepting the standard of one's age. I consider that for any man of culture to accept the standard of his age is a form of the grossest immorality.'

'But, surely, if one lives merely for one's self, Harry, one pays a terrible price for doing so?' suggested the painter.

'Yes, we are overcharged for everything nowadays. I should fancy that the real tragedy of the poor is that they can afford nothing but self-denial. Beautiful sins, like beautiful things, are the privilege of the rich.'

'One has to pay in other ways but money.'

'What sort of ways, Basil?'

'Oh! I should fancy in remorse, in suffering, in . . . well, in the consciousness of degradation.'

Lord Henry shrugged his shoulders. 'My dear fellow, mediæval art is charming, but mediæval emotions are out of date. One can use them in fiction, of course. But then the only things that one can use in fiction are the things that one has ceased to use in fact. Believe me, no civilized man ever regrets a pleasure, and no uncivilized man ever knows what a pleasure is.'

'I know what pleasure is,' cried Dorian Gray. 'It is to adore some one.'

'That is certainly better than being adored,' he answered, toying with some fruits. 'Being adored is a nuisance. Women treat us just as Humanity treats its gods. They worship us, and are always bothering us to do something for them.'

'I should have said that whatever they ask for they had first given to us,' murmured the lad, gravely. 'They create Love in our natures. They have a right to demand it back.'

'That is quite true, Dorian,' cried Hallward.

'Nothing is ever quite true,' said Lord Henry.

'This is,' interrupted Dorian. 'You must admit, Harry, that women give to men the very gold of their lives.'

'Possibly,' he sighed, 'but they invariably want it back in such very small change. That is the worry. Women, as some witty Frenchman once put it, inspire us with the desire to do masterpieces, and always prevent us from carrying them out.'

'Harry, you are dreadful! I don't know why I like you so much.'

'You will always like me, Dorian,' he replied. 'Will you have some coffee, you fellows?—Waiter, bring coffee, and *fine-champagne*,° and some cigarettes. No: don't mind the cigarettes; I have some. Basil, I can't allow you to smoke cigars. You must have a cigarette. A cigarette is the perfect type of a perfect pleasure. It is exquisite, and it leaves one unsatisfied. What more can one want? Yes, Dorian, you will always be fond of me. I represent to you all the sins you have never had the courage to commit.'

'What nonsense you talk, Harry!' cried the lad, taking a light from a fire-breathing silver dragon that the waiter had placed on the table. 'Let us go down to the theatre. When Sibyl comes on the stage you will have a new ideal of life. She will represent something to you that you have never known.'

'I have known everything,' said Lord Henry, with a tired look in his eyes, 'but I am always ready for a new emotion. I am afraid, however, that, for me at any rate, there is no such thing. Still, your wonderful girl may thrill me. I love acting. It is so much more real than life. Let us go. Dorian, you will come with me. I am so sorry, Basil, but there is only room for two in the brougham.° You must follow us in a hansom.'°

They got up and put on their coats, sipping their coffee standing. The painter was silent and preoccupied. There was a gloom over him. He could not bear this marriage, and yet it seemed to him to be better than many other things that might have happened. After a few minutes, they all passed downstairs. He drove off by himself, as had been arranged, and watched the flashing lights of the little brougham in front of him. A strange sense of loss came over him. He felt that Dorian Gray would never again be to him all that he had been in the past. Life had come between them. . . . His eyes darkened, and the crowded, flaring streets became blurred to his eyes. When the cab drew up at the theatre, it seemed to him that he had grown years older.

CHAPTER VII

FOR some reason or other, the house was crowded that night, and the fat Jew manager who met them at the door was beaming from ear to ear with an oily, tremulous smile. He escorted them to their box with a sort of pompous humility, waving his fat jewelled hands, and talking at the top of his voice. Dorian Gray loathed him more than ever. He felt as if he had come to look for Miranda and had been met by Caliban. Lord Henry, upon the other hand, rather liked him. At least he declared he did, and insisted on shaking him by the hand, and assuring him that he was proud to meet a man who had discovered a real genius and gone bankrupt over a poet. Hallward amused himself with watching the faces in the pit. The heat was terribly oppressive, and the huge sunlight flamed like a monstrous dahlia with petals of yellow fire. The youths in the gallery had taken off their coats and waistcoats and hung them over the side. They talked to each other across the theatre, and shared their oranges with the tawdry girls who sat beside them. Some women were laughing in the pit. Their voices were horribly shrill and discordant. The sound of the popping of corks came from the bar.

'What a place to find one's divinity in!' said Lord Henry.

'Yes!' answered Dorian Gray. 'It was here I found her, and she is divine beyond all living things. When she acts you will forget everything. These common, rough people, with their coarse faces and brutal gestures, become quite different when she is on the stage. They sit silently and watch her. They weep and laugh as she wills them to do. She makes them as responsive as a violin. She spiritualizes them, and one feels that they are of the same flesh and blood as one's self.'

'The same flesh and blood as one's self! Oh, I hope not!' exclaimed Lord Henry, who was scanning the occupants of the gallery through his opera-glass.

'Don't pay any attention to him, Dorian,' said the painter. 'I understand what you mean, and I believe in this girl. Any one you love must be marvellous, and any girl that has the effect you describe must be fine and noble. To spiritualize one's age—that is something worth doing. If this girl can give a soul to those who have lived without one, if she can create the sense of beauty in people whose lives have been sordid and ugly, if she can strip them of their selfishness and lend them tears for sorrows that are not their own, she is worthy of all your adoration, worthy of the adoration of the world. This marriage is quite right. I did not think so at first, but I admit it now. The gods made Sibyl Vane for you. Without her you would have been incomplete.'

'Thanks, Basil,' answered Dorian Gray, pressing his hand. 'I knew that you would understand me. Harry is so cynical, he terrifies me. But here is the orchestra. It is quite dreadful, but it only lasts for about five minutes. Then the curtain rises, and you will see the girl to whom I am going to give all my life, to whom I have given everything that is good in me.'

A quarter of an hour afterwards, amidst an extraordinary turmoil of applause, Sibyl Vane stepped on to the stage. Yes, she was certainly lovely to look at—one of the loveliest creatures, Lord Henry thought, that he had ever seen. There was something of the fawn in her shy grace and startled eyes. A faint blush, like the shadow of a rose in a mirror of silver, came to her cheeks as she glanced at the crowded, enthusiastic house. She stepped back a few paces, and her lips seemed to tremble. Basil Hallward leaped to his feet and began to applaud. Motionless, and as one in a dream, sat Dorian Gray, gazing at her. Lord Henry peered through his glasses, murmuring, 'Charming! charming!'

The scene was the hall of Capulet's house, and Romeo in his pilgrim's dress had entered with Mercutio and his other friends. The band, such as it was, struck up a few bars of music, and the dance began. Through the crowd of ungainly, shabbily-dressed actors, Sibyl Vane moved like a creature from a finer world. Her body swayed, while she danced, as a plant sways in the water. The curves of her throat were the curves of a white lily. Her hands seemed to be made of cool ivory.

Yet she was curiously listless. She showed no sign of joy when her eyes rested on Romeo. The few words she had to speak—

> Good pilgrim, you do wrong your hand too much,
> Which mannerly devotion shows in this;
> For saints have hands that pilgrims' hands do touch,
> And palm to palm is holy palmers' kiss—°

with the brief dialogue that follows, were spoken in a thoroughly artificial manner. The voice was exquisite, but from the point of view of tone it was absolutely false. It was wrong in colour. It took away all the life from the verse. It made the passion unreal.

Dorian Gray grew pale as he watched her. He was puzzled and anxious. Neither of his friends dared to say anything to him. She seemed to them to be absolutely incompetent. They were horribly disappointed.

Yet they felt that the true test of any Juliet is the balcony scene of the second act. They waited for that. If she failed there, there was nothing in her.

She looked charming as she came out in the moonlight. That could not be denied. But the staginess of her acting was unbearable, and grew worse as she went on. Her gestures became absurdly artificial. She over-emphasized everything that she had to say. The beautiful passage—

> *Thou knowest the mask of night is on my face,*
> *Else would a maiden blush bepaint my cheek*
> *For that which thou hast heard me speak tonight—*°

was declaimed with the painful precision of a school-girl who has been taught to recite by some second-rate professor of elocution. When she leaned over the balcony and came to those wonderful lines—

> *Although I joy in thee,*
> *I have no joy of this contract tonight:*
> *It is too rash, too unadvised, too sudden;*
> *Too like the lightning, which doth cease to be*
> *Ere one can say, 'It lightens.' Sweet, good-night!*
> *This bud of love by summer's ripening breath*
> *May prove a beauteous flower when next we meet—*°

she spoke the words as though they conveyed no meaning to her. It was not nervousness. Indeed, so far from being nervous, she was absolutely self-contained. It was simply bad art. She was a complete failure.

Even the common, uneducated audience of the pit and gallery lost their interest in the play. They got restless, and began to talk loudly and to whistle. The Jew manager, who was standing at the back of the dress-circle, stamped and swore with rage. The only person unmoved was the girl herself.

When the second act was over there came a storm of hisses, and Lord Henry got up from his chair and put on his coat. 'She is quite beautiful, Dorian,' he said, 'but she can't act. Let us go.'

'I am going to see the play through,' answered the lad, in a hard, bitter voice. 'I am awfully sorry that I have made you waste an evening, Harry. I apologize to you both.'

'My dear Dorian, I should think Miss Vane was ill,' interrupted Hallward. 'We will come some other night.'

'I wish she were ill,' he rejoined. 'But she seems to me to be simply callous and cold. She has entirely altered. Last night she was a great artist. This evening she is merely a commonplace, mediocre actress.'

'Don't talk like that about any one you love, Dorian. Love is a more wonderful thing than Art.'

'They are both simply forms of imitation,' remarked Lord Henry. 'But do let us go. Dorian, you must not stay here any longer. It is not good for one's morals to see bad acting. Besides, I don't suppose you will want your wife to act. So what does it matter if she plays Juliet like a wooden doll? She is very lovely, and if she knows as little about life as she does about acting, she will be a delightful experience. There are only two kinds of people who are really fascinating—people who know absolutely everything, and people who know absolutely nothing.° Good heavens, my dear boy, don't look so tragic! The secret of remaining young is never to have an emotion that is unbecoming. Come to the club with Basil and myself. We will smoke cigarettes and drink to the beauty of Sibyl Vane. She is beautiful. What more can you want?'

'Go away, Harry,' cried the lad. 'I want to be alone. Basil, you must go. Ah! can't you see that my heart is breaking?' The hot tears came to his eyes. His lips trembled, and, rushing to the back of the box, he leaned up against the wall, hiding his face in his hands.

'Let us go, Basil,' said Lord Henry, with a strange tenderness in his voice; and the two young men passed out together.

A few moments afterwards the footlights flared up, and the curtain rose on the third act. Dorian Gray went back to his seat. He looked pale, and proud, and indifferent. The play dragged on, and seemed interminable. Half of the audience went out, tramping in heavy boots, and laughing. The whole thing was a *fiasco*. The last act was played to almost empty benches. The curtain went down on a titter, and some groans.

As soon as it was over, Dorian Gray rushed behind the scenes into the greenroom. The girl was standing there alone, with a look of triumph on her face. Her eyes were lit with an exquisite fire. There was a radiance about her. Her parted lips were smiling over some secret of their own.

When he entered, she looked at him, and an expression of infinite joy came over her. 'How badly I acted tonight, Dorian!' she cried.

'Horribly!' he answered, gazing at her in amazement—'horribly! It was dreadful. Are you ill? You have no idea what it was. You have no idea what I suffered.'

The girl smiled. 'Dorian,' she answered, lingering over his name with long-drawn music in her voice, as though it were sweeter than honey to the red petals of her mouth—'Dorian, you should have understood. But you understand now, don't you?'

'Understand what?' he asked, angrily.

'Why I was so bad tonight. Why I shall always be bad. Why I shall never act well again.'

He shrugged his shoulders. 'You are ill, I suppose. When you are ill you shouldn't act. You make yourself ridiculous. My friends were bored. I was bored.'

She seemed not to listen to him. She was transfigured with joy. An ecstasy of happiness dominated her.

'Dorian, Dorian,' she cried, 'before I knew you, acting was the one reality of my life. It was only in the theatre that I lived. I thought that it was all true. I was Rosalind one night, and Portia the other. The joy of Beatrice was my joy, and the sorrows of Cordelia were mine also. I believed in everything. The common people who acted with me seemed to me to be godlike. The painted scenes were my world. I knew nothing but shadows, and I thought them real. You came—oh, my beautiful love!—and you freed my soul from prison. You taught me what reality really is. Tonight, for the first time in my life, I saw through the hollowness, the sham, the silliness of the empty pageant in which I had always played. Tonight, for the first time, I became conscious that the Romeo was hideous, and old, and painted, that the moonlight in the orchard was false, that the scenery was vulgar, and that the words I had to speak were unreal, were not my words, were not what I wanted to say. You had brought me something higher, something of which all art is but a reflection. You had made me understand what love really is. My love! my love! Prince Charming! Prince of life! I have grown sick of shadows.° You are more to me than all art can ever be. What have I to do with the puppets of a play? When I came on tonight, I could not understand how it was that everything had gone from me. I thought that I was going to be wonderful. I found that I could do nothing. Suddenly it dawned on my soul what it all meant. The knowledge was exquisite to me. I heard them hissing, and I smiled. What could they know of love such as ours? Take me away, Dorian—take me away with you, where we can be quite alone. I hate the stage. I might mimic a passion that I do not feel, but I cannot mimic one that burns me like fire. Oh, Dorian, Dorian, you understand now what it signifies? Even if I could do it, it would be profanation for me to play at being in love. You have made me see that.'

He flung himself down on the sofa, and turned away his face. 'You have killed my love,' he muttered.

She looked at him in wonder, and laughed. He made no answer. She came across to him, and with her little fingers stroked his hair. She knelt down and pressed his hands to her lips. He drew them away, and a shudder ran through him.

Then he leaped up, and went to the door. 'Yes,' he cried, 'you have killed my love. You used to stir my imagination. Now you don't even stir my curiosity. You simply produce no effect. I loved you because you were marvellous, because you had genius and intellect, because you realized the dreams of great poets and gave shape and substance to the shadows

of art. You have thrown it all away. You are shallow and stupid. My God!
how mad I was to love you! What a fool I have been! You are nothing to
me now. I will never see you again. I will never think of you. I will never
mention your name. You don't know what you were to me, once. Why,
once . . . Oh, I can't bear to think of it! I wish I had never laid eyes upon
you! You have spoiled the romance of my life. How little you can know of
love, if you say it mars your art! Without your art you are nothing. I would
have made you famous, splendid, magnificent. The world would have
worshipped you, and you would have borne my name. What are you now?
A third-rate actress with a pretty face.'

The girl grew white, and trembled. She clenched her hands together,
and her voice seemed to catch in her throat. 'You are not serious,
Dorian?' she murmured. 'You are acting.'

'Acting! I leave that to you. You do it so well,' he answered, bitterly.

She rose from her knees, and, with a piteous expression of pain in
her face, came across the room to him. She put her hand upon his
arm, and looked into his eyes. He thrust her back. 'Don't touch me!'
he cried.

A low moan broke from her, and she flung herself at his feet, and lay
there like a trampled flower. 'Dorian, Dorian, don't leave me!' she
whispered. 'I am so sorry I didn't act well. I was thinking of you all the
time. But I will try—indeed, I will try. It came so suddenly across me, my
love for you. I think I should never have known it if you had not kissed
me—if we had not kissed each other. Kiss me again, my love. Don't go
away from me. I couldn't bear it. Oh! don't go away from me. My brother
. . . No; never mind. He didn't mean it. He was in jest. . . . But you, oh!
can't you forgive me for tonight? I will work so hard, and try to improve.
Don't be cruel to me because I love you better than anything in the world.
After all, it is only once that I have not pleased you. But you are quite
right, Dorian. I should have shown myself more of an artist. It was foolish
of me; and yet I couldn't help it. Oh, don't leave me, don't leave me.' A fit
of passionate sobbing choked her. She crouched on the floor like a
wounded thing, and Dorian Gray, with his beautiful eyes, looked down at
her, and his chiselled lips curled in exquisite disdain. There is always
something ridiculous about the emotions of people whom one has ceased
to love. Sibyl Vane seemed to him to be absurdly melodramatic. Her
tears and sobs annoyed him.

'I am going,' he said at last, in his calm, clear voice. 'I don't wish to be
unkind, but I can't see you again. You have disappointed me.'

She wept silently, and made no answer, but crept nearer. Her little
hands stretched blindly out, and appeared to be seeking for him. He

turned on his heel, and left the room. In a few moments he was out of the theatre.

Where he went to he hardly knew. He remembered wandering through dimly-lit streets, past gaunt black-shadowed archways and evil-looking houses. Women with hoarse voices and harsh laughter had called after him. Drunkards had reeled by cursing, and chattering to themselves like monstrous apes. He had seen grotesque children huddled upon doorsteps, and heard shrieks and oaths from gloomy courts.

As the dawn was just breaking he found himself close to Covent Garden.° The darkness lifted, and, flushed with faint fires, the sky hollowed itself into a perfect pearl. Huge carts filled with nodding lilies rumbled slowly down the polished empty street. The air was heavy with the perfume of the flowers, and their beauty seemed to bring him an anodyne for his pain. He followed into the market, and watched the men unloading their waggons. A white-smocked carter offered him some cherries. He thanked him, wondered why he refused to accept any money for them, and began to eat them listlessly. They had been plucked at midnight, and the coldness of the moon had entered into them. A long line of boys carrying crates of striped tulips, and of yellow and red roses, defiled in front of him, threading their way through the huge jade-green piles of vegetables. Under the portico, with its grey sun-bleached pillars, loitered a troop of draggled bareheaded girls, waiting for the auction to be over. Others crowded round the swinging doors of the coffee-house in the Piazza. The heavy cart-horses slipped and stamped upon the rough stones, shaking their bells and trappings. Some of the drivers were lying asleep on a pile of sacks. Iris-necked, and pink-footed, the pigeons ran about picking up seeds.

After a little while, he hailed a hansom, and drove home. For a few moments he loitered upon the doorstep, looking round at the silent Square with its blank close-shuttered windows, and its staring blinds. The sky was pure opal now, and the roofs of the houses glistened like silver against it. From some chimney opposite a thin wreath of smoke was rising. It curled, a violet riband, through the nacre-coloured air.

In the huge gilt Venetian lantern, spoil of some Doge's barge, that hung from the ceiling of the great oak-panelled hall of entrance, lights were still burning from three flickering jets: thin blue petals of flame they seemed, rimmed with white fire. He turned them out, and, having thrown his hat and cape on the table, passed through the library towards the door of his bedroom, a large octagonal chamber on the ground floor that, in his new-born feeling for luxury, he had just had decorated for himself, and hung with some curious Renaissance tapestries that had been discovered stored in a disused attic at Selby Royal. As he was turning the handle of the door, his eye fell upon the portrait Basil Hallward had painted of him. He started back as if in surprise. Then he went on into his own room, looking somewhat puzzled. After he had taken the buttonhole out of his coat, he seemed to hesitate. Finally he came back, went over to the picture, and examined it. In the dim arrested light that struggled through the cream-coloured silk blinds, the face appeared to him to be a little changed. The expression looked different. One would have said that there was a touch of cruelty in the mouth. It was certainly strange.

He turned round, and, walking to the window, drew up the blind. The bright dawn flooded the room, and swept the fantastic shadows into dusky corners, where they lay shuddering. But the strange expression that he had noticed in the face of the portrait seemed to linger there, to be more intensified even. The quivering, ardent sunlight showed him the lines of cruelty round the mouth as clearly as if he had been looking into a mirror after he had done some dreadful thing.

He winced, and, taking up from the table an oval glass framed in ivory Cupids, one of Lord Henry's many presents to him, glanced hurriedly into its polished depths. No line like that warped his red lips. What did it mean?

He rubbed his eyes, and came close to the picture, and examined it again. There were no signs of any change when he looked into the actual painting, and yet there was no doubt that the whole expression had altered. It was not a mere fancy of his own. The thing was horribly apparent.

He threw himself into a chair, and began to think. Suddenly there flashed across his mind what he had said in Basil Hallward's studio the day the picture had been finished. Yes, he remembered it perfectly. He had uttered a mad wish that he himself might remain young, and the portrait grow old; that his own beauty might be untarnished, and the face on the canvas bear the burden of his passions and his sins; that the painted image might be seared with the lines of suffering and thought, and that he might keep all the delicate bloom and loveliness of his then just conscious boyhood. Surely his wish had not been fulfilled? Such things were impossible. It seemed monstrous even to think of them. And, yet, there was the picture before him, with the touch of cruelty in the mouth.

Cruelty! Had he been cruel? It was the girl's fault, not his. He had dreamed of her as a great artist, had given his love to her because he had thought her great. Then she had disappointed him. She had been shallow and unworthy. And, yet, a feeling of infinite regret came over him, as he thought of her lying at his feet sobbing like a little child. He remembered with what callousness he had watched her. Why had he been made like that? Why had such a soul been given to him? But he had suffered also. During the three terrible hours that the play had lasted, he had lived centuries of pain, æon upon æon of torture. His life was well worth hers. She had marred him for a moment, if he had wounded her for an age. Besides, women were better suited to bear sorrow than men. They lived on their emotions. They only thought of their emotions. When they took lovers, it was merely to have some one with whom they could have scenes. Lord Henry had told him that, and Lord Henry knew what women were. Why should he trouble about Sibyl Vane? She was nothing to him now.

But the picture? What was he to say of that? It held the secret of his life, and told his story. It had taught him to love his own beauty. Would it teach him to loathe his own soul? Would he ever look at it again?

No; it was merely an illusion wrought on the troubled senses. The horrible night that he had passed had left phantoms behind it. Suddenly there had fallen upon his brain that tiny scarlet speck that makes men mad. The picture had not changed. It was folly to think so.

Yet it was watching him, with its beautiful marred face and its cruel smile. Its bright hair gleamed in the early sunlight. Its blue eyes met his own. A sense of infinite pity, not for himself, but for the painted image of himself, came over him. It had altered already, and would alter more. Its gold would wither into grey. Its red and white roses would die. For every sin that he committed, a stain would fleck and wreck its fairness. But he would not sin. The picture, changed or unchanged, would be to him the visible emblem of conscience. He would resist temptation. He would not see Lord Henry any more—would not, at any rate, listen to those subtle poisonous theories that in Basil Hallward's garden had first stirred within him the passion for impossible things.° He would go back to Sibyl Vane, make her amends, marry her, try to love her again. Yes, it was his duty to do so. She must have suffered more than he had. Poor child! He had been selfish and cruel to her. The fascination that she had exercised over him would return. They would be happy together. His life with her would be beautiful and pure.

He got up from his chair, and drew a large screen right in front of the portrait, shuddering as he glanced at it. 'How horrible!' he murmured to himself, and he walked across to the window and opened it. When he stepped out on to the grass, he drew a deep breath. The fresh morning air seemed to drive away all his sombre passions. He thought only of

Sibyl. A faint echo of his love came back to him. He repeated her name over and over again. The birds that were singing in the dew-drenched garden seemed to be telling the flowers about her.

CHAPTER VIII

IT was long past noon when he awoke. His valet had crept several times on tiptoe into the room to see if he was stirring, and had wondered what made his young master sleep so late. Finally his bell sounded, and Victor came in softly with a cup of tea, and a pile of letters, on a small tray of old Sèvres china, and drew back the olive-satin curtains, with their shimmering blue lining, that hung in front of the three tall windows.

'Monsieur has well slept this morning,' he said, smiling.

'What o'clock is it, Victor?' asked Dorian Gray, drowsily.

'One hour and a quarter, Monsieur.'

How late it was! He sat up, and, having sipped some tea, turned over his letters. One of them was from Lord Henry, and had been brought by hand that morning. He hesitated for a moment, and then put it aside. The others he opened listlessly. They contained the usual collection of cards, invitations to dinner, tickets for private views, programmes of charity concerts, and the like, that are showered on fashionable young men every morning during the season. There was a rather heavy bill, for a chased silver Louis-Quinze toilet-set, that he had not yet had the courage to send on to his guardians, who were extremely old-fashioned people and did not realize that we live in an age when unnecessary things are our only necessities; and there were several very courteously worded communications from Jermyn Street moneylenders offering to advance any sum of money at a moment's notice and at the most reasonable rates of interest.

After about ten minutes he got up, and, throwing on an elaborate dressing-gown of silk-embroidered cashmere wool, passed into the onyx-paved bath-room. The cool water refreshed him after his long sleep. He seemed to have forgotten all that he had gone through. A dim sense of having taken part in some strange tragedy came to him once or twice, but there was the unreality of a dream about it.

As soon as he was dressed, he went into the library and sat down to a light French breakfast, that had been laid out for him on a small round table close to the open window. It was an exquisite day. The warm air seemed laden with spices. A bee flew in, and buzzed round the blue-dragon bowl that, filled with sulphur-yellow roses, stood before him. He felt perfectly happy.

Suddenly his eye fell on the screen that he had placed in front of the portrait, and he started.

'Too cold for Monsieur?' asked his valet, putting an omelette on the table. 'I shut the window?'

Dorian shook his head. 'I am not cold,' he murmured.

Was it all true? Had the portrait really changed? Or had it been simply his own imagination that had made him see a look of evil where there had been a look of joy? Surely a painted canvas could not alter? The thing was absurd. It would serve as a tale to tell Basil some day. It would make him smile.

And, yet, how vivid was his recollection of the whole thing! First in the dim twilight, and then in the bright dawn, he had seen the touch of cruelty round the warped lips. He almost dreaded his valet leaving the room. He knew that when he was alone he would have to examine the portrait. He was afraid of certainty. When the coffee and cigarettes had been brought and the man turned to go, he felt a wild desire to tell him to remain. As the door was closing behind him he called him back. The man stood waiting for his orders. Dorian looked at him for a moment. 'I am not at home to any one, Victor,' he said, with a sigh. The man bowed and retired.

Then he rose from the table, lit a cigarette, and flung himself down on a luxuriously-cushioned couch that stood facing the screen. The screen was an old one, of gilt Spanish leather, stamped and wrought with a rather florid Louis-Quatorze pattern. He scanned it curiously, wondering if ever before it had concealed the secret of a man's life.

Should he move it aside, after all? Why not let it stay there? What was the use of knowing? If the thing was true, it was terrible. If it was not true, why trouble about it? But what if, by some fate or deadlier chance, eyes other than his spied behind, and saw the horrible change? What should he do if Basil Hallward came and asked to look at his own picture? Basil would be sure to do that. No; the thing had to be examined, and at once. Anything would be better than this dreadful state of doubt.

He got up, and locked both doors. At least he would be alone when he looked upon the mask of his shame. Then he drew the screen aside, and saw himself face to face. It was perfectly true. The portrait had altered.

As he often remembered afterwards, and always with no small wonder, he found himself at first gazing at the portrait with a feeling of almost scientific interest. That such a change should have taken place was incredible to him. And yet it was a fact. Was there some subtle affinity between the chemical atoms, that shaped themselves into form and colour on the canvas, and the soul that was within him? Could it be that what that soul thought, they realized?—that what it dreamed, they made true? Or was there some other, more terrible reason? He shuddered, and felt afraid, and, going back to the couch, lay there, gazing at the picture in sickened horror.

One thing, however, he felt that it had done for him. It had made him conscious how unjust, how cruel, he had been to Sibyl Vane. It was not too late to make reparation for that. She could still be his wife. His unreal and selfish love would yield to some higher influence, would be transformed into some nobler passion, and the portrait that Basil Hallward had painted of him would be a guide to him through life, would be to him what holiness is to some, and conscience to others, and the fear of God to us all. There were opiates for remorse, drugs that could lull the moral sense to sleep. But here was a visible symbol of the degradation of sin. Here was an ever-present sign of the ruin men brought upon their souls.

Three o'clock struck, and four, and the half-hour rang its double chime, but Dorian Gray did not stir. He was trying to gather up the scarlet threads of life, and to weave them into a pattern; to find his way through the sanguine labyrinth of passion through which he was wandering. He did not know what to do, or what to think. Finally, he went over to the table and wrote a passionate letter to the girl he had loved, imploring her forgiveness, and accusing himself of madness. He covered page after page with wild words of sorrow, and wilder words of pain. There is a luxury in self-reproach. When we blame ourselves we feel that no one else has a right to blame us. It is the confession, not the priest, that gives us absolution. When Dorian had finished the letter, he felt that he had been forgiven.

Suddenly there came a knock to the door, and he heard Lord Henry's voice outside. 'My dear boy, I must see you. Let me in at once. I can't bear your shutting yourself up like this.'

He made no answer at first, but remained quite still. The knocking still continued, and grew louder. Yes, it was better to let Lord Henry in, and to explain to him the new life he was going to lead, to quarrel with him if it became necessary to quarrel, to part if parting was inevitable. He jumped up, drew the screen hastily across the picture, and unlocked the door.

'I am so sorry for it all, Dorian,' said Lord Henry, as he entered. 'But you must not think too much about it.'

'Do you mean about Sibyl Vane?' asked the lad.

'Yes, of course,' answered Lord Henry, sinking into a chair, and slowly pulling off his yellow gloves. 'It is dreadful, from one point of view, but it was not your fault. Tell me, did you go behind and see her, after the play was over?'

'Yes.'

'I felt sure you had. Did you make a scene with her?'

'I was brutal, Harry—perfectly brutal. But it is all right now. I am not sorry for anything that has happened. It has taught me to know myself better.'

'Ah, Dorian, I am so glad you take it in that way! I was afraid I would find you plunged in remorse, and tearing that nice curly hair of yours.'

'I have got through all that,' said Dorian, shaking his head, and smiling. 'I am perfectly happy now. I know what conscience is, to begin with. It is not what you told me it was. It is the divinest thing in us. Don't sneer at it, Harry, any more—at least not before me. I want to be good. I can't bear the idea of my soul being hideous.'

'A very charming artistic basis for ethics, Dorian! I congratulate you on it. But how are you going to begin?'

'By marrying Sibyl Vane.'

'Marrying Sibyl Vane!' cried Lord Henry, standing up, and looking at him in perplexed amazement. 'But, my dear Dorian—'

'Yes, Harry, I know what you are going to say. Something dreadful about marriage. Don't say it. Don't ever say things of that kind to me again. Two days ago I asked Sibyl to marry me. I am not going to break my word to her. She is to be my wife.'

'Your wife! Dorian! . . . Didn't you get my letter? I wrote to you this morning, and sent the note down, by my own man.'

'Your letter? Oh, yes, I remember. I have not read it yet, Harry. I was afraid there might be something in it that I wouldn't like. You cut life to pieces with your epigrams.'

'You know nothing then?'

'What do you mean?'

Lord Henry walked across the room, and, sitting down by Dorian Gray, took both his hands in his own, and held them tightly. 'Dorian,' he said, 'my letter—don't be frightened—was to tell you that Sibyl Vane is dead.'

A cry of pain broke from the lad's lips, and he leaped to his feet, tearing his hands away from Lord Henry's grasp. 'Dead! Sibyl dead! It is not true! It is a horrible lie! How dare you say it?'

'It is quite true, Dorian,' said Lord Henry, gravely. 'It is in all the morning papers. I wrote down to you to ask you not to see any one till I came. There will have to be an inquest, of course, and you must not be mixed up in it. Things like that make a man fashionable in Paris. But in

London people are so prejudiced. Here, one should never make one's *début* with a scandal. One should reserve that to give an interest to one's old age. I suppose they don't know your name at the theatre? If they don't, it is all right. Did any one see you going round to her room? That is an important point.'

Dorian did not answer for a few moments. He was dazed with horror. Finally he stammered, in a stifled voice, 'Harry, did you say an inquest? What did you mean by that? Did Sibyl——? Oh, Harry, I can't bear it! But be quick. Tell me everything at once.'

'I have no doubt it was not an accident, Dorian, though it must be put in that way to the public. It seems that as she was leaving the theatre with her mother, about half-past twelve or so, she said she had forgotten something upstairs. They waited some time for her, but she did not come down again. They ultimately found her lying dead on the floor of her dressing-room. She had swallowed something by mistake, some dreadful thing they use at theatres. I don't know what it was, but it had either prussic acid or white lead in it. I should fancy it was prussic acid, as she seems to have died instantaneously.'

'Harry, Harry, it is terrible!' cried the lad.

'Yes; it is very tragic, of course, but you must not get yourself mixed up in it. I see by *The Standard* that she was seventeen. I should have thought she was almost younger than that. She looked such a child, and seemed to know so little about acting. Dorian, you mustn't let this thing get on your nerves. You must come and dine with me, and afterwards we will look in at the Opera: It is a Patti night,° and everybody will be there. You can come to my sister's box. She has got some smart women with her.'

'So I have murdered Sibyl Vane,' said Dorian Gray, half to himself— 'murdered her as surely as if I had cut her little throat with a knife. Yet the roses are not less lovely for all that. The birds sing just as happily in my garden. And tonight I am to dine with you, and then go on to the Opera, and sup somewhere, I suppose, afterwards. How extraordinarily dramatic life is! If I had read all this in a book, Harry, I think I would have wept over it. Somehow, now that it has happened actually, and to me, it seems far too wonderful for tears. Here is the first passionate love-letter I have ever written in my life. Strange, that my first passionate love-letter should have been addressed to a dead girl. Can they feel, I wonder, those white silent people we call the dead? Sibyl! Can she feel, or know, or listen? Oh, Harry, how I loved her once! It seems years ago to me now. She was everything to me. Then came that dreadful night—was it really only last night?—when she played so badly, and my heart almost broke. She explained it all to me. It was terribly pathetic. But I was not moved a bit. I thought her shallow. Suddenly something happened that made me afraid. I can't tell you what it was, but it was terrible. I said I would go back to her. I felt I had done wrong. And now she is dead. My God! my God! Harry, what shall I do? You don't know the danger I am in, and there is nothing to keep me straight. She would have done that for me. She had no right to kill herself. It was selfish of her.'

'My dear Dorian,' answered Lord Henry, taking a cigarette from his case, and producing a gold-latten° matchbox, 'the only way a woman can ever reform a man is by boring him so completely that he loses all possible interest in life. If you had married this girl you would have been wretched. Of course you would have treated her kindly. One can always be kind to people about whom one cares nothing. But she would have soon found out that you were absolutely indifferent to her. And when a woman finds that out about her husband, she either becomes dreadfully dowdy, or wears very smart bonnets that some other woman's husband has to pay for. I say nothing about the social mistake, which would have been abject, which, of course, I would not have allowed, but I assure you that in any case the whole thing would have been an absolute failure.'

'I suppose it would,' muttered the lad, walking up and down the room, and looking horribly pale. 'But I thought it was my duty. It is not my fault that this terrible tragedy has prevented my doing what was right. I remember your saying once that there is a fatality about good resolutions—that they are always made too late. Mine certainly were.'

'Good resolutions are useless attempts to interfere with scientific laws. Their origin is pure vanity. Their result is absolutely *nil*. They give us, now and then, some of those luxurious sterile emotions that have a certain charm for the weak. That is all that can be said for them. They are simply cheques that men draw on a bank where they have no account.'

'Harry,' cried Dorian Gray, coming over and sitting down beside him, 'why is it that I cannot feel this tragedy as much as I want to? I don't think I am heartless. Do you?'

'You have done too many foolish things during the last fortnight to be entitled to give yourself that name, Dorian,' answered Lord Henry, with his sweet, melancholy smile.

The lad frowned. 'I don't like that explanation, Harry,' he rejoined, 'but I am glad you don't think I am heartless. I am nothing of the kind. I know I am not. And yet I must admit that this thing that has happened does not affect me as it should. It seems to me to be simply like a wonderful ending to a wonderful play. It has all the terrible beauty of a Greek tragedy, a tragedy in which I took a great part, but by which I have not been wounded.'

'It is an interesting question,' said Lord Henry, who found an exquisite pleasure in playing on the lad's unconscious egotism—'an extremely interesting question. I fancy that the true explanation is this. It often happens that the real tragedies of life occur in such an inartistic manner that they hurt us by their crude violence, their absolute incoherence, their absurd want of meaning, their entire lack of style. They affect us just as vulgarity affects us. They give us an impression of sheer brute force, and we revolt against that. Sometimes, however, a tragedy that possesses artistic elements of beauty crosses our lives. If these elements of beauty are real, the whole thing simply appeals to our sense of dramatic effect. Suddenly we find that we are no longer the actors, but the spectators of the play. Or rather we are both. We watch ourselves, and the mere wonder of the spectacle enthralls us. In the present case, what is it that has really happened? Some one has killed herself for love of you. I wish that I had ever had such an experience. It would have made me in love with love for the rest of my life. The people who have adored me—there have not been very many, but there have been some—have always insisted on living on, long after I had ceased to care for them, or they to care for me. They have become stout and tedious, and when I meet them they go in at once for reminiscences. That awful memory of woman! What a fearful thing it is! And what an utter intellectual stagnation it reveals! One should absorb the colour of life, but one should never remember its details. Details are always vulgar.'

'I must sow poppies in my garden,' sighed Dorian.

'There is no necessity,' rejoined his companion. 'Life has always poppies in her hands. Of course, now and then things linger. I once wore nothing but violets all through one season, as a form of artistic mourning for a romance that would not die. Ultimately, however, it did die. I forget what killed it. I think it was her proposing to sacrifice the whole world for me. That is always a dreadful moment. It fills one with the terror of eternity. Well—would you believe it?—a week ago, at Lady Hampshire's, I found myself seated at dinner next the lady in question, and she insisted on going over the whole thing again, and digging up the past, and raking up the future. I had buried my romance in a bed of asphodel.° She dragged it out again, and assured me that I had spoiled her life. I am bound to state that she ate an enormous dinner, so I did not feel any anxiety. But what a lack of taste she showed! The one charm of the past is that it is the past. But women never know when the curtain has fallen. They always want a sixth act, and as soon as the interest of the play is entirely over they propose to continue it. If they were allowed their own way, every comedy would have a tragic ending, and every tragedy would culminate in a farce. They are charmingly artificial, but they have no sense of art. You are more fortunate than I am. I assure you, Dorian, that not one of the women I have known would have done for me what Sibyl Vane did for you. Ordinary women always console themselves. Some of them do it by going in for sentimental colours. Never trust a woman who wears mauve, whatever her age may be, or a woman over thirty-five who is fond of pink ribbons. It always means that they have a history. Others find a great consolation in suddenly discovering the good qualities of their husbands. They flaunt their conjugal felicity in one's face, as if it were the most fascinating of sins. Religion consoles some. Its mysteries have all the charm of a flirtation, a woman once told me; and I can quite understand it. Besides, nothing makes one so vain as being told that one is a sinner. Conscience makes egotists of us all.° Yes; there is really no end to the consolations that women find in modern life. Indeed, I have not mentioned the most important one.'

'What is that, Harry?' said the lad, listlessly.

'Oh, the obvious consolation. Taking some one else's admirer when one loses one's own. In good society that always whitewashes a woman. But really, Dorian, how different Sibyl Vane must have been from all the women one meets! There is something to me quite beautiful about her death. I am glad I am living in a century when such wonders happen. They make one believe in the reality of the things we all play with, such as romance, passion, and love.'

'I was terribly cruel to her. You forget that.'

'I am afraid that women appreciate cruelty, downright cruelty, more than anything else. They have wonderfully primitive instincts. We have emancipated them, but they remain slaves looking for their masters, all the same. They love being dominated. I am sure you were splendid. I have never seen you really and absolutely angry, but I can fancy how delightful you looked. And, after all, you said something to me the day before yesterday that seemed to me at the time to be merely fanciful, but that I see now was absolutely true, and it holds the key to everything.'

'What was that, Harry?'

'You said to me that Sibyl Vane represented to you all the heroines of romance—that she was Desdemona one night, and Ophelia the other; that if she died as Juliet, she came to life as Imogen.'

'She will never come to life again now,' muttered the lad, burying his face in his hands.

'No, she will never come to life. She has played her last part. But you must think of that lonely death in the tawdry dressing-room simply as a strange lurid fragment from some Jacobean tragedy, as a wonderful scene from Webster, or Ford, or Cyril Tourneur. The girl never really lived, and so she has never really died. To you at least she was always a dream, a phantom that flitted through Shakespeare's plays and left them lovelier for its presence, a reed through which Shakespeare's music sounded richer and more full of joy. The moment she touched actual life, she marred it, and it marred her, and so she passed away. Mourn for Ophelia, if you like. Put ashes on your head because Cordelia was strangled. Cry out against Heaven because the daughter of Brabantio died. But don't waste your tears over Sibyl Vane. She was less real than they are.'

There was a silence. The evening darkened in the room. Noiselessly, and with silver feet, the shadows crept in from the garden. The colours faded wearily out of things.

After some time Dorian Gray looked up. 'You have explained me to myself, Harry,' he murmured, with something of a sigh of relief. 'I felt all that you have said, but somehow I was afraid of it, and I could not express it to myself. How well you know me! But we will not talk again of what has happened. It has been a marvellous experience. That is all. I wonder if life has still in store for me anything as marvellous.'

'Life has everything in store for you, Dorian. There is nothing that you, with your extraordinary good looks, will not be able to do.'

'But, suppose, Harry, I become haggard, and old, and wrinkled? What then?'

'Ah, then,' said Lord Henry, rising to go—'then, my dear Dorian, you would have to fight for your victories. As it is, they are brought to you. No, you must keep your good looks. We live in an age that reads too much to be wise, and that thinks too much to be beautiful. We cannot spare you. And now you had better dress, and drive down to the club. We are rather late, as it is.'

'I think I shall join you at the Opera, Harry. I feel too tired to eat anything. What is the number of your sister's box?'

'Twenty-seven, I believe. It is on the grand tier. You will see her name on the door. But I am sorry you won't come and dine.'

'I don't feel up to it,' said Dorian, listlessly. 'But I am awfully obliged to you for all that you have said to me. You are certainly my best friend. No one has ever understood me as you have.'

'We are only at the beginning of our friendship, Dorian,' answered Lord Henry, shaking him by the hand. 'Goodbye. I shall see you before nine-thirty, I hope. Remember, Patti is singing.'

As he closed the door behind him, Dorian Gray touched the bell, and in a few minutes Victor appeared with the lamps and drew the blinds down. He waited impatiently for him to go. The man seemed to take an interminable time over everything.

As soon as he had left, he rushed to the screen, and drew it back. No; there was no further change in the picture. It had received the news of Sibyl Vane's death before he had known of it himself. It was conscious of the events of life as they occurred. The vicious cruelty that marred the fine lines of the mouth had, no doubt, appeared at the very moment that the girl had drunk the poison, whatever it was. Or was it indifferent to results? Did it merely take cognizance of what passed within the soul? He wondered, and hoped that some day he would see the change taking place before his very eyes, shuddering as he hoped it.

Poor Sibyl! what a romance it had all been! She had often mimicked death on the stage. Then Death himself had touched her, and taken her with him. How had she played that dreadful last scene? Had she cursed him, as she died? No; she had died for love of him, and love would always be a sacrament to him now. She had atoned for everything, by the sacrifice she had made of her life. He would not think any more of what she had made him go through, on that horrible night at the theatre. When he thought of her, it would be as a wonderful tragic figure sent on to the world's stage to show the supreme reality of Love. A wonderful tragic figure? Tears came to his eyes as he remembered her childlike look and winsome fanciful ways and shy tremulous grace. He brushed them away hastily, and looked again at the picture.

He felt that the time had really come for making his choice. Or had his choice already been made? Yes, life had decided that for him—life, and his own infinite curiosity about life. Eternal youth, infinite passion, pleasures subtle and secret, wild joys and wilder sins—he was to have all these things. The portrait was to bear the burden of his shame: that was all.

A feeling of pain crept over him as he thought of the desecration that was in store for the fair face on the canvas. Once, in boyish mockery of Narcissus, he had kissed, or feigned to kiss, those painted lips that now smiled so cruelly at him. Morning after morning he had sat before the portrait wondering at its beauty, almost enamoured of it, as it seemed to him at times. Was it to alter now with every mood to which he yielded? Was it to become a monstrous and loathsome thing, to be hidden away in a locked room, to be shut out from the sunlight that had so often touched to brighter gold the waving wonder of its hair? The pity of it! the pity of it!°

For a moment he thought of praying that the horrible sympathy that existed between him and the picture might cease. It had changed in answer to a prayer; perhaps in answer to a prayer it might remain unchanged. And, yet, who, that knew anything about Life, would surrender the chance of remaining always young, however fantastic that chance might be, or with what fateful consequences it might be fraught? Besides, was it really under his control? Had it indeed been prayer that had produced the substitution? Might there not be some curious scientific reason for it all? If thought could exercise its influence upon a living organism, might not thought exercise an influence upon dead and inorganic things? Nay, without thought or conscious desire, might not things external to ourselves vibrate in unison with our moods and passions, atom calling to atom in secret love or strange affinity? But the reason was of no importance. He would never again tempt by a prayer any terrible power. If the picture was to alter, it was to alter. That was all. Why inquire too closely into it?

For there would be a real pleasure in watching it. He would be able to follow his mind into its secret places. This portrait would be to him the most magical of mirrors. As it had revealed to him his own body, so it would reveal to him his own soul. And when winter came upon it, he would still be standing where spring trembles on the verge of summer. When the blood crept from its face, and left behind a pallid mask of chalk with leaden eyes, he would keep the glamour of boyhood. Not one blossom of his loveliness would ever fade. Not one pulse of his life would ever weaken. Like the gods of the Greeks, he would be strong, and fleet, and joyous. What did it matter what happened to the coloured image on the canvas? He would be safe. That was everything.

He drew the screen back into its former place in front of the picture, smiling as he did so, and passed into his bedroom, where his valet was already waiting for him. An hour later he was at the Opera, and Lord Henry was leaning over his chair.

CHAPTER IX

As he was sitting at breakfast next morning, Basil Hallward was shown into the room.

'I am so glad I have found you, Dorian,' he said, gravely. 'I called last night, and they told me you were at the Opera. Of course I knew that was impossible. But I wish you had left word where you had really gone to. I passed a dreadful evening, half afraid that one tragedy might be followed by another. I think you might have telegraphed for me when you heard of it first. I read of it quite by chance in a late edition of *The Globe*, that I picked up at the club. I came here at once, and was miserable at not finding you. I can't tell you how heart-broken I am about the whole thing.

I know what you must suffer. But where were you? Did you go down and see the girl's mother? For a moment I thought of following you there. They gave the address in the paper. Somewhere in the Euston Road, isn't it? But I was afraid of intruding upon a sorrow that I could not lighten. Poor woman! What a state she must be in! And her only child, too! What did she say about it all?'

'My dear Basil, how do I know?' murmured Dorian Gray, sipping some pale-yellow wine from a delicate gold-beaded bubble of Venetian glass, and looking dreadfully bored. 'I was at the Opera. You should have come on there. I met Lady Gwendolen, Harry's sister, for the first time. We were in her box. She is perfectly charming; and Patti sang divinely. Don't talk about horrid subjects. If one doesn't talk about a thing, it has never happened. It is simply expression, as Harry says, that gives reality to things. I may mention that she was not the woman's only child. There is a son, a charming fellow, I believe. But he is not on the stage. He is a sailor, or something. And now, tell me about yourself and what you are painting.'

'You went to the Opera?' said Hallward, speaking very slowly, and with a strained touch of pain in his voice. 'You went to the Opera while Sibyl Vane was lying dead in some sordid lodging? You can talk to me of other women being charming, and of Patti singing divinely, before the girl you loved has even the quiet of a grave to sleep in? Why, man, there are horrors in store for that little white body of hers!'

'Stop, Basil! I won't hear it!' cried Dorian, leaping to his feet. 'You must not tell me about things. What is done is done. What is past is past.'

'You call yesterday the past?'

'What has the actual lapse of time got to do with it? It is only shallow people who require years to get rid of an emotion. A man who is master of himself can end a sorrow as easily as he can invent a pleasure. I don't want to be at the mercy of my emotions. I want to use them, to enjoy them, and to dominate them.'

'Dorian, this is horrible! Something has changed you completely. You look exactly the same wonderful boy who, day after day, used to come down to my studio to sit for his picture. But you were simple, natural, and affectionate then. You were the most unspoiled creature in the whole world. Now, I don't know what has come over you. You talk as if you had no heart, no pity in you. It is all Harry's influence. I see that.'

The lad flushed up, and, going to the window, looked out for a few moments on the green, flickering, sun-lashed garden. 'I owe a great deal to Harry, Basil,' he said, at last—'more than I owe to you. You only taught me to be vain.'

'Well, I am punished for that, Dorian—or shall be some day.'

'I don't know what you mean, Basil,' he exclaimed, turning round. 'I don't know what you want. What do you want?'

'I want the Dorian Gray I used to paint,' said the artist, sadly.

'Basil,' said the lad, going over to him, and putting his hand on his shoulder, 'you have come too late. Yesterday when I heard that Sibyl Vane had killed herself——'

'Killed herself! Good heavens! is there no doubt about that?' cried Hallward, looking up at him with an expression of horror.

'My dear Basil! Surely you don't think it was a vulgar accident? Of course she killed herself.'

The elder man buried his face in his hands. 'How fearful,' he muttered, and a shudder ran through him.

'No,' said Dorian Gray, 'there is nothing fearful about it. It is one of the great romantic tragedies of the age. As a rule, people who act lead the most commonplace lives. They are good husbands, or faithful wives, or something tedious. You know what I mean—middle-class virtue, and all that kind of thing. How different Sibyl was! She lived her finest tragedy. She was always a heroine. The last night she played—the night you saw her—she acted badly because she had known the reality of love. When she knew its unreality, she died, as Juliet might have died. She passed again into the sphere of art. There is something of the martyr about her. Her death has all the pathetic uselessness of martyrdom, all its wasted beauty. But, as I was saying, you must not think I have not suffered. If you had come in yesterday at a particular moment—about half-past five, perhaps, or a quarter to six—you would have found me in tears. Even Harry, who was here, who brought me the news, in fact, had no idea what I was going through. I suffered immensely. Then it passed away. I cannot repeat an emotion. No one can, except sentimentalists. And you are awfully unjust, Basil. You come down here to console me. That is charming of you. You find me consoled, and you are furious. How like a sympathetic person! You remind me of a story Harry told me about a certain philanthropist who spent twenty years of his life in trying to get some grievance redressed, or some unjust law altered—I forget exactly what it was. Finally he succeeded, and nothing could exceed his disappointment. He had absolutely nothing to do, almost died of *ennui*, and became a confirmed misanthrope. And besides, my dear old Basil, if you really want to console me, teach me rather to forget what has happened, or to see it from a proper artistic point of view. Was it not Gautier who used to write about *la consolation des arts*?° I remember picking up a little vellum-covered book in your studio one day and chancing on that delightful phrase. Well, I am not like that young man you told me of when we were down at Marlow together, the young man who used to say that yellow satin could console one for all the miseries of life. I love beautiful things that one can touch and handle. Old brocades, green bronzes, lacquerwork, carved ivories, exquisite surroundings, luxury, pomp, there is much to be got from all these. But the artistic temperament that they create, or at any rate reveal, is still more to me. To become the spectator of one's own life, as Harry says, is to escape the suffering of life. I know you are surprised at my talking to you like this. You have not realized how I have developed. I was a schoolboy when you knew me. I am a man now. I have new passions, new thoughts, new ideas. I am different, but you must not like me less. I am changed, but you must always be my friend. Of course I am very fond of Harry. But I know that you are better than he is. You are not stronger—you are too much afraid of life—but you are better. And how happy we used to be together! Don't leave me, Basil, and don't quarrel with me. I am what I am. There is nothing more to be said.'

The painter felt strangely moved. The lad was infinitely dear to him, and his personality had been the great turning-point in his art. He could not bear the idea of reproaching him any more. After all, his indifference was probably merely a mood that would pass away. There was so much in him that was good, so much in him that was noble.

'Well, Dorian,' he said, at length, with a sad smile. 'I won't speak to you again about this horrible thing, after today. I only trust your name won't be mentioned in connection with it. The inquest is to take place this afternoon. Have they summoned you?'

Dorian shook his head, and a look of annoyance passed over his face at the mention of the word 'inquest'. There was something so crude and vulgar about everything of the kind. 'They don't know my name,' he answered.

'But surely she did?'

'Only my Christian name, and that I am quite sure she never mentioned to any one. She told me once that they were all rather curious to learn who I was, and that she invariably told them my name was Prince Charming. It was pretty of her. You must do me a drawing of Sibyl, Basil. I should like to have something more of her than the memory of a few kisses and some broken pathetic words.'

'I will try and do something, Dorian, if it would please you. But you must come and sit to me yourself again. I can't get on without you.'

'I can never sit to you again, Basil. It is impossible!' he exclaimed, starting back.

The painter stared at him. 'My dear boy, what nonsense!' he cried. 'Do you mean to say you don't like what I did of you? Where is it? Why have you pulled the screen in front of it? Let me look at it. It is the best thing I have ever done. Do take the screen away, Dorian. It is simply disgraceful of your servant hiding my work like that. I felt the room looked different as I came in.'

'My servant has nothing to do with it, Basil. You don't imagine I let him arrange my room for me? He settles my flowers for me sometimes—that is all. No; I did it myself. The light was too strong on the portrait.'

'Too strong! Surely not, my dear fellow? It is an admirable place for it. Let me see it.' And Hallward walked towards the corner of the room.

A cry of terror broke from Dorian Gray's lips, and he rushed between the painter and the screen. 'Basil,' he said, looking very pale, 'you must not look at it. I don't wish you to.'

'Not look at my own work! you are not serious. Why shouldn't I look at it?' exclaimed Hallward, laughing.

'If you try to look at it, Basil, on my word of honour I will never speak to you again as long as I live. I am quite serious. I don't offer any explanation, and you are not to ask for any. But, remember, if you touch this screen, everything is over between us.'

Hallward was thunderstruck. He looked at Dorian Gray in absolute amazement. He had never seen him like this before. The lad was actually pallid with rage. His hands were clenched, and the pupils of his eyes were like discs of blue fire. He was trembling all over.

'Dorian!'

'Don't speak!'

'But what is the matter? Of course I won't look at it if you don't want me to,' he said, rather coldly, turning on his heel, and going over towards the window. 'But, really, it seems rather absurd that I shouldn't see my own work, especially as I am going to exhibit it in Paris in the autumn. I shall probably have to give it another coat of varnish before that, so I must see it some day, and why not today?'

'To exhibit it! You want to exhibit it?' exclaimed Dorian Gray, a strange sense of terror creeping over him. Was the world going to be shown his secret? Were people to gape at the mystery of his life? That was impossible. Something—he did not know what—had to be done at once.

'Yes; I don't suppose you will object to that. Georges Petit° is going to collect all my best pictures for a special exhibition in the Rue de Sèze, which will open the first week in October. The portrait will only be away a month. I should think you could easily spare it for that time. In fact, you are sure to be out of town. And if you keep it always behind a screen, you can't care much about it.'

Dorian Gray passed his hand over his forehead. There were beads of perspiration there. He felt that he was on the brink of a horrible danger. 'You told me a month ago that you would never exhibit it,' he cried. 'Why have you changed your mind? You people who go in for being consistent have just as many moods as others have. The only difference is that your moods are rather meaningless. You can't have forgotten that you assured me most solemnly that nothing in the world would induce you to send it to any exhibition. You told Harry exactly the same thing.' He stopped suddenly, and a gleam of light came into his eyes. He remembered that Lord Henry had said to him once, half seriously and half in jest, 'If you want to have a strange quarter of an hour, get Basil to tell you why he won't exhibit your picture. He told me why he wouldn't, and it was a revelation to me.' Yes, perhaps Basil, too, had his secret. He would ask him and try.

'Basil,' he said, coming over quite close, and looking him straight in the face, 'we have each of us a secret. Let me know yours, and I shall tell you mine. What was your reason for refusing to exhibit my picture?'

The painter shuddered in spite of himself. 'Dorian, if I told you, you might like me less than you do, and you would certainly laugh at me. I could not bear your doing either of those two things. If you wish me never to look at your picture again, I am content. I have always you to look at. If you wish the best work I have ever done to be hidden from the world, I am satisfied. Your friendship is dearer to me than any fame or reputation.'

'No, Basil, you must tell me,' insisted Dorian Gray. 'I think I have a right to know.' His feeling of terror had passed away, and curiosity had taken its place. He was determined to find out Basil Hallward's mystery.

'Let us sit down, Dorian,' said the painter, looking troubled. 'Let us sit down. And just answer me one question. Have you noticed in the picture something curious?—something that probably at first did not strike you, but that revealed itself to you suddenly?'

'Basil!' cried the lad, clutching the arms of his chair with trembling hands, and gazing at him with wild, startled eyes.

'I see you did. Don't speak. Wait till you hear what I have to say. Dorian, from the moment I met you, your personality had the most extraordinary influence over me. I was dominated, soul, brain, and power by you. You became to me the visible incarnation of that unseen ideal whose memory haunts us artists like an exquisite dream. I worshipped you. I grew jealous of every one to whom you spoke. I wanted to have you all to myself. I was only happy when I was with you. When you were away from me you were still present in my art. . . . Of course I never let you know anything about this. It would have been impossible. You would not have understood it. I hardly understood it myself. I only knew that I had seen perfection face to face, and that the world had become wonderful to my eyes—too wonderful, perhaps, for in such mad worships there is peril, the peril of losing them, no less than the peril of keeping them. . . . Weeks and weeks went on, and I grew more and more absorbed in you. Then came a new development. I had drawn you as Paris in dainty armour, and as Adonis with huntsman's cloak and polished boar-spear. Crowned with heavy lotus-blossoms you had sat on the prow of Adrian's barge,° gazing across the green turbid Nile. You had leant over the still pool of some Greek woodland, and seen in the water's silent silver the marvel of your own face. And it had all been what art should be, unconscious, ideal, and remote. One day, a fatal day I sometimes think, I determined to paint a wonderful portrait of you as you actually are, not in the costume of dead ages, but in your own dress and in your own time. Whether it was the Realism of the method, or the mere wonder of your own personality, thus directly presented to me without mist or veil, I cannot tell. But I know that as I worked at it, every flake and film of colour seemed to me to reveal my secret. I grew afraid that others would know of my idolatry. I felt, Dorian, that I had told too much, that I had put too much of myself into it. Then it was that I resolved never to allow the picture to be exhibited. You were a little annoyed; but then you did not realize all that it meant to me. Harry, to whom I talked about it, laughed at me. But I did not mind that. When the picture was finished, and I sat alone with it, I felt that I was right. . . . Well, after a few days the thing left my studio, and as soon as I had got rid of the intolerable fascination of its presence it seemed to me that I had been foolish in imagining that I had seen anything in it, more than that you were extremely good-looking and that I could paint. Even now I cannot help feeling that it is a mistake to think that the passion one feels in creation is ever really shown in the work one creates. Art is always more abstract than we fancy. Form and colour tell us of form and colour—that is all. It often seems to me that art conceals the artist far more completely than it ever reveals him. And so when I got this offer from Paris I determined to make your portrait the principal thing in my exhibition. It never occurred to me that you would refuse. I see now that you were right. The picture cannot be shown. You must not be angry with me, Dorian, for what I have told you. As I said to Harry, once, you are made to be worshipped.'

Dorian Gray drew a long breath. The colour came back to his cheeks, and a smile played about his lips. The peril was over. He was safe for the time. Yet he could not help feeling infinite pity for the painter who had just made this strange confession to him, and wondered if he himself would ever be so dominated by the personality of a friend. Lord Henry had the charm of being very dangerous. But that was all. He was too clever and too cynical to be really fond of. Would there ever be some one who would fill him with a strange idolatry? Was that one of the things that life had in store?

'It is extraordinary to me, Dorian,' said Hallward, 'that you should have seen this in the portrait. Did you really see it?'

'I saw something in it,' he answered, 'something that seemed to me very curious.'

'Well, you don't mind my looking at the thing now?'

Dorian shook his head. 'You must not ask me that, Basil. I could not possibly let you stand in front of that picture.'

'You will some day, surely?'

'Never.'

'Well, perhaps you are right. And now goodbye, Dorian. You have been the one person in my life who has really influenced my art. Whatever I have done that is good, I owe to you. Ah! you don't know what it cost me to tell you all that I have told you.'

'My dear Basil,' said Dorian, 'what have you told me? Simply that you felt that you admired me too much. That is not even a compliment.'

'It was not intended as a compliment. It was a confession. Now that I have made it, something seems to have gone out of me. Perhaps one should never put one's worship into words.'

'It was a very disappointing confession.'

'Why, what did you expect, Dorian? You didn't see anything else in the picture, did you? There was nothing else to see?'

'No; there was nothing else to see. Why do you ask? But you mustn't talk about worship. It is foolish. You and I are friends, Basil, and we must always remain so.'

'You have got Harry,' said the painter, sadly.

'Oh, Harry!' cried the lad, with a ripple of laughter. 'Harry spends his days in saying what is incredible, and his evenings in doing what is improbable. Just the sort of life I would like to lead. But still I don't think I would go to Harry if I were in trouble. I would sooner go to you, Basil.'

'You will sit to me again?'

'Impossible!'

'You spoil my life as an artist by refusing, Dorian. No man came across two ideal things. Few come across one.'

'I can't explain it to you, Basil, but I must never sit to you again. There is something fatal about a portrait. It has a life of its own. I will come and have tea with you. That will be just as pleasant.'

'Pleasanter for you, I am afraid,' murmured Hallward, regretfully. 'And now goodbye. I am sorry you won't let me look at the picture once again. But that can't be helped. I quite understand what you feel about it.'

As he left the room, Dorian Gray smiled to himself. Poor Basil! how little he knew of the true reason! And how strange it was that, instead of having been forced to reveal his own secret, he had succeeded almost by chance, in wresting a secret from his friend! How much that strange confession explained to him! The painter's absurd fits of jealousy, his wild devotion, his extravagant panegyrics, his curious reticences—he understood them all now, and he felt sorry. There seemed to him to be something tragic in a friendship so coloured by romance.

He sighed, and touched the bell. The portrait must be hidden away at all costs. He could not run such a risk of discovery again. It had been mad of him to have allowed the thing to remain, even for an hour, in a room to which many of his friends had access.

CHAPTER X

WHEN his servant entered, he looked at him steadfastly, and wondered if he had thought of peering behind the screen. The man was quite impassive, and waited for his orders. Dorian lit a cigarette, and walked over to the glass and glanced into it. He could see the reflection of Victor's face perfectly. It was like a placid mask of servility. There was nothing to be afraid of, there. Yet he thought it best to be on his guard.

Speaking very slowly, he told him to tell the housekeeper that he wanted to see her, and then to go to the frame-maker and ask him to send two of his men round at once. It seemed to him that as the man left the room his eyes wandered in the direction of the screen. Or was that merely his own fancy?

After a few moments, in her black silk dress, with old-fashioned thread mittens on her wrinkled hands, Mrs Leaf bustled into the library. He asked her for the key of the schoolroom.

'The old schoolroom, Mr Dorian?' she exclaimed. 'Why, it is full of dust. I must get it arranged, and put straight before you go into it. It is not fit for you to see, sir. It is not, indeed.'

'I don't want it put straight, Leaf. I only want the key.'

'Well, sir, you'll be covered with cobwebs if you go into it. Why, it hasn't been opened for nearly five years, not since his lordship died.'

He winced at the mention of his grandfather. He had hateful memories of him. 'That does not matter,' he answered. 'I simply want to see the place—that is all. Give me the key.'

'And here is the key, sir,' said the old lady, going over the contents of her bunch with tremulously uncertain hands. 'Here is the key. I'll have it off the bunch in a moment. But you don't think of living up there, sir, and you so comfortable here?'

'No, no,' he cried, petulantly. 'Thank you, Leaf. That will do.'

She lingered for a few moments, and was garrulous over some detail of the household. He sighed, and told her to manage things as she thought best. She left the room, wreathed in smiles.

As the door closed, Dorian put the key in his pocket, and looked round the room. His eye fell on a large purple satin coverlet heavily embroidered with gold, a splendid piece of late seventeenth-century Venetian work that his grandfather had found in a convent near Bologna. Yes, that would serve to wrap the dreadful thing in. It had perhaps served often as a pall for the dead. Now it was to hide something that had a corruption of its own, worse than the corruption of death itself—something that would breed horrors and yet would never die. What the worm was to the corpse, his sins would be to the painted image on the canvas. They would mar its beauty, and eat away its grace. They would defile it, and make it shameful. And yet the thing would still live on. It would be always alive.

He shuddered, and for a moment he regretted that he had not told Basil the true reason why he had wished to hide the picture away. Basil would have helped him to resist Lord Henry's influence, and the still more poisonous influences that came from his own temperament. The love that he bore him°—for it was really love—had nothing in it that was not noble and intellectual. It was not that mere physical admiration of beauty that is born of the senses, and that dies when the senses tire. It was such love as Michael Angelo had known, and Montaigne, and Winckelmann, and Shakespeare himself. Yes, Basil could have saved him. But it was too late now. The past could always be annihilated. Regret, denial, or forgetfulness could do that. But the future was inevitable. There were passions in him that would find their terrible outlet, dreams that would make the shadow of their evil real.

He took up from the couch the great purple-and-gold texture that covered it, and, holding it in his hands, passed behind the screen. Was the face on the canvas viler than before? It seemed to him that it was unchanged; and yet his loathing of it was intensified. Gold hair, blue eyes, and rose-red lips—they all were there. It was simply the expression that had altered. That was horrible in its cruelty. Compared to what he saw in it of censure or rebuke, how shallow Basil's reproaches about Sibyl Vane had been!—how shallow, and of what little account! His own soul was looking out at him from the canvas and calling him to judgment. A look of pain came across him, and he flung the rich pall over the picture. As he did so, a knock came to the door. He passed out as his servant entered.

'The persons are here, Monsieur.'

He felt that the man must be got rid of at once. He must not be allowed to know where the picture was being taken to. There was something sly about him, and he had thoughtful, treacherous eyes. Sitting down at the writing-table, he scribbled a note to Lord Henry, asking him to send him round something to read, and reminding him that they were to meet at eight-fifteen that evening.

'Wait for an answer,' he said, handing it to him, 'and show the men in here.'

In two or three minutes there was another knock, and Mr Hubbard himself, the celebrated frame-maker of South Audley Street, came in with a somewhat rough-looking young assistant. Mr Hubbard was a florid, red-whiskered little man, whose admiration for art was considerably tempered by the inveterate impecuniosity of most of the artists who dealt with him. As a rule, he never left his shop. He waited for people to come to him. But he always made an exception in favour of Dorian Gray. There was something about Dorian that charmed everybody. It was a pleasure even to see him.

'What can I do for you, Mr Gray?' he said, rubbing his fat freckled hands. 'I thought I would do myself the honour of coming round in person. I have just got a beauty of a frame, sir. Picked it up at a sale. Old Florentine. Came from Fonthill,° I believe. Admirably suited for a religious subject, Mr Gray.'

'I am so sorry you have given yourself the trouble of coming round, Mr Hubbard. I shall certainly drop in and look at the frame—though I don't go in much at present for religious art—but today I only want a picture carried to the top of the house for me. It is rather heavy, so I thought I would ask you to lend me a couple of your men.'

'No trouble at all, Mr Gray. I am delighted to be of any service to you. Which is the work of art, sir?'

'This,' replied Dorian, moving the screen back. 'Can you move it, covering and all, just as it is? I don't want it to get scratched going upstairs.'

'There will be no difficulty, sir,' said the genial frame-maker, beginning, with the aid of his assistant, to unhook the picture from the long brass chains by which it was suspended. 'And, now, where shall we carry it to, Mr Gray?'

'I will show you the way, Mr Hubbard, if you will kindly follow me. Or perhaps you had better go in front. I am afraid it is right at the top of the house. We will go up by the front staircase, as it is wider.'

He held the door open for them, and they passed out into the hall and began the ascent. The elaborate character of the frame had made the picture extremely bulky, and now and then, in spite of the obsequious protests of Mr Hubbard, who had the true tradesman's spirited dislike of seeing a gentleman doing anything useful, Dorian put his hand to it so as to help them.

'Something of a load to carry, sir,' gasped the little man, when they reached the top landing. And he wiped his shiny forehead.

'I am afraid it is rather heavy,' murmured Dorian, as he unlocked the door that opened into the room that was to keep for him the curious secret of his life and hide his soul from the eyes of men.

He had not entered the place for more than four years—not, indeed, since he had used it first as a play-room when he was a child, and then as a study when he grew somewhat older. It was a large, well-proportioned room, which had been specially built by the last Lord Kelso for the use of the little grandson whom, for his strange likeness to his mother, and also for other reasons, he had always hated and desired to keep at a distance. It appeared to Dorian to have but little changed. There was the huge Italian *cassone*,° with its fantastically-painted panels and its tarnished gilt mouldings, in which he had so often hidden himself as a boy. There the satinwood bookcase filled with his dog-eared schoolbooks. On the wall behind it was hanging the same ragged Flemish tapestry where a faded king and queen were playing chess in a garden, while a company of hawkers rode by, carrying hooded birds on their gauntleted wrists. How well he remembered it all! Every moment of his lonely childhood came back to him as he looked round. He recalled the stainless purity of his boyish life, and it seemed horrible to him that it was here the fatal portrait was to be hidden away. How little he had thought, in those dead days, of all that was in store for him!

But there was no other place in the house so secure from prying eyes as this. He had the key, and no one else could enter it. Beneath its purple pall, the face painted on the canvas could grow bestial, sodden, and unclean. What did it matter? No one could see it. He himself would not see it. Why should he watch the hideous corruption of his soul? He kept his youth—that was enough. And, besides, might not his nature grow finer, after all? There was no reason that the future should be so full of shame. Some love might come across his life, and purify him, and shield him from those sins that seemed to be already stirring in spirit and in flesh—those curious unpictured sins whose very mystery lent them their subtlety and their charm. Perhaps, some day, the cruel look would have passed away from the scarlet sensitive mouth, and he might show to the world Basil Hallward's masterpiece.

No; that was impossible. Hour by hour, and week by week, the thing upon the canvas was growing old. It might escape the hideousness of sin, but the hideousness of age was in store for it. The cheeks would become hollow or flaccid. Yellow crow's-feet would creep round the fading eyes and make them horrible. The hair would lose its brightness, the mouth would gape or droop, would be foolish or gross, as the mouths of old men are. There would be the wrinkled throat, the cold, blue-veined hands, the twisted body, that he remembered in the grandfather who had been so stern to him in his boyhood. The picture had to be concealed. There was no help for it.

'Bring it in, Mr Hubbard, please,' he said, wearily, turning round. 'I am sorry I kept you so long. I was thinking of something else.'

'Always glad to have a rest, Mr Gray,' answered the frame-maker, who was still gasping for breath. 'Where shall we put it, sir?'

'Oh, anywhere. Here: this will do. I don't want to have it hung up. Just lean it against the wall. Thanks.'

'Might one look at the work of art, sir?'

Dorian started. 'It would not interest you, Mr Hubbard,' he said, keeping his eye on the man. He felt ready to leap upon him and fling him to the ground if he dared to lift the gorgeous hanging that concealed the secret of his life. 'I shan't trouble you any more now. I am much obliged for your kindness in coming round.'

'Not at all, not at all, Mr Gray. Ever ready to do anything for you, sir.' And Mr Hubbard tramped downstairs, followed by the assistant, who glanced back at Dorian with a look of shy wonder in his rough, uncomely face. He had never seen any one so marvellous.

When the sound of their footsteps had died away, Dorian locked the door, and put the key in his pocket. He felt safe now. No one would ever look upon the horrible thing. No eye but his would ever see his shame.

On reaching the library he found that it was just after five o'clock, and that the tea had been already brought up. On a little table of dark perfumed wood thickly incrusted with nacre,° a present from Lady Radley, his guardian's wife, a pretty professional invalid, who had spent the preceding winter in Cairo, was lying a note from Lord Henry, and beside it was a book bound in yellow paper, the cover slightly torn and the edges soiled. A copy of the third edition of *The St James's Gazette* had been placed on the tea-tray. It was evident that Victor had returned. He wondered if he had met the men in the hall as they were leaving the house, and had wormed out of them what they had been doing. He would be sure to miss the picture—had no doubt missed it already, while he had been laying the tea-things. The screen had not been set back, and a blank space was visible on the wall. Perhaps some night he might find him creeping upstairs and trying to force the door of the room. It was a horrible thing to have a spy in one's house. He had heard of rich men who had been blackmailed all their lives by some servant who had read a letter, or overheard a conversation, or picked up a card with an address, or found beneath a pillow a withered flower or a shred of crumpled lace.

He sighed, and, having poured himself out some tea, opened Lord Henry's note. It was simply to say that he sent him round the evening paper, and a book that might interest him, and that he would be at the club at eight-fifteen. He opened *The St James's* languidly, and looked through it. A red pencil-mark on the fifth page caught his eye. It drew attention to the following paragraph:—

INQUEST ON AN ACTRESS.—An inquest was held this morning at the Bell Tavern, Hoxton Road, by Mr Danby, the District Coroner, on the body of Sibyl Vane, a young actress recently engaged at the Royal Theatre, Holborn. A verdict of death by misadventure was returned. Considerable sympathy was expressed for the mother of the deceased, who was greatly affected during the giving of her own evidence, and that of Dr Birrell, who had made the post-mortem examination of the deceased.

He frowned, and, tearing the paper in two went across the room and flung the pieces away. How ugly it all was! And how horribly real ugliness made things! He felt a little annoyed with Lord Henry for having sent him the report. And it was certainly stupid of him to have marked it with red pencil. Victor might have read it. The man knew more than enough English for that.

Perhaps he had read it, and had begun to suspect something. And, yet, what did it matter? What had Dorian Gray to do with Sibyl Vane's death? There was nothing to fear. Dorian Gray had not killed her.

His eye fell on the yellow book that Lord Henry had sent him. What was it, he wondered. He went towards the little pearl-coloured octagonal stand, that had always looked to him like the work of some strange Egyptian bees that wrought in silver, and taking up the volume, flung himself into an arm-chair, and began to turn over the leaves. After a few minutes he became absorbed. It was the strangest book that he had ever read. It seemed to him that in exquisite raiment, and to the delicate sound of flutes, the sins of the world were passing in dumb show before him. Things that he had dimly dreamed of were suddenly made real to him. Things of which he had never dreamed were gradually revealed.

It was a novel without a plot,° and with only one character, being, indeed, simply a psychological study of a certain young Parisian, who spent his life trying to realize in the nineteenth century all the passions and modes of thought that belonged to every century except his own, and to sum up,° as it were, in himself the various moods through which the world-spirit had ever passed, loving for their mere artificiality those renunciations that men have unwisely called virtue, as much as those natural rebellions that wise men still call sin. The style in which it was written was that curious jewelled style, vivid and obscure at once, full of *argot*° and of archaisms, of technical expressions and of elaborate paraphrases, that characterizes the work of some of the finest artists of the French school of *Symbolistes*.° There were in it metaphors as monstrous as orchids, and as subtle in colour. The life of the senses was described in the terms of mystical philosophy. One hardly knew at times whether one was reading the spiritual ecstasies of some mediæval saint or the morbid confessions of a modern sinner. It was a poisonous book. The heavy odour of incense seemed to cling about its pages and to trouble the brain. The mere cadence of the sentences, the subtle monotony of their music, so full as it was of complex refrains and movements elaborately repeated, produced in the mind of the lad, as he passed from chapter to chapter, a form of reverie, a malady of dreaming, that made him unconscious of the falling day and creeping shadows.

Cloudless, and pierced by one solitary star, a copper-green sky gleamed through the windows. He read on by its wan light till he could read no more. Then, after his valet had reminded him several times of the lateness of the hour, he got up, and, going into the next room, placed the book on the little Florentine table that always stood at his bedside, and began to dress for dinner.

It was almost nine o'clock before he reached the club, where he found Lord Henry sitting alone, in the morning-room, looking very much bored.

'I am so sorry, Harry,' he cried, 'but really it is entirely your fault. That book you sent me so fascinated me that I forgot how the time was going.'

'Yes: I thought you would like it,' replied his host, rising from his chair.

'I didn't say I liked it, Harry. I said it fascinated me. There is a great difference.'

'Ah, you have discovered that?' murmured Lord Henry. And they passed into the dining-room.

CHAPTER XI

F O R years, Dorian Gray could not free himself from the influence of this book. Or perhaps it would be more accurate to say that he never sought to free himself from it. He procured from Paris no less than nine large-paper copies of the first edition, and had them bound in different colours, so that they might suit his various moods and the changing fancies of a nature over which he seemed, at times, to have almost entirely lost control. The hero, the wonderful young Parisian, in whom the romantic and the scientific temperaments were so strangely blended, became to him a kind of prefiguring type of himself. And, indeed, the whole book seemed to him to contain the story of his own life, written before he had lived it.

In one point he was more fortunate than the novel's fantastic hero. He never knew—never, indeed, had any cause to know—that somewhat grotesque dread of mirrors, and polished metal surfaces, and still water, which came upon the young Parisian so early in his life, and was occasioned by the sudden decay of a beauty that had once, apparently, been so remarkable. It was with an almost cruel joy—and perhaps in nearly every joy, as certainly in every pleasure, cruelty has its place—that he used to read the latter part of the book, with its really tragic, if somewhat over-emphasized, account of the sorrow and despair of one who had himself lost what in others, and in the world, he had most dearly valued.

For the wonderful beauty that had so fascinated Basil Hallward, and many others besides him, seemed never to leave him. Even those who had heard the most evil things against him, and from time to time strange rumours about his mode of life crept through London and became the chatter of the clubs, could not believe anything to his dishonour when they saw him. He had always the look of one who had kept himself unspotted from the world.° Men who talked grossly became silent when Dorian Gray entered the room. There was something in the purity of his face that rebuked them. His mere presence seemed to recall to them the memory of the innocence that they had tarnished. They wondered how one so charming and graceful as he was could have escaped the stain of an age that was at once sordid and sensual.

Often, on returning home from one of those mysterious and prolonged absences that gave rise to such strange conjecture among those who were his friends, or thought that they were so, he himself would creep upstairs to the locked room, open the door with the key that never left him now, and stand, with a mirror, in front of the portrait that Basil Hallward had painted of him, looking now at the evil and aging face on the canvas, and now at the fair young face that laughed back at him from the polished glass. The very sharpness of the contrast used to quicken his sense of pleasure. He grew more and more enamoured of his own beauty, more and more interested in the corruption of his own soul. He would examine with minute care, and sometimes with a monstrous and terrible delight, the hideous lines that seared the wrinkling forehead or crawled around the heavy sensual mouth, wondering sometimes which were the more horrible, the signs of sin or the signs of age. He would place his white hands beside the coarse bloated hands of the picture, and smile. He mocked the misshapen body and the failing limbs.

There were moments, indeed, at night, when, lying sleepless in his own delicately-scented chamber, or in the sordid room of the little ill-famed tavern near the Docks, which, under an assumed name, and in disguise, it was his habit to frequent, he would think of the ruin he had brought upon his soul, with a pity that was all the more poignant because it was purely selfish. But moments such as these were rare. That curiosity about life which Lord Henry had first stirred in him, as they sat together in the garden of their friend, seemed to increase with gratification.° The more he knew, the more he desired to know. He had mad hungers that grew more ravenous as he fed them.

Yet he was not really reckless, at any rate in his relations to society. Once or twice every month during the winter, and on each Wednesday evening while the season lasted, he would throw open to the world his beautiful house and have the most celebrated musicians of the day to charm his guests with the wonders of their art. His little dinners, in the settling of which Lord Henry always assisted him, were noted as much for the careful selection and placing of those invited, as for the exquisite taste shown in the decoration of the table, with its subtle symphonic arrangements of exotic flowers, and embroidered cloths, and antique plate of gold and silver. Indeed, there were many, especially among the very young men, who saw, or fancied that they saw, in Dorian Gray the true realization of a type of which they had often dreamed in Eton or Oxford days, a type that was to combine something of the real culture of the scholar with all the grace and distinction and perfect manner of a citizen of the world. To them he seemed to be of the company of those whom Dante describes as having sought to 'make themselves perfect by the worship of beauty'.° Like Gautier, he was one for whom 'the visible world existed'.°

And, certainly, to him Life itself was the first, the greatest, of the arts, and for it all the other arts seemed to be but a preparation. Fashion, by which what is really fantastic becomes for a moment universal, and Dandyism, which, in its own way, is an attempt to assert the absolute modernity of beauty, had, of course, their fascination for him. His mode of dressing, and the particular styles that from time to time he affected, had their marked influence on the young exquisites of the Mayfair balls and Pall Mall club windows, who copied him in everything that he did, and tried to reproduce the accidental charm of his graceful, though to him only half-serious, fopperies.

For, while he was but too ready to accept the position that was almost immediately offered to him on his coming of age, and found, indeed, a subtle pleasure in the thought that he might really become to the London of his own day what to imperial Neronian Rome the author of the 'Satyricon'° once had been, yet in his inmost heart he desired to be something more than a mere *arbiter elegantiarum*, to be consulted on the wearing of a jewel, or the knotting of a necktie, or the conduct of a cane. He sought to elaborate some new scheme of life that would have its reasoned philosophy and its ordered principles, and find in the spiritu-alizing of the senses its highest realization.

The worship of the senses has often, and with much justice, been decried, men feeling a natural instinct of terror about passions and sensations that seem stronger than themselves, and that they are conscious of sharing with the less highly organized forms of existence. But it appeared to Dorian Gray that the true nature of the senses had never been understood, and that they had remained savage and animal merely because the world had sought to starve them into submission or to kill them by pain, instead of aiming at making them elements of a new spirituality, of which a fine instinct for beauty was to be the dominant characteristic. As he looked back upon man moving through History, he was haunted by a feeling of loss. So much had been surrendered! and to such little purpose! There had been mad wilful rejections, monstrous forms of self-torture and self-denial, whose origin was fear, and whose result was a degradation infinitely more terrible than that fancied degradation from which, in their ignorance, they had sought to escape, Nature, in her wonderful irony, driving out the anchorite to feed with the wild animals of the desert and giving to the hermit the beasts of the field as his companions.

Yes: there was to be, as Lord Henry had prophesied, a new Hedonism° that was to recreate life, and to save it from that harsh, uncomely puritanism that is having, in our own day, its curious revival. It was to have its service of the intellect, certainly; yet, it was never to accept any theory or system that would involve the sacrifice of any mode of passionate experience. Its aim, indeed, was to be experience itself, and not the fruits of experience, sweet or bitter as they might be. Of the asceticism that deadens the senses, as of the vulgar profligacy that dulls them, it was to know nothing. But it was to teach man to concentrate himself upon the moments of a life that is itself but a moment.

There are few of us who have not sometimes wakened before dawn, either after one of those dreamless nights that make us almost enamoured of death, or one of those nights of horror and misshapen joy, when through the chambers of the brain sweep phantoms more terrible than reality itself, and instinct with that vivid life that lurks in all grotesques, and that lends to Gothic art its enduring vitality, this art being, one might fancy, especially the art of those whose minds have been troubled with the malady of reverie. Gradually white fingers creep through the curtains, and they appear to tremble. In black fantastic shapes, dumb shadows crawl into the corners of the room, and crouch there. Outside, there is the stirring of birds among the leaves, or the sound of men going forth to their work, or the sigh and sob of the wind coming down from the hills, and wandering round the silent house, as though it feared to wake the sleepers, and yet must needs call forth sleep from her purple cave. Veil after veil of thin dusky gauze is lifted, and by degrees the forms and colours of things are restored to them, and we watch the dawn remaking the world in its antique pattern. The wan mirrors get back their mimic life. The flameless tapers stand where we had left them, and beside them lies the half-cut book that we had been studying, or the wired flower that we had worn at the ball, or the letter that we had been afraid to read, or that we had read too often. Nothing seems to us changed. Out of the unreal shadows of the night comes back the real life that we had known. We have to resume it where we had left off, and there steals over us a terrible sense of the necessity for the continuance of energy in the same wearisome round of stereotyped habits, or a wild longing, it may be, that our eyelids might open some morning upon a world that had been refashioned anew in the darkness for our pleasure, a world in which things would have fresh shapes and colours, and be changed, or have other secrets, a world in which the past would have little or no place, or survive, at any rate, in no conscious form of obligation or regret, the remembrance even of joy having its bitterness, and the memories of pleasure their pain.

It was the creation of such worlds as these that seemed to Dorian Gray to be the true object, or amongst the true objects, of life; and in his search for sensations that would be at once new and delightful, and possess that element of strangeness that is so essential to romance, he would often adopt certain modes of thought that he knew to be really alien to his nature, abandon himself to their subtle influences, and then, having, as it were, caught their colour and satisfied his intellectual curiosity, leave them with that curious indifference that is not incompatible with a real ardour of temperament, and that indeed, according to certain modern psychologists, is often a condition of it.

It was rumoured of him once that he was about to join the Roman Catholic communion; and certainly the Roman ritual had always a great attraction for him. The daily sacrifice, more awful really than all the sacrifices of the antique world, stirred him as much by its superb rejection of the evidence of the senses as by the primitive simplicity of its elements and the eternal pathos of the human tragedy that it sought to symbolize. He loved to kneel down on the cold marble pavement, and watch the priest, in his stiff flowered dalmatic,° slowly and with white hands moving aside the veil of the tabernacle, or raising aloft the jewelled lantern-shaped monstrance with that pallid wafer that at times, one would fain think, is indeed the '*panis cœlestis*', the bread of angels, or, robed in the garments of the Passion of Christ, breaking the Host into the chalice, and smiting his breast for his sins. The fuming censers, that the grave boys, in their lace and scarlet, tossed into the air like great gilt flowers, had their subtle fascination for him. As he passed out, he used to look with wonder at the black confessionals, and long to sit in the dim shadow of one of them and listen to men and women whispering through the worn grating the true story of their lives.

But he never fell into the error of arresting his intellectual development by any formal acceptance of creed or system, or of mistaking, for a house in which to live, an inn that is but suitable for the sojourn of a night, or for a few hours of a night in which there are no stars and the moon is in travail. Mysticism, with its marvellous power of making common things strange to us, and the subtle antinomianism° that always seems to accompany it, moved him for a season; and for a season he inclined to the materialistic doctrines of the *Darwinismus* movement° in Germany, and found a curious pleasure in tracing the thoughts and passions of men to some pearly cell in the brain, or some white nerve in the body, delighting in the conception of the absolute dependence of the spirit on certain physical conditions, morbid or healthy, normal or diseased. Yet, as has been said of him before, no theory of life seemed to him to be of any importance compared with life itself. He felt keenly conscious of how barren all intellectual speculation is when separated from action and experiment. He knew that the senses, no less than the soul, have their spiritual mysteries to reveal.

And so he would now study perfumes,° and the secrets of their manufacture, distilling heavily-scented oils, and burning odorous gums from the East. He saw that there was no mood of the mind that had not its counterpart in the sensuous life, and set himself to discover their true relations, wondering what there was in frankincense that made one mystical, and in ambergris that stirred one's passions, and in violets that woke the memory of dead romances, and in musk that troubled the brain, and in champak that stained the imagination; and seeking often to elaborate a real psychology of perfumes, and to estimate the several influences of sweet-smelling roots, and scented pollen-laden flowers, of aromatic balms, and of dark and fragrant woods, of spikenard that sickens, of hovenia that makes men mad, and of aloes that are said to be able to expel melancholy from the soul.

At another time he devoted himself entirely to music, and in a long latticed room, with a vermilion-and-gold ceiling and walls of olive-green lacquer, he used to give curious concerts in which mad gypsies tore wild music from little zithers, or grave yellow-shawled Tunisians plucked at the strained strings of monstrous lutes, while grinning negroes beat monotonously upon copper drums, and, crouching upon scarlet mats, slim turbaned Indians blew through long pipes of reed or brass, and charmed, or feigned to charm, great hooded snakes and horrible horned adders. The harsh intervals and shrill discords of barbaric music stirred him at times when Schubert's grace, and Chopin's beautiful sorrows, and the mighty harmonies of Beethoven himself, fell unheeded on his ear. He collected together from all parts of the world the strangest instruments° that could be found, either in the tombs of dead nations or among the few savage tribes that have survived contact with Western civilizations, and loved to touch and try them. He had the mysterious *juruparis* of the Rio Negro Indians, that women are not allowed to look at, and that even youths may not see till they have been subjected to fasting and scourging, and the earthen jars of the Peruvians that have the shrill cries of birds, and flutes of human bones such as Alfonso de Ovalle heard in Chili, and the sonorous green jaspers that are found near Cuzco and give forth a note of singular sweetness. He had painted gourds filled with pebbles that rattled when they were shaken; the long *clarin* of the

Mexicans, into which the performer does not blow, but through which he inhales the air; the harsh *turé* of the Amazon tribes, that is sounded by the sentinels who sit all day long in high trees, and can be heard, it is said, at a distance of three leagues; the *teponaztli*, that has two vibrating tongues of wood, and is beaten with sticks that are smeared with an elastic gum obtained from the milky juice of plants; the *yotl*-bells of the Aztecs, that are hung in clusters like grapes; and a huge cylindrical drum, covered with the skins of great serpents, like the one that Bernal Diaz saw when he went with Cortes into the Mexican temple, and of whose doleful sound he has left us so vivid a description. The fantastic character of these instruments fascinated him, and he felt a curious delight in the thought that Art, like Nature, has her monsters, things of bestial shape and with hideous voices. Yet, after some time, he wearied of them, and would sit in his box at the Opera, either alone or with Lord Henry, listening in rapt pleasure to 'Tannhäuser', and seeing in the prelude to that great work of art a presentation of the tragedy of his own soul.°

On one occasion he took up the study of jewels, and appeared at a costume ball as Anne de Joyeuse,° Admiral of France, in a dress covered with five hundred and sixty pearls. This taste enthralled him for years, and, indeed, may be said never to have left him. He would often spend a whole day settling and resettling in their cases the various stones that he had collected,° such as the olive-green chrysoberyl that turns red by lamplight, the cymophane with its wire-like line of silver, the pistachio-coloured peridot, rose-pink and wine-yellow topazes, carbuncles of fiery scarlet with tremulous four-rayed stars, flame-red cinnamon-stones, orange and violet spinels, and amethysts with their alternate layers of ruby and sapphire. He loved the red gold of the sunstone, and the moonstone's pearly whiteness, and the broken rainbow of the milky opal. He procured from Amsterdam three emeralds of extraordinary size and richness of colour, and had a turquoise *de la vieille roche* that was the envy of all the connoisseurs.

He discovered wonderful stories, also, about jewels.° In Alphonso's 'Clericalis Disciplina' a serpent was mentioned with eyes of real jacinth, and in the romantic history of Alexander, the Conqueror of Emathia was said to have found in the vale of Jordan snakes 'with collars of real emeralds growing on their backs'. There was a gem in the brain of the dragon, Philostratus told us, and 'by the exhibition of golden letters and a scarlet robe' the monster could be thrown into a magical sleep, and slain. According to the great alchemist, Pierre de Boniface, the diamond rendered a man invisible, and the agate of India made him eloquent. The cornelian appeased anger, and the hyacinth provoked sleep, and the amethyst drove away the fumes of wine. The garnet cast out demons, and the hydropicus deprived the moon of her colour. The selenite waxed and waned with the moon, and the meloceus, that discovers thieves, could be affected only by the blood of kids. Leonardus Camillus had seen a white stone taken from the brain of a newly-killed toad, that was a certain antidote against poison. The bezoar, that was found in the heart of the Arabian deer, was a charm that could cure the plague. In the nests of Arabian birds was the aspilates, that, according to Democritus, kept the wearer from any danger by fire.

The King of Ceilan rode through his city with a large ruby in his hands, at the ceremony of his coronation. The gates of the palace of John the Priest were 'made of sardius, with the horn of the horned snake inwrought, so that no man might bring poison within'. Over the gable were 'two golden apples, in which were two carbuncles', so that the gold might shine by day, and the carbuncles by night. In Lodge's strange romance 'A Margarite of America' it was stated that in the chamber of the queen one could behold 'all the chaste ladies of the world, inchased out of silver, looking through fair mirrours of chrysolites, carbuncles, saphhires, and greene emeraults'. Marco Polo had seen the inhabitants of Zipangu place rose-coloured pearls in the mouths of the dead. A sea-monster had been enamoured of the pearl that the diver brought to King Perozes, and had slain the thief, and mourned for seven moons over its loss. When the Huns lured the king into the great pit, he flung it away—Procopius tells the story—nor was it ever found again, though the Emperor Anastasius offered five hundred-weight of gold pieces for it. The King of Malabar had shown to a certain Venetian a rosary of three hundred and four pearls, one for every god that he worshipped.

When the Duke de Valentinois, son of Alexander VI, visited Louis XII of France, his horse was loaded with gold leaves, according to Brantôme, and his cap had double rows of rubies that threw out a great light. Charles of England had ridden in stirrups hung with four hundred and twenty-one diamonds. Richard II had a coat, valued at thirty thousand marks, which was covered with balas rubies. Hall described Henry VIII, on his way to the Tower previous to his coronation, as wearing 'a jacket of raised gold, the placard embroidered with diamonds and other rich stones, and a great bauderike about his neck of large balasses'. The favourites of James I wore ear-rings of emeralds set in gold filigrane. Edward II gave to Piers Gaveston a suit of red-gold armour studded with jacinths, a collar of gold roses set with turquoise-stones, and a skull-cap *parsemé* with pearls. Henry II wore jewelled gloves reaching to the elbow, and had a hawk-glove sewn with twelve rubies and fifty-two great orients. The ducal hat of Charles the Rash, the last Duke of Burgundy of his race, was hung with pear-shaped pearls, and studded with sapphires. How exquisite life had once been! How gorgeous in its pomp and decoration! Even to read of the luxury of the dead was wonderful.

Then he turned his attention to embroideries,° and to the tapestries that performed the office of frescoes in the chill rooms of the Northern nations of Europe. As he investigated the subject—and he always had an extraordinary faculty of becoming absolutely absorbed for the moment in whatever he took up—he was almost saddened by the reflection of the ruin that Time brought on beautiful and wonderful things. He, at any rate, had escaped that. Summer followed summer, and the yellow jonquils bloomed and died many times, and nights of horror repeated the story of their shame, but he was unchanged. No winter marred his face or stained his flower-like bloom. How different it was with material things! Where had they passed to? Where was the great crocus-coloured robe, on which the gods fought against the giants, that had been worked by brown girls for the pleasure of Athena? Where, the huge velarium that Nero had stretched across the Colosseum at Rome, that Titan sail of purple on which was represented the starry sky, and Apollo driving a chariot drawn by white gilt-reined steeds? He longed to see the curious table-napkins wrought for the Priest of the Sun, on which were displayed all the dainties and viands that could be wanted for a feast; the mortuary cloth of King Chilperic, with its three hundred golden bees; the fantastic robes that excited the indignation of the Bishop of Pontus, and were figured with 'lions, panthers, bears, dogs, forests, rocks, hunters—all, in fact, that a painter can copy from nature'; and the coat that Charles of Orleans once wore, on the sleeves of which were embroidered the verses of a song beginning '*Madame, je suis tout joyeux*', the musical accompaniment of the words being wrought in gold thread, and each note, of square shape in those days, formed with four pearls. He read of the room that was prepared at the palace of Rheims for the use of Queen Joan of Burgundy, and was decorated with 'thirteen hundred and twenty-one parrots, made in broidery, and blazoned with the king's arms, and five hundred and sixty-one butterflies, whose wings were similarly ornamented with the arms of the queen, the whole worked in gold'. Catherine de Médicis had a mourning-bed made for her of black velvet powdered with crescents and suns. Its curtains were of damask, with leafy wreaths and garlands, figured upon a gold and silver ground, and fringed along the edges with broideries of pearls, and it stood in a room hung with rows of the queen's devices in cut black velvet upon cloth of silver. Louis XIV had gold-embroidered caryatides fifteen feet high in his apartment. The state bed of Sobieski, King of Poland, was made of Smyrna gold brocade embroidered in turquoises with verses from the Koran. Its supports were of silver gilt, beautifully chased, and profusely set with enamelled and jewelled medallions. It had been taken from the Turkish camp before Vienna, and the standard of Mohammed had stood beneath the tremulous gilt of its canopy.

And so, for a whole year, he sought to accumulate the most exquisite specimens that he could find of textile and embroidered work, getting the dainty Delhi muslins, finely wrought with gold-thread palmates, and stitched over with iridescent beetles' wings; the Dacca gauzes, that from their transparency are known in the East as 'woven air', and 'running water', and 'evening dew'; strange figured cloths from Java; elaborate yellow Chinese hangings; books bound in tawny satins or fair blue silks, and wrought with *fleurs de lys*, birds, and images; veils of *lacis* worked in Hungary point; Sicilian brocades, and stiff Spanish velvets; Georgian work with its gilt coins, and Japanese *Foukousas* with their green-toned golds and their marvellously-plumaged birds.

He had a special passion, also, for ecclesiastical vestments,° as indeed he had for everything connected with the service of the Church. In the long cedar chests that lined the west gallery of his house he had stored away many rare and beautiful specimens of what is really the raiment of the Bride of Christ, who must wear purple and jewels and fine linen that she may hide the pallid macerated body that is worn by the suffering that she seeks for, and wounded by self-inflicted pain. He possessed a gorgeous cope of crimson silk and gold-thread damask, figured with a repeating pattern of golden pomegranates set in six-petalled formal blossoms, beyond which on either side was the pine-apple device wrought in seed-pearls. The orphreys were divided into panels representing scenes from the life of the Virgin, and the coronation of the Virgin was figured in coloured silks upon the hood. This was Italian work of the fifteenth century. Another cope was of green velvet, embroidered with heart-shaped groups of acanthus-leaves, from which spread long-stemmed white blossoms, the details of which were picked out with silver thread and coloured crystals. The morse bore a seraph's head in gold-thread raised work. The orphreys were woven in a diaper of red and gold silk, and were starred with medallions of many saints and martyrs, among whom was St Sebastian. He had chasubles, also, of amber-coloured silk, and blue silk and gold brocade, and yellow silk damask and cloth of gold, figured with representations of the Passion and Crucifixion of Christ, and embroidered with lions and peacocks and other emblems; dalmatics of white satin and pink silk damask, decorated with tulips and dolphins and *fleurs de lys*; altar frontals of crimson velvet and blue linen; and many corporals, chalice-veils, and sudaria. In the mystic offices to which such things were put, there was something that quickened his imagination.

For these treasures, and everything that he collected in his lovely house, were to be to him means of forgetfulness, modes by which he could escape, for a season, from the fear that seemed to him at times to be almost too great to be borne. Upon the walls of the lonely locked room where he had spent so much of his boyhood, he had hung with his own hands the terrible portrait whose changing features showed him the real degradation of his life, and in front of it had draped the purple-and-gold pall as a curtain. For weeks he would not go there, would forget the hideous painted thing, and get back his light heart, his wonderful joyousness, his passionate absorption in mere existence. Then, suddenly, some night he would creep out of the house, go down to dreadful places near Blue Gate Fields, and stay there, day after day, until he was driven away. On his return he would sit in front of the picture, sometimes loathing it and himself, but filled, at other times, with that pride of individualism that is half the fascination of sin, and smiling, with secret pleasure, at the misshapen shadow that had to bear the burden that should have been his own.

After a few years he could not endure to be long out of England, and gave up the villa that he had shared at Trouville with Lord Henry, as well as the little white walled-in house at Algiers where they had more than once spent the winter. He hated to be separated from the picture that was such a part of his life, and was also afraid that during his absence some one might gain access to the room, in spite of the elaborate bars that he had caused to be placed upon the door.

He was quite conscious that this would tell them nothing. It was true that the portrait still preserved, under all the foulness and ugliness of the face, its marked likeness to himself; but what could they learn from that? He would laugh at any one who tried to taunt him. He had not painted it. What was it to him how vile and full of shame it looked? Even if he told them, would they believe it?

Yet he was afraid. Sometimes when he was down at his great house in Nottinghamshire, entertaining the fashionable young men of his own rank who were his chief companions, and astounding the country by the wanton luxury and gorgeous splendour of his mode of life, he would suddenly leave his guests and rush back to town to see that the door had not been tampered with, and that the picture was still there. What if it should be stolen? The mere thought made him cold with horror. Surely the world would know his secret then. Perhaps the world already suspected it.

For, while he fascinated many, there were not a few who distrusted him. He was very nearly blackballed° at a West End club of which his birth and social position fully entitled him to become a member, and it was said that on one occasion, when he was brought by a friend into the smoking-room of the Churchill, the Duke of Berwick and another gentleman got up in a marked manner and went out. Curious stories became current about him after he had passed his twenty-fifth year. It was rumoured that he had been seen brawling with foreign sailors in a low den in the distant parts of Whitechapel, and that he consorted with thieves and coiners and knew the mysteries of their trade. His extraordinary absences became notorious, and, when he used to reappear again in society, men would whisper to each other in corners, or pass him with a sneer, or look at him with cold searching eyes, as though they were determined to discover his secret.

Of such insolences and attempted slights he, of course, took no notice, and in the opinion of most people his frank debonnair manner, his charming boyish smile, and the infinite grace of that wonderful youth that seemed never to leave him, were in themselves a sufficient answer to the calumnies, for so they termed them, that were circulated about him. It was remarked, however, that some of those who had been most intimate with him appeared, after a time, to shun him. Women who had wildly adored him, and for his sake had braved all social censure and set convention at defiance, were seen to grow pallid with shame or horror if Dorian Gray entered the room.

Yet these whispered scandals only increased, in the eyes of many, his strange and dangerous charm. His great wealth was a certain element of security. Society, civilized society at least, is never very ready to believe anything to the detriment of those who are both rich and fascinating. It feels instinctively that manners are of more importance than morals,° and, in its opinion, the highest respectability is of much less value than the possession of a good *chef*. And, after all, it is a very poor consolation to be told that the man who has given one a bad dinner, or poor wine, is irreproachable in his private life. Even the cardinal virtues cannot atone for half-cold *entrées*, as Lord Henry remarked once, in a discussion on the subject; and there is possibly a good deal to be said for his view. For the canons of good society are, or should be, the same as the canons of art. Form is absolutely essential to it. It should have the dignity of a ceremony, as well as its unreality, and should combine the insincere character of a romantic play with the wit and beauty that make such plays delightful to us. Is insincerity such a terrible thing?° I think not. It is merely a method by which we can multiply our personalities.

Such, at any rate, was Dorian Gray's opinion. He used to wonder at the shallow psychology of those who conceive the Ego in man as a thing simple, permanent, reliable, and of one essence. To him, man was a being with myriad lives and myriad sensations,° a complex multiform creature that bore within itself strange legacies of thought and passion, and whose very flesh was tainted with the monstrous maladies of the dead. He loved to stroll through the gaunt cold picture-gallery of his country house and look at the various portraits of those whose blood flowed in his veins. Here was Philip Herbert, described by Francis Osborne, in his 'Memoires on the Reigns of Queen Elizabeth and King James', as one who was 'caressed by the Court for his handsome face,° which kept him not long company'. Was it young Herbert's life that he sometimes led? Had some strange poisonous germ crept from body to body till it had reached his own? Was it some dim sense of that ruined grace that had made him so suddenly, and almost without cause, give utterance, in Basil Hallward's studio, to the mad prayer that had so changed his life? Here, in gold-embroidered red doublet, jewelled surcoat, and gilt-edged ruff and wrist-bands, stood Sir Anthony Sherard, with his silver-and-black armour piled at his feet. What had this man's legacy been? Had the lover of Giovanna of Naples bequeathed him some inheritance of sin and shame? Were his own actions merely the dreams that the dead man had not dared to realize? Here, from the fading canvas, smiled Lady Elizabeth Devereux, in her gauze hood, pearl stomacher, and pink slashed sleeves. A flower was in her right hand, and her left clasped an enamelled collar of white and damask roses. On a table by her side lay a mandolin and an apple. There were large green rosettes upon her little pointed shoes. He knew her life, and the strange stories that were told about her lovers. Had he something of her temperament in him? These oval heavy-lidded eyes seemed to look curiously at him. What of George Willoughby, with his powdered hair and fantastic patches? How evil he looked! The face was saturnine and swarthy, and the sensual lips seemed to be twisted with disdain. Delicate lace ruffles fell over the lean yellow hands that were so overladen with rings. He had been a macaroni of the eighteenth century, and the friend, in his youth, of Lord Ferrars. What of the second Lord Beckenham, the companion of the Prince Regent in his wildest days, and one of the witnesses at the secret marriage with Mrs Fitzherbert? How proud and handsome he was, with his chestnut curls and insolent pose! What passions had he bequeathed? The world had looked upon him as infamous. He had led the orgies at Carlton House.° The star of the Garter glittered upon his breast. Beside him hung the portrait of his wife, a pallid, thin-lipped woman in black. Her blood, also, stirred within him. How curious it all seemed! And his mother with her Lady Hamilton face, and her moist wine-dashed lips—he knew what he had got from her. He had got from her his beauty, and his passion for the beauty of others. She laughed at him in her loose Bacchante dress. There were vine leaves in her hair. The purple spilled from the cup she was holding. The carnations of the painting had withered, but the eyes were still wonderful in their depth and brilliancy of colour. They seemed to follow him wherever he went.

Yet one had ancestors in literature, as well as in one's own race, nearer perhaps in type and temperament, many of them, and certainly with an influence of which one was more absolutely conscious. There were times when it appeared to Dorian Gray that the whole of history was merely the record of his own life, not as he had lived it in act and circumstance, but as his imagination had created it for him, as it had been in his brain and in his passions. He felt that he had known them all, those strange terrible figures that had passed across the stage of the world and made sin so marvellous and evil so full of subtlety. It seemed to him that in some mysterious way their lives had been his own.

The hero of the wonderful novel that had so influenced his life had himself known this curious fancy. In the seventh chapter he tells how, crowned with laurel, lest lightning might strike him, he had sat, as Tiberius,° in a garden at Capri, reading the shameful books of Elephantis, while dwarfs and peacocks strutted round him and the flute-player mocked the swinger of the censer; and, as Caligula, had caroused with the green-shirted jockeys in their stables, and supped in an ivory manger with a jewel-frontleted horse; and, as Domitian, had wandered through a corridor lined with marble mirrors, looking round with haggard eyes for the reflection of the dagger that was to end his days, and sick with that ennui, that terrible *tædium vitæ*, that comes on those to whom life denies nothing; and had peered through a clear emerald at the red shambles of the Circus, and then, in a litter of pearl and purple drawn by silver-shod mules, been carried through the Street of Pomegranates to a House of Gold, and heard men cry on Nero Cæsar as he passed by; and, as Elagabalus, had painted his face with colours, and plied the distaff among the women, and brought the Moon from Carthage, and given her in mystic marriage to the Sun.

Over and over again Dorian used to read this fantastic chapter, and the two chapters immediately following, in which, as in some curious tapestries or cunningly-wrought enamels, were pictured the awful and beautiful forms of those whom Vice and Blood and Weariness had made monstrous or mad:° Filippo, Duke of Milan, who slew his wife, and painted her lips with a scarlet poison that her lover might suck death from the dead thing he fondled; Pietro Barbi, the Venetian, known as Paul the Second, who sought in his vanity to assume the title of Formosus, and whose tiara, valued at two hundred thousand florins, was bought at the price of a terrible sin; Gian Maria Visconti, who used hounds to chase living men, and whose murdered body was covered with roses by a harlot who had loved him; the Borgia on his white horse, with Fratricide riding beside him, and his mantle stained with the blood of Perotto; Pietro Riario, the young Cardinal Archbishop of Florence, child and minion of Sixtus IV, whose beauty was equalled only by his debauchery, and who received Leonora of Aragon in a pavilion of white and crimson silk, filled with nymphs and centaurs, and gilded a boy that he might serve at the feast as Ganymede or Hylas; Ezzelin, whose melancholy could be cured only by the spectacle of death, and who had a passion for red blood, as other men have for red wine—the son of the Fiend, as was reported, and one who had cheated his father at dice when gambling with him for his own soul; Giambattista Cibo, who in mockery took the name of Innocent, and into whose torpid veins the blood of three lads was infused by a Jewish doctor; Sigismondo Malatesta, the lover of Isotta, and the lord of Rimini, whose effigy was burned at Rome as the enemy of God and man, who strangled Polyssena with a napkin, and gave poison to Ginevra d'Este in a cup of emerald, and in honour of a shameful passion built a pagan church for Christian worship; Charles VI, who had so wildly adored his brother's wife that a leper had warned him of the insanity that was coming on him, and who, when his brain had sickened and grown strange, could only be soothed by Saracen cards painted with the images of Love and Death and Madness; and, in his trimmed jerkin and jewelled cap and acanthus-like curls, Grifonetto Baglioni, who slew Astorre with his bride, and Simonetto with his page, and whose comeliness was such that, as he lay dying in the yellow piazza of Perugia, those who had hated him could not choose but weep, and Atalanta, who had cursed him, blessed him.

There was a horrible fascination in them all. He saw them at night, and they troubled his imagination in the day. The Renaissance knew of strange manners of poisoning—poisoning by a helmet and a lighted torch, by an embroidered glove and a jewelled fan, by a gilded pomander and by an amber chain. Dorian Gray had been poisoned by a book.°

There were moments when he looked on evil simply as a mode through which he could realize his conception of the beautiful.

CHAPTER XII

It was on the ninth of November, the eve of his own thirty-eighth birthday, as he often remembered afterwards.

He was walking home about eleven o'clock from Lord Henry's, where he had been dining, and was wrapped in heavy furs, as the night was cold and foggy. At the corner of Grosvenor Square and South Audley Street a man passed him in the mist, walking very fast, and with the collar of his grey ulster° turned up. He had a bag in his hand. Dorian recognized him. It was Basil Hallward. A strange sense of fear, for which he could not account, came over him. He made no sign of recognition, and went on quickly, in the direction of his own house.

But Hallward had seen him. Dorian heard him first stopping on the pavement and then hurrying after him. In a few moments his hand was on his arm.

'Dorian! What an extraordinary piece of luck! I have been waiting for you in your library ever since nine o'clock. Finally I took pity on your tired servant, and told him to go to bed, as he let me out. I am off to Paris by the midnight train, and I particularly wanted to see you before I left. I thought it was you, or rather your fur coat, as you passed me. But I wasn't quite sure. Didn't you recognize me?'

'In this fog, my dear Basil? Why, I can't even recognize Grosvenor Square. I believe my house is somewhere about here, but I don't feel at all certain about it. I am sorry you are going away, as I have not seen you for ages. But I suppose you will be back soon?'

'No: I am going to be out of England for six months. I intend to take a studio in Paris, and shut myself up till I have finished a great picture I have in my head. However, it wasn't about myself I wanted to talk. Here we are at your door. Let me come in for a moment. I have something to say to you.'

'I shall be charmed. But won't you miss your train?' said Dorian Gray, languidly, as he passed up the steps and opened the door with his latch-key.

The lamp-light struggled out through the fog, and Hallward looked at his watch. 'I have heaps of time,' he answered. 'The train doesn't go till twelve-fifteen, and it is only just eleven. In fact, I was on my way to the club to look for you, when I met you. You see, I shan't have any delay about luggage, as I have sent on my heavy things. All I have with me is in this bag, and I can easily get to Victoria in twenty minutes.'

Dorian looked at him and smiled. 'What a way for a fashionable painter to travel! A Gladstone bag, and an ulster! Come in, or the fog will get into the house. And mind you don't talk about anything serious. Nothing is serious nowadays. At least nothing should be.'

Hallward shook his head, as he entered, and followed Dorian into the library. There was a bright wood fire blazing in the large open hearth. The lamps were lit, and an open Dutch silver spirit-case stood, with some siphons of soda-water and large cut-glass tumblers, on a little marqueterie table.

'You see your servant made me quite at home, Dorian. He gave me everything I wanted, including your best gold-tipped cigarettes. He is a most hospitable creature. I like him much better than the Frenchman you used to have. What has become of the Frenchman, by the bye?'

Dorian shrugged his shoulders. 'I believe he married Lady Radley's maid, and has established her in Paris as an English dressmaker. *Anglomanie* is very fashionable over there now, I hear. It seems silly of the French, doesn't it? But—do you know?—he was not at all a bad servant. I never liked him, but I had nothing to complain about. One often imagines things that are quite absurd. He was really very devoted to me, and seemed quite sorry when he went away. Have another brandy-and-soda? Or would you like hock-and-seltzer? I always take hock-and-seltzer myself. There is sure to be some in the next room.'

'Thanks, I won't have anything more,' said the painter, taking his cap and coat off, and throwing them on the bag that he had placed in the corner. 'And now, my dear fellow, I want to speak to you seriously. Don't frown like that. You make it so much more difficult for me.'

'What is it all about?' cried Dorian, in his petulant way, flinging himself down on the sofa. 'I hope it is not about myself. I am tired of myself tonight. I should like to be somebody else.'

'It is about yourself,' answered Hallward, in his grave, deep voice, 'and I must say it to you. I shall only keep you half an hour.'

Dorian sighed, and lit a cigarette. 'Half an hour!' he murmured.

'It is not much to ask of you, Dorian, and it is entirely for your own sake that I am speaking. I think it right that you should know that the most dreadful things are being said against you in London.'

'I don't wish to know anything about them. I love scandals about other people, but scandals about myself don't interest me. They have not got the charm of novelty.'

'They must interest you, Dorian. Every gentleman is interested in his good name. You don't want people to talk of you as something vile and degraded. Of course you have your position, and your wealth, and all that kind of thing. But position and wealth are not everything. Mind you, I don't believe these rumours at all. At least, I can't believe them when I see you. Sin is a thing that writes itself across a man's face. It cannot be concealed. People talk sometimes of secret vices. There are no such things. If a wretched man has a vice, it shows itself in the lines of his mouth, the droop of his eyelids, the moulding of his hands even. Somebody—I won't mention his name, but you know him—came to me last year to have his portrait done. I had never seen him before, and had never heard anything about him at the time, though I have heard a good deal since. He offered an extravagant price. I refused him. There was something in the shape of his fingers that I hated. I know now that I was quite right in what I fancied about him. His life is dreadful. But you, Dorian, with your pure, bright, innocent face, and your marvellous untroubled youth—I can't believe anything against you. And yet I see you very seldom, and you never come down to the studio now, and when I am away from you, and I hear all these hideous things that people are whispering about you, I don't know what to say. Why is it, Dorian, that a man like the Duke of Berwick leaves the room of a club when you enter it? Why is it that so many gentlemen in London will neither go to your house nor invite you to theirs? You used to be a friend of Lord Staveley. I met him at dinner last week. Your name happened to come up in conversation, in connection with the miniatures you have lent to the exhibition at the Dudley.° Staveley curled his lip, and said that you might have the most artistic tastes, but that you were a man whom no pure-minded girl should be allowed to know, and whom no chaste woman should sit in the same room with. I reminded him that I was a friend of yours, and asked him what he meant. He told me. He told me right out before everybody. It was horrible! Why is your friendship so fatal to young men? There was that wretched boy in the Guards who committed suicide. You were his great friend. There was Sir Henry Ashton, who had to leave England, with a tarnished name. You and he were inseparable. What about Adrian Singleton, and his dreadful end? What about Lord Kent's only son, and his career? I met his father yesterday in St James's Street. He seemed broken with shame and sorrow. What about the young Duke of Perth? What sort of life has he got now? What gentleman would associate with him?'

'Stop, Basil. You are talking about things of which you know nothing,' said Dorian Gray, biting his lip, and with a note of infinite contempt in his voice. 'You ask me why Berwick leaves a room when I enter it. It is because I know everything about his life, not because he knows anything about mine. With such blood as he has in his veins, how could his record be clean? You ask me about Henry Ashton and young Perth. Did I teach the one his vices, and the other his debauchery? If Kent's silly son takes his wife from the streets, what is that to me? If Adrian Singleton writes his friend's name across a bill, am I his keeper? I know how people chatter in England. The middle classes air their moral prejudices over their gross dinner-tables, and whisper about what they call the profligacies of their betters in order to try and pretend that they are in smart society, and on intimate terms with the people they slander. In this country it is enough for a man to have distinction and brains for every common tongue to wag against him. And what sort of lives do these people, who pose as being moral, lead themselves? My dear fellow, you forget that we are in the native land of the hypocrite.'

'Dorian,' cried Hallward, 'that is not the question. England is bad enough I know, and English society is all wrong. That is the reason why I want you to be fine. You have not been fine. One has a right to judge of a man by the effect he has over his friends. Yours seem to lose all sense of honour, of goodness, of purity. You have filled them with a madness for pleasure. They have gone down into the depths. You led them there. Yes: you led them there, and yet you can smile, as you are smiling now. And there is worse behind. I know you and Harry are inseparable. Surely for that reason, if for none other, you should not have made his sister's name a by-word.'

'Take care, Basil. You go too far.'

'I must speak, and you must listen. You shall listen. When you met Lady Gwendolen, not a breath of scandal had ever touched her. Is there a single decent woman in London now who would drive with her in the Park? Why, even her children are not allowed to live with her. Then there are other stories—stories that you have been seen creeping at dawn out of dreadful houses and slinking in disguise into the foulest dens in London. Are they true? Can they be true? When I first heard them, I laughed. I hear them now, and they make me shudder. What about your country house, and the life that is led there? Dorian, you don't know what is said about you. I won't tell you that I don't want to preach to you. I remember Harry saying once that every man who turned himself into an amateur curate for the moment always began by saying that, and then proceeded to break his word. I do want to preach to you. I want you to lead such a life as will make the world respect you. I want you to have a clean name and a fair record. I want you to get rid of the dreadful people you associate with. Don't shrug your shoulders like that. Don't be so indifferent. You have a wonderful influence. Let it be for good, not for evil. They say that you corrupt every one with whom you become intimate, and that it is quite sufficient for you to enter a house, for shame of some kind to follow after. I don't know whether it is so or not. How should I know? But it is said of you. I am told things that it seems impossible to doubt. Lord Gloucester was one of my greatest friends at Oxford. He showed me a letter that his wife had written to him when she was dying alone in her villa at Mentone. Your name was implicated in the most terrible confession I ever read. I told him that it was absurd—that I knew you thoroughly, and that you were incapable of anything of the kind. Know you? I wonder do I know you? Before I could answer that, I should have to see your soul.'

'To see my soul!' muttered Dorian Gray, starting up from the sofa and turning almost white from fear.

'Yes,' answered Hallward, gravely, and with deep-toned sorrow in his voice—'to see your soul. But only God can do that.'

A bitter laugh of mockery broke from the lips of the younger man. 'You shall see it yourself, tonight!' he cried, seizing a lamp from the table. 'Come: it is your own handiwork. Why shouldn't you look at it? You can tell the world all about it afterwards, if you choose. Nobody would believe you. If they did believe you, they would like me all the better for it. I know the age better than you do, though you will prate about it so tediously. Come, I tell you. You have chattered enough about corruption. Now you shall look on it face to face.'

There was the madness of pride in every word he uttered. He stamped his foot upon the ground in his boyish insolent manner. He felt a terrible joy at the thought that some one else was to share his secret, and that the man who had painted the portrait that was the origin of all his shame was to be burdened for the rest of his life with the hideous memory of what he had done.

'Yes,' he continued, coming closer to him, and looking steadfastly into his stern eyes, 'I shall show you my soul. You shall see the thing that you fancy only God can see.'

Hallward started back. 'This is blasphemy, Dorian!' he cried. 'You must not say things like that. They are horrible, and they don't mean anything.'

'You think so?' He laughed again.

'I know so. As for what I said to you tonight, I said it for your good. You know I have been always a staunch friend to you.'

'Don't touch me. Finish what you have to say.'

A twisted flash of pain shot across the painter's face. He paused for a moment, and a wild feeling of pity came over him. After all, what right had he to pry into the life of Dorian Gray? If he had done a tithe of what was rumoured about him, how much he must have suffered! Then he straightened himself up, and walked over to the fireplace, and stood there, looking at the burning logs with their frost-like ashes and their throbbing cores of flame.

'I am waiting, Basil,' said the young man, in a hard, clear voice.

He turned round. 'What I have to say is this,' he cried. 'You must give me some answer to these horrible charges that are made against you. If you tell me that they are absolutely untrue from beginning to end, I shall believe you. Deny them, Dorian, deny them! Can't you see what I am going through? My God! don't tell me that you are bad, and corrupt, and shameful.'

Dorian Gray smiled. There was a curl of contempt in his lips. 'Come upstairs, Basil,' he said, quietly. 'I keep a diary of my life from day to day, and it never leaves the room in which it is written. I will show it to you if you come with me.'

'I will come with you, Dorian, if you wish it. I see I have missed my train. That makes no matter. I can go tomorrow. But don't ask me to read anything tonight. All I want is a plain answer to my question.'

'That shall be given to you upstairs. I could not give it here. You will not have to read long.'

CHAPTER XIII

HE passed out of the room, and began the ascent, Basil Hallward following close behind. They walked softly, as men do instinctively at night. The lamp cast fantastic shadows on the wall and staircase. A rising wind made some of the windows rattle.

When they reached the top landing, Dorian set the lamp down on the floor, and taking out the key turned it in the lock. 'You insist on knowing, Basil?' he asked, in a low voice.

'Yes.'

'I am delighted,' he answered, smiling. Then he added, somewhat harshly, 'You are the one man in the world who is entitled to know everything about me. You have had more to do with my life than you think': and, taking up the lamp, he opened the door and went in. A cold current of air passed them, and the light shot up for a moment in a flame of murky orange. He shuddered. 'Shut the door behind you,' he whispered, as he placed the lamp on the table.

Hallward glanced round him, with a puzzled expression. The room looked as if it had not been lived in for years. A faded Flemish tapestry, a curtained picture, an old Italian *cassone*, and an almost empty bookcase—that was all that it seemed to contain, besides a chair and a table. As Dorian Gray was lighting a half-burned candle that was standing on the mantelshelf, he saw that the whole place was covered with dust, and that the carpet was in holes. A mouse ran scuffling behind the wainscoting. There was a damp odour of mildew.

'So you think that it is only God who sees the soul, Basil? Draw that curtain back, and you will see mine.'

The voice that spoke was cold and cruel. 'You are mad, Dorian, or playing a part,' muttered Hallward, frowning.

'You won't? Then I must do it myself,' said the young man; and he tore the curtain from its rod, and flung it on the ground.

An exclamation of horror broke from the painter's lips as he saw in the dim light the hideous face on the canvas grinning at him. There was something in its expression that filled him with disgust and loathing. Good heavens! it was Dorian Gray's own face that he was looking at! The horror, whatever it was, had not yet entirely spoiled that marvellous beauty. There was still some gold in the thinning hair and some scarlet on the sensual mouth. The sodden eyes had kept something of the loveliness of their blue, the noble curves had not yet completely passed away from chiselled nostrils and from plastic throat. Yes, it was Dorian himself. But who had done it? He seemed to recognize his own brushwork, and the frame was his own design. The idea was monstrous, yet he felt afraid. He seized the lighted candle, and held it to the picture. In the left-hand corner was his own name, traced in long letters of bright vermilion.

It was some foul parody, some infamous, ignoble satire. He had never done that. Still, it was his own picture. He knew it, and he felt as if his blood had changed in a moment from fire to sluggish ice. His own picture! What did it mean? Why had it altered? He turned, and looked at Dorian Gray with the eyes of a sick man. His mouth twitched, and his parched tongue seemed unable to articulate. He passed his hand across his forehead. It was dank with clammy sweat.

The young man was leaning against the mantelshelf, watching him with that strange expression that one sees on the faces of those who are absorbed in a play when some great artist is acting. There was neither real sorrow in it nor real joy. There was simply the passion of the spectator, with perhaps a flicker of triumph in his eyes. He had taken the flower out of his coat, and was smelling it, or pretending to do so.

'What does this mean?' cried Hallward, at last. His own voice sounded shrill and curious in his ears.

'Years ago, when I was a boy,' said Dorian Gray, crushing the flower in his hand, 'you met me, flattered me, and taught me to be vain of my good looks. One day you introduced me to a friend of yours, who explained to me the wonder of youth, and you finished a portrait of me that revealed to me the wonder of beauty. In a mad moment, that, even now, I don't know whether I regret or not, I made a wish, perhaps you would call it a prayer . . .'

'I remember it! Oh, how well I remember it! No! the thing is impossible. The room is damp. Mildew has got into the canvas. The paints I used had some wretched mineral poison in them. I tell you the thing is impossible.'

'Ah, what is impossible?' murmured the young man, going over to the window, and leaning his forehead against the cold, mist-stained glass.

'You told me you had destroyed it.'

'I was wrong. It has destroyed me.'

'I don't believe it is my picture.'

'Can't you see your ideal in it?' said Dorian, bitterly.

'My ideal, as you call it . . .'

'As you called it.'

'There was nothing evil in it, nothing shameful. You were to me such an ideal as I shall never meet again. This is the face of a satyr.'

'It is the face of my soul.'

'Christ! what a thing I must have worshipped! It has the eyes of a devil.'

'Each of us has Heaven and Hell in him, Basil,' cried Dorian, with a wild gesture of despair.

Hallward turned again to the portrait, and gazed at it. 'My God! if it is true,' he exclaimed, 'and this is what you have done with your life, why, you must be worse even than those who talk against you fancy you to be!' He held the light up again to the canvas, and examined it. The surface seemed to be quite undisturbed, and as he had left it. It was from within, apparently, that the foulness and horror had come. Through some strange quickening of inner life the leprosies of sin were slowly eating the thing away. The rotting of a corpse in a watery grave was not so fearful.

His hand shook, and the candle fell from its socket on the floor, and lay there sputtering. He placed his foot on it and put it out. Then he flung himself into the rickety chair that was standing by the table and buried his face in his hands.

'Good God, Dorian, what a lesson! what an awful lesson!'° There was no answer, but he could hear the young man sobbing at the window. 'Pray, Dorian, pray,' he murmured. 'What is it that one was taught to say in one's boyhood? "Lead us not into temptation. Forgive us our sins. Wash away our iniquities." Let us say that together. The prayer of your pride has been answered. The prayer of your repentance will be answered also. I worshipped you too much. I am punished for it. You worshipped yourself too much. We are both punished.'

Dorian Gray turned slowly around, and looked at him with tear-dimmed eyes. 'It is too late, Basil,' he faltered.

'It is never too late, Dorian. Let us kneel down and try if we cannot remember a prayer. Isn't there a verse somewhere, "Though your sins be as scarlet, yet I will make them as white as snow"?'°

'Those words mean nothing to me now.'

'Hush! don't say that. You have done enough evil in your life. My God! don't you see that accursed thing leering at us?'

Dorian Gray glanced at the picture, and suddenly an uncontrollable feeling of hatred for Basil Hallward came over him, as though it had been suggested to him by the image on the canvas, whispered into his ear by those grinning lips. The mad passions of a hunted animal stirred within him, and he loathed the man who was seated at the table, more than in his whole life he had ever loathed anything. He glanced wildly around. Something glimmered on the top of the painted chest that faced him. His eye fell on it. He knew what it was. It was a knife that he had brought up, some days before, to cut a piece of cord, and had forgotten to take away with him. He moved slowly towards it, passing Hallward as he did so. As soon as he got behind him, he seized it, and turned round. Hallward stirred in his chair as if he was going to rise. He rushed at him, and dug the knife into the great vein that is behind the ear, crushing the man's head down on the table, and stabbing again and again.

There was a stifled groan, and the horrible sound of some one choking with blood. Three times the outstretched arms shot up convulsively, waving grotesque stiff-fingered hands in the air. He stabbed him twice more, but the man did not move. Something began to trickle on the floor. He waited for a moment, still pressing the head down. Then he threw the knife on the table, and listened.

He could hear nothing, but the drip, drip on the threadbare carpet. He opened the door and went out on the landing. The house was absolutely quiet. No one was about. For a few seconds he stood bending over the balustrade, and peering down into the black seething well of darkness. Then he took out the key and returned to the room, locking himself in as he did so.

The thing was still seated in the chair, straining over the table with bowed head, and humped back, and long fantastic arms. Had it not been for the red jagged tear in the neck, and the clotted black pool that was slowly widening on the table, one would have said that the man was simply asleep.

How quickly it had all been done! He felt strangely calm, and, walking over to the window, opened it, and stepped out on the balcony. The wind had blown the fog away, and the sky was like a monstrous peacock's tail, starred with myriads of golden eyes. He looked down, and saw the policeman going his rounds and flashing the long beam of his lantern on the doors of the silent houses. The crimson spot of a prowling hansom gleamed at the corner, and then vanished. A woman in a fluttering shawl was creeping slowly by the railings, staggering as she went. Now and then she stopped, and peered back. Once, she began to sing in a hoarse voice. The policeman strolled over and said something to her. She stumbled away, laughing. A bitter blast swept across the Square. The gas-lamps flickered, and became blue, and the leafless trees shook their black iron branches to and fro. He shivered, and went back, closing the window behind him.

Having reached the door, he turned the key, and opened it. He did not even glance at the murdered man. He felt that the secret of the whole thing was not to realize the situation. The friend who had painted the fatal portrait to which all his misery had been due, had gone out of his life. That was enough.

Then he remembered the lamp. It was a rather curious one of Moorish workmanship, made of dull silver inlaid with arabesques of burnished steel, and studded with coarse turquoises. Perhaps it might be missed by his servant, and questions would be asked. He hesitated for a moment, then he turned back and took it from the table. He could not help seeing the dead thing. How still it was! How horribly white the long hands looked! It was like a dreadful wax image.

Having locked the door behind him, he crept quietly downstairs. The woodwork creaked, and seemed to cry out as if in pain. He stopped several times, and waited. No: everything was still. It was merely the sound of his own footsteps.

When he reached the library, he saw the bag and coat in the corner. They must be hidden away somewhere. He unlocked a secret press that was in the wainscoting, a press in which he kept his own curious disguises, and put them into it. He could easily burn them afterwards. Then he pulled out his watch. It was twenty minutes to two.

He sat down, and began to think. Every year—every month, almost—

men were strangled in England for what he had done. There had been a madness of murder in the air. Some red star° had come too close to the earth. . . . And yet what evidence was there against him? Basil Hallward had left the house at eleven. No one had seen him come in again. Most of the servants were at Selby Royal. His valet had gone to bed. . . . Paris! Yes. It was to Paris that Basil had gone, and by the midnight train, as he had intended. With his curious reserved habits, it would be months before any suspicions would be aroused. Months! Everything could be destroyed long before then.

A sudden thought struck him. He put on his fur coat and hat, and went out into the hall. There he paused, hearing the slow heavy tread of the policeman on the pavement outside, and seeing the flash of the bull's-eye° reflected in the window. He waited, and held his breath.

After a few moments he drew back the latch, and slipped out, shutting the door very gently behind him. Then he began ringing the bell. In about five minutes his valet appeared, half dressed, and looking very drowsy.

'I am sorry to have had to wake you up, Francis,' he said, stepping in; 'but I had forgotten my latch-key. What time is it?'

'Ten minutes past two, sir,' answered the man, looking at the clock and blinking.

'Ten minutes past two? How horribly late! You must wake me at nine tomorrow. I have some work to do.'

'All right, sir.'

'Did any one call this evening?'

'Mr Hallward, sir. He stayed here till eleven, and then he went away to catch his train.'

'Oh! I am sorry I didn't see him. Did he leave any message?'

'No, sir, except that he would write to you from Paris, if he did not find you at the club.'

'That will do, Francis. Don't forget to call me at nine tomorrow.'

'No, sir.'

The man shambled down the passage in his slippers.

Dorian Gray threw his hat and coat upon the table, and passed into the library. For a quarter of an hour he walked up and down the room biting his lip, and thinking. Then he took down the Blue Book° from one of the shelves, and began to turn over the leaves. 'Alan Campbell, 152, Hertford Street, Mayfair.' Yes; that was the man he wanted.

CHAPTER XIV

AT nine o'clock the next morning his servant came in with a cup of chocolate on a tray, and opened the shutters. Dorian was sleeping quite peacefully, lying on his right side, with one hand underneath his cheek. He looked like a boy who had been tired out with play, or study.

The man had to touch him twice on the shoulder before he woke, and as he opened his eyes a faint smile passed across his lips, as though he had been lost in some delightful dream. Yet he had not dreamed at all. His night had been untroubled by any images of pleasure or of pain. But youth smiles without any reason. It is one of its chiefest charms.

He turned round, and, leaning upon his elbow, began to sip his chocolate. The mellow November sun came streaming into the room. The sky was bright, and there was a genial warmth in the air. It was almost like a morning in May.

Gradually the events of the preceding night crept with silent blood-stained feet into his brain, and reconstructed themselves there with terrible distinctness. He winced at the memory of all that he had suffered, and for a moment the same curious feeling of loathing for Basil Hallward, that had made him kill him as he sat in the chair, came back to him, and he grew cold with passion. The dead man was still sitting there, too, and in the sunlight now. How horrible that was! Such hideous things were for the darkness, not for the day.

He felt that if he brooded on what he had gone through he would sicken or grow mad. There were sins whose fascination was more in the memory than in the doing of them, strange triumphs that gratified the pride more than the passions, and gave to the intellect a quickened sense of joy, greater than any joy they brought, or could ever bring, to the senses. But this was not one of them. It was a thing to be driven out of the mind, to be drugged with poppies, to be strangled lest it might strangle one itself.

When the half-hour struck, he passed his hand across his forehead, and then got up hastily, and dressed himself with even more than his usual care, giving a good deal of attention to the choice of his necktie and scarf-pin, and changing his rings more than once. He spent a long time also over breakfast, tasting the various dishes, talking to his valet about some new liveries that he was thinking of getting made for the servants at Selby, and going through his correspondence. At some of the letters he smiled. Three of them bored him. One he read several times over, and then tore up with a slight look of annoyance in his face. 'That awful thing, a woman's memory!'° as Lord Henry had once said.

After he had drunk his cup of black coffee, he wiped his lips slowly with a napkin, motioned to his servant to wait, and going over to the table sat down and wrote two letters. One he put in his pocket, the other he handed to the valet.

'Take this round to 152, Hertford Street, Francis, and if Mr Campbell is out of town, get his address.'

As soon as he was alone, he lit a cigarette, and began sketching upon a piece of paper, drawing first flowers, and bits of architecture, and then human faces. Suddenly he remarked that every face that he drew seemed to have a fantastic likeness to Basil Hallward.° He frowned, and, getting up, went over to the bookcase and took out a volume at hazard. He was determined that he would not think about what had happened until it became absolutely necessary that he should do so.

When he had stretched himself on the sofa, he looked at the title-page of the book. It was Gautier's 'Émaux et Camées',° Charpentier's Japanese-paper edition, with the Jacquemart etching. The binding was of citron-green leather, with a design of gilt trellis-work and dotted pomegranates. It had been given to him by Adrian Singleton. As he turned over the pages his eye fell on the poem about the hand of Lacenaire, the cold yellow hand *'du supplice encore mal lavée'*, with its downy red hairs and its *'doigts de faune'*. He glanced at his own white taper fingers, shuddering slightly in spite of himself, and passed on, till he came to those lovely stanzas upon Venice:—°

> *Sur une gamme chromatique,*
> *Le sein de perles ruisselant,*
> *La Vénus de l'Adriatique*
> *Sort de l'eau son corps rose et blanc.*
>
> *Les dômes, sur l'azur des ondes*
> *Suivant la phrase au pur contour,*
> *S'enflent comme des gorges rondes*
> *Que soulève un soupir d'amour.*
>
> *L'esquif aborde et me dépose,*
> *Jetant son amarre au pilier,*
> *Devant une façade rose,*
> *Sur le marbre d'un escalier.*

How exquisite they were! As one read them, one seemed to be floating down the green waterways of the pink and pearl city, seated in a black gondola with silver prow and trailing curtains. The mere lines looked to him like those straight lines of turquoise-blue that follow one as one pushes out to the Lido. The sudden flashes of colour reminded him of the gleam of the opal-and-iris-throated birds that flutter round the tall honey-combed Campanile, or stalk, with such stately grace, through the dim, dust-stained arcades. Leaning back with half-closed eyes, he kept saying over and over to himself:—

> *Devant une façade rose,*
> *Sur le marbre d'un escalier.*

The whole of Venice was in those two lines. He remembered the autumn that he had passed there, and a wonderful love that had stirred him to mad, delightful follies. There was romance in every place. But Venice, like Oxford, had kept the background for romance, and, to the true romantic, background was everything, or almost everything. Basil had been with him part of the time, and had gone wild over Tintoret. Poor Basil! what a horrible way for a man to die!

He sighed, and took up the volume again, and tried to forget. He read of the swallows° that fly in and out of the little café at Smyrna where the Hadjis sit counting their amber beads and the turbaned merchants smoke their long tasselled pipes and talk gravely to each other; he read of the Obelisk° in the Place de la Concorde that weeps tears of granite in its lonely sunless exile, and longs to be back by the hot lotus-covered Nile, where there are Sphinxes, and rose-red ibises, and white vultures with gilded claws, and crocodiles, with small beryl eyes, that crawl over the green steaming mud; he began to brood over those verses which, drawing music from kiss-stained marble, tell of that curious statue that Gautier compares to a contralto voice, the '*monstre charmant*' that couches in the porphyry-room of the Louvre.° But after a time the book fell from his hand. He grew nervous, and a horrible fit of terror came over him. What if Alan Campbell should be out of England? Days would elapse before he could come back. Perhaps he might refuse to come. What could he do then? Every moment was of vital importance.

They had been great friends once, five years before—almost inseparable, indeed. Then the intimacy had come suddenly to an end. When they met in society now, it was only Dorian Gray who smiled: Alan Campbell never did.

He was an extremely clever young man, though he had no real appreciation of the visible arts, and whatever little sense of the beauty of poetry he possessed he had gained entirely from Dorian. His dominant intellectual passion was for science. At Cambridge he had spent a great deal of his time working in the Laboratory, and had taken a good class in the Natural Science Tripos of his year. Indeed, he was still devoted to the study of chemistry, and had a laboratory of his own, in which he used to shut himself up all day long, greatly to the annoyance of his mother, who had set her heart on his standing for Parliament and had a vague idea that a chemist was a person who made up prescriptions. He was an excellent musician, however, as well, and played both the violin and the piano better than most amateurs. In fact, it was music that had first brought him and Dorian Gray together—music and that indefinable attraction that Dorian seemed to be able to exercise whenever he wished, and indeed exercised often without being conscious of it. They had met at Lady Berkshire's the night that Rubinstein° played there, and after that used to be always seen together at the Opera, and wherever good music was going on. For eighteen months their intimacy lasted. Campbell was always either at Selby Royal or in Grosvenor Square. To him, as to many others, Dorian Gray was the type of everything that is wonderful and fascinating in life. Whether or not a quarrel had taken place between them no one ever knew. But suddenly people remarked that they scarcely spoke when they met, and that Campbell seemed always to go away early from any party at which Dorian Gray was present. He had changed, too—was strangely melancholy at times, appeared almost to dislike hearing music, and would never himself play, giving as his excuse, when he was called upon, that he was so absorbed in science that he had no time left in which to practise. And this was certainly true. Every day he seemed to become more interested in biology, and his name appeared once or twice in some of the scientific reviews, in connection with certain curious experiments.

This was the man Dorian Gray was waiting for. Every second he kept glancing at the clock. As the minutes went by he became horribly agitated. At last he got up, and began to pace up and down the room, looking like a beautiful caged thing. He took long stealthy strides. His hands were curiously cold.

The suspense became unbearable. Time seemed to him to be crawling with feet of lead, while he by monstrous winds was being swept towards the jagged edge of some black cleft or precipice. He knew what was waiting for him there; saw it indeed, and, shuddering, crushed with dank hands his burning lids as though he would have robbed the very brain of sight, and driven the eyeballs back into their cave. It was useless. The brain had its own food on which it battened, and the imagination, made grotesque by terror, twisted and distorted as a living thing by pain, danced like some foul puppet on a stand, and grinned through moving masks. Then, suddenly, Time stopped for him. Yes: that blind, slow-breathing thing crawled no more, and horrible thoughts, Time being dead, raced nimbly on in front, and dragged a hideous future from its grave, and showed it to him. He stared at it. Its very horror made him stone.

At last the door opened, and his servant entered. He turned glazed eyes upon him.

'Mr Campbell, sir,' said the man.

A sigh of relief broke from his parched lips, and the colour came back to his cheeks.

'Ask him to come in at once, Francis.' He felt that he was himself again. His mood of cowardice had passed away.

The man bowed, and retired. In a few moments Alan Campbell walked in, looking very stern and rather pale, his pallor being intensified by his coal-black hair and dark eyebrows.

'Alan! this is kind of you. I thank you for coming.'

'I had intended never to enter your house again, Gray. But you said it was a matter of life and death.' His voice was hard and cold. He spoke with slow deliberation. There was a look of contempt in the steady searching gaze that he turned on Dorian. He kept his hands in the pockets of his Astrakhan coat, and seemed not to have noticed the gesture with which he had been greeted.

'Yes: it is a matter of life and death, Alan, and to more than one person. Sit down.'

Campbell took a chair by the table, and Dorian sat opposite to him. The two men's eyes met. In Dorian's there was infinite pity. He knew that what he was going to do was dreadful.

After a strained moment of silence, he leaned across and said, very quietly, but watching the effect of each word upon the face of him he had sent for, 'Alan, in a locked room at the top of this house, a room to which nobody but myself has access, a dead man is seated at a table. He has been dead ten hours now. Don't stir, and don't look at me like that. Who the man is, why he died, how he died, are matters that do not concern you. What you have to do is this——'

'Stop, Gray. I don't want to know anything further. Whether what you have told me is true or not true, doesn't concern me. I entirely decline to be mixed up in your life. Keep your horrible secrets to yourself. They don't interest me any more.'

'Alan, they will have to interest you. This one will have to interest you. I am awfully sorry for you, Alan. But I can't help myself. You are the one man who is able to save me. I am forced to bring you into the matter. I have no option. Alan, you are scientific. You know about chemistry, and things of that kind. You have made experiments. What you have got to do is to destroy the thing that is upstairs—to destroy it so that not a vestige of it will be left. Nobody saw this person come into the house. Indeed, at the present moment he is supposed to be in Paris. He will not be missed for months. When he is missed, there must be no trace of him found here. You, Alan, you must change him, and everything that belongs to him, into a handful of ashes that I may scatter in the air.'

'You are mad, Dorian.'

'Ah! I was waiting for you to call me Dorian.'

'You are mad, I tell you—mad to imagine that I would raise a finger to help you, mad to make this monstrous confession. I will have nothing to do with this matter, whatever it is. Do you think I am going to peril my reputation for you? What is it to me what devil's work you are up to?'

'It was suicide, Alan.'

'I am glad of that. But who drove him to it? You, I should fancy.'

'Do you still refuse to do this for me?'

'Of course I refuse. I will have absolutely nothing to do with it. I don't care what shame comes on you. You deserve it all. I should not be sorry to see you disgraced, publicly disgraced. How dare you ask me, of all men in the world, to mix myself up in this horror? I should have thought you knew more about people's characters. Your friend Lord Henry Wotton can't have taught you much about psychology, whatever else he has taught you. Nothing will induce me to stir a step to help you. You have come to the wrong man. Go to some of your friends. Don't come to me.'

'Alan, it was murder. I killed him. You don't know what he had made me suffer. Whatever my life is, he had more to do with the making or the marring of it than poor Harry has had. He may not have intended it, the result was the same.'

'Murder! Good God, Dorian, is that what you have come to? I shall not inform upon you. It is not my business. Besides, without my stirring in the matter, you are certain to be arrested. Nobody ever commits a crime without doing something stupid. But I will have nothing to do with it.'

'You must have something to do with it. Wait, wait a moment; listen to me. Only listen, Alan. All I ask of you is to perform a certain scientific experiment. You go to hospitals and dead-houses, and the horrors that you do there don't affect you. If in some hideous dissecting-room or fetid laboratory you found this man lying on a leaden table with red gutters scooped out in it for the blood to flow through, you would simply look upon him as an admirable subject. You would not turn a hair. You would not believe that you were doing anything wrong. On the contrary, you would probably feel that you were benefiting the human race, or increasing the sum of knowledge in the world, or gratifying intellectual curiosity, or something of that kind. What I want you to do is merely what you have often done before. Indeed, to destroy a body must be far less horrible than what you are accustomed to work at. And, remember, it is the only piece of evidence against me. If it is discovered, I am lost; and it is sure to be discovered unless you help me.'

'I have no desire to help you. You forget that. I am simply indifferent to the whole thing. It has nothing to do with me.'

'Alan, I entreat you. Think of the position I am in. Just before you came I almost fainted with terror. You may know terror yourself some day. No! don't think of that. Look at the matter purely from the scientific point of view. You don't inquire where the dead things on which you experiment come from. Don't inquire now. I have told you too much as it is. But I beg of you to do this. We were friends once, Alan.'

'Don't speak about those days, Dorian: they are dead.'

'The dead linger sometimes. The man upstairs will not go away. He is sitting at the table with bowed head and outstretched arms. Alan! Alan! if you don't come to my assistance I am ruined. Why, they will hang me, Alan! Don't you understand? They will hang me for what I have done.'

'There is no good in prolonging this scene. I absolutely refuse to do anything in the matter. It is insane of you to ask me.'

'You refuse?'

'Yes.'

'I entreat you, Alan.'

'It is useless.'

The same look of pity came into Dorian Gray's eyes. Then he stretched out his hand, took a piece of paper, and wrote something on it. He read it over twice, folded it carefully, and pushed it across the table. Having done this, he got up, and went over to the window.

Campbell looked at him in surprise, and then took up the paper, and opened it. As he read it, his face became ghastly pale, and he fell back in his chair. A horrible sense of sickness came over him. He felt as if his heart was beating itself to death in some empty hollow.

After two or three minutes of terrible silence, Dorian turned round, and came and stood behind him, putting his hand upon his shoulder.

'I am so sorry for you, Alan,' he murmured, 'but you leave me no alternative. I have a letter written already. Here it is. You see the address. If you don't help me, I must send it. If you don't help me, I will send it. You know what the result will be. But you are going to help me. It is impossible for you to refuse now. I tried to spare you. You will do me the justice to admit that. You were stern, harsh, offensive. You treated me as no man has ever dared to treat me—no living man, at any rate. I bore it all. Now it is for me to dictate terms.'

Campbell buried his face in his hands, and a shudder passed through him.

'Yes, it is my turn to dictate terms, Alan. You know what they are. The thing is quite simple. Come, don't work yourself into this fever. The thing has to be done. Face it, and do it.'

A groan broke from Campbell's lips, and he shivered all over. The ticking of the clock on the mantelpiece seemed to him to be dividing Time into separate atoms of agony, each of which was too terrible to be borne. He felt as if an iron ring was being slowly tightened round his forehead, as if the disgrace with which he was threatened had already come upon him. The hand upon his shoulder weighed like a hand of lead. It was intolerable. It seemed to crush him.

'Come, Alan, you must decide at once.'

'I cannot do it,' he said, mechanically, as though words could alter things.

'You must. You have no choice. Don't delay.'

He hesitated a moment. 'Is there a fire in the room upstairs?'

'Yes, there is a gas-fire with asbestos.'

'I shall have to go home and get some things from the laboratory.'

'No, Alan, you must not leave the house. Write out on a sheet of note-paper what you want, and my servant will take a cab and bring the things back to you.'

Campbell scrawled a few lines, blotted them, and addressed an envelope to his assistant. Dorian took the note up and read it carefully. Then he rang the bell, and gave it to his valet, with orders to return as soon as possible, and to bring the things with him.

As the hall door shut, Campbell started nervously, and, having got up from the chair, went over to the chimney-piece. He was shivering with a kind of ague. For nearly twenty minutes, neither of the men spoke. A fly buzzed noisily about the room, and the ticking of the clock was like the beat of a hammer.

As the chime struck one, Campbell turned round, and, looking at Dorian Gray, saw that his eyes were filled with tears. There was something in the purity and refinement of that sad face that seemed to enrage him. 'You are infamous, absolutely infamous!' he muttered.

'Hush, Alan: you have saved my life,' said Dorian.

'Your life? Good heavens! what a life that is! You have gone from corruption to corruption, and now you have culminated in crime. In doing what I am going to do, what you force me to do, it is not of your life that I am thinking.'

'Ah, Alan,' murmured Dorian, with a sigh, 'I wish you had a

thousandth part of the pity for me that I have for you.' He turned away as he spoke, and stood looking at the garden. Campbell made no answer.

After about ten minutes a knock came to the door, and the servant entered, carrying a large mahogany chest of chemicals, with a long coil of steel and platinum wire and two rather curiously-shaped iron clamps.

'Shall I leave the things here, sir?' he asked Campbell.

'Yes,' said Dorian. 'And I am afraid, Francis, that I have another errand for you. What is the name of the man at Richmond who supplies Selby with orchids?'

'Harden, sir.'

'Yes—Harden. You must go down to Richmond at once, see Harden personally, and tell him to send twice as many orchids as I ordered, and to have as few white ones as possible. In fact, I don't want any white ones. It is a lovely day, Francis, and Richmond is a very pretty place, otherwise I wouldn't bother you about it.'

'No trouble, sir. At what time shall I be back?'

Dorian looked at Campbell. 'How long will your experiment take, Alan?' he said, in a calm, indifferent voice. The presence of a third person in the room seemed to give him extraordinary courage.

Campbell frowned, and bit his lip. 'It will take about five hours,' he answered.

'It will be time enough, then, if you are back at half-past seven, Francis. Or stay: just leave my things out for dressing. You can have the evening to yourself. I am not dining at home, so I shall not want you.'

'Thank you, sir,' said the man, leaving the room.

'Now, Alan, there is not a moment to be lost. How heavy this chest is! I'll take it for you. You bring the other things.' He spoke rapidly, and in an authoritative manner. Campbell felt dominated by him. They left the room together.

When they reached the top landing, Dorian took out the key and turned it in the lock. Then he stopped, and a troubled look came into his eyes. He shuddered. 'I don't think I can go in, Alan,' he murmured.

'It is nothing to me. I don't require you,' said Campbell, coldly.

Dorian half opened the door. As he did so, he saw the face of his portrait leering in the sunlight. On the floor in front of it the torn curtain was lying. He remembered that the night before he had forgotten, for the first time in his life, to hide the fatal canvas, and was about to rush forward, when he drew back with a shudder.

What was that loathsome red dew that gleamed, wet and glistening, on one of the hands, as though the canvas had sweated blood? How horrible it was!—more horrible, it seemed to him for the moment, than the silent thing that he knew was stretched across the table, the thing whose grotesque misshapen shadow on the spotted carpet showed him that it had not stirred, but was still there, as he had left it.

He heaved a deep breath, opened the door a little wider, and with half-closed eyes and averted head walked quickly in, determined that he would not look even once upon the dead man. Then, stooping down, and taking up the gold-and-purple hanging, he flung it right over the picture.

There he stopped, feeling afraid to turn round, and his eyes fixed themselves on the intricacies of the pattern before him. He heard Campbell bringing in the heavy chest, and the irons, and the other things that he had required for his dreadful work. He began to wonder if he and Basil Hallward had ever met, and, if so, what they had thought of each other.

'Leave me now,' said a stern voice behind him.

He turned and hurried out, just conscious that the dead man had been thrust back into the chair, and that Campbell was gazing into a glistening yellow face. As he was going downstairs he heard the key being turned in the lock.

It was long after seven when Campbell came back into the library. He was pale, but absolutely calm. 'I have done what you asked me to do,' he muttered. 'And now, goodbye. Let us never see each other again.'

'You have saved me from ruin, Alan. I cannot forget that,' said Dorian, simply.

As soon as Campbell had left, he went upstairs. There was a horrible smell of nitric acid in the room. But the thing that had been sitting at the table was gone.

CHAPTER XV

THAT evening, at eight-thirty, exquisitely dressed, and wearing a large buttonhole of Parma violets, Dorian Gray was ushered into Lady Narborough's drawing-room by bowing servants. His forehead was throbbing with maddened nerves, and he felt wildly excited, but his manner as he bent over his hostess's hand was as easy and graceful as ever. Perhaps one never seems so much at one's ease as when one has to play a part. Certainly no one looking at Dorian Gray that night could have believed that he had passed through a tragedy as horrible as any tragedy of our age. Those finely-shaped fingers could never have clutched a knife for sin, nor those smiling lips have cried out on God and goodness. He himself could not help wondering at the calm of his demeanour, and for a moment felt keenly the terrible pleasure of a double life.

It was a small party, got up rather in a hurry by Lady Narborough, who was a very clever woman, with what Lord Henry used to describe as the remains of really remarkable ugliness. She had proved an excellent wife to one of our most tedious ambassadors, and having buried her husband properly in a marble mausoleum, which she had herself designed, and married off her daughters to some rich, rather elderly men, she devoted herself now to the pleasures of French fiction, French cookery, and French *esprit* when she could get it.

Dorian was one of her especial favourites, and she always told him that she was extremely glad she had not met him in early life. 'I know, my dear, I should have fallen madly in love with you,' she used to say, 'and thrown my bonnet right over the mills for your sake. It is most fortunate that you were not thought of at the time. As it was, our bonnets were so unbecoming, and the mills were so occupied in trying to raise the wind, that I never had even a flirtation with anybody. However, that was all Narborough's fault. He was dreadfully short-sighted, and there is no pleasure in taking in a husband who never sees anything.'

Her guests this evening were rather tedious. The fact was, as she explained to Dorian, behind a very shabby fan, one of her married daughters had come up quite suddenly to stay with her, and, to make matters worse, had actually brought her husband with her. 'I think it is most unkind of her, my dear,' she whispered. 'Of course I go and stay with them every summer after I come from Homburg, but then an old woman like me must have fresh air sometimes, and besides, I really wake them up. You don't know what an existence they lead down there. It is pure unadulterated country life. They get up early, because they have so much to do, and go to bed early because they have so little to think about. There has not been a scandal in the neighbourhood since the time of Queen Elizabeth, and consequently they all fall asleep after dinner. You shan't sit next either of them. You shall sit by me, and amuse me.'

Dorian murmured a graceful compliment, and looked round the room. Yes: it was certainly a tedious party. Two of the people he had never seen before, and the others consisted of Ernest Harrowden, one of those middle-aged mediocrities so common in London clubs who have no enemies, but are thoroughly disliked by their friends; Lady Ruxton, an overdressed woman of forty-seven, with a hooked nose, who was always trying to get herself compromised, but was so peculiarly plain that to her great disappointment no one would ever believe anything against her; Mrs Erlynne, a pushing nobody, with a delightful lisp, and

Venetian-red hair; Lady Alice Chapman, his hostess's daughter, a dowdy dull girl, with one of those characteristic British faces, that, once seen, are never remembered; and her husband, a red-cheeked, white-whiskered creature who, like so many of his class, was under the impression that inordinate joviality can atone for an entire lack of ideas.

He was rather sorry he had come, till Lady Narborough, looking at the great ormolu gilt clock that sprawled in gaudy curves on the mauve-draped mantelshelf, exclaimed: 'How horrid of Henry Wotton to be so late! I sent round to him this morning on chance, and he promised faithfully not to disappoint me.'

It was some consolation that Harry was to be there, and when the door opened and he heard his slow musical voice lending charm to some insincere apology, he ceased to feel bored.

But at dinner he could not eat anything. Plate after plate went away untasted. Lady Narborough kept scolding him for what she called 'an insult to poor Adolphe, who invented the *menu* specially for you,' and now and then Lord Henry looked across at him, wondering at his silence and abstracted manner. From time to time the butler filled his glass with champagne. He drank eagerly, and his thirst seemed to increase.

'Dorian,' said Lord Henry, at last, as the *chaudfroid*° was being handed round, 'what is the matter with you tonight? You are quite out of sorts.'

'I believe he is in love,' cried Lady Narborough, 'and that he is afraid to tell me for fear I should be jealous. He is quite right. I certainly should.'

'Dear Lady Narborough,' murmured Dorian, smiling, 'I have not been in love for a whole week—not, in fact, since Madame de Ferrol left town.'

'How you men can fall in love with that woman!' exclaimed the old lady. 'I really cannot understand it.'

'It is simply because she remembers you when you were a little girl, Lady Narborough,' said Lord Henry. 'She is the one link between us and your short frocks.'

'She does not remember my short frocks at all, Lord Henry. But I remember her very well at Vienna thirty years ago, and how *décolletée* she was then.'

'She is still *décolletée*,' he answered, taking an olive in his long fingers; 'and when she is in a very smart gown she looks like an *édition de luxe* of a bad French novel. She is really wonderful, and full of surprises. Her capacity for family affection is extraordinary. When her third husband died, her hair turned quite gold from grief.'

'How can you, Harry!' cried Dorian.

'It is a most romantic explanation,' laughed the hostess. 'But her third husband, Lord Henry! You don't mean to say Ferrol is the fourth?'

'Certainly, Lady Narborough.'

'I don't believe a word of it.'

'Well, ask Mr Gray. He is one of her most intimate friends.'

'Is it true, Mr Gray?'

'She assures me so, Lady Narborough,' said Dorian. 'I asked her whether, like Marguerite de Navarre,° she had their hearts embalmed and hung at her girdle. She told me she didn't, because none of them had had any hearts at all.'

'Four husbands! Upon my word that is *trop de zêle.*'

'*Trop d'audace*, I tell her,' said Dorian.

'Oh! she is audacious enough for anything, my dear. And what is Ferrol like? I don't know him.'

'The husbands of very beautiful women belong to the criminal classes,' said Lord Henry, sipping his wine.

Lady Narborough hit him with her fan. 'Lord Henry, I am not at all surprised that the world says that you are extremely wicked.'

'But what world says that?' asked Lord Henry, elevating his eyebrows. 'It can only be the next world. This world and I are on excellent terms.'

'Everybody I know says you are very wicked,' cried the old lady, shaking her head.

Lord Henry looked serious for some moments. 'It is perfectly monstrous,' he said, at last, 'the way people go about nowadays saying things against one behind one's back that are absolutely and entirely true.'

'Isn't he incorrigible?' cried Dorian, leaning forward in his chair.

'I hope so,' said his hostess laughing. 'But really if you all worship Madame de Ferrol in this ridiculous way, I shall have to marry again so as to be in the fashion.'

'You will never marry again, Lady Narborough,' broke in Lord Henry. 'You were far too happy. When a woman marries again it is because she detested her first husband. When a man marries again, it is because he adored his first wife. Women try their luck; men risk theirs.'

'Narborough wasn't perfect,' cried the old lady.

'If he had been, you would not have loved him, my dear lady,' was the rejoinder. 'Women love us for our defects. If we have enough of them they will forgive us everything, even our intellects. You will never ask me to dinner again, after saying this, I am afraid, Lady Narborough; but it is quite true.'

'Of course it is true, Lord Henry. If we women did not love you for your defects, where would you all be? Not one of you would ever be married. You would be a set of unfortunate bachelors. Not, however, that that would alter you much. Nowadays all the married men live like bachelors, and all the bachelors like married men.'

'*Fin de siècle*,' murmured Lord Henry.

'*Fin du globe*,' answered his hostess.

'I wish it were *fin du globe*,' said Dorian, with a sigh. 'Life is a great disappointment.'

'Ah, my dear,' cried Lady Narborough, putting on her gloves, 'don't tell me that you have exhausted Life. When a man says that one knows that Life has exhausted him. Lord Henry is very wicked, and I sometimes wish that I had been; but you are made to be good—you look so good. I must find you a nice wife. Lord Henry, don't you think that Mr Gray should get married?'

'I am always telling him so, Lady Narborough,' said Lord Henry, with a bow.

'Well, we must look out for a suitable match for him. I shall go through Debrett° carefully tonight, and draw out a list of all the eligible young ladies.'

'With their ages, Lady Narborough?' asked Dorian.

'Of course, with their ages, slightly edited. But nothing must be done in a hurry. I want it to be what *The Morning Post* calls a suitable alliance, and I want you both to be happy.'

'What nonsense people talk about happy marriages!' exclaimed Lord Henry. 'A man can be happy with any woman, as long as he does not love her.'

'Ah! what a cynic you are!' cried the old lady, pushing back her chair, and nodding to Lady Ruxton. 'You must come and dine with me soon again. You are really an admirable tonic, much better than what Sir Andrew prescribes for me. You must tell me what people you would like to meet, though. I want it to be a delightful gathering.'

'I like men who have a future, and women who have a past,' he answered. 'Or do you think that would make it a petticoat party?'

'I fear so,' she said, laughing, as she stood up. 'A thousand pardons, my dear Lady Ruxton,' she added, 'I didn't see you hadn't finished your cigarette.'

'Never mind, Lady Narborough. I smoke a great deal too much. I am going to limit myself, for the future.'

'Pray don't, Lady Ruxton,' said Lord Henry. 'Moderation is a fatal thing. Enough is as bad as a meal. More than enough is as good as a feast.'

Lady Ruxton glanced at him curiously. 'You must come and explain that to me some afternoon, Lord Henry. It sounds a fascinating theory,' she murmured, as she swept out of the room.

'Now, mind you don't stay too long over your politics and scandal,' cried Lady Narborough from the door. 'If you do, we are sure to squabble upstairs.'

The men laughed, and Mr Chapman got up solemnly from the foot of the table and came up to the top. Dorian Gray changed his seat, and went and sat by Lord Henry. Mr Chapman began to talk in a loud voice about the situation in the House of Commons. He guffawed at his adversaries. The word *doctrinaire*°—word full of terror to the British mind—reappeared from time to time between his explosions. An alliterative prefix served as an ornament of oratory. He hoisted the Union Jack on the pinnacles of Thought. The inherited stupidity of the race—sound English common sense he jovially termed it—was shown to be the proper bulwark for Society.

A smile curved Lord Henry's lips, and he turned round and looked at Dorian.

'Are you better, my dear fellow?' he asked. 'You seemed rather out of sorts at dinner.'

'I am quite well, Harry. I am tired. That is all.'

'You were charming last night. The little Duchess is quite devoted to you. She tells me she is going down to Selby.'

'She has promised to come on the twentieth.'

'Is Monmouth to be there too?'

'Oh, yes, Harry.'

'He bores me dreadfully, almost as much as he bores her. She is very clever, too clever for a woman. She lacks the indefinable charm of weakness. It is the feet of clay that make the gold of the image precious.° Her feet are very pretty, but they are not feet of clay. White porcelain feet, if you like. They have been through the fire, and what fire does not destroy, it hardens. She has had experiences.'

'How long has she been married?' asked Dorian.

'An eternity, she tells me. I believe, according to the Peerage, it is ten years, but ten years with Monmouth must have been like eternity, with time thrown in. Who else is coming?'

'Oh, the Willoughbys, Lord Rugby and his wife, our hostess, Geoffrey Clouston, the usual set. I have asked Lord Grotrian.'

'I like him,' said Lord Henry. 'A great many people don't, but I find him charming. He atones for being occasionally somewhat over-dressed, by being always absolutely over-educated.° He is a very modern type.'

'I don't know if he will be able to come, Harry. He may have to go to Monte Carlo with his father.'

'Ah! what a nuisance people's people are! Try and make him come. By the way, Dorian, you ran off very early last night. You left before eleven. What did you do afterwards? Did you go straight home?'

Dorian glanced at him hurriedly, and frowned. 'No, Harry,' he said at last, 'I did not get home till nearly three.'

'Did you go to the club?'

'Yes,' he answered. Then he bit his lip. 'No, I don't mean that. I didn't go to the club. I walked about. I forget what I did. . . . How inquisitive you are, Harry! You always want to know what one has been doing. I always want to forget what I have been doing. I came in at half-past two, if you wish to know the exact time. I had left my latch-key at home, and my servant had to let me in. If you want any corroborative evidence on the subject you can ask him.'

Lord Henry shrugged his shoulders. 'My dear fellow, as if I cared! Let us go up to the drawing-room. No sherry, thank you, Mr Chapman. Something has happened to you, Dorian. Tell me what it is. You are not yourself tonight.'

'Don't mind me, Harry. I am irritable, and out of temper. I shall come round and see you tomorrow, or next day. Make my excuses to Lady Narborough. I shan't go upstairs. I shall go home. I must go home.'

'All right, Dorian. I dare say I shall see you tomorrow at tea-time. The Duchess is coming.'

'I will try to be there, Harry,' he said, leaving the room. As he drove back to his own house he was conscious that the sense of terror he thought he had strangled had come back to him. Lord Henry's casual questioning had made him lose his nerves for the moment, and he wanted his nerve still. Things that were dangerous had to be destroyed. He winced. He hated the idea of even touching them.

Yet it had to be done. He realized that, and when he had locked the door of his library, he opened the secret press into which he had thrust Basil Hallward's coat and bag. A huge fire was blazing. He piled another log on it. The smell of the singeing clothes and burning leather was horrible. It took him three-quarters of an hour to consume everything. At the end he felt faint and sick, and having lit some Algerian pastilles in a pierced copper brazier, he bathed his hands and forehead with a cool musk-scented vinegar.

Suddenly he started.° His eyes grew strangely bright, and he gnawed nervously at his under-lip. Between two of the windows stood a large Florentine cabinet, made out of ebony, and inlaid with ivory and blue lapis. He watched it as though it were a thing that could fascinate and make afraid, as though it held something that he longed for and yet almost loathed. His breath quickened. A mad craving came over him. He lit a cigarette and then threw it away. His eyelids drooped till the long fringed lashes almost touched his cheek. But he still watched the cabinet. At last he got up from the sofa on which he had been lying, went over to it, and, having unlocked it, touched some hidden spring. A triangular drawer passed slowly out. His fingers moved instinctively towards it, dipped in, and closed on something. It was a small Chinese box of black and gold-dust lacquer, elaborately wrought, the sides patterned with curved waves, and the silken cords hung with round crystals and tasselled in plaited metal threads. He opened it. Inside was a green paste waxy in lustre, the odour curiously heavy and persistent.

He hesitated for some moments, with a strangely immobile smile upon his face. Then shivering, though the atmosphere of the room was terribly hot, he drew himself up, and glanced at the clock. It was twenty minutes to twelve. He put the box back, shutting the cabinet doors as he did so, and went into his bedroom.

As midnight was striking bronze blows upon the dusky air, Dorian Gray, dressed commonly, and with a muffler wrapped round his throat, crept quietly out of his house. In Bond Street he found a hansom with a good horse. He hailed it, and in a low voice gave the driver an address.

The man shook his head. 'It is too far for me,' he muttered.

'Here is a sovereign for you,' said Dorian. 'You shall have another if you drive fast.'

'All right, sir,' answered the man, 'you will be there in an hour,' and after his fare had got in he turned his horse round, and drove rapidly towards the river.

CHAPTER XVI

A COLD rain began to fall, and the blurred street-lamps looked ghastly in the dripping mist. The public-houses were just closing, and dim men and women were clustering in broken groups round their doors. From some of the bars came the sound of horrible laughter. In others, drunkards brawled and screamed.

Lying back in the hansom, with his hat pulled over his forehead, Dorian Gray watched with listless eyes the sordid shame of the great city, and now and then he repeated to himself the words that Lord Henry had said to him on the first day they had met, 'To cure the soul by means of the senses, and the senses by means of the soul.' Yes, that was the secret.

He had often tried it, and would try it again now. There were opium-dens, where one could buy oblivion, dens of horror where the memory of old sins could be destroyed by the madness of sins that were new.

The moon hung low in the sky like a yellow skull. From time to time a huge misshapen cloud stretched a long arm across and hid it. The gas-lamps grew fewer, and the streets more narrow and gloomy. Once the man lost his way, and had to drive back half a mile. A steam rose from the horse as it splashed up the puddles. The side-windows of the hansom were clogged with a grey-flannel mist.

'To cure the soul by means of the senses, and the senses by means of the soul'! How the words rang in his ears! His soul, certainly, was sick to death. Was it true that the senses could cure it? Innocent blood had been spilt. What could atone for that? Ah! for that there was no atonement; but though forgiveness was impossible, forgetfulness was possible still, and he was determined to forget, to stamp the thing out, to crush it as one would crush the adder that had stung one. Indeed, what right had Basil to have spoken to him as he had done? Who had made him a judge over others? He had said things that were dreadful, horrible, not to be endured.

On and on plodded the hansom, going slower, it seemed to him, at each step. He thrust up the trap, and called to the man to drive faster. The hideous hunger for opium began to gnaw at him. His throat burned, and his delicate hands twitched nervously together. He struck at the horse madly with his stick. The driver laughed, and whipped up. He laughed in answer, and the man was silent.

The way seemed interminable, and the streets like the black web of some sprawling spider. The monotony became unbearable, and, as the mist thickened, he felt afraid.

Then they passed by lonely brickfields. The fog was lighter here, and he could see the strange bottle-shaped kilns with their orange fan-like tongues of fire. A dog barked as they went by, and far away in the darkness some wandering seagull screamed. The horse stumbled in a rut, then swerved aside, and broke into a gallop.

After some time they left the clay road, and rattled again over rough-paven streets. Most of the windows were dark, but now and then fantastic shadows were silhouetted against some lamp-lit blind.° He watched them curiously. They moved like monstrous marionettes, and made gestures like live things. He hated them. A dull rage was in his heart. As they turned a corner a woman yelled something at them from an open door, and two men ran after the hansom for about a hundred yards. The driver beat at them with his whip.

It is said that passion makes one think in a circle. Certainly with hideous iteration the bitten lips of Dorian Gray shaped and reshaped those subtle words that dealt with soul and sense, till he had found in them the full expression, as it were, of his mood, and justified, by intellectual approval, passions that without such justification would still have dominated his temper. From cell to cell of his brain crept the one thought; and the wild desire to live, most terrible of all man's appetites, quickened into force each trembling nerve and fibre. Ugliness that had once been hateful to him because it made things real, became dear to him now for that very reason. Ugliness was the one reality. The coarse brawl, the loathsome den, the crude violence of disordered life, the very vileness of thief and outcast, were more vivid, in their intense actuality of impression, than all the gracious shapes of Art, the dreamy shadows of Song. They were what he needed for forgetfulness. In three days he would be free.

Suddenly the man drew up with a jerk at the top of a dark lane. Over the low roofs and jagged chimney-stacks of the houses rose the black masts of ships. Wreaths of white mist clung like ghostly sails to the yards.

'Somewhere about here, sir, ain't it?' he asked huskily through the trap.

Dorian started, and peered round. 'This will do,' he answered, and, having got out hastily, and given the driver the extra fare he had promised him, he walked quickly in the direction of the quay. Here and there a lantern gleamed at the stern of some huge merchantman. The light shook and splintered in the puddles. A red glare came from an outward-bound steamer that was coaling. The slimy pavement looked like a wet mackintosh.

He hurried on towards the left, glancing back now and then to see if he was being followed. In about seven or eight minutes he reached a small shabby house, that was wedged in between two gaunt factories. In one of the top windows stood a lamp. He stopped, and gave a peculiar knock.

After a little time he heard steps in the passage, and the chain being unhooked. The door opened quietly, and he went in without saying a word to the squat misshapen figure that flattened itself into the shadow as he passed. At the end of the hall hung a tattered green curtain that swayed and shook in the gusty wind which had followed him in from the street. He dragged it aside, and entered a long, low room which looked as if it had once been a third-rate dancing-saloon. Shrill flaring gas-jets, dulled and distorted in the fly-blown mirrors that faced them, were ranged round the walls. Greasy reflectors of ribbed tin backed them, making quivering discs of light. The floor was covered with ochre-coloured sawdust, trampled here and there into mud, and stained with dark rings of spilt liquor. Some Malays were crouching by a little charcoal stove playing with bone counters, and showing their white teeth as they chattered. In one corner with his head buried in his arms, a sailor sprawled over a table, and by the tawdrily-painted bar that ran across one complete side stood two haggard women mocking an old man who was brushing the sleeves of his coat with an expression of disgust. 'He thinks he's got red ants on him,' laughed one of them, as Dorian passed by. The man looked at her in terror, and began to whimper.

At the end of the room there was a little staircase, leading to a darkened chamber. As Dorian hurried up its three rickety steps, the heavy odour of opium met him. He heaved a deep breath, and his nostrils quivered with pleasure. When he entered, a young man with smooth yellow hair, who was bending over a lamp lighting a long thin pipe, looked up at him, and nodded in a hesitating manner.

'You here, Adrian?' muttered Dorian.

'Where else should I be?' he answered, listlessly. 'None of the chaps will speak to me now.'

'I thought you had left England.'

'Darlington is not going to do anything. My brother paid the bill at last. George doesn't speak to me either. . . . I don't care,' he added, with a sigh. 'As long as one has this stuff, one doesn't want friends. I think I have had too many friends.'

Dorian winced, and looked round at the grotesque things that lay in such fantastic postures on the ragged mattresses. The twisted limbs, the gaping mouths, the staring lustreless eyes, fascinated him. He knew in what strange heavens they were suffering, and what dull hells were teaching them the secret of some new joy. They were better off than he was. He was prisoned in thought. Memory, like a horrible malady, was eating his soul away. From time to time he seemed to see the eyes of Basil Hallward looking at him. Yet he felt he could not stay. The presence of Adrian Singleton troubled him. He wanted to be where no one would know who he was. He wanted to escape from himself.

'I am going on to the other place,' he said, after a pause.

'On the wharf?'

'Yes.'

'That mad-cat is sure to be there. They won't have her in this place now.'

Dorian shrugged his shoulders. 'I am sick of women who love one. Women who hate one are much more interesting. Besides, the stuff is better.'

'Much the same.'

'I like it better. Come and have something to drink. I must have something.'

'I don't want anything,' murmured the young man.

'Never mind.'

Adrian Singleton rose up wearily, and followed Dorian to the bar. A half-caste, in a ragged turban and a shabby ulster, grinned a hideous greeting as he thrust a bottle of brandy and two tumblers in front of them. The women sidled up, and began to chatter. Dorian turned his back on them, and said something in a low voice to Adrian Singleton.

A crooked smile, like a Malay crease, writhed across the face of one of the women. 'We are very proud tonight,' she sneered.

'For God's sake don't talk to me,' cried Dorian, stamping his foot on the ground. 'What do you want? Money? Here it is. Don't ever talk to me again.'

Two red sparks flashed for a moment in the woman's sodden eyes, then flickered out, and left them dull and glazed. She tossed her head, and raked the coins off the counter with greedy fingers. Her companion watched her enviously.

'It's no use,' sighed Adrian Singleton. 'I don't care to go back. What does it matter? I am quite happy here.'

'You will write to me if you want anything, won't you?' said Dorian, after a pause.

'Perhaps.'

'Goodnight, then.'

'Goodnight,' answered the young man, passing up the steps, and wiping his parched mouth with a handkerchief.

Dorian walked to the door with a look of pain in his face. As he drew the curtain aside a hideous laugh broke from the painted lips of the woman who had taken his money. 'There goes the devil's bargain!' she hiccoughed, in a hoarse voice.

'Curse you!' he answered, 'don't call me that.'

She snapped her fingers. 'Prince Charming is what you like to be called, ain't it?' she yelled after him.

The drowsy sailor leapt to his feet as she spoke, and looked wildly round. The sound of the shutting of the hall door fell on his ear. He rushed out as if in pursuit.

Dorian Gray hurried along the quay through the drizzling rain. His meeting with Adrian Singleton had strangely moved him, and he wondered if the ruin of that young life was really to be laid at his door, as Basil Hallward had said to him with such infamy of insult. He bit his lip, and for a few seconds his eyes grew sad. Yet, after all, what did it matter to him? One's days were too brief to take the burden of another's errors on one's shoulders. Each man lived his own life, and paid his own price for living it. The only pity was one had to pay so often for a single fault. One had to pay over and over again, indeed. In her dealings with man Destiny never closed her accounts.

There are moments, psychologists tell us, when the passion for sin, or for what the world calls sin, so dominates a nature, that every fibre of the body, as every cell of the brain, seems to be instinct with fearful impulses. Men and women at such moments lose the freedom of their will. They move to their terrible end as automatons move. Choice is taken from them, and conscience is either killed, or, if it lives at all, lives but to give rebellion its fascination, and disobedience its charm. For all sins, as theologians weary not of reminding us, are sins of disobedience. When that high spirit, that morning-star of evil, fell from heaven, it was as a rebel that he fell.

Callous, concentrated on evil, with stained mind and soul hungry for rebellion, Dorian Gray hastened on, quickening his step as he went, but as he darted aside into a dim archway, that had served him often as a short cut to the ill-famed place where he was going, he felt himself suddenly seized from behind, and before he had time to defend himself he was thrust back against the wall, with a brutal hand round his throat.

He struggled madly for life, and by a terrible effort wrenched the tightening fingers away. In a second he heard the click of a revolver, and saw the gleam of a polished barrel pointing straight at his head, and the dusky form of a short thick-set man facing him.

'What do you want?' he gasped.

'Keep quiet,' said the man. 'If you stir, I shoot you.'

'You are mad. What have I done to you?'

'You wrecked the life of Sibyl Vane,' was the answer, 'and Sibyl Vane was my sister. She killed herself. I know it. Her death is at your door. I swore I would kill you in return. For years I have sought you. I had no clue, no trace. The two people who could have described you were dead. I knew nothing of you but the pet name she used to call you. I heard it tonight by chance. Make your peace with God, for tonight you are going to die.'

Dorian Gray grew sick with fear. 'I never knew her,' he stammered. 'I never heard of her. You are mad.'

'You had better confess your sin, for as sure as I am James Vane, you are going to die.' There was a horrible moment. Dorian did not know what to say or do. 'Down on your knees!' growled the man. 'I give you one minute to make your peace—no more. I go on board tonight for India, and I must do my job first. One minute. That's all.'

Dorian's arms fell to his side. Paralysed with terror, he did not know what to do. Suddenly a wild hope flashed across his brain. 'Stop,' he cried. 'How long ago is it since your sister died? Quick, tell me!'

'Eighteen years,' said the man. 'Why do you ask me? What do years matter?'

'Eighteen years,' laughed Dorian Gray, with a touch of triumph in his voice. 'Eighteen years! Set me under the lamp and look at my face!'

James Vane hesitated for a moment, not understanding what was meant. Then he seized Dorian Gray and dragged him from the archway.

Dim and wavering as was the windblown light, yet it served to show him the hideous error, as it seemed, into which he had fallen, for the face of the man he had sought to kill had all the bloom of boyhood, all the unstained purity of youth. He seemed little more than a lad of twenty summers, hardly older, if older indeed at all, than his sister had been when they had parted so many years ago. It was obvious that this was not the man who had destroyed her life.

He loosened his hold and reeled back. 'My God! my God!' he cried, 'and I would have murdered you!'

Dorian Gray drew a long breath. 'You have been on the brink of committing a terrible crime, my man,' he said, looking at him sternly. 'Let this be a warning to you not to take vengeance into your own hands.'

'Forgive me, sir,' muttered James Vane. 'I was deceived. A chance word I heard in that damned den set me on the wrong track.'

'You had better go home, and put that pistol away, or you may get into trouble,' said Dorian, turning on his heel, and going slowly down the street.

James Vane stood on the pavement in horror. He was trembling from head to foot. After a little while a black shadow that had been creeping along the dripping wall, moved out into the light and came close to him with stealthy footsteps. He felt a hand laid on his arm and looked round with a start. It was one of the women who had been drinking at the bar.

'Why didn't you kill him?' she hissed out, putting her haggard face quite close to his. 'I knew you were following him when you rushed out from Daly's. You fool! You should have killed him. He has lots of money, and he's as bad as bad.'

'He is not the man I am looking for,' he answered, 'and I want no man's money. I want a man's life. The man whose life I want must be nearly forty now. This one is little more than a boy. Thank God, I have not got his blood upon my hands.'

The woman gave a bitter laugh. 'Little more than a boy!' she sneered. 'Why, man, it's nigh on eighteen years since Prince Charming made me what I am.'

'You lie!' cried James Vane.

She raised her hand up to heaven. 'Before God I am telling the truth,' she cried.

'Before God?'

'Strike me dumb if it ain't so. He is the worst one that comes here. They say he has sold himself to the devil for a pretty face. It's nigh on eighteen years since I met him. He hasn't changed much since then. I have though,' she added, with a sickly leer.

'You swear this?'

'I swear it,' came in hoarse echo from her flat mouth. 'But don't give me away to him,' she whined; 'I am afraid of him. Let me have some money for my night's lodging.'

He broke from her with an oath, and rushed to the corner of the street, but Dorian Gray had disappeared. When he looked back, the woman had vanished also.

CHAPTER XVII

A WEEK later Dorian Gray was sitting in the conservatory at Selby Royal talking to the pretty Duchess of Monmouth, who with her husband, a jaded-looking man of sixty, was amongst his guests. It was tea-time, and the mellow light of the huge lace-covered lamp that stood on the table lit up the delicate china and hammered silver of the service at which the Duchess was presiding. Her white hands were moving daintily among the cups, and her full red lips were smiling at something that Dorian had whispered to her. Lord Henry was lying back in a silk-draped wicker chair looking at them. On a peach-coloured divan sat Lady Narborough pretending to listen to the Duke's description of the last Brazilian beetle that he had added to his collection. Three young men in elaborate smoking-suits were handing tea-cakes to some of the women. The house-party consisted of twelve people, and there were more expected to arrive on the next day.

'What are you two talking about?' said Lord Henry, strolling over to the table, and putting his cup down. 'I hope Dorian has told you about my plan for rechristening everything, Gladys. It is a delightful idea.'

'But I don't want to be rechristened, Harry,' rejoined the Duchess, looking up at him with her wonderful eyes. 'I am quite satisfied with my own name, and I am sure Mr Gray should be satisfied with his.'

'My dear Gladys, I would not alter either name for the world. They are both perfect. I was thinking chiefly of flowers. Yesterday I cut an orchid, for my buttonhole. It was a marvellous spotted thing, as effective as the seven deadly sins. In a thoughtless moment I asked one of the gardeners what it was called. He told me it was a fine specimen of *Robinsoniana*, or something dreadful of that kind. It is a sad truth, but we have lost the faculty of giving lovely names to things. Names are everything. I never quarrel with actions. My one quarrel is with words. That is the reason I hate vulgar realism in literature. The man who could call a spade a spade should be compelled to use one. It is the only thing he is fit for.'

'Then what should we call you, Harry?' she asked.

'His name is Prince Paradox,' said Dorian.

'I recognize him in a flash,' exclaimed the Duchess.

'I won't hear of it,' laughed Lord Henry, sinking into a chair. 'From a label there is no escape! I refuse the title.'

'Royalties may not abdicate,' fell as a warning from pretty lips.

'You wish me to defend my throne, then?'

'Yes.'

'I give the truths of tomorrow.'

'I prefer the mistakes of today,' she answered.

'You disarm me, Gladys,' he cried, catching the wilfulness of her mood.

'Of your shield, Harry: not of your spear.'

'I never tilt against Beauty,' he said, with a wave of his hand.

'That is your error, Harry, believe me. You value beauty far too much.'

'How can you say that? I admit that I think that it is better to be beautiful than to be good. But on the other hand no one is more ready than I am to acknowledge that it is better to be good than to be ugly.'

'Ugliness is one of the seven deadly sins, then?' cried the Duchess. 'What becomes of your simile about the orchid?'

'Ugliness is one of the seven deadly virtues, Gladys. You, as a good Tory, must not underrate them. Beer, the Bible, and the seven deadly virtues have made our England what she is.'

'You don't like your country, then?' she asked.

'I live in it.'

'That you may censure it the better.'

'Would you have me take the verdict of Europe on it?' he enquired.

'What do they say of us?'

'That Tartuffe° has emigrated to England and opened a shop.'

'Is that yours, Harry?'

'I give it to you.'

'I could not use it. It is too true.'

'You need not be afraid. Our countrymen never recognize a description.'

'They are practical.'

'They are more cunning than practical. When they make up their ledger, they balance stupidity by wealth, and vice by hypocrisy.'

'Still, we have done great things.'

'Great things have been thrust on us, Gladys.'

'We have carried their burden.'

'Only as far as the Stock Exchange.'

She shook her head. 'I believe in the race,' she cried.

'It represents the survival of the pushing.'

'It has development.'

'Decay fascinates me more.'

'What of Art?' she asked.

'It is a malady.'

'Love?'

'An illusion.'

'Religion?'

'The fashionable substitute for Belief.'

'You are a sceptic.'

'Never! Scepticism is the beginning of Faith.'

'What are you?'

'To define is to limit.'

'Give me a clue.'

'Threads snap. You would lose your way in the labyrinth.'

'You bewilder me. Let us talk of some one else.'

'Our host is a delightful topic. Years ago he was christened Prince Charming.'

'Ah! don't remind me of that,' cried Dorian Gray.

'Our host is rather horrid this evening,' answered the Duchess, colouring. 'I believe he thinks that Monmouth married me on purely scientific principles as the best specimen he could find of a modern butterfly.'

'Well, I hope he won't stick pins into you, Duchess,' laughed Dorian.

'Oh! my maid does that already, Mr Gray, when she is annoyed with me.'

'And what does she get annoyed with you about, Duchess?'

'For the most trivial things, Mr Gray, I assure you. Usually because I come in at ten minutes to nine and tell her that I must be dressed by half-past eight.'

'How unreasonable of her! You should give her warning.'

'I daren't, Mr Gray. Why, she invents hats for me. You remember the one I wore at Lady Hilstone's garden-party? You don't, but it is nice of you to pretend that you do. Well, she made it out of nothing. All good hats are made out of nothing.'

'Like all good reputations, Gladys,' interrupted Lord Henry. 'Every effect that one produces gives one an enemy. To be popular one must be a mediocrity.'

'Not with women,' said the Duchess, shaking her head; 'and women rule the world. I assure you we can't bear mediocrities. We women, as some one says, love with our ears, just as you men love with your eyes, if you ever love at all.'

'It seems to me that we never do anything else,' murmured Dorian.

'Ah! then, you never really love, Mr Gray,' answered the Duchess, with mock sadness.

'My dear Gladys!' cried Lord Henry. 'How can you say that? Romance lives by repetition, and repetition converts an appetite into an art. Besides, each time that one loves is the only time one has ever loved. Difference of object does not alter singleness of passion. It merely intensifies it. We can have in life but one great experience at best, and the secret of life is to reproduce that experience as often as possible.'

'Even when one has been wounded by it, Harry?' asked the Duchess, after a pause.

'Especially when one has been wounded by it,' answered Lord Henry.

The Duchess turned and looked at Dorian Gray with a curious expression in her eyes. 'What do you say to that, Mr Gray?' she enquired.

Dorian hesitated for a moment. Then he threw his head back and laughed. 'I always agree with Harry, Duchess.'

'Even when he is wrong?'

'Harry is never wrong, Duchess.'

'And does his philosophy make you happy?'

'I have never searched for happiness. Who wants happiness? I have searched for pleasure.'

'And found it, Mr Gray?'

'Often. Too often.'

The Duchess sighed. 'I am searching for peace,' she said, 'and if I don't go and dress, I shall have none this evening.'

'Let me get you some orchids, Duchess,' cried Dorian, starting to his feet, and walking down the conservatory.

'You are flirting disgracefully with him,' said Lord Henry to his cousin. 'You had better take care. He is very fascinating.'

'If he were not, there would be no battle.'

'Greek meets Greek, then?'

'I am on the side of the Trojans. They fought for a woman.'

'They were defeated.'

'There are worse things than capture,' she answered.

'You gallop with a loose rein.'

'Pace gives life,' was the *riposte*.

'I shall write it in my diary tonight.'

'What?'

'That a burnt child loves the fire.'

'I am not even singed. My wings are untouched.'

'You use them for everything, except flight.'

'Courage has passed from men to women. It is a new experience for us.'

'You have a rival.'

'Who?'

He laughed. 'Lady Narborough,' he whispered. 'She perfectly adores him.'

'You fill me with apprehension. The appeal to Antiquity is fatal to us who are romanticists.'

'Romanticists! You have all the methods of science.'

'Men have educated us.'

'But not explained you.'

'Describe us as a sex,' was her challenge.

'Sphinxes without secrets.'°

She looked at him, smiling. 'How long Mr Gray is!' she said. 'Let us go and help him. I have not yet told him the colour of my frock.'

'Ah! you must suit your frock to his flowers, Gladys.'

'That would be a premature surrender.'

'Romantic Art begins with its climax.'

'I must keep an opportunity for retreat.'

'In the Parthian manner?'°

'They found safety in the desert. I could not do that.'

'Women are not always allowed a choice,' he answered, but hardly had he finished the sentence before from the far end of the conservatory came a stifled groan, followed by the dull sound of a heavy fall. Everybody started up. The Duchess stood motionless in horror. And with fear in his eyes Lord Henry rushed through the flapping palms, to find Dorian Gray lying face downwards on the tiled floor in a death-like swoon.

He was carried at once into the blue drawing-room, and laid upon one of the sofas. After a short time he came to himself, and looked round with a dazed expression.

'What has happened?' he asked. 'Oh! I remember. Am I safe here, Harry?' He began to tremble.

'My dear Dorian,' answered Lord Henry, 'you merely fainted. That was all. You must have overtired yourself. You had better not come down to dinner. I will take your place.'

'No, I will come down,' he said, struggling to his feet. 'I would rather come down. I must not be alone.'

He went to his room and dressed. There was a wild recklessness of gaiety in his manner as he sat at table, but now and then a thrill of terror ran through him when he remembered that, pressed against the window of the conservatory like a white handkerchief, he had seen the face of James Vane watching him.

CHAPTER XVIII

THE next day he did not leave the house, and, indeed, spent most of the time in his own room, sick with a wild terror of dying, and yet indifferent to life itself. The consciousness of being hunted, snared, tracked down, had begun to dominate him. If the tapestry did but tremble in the wind, he shook. The dead leaves that were blown against the leaded panes seemed to him like his own wasted resolutions and wild regrets. When he closed his eyes, he saw again the sailor's face peering through the mist-stained glass, and horror seemed once more to lay its hand upon his heart.

But perhaps it had been only his fancy that had called vengeance out of the night, and set the hideous shapes of punishment before him. Actual life was chaos, but there was something terribly logical in the imagination. It was the imagination that set remorse to dog the feet of sin. It was the imagination that made each crime bear its misshapen brood. In the common world of fact the wicked were not punished, nor the good rewarded. Success was given to the strong, failure thrust upon the weak. That was all. Besides, had any stranger been prowling round the house he would have been seen by the servants or the keepers. Had any footmarks been found on the flower-beds, the gardeners would have reported it. Yes: it had been merely fancy. Sibyl Vane's brother had not come back to kill him. He had sailed away in his ship to founder in some winter sea. From him, at any rate, he was safe. Why, the man did not know who he was, could not know who he was. The mask of youth had saved him.

And yet if it had been merely an illusion, how terrible it was to think that conscience could raise such fearful phantoms, and give them visible form, and make them move before one! What sort of life would his be if, day and night, shadows of his crime were to peer at him from silent corners, to mock him from secret places, to whisper in his ear as he sat at the feast, to wake him with icy fingers as he lay asleep! As the thought crept through his brain, he grew pale with terror, and the air seemed to him to have become suddenly colder. Oh! in what a wild hour of madness he had killed his friend! How ghastly the mere memory of the scene! He saw it all again. Each hideous detail came back to him with added horror. Out of the black cave of Time, terrible and swathed in scarlet, rose the image of his sin. When Lord Henry came in at six o'clock, he found him crying as one whose heart will break.

It was not till the third day that he ventured to go out. There was something in the clear, pine-scented air of that winter morning that seemed to bring him back his joyousness and his ardour for life. But it was not merely the physical conditions of environment that had caused the change. His own nature had revolted against the excess of anguish that had sought to maim and mar the perfection of its calm. With subtle and finely-wrought temperaments it is always so. Their strong passions must either bruise or bend. They either slay the man, or themselves die. Shallow sorrows and shallow loves live on. The loves and sorrows that are great are destroyed by their own plenitude. Besides, he had convinced himself that he had been the victim of a terror-stricken imagination, and looked back now on his fears with something of pity and not a little of contempt.

After breakfast he walked with the Duchess for an hour in the garden, and then drove across the park to join the shooting-party. The crisp frost lay like salt upon the grass. The sky was an inverted cup of blue metal. A thin film of ice bordered the flat reed-grown lake.

At the corner of the pine-wood he caught sight of Sir Geoffrey Clouston, the Duchess's brother, jerking two spent cartridges out of his gun. He jumped from the cart, and having told the groom to take the mare home, made his way towards his guest through the withered bracken and rough undergrowth.

'Have you had good sport, Geoffrey?' he asked.

'Not very good, Dorian. I think most of the birds have gone to the open. I dare say it will be better after lunch, when we get to new ground.'

Dorian strolled along by his side. The keen aromatic air, the brown and red lights that glimmered in the wood, the hoarse cries of the beaters ringing out from time to time, and the sharp snaps of the guns that followed, fascinated him, and filled him with a sense of delightful freedom. He was dominated by the carelessness of happiness, by the high indifference of joy.

Suddenly from a lumpy tussock of old grass, some twenty yards in front of them, with black-tipped ears erect, and long hinder limbs throwing it forward, started a hare. It bolted for a thicket of alders. Sir Geoffrey put his gun to his shoulder, but there was something in the animal's grace of movement that strangely charmed Dorian Gray, and he cried out at once, 'Don't shoot it, Geoffrey. Let it live.'

'What nonsense, Dorian!' laughed his companion, and as the hare bounded into the thicket he fired. There were two cries heard, the cry of a hare in pain, which is dreadful, the cry of a man in agony, which is worse.

'Good heavens! I have hit a beater!' exclaimed Sir Geoffrey. 'What an ass the man was to get in front of the guns! Stop shooting there!' he called out at the top of his voice. 'A man is hurt.'

The head-keeper came running up with a stick in his hand.

'Where, sir? Where is he?' he shouted. At the same time the firing ceased along the line.

'Here,' answered Sir Geoffrey, angrily, hurrying towards the thicket. 'Why on earth don't you keep your men back? Spoiled my shooting for the day.'

Dorian watched them as they plunged into the alder-clump, brushing the lithe, swinging branches aside. In a few moments they emerged, dragging a body after them into the sunlight. He turned away in horror. It seemed to him that misfortune followed wherever he went. He heard Sir Geoffrey ask if the man was really dead, and the affirmative answer of the keeper. The wood seemed to him to have become suddenly alive with faces. There was the trampling of myriad feet, and the low buzz of voices. A great copper-breasted pheasant came beating through the boughs overhead.

After a few moments, that were to him, in his perturbed state, like endless hours of pain, he felt a hand laid on his shoulder. He started, and looked round.

'Dorian,' said Lord Henry, 'I had better tell them that the shooting is stopped for today. It would not look well to go on.'

'I wish it were stopped for ever, Harry,' he answered, bitterly. 'The whole thing is hideous and cruel. Is the man . . . ?'

He could not finish the sentence.

'I am afraid so,' rejoined Lord Henry. 'He got the whole charge of shot in his chest. He must have died almost instantaneously. Come; let us go home.'

They walked side by side in the direction of the avenue for nearly fifty yards without speaking. Then Dorian looked at Lord Henry, and said, with a heavy sigh, 'It is a bad omen, Harry, a very bad omen.'

'What is?' asked Lord Henry. 'Oh! this accident, I suppose. My dear fellow, it can't be helped. It was the man's own fault. Why did he get in front of the guns? Besides, it is nothing to us. It is rather awkward for Geoffrey, of course. It does not do to pepper beaters. It makes people think that one is a wild shot. And Geoffrey is not; he shoots very straight. But there is no use talking about the matter.'

Dorian shook his head. 'It is a bad omen, Harry. I feel as if something horrible were going to happen to some of us. To myself, perhaps,' he added, passing his hand over his eyes, with a gesture of pain.

The elder man laughed. 'The only horrible thing in the world is *ennui*, Dorian. That is the one sin for which there is no forgiveness. But we are not likely to suffer from it, unless these fellows keep chattering about this thing at dinner. I must tell them that the subject is to be tabooed. As for omens, there is no such thing as an omen. Destiny does not send us heralds. She is too wise or too cruel for that. Besides, what on earth could happen to you, Dorian? You have everything in the world that a man can want. There is no one who would not be delighted to change places with you.'

'There is no one with whom I would not change places, Harry. Don't laugh like that. I am telling you the truth. The wretched peasant who has just died is better off than I am. I have no terror of Death. It is the coming of Death that terrifies me. Its monstrous wings seem to wheel in the leaden air around me. Good heavens! don't you see a man moving behind the trees there, watching me, waiting for me?'

Lord Henry looked in the direction in which the trembling gloved hand was pointing. 'Yes,' he said, smiling, 'I see the gardener waiting for you. I suppose he wants to ask you what flowers you wish to have on the table tonight. How absurdly nervous you are, my dear fellow! You must come and see my doctor, when we get back to town.'

Dorian heaved a sigh of relief as he saw the gardener approaching. The man touched his hat, glanced for a moment at Lord Henry in a hesitating manner, and then produced a letter, which he handed to his master. 'Her Grace told me to wait for an answer,' he murmured.

Dorian put the letter into his pocket. 'Tell her Grace that I am coming in,' he said, coldly. The man turned round, and went rapidly in the direction of the house.

'How fond women are of doing dangerous things!' laughed Lord Henry. 'It is one of the qualities in them that I admire most. A woman will flirt with anybody in the world as long as other people are looking on.'

'How fond you are of saying dangerous things, Harry! In the present instance you are quite astray. I like the Duchess very much, but I don't love her.'

'And the Duchess loves you very much, but she likes you less, so you are excellently matched.'

'You are talking scandal, Harry, and there is never any basis for scandal.'

'The basis of every scandal is an immoral certainty,' said Lord Henry, lighting a cigarette.

'You would sacrifice anybody, Harry, for the sake of an epigram.'

'The world goes to the altar of its own accord,' was the answer.

'I wish I could love,' cried Dorian Gray, with a deep note of pathos in his voice. 'But I seem to have lost the passion, and forgotten the desire. I am too much concentrated on myself. My own personality has become a burden to me. I want to escape, to go away, to forget. It was silly of me to come down here at all. I think I shall send a wire to Harvey to have the yacht got ready. On a yacht one is safe.'

'Safe from what, Dorian? You are in some trouble. Why not tell me what it is? You know I would help you.'

'I can't tell you, Harry,' he answered, sadly. 'And I dare say it is only a fancy of mine. This unfortunate accident has upset me. I have a horrible presentiment that something of the kind may happen to me.'

'What nonsense!'

'I hope it is, but I can't help feeling it. Ah! here is the Duchess, looking like Artemis in a tailor-made gown. You see we have come back, Duchess.'

'I have heard all about it, Mr Gray,' she answered. 'Poor Geoffrey is terribly upset. And it seems that you asked him not to shoot the hare. How curious!'

'Yes, it was very curious. I don't know what made me say it. Some whim, I suppose. It looked the loveliest of little live things. But I am sorry they told you about the man. It is a hideous subject.'

'It is an annoying subject,' broke in Lord Henry. 'It has no psychological value at all. Now if Geoffrey had done the thing on purpose, how interesting he would be! I should like to know some one who had committed a real murder.'

'How horrid of you, Harry!' cried the Duchess. 'Isn't it, Mr Gray? Harry, Mr Gray is ill again. He is going to faint.'

Dorian drew himself up with an effort, and smiled. 'It is nothing, Duchess,' he murmured; 'my nerves are dreadfully out of order. That is all. I am afraid I walked too far this morning. I didn't hear what Harry said. Was it very bad? You must tell me some other time. I think I must go and lie down. You will excuse me, won't you?'

They had reached the great flight of steps that led from the conservatory on to the terrace. As the glass door closed behind Dorian, Lord Henry turned and looked at the Duchess with his slumberous eyes. 'Are you very much in love with him?' he asked.

She did not answer for some time, but stood gazing at the landscape. 'I wish I knew,' she said at last.

He shook his head. 'Knowledge would be fatal. It is the uncertainty that charms one. A mist makes things wonderful.'

'One may lose one's way.'

'All ways end at the same point, my dear Gladys.'

'What is that?'

'Disillusion.'

'It was my *début* in life,' she sighed.

'It came to you crowned.'

'I am tired of strawberry leaves.'°

'They become you.'

'Only in public.'

'You would miss them,' said Lord Henry.

'I will not part with a petal.'

'Monmouth has ears.'

'Old age is dull of hearing.'

'Has he never been jealous?'

'I wish he had been.'

He glanced about as if in search of something. 'What are you looking for?' she enquired.

'The button from your foil,' he answered. 'You have dropped it.'

She laughed. 'I have still the mask.'

'It makes your eyes lovelier,' was his reply.

She laughed again. Her teeth showed like white seeds in a scarlet fruit.

Upstairs, in his own room, Dorian Gray was lying on a sofa, with terror in every tingling fibre of his body. Life had suddenly become too hideous a burden for him to bear. The dreadful death of the unlucky beater, shot in the thicket like a wild animal, had seemed to him to prefigure death for himself also. He had nearly swooned at what Lord Henry had said in a chance mood of cynical jesting.

At five o'clock he rang his bell for his servant and gave him orders to pack his things for the night-express to town, and to have the brougham at the door by eight-thirty. He was determined not to sleep another night at Selby Royal. It was an ill-omened place. Death walked there in the sunlight. The grass of the forest had been spotted with blood.

Then he wrote a note to Lord Henry, telling him that he was going up to town to consult his doctor, and asking him to entertain his guests in his absence. As he was putting it into the envelope, a knock came to the door, and his valet informed him that the head-keeper wished to see him. He frowned, and bit his lip. 'Send him in,' he muttered, after some moments' hesitation.

As soon as the man entered Dorian pulled his cheque-book out of a drawer, and spread it out before him.

'I suppose you have come about the unfortunate accident of this morning, Thornton?' he said, taking up a pen.

'Yes, sir,' answered the gamekeeper.

'Was the poor fellow married? Had he any people dependent on him?' asked Dorian, looking bored. 'If so, I should not like them to be left in want, and will send them any sum of money you may think necessary.'

'We don't know who he is, sir. That is what I took the liberty of coming to you about.'

'Don't know who he is?' said Dorian, listlessly. 'What do you mean? Wasn't he one of your men?'

'No, sir. Never saw him before. Seems like a sailor, sir.'

The pen dropped from Dorian Gray's hand, and he felt as if his heart had suddenly stopped beating. 'A sailor?' he cried out. 'Did you say a sailor?'

'Yes, sir. He looks as if he had been a sort of sailor; tattooed on both arms, and that kind of thing.'

'Was there anything found on him?' said Dorian, leaning forward and looking at the man with startled eyes. 'Anything that would tell his name?'

'Some money, sir—not much, and a six-shooter. There was no name of any kind. A decent-looking man, sir, but rough-like. A sort of sailor we think.'

Dorian started to his feet. A terrible hope fluttered past him. He clutched at it madly. 'Where is the body?' he exclaimed. 'Quick! I must see it at once.'

'It is in an empty stable in the Home Farm, sir. The folk don't like to have that sort of thing in their houses. They say a corpse brings bad luck.'

'The Home Farm! Go there at once and meet me. Tell one of the grooms to bring my horse round. No. Never mind. I'll go to the stables myself. It will save time.'

In less than a quarter of an hour Dorian Gray was galloping down the long avenue as hard as he could go. The trees seemed to sweep past him in spectral procession, and wild shadows to fling themselves across his path. Once the mare swerved at a white gate-post and nearly threw him. He lashed her across the neck with his crop. She cleft the dusky air like an arrow. The stones flew from her hoofs.

At last he reached the Home Farm. Two men were loitering in the yard. He leapt from the saddle and threw the reins to one of them. In the farthest stable a light was glimmering. Something seemed to tell him that the body was there, and he hurried to the door, and put his hand upon the latch.

There he paused for a moment, feeling that he was on the brink of a discovery that would either make or mar his life. Then he thrust the door open, and entered.

On a heap of sacking in the far corner was lying the dead body of a man dressed in a coarse shirt and a pair of blue trousers. A spotted handkerchief had been placed over the face. A coarse candle, stuck in a bottle, sputtered beside it.

Dorian Gray shuddered. He felt that his could not be the hand to take the handkerchief away, and called out to one of the farm-servants to come to him.

'Take that thing off the face. I wish to see it,' he said, clutching at the doorpost for support.

When the farm-servant had done so, he stepped forward. A cry of joy broke from his lips. The man who had been shot in the thicket was James Vane.

He stood there for some minutes looking at the dead body. As he rode home, his eyes were full of tears, for he knew he was safe.

CHAPTER XIX

'THERE is no use your telling me that you are going to be good,' cried Lord Henry, dipping his white fingers into a red copper bowl filled with rose-water. 'You are quite perfect. Pray, don't change.'

Dorian Gray shook his head. 'No, Harry, I have done too many dreadful things in my life. I am not going to do any more. I began my good actions yesterday.'

'Where were you yesterday?'

'In the country, Harry. I was staying at a little inn by myself.'

'My dear boy,' said Lord Henry, smiling, 'anybody can be good in the country. There are no temptations there. That is the reason why people who live out of town are so absolutely uncivilized. Civilization is not by any means an easy thing to attain to. There are only two ways by which man can reach it. One is by being cultured, the other by being corrupt. Country people have no opportunity of being either, so they stagnate.'

'Culture and corruption,' echoed Dorian. 'I have known something of both. It seems terrible to me now that they should ever be found together. For I have a new ideal, Harry. I am going to alter. I think I have altered.'

'You have not yet told me what your good action was. Or did you say you had done more than one?' asked his companion, as he spilt into his plate a little crimson pyramid of seeded strawberries, and through a perforated shell-shaped spoon snowed white sugar upon them.

'I can tell you, Harry. It is not a story I could tell to any one else. I spared somebody. It sounds vain, but you understand what I mean. She was quite beautiful, and wonderfully like Sibyl Vane. I think it was that which first attracted me to her. You remember Sibyl, don't you? How long ago that seems! Well, Hetty was not one of our own class, of course. She was simply a girl in a village. But I really loved her. I am quite sure that I loved her. All during this wonderful May that we have been having, I used to run down and see her two or three times a week. Yesterday she met me in a little orchard. The apple-blossoms kept tumbling down on her hair, and she was laughing. We were to have gone away together this morning at dawn. Suddenly I determined to leave her as flower-like as I had found her.'

'I should think the novelty of the emotion must have given you a thrill of real pleasure, Dorian,' interrupted Lord Henry. 'But I can finish your idyll for you. You gave her good advice, and broke her heart. That was the beginning of your reformation.'

'Harry, you are horrible! You mustn't say these dreadful things. Hetty's heart is not broken. Of course she cried, and all that. But there is no disgrace upon her. She can live, like Perdita, in her garden of mint and marigold.'

'And weep over a faithless Florizel,'° said Lord Henry, laughing, as he leant back in his chair. 'My dear Dorian, you have the most curiously boyish moods. Do you think this girl will ever be really contented now with any one of her own rank? I suppose she will be married some day to a rough carter or a grinning ploughman. Well, the fact of having met you, and loved you, will teach her to despise her husband, and she will be wretched. From a moral point of view, I cannot say that I think much of your great renunciation. Even as a beginning, it is poor. Besides, how do you know that Hetty isn't floating at the present moment in some star-lit mill-pond, wilth lovely water-lilies round her, like Ophelia?'

'I can't bear this, Harry! You mock at everything, and then suggest the most serious tragedies. I am sorry I told you now. I don't care what you say to me. I know I was right in acting as I did. Poor Hetty! As I rode past the farm this morning, I saw her white face at the window, like a spray of jasmine. Don't let us talk about it any more, and don't try to persuade me that the first good action I have done for years, the first little bit of self-sacrifice I have ever known, is really a sort of sin. I want to be better. I am going to be better. Tell me something about yourself. What is going on in town? I have not been to the club for days.'

'The people are still discussing poor Basil's disappearance.'

'I should have thought they had got tired of that by this time,' said Dorian, pouring himself out some wine, and frowning slightly.

'My dear boy, they have only been talking about it for six weeks, and the British public are really not equal to the mental strain of having more than one topic every three months. They have been very fortunate lately, however. They have had my own divorce-case, and Alan Campbell's suicide. Now they have got the mysterious disappearance of an artist. Scotland Yard still insists that the man in the grey ulster who left for Paris by the midnight train on the ninth of November was poor Basil, and the French police declare that Basil never arrived in Paris at all. I suppose in about a fortnight we shall be told that he has been seen in San Francisco. It is an odd thing, but every one who disappears is said to be seen at San Francisco. It must be a delightful city, and possess all the attractions of the next world.'

'What do you think has happened to Basil?' asked Dorian, holding up his Burgundy against the light, and wondering how it was that he could discuss the matter so calmly.

'I have not the slightest idea. If Basil chooses to hide himself, it is no business of mine. If he is dead, I don't want to think about him. Death is the only thing that ever terrifies me. I hate it.'

'Why?' said the younger man, wearily.

'Because,' said Lord Henry, passing beneath his nostrils the gilt trellis of an open vinaigrette box,° 'one can survive everything nowadays except that. Death and vulgarity are the only two facts in the nineteenth century that one cannot explain away. Let us have our coffee in the music-room, Dorian. You must play Chopin to me. The man with whom my wife ran away played Chopin exquisitely. Poor Victoria! I was very fond of her. The house is rather lonely without her. Of course married life is merely a habit, a bad habit. But then one regrets the loss even of one's worst habits. Perhaps one regrets them the most. They are such an essential part of one's personality.'

Dorian said nothing, but rose from the table, and, passing into the next room, sat down to the piano and let his fingers stray across the white and black ivory of the keys. After the coffee had been brought in, he stopped, and, looking over at Lord Henry, said, 'Harry, did it ever occur to you that Basil was murdered?'

Lord Henry yawned. 'Basil was very popular, and always wore a Waterbury watch.° Why should he have been murdered? He was not clever enough to have enemies. Of course he had a wonderful genius for painting. But a man can paint like Velasquez and yet be as dull as possible. Basil was really rather dull. He only interested me once, and that was when he told me, years ago, that he had a wild adoration for you, and that you were the dominant motive of his art.'

'I was very fond of Basil,' said Dorian, with a note of sadness in his voice. 'But don't people say that he was murdered?'

'Oh, some of the papers do. It does not seem to me to be at all probable. I know there are dreadful places in Paris, but Basil was not the sort of man to have gone to them. He had no curiosity. It was his chief defect.'

'What would you say, Harry, if I told you that I had murdered Basil?' said the younger man. He watched him intently after he had spoken.

'I would say, my dear fellow, that you were posing for a character that doesn't suit you. All crime is vulgar, just as all vulgarity is crime. It is not in you, Dorian, to commit a murder. I am sorry if I hurt your vanity by saying so, but I assure you it is true. Crime belongs exclusively to the lower orders. I don't blame them in the smallest degree. I should fancy that crime was to them what art is to us, simply a method of procuring extraordinary sensations.'

'A method of procuring sensations? Do you think, then, that a man who has once committed a murder could possibly do the same crime again? Don't tell me that.'

'Oh! anything becomes a pleasure if one does it too often,' cried Lord Henry, laughing. 'That is one of the most important secrets of life. I should fancy, however, that murder is always a mistake. One should never do anything that one cannot talk about after dinner. But let us pass from poor Basil. I wish I could believe that he had come to such a really romantic end as you suggest; but I can't. I dare say he fell into the Seine off an omnibus, and that the conductor hushed up the scandal. Yes: I should fancy that was his end. I see him lying now on his back under those dull-green waters with the heavy barges floating over him, and long weeds catching in his hair. Do you know, I don't think he would have done much more good work. During the last ten years his painting had gone off very much.'

Dorian heaved a sigh, and Lord Henry strolled across the room and began to stroke the head of a curious Java parrot, a large grey-plumaged bird, with pink crest and tail, that was balancing itself upon a bamboo perch. As his pointed fingers touched it, it dropped the white scurf of crinkled lids over black glass-like eyes, and began to sway backwards and forwards.

'Yes,' he continued, turning round, and taking his handkerchief out of his pocket; 'his painting had quite gone off. It seemed to me to have lost something. It had lost an ideal. When you and he ceased to be great friends, he ceased to be a great artist. What was it separated you? I suppose he bored you. If so, he never forgave you. It's a habit bores have. By the way, what has become of that wonderful portrait he did of you? I don't think I have ever seen it since he finished it. Oh! I remember your telling me years ago that you had sent it down to Selby, and that it had got mislaid or stolen on the way. You never got it back? What a pity! It was really a masterpiece. I remember I wanted to buy it. I wish I had now. It belonged to Basil's best period. Since then, his work was that curious mixture of bad painting and good intentions that always entitles a man to be called a representative British artist. Did you advertise for it? You should.'

'I forget,' said Dorian. 'I suppose I did. But I never really liked it. I am sorry I sat for it. The memory of the thing is hateful to me. Why do you talk of it? It used to remind me of those curious lines in some play— "Hamlet", I think—how do they run?—

> Like the painting of a sorrow,
> A face without a heart.°

Yes: that is what it was like.'

Lord Henry laughed. 'If a man treats life artistically, his brain is his heart,' he answered, sinking into an arm-chair.

Dorian Gray shook his head, and struck some soft chords on the piano. '"Like the painting of a sorrow,"' he repeated, '"a face without a heart".'

The elder man lay back and looked at him with half-closed eyes. 'By the way, Dorian,' he said, after a pause, '"what does it profit a man if he gain the whole world and lose—how does the quotation run?—his own soul"?'°

The music jarred and Dorian Gray started, and stared at his friend. 'Why do you ask me that, Harry?'

'My dear fellow,' said Lord Henry, elevating his eyebrows in surprise, 'I asked you because I thought you might be able to give me an answer. That is all. I was going through the Park last Sunday, and close by the Marble Arch there stood a little crowd of shabby-looking people listening to some vulgar street-preacher. As I passed by, I heard the man yelling out that question to his audience. It struck me as being rather dramatic. London is very rich in curious effects of that kind. A wet Sunday, an uncouth Christian in a mackintosh, a ring of sickly white faces under a broken roof of dripping umbrellas, and a wonderful phrase flung into the air by shrill, hysterical lips—it was really very good in its way, quite a suggestion. I thought of telling the prophet that Art had a soul, but that man had not. I am afraid, however, he would not have understood me.'

'Don't, Harry. The soul is a terrible reality. It can be bought, and sold, and bartered away. It can be poisoned, or made perfect. There is a soul in each one of us. I know it.'

'Do you feel quite sure of that, Dorian?'

'Quite sure.'

'Ah! then it must be an illusion. The things one feels absolutely certain about are never true. That is the fatality of Faith, and the lesson of Romance. How grave you are! Don't be so serious. What have you or I to do with the superstitions of our age? No: we have given up our belief in the soul. Play me something. Play me a nocturne, Dorian, and, as you play, tell me, in a low voice, how you have kept your youth. You must have some secret. I am only ten years older than you are, and I am wrinkled, and worn, and yellow. You are really wonderful, Dorian. You have never looked more charming than you do tonight. You remind me of the day I saw you first. You were rather cheeky, very shy, and absolutely extraordinary. You have changed, of course, but not in appearance. I wish you would tell me your secret. To get back my youth I would do anything in the world, except take exercise, get up early, or be respectable. Youth! There is nothing like it. It's absurd to talk of the ignorance of youth. The only people to whose opinions I listen now with any respect are people much younger than myself. They seem in front of me. Life has revealed to them her latest wonder. As for the aged, I always contradict the aged. I do it on principle. If you ask them their opinion on something that happened yesterday, they solemnly give you the opinions current in 1820, when people wore high stocks, believed in everything, and knew absolutely nothing. How lovely that thing you are playing is! I wonder did

Chopin write it at Majorca, with the sea weeping round the villa, and the salt spray dashing against the panes? It is marvellously romantic. What a blessing it is that there is one art left to us that is not imitative! Don't stop. I want music tonight. It seems to me that you are the young Apollo, and that I am Marsyas° listening to you. I have sorrows, Dorian, of my own, that even you know nothing of. The tragedy of old age is not that one is old, but that one is young. I am amazed sometimes at my own sincerity. Ah, Dorian, how happy you are! What an exquisite life you have had! You have drunk deeply of everything. You have crushed the grapes against your palate. Nothing has been hidden from you. And it has all been to you no more than the sound of music.° It has not marred you. You are still the same.'

'I am not the same, Harry.'

'Yes: you are the same. I wonder what the rest of your life will be. Don't spoil it by renunciations. At present you are a perfect type. Don't make yourself incomplete. You are quite flawless now. You need not shake your head: you know you are. Besides, Dorian, don't deceive yourself. Life is not governed by will or intention. Life is a question of nerves, and fibres, and slowly built-up cells in which thought hides itself and passion has its dreams. You may fancy yourself safe, and think yourself strong. But a chance tone of colour in a room or a morning sky, a particular perfume that you had once loved and that brings subtle memories with it, a line from a forgotten poem that you had come across again, a cadence from a piece of music that you had ceased to play—I tell you, Dorian, that it is on things like these that our lives depend. Browning writes about that somewhere,° but our own senses will imagine them for us. There are moments when the odour of *lilas blanc* passes suddenly across me, and I have to live the strangest month of my life over again. I wish I could change places with you, Dorian. The world has cried out against us both, but it has always worshipped you. It always will worship you. You are the type of what the age is searching for, and what it is afraid it has found. I am so glad that you have never done anything, never carved a statue, or painted a picture, or produced anything outside of yourself! Life has been your art. You have set yourself to music. Your days are your sonnets.'

Dorian rose up from the piano, and passed his hand through his hair. 'Yes, life has been exquisite,' he murmured, 'but I am not going to have the same life, Harry. And you must not say these extravagant things to me. You don't know everything about me. I think that if you did, even you would turn from me. You laugh. Don't laugh.'

'Why have you stopped playing, Dorian? Go back and give me the nocturne over again. Look at that great honey-coloured moon that hangs in the dusky air. She is waiting for you to charm her, and if you play she will come closer to the earth. You won't? Let us go to the club, then. It has been a charming evening, and we must end it charmingly. There is some one at White's who wants immensely to know you—young Lord Poole, Bournemouth's eldest son. He has already copied your neckties, and has begged me to introduce him to you. He is quite delightful, and rather reminds me of you.'

'I hope not,' said Dorian, with a sad look in his eyes. 'But I am tired tonight, Harry. I shan't go to the club. It is nearly eleven, and I want to go to bed early.'

'Do stay. You have never played so well as tonight. There was something in your touch that was wonderful. It had more expression than I had ever heard from it before.'

'It is because I am going to be good,' he answered, smiling. 'I am a little changed already.'

'You cannot change to me, Dorian,' said Lord Henry. 'You and I will always be friends.'

'Yet you poisoned me with a book once. I should not forgive that. Harry, promise me that you will never lend that book to any one. It does harm.'

'My dear boy, you are really beginning to moralize. You will soon be going about like the converted, and the revivalist, warning people against all the sins of which you have grown tired. You are much too delightful to do that. Besides, it is no use. You and I are what we are, and will be what we will be. As for being poisoned by a book, there is no such thing as that. Art has no influence upon action. It annihilates the desire to act. It is superbly sterile. The books that the world calls immoral are books that show the world its own shame. That is all. But we won't discuss literature. Come round tomorrow. I am going to ride at eleven. We might go together, and I will take you to lunch afterwards with Lady Branksome. She is a charming woman, and wants to consult you about some tapestries she is thinking of buying. Mind you come. Or shall we lunch with our little Duchess? She says she never sees you now. Perhaps you are tired of Gladys? I thought you would be. Her clever tongue gets on one's nerves. Well, in any case, be here at eleven.'

'Must I really come, Harry?'

'Certainly. The Park is quite lovely now. I don't think there have been such lilacs since the year I met you.'

'Very well. I shall be here at eleven,' said Dorian. 'Goodnight, Harry.'

As he reached the door he hesitated for a moment, as if he had something more to say. Then he sighed and went out.

CHAPTER XX

IT was a lovely night, so warm that he threw his coat over his arm, and did not even put his silk scarf round his throat. As he strolled home, smoking his cigarette, two young men in evening dress passed him. He heard one of them whisper to the other, 'That is Dorian Gray.' He remembered how pleased he used to be when he was pointed out, or stared at, or talked about. He was tired of hearing his own name now. Half the charm of the little village where he had been so often lately was that no one knew who he was. He had often told the girl whom he had lured to love him that he was poor, and she had believed him. He had told her once that he was wicked, and she had laughed at him, and answered that wicked people were always very old and very ugly. What a laugh she had!—just like a thrush singing. And how pretty she had been in her cotton dresses and her large hats! She knew nothing, but she had everything that he had lost.

When he reached home, he found his servant waiting up for him. He sent him to bed, and threw himself down on the sofa in the library, and began to think over some of the things that Lord Henry had said to him.

Was it really true that one could never change? He felt a wild longing for the unstained purity of his boyhood—his rose-white boyhood, as Lord Henry had once called it. He knew that he had tarnished himself, filled his mind with corruption and given horror to his fancy; that he had been an evil influence to others, and had experienced a terrible joy in being so; and that of the lives that had crossed his own it had been the fairest and the most full of promise that he had brought to shame. But was it all irretrievable? Was there no hope for him?

Ah! in what a monstrous moment of pride and passion he had prayed that the portrait should bear the burden of his days, and he keep the unsullied splendour of eternal youth! All his failure had been due to that. Better for him that each sin of his life had brought its sure, swift penalty along with it. There was purification in punishment. Not 'Forgive us our sins', but 'Smite us for our iniquities', should be the prayer of man to a most just God.

The curiously-carved mirror that Lord Henry had given to him, so many years ago now, was standing on the table, and the white-limbed Cupids laughed round as of old. He took it up, as he had done on that night of horror, when he had first noted the change in the fatal picture, and with wild tear-dimmed eyes looked into its polished shield. Once, some one who had terribly loved him, had written to him a mad letter° ending with these idolatrous words: 'The world is changed because you are made of ivory and gold. The curves of your lips rewrite history.' The phrases came back to his memory, and he repeated them over and over to himself. Then he loathed his own beauty, and flinging the mirror on the floor crushed it into silver splinters beneath his heel. It was his beauty that had ruined him, his beauty and the youth that he had prayed for. But for those two things, his life might have been free from stain. His beauty had been to him but a mask, his youth but a mockery. What was youth at best? A green, and unripe time, a time of shallow moods, and sickly thoughts. Why had he worn its livery? Youth had spoiled him.

It was better not to think of the past. Nothing could alter that. It was of himself, and of his own future, that he had to think. James Vane was hidden in a nameless grave in Selby churchyard. Alan Campbell had shot himself one night in his laboratory, but had not revealed the secret that he had been forced to know. The excitement, such as it was, over Basil Hallward's disappearance, would soon pass away. It was already waning. He was perfectly safe there. Nor, indeed, was it the death of Basil Hallward that weighed most upon his mind. It was the living death of his own soul that troubled him. Basil had painted the portrait that had marred his life. He could not forgive him that. It was the portrait that had done everything. Basil had said things to him that were unbearable, and that he had yet borne with patience. The murder had been simply the madness of a moment. As for Alan Campbell, his suicide had been his own act. He had chosen to do it. It was nothing to him.

A new life! That was what he wanted. That was what he was waiting for. Surely he had begun it already. He had spared one innocent thing, at any rate. He would never again tempt innocence. He would be good.

As he thought of Hetty Merton, he began to wonder if the portrait in the locked room had changed. Surely it was not still so horrible as it had been? Perhaps if his life became pure, he would be able to expel every sign of evil passion from the face. Perhaps the signs of evil had already gone away. He would go and look.

He took the lamp from the table and crept upstairs. As he unbarred the door, a smile of joy flitted across his strangely young-looking face and lingered for a moment about his lips. Yes, he would be good, and the hideous thing that he had hidden away would no longer be a terror to him. He felt as if the load had been lifted from him already.

He went in quietly, locking the door behind him, as was his custom, and dragged the purple hanging from the portrait. A cry of pain and indignation broke from him. He could see no change, save that in the eyes there was a look of cunning, and in the mouth the curved wrinkle of the hypocrite. The thing was still loathsome—more loathsome, if possible, than before—and the scarlet dew that spotted the hand seemed brighter, and more like blood newly spilt. Then he trembled. Had it been merely vanity that had made him do his one good deed? Or the desire for a new sensation, as Lord Henry had hinted, with his mocking laugh? Or that passion to act a part that sometimes makes us do things finer than we are ourselves? Or, perhaps, all these? And why was the red stain larger than it had been? It seemed to have crept like a horrible disease over the wrinkled fingers. There was blood on the painted feet, as though the thing had dripped—blood even on the hand that had not held the knife. Confess? Did it mean that he was to confess? To give himself up, and be put to death? He laughed. He felt that the idea was monstrous. Besides, even if he did confess, who would believe him? There was no trace of the murdered man anywhere. Everything belonging to him had been destroyed. He himself had burned what had been below-stairs. The world would simply say that he was mad. They would shut him up if he persisted in his story. . . . Yet it was his duty to confess, to suffer public shame, and to make public atonement. There was a God who called upon men to tell their sins to earth as well as to heaven. Nothing that he could do would cleanse him till he had told his own sin. His sin? He shrugged his shoulders. The death of Basil Hallward seemed very little to him. He was thinking of Hetty Merton. For it was an unjust mirror, this mirror of his soul that he was looking at. Vanity? Curiosity? Hypocrisy? Had there been nothing more in his renunciation than that? There had been something more. At least he thought so. But who could tell? . . . No. There had been nothing more. Through vanity he had spared her. In hypocrisy he had worn the mask of goodness. For curiosity's sake he had tried the denial of self. He recognized that now.

But this murder—was it to dog him all his life? Was he always to be burdened by his past? Was he really to confess? Never. There was only one bit of evidence left against him. The picture itself—that was evidence. He would destroy it. Why had he kept it so long? Once it had given him pleasure to watch it changing and growing old. Of late he had felt no such pleasure. It had kept him awake at night. When he had been away, he had been filled with terror lest other eyes should look upon it. It had brought melancholy across his passions. Its mere memory had marred many moments of joy. It had been like conscience to him. Yes, it had been conscience. He would destroy it.

He looked round, and saw the knife that had stabbed Basil Hallward.

He had cleaned it many times, till there was no stain left upon it. It was bright, and glistened. As it had killed the painter, so it would kill the painter's work, and all that that meant. It would kill the past, and when that was dead he would be free. It would kill this monstrous soul-life, and, without its hideous warnings, he would be at peace. He seized the thing, and stabbed the picture with it.

There was a cry heard, and a crash. The cry was so horrible in its agony that the frightened servants woke, and crept out of their rooms. Two gentlemen, who were passing in the Square below, stopped, and looked up at the great house. They walked on till they met a policeman, and brought him back. The man rang the bell several times, but there was no answer. Except for a light in one of the top windows, the house was all dark. After a time, he went away, and stood in an adjoining portico and watched.

'Whose house is that, constable?' asked the elder of the two gentlemen.

'Mr Dorian Gray's, sir,' answered the policeman.

They looked at each other, as they walked away, and sneered. One of them was Sir Henry Ashton's uncle.

Inside, in the servants' part of the house, the half-clad domestics were talking in low whispers to each other. Old Mrs Leaf was crying, and wringing her hands. Francis was as pale as death.

After about a quarter of an hour, he got the coachman and one of the footmen and crept upstairs. They knocked, but there was no reply. They called out. Everything was still. Finally, after vainly trying to force the door, they got on the roof, and dropped down on to the balcony. The windows yielded easily: their bolts were old.

When they entered, they found hanging upon the wall a splendid portrait of their master as they had last seen him, in all the wonder of his exquisite youth and beauty. Lying on the floor was a dead man, in evening dress, with a knife in his heart. He was withered, wrinkled, and loathsome of visage. It was not till they had examined the rings that they recognized who it was.

THE END.

THE DECAY OF LYING

An Observation

A dialogue. Persons: Cyril and Vivian. Scene: the library of a country house in Nottinghamshire.

Cyril (coming in through the open window from the terrace). My dear Vivian, don't coop yourself up all day in the library. It is a perfectly lovely afternoon. The air is exquisite. There is a mist upon the woods, like the purple bloom upon a plum. Let us go and lie on the grass, and smoke cigarettes, and enjoy Nature.

Vivian. Enjoy Nature! I am glad to say that I have entirely lost that faculty. People tell us that Art makes us love Nature more than we loved her before; that it reveals her secrets to us; and that after a careful study of Corot and Constable we see things in her that had escaped our observation. My own experience is that the more we study Art, the less we care for Nature. What Art really reveals to us is Nature's lack of design, her curious crudities, her extraordinary monotony, her absolutely unfinished condition. Nature has good intentions, of course, but, as Aristotle once said,° she cannot carry them out. When I look at a landscape I cannot help seeing all its defects. It is fortunate for us, however, that Nature is so imperfect, as otherwise we should have had no art at all. Art is our spirited protest, our gallant attempt to teach Nature her proper place. As for the infinite variety of Nature, that is a pure myth. It is not to be found in Nature herself. It resides in the imagination, or fancy, or cultivated blindness of the man who looks at her.

Cyril. Well, you need not look at the landscape. You can lie on the grass and smoke and talk.

Vivian. But Nature is so uncomfortable. Grass is hard and lumpy and damp, and full of dreadful black insects. Why, even Morris' poorest workman° could make you a more comfortable seat than the whole of Nature can. Nature pales before the furniture of 'the street which from Oxford has borrowed its name', as the poet you love so much once vilely phrased it.° I don't complain. If Nature had been comfortable, mankind would never have invented architecture, and I prefer houses to the open air. In a house we all feel of the proper proportions. Everything is subordinated to us, fashioned for our use and our pleasure. Egotism itself, which is so necessary to a proper sense of human dignity, is entirely the result of indoor life. Out of doors one becomes abstract and impersonal. One's individuality absolutely leaves one. And then Nature is so indifferent, so unappreciative. Whenever I am walking in the park here, I always feel that I am no more to her than the cattle that browse on the slope, or the burdock that blooms in the ditch. Nothing is more evident than that Nature hates Mind. Thinking is the most unhealthy thing in the world, and people die of it just as they die of any other disease. Fortunately, in England at any rate, thought is not catching. Our splendid physique as a people is entirely due to our national stupidity. I only hope we shall be able to keep this great historic bulwark of our happiness for many years to come; but I am afraid that we are beginning to be over-educated; at least everybody who is incapable of learning has taken to teaching—that is really what our enthusiasm for education has come to. In the meantime, you had better go back to your wearisome uncomfortable Nature, and leave me to correct my proofs.

Cyril. Writing an article! That is not very consistent after what you have just said.

Vivian. Who wants to be consistent? The dullard and the doctrinaire, the tedious people who carry out their principles to the bitter end of action, to the *reductio ad absurdum* of practice. Not I. Like Emerson, I write over the door of my library the word 'Whim'.° Besides, my article is really a most salutary and valuable warning. If it is attended to, there may be a new Renaissance of Art.

Cyril. What is the subject?

Vivian. I intend to call it 'The Decay of Lying: A Protest'.

Cyril. Lying! I should have thought that our politicians kept up that habit.

Vivian. I assure you that they do not. They never rise beyond the level of misrepresentation, and actually condescend to prove, to discuss, to argue. How different from the temper of the true liar, with his frank, fearless statements, his superb irresponsibility, his healthy, natural disdain of proof of any kind! After all, what is a fine lie? Simply that which is its own evidence. If a man is sufficiently unimaginative to produce evidence in support of a lie, he might just as well speak the truth at once. No, the politicians won't do. Something may, perhaps, be urged on behalf of the Bar. The mantle of the Sophist° has fallen on its members. Their feigned ardours and unreal rhetoric are delightful. They can make the worse appear the better cause, as though they were fresh from Leontine schools,° and have been known to wrest from reluctant juries triumphant verdicts of acquittal for their clients, even when those clients, as often happens, were clearly and unmistakeably innocent. But they are briefed by the prosaic, and are not ashamed to appeal to precedent. In spite of their endeavours, the truth will out. Newspapers, even, have degenerated. They may now be absolutely relied upon. One feels it as one wades through their columns. It is always the unreadable that occurs. I am afraid that there is not much to be said in favour of either the lawyer or the journalist. Besides, what I am pleading for is Lying in art. Shall I read you what I have written? It might do you a great deal of good.

Cyril. Certainly, if you give me a cigarette. Thanks. By the way, what magazine do you intend it for?

Vivian. For the *Retrospective Review.*° I think I told you that the elect had revived it.

Cyril. Whom do you mean by 'the elect'?

Vivian. Oh, The Tired Hedonists° of course. It is a club to which I belong. We are supposed to wear faded roses in our button-holes when we meet, and to have a sort of cult for Domitian. I am afraid you are not eligible. You are too fond of simple pleasures.

Cyril. I should be black-balled on the ground of animal spirits, I suppose?

Vivian. Probably. Besides, you are a little too old. We don't admit anybody who is of the usual age.

Cyril. Well, I should fancy you are all a good deal bored with each other.

Vivian. We are. That is one of the objects of the club. Now, if you promise not to interrupt too often, I will read you my article.

Cyril. You will find me all attention.

Vivian (reading in a very clear, musical voice). 'THE DECAY OF LYING: A PROTEST.—One of the chief causes that can be assigned for the curiously commonplace character of most of the literature of our age is undoubtedly the decay of Lying as an art, a science, and a social pleasure. The ancient historians gave us delightful fiction in the form of fact; the modern novelist presents us with dull facts under the guise of fiction. The Blue-Book° is rapidly becoming his ideal both for method and manner. He has his tedious "*document humain*", his miserable little "*coin de la création*",° into which he peers with his microscope. He is to be found at the Librairie Nationale, or at the British Museum, shamelessly reading up his subject. He has not even the courage of other people's ideas,° but insists on going directly to life for everything, and ultimately, between encyclopædias and personal experience, he comes to the ground, having drawn his types from the family circle or from the weekly washerwoman, and having acquired an amount of useful information from which never, even in his most meditative moments, can he thoroughly free himself.

'The loss that results to literature in general from this false ideal of our time can hardly be overestimated. People have a careless way of talking about a "born liar", just as they talk about a "born poet". But in both cases they are wrong. Lying and poetry are arts—arts, as Plato saw,° not unconnected with each other—and they require the most careful study, the most disinterested devotion. Indeed, they have their technique, just as the more material arts of painting and sculpture have, their subtle secrets of form and colour, their craft-mysteries, their deliberate artistic methods. As one knows the poet by his fine music, so one can recognize the liar by his rich rhythmic utterance, and in neither case will the casual inspiration of the moment suffice. Here, as elsewhere, practice must precede perfection. But in modern days while the fashion of writing poetry has become far too common, and should, if possible, be discouraged, the fashion of lying has almost fallen into disrepute. Many a young man starts in life with a natural gift for exaggeration which, if nurtured in congenial and sympathetic surroundings, or by the imitation of the best models, might grow into something really great and wonderful. But, as a rule, he comes to nothing. He either falls into careless habits of accuracy——'

Cyril. My dear fellow!

Vivian. Please don't interrupt in the middle of a sentence. 'He either falls into careless habits of accuracy, or takes to frequenting the society of the aged and the well-informed. Both things are equally fatal to his imagination, as indeed they would be fatal to the imagination of anybody, and in a short time he develops a morbid and unhealthy faculty of truth-telling, begins to verify all statements made in his presence, has no hesitation in contradicting people who are much younger than himself, and often ends by writing novels which are so like life that no one can possibly believe in their probability. This is no isolated instance that we are giving. It is simply one example out of many; and if something cannot be done to check, or at least to modify, our monstrous worship of facts, Art will become sterile, and Beauty will pass away from the land.

'Even Mr Robert Louis Stevenson,° that delightful master of delicate and fanciful prose, is tainted with this modern vice, for we know positively no other name for it. There is such a thing as robbing a story of its reality by trying to make it too true, and *The Black Arrow* is so inartistic as not to contain a single anachronism to boast of, while the transformation of Dr Jekyll reads dangerously like an experiment out of the *Lancet*.° As for Mr Rider Haggard,° who really has, or had once, the makings of a perfectly magnificent liar, he is now so afraid of being suspected of genius that when he does tell us anything marvellous, he feels bound to invent a personal reminiscence, and to put it into a footnote as a kind of cowardly corroboration. Nor are our other novelists much better. Mr Henry James° writes fiction as if it were a painful duty, and wastes upon mean motives and imperceptible "points of view" his neat literary style, his felicitous phrases, his swift and caustic satire. Mr Hall Caine,° it is true, aims at the grandiose, but then he writes at the top of his voice. He is so loud that one cannot hear what he says. Mr James Payn° is an adept in the art of concealing what is not worth finding. He hunts down the obvious with the enthusiasm of a short-sighted detective. As one turns over the pages, the suspense of the author becomes almost unbearable. The horses of Mr William Black's° phaeton do not soar towards the sun. They merely frighten the sky at evening into violent chromolithographic effects. On seeing them approach, the peasants take refuge in dialect. Mrs Oliphant° prattles pleasantly about curates, lawn-tennis parties, domesticity, and other wearisome things. Mr Marion Crawford° has immolated himself upon the altar of local colour. He is like the lady in the French comedy who keeps talking about "le beau ciel d'Italie".° Besides, he has fallen into a bad habit of uttering moral platitudes. He is always telling us that to be good is to be good, and that to be bad is to be wicked. At times he is almost edifying. *Robert Elsmere°* is of course a masterpiece—a masterpiece of the "genre ennuyeux", the one form of literature that the English people seem to thoroughly enjoy. A thoughtful young friend of ours once told us that it reminded him of the sort of conversation that goes on at a meat tea in the house of a serious Nonconformist family, and we can quite believe it. Indeed it is only in England that such a book could be produced. England is the home of lost ideas.° As for that great and daily increasing school of novelists for whom the sun always rises in the East End, the only thing that can be said about them is that they find life crude, and leave it raw.

'In France, though nothing so deliberately tedious as *Robert Elsmere* has been produced, things are not much better. M. Guy de Maupassant,° with his keen mordant irony and his hard vivid style, strips life of the few poor rags that still cover her, and shows us foul sore and festering wound. He writes lurid little tragedies in which everybody is ridiculous; bitter comedies at which one cannot laugh for very tears. M. Zola,° true to the lofty principle that he lays down in one of his pronunciamientos° on literature, "L'homme de génie n'a jamais d'esprit", is determined to show that, if he has not got genius, he can at least be dull. And how well he succeeds! He is not without power. Indeed at times, as in *Germinal*, there is something almost epic in his work. But his work is entirely wrong from beginning to end, and wrong not on the ground of morals, but on the ground of art. From any ethical standpoint it is just what it should be.

The author is perfectly truthful, and describes things exactly as they happen. What more can any moralist desire? We have no sympathy at all with the moral indignation of our time against M. Zola. It is simply the indignation of Tartuffe° on being exposed. But from the standpoint of art, what can be said in favour of the author of *L'Assommoir*, *Nana*, and *Pot-Bouille*? Nothing. Mr Ruskin once described the characters in George Eliot's novels as being like the sweepings of a Pentonville omnibus,° but M. Zola's characters are much worse. They have their dreary vices, and their drearier virtues. The record of their lives is absolutely without interest. Who cares what happens to them? In literature we require distinction, charm, beauty, and imaginative power. We don't want to be harrowed and disgusted with an account of the doings of the lower orders. M. Daudet° is better. He has wit, a light touch, and an amusing style. But he has lately committed literary suicide. Nobody can possibly care for Delobelle with his "Il faut lutter pour l'art", or for Valmajour with his eternal refrain about the nightingale, or for the poet in *Jack* with his "mots cruels", now that we have learned from *Vingt Ans de ma Vie littéraire* that these characters were taken directly from life. To us they seem to have suddenly lost all their vitality, all the few qualities they ever possessed. The only real people are the people who never existed, and if a novelist is base enough to go to life for his personages he should at least pretend that they are creations, and not boast of them as copies. The justification of a character in a novel is not that other persons are what they are, but that the author is what he is. Otherwise the novel is not a work of art. As for M. Paul Bourget,° the master of the *roman psychologique*, he commits the error of imagining that the men and women of modern life are capable of being infinitely analysed for an innumerable series of chapters. In point of fact what is interesting about people in good society—and M. Bourget rarely moves out of the Faubourg St Germain,° except to come to London,—is the mask that each one of them wears, not the reality that lies behind the mask. It is a humiliating confession, but we are all of us made out of the same stuff. In Falstaff there is something of Hamlet, in Hamlet there is not a little of Falstaff. The fat knight has his moods of melancholy, and the young prince his moments of coarse humour. Where we differ from each other is purely in accidentals: in dress, manner, tone of voice, religious opinions,° personal appearance, tricks of habit, and the like. The more one analyses people, the more all reasons for analysis disappear. Sooner or later one comes to that dreadful universal thing called human nature. Indeed, as any one who has ever worked among the poor knows only too well, the brotherhood of man is no mere poet's dream, it is a most depressing and humiliating reality; and if a writer insists upon analysing the upper classes, he might just as well write of match-girls and costermongers at once.' However, my dear Cyril, I will not detain you any further just here. I quite admit that modern novels have many good points. All I insist on is that, as a class, they are quite unreadable.

Cyril. That is certainly a very grave qualification, but I must say that I think you are rather unfair in some of your strictures. I like *The Deemster,*° and *The Daughter of Heth*, and *Le Disciple*, and *Mr Isaacs*, and as for *Robert Elsmere* I am quite devoted to it. Not that I can look upon it as a serious work. As a statement of the problems that confront the earnest Christian it is ridiculous and antiquated. It is simply Arnold's *Literature and Dogma*° with the literature left out. It is as much behind the age as Paley's *Evidences,*° or Colenso's° method of Biblical exegesis. Nor could anything be less impressive than the unfortunate hero gravely heralding a dawn that rose long ago, and so completely missing its true significance that he proposes to carry on the business of the old firm under the new name. On the other hand, it contains several clever caricatures, and a heap of delightful quotations, and Green's° philosophy very pleasantly sugars the somewhat bitter pill of the author's fiction. I also cannot help expressing my surprise that you have said nothing about the two novelists whom you are always reading, Balzac and George Meredith. Surely they are realists, both of them?

Vivian. Ah! Meredith!° Who can define him? His style is chaos illumined by flashes of lightning. As a writer he has mastered everything except language: as a novelist he can do everything, except tell a story: as an artist he is everything, except articulate. Somebody in Shakespeare—Touchstone,° I think—talks about a man who is always breaking his shins over his own wit, and it seems to me that this might serve as the basis for a criticism of Meredith's method. But whatever he is, he is not a realist. Or rather I would say that he is a child of realism who is not on speaking terms with his father. By deliberate choice he has made himself a romanticist. He has refused to bow the knee to Baal,° and after all, even if the man's fine spirit did not revolt against the noisy assertions of realism, his style would be quite sufficient of itself to keep life at a respectful distance. By its means he has planted round his garden a hedge full of thorns, and red with wonderful roses. As for Balzac,° he was a most remarkable combination of the artistic temperament with the scientific spirit. The latter he bequeathed to his disciples: the former was entirely his own. The difference between such a book as M. Zola's *L'Assommoir* and Balzac's *Illusions Perdues* is the difference between unimaginative realism and imaginative reality. 'All Balzac's characters,' said Baudelaire, 'are gifted with the same ardour of life that animated himself. All his fictions are as deeply coloured as dreams. Each mind is a weapon loaded to the muzzle with will. The very scullions have genius.'° A steady course of Balzac reduces our living friends to shadows, and our acquaintances to the shadows of shades. His characters have a kind of fervent fiery-coloured existence. They dominate us, and defy scepticism. One of the greatest tragedies of my life is the death of Lucien de Rubempré. It is a grief from which I have never been able to completely rid myself. It haunts me in my moments of pleasure. I remember it when I laugh. But Balzac is no more a realist than Holbein° was. He created life, he did not copy it. I admit, however, that he set far too high a value on modernity of form, and that, consequently, there is no book of his that, as an artistic masterpiece, can rank with *Salammbô*° or *Esmond*, or *The Cloister and the Hearth*, or the *Vicomte de Bragelonne*.

Cyril. Do you object to modernity of form, then?

Vivian. Yes. It is a huge price to pay for a very poor result. Pure modernity of form is always somewhat vulgarizing. It cannot help being so. The public imagine that, because they are interested in their immediate surroundings, Art should be interested in them also, and should take them as her subject-matter. But the mere fact that they are interested in these things makes them unsuitable subjects for Art. The only beautiful things, as somebody once said,° are the things that do not concern us. As long as a thing is useful or necessary to us, or affects us in any way, either for pain or for pleasure, or appeals strongly to our sympathies, or is a vital part of the environment in which we live, it is outside the proper sphere of art. To art's subject-matter we should be more or less indifferent. We should, at any rate, have no preferences, no prejudices, no partisan feeling of any kind. It is exactly because Hecuba° is nothing to us that her sorrows are such an admirable motive for a tragedy. I do not know anything in the whole history of literature sadder than the artistic career of Charles Reade.° He wrote one beautiful book, *The Cloister and the Hearth*, a book as much above *Romola*° as *Romola* is above *Daniel Deronda*, and wasted the rest of his life in a foolish attempt to be modern, to draw public attention to the state of our convict prisons, and the management of our private lunatic asylums. Charles Dickens° was depressing enough in all conscience when he tried to arouse our sympathy for the victims of the poor-law administration; but Charles Reade, an artist, a scholar, a man with a true sense of beauty, raging and roaring over the abuses of contemporary life like a common pamphleteer or a sensational journalist, is really a sight for the angels to weep over.

Believe me, my dear Cyril, modernity of form and modernity of subject-matter are entirely and absolutely wrong. We have mistaken the common livery of the age for the vesture of the Muses, and spend our days in the sordid streets and hideous suburbs of our vile cities when we should be out on the hillside with Apollo. Certainly we are a degraded race, and have sold our birthright for a mess of facts.°

Cyril. There is something in what you say, and there is no doubt that whatever amusement we may find in reading a purely modern novel, we have rarely any artistic pleasure in re-reading it. And this is perhaps the best rough test of what is literature and what is not. If one cannot enjoy reading a book over and over again, there is no use reading it at all. But what do you say about the return to Life and Nature? This is the panacea that is always being recommended to us.

Vivian. I will read you what I say on that subject. The passage comes later on in the article, but I may as well give it to you now:—

'The popular cry of our time is "Let us return to Life and Nature; they will recreate Art for us, and send the red blood coursing through her veins; they will shoe her feet with swiftness and make her hand strong." But, alas! we are mistaken in our amiable and well-meaning efforts. Nature is always behind the age. And as for Life, she is the solvent that breaks up Art, the enemy that lays waste her house.'

Cyril. What do you mean by saying that Nature is always behind the age?

Vivian. Well, perhaps that is rather cryptic. What I mean is this. If we take Nature to mean natural simple instinct as opposed to self-conscious culture, the work produced under this influence is always old-fashioned, antiquated, and out of date. One touch of Nature may make the whole world kin, but two touches of Nature will destroy any work of Art.° If, on the other hand, we regard Nature as the collection of phenomena external to man, people only discover in her what they bring to her. She has no suggestions of her own. Wordsworth went to the lakes, but he was never a lake poet. He found in stones the sermons° he had already hidden there. He went moralizing about the district, but his good work was produced when he returned, not to Nature but to poetry. Poetry gave him 'Laodamia', and the fine sonnets, and the great Ode,° such as it is. Nature gave him 'Martha Ray' and 'Peter Bell', and the address to Mr Wilkinson's spade.

Cyril. I think that view might be questioned. I am rather inclined to believe in the 'impulse from a vernal wood',° though of course the artistic value of such an impulse depends entirely on the kind of temperament that receives it, so that the return to Nature would come to mean simply the advance to a great personality. You would agree with that, I fancy. However, proceed with your article.

Vivian (*reading*). 'Art begins with abstract decoration with purely imaginative and pleasurable work dealing with what is unreal and non-existent.° This is the first stage. Then Life becomes fascinated with this new wonder, and asks to be admitted into the charmed circle. Art takes life as part of her rough material, recreates it, and refashions it in fresh forms, is absolutely indifferent to fact, invents, imagines, dreams, and keeps between herself and reality the impenetrable barrier of beautiful style, of decorative or ideal treatment. The third stage is when Life gets the upper hand, and drives Art out into the wilderness. This is the true decadence,° and it is from this that we are now suffering.

'Take the case of the English drama. At first in the hands of the monks Dramatic Art was abstract, decorative, and mythological. Then she enlisted Life in her service, and using some of life's external forms, she created an entirely new race of beings, whose sorrows were more terrible than any sorrow man has ever felt, whose joys were keener than lover's joys, who had the rage of the Titans° and the calm of the gods, who had monstrous and marvellous sins, monstrous and marvellous virtues. To them she gave a language different from that of actual use, a language full of resonant music and sweet rhythm, made stately by solemn cadence, or made delicate by fanciful rhyme, jewelled with wonderful words, and enriched with lofty diction. She clothed her children in strange raiment and gave them masks, and at her bidding the antique world rose from its marble tomb. A new Caesar stalked through the streets of risen Rome, and with purple sail and flute-led oars another Cleopatra passed up the river to Antioch. Old myth and legend and dream took shape and substance. History was entirely re-written, and there was hardly one of the dramatists who did not recognize that the object of Art is not simple truth but complex beauty.° In this they were perfectly right. Art itself is really a form of exaggeration; and selection, which is the very spirit of art, is nothing more than an intensified mode of over-emphasis.

'But Life soon shattered the perfection of the form. Even in Shakespeare we can see the beginning of the end. It shows itself by the gradual breaking up of the blank-verse in the later plays, by the predominance given to prose, and by the over-importance assigned to characterization. The passages in Shakespeare—and they are many—where the language is uncouth, vulgar, exaggerated, fantastic, obscene even, are entirely due to Life calling for an echo of her own voice, and rejecting the intervention of beautiful style, through which alone should Life be suffered to find expression. Shakespeare is not by any means a flawless artist. He is too fond of going directly to life, and borrowing life's natural utterance. He forgets that when Art surrenders her imaginative medium she surrenders everything.° Goethe says, somewhere—

In der Beschränkung zeigt sich erst der Meister,°

"It is in working within limits that the master reveals himself", and the limitation, the very condition of any art is style. However, we need not linger any longer over Shakespeare's realism. *The Tempest* is the most perfect of palinodes.° All that we desired to point out was, that the magnificent work of the Elizabethan and Jacobean artists contained within itself the seeds of its own dissolution, and that, if it drew some of its strength from using life as rough material, it drew all its weakness from using life as an artistic method. As the inevitable result of this substitution of an imitative for a creative medium, this surrender of an imaginative form, we have the modern English melodrama. The characters in these plays talk on the stage exactly as they would talk off it; they have neither aspirations nor aspirates; they are taken directly from life and reproduce its vulgarity down to the smallest detail; they present the gait, manner, costume, and accent of real people; they would pass unnoticed in a third-class railway carriage. And yet how wearisome the plays are! They do not succeed in producing even that impression of reality at which they aim, and which is their only reason for existing. As a method, realism is a complete failure.

'What is true about the drama and the novel is no less true about those arts that we call the decorative arts. The whole history of these arts in Europe is the record of the struggle between Orientalism, with its frank rejection of imitation, its love of artistic convention, its dislike to the actual representation of any object in Nature, and our own imitative spirit. Wherever the former has been paramount, as in Byzantium, Sicily, and Spain, by actual contact, or in the rest of Europe by the influence of the Crusades, we have had beautiful and imaginative work in which the visible things of life are transmuted into artistic conventions, and the things that Life has not are invented and fashioned for her delight. But wherever we have returned to Life and Nature, our work has always become vulgar, common, and uninteresting. Modern tapestry, with its aërial effects, its elaborate perspective, its broad expanses of waste sky, its faithful and laborious realism, has no beauty whatsoever. The pictorial glass of Germany is absolutely detestable. We are beginning to weave possible carpets in England, but only because we have returned to the method and spirit of the East. Our rugs and carpets of twenty years ago, with their solemn depressing truths, their inane worship of Nature, their sordid reproductions of visible objects, have become, even to the Philistine,° a source of laughter. A cultured Mahomedan once remarked to us, "You Christians are so occupied in misinterpreting the fourth commandment that you have never thought of making an artistic application of the second.'"° He was perfectly right, and the whole truth of the matter is this: The proper school to learn art in is not Life but Art.'°

And now let me read you a passage which seems to me to settle the question very completely.

'It was not always thus. We need not say anything about the poets, for they, with the unfortunate exception of Mr Wordsworth, have been really faithful to their high mission, and are universally recognized as being absolutely unreliable. But in the works of Herodotus,° who, in spite of the shallow and ungenerous attempts of modern sciolists° to verify his history, may justly be called the "Father of Lies"; in the published speeches of Cicero° and the biographies of Suetonius;° in Tacitus° at his best; in Pliny's° *Natural History*; in Hanno's° *Periplus*; in all the early chronicles; in the Lives of the Saints; in Froissart° and Sir Thomas Mallory;° in the travels of Marco Polo;° in Olaus Magnus,° and Aldrovandus,° and Conrad Lycosthenes,° with his magnificent *Prodigiorum et Ostentorum Chronicon*; in the autobiography of Benvenuto Cellini;° in the memoirs of Casanuova;° in Defoe's° *History of the Plague*; in Boswell's° *Life of Johnson*; in Napoleon's° despatches, and in the works of our own Carlyle,° whose *French Revolution* is one of the most fascinating historical novels ever written, facts are either kept in their proper subordinate position, or else entirely excluded on the general ground of dulness. Now, everything is changed. Facts are not merely finding a footing-place in history, but they are usurping the domain of Fancy, and have invaded the kingdom of Romance. Their chilling touch is over everything. They are vulgarizing mankind. The crude commercialism of America, its materializing spirit, its indifference to the poetical side of things, and its lack of imagination and of high unattainable ideals, are entirely due to that country having adopted for its national hero a man, who according to his own confession, was incapable of telling a lie, and it is not too much to say that the story of George Washington° and the cherry-tree has done more harm, and in a shorter space of time, than any other moral tale in the whole of literature.'

Cyril. My dear boy!

Vivian. I assure you it is the case, and the amusing part of the whole thing is that the story of the cherry-tree is an absolute myth. However, you must not think that I am too despondent about the artistic future either of America or of our own country. Listen to this:—

'That some change will take place before this century has drawn to its close we have no doubt whatsoever. Bored by the tedious and improving conversation of those who have neither the wit to exaggerate nor the genius to romance, tired of the intelligent person whose reminiscences are always based upon memory, whose statements are invariably limited by probability, and who is at any time liable to be corroborated by the merest Philistine° who happens to be present, Society sooner or later must return to its lost leader, the cultured and fascinating liar. Who he was who first, without ever having gone out to the rude chase, told the wondering cavemen at sunset how he had dragged the Megatherium° from the purple darkness of its jasper cave, or slain the Mammoth in single combat and brought back its gilded tusks, we cannot tell, and not one of our modern anthropologists, for all their much-boasted science, has had the ordinary courage to tell us. Whatever was his name or race, he certainly was the true founder of social intercourse. For the aim of the liar is simply to charm, to delight, to give pleasure. He is the very basis of civilized society, and without him a dinner party, even at the mansions of the great, is as dull as a lecture at the Royal Society,° or a debate at the Incorporated Authors,° or one of Mr Burnand's° farcical comedies.

'Nor will he be welcomed by society alone. Art, breaking from the prison-house of realism, will run to greet him, and will kiss his false, beautiful lips, knowing that he alone is in possession of the great secret of all her manifestations, the secret that Truth is entirely and absolutely a matter of style; while Life—poor, probable, uninteresting human life— tired of repeating herself for the benefit of Mr Herbert Spencer,° scientific historians, and the compilers of statistics in general, will follow meekly after him, and try to reproduce, in her own simple and untutored way, some of the marvels of which he talks.

'No doubt there will always be critics who, like a certain writer in the *Saturday Review*,° will gravely censure the teller of fairy tales for his defective knowledge of natural history, who will measure imaginative work by their own lack of any imaginative faculty, and will hold up their inkstained hands in horror if some honest gentleman, who has never been farther than the yew-trees of his own garden, pens a fascinating book of travels like Sir John Mandeville, or, like great Raleigh, writes a whole history of the world, without knowing anything whatsoever about the past. To excuse themselves they will try and shelter under the shield of him who made Prospero the magician, and gave him Caliban and Ariel as his servants, who heard the Tritons blowing their horns round the coral reefs of the Enchanted Isle, and the fairies singing to each other in a wood near Athens, who led the phantom kings in dim procession across the misty Scottish heath, and hid Hecate in a cave with the weird sisters. They will call upon Shakespeare—they always do—and will quote that hackneyed passage about Art holding the mirror up to Nature,° forgetting that this unfortunate aphorism is deliberately said by Hamlet in order to convince the bystanders of his absolute insanity in all art-matters.'

Cyril. Ahem! Another cigarette, please.

Vivian. My dear fellow, whatever you may say, it is merely a dramatic utterance, and no more represents Shakespeare's real views upon art than the speeches of Iago represent his real views upon morals. But let me get to the end of the passage:

'Art finds her own perfection within, and not outside of, herself. She is not to be judged by any external standard of resemblance. She is a veil, rather than a mirror. She has flowers that no forests know of, birds that no woodland possesses. She makes and unmakes many worlds, and can draw the moon from heaven with a scarlet thread. Hers are the "forms more real than living man",° and hers the great archetypes of which things that have existence are but unfinished copies. Nature has, in her eyes, no laws, no uniformity. She can work miracles at her will, and when she calls monsters from the deep they come. She can bid the almond tree blossom in winter, and send the snow upon the ripe cornfield. At her word the frost lays its silver finger on the burning mouth of June, and the winged lions creep out from the hollows of the Lydian hills. The dryads peer from the thicket as she passes by, and the brown fauns smile strangely at her when she comes near them. She has hawk-faced gods that worship her, and the centaurs gallop at her side.'

Cyril. I like that. I can see it. Is that the end?

Vivian. No. There is one more passage, but it is purely practical. It simply suggests some methods by which we could revive this lost art of Lying.

Cyril. Well, before you read it to me, I should like to ask you a question. What do you mean by saying that life, 'poor, probable, uninteresting human life', will try to reproduce the marvels of art? I can quite understand your objection to art being treated as a mirror. You think it would reduce genius to the position of a cracked looking-glass. But you don't mean to say that you seriously believe that Life imitates Art, that Life in fact is the mirror, and Art the reality?

Vivian. Certainly I do. Paradox though it may seem—and paradoxes are always dangerous things—it is none the less true that Life imitates art far more than Art imitates life.° We have all seen in our own day in England how a certain curious and fascinating type of beauty, invented and emphasized by two imaginative painters,° has so influenced Life that whenever one goes to a private view or to an artistic salon one sees, here the mystic eyes of Rossetti's dream, the long ivory throat, the strange square-cut jaw, the loosened shadowy hair that he so ardently loved, there the sweet maidenhood of 'The Golden Stair', the blossom-like mouth and weary loveliness of the 'Laus Amoris', the passion-pale face of Andromeda, the thin hands and lithe beauty of the Vivien in 'Merlin's Dream'. And it has always been so. A great artist invents a type, and Life tries to copy it, to reproduce it in a popular form, like an enterprising publisher. Neither Holbein nor Vandyck found in England what they have given us. They brought their types with them, and Life with her keen imitative faculty set herself to supply the master with models. The Greeks, with their quick artistic instinct, understood this, and set in the bride's chamber the statue of Hermes or of Apollo, that she might bear children as lovely as the works of art that she looked at in her rapture or her pain. They knew that Life gains from Art not merely spirituality, depth of thought and feeling, soul-turmoil or soul-peace, but that she can form herself on the very lines and colours of art, and can reproduce the dignity of Pheidias as well as the grace of Praxiteles.° Hence came their objection to realism. They disliked it on purely social grounds. They felt that it inevitably makes people ugly, and they were perfectly right. We try to improve the conditions of the race by means of good air, free sunlight, wholesome water, and hideous bare buildings for the better housing of the lower orders. But these things merely produce health, they do not produce beauty. For this, Art is required, and the true disciples of the great artist are not his studio-imitators, but those who become like his works of art, be they plastic as in Greek days, or pictorial as in modern times; in a word, Life is Art's best, Art's only pupil.

As it is with the visible arts, so it is with literature. The most obvious and the vulgarest form in which this is shown is in the case of the silly boys who, after reading the adventures of Jack Sheppard or Dick Turpin,° pillage the stalls of unfortunate apple-women, break into sweet-shops at night, and alarm old gentlemen who are returning home from the city by leaping out on them in suburban lanes, with black masks and unloaded revolvers. This interesting phenomenon, which always occurs after the appearance of a new edition of either of the books I have alluded to, is usually attributed to the influence of literature on the imagination. But this is a mistake. The imagination is essentially creative and always seeks for a new form. The boy-burglar is simply the inevitable result of life's imitative instinct. He is Fact, occupied as Fact usually is, with trying to reproduce Fiction, and what we see in him is repeated on an extended scale throughout the whole of life. Schopenhauer° has analysed the pessimism that characterizes modern thought, but Hamlet invented it. The world has become sad because a puppet was once melancholy. The Nihilist,° that strange martyr who has no faith, who goes to the stake without enthusiasm, and dies for what he does not believe in, is a purely literary product. He was invented by Tourgénieff, and completed by Dostoieffski. Robespierre came out of the pages of Rousseau° as surely as the People's Palace° rose out of the *débris* of a novel. Literature always anticipates life. It does not copy it, but moulds it to its purpose. The nineteenth century, as we know it, is largely an invention of Balzac.° Our Luciens de Rubempré, our Rastignacs, and De Marsays made their first appearance on the stage of the *Comédie Humaine*. We are merely carrying out, with footnotes and unnecessary additions, the whim or fancy or creative vision of a great novelist. I once asked a lady, who knew Thackeray intimately, whether he had had any model for Becky Sharp.° She told me that Becky was an invention, but that the idea of the character had been partly suggested by a governess who lived in the neighbourhood of Kensington Square, and was the companion of a very selfish and rich old woman. I inquired what became of the governess, and she replied that, oddly enough, some years after the appearance of *Vanity Fair*, she ran away with the nephew of the lady with whom she was living, and for a short time made a great splash in society, quite in Mrs Rawdon Crawley's style, and entirely by Mrs Rawdon Crawley's methods. Ultimately she came to grief, disappeared to the Continent, and used to be occasionally seen at Monte Carlo and other gambling places. The noble gentleman from whom the same great sentimentalist drew Colonel Newcome died, a few months after *The Newcomes* had reached a fourth edition, with the word 'Adsum' on his lips. Shortly after Mr Stevenson published his curious psychological story of transformation,° a friend of mine, called Mr Hyde, was in the north of London, and being anxious to get to a railway station, took what he thought would be a short cut, lost his way, and found himself in a network of mean, evil-looking streets. Feeling rather nervous he began to walk extremely fast, when suddenly out of an archway ran a child right between his legs. It fell on the pavement, he tripped over it, and trampled upon it. Being of course very much frightened and a little hurt, it began to scream, and in a few seconds the whole street was full of rough people who came pouring out of the houses like ants. They surrounded him, and asked him his name. He was just about to give it when he suddenly remembered the opening incident in Mr Stevenson's story. He was so filled with horror at having realized in his own person that terrible and well written scene, and at having done accidentally, though in fact, what the Mr Hyde of fiction had done with deliberate intent, that he ran away as hard as he could go. He was, however, very closely followed, and finally he took refuge in a surgery, the door of which happened to be open, where he explained to a young assistant, who happened to be there, exactly what had occurred. The humanitarian crowd were induced to go away on his giving them a small sum of money, and as soon as the coast was clear he left. As he passed out, the name on the brass door-plate of the surgery caught his eye. It was 'Jekyll'. At least it should have been.

Here the imitation, as far as it went, was of course accidental. In the following case the imitation was self-conscious. In the year 1879, just after I had left Oxford, I met at a reception at the house of one of the Foreign Ministers a woman of very curious exotic beauty. We became great friends, and were constantly together. And yet what interested most in her was not her beauty, but her character, her entire vagueness of character.° She seemed to have no personality at all, but simply the possibility of many types. Sometimes she would give herself up entirely to art, turn her drawing-room into a studio, and spend two or three days a week at picture-galleries or museums. Then she would take to attending race-meetings, wear the most horsey clothes, and talk about nothing but betting. She abandoned religion for mesmerism, mesmerism for politics, and politics for the melodramatic excitements of philanthropy. In fact, she was a kind of Proteus, and as much a failure in all her transformations as was that wondrous sea-god when Odysseus° laid hold of him. One day a serial began in one of the French magazines. At that time I used to read serial stories, and I well remember the shock of surprise I felt when I came to the description of the heroine. She was so like my friend that I brought her the magazine, and she recognized herself in it immediately, and seemed fascinated by the resemblance. I should tell you, by the way, that the story was translated from some dead Russian writer, so that the author had not taken his type from my friend. Well, to put the matter briefly, some months afterwards I was in Venice, and finding the magazine in the reading-room of the hotel, I took it up casually to see what had become of the heroine. It was a most piteous tale, as the girl had ended by running away with a man absolutely inferior to her, not merely in social station, but in character and intellect also. I wrote to my friend that evening about my views on John Bellini,° and the admirable ices at Florio's,° and the artistic value of gondolas, but added a postscript to the effect that her double in the story had behaved in a very silly manner. I don't know why I added that, but I remember I had a sort of dread over me that she might do the same thing. Before my letter had reached her, she had run away with a man who deserted her in six months. I saw her in 1884 in Paris, where she was living with her mother, and I asked her whether the story had had anything to do with her action. She told me that she had felt an absolutely irresistible impulse to follow the heroine step by step in her strange and fatal progress, and that it was with a feeling of real terror that she had looked forward to the last few chapters of the story. When they appeared, it seemed to her that she was compelled to reproduce them in life, and she did so. It was a most clear example of this imitative instinct of which I was speaking, and an extremely tragic one.

However, I do not wish to dwell any further upon individual instances. Personal experience is a most vicious and limited circle. All that I desire to point out is the general principle that Life imitates Art far more than Art imitates Life, and I feel sure that if you think seriously about it you will find that it is true. Life holds the mirror up to Art, and either reproduces some strange type imagined by painter or sculptor, or realizes in fact what has been dreamed in fiction. Scientifically speaking, the basis of life—the energy of life, as Aristotle° would call it—is simply the desire for expression, and Art is always presenting various forms through which this expression can be attained. Life seizes on them and uses them, even if they be to her own hurt. Young men have committed suicide because Rolla° did so, have died by their own hand because by his own hand Werther° died. Think of what we owe to the imitation of Christ, of what we owe to the imitation of Cæsar.

Cyril. The theory is certainly a very curious one,° but to make it complete you must show that Nature, no less than Life, is an imitation of Art. Are you prepared to prove that?

Vivian. My dear fellow, I am prepared to prove anything.

Cyril. Nature follows the landscape painter then, and takes her effects from him?

Vivian. Certainly. Where, if not from the Impressionists,° do we get those wonderful brown fogs that come creeping down our streets, blurring the gas-lamps and changing the houses into monstrous shadows? To whom, if not to them and their master, do we owe the lovely silver mists that brood over our river, and turn to faint forms of fading grace curved bridge and swaying barge? The extraordinary change that has taken place in the climate of London during the last ten years is entirely due to this particular school of Art. You smile. Consider the matter from a scientific or a metaphysical point of view, and you will find that I am right. For what is Nature? Nature is no great mother who has borne us. She is our creation. It is in our brain that she quickens to life.

Things are because we see them, and what we see, and how we see it, depends on the Arts that have influenced us. To look at a thing is very different from seeing a thing. One does not see anything until one sees its beauty. Then, and then only, does it come into existence. At present, people see fogs, not because there are fogs, but because poets and painters have taught them the mysterious loveliness of such effects. There may have been fogs for centuries in London. I dare say there were. But no one saw them, and so we do not know anything about them. They did not exist till Art had invented them. Now, it must be admitted, fogs are carried to excess. They have become the mere mannerism of a clique, and the exaggerated realism of their method gives dull people bronchitis. Where the cultured catch an effect, the uncultured catch cold. And so, let us be humane, and invite Art to turn her wonderful eyes elsewhere. She has done so already, indeed. That white quivering sunlight that one sees now in France, with its strange blotches of mauve, and its restless violet shadows, is her latest fancy, and, on the whole, Nature reproduces it quite admirably. Where she used to give us Corots and Daubignys,° she gives us now exquisite Monets and entrancing Pisaros.° Indeed there are moments, rare, it is true, but still to be observed from time to time, when Nature becomes absolutely modern. Of course she is not always to be relied upon. The fact is that she is in this unfortunate position. Art creates an incomparable and unique effect, and, having done so, passes on to other things. Nature, upon the other hand, forgetting that imitation can be made the sincerest form of insult, keeps on repeating this effect until we all become absolutely wearied of it. Nobody of any real culture, for instance, ever talks nowadays about the beauty of a sunset. Sunsets are quite old-fashioned. They belong to the time when Turner° was the last note in art. To admire them is a distinct sign of provincialism of temperament. Upon the other hand they go on. Yesterday evening Mrs Arundel insisted on my going to the window, and looking at the glorious sky, as she called it. Of course I had to look at it. She is one of those absurdly pretty Philistines, to whom one can deny nothing. And what was it? It was simply a very second-rate Turner, a Turner of a bad period, with all the painter's worst faults exaggerated and over-emphasized. Of course, I am quite ready to admit that Life very often commits the same error. She produces her false Renés° and her sham Vautrins,° just as Nature gives us, on one day a doubtful Cuyp,° and on another a more than questionable Rousseau.° Still, Nature irritates one more when she does things of that kind. It seems so stupid, so obvious, so unnecessary. A false Vautrin might be delightful. A doubtful Cuyp is unbearable. However, I don't want to be too hard on Nature. I wish the Channel, especially at Hastings, did not look quite so often like a Henry Moore,° grey pearl with yellow lights, but then, when Art is more varied, Nature will, no doubt, be more varied also. That she imitates Art, I don't think even her worst enemy would deny now. It is the one thing that keeps her in touch with civilized man. But have I proved my theory to your satisfaction?

Cyril. You have proved it to my dissatisfaction, which is better. But even admitting this strange imitative instinct in Life and Nature, surely you would acknowledge that Art expresses the temper of its age, the spirit of its time, the moral and social conditions that surround it, and under whose influence it is produced.

Vivian. Certainly not! Art never expresses anything but itself.° This is the principle of my new æsthetics; and it is this, more than that vital connection between form and substance, on which Mr Pater° dwells, that makes music the type of all the arts. Of course, nations and individuals, with that healthy natural vanity which is the secret of existence, are always under the impression that it is of them that the Muses are talking, always trying to find in the calm dignity of imaginative art some mirror of their own turbid passions, always forgetting that the singer of life is not Apollo, but Marsyas.° Remote from reality, and with her eyes turned away from the shadows of the cave,° Art reveals her own perfection, and the wondering crowd that watches the opening of the marvellous, many-petalled rose° fancies that it is its own history that is being told to it, its own spirit that is finding expression in a new form. But it is not so. The highest art rejects the burden of the human spirit, and gains more from a new medium or a fresh material than she does from any enthusiasm for art, or from any lofty passion, or from any great awakening of the human consciousness. She develops purely on her own lines. She is not symbolic of any age. It is the ages that are her symbols.

Even those who hold that Art is representative of time and place and people, cannot help admitting that the more imitative an art is, the less it represents to us the spirit of its age. The evil faces of the Roman emperors look out at us from the foul porphyry and spotted jasper in which the realistic artists of the day delighted to work, and we fancy that in those cruel lips and heavy sensual jaws we can find the secret of the ruin of the Empire. But it was not so. The vices of Tiberius° could not destroy that supreme civilization, any more than the virtues of the Antonines° could save it. It fell for other, for less interesting reasons. The sibyls and prophets of the Sistine° may indeed serve to interpret for some that new birth of the emancipated spirit that we call the Renaissance; but what do the drunken boors and brawling peasants of Dutch art tell us about the great soul of Holland? The more abstract, the more ideal an art is, the more it reveals to us the temper of its age. If we wish to understand a nation by means of its art, let us look at its architecture or its music.

Cyril. I quite agree with you there. The spirit of an age may be best expressed in the abstract ideal arts, for the spirit itself is abstract and ideal. Upon the other hand, for the visible aspect of an age, for its look, as the phrase goes, we must of course go to the arts of imitation.

Vivian. I don't think so. After all, what the imitative arts really give us are merely the various styles of particular artists, or of certain schools of artists. Surely you don't imagine that the people of the Middle Ages bore any resemblance at all to the figures on mediæval stained glass, or in mediæval stone and wood carving, or on mediæval metal-work, or tapestries, or illuminated MSS.° They were probably very ordinary-looking people, with nothing grotesque, or remarkable, or fantastic in their appearance. The Middle Ages, as we know them in art, are simply a definite form of style, and there is no reason at all why an artist with this style should not be produced in the nineteenth century. No great artist ever sees things as they really are. If he did, he would cease to be an artist. Take an example from our own day. I know that you are fond of Japanese things. Now, do you really imagine that the Japanese people, as they are presented to us in art, have any existence? If you do, you have never understood Japanese art at all. The Japanese people are the deliberate self-conscious creation of certain individual artists. If you set a picture by Hokusai,° or Hokkei, or any of the great native painters, beside a real Japanese gentleman or lady, you will see that there is not the slightest resemblance between them. The actual people who live in Japan are not unlike the general run of English people; that is to say, they are extremely commonplace, and have nothing curious or extraordinary about them. In fact the whole of Japan is a pure invention. There is no such country, there are no such people. One of our most charming painters° went recently to the Land of the Chrysanthemum in the foolish hope of seeing the Japanese. All he saw, all he had the chance of painting, were a few lanterns and some fans. He was quite unable to discover the inhabitants, as his delightful exhibition at Messrs Dowdeswell's Gallery showed only too well. He did not know that the Japanese people are, as I have said, simply a mode of style, an exquisite fancy of art. And so, if you desire to see a Japanese effect, you will not behave like a tourist and go to Tokio. On the contrary, you will stay at home, and steep yourself in the work of certain Japanese artists, and then, when you have absorbed the spirit of their style, and caught their imaginative manner of vision, you will go some afternoon and sit in the Park or stroll down Piccadilly, and if you cannot see an absolutely Japanese effect there, you will not see it anywhere. Or, to return again to the past, take as another instance the ancient Greeks. Do you think that Greek art ever tells us what the Greek people were like? Do you believe that the Athenian women were like the stately dignified figures of the Parthenon frieze, or like those marvellous goddesses who sat in the triangular pediments of the same building? If you judge from the art, they certainly were so. But read an authority, like Aristophanes° for instance. You will find that the Athenian ladies laced tightly, wore high-heeled shoes, dyed their hair yellow, painted and rouged their faces, and were exactly like any silly fashionable or fallen creature of our own day. The fact is that we look back on the ages entirely through the medium of Art, and Art, very fortunately, has never once told us the truth.

Cyril. But modern portraits by English painters, what of them? Surely they are like the people they pretend to represent?

Vivian. Quite so. They are so like them that a hundred years from now no one will believe in them. The only portraits in which one believes are portraits where there is very little of the sitter, and a very great deal of the artist. Holbein's drawings of the men and women of his time impress us with a sense of their absolute reality. But this is simply because Holbein compelled life to accept his conditions, to restrain itself within his limitations, to reproduce his type, and to appear as he wished it to appear. It is style that makes us believe in a thing—nothing but style. Most of our modern portrait painters are doomed to absolute oblivion. They never paint what they see. They paint what the public sees, and the public never sees anything.°

Cyril. Well, after that I think I should like to hear the end of your article.

Vivian. With pleasure. Whether it will do any good I really cannot say. Ours is certainly the dullest and most prosaic century possible. Why, even Sleep has played us false, and has closed up the gates of ivory, and opened the gates of horn.° The dreams of the great middle classes of this country, as recorded in Mr Myers's two bulky volumes° on the subject and in the Transactions of the Psychical Society, are the most depressing things that I have ever read. There is not even a fine nightmare among them. They are commonplace, sordid, and tedious. As for the Church I cannot conceive anything better for the culture of a country than the presence in it of a body of men whose duty it is to believe in the supernatural, to perform daily miracles, and to keep alive that mythopœic faculty which is so essential for the imagination. But in the English

Church a man succeeds, not through his capacity for belief, but through his capacity for disbelief. Ours is the only Church where the sceptic stands at the altar, and where St Thomas° is regarded as the ideal apostle. Many a worthy clergyman, who passes his life in admirable works of kindly charity, lives and dies unnoticed and unknown; but it is sufficient for some shallow uneducated passman out of either University° to get up in his pulpit and express his doubts about Noah's ark, or Balaam's ass, or Jonah and the whale, for half of London to flock to hear him, and to sit open-mouthed in rapt admiration at his superb intellect. The growth of common sense in the English Church is a thing very much to be regretted. It is really a degrading concession to a low form of realism. It is silly, too. It springs from an entire ignorance of psychology. Man can believe the impossible, but man can never believe the improbable. However, I must read the end of my article:—

'What we have to do, what at any rate it is our duty to do, is to revive this old art of Lying. Much of course may be done, in the way of educating the public, by amateurs in the domestic circle, at literary lunches, and at afternoon teas. But this is merely the light and graceful side of lying, such as was probably heard at Cretan dinner parties. There are many other forms. Lying for the sake of gaining some immediate personal advantage, for instance—lying with a moral purpose, as it is usually called—though of late it has been rather looked down upon, was extremely popular with the antique world. Athena laughs when Odysseus tells her "his words of sly devising",° as Mr William Morris phrases it, and the glory of mendacity illumines the pale brow of the stainless hero of Euripidean tragedy,° and sets among the noble women of the past the young bride of one of Horace's most exquisite odes.° Later on, what at first had been merely a natural instinct was elevated into a self-conscious science. Elaborate rules were laid down for the guidance of mankind, and an important school of literature grew up round the subject. Indeed, when one remembers the excellent philosophical treatise of Sanchez° on the whole question, one cannot help regretting that no one has ever thought of publishing a cheap and condensed edition of the works of that great casuist. A short primer, "When to Lie and How", if brought out in an attractive and not too expensive a form, would no doubt command a large sale, and would prove of real practical service to many earnest and deep-thinking people. Lying for the sake of the improvement of the young, which is the basis of home education, still lingers amongst us, and its advantages are so admirably set forth in the early books of Plato's *Republic*° that it is unnecessary to dwell upon them here. It is a mode of lying for which all good mothers have peculiar capabilities, but it is capable of still further development, and has been sadly overlooked by the School Board. Lying for the sake of a monthly salary is of course well known in Fleet Street, and the profession of a political leader-writer is not without its advantages. But it is said to be a somewhat dull occupation, and it certainly does not lead to much beyond a kind of ostentatious obscurity. The only form of lying that is absolutely beyond reproach is Lying for its own sake, and the highest development of this is, as we have already pointed out, Lying in Art. Just as those who do not love Plato more than Truth cannot pass beyond the threshold of the Academe,° so those who do not love Beauty more than Truth never know the inmost shrine of Art. The solid stolid British intellect lies in the desert sands like the Sphinx in Flaubert's marvellous tale,° and fantasy, *La Chimère*, dances round it, and calls to it with her false, flute-toned voice. It may not hear her now, but surely some day, when we are all bored to death with the commonplace character of modern fiction, it will hearken to her and try to borrow her wings.

'And when that day dawns, or sunset reddens, how joyous we shall all be! Facts will be regarded as discreditable, Truth will be found mourning over her fetters, and Romance, with her temper of wonder, will return to the land. The very aspect of the world will change to our startled eyes. Out of the sea will rise Behemoth and Leviathan,° and sail round the high-pooped galleys, as they do on the delightful maps of those ages when books on geography were actually readable. Dragons will wander about the waste places, and the phœnix will soar from her nest of fire into the air. We shall lay our hands upon the basilisk, and see the jewel in the toad's head. Champing his gilded oats, the Hippogriff will stand in our stalls, and over our heads will float the Blue Bird° singing of beautiful and impossible things, of things that are lovely and that never happen, of things that are not and that should be. But before this comes to pass we must cultivate the lost art of Lying.'

Cyril. Then we must certainly cultivate it at once. But in order to avoid making any error I want you to tell me briefly the doctrines of the new æsthetics.

Vivian. Briefly, then, they are these. Art never expresses anything but itself. It has an independent life, just as Thought has, and develops purely on its own lines. It is not necessarily realistic in an age of realism, nor spiritual in an age of faith. So far from being the creation of its time, it is usually in direct opposition to it, and the only history that it preserves for us is the history of its own progress. Sometimes it returns upon its footsteps, and revives some antique form, as happened in the archaistic movement of late Greek Art, and in the pre-Raphaelite movement of our own day. At other times it entirely anticipates its age, and produces in one century work that it takes another century to understand, to appreciate, and to enjoy. In no case does it reproduce its age. To pass from the art of a time to the time itself is the great mistake that all historians commit.

The second doctrine is this. All bad art comes from returning to Life and Nature, and elevating them into ideals. Life and Nature may sometimes be used as part of Art's rough material, but before they are of any real service to art they must be translated into artistic conventions. The moment Art surrenders its imaginative medium it surrenders everything. As a method Realism is a complete failure, and the two things that every artist should avoid are modernity of form and modernity of subject-matter. To us, who live in the nineteenth century, any century is a suitable subject for art except our own. The only beautiful things are the things that do not concern us. It is, to have the pleasure of quoting myself, exactly because Hecuba is nothing to us that her sorrows are so suitable a motive for a tragedy. Besides, it is only the modern that ever becomes old-fashioned. M. Zola sits down to give us a picture of the Second Empire.° Who cares for the Second Empire now? It is out of date. Life goes faster than Realism, but Romanticism is always in front of Life.

The third doctrine is that Life imitates Art far more than Art imitates Life. This results not merely from Life's imitative instinct, but from the fact that the self-conscious aim of Life is to find expression, and that Art offers it certain beautiful forms through which it may realize that energy. It is a theory that has never been put forward before, but it is extremely fruitful, and throws an entirely new light upon the history of Art.

It follows, as a corollary from this, that external Nature also imitates Art. The only effects that she can show us are effects that we have already seen through poetry, or in paintings. This is the secret of Nature's charm, as well as the explanation of Nature's weakness.

The final revelation is that Lying, the telling of beautiful untrue things, is the proper aim of Art. But of this I think I have spoken at sufficient length. And now let us go out on the terrace, where 'droops the milk-white peacock like a ghost',° while the evening star 'washes the dusk with silver'.° At twilight nature becomes a wonderfully suggestive effect, and is not without loveliness, though perhaps its chief use is to illustrate quotations from the poets. Come! We have talked long enough.

THE CRITIC AS ARTIST

With some remarks upon the importance of doing nothing°

A Dialogue. Part I. Persons: Gilbert and Ernest.° Scene: the library of a house in Piccadilly, overlooking the Green Park.

THE CRITIC AS ARTIST

Gilbert (*at the piano*). My dear Ernest, what are you laughing at?

Ernest (*looking up*). At a capital story that I have just come across in this volume of Reminiscences that I have found on your table.

Gilbert. What is the book? Ah! I see. I have not read it yet. Is it good?

Ernest. Well, while you have been playing, I have been turning over the pages with some amusement, though, as a rule, I dislike modern memoirs. They are generally written by people who have either entirely lost their memories, or have never done anything worth remembering; which, however, is, no doubt, the true explanation of their popularity, as the English public always feels perfectly at its ease when a mediocrity is talking to it.

Gilbert. Yes: the public is wonderfully tolerant. It forgives everything except genius. But I must confess that I like all memoirs. I like them for their form, just as much as for their matter. In literature mere egotism is delightful. It is what fascinates us in the letters of personalities so different as Cicero and Balzac, Flaubert and Berlioz, Byron and Madame de Sévigné.° Whenever we come across it, and, strangely enough, it is rather rare, we cannot but welcome it, and do not easily forget it. Humanity will always love Rousseau° for having confessed his sins, not to a priest, but to the world, and the couchant nymphs that Cellini° wrought in bronze for the castle of King Francis, the green and gold Perseus, even, that in the open Loggia at Florence shows the moon the dead terror that once turned life to stone,° have not given it more pleasure than has that autobiography in which the supreme scoundrel of the Renaissance relates the story of his splendour and his shame. The opinions, the character, the achievements of the man, matter very little. He may be a sceptic like the gentle Sieur de Montaigne,° or a saint like the bitter son of Monica,° but when he tells us his own secrets he can always charm our ears to listening, and our lips to silence. The mode of thought that Cardinal Newman° represented—if that can be called a mode of thought which seeks to solve intellectual problems by a denial of the supremacy of the intellect—may not, cannot, I think, survive. But the world will never weary of watching that troubled soul in its progress from darkness to darkness. The lonely church at Littlemore, where 'the breath of the morning is damp, and worshippers are few', will always be dear to it, and whenever men see the yellow snapdragon blossoming on the wall of Trinity they will think of that gracious undergraduate who saw in the flower's sure recurrence a prophecy that he would abide for ever with the Benign Mother of his days—a prophecy that Faith, in her wisdom or her folly, suffered not to be fulfilled. Yes; autobiography is irresistible. Poor, silly, conceited Mr Secretary Pepys° has chattered his way into the circle of the Immortals, and, conscious that indiscretion is the better part of valour,° bustles about among them in that 'shaggy purple gown with gold buttons and looped lace' which he is so fond of describing to us, perfectly at his ease, and prattling, to his own and our infinite pleasure, of the Indian blue petticoat that he bought for his wife, of the 'good hog's harslet', and the 'pleasant French fricassee of veal' that he loved to eat, of his game of bowls with Will Joyce, and his 'gadding after beauties', and his reciting of *Hamlet* on a Sunday, and his playing of the viol on week days, and other wicked or trivial things. Even in actual life egotism is not without its attractions. When people talk to us about others they are usually dull. When they talk to us about themselves they are nearly always interesting, and if one could shut them up, when they become wearisome, as easily as one can shut up a book of which one has grown wearied, they would be perfect absolutely.

Ernest. There is much virtue in that If, as Touchstone would say.° But do you seriously propose that every man should become his own Boswell?° What would become of our industrious compilers of Lives and Recollections in that case?

Gilbert. What has become of them? They are the pest of the age, nothing more and nothing less. Every great man nowadays has his disciples, and it is always Judas who writes the biography.°

Ernest. My dear fellow!

Gilbert. I am afraid it is true. Formerly we used to canonize our heroes. The modern method is to vulgarize them.° Cheap editions of great books may be delightful, but cheap editions of great men are absolutely detestable.

Ernest. May I ask, Gilbert, to whom you allude?

Gilbert. Oh! to all our second-rate *litterateurs*. We are overrun by a set of people who, when poet or painter passes away, arrive at the house along with the undertaker,° and forget that their one duty is to behave as mutes. But we won't talk about them. They are the mere body-snatchers of literature. The dust is given to one, and the ashes to another, and the soul is out of their reach. And now, let me play Chopin to you, or Dvorák? Shall I play you a fantasy by Dvorák? He writes passionate, curiously-coloured things.

Ernest. No; I don't want music just at present. It is far too indefinite. Besides, I took the Baroness Bernstein down to dinner last night, and, though absolutely charming in every other respect, she insisted on discussing music as if it were actually written in the German language. Now, whatever music sounds like, I am glad to say that it does not sound in the smallest degree like German. There are forms of patriotism that are really quite degrading. No; Gilbert, don't play any more. Turn round and talk to me. Talk to me till the white-horned day comes into the room. There is something in your voice that is wonderful.

Gilbert (*rising from the piano*). I am not in a mood for talking tonight. How horrid of you to smile! I really am not. Where are the cigarettes? Thanks. How exquisite these single daffodils are! They seem to be made of amber and cool ivory. They are like Greek things of the best period. What was the story in the confessions of the remorseful Academician° that made you laugh? Tell it to me. After playing Chopin, I feel as if I had been weeping over sins that I had never committed, and mourning over tragedies that were not my own. Music always seems to me to produce that effect. It creates for one a past of which one has been ignorant, and fills one with a sense of sorrows that have been hidden from one's tears.° I can fancy a man who had led a perfectly commonplace life, hearing by chance some curious piece of music, and suddenly discovering that his soul, without his being conscious of it, had passed through terrible experiences, and known fearful joys, or wild romantic loves, or great renunciations. And so, tell me this story, Ernest. I want to be amused.

Ernest. Oh! I don't know that it is of any importance. But I thought it a really admirable illustration of the true value of ordinary art-criticism. It seems that a lady once gravely asked the remorseful Academician, as you call him, if his celebrated picture of 'A Spring-Day at Whiteley's', or 'Waiting for the Last Omnibus', or some subject of that kind, was all painted by hand?

Gilbert. And was it?

Ernest. You are quite incorrigible. But, seriously speaking, what is the use of art-criticism? Why cannot the artist be left alone, to create a new world if he wishes it, or, if not, to shadow forth the world which we

already know, and of which, I fancy, we would each one of us be wearied
if Art, with her fine spirit of choice and delicate instinct of selection, did
not, as it were, purify it for us, and give to it a momentary perfection. It
seems to me that the imagination spreads, or should spread, a solitude
around it, and works best in silence and in isolation. Why should the
artist be troubled by the shrill clamour of criticism? Why should those
who cannot create take upon themselves to estimate the value of creative
work? What can they know about it? If a man's work is easy to
understand, an explanation is unnecessary. . . .

Gilbert. And if his work is incomprehensible, an explanation is
wicked.

Ernest. I did not say that.

Gilbert. Ah! but you should have. Nowadays, we have so few mysteries
left to us that we cannot afford to part with one of them. The members of
the Browning Society,° like the theologians of the Broad Church Party,°
or the authors of Mr Walter Scott's Great Writers' Series,° seem to me to
spend their time in trying to explain their divinity away. Where one had
hoped that Browning was a mystic, they have sought to show that he was
simply inarticulate. Where one had fancied that he had something to
conceal, they have proved that he had but little to reveal. But I speak
merely of his incoherent work. Taken as a whole, the man was great. He
did not belong to the Olympians, and had all the incompleteness of the
Titans.° He did not survey, and it was but rarely that he could sing. His
work is marred by struggle, violence and effort, and he passed not from
emotion to form, but from thought to chaos. Still, he was great. He has
been called a thinker, and was certainly a man who was always thinking,
and always thinking aloud; but it was not thought that fascinated him, but
rather the processes by which thought moves. It was the machine he
loved, not what the machine makes. The method by which the fool
arrives at his folly was as dear to him as the ultimate wisdom of the wise.
So much, indeed, did the subtle mechanism of mind fascinate him that
he despised language, or looked upon it as an incomplete instrument of
expression. Rhyme, that exquisite echo which in the Muse's hollow hill°
creates and answers its own voice; rhyme, which in the hands of the real
artist becomes not merely a material element of metrical beauty, but a
spiritual element of thought and passion also, waking a new mood, it may
be, or stirring a fresh train of ideas, or opening by mere sweetness and
suggestion of sound some golden door at which the Imagination itself
had knocked in vain; rhyme, which can turn man's utterance to the
speech of gods; rhyme, the one chord we have added to the Greek lyre,
became in Robert Browning's hands a grotesque, misshapen thing,

which at times made him masquerade in poetry as a low comedian, and ride Pegasus° too often with his tongue in his cheek. There are moments when he wounds us by monstrous music. Nay, if he can only get his music by breaking the strings of his lute, he breaks them, and they snap in discord, and no Athenian tettix,° making melody from tremulous wings, lights on the ivory horn to make the movement perfect, or the interval less harsh. Yet, he was great: and though he turned language into ignoble clay, he made from it men and women that live.° He is the most Shakespearian creature since Shakespeare. If Shakespeare could sing with myriad lips, Browning could stammer through a thousand mouths. Even now, as I am speaking, and speaking not against him but for him, there glides through the room the pageant of his persons. There, creeps Fra Lippo Lippi with his cheeks still burning from some girl's hot kiss. There, stands dread Saul with the lordly male-sapphires gleaming in his turban. Mildren Tresham is there, and the Spanish monk, yellow with hatred, and Blougram, and Ben Ezra, and the Bishop of St Praxed's. The spawn of Setebos gibbers in the corner, and Sebald, hearing Pippa pass by, looks on Ottima's haggard face, and loathes her and his own sin, and himself. Pale as the white satin of his doublet, the melancholy king watches with dreamy treacherous eyes too loyal Strafford pass forth to his doom, and Andrea shudders as he hears the cousin's whistle in the garden, and bids his perfect wife go down. Yes, Browning was great. And as what will he be remembered? As a poet? Ah, not as a poet! He will be remembered as a writer of fiction, as the most supreme writer of fiction, it may be, that we have ever had. His sense of dramatic situation was unrivalled, and, if he could not answer his own problems, he could at least put problems forth, and what more should an artist do? Considered from the point of view of a creator of character he ranks next to him who made Hamlet. Had he been articulate, he might have sat beside him. The only man who can touch the hem of his garment is George Meredith.° Meredith is a prose Browning, and so is Browning. He used poetry as a medium for writing in prose.

Ernest. There is something in what you say, but there is not everything in what you say. In many points you are unjust.

Gilbert. It is difficult not to be unjust to what one loves. But let us return to the particular point at issue. What was it that you said?

Ernest. Simply this: that in the best days of art there were no art-critics.

Gilbert. I seem to have heard that observation before, Ernest. It has all the vitality of error and all the tediousness of an old friend.°

Ernest. It is true. Yes: there is no use your tossing your head in that petulant manner. It is quite true. In the best days of art there were no art-critics. The sculptor hewed from the marble block the great white-limbed Hermes° that slept within it. The waxers and gilders of images gave tone and texture to the statue, and the world, when it saw it, worshipped and was dumb. He poured the glowing bronze into the mould of sand, and the river of red metal cooled into noble curves and took the impress of the body of a god. With enamel or polished jewels he gave sight to the sightless eyes. The hyacinth-like curls grew crisp beneath his graver. And when, in some dim frescoed fane, or pillared sunlit portico, the child of Leto° stood upon his pedestal, those who had passed by, ἁβρῶς βαίνοντες διὰ λαμπροτάτου αἰθέρος,° became conscious of a new influence that had come across their lives, and dreamily, or with a sense of strange and quickening joy, went to their homes or daily labour, or wandered, it may be, through the city gates to that nymph-haunted meadow where young Phædrus° bathed his feet, and, lying there on the soft grass, beneath the tall wind-whispering planes and flowering *agnus castus*,° began to think of the wonder of beauty, and grew silent with unaccustomed awe. In those days the artist was free. From the river valley he took the fine clay in his fingers, and with a little tool of wood or bone, fashioned it into forms so exquisite that the people gave them to the dead as their playthings, and we find them still in the dusty tombs on the yellow hillside by Tanagra,° with the faint gold and the fading crimson still lingering about hair and lips and raiment. On a wall of fresh plaster, stained with bright sandyx or mixed with milk and saffron, he pictured one who trod with tired feet the purple white-starred fields of asphodel,° one 'in whose eyelids lay the whole of the Trojan War', Polyxena,° the daughter of Priam; or figured Odysseus, the wise and cunning, bound by tight cords to the mast-step, that he might listen without hurt to the singing of the Sirens, or wandering by the clear river of Acheron, where the ghosts of fishes flitted over the pebbly bed; or showed the Persian in trews and mitre flying before the Greek at Marathon,° or the galleys clashing their beaks of brass in the little Salaminian bay.° He drew with silver-point and charcoal upon parchment and prepared cedar. Upon ivory and rose-coloured terra-cotta he painted with wax, making the wax fluid with juice of olives, and with heated irons making it firm. Panel and marble and linen canvas became wonderful as his brush swept across them; and life seeing her own image, was still, and dared not speak. All life, indeed, was his, from the merchants seated in the market-place to the cloaked shepherd lying on the hill; from the nymph hidden in the laurels and the faun that pipes at noon, to the king whom, in long green-curtained litter, slaves bore upon oil-bright shoulders, and fanned with peacock fans. Men and women, with pleasure or sorrow in their faces, passed before him. He watched them, and their secret became his. Through form and colour he recreated a world.

All subtle arts belonged to him also. He held the gem against the revolving disk, and the amethyst became the purple couch for Adonis, and across the veined sardonyx sped Artemis with her hounds. He beat out the gold into roses, and strung them together for necklace or armlet. He beat out the gold into wreaths for the conqueror's helmet, or into palmates° for the Tyrian robe, or into masks for the royal dead. On the back of the silver mirror he graved Thetis° borne by her Nereids, or love-sick Phædra° with her nurse, or Persephone,° weary of memory, putting poppies in her hair. The potter sat in his shed, and, flower-like from the silent wheel, the vase rose up beneath his hands. He decorated the base and stem and ears with pattern of dainty olive-leaf, or foliated acanthus, or curved and crested wave. Then in black or red he painted lads wrestling, or in the race: knights in full armour, with strange heraldic shields and curious visors, leaning from shell-shaped chariot over rearing steeds: the gods seated at the feast or working their miracles: the heroes in their victory or in their pain. Sometimes he would etch in thin vermilion lines upon a ground of white the languid bridegroom and his bride, with Eros hovering round them—an Eros like one of Donatello's angels, a little laughing thing with gilded or with azure wings. On the curved side he would write the name of his friend. ΚΑΛΟΣ ΑΛΚΙΒΙΑΔΗΣ or ΚΑΛΟΣ ΧΑΡΜΙΔΗΣ° tells us the story of his days. Again, on the rim of the wide flat cup he would draw the stag browsing, or the lion at rest, as his fancy willed it. From the tiny perfume-bottle laughed Aphrodite at her toilet, and, with bare-limbed Mænads in his train, Dionysus° danced round the wine-jar on naked must-stained° feet, while, satyr-like, the old Silenus° sprawled upon the bloated skins, or shook that magic spear which was tipped with a fretted fir-cone, and wreathed with dark ivy. And no one came to trouble the artist at his work. No irresponsible chatter disturbed him. He was not worried by opinions. By the Ilyssus, says Arnold somewhere, there was no Higginbotham.° By the Ilyssus, my dear Gilbert, there were no silly art-congresses,° bringing provincialism to the provinces and teaching the mediocrity how to mouth. By the Ilyssus there were no tedious magazines about art, in which the industrious prattle of what they do not understand. On the reed-grown banks of that little stream strutted no ridiculous journalism monopolizing the seat of judgment when it should be apologizing in the dock. The Greeks had no art-critics.

Gilbert. Ernest, you are quite delightful, but your views are terribly unsound. I am afraid that you have been listening to the conversation of someone older than yourself. That is always a dangerous thing to do, and if you allow it to degenerate into a habit, you will find it absolutely fatal to any intellectual development. As for modern journalism, it is not my business to defend it. It justifies its own existence by the great Darwinian principle° of the survival of the vulgarest. I have merely to do with literature.

Ernest. But what is the difference between literature and journalism?

Gilbert. Oh! journalism is unreadable, and literature is not read. That is all. But with regard to your statement that the Greeks had no art-critics, I assure you that is quite absurd. It would be more just to say that the Greeks were a nation of art-critics.

Ernest. Really?

Gilbert. Yes, a nation of art-critics. But I don't wish to destroy the delightfully unreal picture that you have drawn of the relation of the Hellenic artist to the intellectual spirit of his age. To give an accurate description of what has never occurred is not merely the proper occupation of the historian, but the inalienable privilege of any man of parts and culture. Still less do I desire to talk learnedly. Learned conversation is either the affectation of the ignorant or the profession of the mentally unemployed. And, as for what is called improving conversation, that is merely the foolish method by which the still more foolish philanthropist feebly tries to disarm the just rancour of the criminal classes. No: let me play to you some mad scarlet thing by Dvorák. The pallid figures on the tapestry are smiling at us, and the heavy eyelids of my bronze Narcissus are folded in sleep. Don't let us discuss anything solemnly. I am but too conscious of the fact that we are born in an age when only the dull are treated seriously, and I live in terror of not being misunderstood.° Don't degrade me into the position of giving you useful information. Education is an admirable thing, but it is well to remember from time to time that nothing that is worth knowing can be taught.° Through the parted curtains of the window I see the moon like a clipped piece of silver. Like gilded bees the stars cluster round her. The sky is a hard hollow sapphire. Let us go out into the night. Thought is wonderful, but adventure is more wonderful still. Who knows but we may meet Prince Florizel of Bohemia,° and hear the fair Cuban tell us that she is not what she seems?

Ernest. You are horribly wilful. I insist on your discussing this matter with me. You have said that the Greeks were a nation of art-critics. What art-criticism have they left us?

Gilbert. My dear Ernest, even if not a single fragment of art-criticism had come down to us from Hellenic or Hellenistic days, it would be none the less true that the Greeks were a nation of art-critics, and that they invented the criticism of art just as they invented the criticism of everything else. For, after all, what is our primary debt to the Greeks? Simply the critical spirit. And, this spirit, which they exercised on questions of religion and science, of ethics and metaphysics, of politics and education, they exercised on questions of art also, and, indeed, of the two supreme and highest arts, they have left us the most flawless system of criticism that the world has ever seen.

Ernest. But what are the two supreme and highest arts?

Gilbert. Life and Literature, life and the perfect expression of life. The principles of the former, as laid down by the Greeks, we may not realize in an age so marred by false ideals as our own. The principles of the latter, as they laid them down, are, in many cases, so subtle that we can hardly understand them. Recognizing that the most perfect art is that which most fully mirrors man in all his infinite variety, they elaborated the criticism of language, considered in the light of the mere material of that art, to a point to which we, with our accentual system of reasonable or emotional emphasis, can barely if at all attain; studying, for instance, the metrical movements of a prose as scientifically as a modern musician studies harmony and counterpoint, and, I need hardly say, with much keener æsthetic instinct. In this they were right, as they were right in all things. Since the introduction of printing, and the fatal development of the habit of reading amongst the middle and lower classes of this country, there has been a tendency in literature to appeal more and more to the eye, and less and less to the ear which is really the sense which, from the standpoint of pure art, it should seek to please, and by whose canons of pleasure it should abide always. Even the work of Mr Pater, who is, on the whole, the most perfect master of English prose now creating amongst us, is often far more like a piece of mosaic than a passage in music, and seems, here and there, to lack the true rhythmical life of words and the fine freedom and richness of effect that such rhythmical life produces. We, in fact, have made writing a definite mode of composition, and have treated it as a form of elaborate design. The Greeks, upon the other hand, regarded writing simply as a method of chronicling. Their test was always the spoken word in its musical and metrical relations. The voice was the medium, and the ear the critic. I have sometimes thought that the story of Homer's blindness might be really an artistic myth, created in critical days, and serving to remind us, not merely that the great poet is always a seer, seeing less with the eyes of the body than he does with the eyes of the soul, but that he is a true singer also, building his song out of music, repeating each line over and over again to himself till he has caught the secret of its melody, chaunting in darkness the words that are winged with light. Certainly, whether this be so or not, it was to his blindness, as an occasion if not as a cause, that England's great poet owed much of the majestic movement and sonorous splendour of his later verse. When Milton could no longer write, he began to sing. Who would match the measures of *Comus* with the measures of *Samson Agonistes*, or of *Paradise Lost* or *Regained?* When Milton became blind he composed, as everyone should compose, with the voice purely, and so the pipe or reed of earlier days became that mighty many-stopped organ whose rich reverberant music has all the stateliness of Homeric verse, if it seeks not to have its swiftness, and is the one imperishable inheritance of English literature, sweeping through all the ages, because above them, and abiding with us ever, being immortal in its form. Yes: writing has done much harm to writers. We must return to the voice. That must be our test, and perhaps then we shall be able to appreciate some of the subtleties of Greek art-criticism.

As it now is, we cannot do so. Sometimes, when I have written a piece of prose that I have been modest enough to consider absolutely free from fault, a dreadful thought comes over me that I may have been guilty of the immoral effeminacy of using trochaic and tribrachic movements, a crime for which a learned critic of the Augustan age censures with most just severity the brilliant if somewhat paradoxical Hegesias.° I grow cold when I think of it, and wonder to myself if the admirable ethical effect of the prose of that charming writer, who once in a spirit of reckless generosity towards the uncultivated portion of our community pro- claimed the monstrous doctrine that conduct is three-fourths of life,° will not some day be entirely annihilated by the discovery that the pæons° have been wrongly placed.

Ernest. Ah! Now you are flippant.

Gilbert. Who would not be flippant when he is gravely told that the Greeks had no art-critics? I can understand it being said that the constructive genius of the Greeks lost itself in criticism, but not that the race to whom we owe the critical spirit did not criticize. You will not ask me to give you a survey of Greek art criticism from Plato to Plotinus. The night is too lovely for that, and the moon, if she heard us, would put more ashes on her face than are there already. But think merely of one perfect little work of æsthetic criticism, Aristotle's *Treatise on Poetry*. It is not perfect in form, for it is badly written, consisting perhaps of notes jotted down for an art lecture, or of isolated fragments destined for some larger book, but in temper and treatment it is perfect absolutely. The ethical effect of art, its importance to culture, and its place in the formation of character, had been done once for all by Plato; but here we have art treated, not from the moral, but from the purely æsthetic point of view. Plato had, of course, dealt with many definitely artistic subjects, such as the importance of unity in a work of art, the necessity for tone and harmony, the æsthetic value of appearances, the relation of the visible arts to the external world, and the relation of fiction to fact. He first perhaps stirred in the soul of man that desire which we have not yet satisfied, the desire to know the connection between Beauty and Truth, and the place of Beauty in the moral and intellectual order of the Kosmos. The problems of idealism and realism, as he sets them forth, may seem to many to be somewhat barren of result in the metaphysical sphere of abstract being in which he places them, but transfer them to the sphere of art, and you will find that they are still vital and full of meaning. It may be that it is as a critic of Beauty that Plato is destined to live, and that by altering the name of the sphere of his speculation we shall find a new philosophy. But Aristotle, like Goethe, deals with art primarily in its concrete manifestations, taking Tragedy, for instance, and investigating the material it uses, which is language, its subject-matter, which is life, the method by which it works, which is action, the conditions under which it reveals itself, which are those of theatric presentation, its logical structure, which is plot, and its final æsthetic appeal, which is to the sense of beauty realized through the passions of pity and awe. That purification and spiritualizing of the nature which he calls κάθαρσις° is, as Goethe saw, essentially æsthetic, and is not moral, as Lessing fancied. Concerning himself primarily with the impression that the work of art produces,° Aristotle sets himself to analyse that impression, to investigate its source, to see how it is engendered. As a physiologist and psychologist, he knows that the health of a function resides in energy. To have a capacity for a passion and not to realize it, is to make oneself incomplete and limited. The mimic spectacle of life that Tragedy affords cleanses the bosom of much 'perilous stuff',° and by presenting high and worthy objects for the exercise of the emotions purifies and spiritualizes the man; nay, not merely does it spiritualize him, but it initiates him also into noble feelings of which he might else have known nothing, the word κάθαρσις having, it has sometimes seemed to me, a definite allusion to the rite of initiation, if indeed that be not, as I am occasionally tempted to fancy, its true and only meaning here. This is of course a mere outline of the book. But you see what a perfect piece of æsthetic criticism it is. Who indeed but a Greek could have analysed art so well? After reading it, one does not wonder any longer that Alexandria° devoted itself so largely to art-criticism, and that we find the artistic temperaments of the day investigating every question of style and manner, discussing the great Academic schools of painting, for instance, such as the school of Sicyon,° that sought to preserve the dignified traditions of the antique mode, or the realistic and impressionist schools, that aimed at reproducing actual life, or the elements of ideality in portraiture, or the artistic value of the epic form in an age so modern as theirs, or the proper subject-matter for the artist. Indeed, I fear that the inartistic temperaments of the day busied themselves also in matters of literature and art, for the accusations of plagiarism° were endless, and such accusations proceed either from the thin colourless lips of impotence, or from the grotesque mouths of those who, possessing nothing of their own, fancy that they can gain a reputation for wealth by crying out that they have been robbed. And I assure you, my dear Ernest, that the Greeks chattered about painters quite as much as people do nowadays, and had their private views, and shilling exhibitions, and Arts and Crafts guilds, and Pre-Raphaelite movements, and movements towards realism, and lectured about art, and wrote essays on art, and produced their art-historians, and their archæologists, and all the rest of it. Why, even the theatrical managers of travelling companies brought their dramatic critics with them when they went on tour, and paid them very handsome salaries for writing laudatory notices. Whatever, in fact, is modern in our life we owe to the Greeks. Whatever is an anachronism is due to mediævalism.° It is the Greeks who have given us the whole system of art-criticism, and how fine their critical instinct was, may be seen from the fact that the material they criticized with most care was, as I have already said, language. For the material that painter or sculptor uses is meagre in comparison with that of words. Words have not merely music as sweet as that of viol and lute, colour as rich and vivid as any that makes lovely for us the canvas of the Venetian or the Spaniard, and plastic form no less sure and certain than that which reveals itself in marble or in bronze, but thought and passion and spirituality are theirs also, are theirs indeed alone. If the Greeks had criticized nothing but language, they would still have been the great art-critics of the world. To know the principles of the highest art, is to know the principles of all the arts.

But I see that the moon is hiding behind a sulphur-coloured cloud. Out of a tawny mane of drift she gleams like a lion's eye. She is afraid that I will talk to you of Lucian and Longinus, of Quinctilian and Dionysius, of Pliny and Fronto and Pausanias, of all those who in the antique world wrote or lectured upon art-matters. She need not be afraid. I am tired of my expedition into the dim, dull abyss of facts. There is nothing left for me now but the divine μονόχρονος ἡδονή° of another cigarette. Cigarettes have at least the charm of leaving one unsatisfied.

Ernest. Try one of mine. They are rather good. I get them direct from Cairo. The only use of our *attachés* is that they supply their friends with excellent tobacco. And as the moon has hidden herself, let us talk a little longer. I am quite ready to admit that I was wrong in what I said about the Greeks. They were, as you have pointed out, a nation of art-critics. I acknowledge it, and I feel a little sorry for them. For the creative faculty is higher than the critical.° There is really no comparison between them.

Gilbert. The antithesis between them is entirely arbitrary. Without the critical faculty, there is no artistic creation at all, worthy of the name. You spoke a little while ago of that fine spirit of choice and delicate instinct of selection by which the artist realizes life for us, and gives to it a momentary perfection. Well, that spirit of choice, that subtle tact of omission, is really the critical faculty in one of its most characteristic moods, and no one who does not possess this critical faculty can create anything at all in art. Arnold's definition of literature as a criticism of life,° was not very felicitous in form, but it showed how keenly he recognized the importance of the critical element in all creative work.

Ernest. I should have said that great artists worked unconsciously, that they were 'wiser than they knew',° as, I think, Emerson remarks somewhere.

Gilbert. It is really not so, Ernest. All fine imaginative work is self-conscious and deliberate. No poet sings because he must sing. At least, no great poet does. A great poet sings because he chooses to sing. It is so now, and it has always been so. We are sometimes apt to think that the voices that sounded at the dawn of poetry were simpler, fresher, and more natural than ours, and that the world which the early poets looked at, and through which they walked, had a kind of poetical quality of its own, and almost without changing could pass into song. The snow lies thick now upon Olympus, and its steep scarped sides are bleak and barren, but once, we fancy, the white feet of the Muses brushed the dew from the anemones in the morning, and at evening came Apollo to sing to the shepherds in the vale. But in this we are merely lending to other ages what we desire, or think we desire, for our own. Our historical sense is at fault. Every century that produces poetry is, so far, an artificial century, and the work that seems to us to be the most natural and simple product of its time is always the result of the most self-conscious effort. Believe me, Ernest, there is no fine art without self-consciousness, and self-consciousness and the critical spirit are one.

Ernest. I see what you mean, and there is much in it. But surely you would admit that the great poems of the early world, the primitive, anonymous collective poems, were the result of the imagination of races, rather than of the imagination of individuals?

Gilbert. Not when they became poetry. Not when they received a beautiful form. For there is no art where there is no style, and no style where there is no unity, and unity is of the individual. No doubt Homer had old ballads and stories to deal with, as Shakespeare had chronicles and plays and novels from which to work, but they were merely his rough material. He took them, and shaped them into song. They become his, because he made them lovely. They were built out of music,

> And so not built at all,
> And therefore built for ever.°

The longer one studies life and literature, the more strongly one feels that behind everything that is wonderful stands the individual, and that it is not the moment that makes the man, but the man who creates the age.° Indeed, I am inclined to think that each myth and legend that seems to us to spring out of the wonder, or terror, or fancy of tribe and nation, was in its origin the invention of one single mind. The curiously limited number of the myths seems to me to point to this conclusion. But we must not go off into questions of comparative mythology. We must keep to criticism. And what I want to point out is this. An age that has no criticism is either an age in which art is immobile, hieratic, and confined to the reproduction of formal types, or an age that possesses no art at all. There have been critical ages that have not been creative, in the ordinary sense of the word, ages in which the spirit of man has sought to set in order the treasures of his treasure-house, to separate the gold from the silver, and the silver from the lead, to count over the jewels, and to give names to the pearls. But there has never been a creative age that has not been critical also. For it is the critical faculty that invents fresh forms. The tendency of creation is to repeat itself. It is to the critical instinct that we owe each new school that springs up, each new mould that art finds ready to its hand. There is really not a single form that art now uses that does not come to us from the critical spirit of Alexandria,° where these forms were either stereotyped, or invented, or made perfect. I say Alexandria, not merely because it was there that the Greek spirit became most self-conscious, and indeed ultimately expired in scepticism and theology, but because it was to that city, and not to Athens, that Rome turned for her models, and it was through the survival, such as it was, of the Latin language that culture lived at all. When, at the Renaissance, Greek literature dawned upon Europe, the soil had been in some measure prepared for it. But, to get rid of the details of history, which are always wearisome and usually inaccurate, let us say generally, that the forms of art have been due to the Greek critical spirit. To it we owe the epic, the lyric, the entire drama in every one of its developments, including burlesque, the idyll, the romantic novel, the novel of adventure, the essay, the dialogue, the oration, the lecture, for which perhaps we should not forgive them, and the epigram, in all the wide meaning of that word. In fact, we owe it everything, except the sonnet, to which, however, some curious parallels of thought-movement may be traced in the Anthology,° American journalism, to which no parallel can be found anywhere, and the ballad in sham Scotch dialect,° which one of our most industrious writers has recently proposed should be made the basis for a final and unanimous effort on the part of our second-rate poets to make themselves really romantic. Each new school, as it appears, cries out against criticism, but it is to the critical faculty in man that it owes its origin. The mere creative instinct does not innovate, but reproduces.

Ernest. You have been talking of criticism as an essential part of the creative spirit, and I now fully accept your theory. But what of criticism outside creation? I have a foolish habit of reading periodicals, and it seems to me that most modern criticism is perfectly valueless.

Gilbert. So is most modern creative work also. Mediocrity weighing mediocrity in the balance, and incompetence applauding its brother— that is the spectacle which the artistic activity of England affords us from time to time. And yet, I feel I am a little unfair in this matter. As a rule, the critics—I speak, of course, of the higher class, of those in fact who write for the sixpenny papers—are far more cultured than the people whose work they are called upon to review. This is, indeed, only what one would expect, for criticism demands infinitely more cultivation than creation does.

Ernest. Really?

Gilbert. Certainly. Anybody can write a three-volumed novel.° It merely requires a complete ignorance of both life and literature. The difficulty that I should fancy the reviewer feels is the difficulty of sustaining any standard. Where there is no style a standard must be impossible. The poor reviewers are apparently reduced to be the reporters of the police-court of literature, the chroniclers of the doings of the habitual criminals of art. It is sometimes said of them that they do not read all through the works they are called upon to criticize. They do not. Or at least they should not. If they did so, they would become confirmed misanthropes, or if I may borrow a phrase from one of the pretty

Newnham graduates,° confirmed womanthropes for the rest of their lives. Nor is it necessary. To know the vintage and quality of a wine one need not drink the whole cask. It must be perfectly easy in half an hour to say whether a book is worth anything or worth nothing. Ten minutes are really sufficient, if one has the instinct for form. Who wants to wade through a dull volume? One tastes it, and that is quite enough—more than enough, I should imagine. I am aware that there are many honest workers in painting as well as in literature who object to criticism entirely. They are quite right. Their work stands in no intellectual relation to their age. It brings us no new element of pleasure. It suggests no fresh departure of thought, or passion, or beauty. It should not be spoken of. It should be left to the oblivion that it deserves.

Ernest. But, my dear fellow—excuse me for interrupting you—you seem to me to be allowing your passion for criticism to lead you a great deal too far. For, after all, even you must admit that it is much more difficult to do a thing than to talk about it.

Gilbert. More difficult to do a thing than to talk about it? Not at all. That is a gross popular error. It is very much more difficult to talk about a thing than to do it. In the sphere of actual life that is of course obvious. Anybody can make history. Only a great man can write it. There is no mode of action, no form of emotion, that we do not share with the lower animals. It is only by language that we rise above them, or above each other—by language, which is the parent, and not the child, of thought. Action, indeed, is always easy, and when presented to us in its most aggravated, because most continuous form, which I take to be that of real industry, becomes simply the refuge of people who have nothing whatsoever to do. No, Ernest, don't talk about action. It is a blind thing dependent on external influences, and moved by an impulse of whose nature it is unconscious. It is a thing incomplete in its essence, because limited by accident, and ignorant of its direction, being always at variance with its aim. Its basis is the lack of imagination. It is the last resource of those who know not how to dream.

Ernest. Gilbert, you treat the world as if it were a crystal ball. You hold it in your hand, and reverse it to please a wilful fancy. You do nothing but rewrite history.

Gilbert. The one duty we owe to history is to rewrite it. That is not the least of the tasks in store for the critical spirit. When we have fully discovered the scientific laws that govern life, we shall realize that the one person who has more illusions than the dreamer is the man of action. He, indeed, knows neither the origin of his deeds nor their results. From the field in which he thought that he had sown thorns, we have gathered our vintage, and the fig-tree that he planted for our pleasure is as barren as the thistle,° and more bitter. It is because Humanity has never known where it was going that it has been able to find its way.

Ernest. You think, then, that in the sphere of action a conscious aim is a delusion?

Gilbert. It is worse than a delusion. If we lived long enough to see the results of our actions it may be that those who call themselves good would be sickened with a dull remorse, and those whom the world calls evil stirred by a noble joy. Each little thing that we do passes into the great machine of life which may grind our virtues to powder and make them worthless, or transform our sins into elements of a new civilization, more marvellous and more splendid than any that has gone before. But men are the slaves of words. They rage against Materialism, as they call it, forgetting that there has been no material improvement that has not spiritualized the world, and that there have been few, if any, spiritual awakenings that have not wasted the world's faculties in barren hopes, and fruitless aspirations, and empty or trammelling creeds. What is termed Sin is an essential element of progress. Without it the world would stagnate, or grow old, or become colourless. By its curiosity, Sin increases the experience of the race. Through its intensified assertion of individualism, it saves us from monotony of type. In its rejection of the current notions about morality, it is one with the higher ethics. And as for the virtues! What are the virtues? Nature, M. Renan tells us, cares little about chastity,° and it may be that it is to the shame of the Magdalen,° and not to their own purity, that the Lucretias° of modern life owe their freedom from stain. Charity, as even those of whose religion it makes a formal part have been compelled to acknowledge, creates a multitude of evils.° The mere existence of conscience, that faculty of which people prate so much nowadays, and are so ignorantly proud, is a sign of our imperfect development. It must be merged in instinct before we become fine. Self-denial is simply a method by which man arrests his progress, and self-sacrifice a survival of the mutilation of the savage, part of that old worship of pain which is so terrible a factor in the history of the world, and which even now makes its victims day by day, and has its altars in the land. Virtues! Who knows what the virtues are? Not you. Not I. Not anyone. It is well for our vanity that we slay the criminal, for if we suffered him to live he might show us what we had gained by his crime. It is well for his peace that the saint goes to his martyrdom. He is spared the sight of the horror of his harvest.

Ernest. Gilbert, you sound too harsh a note. Let us go back to the more gracious fields of literature. What was it you said? That it was more difficult to talk about a thing than to do it?

Gilbert (after a pause). Yes: I believe I ventured upon that simple truth. Surely you see now that I am right? When man acts he is a puppet. When he describes he is a poet. The whole secret lies in that. It was easy enough on the sandy plains by windy Ilion° to send the notched arrow from the painted bow, or to hurl against the shield of hide and flamelike brass the long ash-handled spear. It was easy for the adulterous queen to spread the Tyrian carpets for her lord, and then, as he lay couched in the marble bath, to throw over his head the purple net, and call to her smooth-faced lover to stab through the meshes at the heart that should have broken at Aulis.° For Antigone° even, with Death waiting for her as her bridegroom, it was easy to pass through the tainted air at noon, and climb the hill, and strew with kindly earth the wretched naked corse that had no tomb. But what of those who wrote about these things? What of those who gave them reality, and made them live for ever? Are they not greater than the men and women they sing of? 'Hector that sweet knight is dead',° and Lucian tells us how in the dim underworld Menippus saw the bleaching skull of Helen,° and marvelled that it was for so grim a favour that all those horned ships were launched, those beautiful mailed men laid low, those towered cities brought to dust. Yet, every day the swanlike daughter of Leda° comes out on the battlements, and looks down at the tide of war. The greybeards wonder at her loveliness, and she stands by the side of the king. In his chamber of stained ivory lies her leman. He is polishing his dainty armour, and combing the scarlet plume. With squire and page, her husband passes from tent to tent. She can see his bright hair, and hears, or fancies that she hears, that clear cold voice. In the courtyard below, the son of Priam is buckling on his brazen cuirass. The white arms of Andromache are around his neck. He sets his helmet on the ground, lest their babe should be frightened. Behind the embroidered curtains of his pavilion sits Achilles, in perfumed raiment, while in harness of gilt and silver the friend of his soul arrays himself to go forth to the fight. From a curiously carven chest that his mother Thetis had brought to his ship-side, the Lord of the Myrmidons° takes out that mystic chalice that the lip of man had never touched, and cleanses it with brimstone, and with fresh water cools it, and, having washed his hands, fills with black wine its burnished hollow, and spills the thick grape-blood upon the ground in honour of Him whom at Dodona° barefooted prophets worshipped, and prays to Him, and knows not that he prays in vain, and that by the hands of two knights from Troy, Panthous' son, Euphorbus,° whose lovelocks were looped with gold, and the Priamid, the lion-hearted, Patroklus, the comrade of comrades, must meet his doom. Phantoms, are they? Heroes of mist and mountain? Shadows in a song? No: they are real. Action! What is action? It dies at the moment of its energy. It is a base concession to fact. The world is made by the singer for the dreamer.

Ernest. While you talk it seems to me to be so.

Gilbert. It is so in truth. On the mouldering citadel of Troy lies the lizard like a thing of green bronze. The owl has built her nest in the palace of Priam. Over the empty plain wander shepherd and goatherd with their flocks, and where, on the wine-surfaced, oily sea, οἶνοψ πόντος,° as Homer calls it, copper-prowed and streaked with vermilion, the great galleys of the Danaoi° came in their gleaming crescent, the lonely tunny-fisher sits in his little boat and watches the bobbing corks of his net. Yet, every morning the doors of the city are thrown open, and on foot, or in horse-drawn chariot, the warriors go forth to battle, and mock their enemies from behind their iron masks. All day long the fight rages, and when night comes the torches gleam by the tents, and the cresset burns in the hall. Those who live in marble or on painted panel, know of life but a single exquisite instant, eternal indeed in its beauty, but limited to one note of passion or one mood of calm. Those whom the poet makes live have their myriad emotions of joy and terror, of courage and despair, of pleasure and of suffering. The seasons come and go in glad or saddening pageant, and with winged or leaden feet the years pass by before them. They have their youth and their manhood, they are children, and they grow old. It is always dawn for St Helena, as Veronese° saw her at the window. Through the still morning air the angels bring her the symbol of God's pain. The cool breezes of the morning lift the gilt threads from her brow. On that little hill by the city of Florence, where the lovers of Giorgione are lying, it is always the solstice of noon, of noon made so languorous by summer suns that hardly can the slim naked girl dip into the marble tank the round bubble of clear glass, and the long fingers of the lute-player rest idly upon the chords.° It is twilight always for the dancing nymphs whom Corot° set free among the silver poplars of France. In eternal twilight they move, those frail diaphanous figures, whose tremulous white feet seem not to touch the dew-drenched grass they tread on. But those who walk in epos, drama, or romance, see through the labouring months the young moons wax and wane, and watch the night from evening unto morning star, and from sunrise unto sunsetting can note the shifting day with all its gold and shadow. For them, as for us, the flowers bloom and wither, and the Earth, that Green-tressed Goddess° as Coleridge calls her, alters her raiment for their pleasure. The statue is concentrated to one moment of perfection. The image stained upon the canvas possesses no spiritual element of growth or change. If they know nothing of death, it is because they know little of life, for the secrets of life and death belong to those, and those only, whom the sequence of time affects, and who possess not merely the present but the future, and can rise or fall from a past of glory or of shame. Movement, that problem of the visible arts, can be truly realized by Literature alone. It is Literature that shows us the body in its swiftness and the soul in its unrest.

Ernest. Yes; I see now what you mean. But, surely, the higher you place the creative artist, the lower must the critic rank.

Gilbert. Why so?

Ernest. Because the best that he can give us will be but an echo of rich music, a dim shadow of clear-outlined form. It may, indeed, be that life is chaos, as you tell me that it is; that its martyrdoms are mean and its heroisms ignoble; and that it is the function of Literature to create, from the rough material of actual existence, a new world that will be more marvellous, more enduring, and more true than the world that common eyes look upon, and through which common natures seek to realize their perfection. But surely, if this new world has been made by the spirit and touch of a great artist, it will be a thing so complete and perfect that there will be nothing left for the critic to do. I quite understand now, and indeed admit most readily, that it is far more difficult to talk about a thing than to do it. But it seems to me that this sound and sensible maxim, which is really extremely soothing to one's feelings, and should be adopted as its motto by every Academy of Literature all over the world, applies only to the relations that exist between Art and Life, and not to any relations that there may be between Art and Criticism.

Gilbert. But, surely, Criticism is itself an art. And just as artistic creation implies the working of the critical faculty, and, indeed, without it cannot be said to exist at all, so Criticism is really creative in the highest sense of the word. Criticism is, in fact, both creative and independent.

Ernest. Independent?

Gilbert. Yes; independent. Criticism is no more to be judged by any low standard of imitation or resemblance than is the work of poet or sculptor. The critic occupies the same relation to the work of art that he criticizes as the artist does to the visible world of form and colour, or the unseen world of passion and of thought. He does not even require for the perfection of his art the finest materials. Anything will serve his purpose. And just as out of the sordid and sentimental amours of the silly wife of a small country doctor in the squalid village of Yonville-l'Abbaye, near

Rouen, Gustave Flaubert was able to create a classic, and make a masterpiece of style,° so, from subjects of little or of no importance, such as the pictures in this year's Royal Academy, or in any year's Royal Academy for that matter, Mr Lewis Morris's poems,° M. Ohnet's novels,° or the plays of Mr Henry Arthur Jones,° the true critic can, if it be his pleasure so to direct or waste his faculty of contemplation, produce work that will be flawless in beauty and instinct with intellectual subtlety. Why not? Dulness is always an irresistible temptation for brilliancy, and stupidity is the permanent *Bestia Trionfans*° that calls wisdom from its cave. To an artist so creative as the critic, what does subject-matter signify? No more and no less than it does to the novelist and the painter. Like them, he can find his motives everywhere. Treatment is the test. There is nothing that has not in it suggestion or challenge.

Ernest. But is Criticism really a creative art?

Gilbert. Why should it not be? It works with materials, and puts them into a form that is at once new and delightful. What more can one say of poetry? Indeed, I would call criticism a creation within a creation. For just as the great artists, from Homer and Æschylus, down to Shakespeare and Keats, did not go directly to life for their subject-matter, but sought for it in myth, and legend and ancient tale, so the critic deals with materials that others have, as it were, purified for him, and to which imaginative form and colour have been already added. Nay, more, I would say that the highest Criticism, being the purest form of personal impression, is in its way more creative than creation, as it has least reference to any standard external to itself, and is, in fact, its own reason for existing, and, as the Greeks would put it, in itself, and to itself, an end. Certainly, it is never trammelled by any shackles of verisimilitude. No ignoble considerations of probability, that cowardly concession to the tedious repetitions of domestic or public life, affect it ever. One may appeal from fiction unto fact. But from the soul there is no appeal.

Ernest. From the soul?

Gilbert. Yes, from the soul. That is what the highest criticism really is, the record of one's own soul.° It is more fascinating than history, as it is concerned simply with oneself. It is more delightful than philosophy, as its subject is concrete and not abstract, real and not vague. It is the only civilized form of autobiography, as it deals not with the events, but with the thoughts of one's life; not with life's physical accidents of deed or circumstance, but with the spiritual moods and imaginative passions of the mind. I am always amused by the silly vanity of those writers and artists of our day who seem to imagine that the primary function of the critic is to chatter about their second-rate work. The best that one can say of most modern creative art is that it is just a little less vulgar than reality, and so the critic, with his fine sense of distinction and sure instinct of delicate refinement, will prefer to look into the silver mirror or through the woven veil, and will turn his eyes away from the chaos and clamour of actual existence, though the mirror be tarnished and the veil be torn. His sole aim is to chronicle his own impressions.° It is for him that pictures are painted, books written, and marble hewn into form.

Ernest. I seem to have heard another theory of Criticism.

Gilbert. Yes: it has been said by one whose gracious memory we all revere, and the music of whose pipe once lured Proserpina from her Sicilian fields, and made those white feet stir, and not in vain, the Cumnor cowslips,° that the proper aim of Criticism is to see the object as in itself it really is. But this is a very serious error, and takes no cognizance of Criticism's most perfect form, which is in its essence purely subjective, and seeks to reveal its own secret and not the secret of another. For the highest Criticism deals with art not as expressive but as impressive purely.

Ernest. But is that really so?

Gilbert. Of course it is. Who cares whether Mr Ruskin's views on Turner° are sound or not? What does it matter? That mighty and majestic prose of his, so fervid and so fiery-coloured in its noble eloquence, so rich in its elaborate symphonic music, so sure and certain, at its best, in subtle choice of word and epithet, is at least as great a work of art as any of those wonderful sunsets that bleach or rot on their corrupted canvases in England's Gallery; greater indeed, one is apt to think at times, not merely because its equal beauty is more enduring, but on account of the fuller variety of its appeal, soul speaking to soul in those long-cadenced lines, not through form and colour alone, though through these, indeed, completely and without loss, but with intellectual and emotional utterance, with lofty passion and with loftier thought, with imaginative insight, and with poetic aim; greater, I always think, even as Literature is the greater art. Who, again, cares whether Mr Pater has put into the portrait of Monna Lisa something that Lionardo never dreamed of?° The painter may have been merely the slave of an archaic smile, as some have fancied, but whenever I pass into the cool galleries of the Palace of the Louvre, and stand before that strange figure 'set in its marble chair in that cirque of fantastic rocks, as in some faint light under sea', I murmur to myself, 'She is older than the rocks among which she sits; like the vampire, she has been dead many times, and learned the secrets of the grave; and has been a diver in deep seas, and keeps their fallen day about her; and trafficked for strange webs with Eastern merchants; and, as Leda, was the mother of Helen of Troy, and, as St Anne, the mother of Mary; and all this has been to her but as the sound of lyres and flutes, and lives only in the delicacy with which it has moulded the changing lineaments, and tinged the eyelids and the hands.' And I say to my friend, 'The presence that thus so strangely rose beside the waters is expressive of what in the ways of a thousand years man had come to desire;' and he answers me, 'Hers is the head upon which all "the ends of the world are come",° and the eyelids are a little weary'.

And so the picture becomes more wonderful to us than it really is, and reveals to us a secret of which, in truth, it knows nothing, and the music of the mystical prose is as sweet in our ears as was that flute-player's music that lent to the lips of La Gioconda those subtle and poisonous curves. Do you ask me what Lionardo would have said had anyone told him of this picture that 'all the thoughts and experience of the world had etched and moulded there in that which they had of power to refine and make expressive the outward form, the animalism of Greece, the lust of Rome, the reverie of the Middle Age with its spiritual ambition and imaginative loves, the return of the Pagan world, the sins of the Borgias'? He would probably have answered that he had contemplated none of these things, but had concerned himself simply with certain arrangements of lines and masses, and with new and curious colour-harmonies of blue and green. And it is for this very reason that the criticism which I have quoted is criticism of the highest kind. It treats the work of art simply as a starting-point for a new creation. It does not confine itself— let us at least suppose so for the moment—to discovering the real intention of the artist and accepting that as final. And in this it is right, for the meaning of any beautiful created thing is, at least, as much in the soul of him who looks at it, as it was in his soul who wrought it. Nay, it is rather the beholder who lends to the beautiful thing its myriad meanings, and makes it marvellous for us, and sets it in some new relation to the age, so that it becomes a vital portion of our lives, and a symbol of what we pray for, or perhaps of what, having prayed for, we fear that we may receive. The longer I study, Ernest, the more clearly I see that the beauty of the visible arts is, as the beauty of music, impressive primarily, and that it may be marred, and indeed often is so, by any excess of intellectual intention on the part of the artist. For when the work is finished it has, as it were, an independent life of its own, and may deliver a message far other than that which was put into its lips to say. Sometimes, when I listen to the overture to *Tannhäuser*,° I seem indeed to see that comely knight treading delicately on the flower-strewn grass, and to hear the voice of Venus calling to him from the caverned hill. But at other times it speaks to me of a thousand different things,° of myself, it may be, and my own life, or of the lives of others whom one has loved and grown weary of loving, or of the passions that man has known, or of the passions that man has not known, and so has sought for. Tonight it may fill one with that ΕΡΩΣ ΤΩΝ ΑΔΥΝΑΤΩΝ,° that *Amour de l'Impossible*, which falls like a madness on many who think they live securely and out of reach of harm, so that they sicken suddenly with the poison of unlimited desire, and, in the infinite pursuit of what they may not obtain, grow faint and swoon or stumble. Tomorrow, like the music of which Aristotle and Plato tell us, the noble Dorian music of the Greek, it may perform the office of a physician, and give us an anodyne against pain, and heal the spirit that is wounded, and 'bring the soul into harmony with all right things'.° And what is true about music is true about all the arts. Beauty has as many meanings as man has moods. Beauty is the symbol of symbols. Beauty reveals everything, because it expresses nothing. When it shows us itself, it shows us the whole fiery-coloured world.

Ernest. But is such work as you have talked about really criticism?

Gilbert. It is the highest Criticism, for it criticizes not merely the individual work of art, but Beauty itself, and fills with wonder a form which the artist may have left void, or not understood, or understood incompletely.

Ernest. The highest Criticism, then, is more creative than creation, and the primary aim of the critic is to see the object as in itself it really is not; that is your theory, I believe?

Gilbert. Yes, that is my theory. To the critic the work of art is simply a suggestion for a new work of his own, that need not necessarily bear any obvious resemblance to the thing it criticizes. The one characteristic of a beautiful form is that one can put into it whatever one wishes, and see in it whatever one chooses to see; and the Beauty, that gives to creation its universal and æsthetic element, makes the critic a creator in his turn, and whispers of a thousand different things which were not present in the mind of him who carved the statue or painted the panel or graved the gem.

It is sometimes said by those who understand neither the nature of the highest Criticism nor the charm of the highest Art, that the pictures that the critic loves most to write about are those that belong to the anecdotage of painting, and that deal with scenes taken out of literature or history. But this is not so. Indeed, pictures of this kind are far too intelligible. As a class, they rank with illustrations, and even considered from this point of view are failures, as they do not stir the imagination, but set definite bounds to it. For the domain of the painter is, as I suggested before, widely different from that of the poet. To the latter belongs life in its full and absolute entirety; not merely the beauty that men look at, but the beauty that men listen to also; not merely the momentary grace of form or the transient gladness of colour, but the whole sphere of feeling, the perfect cycle of thought. The painter is so far limited that it is only through the mask of the body that he can show us the mystery of the soul; only through conventional images that he can handle ideas; only through its physical equivalents that he can deal with psychology. And how inadequately does he do it then, asking us to accept the torn turban of the Moor for the noble rage of Othello, or a dotard in a storm for the wild madness of Lear!° Yet it seems as if nothing could stop him. Most of our elderly English painters spend their wicked and wasted lives in poaching upon the domain of the poets, marring their motives by clumsy treatment, and striving to render, by visible form or colour, the marvel of what is invisible, the splendour of what is not seen. Their pictures are, as a natural consequence, insufferably tedious. They have degraded the visible arts into the obvious arts, and the one thing not worth looking at is the obvious. I do not say that poet and painter may not treat of the same subject. They have always done so, and will always do so. But while the poet can be pictorial or not, as he chooses, the painter must be pictorial always. For a painter is limited, not to what he sees in nature, but to what upon canvas may be seen.

And so, my dear Ernest, pictures of this kind will not really fascinate the critic. He will turn from them to such works as make him brood and dream and fancy, to works that possess the subtle quality of suggestion, and seem to tell one that even from them there is an escape into a wider world. It is sometimes said that the tragedy of an artist's life is that he cannot realize his ideal. But the true tragedy that dogs the steps of most artists is that they realize their ideal too absolutely. For, when the ideal is realized, it is robbed of its wonder and its mystery, and becomes simply a new starting-point for an ideal that is other than itself. This is the reason why music is the perfect type of art. Music can never reveal its ultimate secret. This, also, is the explanation of the value of limitations in art. The sculptor gladly surrenders imitative colour, and the painter the actual dimensions of form, because by such renunciations they are able to avoid too definite a presentation of the Real, which would be mere imitation, and too definite a realization of the Ideal, which would be too purely intellectual. It is through its very incompleteness that Art becomes complete in beauty, and so addresses itself, not to the faculty of recognition nor to the faculty of reason, but to the æsthetic sense alone, which, while accepting both reason and recognition as stages of apprehension, subordinates them both to a pure synthetic impression of the work of art as a whole, and, taking whatever alien emotional elements the work may possess, uses their very complexity as a means by which a richer unity may be added to the ultimate impression itself. You see, then, how it is that the æsthetic critic rejects those obvious modes of art that have but one message to deliver, and having delivered it become dumb and sterile, and seeks rather for such modes as suggest reverie and mood, and by their imaginative beauty make all interpretations true and no interpretation final. Some resemblance, no doubt, the creative work of the critic will have to the work that has stirred him to creation, but it will be such resemblance as exists, not between Nature and the mirror that the painter of landscape or figure may be supposed to hold up to her, but between Nature and the work of the decorative artist. Just as on the flowerless carpets of Persia, tulip and rose blossom indeed and are lovely to look on, though they are not reproduced in visible shape or line; just as the pearl and purple of the sea-shell is echoed in the church of St Mark at Venice; just as the vaulted ceiling of the wondrous chapel of Ravenna is made gorgeous by the gold and green and sapphire of the peacock's tail, though the birds of Juno fly not across it;° so the critic reproduces the work that he criticizes in a mode that is never imitative, and part of whose charm may really consist in the rejection of resemblance, and shows us in this way not merely the meaning but also the mystery of Beauty, and, by transforming each art into literature, solves once for all the problem of Art's unity.

But I see it is time for supper. After we have discussed some Chambertin and a few ortolans,° we will pass on to the question of the critic considered in the light of the interpreter.

Ernest. Ah! you admit, then, that the critic may occasionally be allowed to see the object as in itself it really is.

Gilbert. I am not quite sure. Perhaps I may admit it after supper. There is a subtle influence in supper.

THE CRITIC AS ARTIST

With some remarks upon the importance of discussing everything°

———

A Dialogue. Part II. Persons: the same. Scene: the same.

———

THE CRITIC AS ARTIST

Ernest. The ortolans were delightful, and the Chambertin perfect. And now let us return to the point at issue.

Gilbert. Ah! don't let us do that. Conversation should touch everything, but should concentrate itself on nothing. Let us talk about *Moral Indignation, its Cause and Cure*, a subject on which I think of writing: or about *The Survival of Thersites,*° as shown by the English comic papers; or about any topic that may turn up.

Ernest. No: I want to discuss the critic and criticism. You have told me that the highest criticism deals with art, not as expressive, but as impressive purely, and is consequently both creative and independent, is in fact an art by itself, occupying the same relation to creative work that creative work does to the visible world of form and colour, or the unseen world of passion and of thought. Well, now tell me, will not the critic be sometimes a real interpreter?

Gilbert. Yes; the critic will be an interpreter, if he chooses. He can pass from his synthetic impression of the work of art as a whole, to an analysis or exposition of the work itself, and in this lower sphere, as I hold it to be, there are many delightful things to be said and done. Yet his object will not always be to explain the work of art. He may seek rather to deepen its mystery, to raise round it, and round its maker, that mist of wonder which is dear to both gods and worshippers alike. Ordinary people are 'terribly at ease in Zion'.° They propose to walk arm in arm with the poets, and have a glib ignorant way of saying 'Why should we read what is written about Shakespeare and Milton? We can read the plays and the poems. That is enough.' But an appreciation of Milton is, as the late Rector of Lincoln° remarked once, the reward of consummate scholarship. And he who desires to understand Shakespeare truly must understand the relations in which Shakespeare stood to the Renaissance and the Reformation, to the age of Elizabeth and the age of James; he must be familiar with the history of the struggle for supremacy between the old classical forms and the new spirit of romance, between the school of Sidney, and Daniel, and Jonson, and the school of Marlowe and Marlowe's greater son; he must know the materials that were at Shakespeare's disposal, and the method in which he used them, and the conditions of theatric presentation in the sixteenth and seventeenth century, their limitations and their opportunities for freedom, and the literary criticism of Shakespeare's day, its aims and modes and canons; he must study the English language in its progress, and blank or rhymed verse in its various developments; he must study the Greek drama, and the connection between the art of the creator of the Agamemnon° and the art of the creator of Macbeth; in a word, he must be able to bind Elizabethan London to the Athens of Pericles,° and to learn Shakespeare's true position in the history of European drama and the drama of the world. The critic will certainly be an interpreter, but he will not treat Art as a riddling Sphinx, whose shallow secret may be guessed and revealed by one whose feet are wounded and who knows not his name.° Rather, he will look upon Art as a goddess whose mystery it is his province to intensify, and whose majesty his privilege to make more marvellous in the eyes of men.

And here, Ernest, this strange thing happens. The critic will indeed be an interpreter, but he will not be an interpreter in the sense of one who simply repeats in another form a message that has been put into his lips to say. For, just as it is only by contact with the art of foreign nations that the art of a country gains that individual and separate life that we call nationality, so, by curious inversion, it is only by intensifying his own personality that the critic can interpret the personality and work of others,° and the more strongly this personality enters into the interpretation the more real the interpretation becomes, the more satisfying, the more convincing, and the more true.

Ernest. I would have said that personality would have been a disturbing element.

Gilbert. No; it is an element of revelation. If you wish to understand others you must intensify your own individualism.

Ernest. What, then, is the result?

Gilbert. I will tell you, and perhaps I can tell you best by definite example. It seems to me that, while the literary critic stands of course first, as having the wider range, and larger vision, and nobler material, each of the arts has a critic, as it were, assigned to it. The actor is a critic of the drama. He shows the poet's work under new conditions, and by a method special to himself. He takes the written word, and action, gesture, and voice become the media of revelation. The singer, or the player on lute and viol, is the critic of music. The etcher of a picture robs the painting of its fair colours, but shows us by the use of a new material its true colour-quality, its tones and values, and the relations of its masses, and so is, in his way, a critic of it, for the critic is he who exhibits to us a work of art in a form different from that of the work itself, and the employment of a new material is a critical as well as a creative element. Sculpture, too, has its critic, who may be either the carver of a gem, as he was in Greek days, or some painter like Mantegna,° who sought to reproduce on canvas the beauty of plastic line and the symphonic dignity of processional bas-relief. And in the case of all these creative critics of art it is evident that personality is an absolute essential for any real interpretation. When Rubinstein° plays to us the *Sonata Appassionata* of Beethoven, he gives us not merely Beethoven, but also himself, and so gives us Beethoven absolutely—Beethoven reinterpreted through a rich artistic nature, and made vivid and wonderful to us by a new and intense personality. When a great actor plays Shakespeare we have the same experience. His own individuality becomes a vital part of the interpretation. People sometimes say that actors give us their own Hamlets, and not Shakespeare's; and this fallacy—for it is a fallacy—is, I regret to say, repeated by that charming and graceful writer who has lately deserted the turmoil of literature for the peace of the House of Commons, I mean the author of *Obiter Dicta.*° In point of fact, there is no such thing as Shakespeare's Hamlet. If Hamlet has something of the definiteness of a work of art, he has also all the obscurity that belongs to life. There are as many Hamlets as there are melancholies.

Ernest. As many Hamlets as there are melancholies?

Gilbert. Yes: and as art springs from personality, so it is only to personality that it can be revealed, and from the meeting of the two comes right interpretative criticism.

Ernest. The critic, then, considered as the interpreter, will give no less than he receives, and lend as much as he borrows?

Gilbert. He will be always showing us the work of art in some new relation to our age. He will always be reminding us that great works of art are living things—are, in fact, the only things that live. So much, indeed, will he feel this, that I am certain that, as civilization progresses and we become more highly organized, the elect spirits of each age, the critical and cultured spirits, will grow less and less interested in actual life, and *will seek to gain their impressions almost entirely from what Art has touched.*° For Life is terribly deficient in form. Its catastrophes happen in the wrong way and to the wrong people. There is a grotesque horror about its comedies, and its tragedies seem to culminate in farce. One is always wounded when one approaches it. Things last either too long, or not long enough.

Ernest. Poor life! Poor human life! Are you not even touched by the tears that the Roman poet° tells us are part of its essence?

Gilbert. Too quickly touched by them, I fear. For when one looks back upon the life that was so vivid in its emotional intensity, and filled with such fervent moments of ecstasy or of joy, it all seems to be a dream and an illusion. What are the unreal things, but the passions that once burned one like fire? What are the incredible things, but the things that one has faithfully believed? What are the improbable things? The things that one has done oneself. No, Ernest; life cheats us with shadows, like a puppet-master. We ask it for pleasure. It gives it to us, with bitterness and disappointment in its train. We come across some noble grief that we think will lend the purple dignity of tragedy to our days, but it passes away from us, and things less noble take its place, and on some grey windy dawn, or odorous eve of silence and of silver, we find ourselves looking with callous wonder, or dull heart of stone, at the tress of gold-flecked hair that we had once so wildly worshipped and so madly kissed.

Ernest. Life then is a failure?

Gilbert. From the artistic point of view, certainly. And the chief thing that makes life a failure from this artistic point of view is the thing that lends to life its sordid security, the fact that one can never repeat exactly the same emotion. How different it is in the world of Art! On a shelf of the bookcase behind you stands the *Divine Comedy,*° and I know that, if I open it at a certain place, I shall be filled with a fierce hatred of some one who has never wronged me, or stirred by a great love for some one whom I shall never see. There is no mood or passion that Art cannot give us, and those of us who have discovered her secret can settle beforehand what our experiences are going to be. We can choose our day and select our hour. We can say to ourselves, 'Tomorrow, at dawn, we shall walk with grave Virgil through the valley of the shadow of death,' and lo! the dawn finds us in the obscure wood, and the Mantuan stands by our side. We pass through the gate of the legend fatal to hope, and with pity or with joy behold the horror of another world. The hypocrites go by, with their painted faces and their cowls of gilded lead. Out of the ceaseless winds that drive them, the carnal look at us, and we watch the heretic rending his flesh, and the glutton lashed by the rain. We break the withered branches from the tree in the grove of the Harpies, and each dull-hued poisonous twig bleeds with red blood before us, and cries aloud with bitter cries. Out of a horn of fire Odysseus speaks to us, and when from his sepulchre of flame the great Ghibelline rises, the pride that triumphs over the torture of that bed becomes ours for a moment. Through the dim purple air fly those who have stained the world with the beauty of their sin, and in the pit of loathsome disease, dropsy-stricken and swollen of body into the semblance of a monstrous lute, lies Adamo di Brescia, the coiner of false coin. He bids us listen to his misery; we stop, and with dry and gaping lips he tells us how he dreams day and night of the brooks of clear water that in cool dewy channels gush down the green Casentine hills. Sinon, the false Greek of Troy, mocks at him. He smites him in the face, and they wrangle. We are fascinated by their shame, and loiter, till Virgil chides us and leads us away to that city turreted by giants where great Nimrod blows his horn. Terrible things are in store for us, and we go to meet them in Dante's raiment and with Dante's heart. We traverse the marshes of the Styx, and Argenti swims to the boat through the slimy waves. He calls to us, and we reject him. When we hear the voice of his agony we are glad, and Virgil praises us for the bitterness of our scorn. We tread upon the cold crystal of Cocytus, in which traitors stick like straws in glass. Our foot strikes against the head of Bocca. He will not tell us his name, and we tear the hair in handfuls from the screaming skull. Alberigo prays us to break the ice upon his face that he may weep a little. We pledge our word to him, and when he has uttered his dolorous tale we deny the word that we have spoken, and pass from him; such cruelty being courtesy indeed, for who more base than he who has mercy for the condemned of God? In the jaws of Lucifer we see the man who sold Christ, and in the jaws of Lucifer the men who slew Cæsar. We tremble, and come forth to rebehold the stars.

In the land of Purgation the air is freer, and the holy mountain rises into the pure light of day. There is peace for us, and for those who for a season abide in it there is some peace also, though, pale from the poison of the Maremma, Madonna Pia passes before us, and Ismene, with the sorrow of earth still lingering about her, is there. Soul after soul makes us share in some repentance or some joy. He whom the mourning of his widow taught to drink the sweet wormwood of pain, tells us of Nella praying in her lonely bed, and we learn from the mouth of Buonconte how a single tear may save a dying sinner from the fiend. Sordello, that noble and disdainful Lombard, eyes us from afar like a couchant lion. When he learns that Virgil is one of Mantua's citizens, he falls upon his neck, and when he learns that he is the singer of Rome he falls before his feet. In that valley whose grass and flowers are fairer than cleft emerald and Indian wood, and brighter than scarlet and silver, they are singing who in the world were kings; but the lips of Rudolph of Hapsburg do not move to the music of the others, and Philip of France beats his breast and Henry of England sits alone. On and on we go, climbing the marvellous stair, and the stars become larger than their wont, and the song of the kings grows faint, and at length we reach the seven trees of gold and the garden of the Earthly Paradise. In a griffin-drawn chariot appears one whose brows are bound with olive, who is veiled in white, and mantled in green, and robed in a vesture that is coloured like live fire. The ancient flame wakes within us. Our blood quickens through terrible pulses. We recognize her. It is Beatrice, the woman we have worshipped. The ice congealed about our heart melts. Wild tears of anguish break from us, and we bow our forehead to the ground, for we know that we have sinned. When we have done penance, and are purified, and have drunk of the fountain of Lethe and bathed in the fountain of Eunoe, the mistress of our soul raises us to the Paradise of Heaven. Out of that eternal pearl, the moon, the face of Piccarda Donati leans to us. Her beauty troubles us for a moment, and when, like a thing that falls through water, she passes away, we gaze after her with wistful eyes. The sweet planet of Venus is full of lovers. Cunizza, the sister of Ezzelin, the lady of Sordello's heart, is there, and Folco, the passionate singer of Provence, who in sorrow for Azalais forsook the world, and the Canaanitish harlot whose soul was the first that Christ redeemed. Joachim of Flora stands in the sun, and, in the sun, Aquinas recounts the story of St Francis and Bonaventure the story of St Dominic. Through the burning rubies of Mars, Cacciaguida approaches. He tells us of the arrow that is shot from the bow of exile, and how salt tastes the bread of another, and how steep are the stairs in the house of a stranger. In Saturn the souls sing not, and even she who guides us dare not smile. On a ladder of gold the flames rise and fall. At last, we see the pageant of the Mystical Rose. Beatrice fixes her eyes upon the face of God to turn them not again. The beatific vision is granted to us; we know the Love that moves the sun and all the stars.

Yes, we can put the earth back six hundred courses and make ourselves one with the great Florentine,° kneel at the same altar with him, and share his rapture and his scorn. And if we grow tired of an antique time, and desire to realize our own age in all its weariness and sin, are there not books that can make us live more in one single hour than life can make us live in a score of shameful years? Close to your hand lies a little volume, bound in some Nile-green skin that has been powdered with gilded nenuphars and smoothed with hard ivory. It is the book that Gautier loved, it is Baudelaire's masterpiece.° Open it at that sad madrigal that begins

Que m'importe que tu sois sage?
Sois belle! et sois triste!

and you will find yourself worshipping sorrow as you have never worshipped joy. Pass on to the poem on the man who tortures himself, let its subtle music steal into your brain and colour your thoughts, and you will become for a moment what he was who wrote it; nay, not for a moment only, but for many barren moonlit nights and sunless sterile days will a despair that is not your own make its dwelling within you, and the misery of another gnaw your heart away. Read the whole book, suffer it to tell even one of its secrets to your soul, and your soul will grow eager to know more, and will feed upon poisonous honey,° and seek to repent of strange crimes of which it is guiltless, and to make atonement for terrible pleasures that it has never known. And then, when you are tired of these flowers of evil, turn to the flowers that grow in the garden of Perdita,° and in their dew-drenched chalices cool your fevered brow, and let their loveliness heal and restore your soul; or wake from his forgotten tomb the sweet Syrian, Meleager,° and bid the lover of Heliodore make you music, for he too has flowers in his song, red pomegranate-blossoms, and irises that smell of myrrh, ringed daffodils and dark-blue hyacinths, and marjoram and crinkled ox-eyes. Dear to him was the perfume of the bean-field at evening, and dear to him the odorous eared-spikenard that grew on the Syrian hills, and the fresh green thyme, the wine-cup's charm. The feet of his love as she walked in the garden were like lilies set upon lilies. Softer than sleep-laden poppy petals were her lips, softer than violets and as scented. The flame-like crocus sprang from the grass to look at her. For her the slim narcissus stored the cool rain; and for her the anemones forgot the Sicilian winds that wooed them. And neither crocus, nor anemone, nor narcissus was as fair as she was.

It is a strange thing, this transference of emotion. We sicken with the same maladies as the poets, and the singer lends us his pain. Dead lips have their message for us, and hearts that have fallen to dust can communicate their joy. We run to kiss the bleeding mouth of Fantine,° and we follow Manon Lescaut° over the whole world. Ours is the love-madness of the Tyrian,° and the terror of Orestes° is ours also. There is no passion that we cannot feel, no pleasure that we may not gratify, and we can choose the time of our initiation and the time of our freedom also. Life! Life! Don't let us go to life for our fulfilment or our experience. It is a thing narrowed by circumstances, incoherent in its utterance, and without that fine correspondence of form and spirit which is the only thing that can satisfy the artistic and critical temperament. It makes us pay too high a price for its wares, and we purchase the meanest of its secrets at a cost that is monstrous and infinite.

Ernest. Must we go, then, to Art for everything?

Gilbert. For everything. Because Art does not hurt us. The tears that we shed at a play are a type of the exquisite sterile emotions that it is the function of Art to awaken. We weep, but we are not wounded. We grieve, but our grief is not bitter. In the actual life of man, sorrow, as Spinoza° says somewhere, is a passage to a lesser perfection. But the sorrow with which Art fills us both purifies and initiates, if I may quote once more from the great art-critic of the Greeks.° It is through Art, and through Art only, that we can realize our perfection; through Art, and through Art only, that we can shield ourselves from the sordid perils of actual existence. This results not merely from the fact that nothing that one can imagine is worth doing, and that one can imagine everything, but from the subtle law that emotional forces, like the forces of the physical sphere, are limited in extent and energy. One can feel so much, and no more. And how can it matter with what pleasure life tries to tempt one, or with what pain it seeks to maim and mar one's soul, if in the spectacle of the lives of those who have never existed one has found the true secret of joy, and wept away one's tears over their deaths who, like Cordelia and the daughter of Brabantio,° can never die?

Ernest. Stop a moment. It seems to me that in everything that you have said there is something radically immoral.

Gilbert. All art is immoral.

Ernest. All art?

Gilbert. Yes. For emotion for the sake of emotion is the aim of art, and emotion for the sake of action is the aim of life, and of that practical organization of life that we call society.° Society, which is the beginning and basis of morals, exists simply for the concentration of human energy, and in order to ensure its own continuance and healthy stability it demands, and no doubt rightly demands, of each of its citizens that he should contribute some form of productive labour to the common weal, and toil and travail that the day's work may be done. Society often forgives the criminal; it never forgives the dreamer. The beautiful sterile emotions that art excites in us, are hateful in its eyes, and so completely are people dominated by the tyranny of this dreadful social ideal that they are always coming shamelessly up to one at Private Views and other places that are open to the general public, and saying in a loud stentorian voice, 'What are you doing?' whereas 'What are you thinking?' is the only question that any single civilized being should ever be allowed to whisper to another. They mean well, no doubt, these honest beaming folk. Perhaps that is the reason why they are so excessively tedious. But some one should teach them that while, in the opinion of society, Contemplation is the gravest sin of which any citizen can be guilty, in the opinion of the highest culture it is the proper occupation of man.

Ernest. Contemplation?

Gilbert. Contemplation. I said to you some time ago that it was far more difficult to talk about a thing than to do it. Let me say to you now that to do nothing at all is the most difficult thing in the world, the most difficult and the most intellectual.° To Plato, with his passion for wisdom, this was the noblest form of energy. To Aristotle, with his passion for knowledge, this was the noblest form of energy also.° It was to this that the passion for holiness led the saint and the mystic of mediæval days.

Ernest. We exist, then, to do nothing?

Gilbert. It is to do nothing that the elect exist. Action is limited and relative. Unlimited and absolute is the vision of him who sits at ease and watches, who walks in loneliness and dreams. But we who are born at the close of this wonderful age, are at once too cultured and too critical, too intellectually subtle and too curious of exquisite pleasures, to accept any speculations about life in exchange for life itself. To us the *città divina°* is colourless, and the *fruitio Dei°* without meaning. Metaphysics do not satisfy our temperaments, and religious ecstasy is out of date. The world through which the Academic philosopher° becomes 'the spectator of all time and of all existence' is not really an ideal world, but simply a world of abstract ideas. When we enter it, we starve amidst the chill mathematics of thought. The courts of the city of God are not open to us now. Its gates are guarded by Ignorance, and to pass them we have to surrender all that in our nature is most divine. It is enough that our fathers believed. They have exhausted the faith-faculty of the species. Their legacy to us is the scepticism of which they were afraid. Had they put it into words, it might not live within us as thought. No, Ernest, no. We cannot go back to the saint. There is far more to be learned from the sinner. We cannot go back to the philosopher, and the mystic leads us astray. Who, as Mr Pater suggests somewhere, would exchange the curve of a single rose-leaf for that formless intangible Being which Plato rates so high?° What to us is the Illumination of Philo,° the Abyss of Eckhart,° the Vision of Böhme,° the monstrous Heaven itself that was revealed to Swedenborg's° blinded eyes? Such things are less than the yellow trumpet of one daffodil of the field, far less than the meanest of the visible arts; for, just as Nature is matter struggling into mind, so Art is mind expressing itself under the conditions of matter, and thus, even in the lowliest of her manifestations, she speaks to both sense and soul alike. To the æsthetic temperament the vague is always repellent. The Greeks were a nation of artists, because they were spared the sense of the infinite. Like Aristotle, like Goethe after he had read Kant,° we desire the concrete, and nothing but the concrete can satisfy us.

Ernest. What then do you propose?

Gilbert. It seems to me that with the development of the critical spirit we shall be able to realize, not merely our own lives, but the collective life of the race, and so to make ourselves absolutely modern, in the true meaning of the word modernity. For he to whom the present is the only thing that is present, knows nothing of the age in which he lives. To realize the nineteenth century, one must realize every century that has preceded it and that has contributed to its making. To know anything about oneself, one must know all about others. There must be no mood with which one cannot sympathize, no dead mode of life that one cannot make alive.° Is this impossible? I think not. By revealing to us the absolute mechanism of all action, and so freeing us from the self-imposed and trammelling burden of moral responsibility, the scientific principle of Heredity has become, as it were, the warrant for the contemplative life. It has shown us that we are never less free than when we try to act. It has hemmed us round with the nets of the hunter, and written upon the wall the prophecy of our doom.° We may not watch it, for it is within us. We may not see it, save in a mirror that mirrors the soul. It is Nemesis° without her mask. It is the last of the Fates,° and the most terrible. It is the only one of the Gods whose real name we know.

And yet, while in the sphere of practical and external life it has robbed energy of its freedom and activity of its choice, in the subjective sphere, where the soul is at work, it comes to us, this terrible shadow, with many gifts in its hands, gifts of strange temperaments and subtle suscepti-bilities, gifts of wild ardours and chill moods of indifference, complex multiform gifts of thoughts that are at variance with each other, and passions that war against themselves. And so, it is not our own life that we live, but the lives of the dead,° and the soul that dwells within us is no single spiritual entity, making us personal and individual, created for our service, and entering into us for our joy. It is something that has dwelt in fearful places, and in ancient sepulchres has made its abode. It is sick with many maladies, and has memories of curious sins. It is wiser than we are, and its wisdom is bitter. It fills us with impossible desires, and makes us follow what we know we cannot gain. One thing, however, Ernest, it can do for us. It can lead us away from surroundings whose beauty is dimmed to us by the mist of familiarity, or whose ignoble ugliness and sordid claims are marring the perfection of our development. It can help us to leave the age in which we were born, and to pass into other ages, and find ourselves not exiled from their air. It can teach us how to escape from our experience, and to realize the experiences of those who are greater than we are. The pain of Leopardi° crying out against life becomes our pain. Theocritus° blows on his pipe, and we laugh with the lips of nymph and shepherd. In the wolfskin of Pierre Vidal° we flee before the hounds, and in the armour of Lancelot° we ride from the bower of the Queen. We have whispered the secret of our love beneath the cowl of Abelard,° and in the stained raiment of Villon have put our shame into song. We can see the dawn through Shelley's eyes, and when we wander with Endymion° the Moon grows amorous of our youth. Ours is the anguish of Atys,° and ours the weak rage and noble sorrows of the Dane.° Do you think that it is the imagination that enables us to live these countless lives? Yes: it is the imagination; and the imagination is the result of heredity. It is simply concentrated race-experience.

Ernest. But where in this is the function of the critical spirit?

Gilbert. The culture that this transmission of racial experiences makes possible can be made perfect by the critical spirit alone, and indeed may be said to be one with it. For who is the true critic but he who bears within himself the dreams, and ideas, and feelings of myriad generations, and to whom no form of thought is alien, no emotional impulse obscure? And who the true man of culture, if not he who by fine scholarship and fastidious rejection has made instinct self-conscious and intelligent, and can separate the work that has distinction from the work that has it not, and so by contact and comparison makes himself master of the secrets of style and school, and understands their meanings, and listens to their voices, and develops that spirit of disinterested curiosity which is the real root, as it is the real flower, of the intellectual life, and thus attains to intellectual clarity, and, having learned 'the best that is known and thought in the world',° lives—it is not fanciful to say so—with those who are the Immortals.

Yes, Ernest: the contemplative life, the life that has for its aim not *doing* but *being,*° and not *being* merely, but *becoming*—that is what the critical spirit can give us. The gods live thus: either brooding over their own perfection, as Aristotle tells us, or, as Epicurus fancied, watching with the calm eyes of the spectator the tragi-comedy of the world that they have made. We, too, might live like them, and set ourselves to witness with appropriate emotions the varied scenes that man and nature afford. We might make ourselves spiritual by detaching ourselves from action, and become perfect by the rejection of energy. It has often seemed to me that Browning felt something of this. Shakespeare hurls Hamlet into active life, and makes him realize his mission by effort. Browning might have given us a Hamlet who would have realized his mission by thought. Incident and event were to him unreal or unmeaning. He made the soul the protagonist of life's tragedy, and looked on action as the one undramatic element of a play. To us, at any rate, the ΒΙΟΣ ΘΕΩΡΗΤΙΚΟΣ° is the true ideal. From the high tower of Thought we can look out at the world. Calm, and self-centred,° and complete, the æsthetic critic contemplates life, and no arrow drawn at a venture can pierce between the joints of his harness.° He at least is safe. He has discovered how to live.

Is such a mode of life immoral? Yes: all the arts are immoral, except those baser forms of sensual or didactic art that seek to excite to action of evil or of good. For action of every kind belongs to the sphere of ethics. The aim of art is simply to create a mood.° Is such a mode of life unpractical? Ah! it is not so easy to be unpractical as the ignorant Philistine imagines. It were well for England if it were so. There is no country in the world so much in need of unpractical people as this country of ours. With us, Thought is degraded by its constant association with practice. Who that moves in the stress and turmoil of actual existence, noisy politician, or brawling social reformer, or poor narrow-minded priest blinded by the sufferings of that unimportant section of the community among whom he has cast his lot, can seriously claim to be able to form a disinterested° intellectual judgment about any one thing? Each of the professions means a prejudice. The necessity for a career forces every one to take sides. We live in the age of the overworked, and the under-educated; the age in which people are so industrious that they become absolutely stupid. And, harsh though it may sound, I cannot help saying that such people deserve their doom. The sure way of knowing nothing about life is to try to make oneself useful.°

Ernest. A charming doctrine, Gilbert.

Gilbert. I am not sure about that, but it has at least the minor merit of being true. That the desire to do good to others produces a plentiful crop of prigs is the least of the evils of which it is the cause. The prig is a very interesting psychological study, and though of all poses a moral pose is the most offensive, still to have a pose at all is something. It is a formal recognition of the importance of treating life from a definite and reasoned standpoint. That Humanitarian Sympathy wars against Nature, by securing the survival of the failure,° may make the man of science loathe its facile virtues. The political economist may cry out against it for putting the improvident on the same level as the provident, and so robbing life of the strongest, because most sordid, incentive to industry. But, in the eyes of the thinker, the real harm that emotional sympathy does is that it limits knowledge, and so prevents us from solving any single social problem. We are trying at present to stave off the coming crisis, the coming revolution as my friends the Fabianists° call it, by means of doles and alms. Well, when the revolution or crisis arrives, we shall be powerless because we shall know nothing. And so, Ernest, let us not be deceived. England will never be civilized till she has added Utopia° to her dominions. There is more than one of her colonies that she might with advantage surrender for so fair a land. What we want are unpractical people who see beyond the moment, and think beyond the day. Those who try to lead the people can only do so by following the mob. It is through the voice of one crying in the wilderness° that the ways of the gods must be prepared.

But perhaps you think that in beholding for the mere joy of beholding, and contemplating for the sake of contemplation, there is something that is egotistic. If you think so, do not say so. It takes a thoroughly selfish age, like our own, to deify self-sacrifice. It takes a thoroughly grasping age, such as that in which we live, to set above the fine intellectual virtues, those shallow and emotional virtues that are an immediate practical benefit to itself. They miss their aim, too, these philanthropists and sentimentalists of our day, who are always chattering to one about one's duty to one's neighbour. For the development of the race depends on the development of the individual, and where self-culture has ceased to be the ideal, the intellectual standard is instantly lowered, and, often, ultimately lost. If you meet at dinner a man who has spent his life in educating himself—a rare type in our time, I admit, but still one occasionally to be met with—you rise from table richer, and conscious that a high ideal has for a moment touched and sanctified your days. But oh! my dear Ernest, to sit next a man who has spent his life in trying to educate others!° What a dreadful experience that is! How appalling is that ignorance which is the inevitable result of the fatal habit of imparting opinions! How limited in range the creature's mind proves to be! How it wearies us, and must weary himself, with its endless repetitions and sickly reiteration! How lacking it is in any element of intellectual growth! In what a vicious circle it always moves!

Ernest. You speak with strange feeling, Gilbert. Have you had this dreadful experience, as you call it, lately?

Gilbert. Few of us escape it. People say that the schoolmaster is abroad.° I wish to goodness he were. But the type of which, after all, he is only one, and certainly the least important, of the representatives, seems to me to be really dominating our lives; and just as the philanthropist is the nuisance of the ethical sphere, so the nuisance of the intellectual sphere is the man who is so occupied in trying to educate others, that he has never had any time to educate himself. No, Ernest, self-culture is the true ideal of man. Goethe saw it,° and the immediate debt that we owe to Goethe is greater than the debt we owe to any man since Greek days. The Greeks saw it, and have left us, as their legacy to modern thought, the conception of the contemplative life as well as the critical method by which alone can that life be truly realized. It was the one thing that made the Renaissance great, and gave us Humanism. It is the one thing that could make our own age great also; for the real weakness of England lies, not in incomplete armaments or unfortified coasts, not in the poverty that creeps through sunless lanes, or the drunkenness that brawls in loath-some courts, but simply in the fact that her ideals are emotional and not intellectual.

I do not deny that the intellectual ideal is difficult of attainment, still less that it is, and perhaps will be for years to come, unpopular with the crowd. It is so easy for people to have sympathy with suffering. It is so difficult for them to have sympathy with thought. Indeed, so little do ordinary people understand what thought really is, that they seem to imagine that, when they have said that a theory is dangerous, they have pronounced its condemnation, whereas it is only such theories that have any true intellectual value. An idea that is not dangerous is unworthy of being called an idea at all.°

Ernest. Gilbert, you bewilder me. You have told me that all art is, in its essence, immoral. Are you going to tell me now that all thought is, in its essence, dangerous?

Gilbert. Yes, in the practical sphere it is so. The security of society lies in custom and unconscious instinct, and the basis of the stability of society, as a healthy organism, is the complete absence of any intelligence amongst its members. The great majority of people being fully aware of this, rank themselves naturally on the side of that splendid system that elevates them to the dignity of machines, and rage so wildly against the intrusion of the intellectual faculty into any question that concerns life, that one is tempted to define man as a rational animal° who always loses his temper when he is called upon to act in accordance with the dictates of reason. But let us turn from the practical sphere, and say no more about the wicked philanthropists, who, indeed, may well be left to the mercy of the almond-eyed sage of the Yellow River, Chuang Tsŭ° the wise, who has proved that such well-meaning and offensive busybodies have destroyed the simple and spontaneous virtue that there is in man. They are a wearisome topic, and I am anxious to get back to the sphere in which criticism is free.

Ernest. The sphere of the intellect?

Gilbert. Yes. You remember that I spoke of the critic as being in his own way as creative as the artist, whose work, indeed, may be merely of value in so far as it gives to the critic a suggestion for some new mood of thought and feeling which he can realize with equal, or perhaps greater, distinction of form, and, through the use of a fresh medium of expression, make differently beautiful and more perfect. Well, you seemed to me to be a little sceptical about the theory. But perhaps I wronged you?

Ernest. I am not really sceptical about it, but I must admit that I feel very strongly that such work as you describe the critic producing—and creative such work must undoubtedly be admitted to be—is, of necessity, purely subjective, whereas the greatest work is objective always, objective and impersonal.

Gilbert. The difference between objective and subjective work is one of external form merely.° It is accidental, not essential. All artistic creation is absolutely subjective. The very landscape that Corot looked at was, as he said himself, but a mood of his own mind;° and those great figures of Greek or English drama that seem to us to possess an actual existence of their own, apart from the poets who shaped and fashioned them, are, in their ultimate analysis, simply the poets themselves, not as they thought they were, but as they thought they were not; and by such thinking came in strange manner, though but for a moment, really so to be. For out of ourselves we can never pass, nor can there be in creation what in the creator was not. Nay, I would say that the more objective a creation appears to be, the more subjective it really is. Shakespeare might have met Rosencrantz and Guildenstern in the white streets of London, or seen the serving-men of rival houses bite their thumbs at each other in the open square; but Hamlet came out of his soul, and Romeo out of his passion. They were elements of his nature to which he gave visible form, impulses that stirred so strongly within him that he had, as it were perforce, to suffer them to realize their energy, not on the lower plane of actual life, where they would have been trammelled and constrained and so made imperfect, but on that imaginative plane of art where Love can indeed find in Death its rich fulfilment, where one can stab the eavesdropper behind the arras, and wrestle in a new-made grave, and make a guilty king drink his own hurt, and see one's father's spirit, beneath the glimpses of the moon, stalking in complete steel from misty wall to wall. Action being limited would have left Shakespeare unsatisfied and unexpressed; and, just as it is because he did nothing that he has been able to achieve everything, so it is because he never speaks to us of himself in his plays that his plays reveal him to us absolutely, and show us his true nature and temperament far more completely than do those strange and exquisite sonnets, even, in which he bares to crystal eyes the secret closet of his heart. Yes, the objective form is the most subjective in matter. Man is least himself when he talks in his own person. Give him a mask, and he will tell you the truth.

Ernest. The critic, then, being limited to the subjective form, will necessarily be less able to fully express himself than the artist, who has always at his disposal the forms that are impersonal and objective.

Gilbert. Not necessarily, and certainly not at all if he recognizes that each mode of criticism is, in its highest development, simply a mood, and that we are never more true to ourselves than when we are inconsistent. The æsthetic critic, constant only to the principle of beauty in all things, will ever be looking for fresh impressions,° winning from the various schools the secret of their charm, bowing, it may be, before foreign altars, or smiling, if it be his fancy, at strange new gods. What other people call one's past has, no doubt, everything to do with them, but has absolutely nothing to do with oneself. The man who regards his past is a man who deserves to have no future to look forward to. When one has found expression for a mood, one has done with it. You laugh; but believe me it is so. Yesterday it was Realism that charmed one. One gained from it that *nouveau frisson*° which it was its aim to produce. One analysed it, explained it, and wearied of it. At sunset came the *Luministe*° in painting, and the *Symboliste* in poetry,° and the spirit of mediævalism, that spirit which belongs not to time but to temperament, woke suddenly in wounded Russia,° and stirred us for a moment by the terrible fascination of pain. Today the cry is for Romance, and already the leaves are tremulous in the valley, and on the purple hill-tops walks Beauty with slim gilded feet. The old modes of creation linger, of course. The artists reproduce either themselves or each other, with wearisome iteration. But Criticism is always moving on, and the critic is always developing.

Nor, again, is the critic really limited to the subjective form of expression. The method of the drama is his, as well as the method of the epos. He may use dialogue, as he did who set Milton talking to Marvel on the nature of comedy and tragedy, and made Sidney and Lord Brooke discourse on letters beneath the Penshurst oaks;° or adopt narration, as Mr Pater is fond of doing, each of whose Imaginary Portraits°—is not that the title of the book?—presents to us, under the fanciful guise of fiction, some fine and exquisite piece of criticism, one on the painter

Watteau, another on the philosophy of Spinoza, a third on the Pagan elements of the early Renaissance, and the last, and in some respects the most suggestive, on the source of that Aufklärung, that enlightening which dawned on Germany in the last century, and to which our own culture owes so great a debt. Dialogue, certainly, that wonderful literary form which, from Plato to Lucian,° and from Lucian to Giordano Bruno,° and from Bruno to that grand old Pagan° in whom Carlyle took such delight, the creative critics of the world have always employed, can never lose for the thinker its attraction as a mode of expression. By its means he can both reveal and conceal himself, and give form to every fancy, and reality to every mood. By its means he can exhibit the object from each point of view, and show it to us in the round, as a sculptor shows us things, gaining in this manner all the richness and reality of effect that comes from those side issues that are suddenly suggested by the central idea in its progress, and really illumine the idea more completely, or from those felicitous after-thoughts that give a fuller completeness to the central scheme, and yet convey something of the delicate charm of chance.

Ernest. By its means, too, he can invent an imaginary antagonist, and convert him when he chooses by some absurdly sophistical argument.

Gilbert. Ah! it is so easy to convert others. It is so difficult to convert oneself. To arrive at what one really believes, one must speak through lips different from one's own. To know the truth one must imagine myriads of falsehoods. For what is Truth? In matters of religion, it is simply the opinion that has survived. In matters of science, it is the ultimate sensation. In matters of art, it is one's last mood. And you see now, Ernest, that the critic has at his disposal as many objective forms of expression as the artist has. Ruskin put his criticism into imaginative prose, and is superb in his changes and contradictions; and Browning put his into blank verse, and made painter and poet° yield us their secret; and M. Renan° uses dialogue, and Mr Pater fiction, and Rossetti translated into sonnet-music the colour of Giorgione and the design of Ingres, and his own design and colour also,° feeling, with the instinct of one who had many modes of utterance, that the ultimate art is literature, and the finest and fullest medium that of words.

Ernest. Well, now that you have settled that the critic has at his disposal all objective forms, I wish you would tell me what are the qualities that should characterize the true critic.

Gilbert. What would you say they were?

Ernest. Well, I should say that a critic should above all things be fair.

Gilbert. Ah! not fair. A critic cannot be fair in the ordinary sense of the word. It is only about things that do not interest one that one can give a really unbiased opinion, which is no doubt the reason why an unbiased opinion is always absolutely valueless. The man who sees both sides of a question, is a man who sees absolutely nothing at all. Art is a passion, and, in matters of art, Thought is inevitably coloured by emotion, and so is fluid rather than fixed, and, depending upon fine moods and exquisite moments, cannot be narrowed into the rigidity of a scientific formula or a theological dogma. It is to the soul that Art speaks, and the soul may be made the prisoner of the mind as well as of the body. One should, of course, have no prejudices; but, as a great Frenchman remarked a hundred years ago, it is one's business in such matters to have prefer-ences, and when one has preferences one ceases to be fair. It is only an auctioneer who can equally and impartially admire all schools of Art.° No: fairness is not one of the qualities of the true critic. It is not even a condition of criticism. Each form of Art with which we come in contact dominates us for the moment to the exclusion of every other form. We must surrender ourselves absolutely to the work in question, whatever it may be, if we wish to gain its secret. For the time, we must think of nothing else, can think of nothing else, indeed.

    Ernest. The true critic will be rational, at any rate, will he not?

    Gilbert. Rational? There are two ways of disliking art, Ernest. One is to dislike it. The other, to like it rationally. For Art, as Plato saw,° and not without regret, creates in listener and spectator a form of divine madness. It does not spring from inspiration, but it makes others inspired. Reason is not the faculty to which it appeals. If one loves Art at all, one must love it beyond all other things in the world, and against such love, the reason, if one listened to it, would cry out. There is nothing sane about the worship of beauty. It is too splendid to be sane. Those of whose lives it forms the dominant note will always seem to the world to be pure visionaries.

    Ernest. Well, at least, the critic will be sincere.

    Gilbert. A little sincerity is a dangerous thing,° and a great deal of it is absolutely fatal. The true critic will, indeed, always be sincere in his devotion to the principle of beauty, but he will seek for beauty in every age and in each school, and will never suffer himself to be limited to any settled custom of thought, or stereotyped mode of looking at things.° He will realize himself in many forms, and by a thousand different ways, and will ever be curious of new sensations and fresh points of view. Through constant change, and through constant change alone, he will find his true unity. He will not consent to be the slave of his own opinions.° For what is mind but motion in the intellectual sphere? The essence of thought, as the essence of life, is growth. You must not be frightened by words, Ernest. What people call insincerity is simply a method by which we can multiply our personalities.

Ernest. I am afraid I have not been fortunate in my suggestions.

Gilbert. Of the three qualifications you mentioned, two, sincerity and fairness, were, if not actually moral,° at least on the border-land of morals, and the first condition of criticism is that the critic should be able to recognize that the sphere of Art and the sphere of Ethics are absolutely distinct and separate. When they are confused, Chaos has come again.° They are too often confused in England now, and though our modern Puritans cannot destroy a beautiful thing, yet, by means of their extraordinary prurience, they can almost taint beauty for a moment. It is chiefly, I regret to say, through journalism that such people find expression. I regret it because there is much to be said in favour of modern journalism. By giving us the opinions of the uneducated, it keeps us in touch with the ignorance of the community. By carefully chronicling the current events of contemporary life, it shows us of what very little importance such events really are. By invariably discussing the unnecessary, it makes us understand what things are requisite for culture, and what are not. But it should not allow poor Tartuffe° to write articles upon modern art. When it does this it stultifies itself. And yet Tartuffe's articles, and Chadband's° notes do this good, at least. They serve to show how extremely limited is the area over which ethics, and ethical considerations, can claim to exercise influence. Science is out of the reach of morals, for her eyes are fixed upon eternal truths. Art is out of the reach of morals, for her eyes are fixed upon things beautiful and immortal and ever-changing. To morals belong the lower and less intellectual spheres. However, let these mouthing Puritans pass; they have their comic side. Who can help laughing when an ordinary journalist seriously proposes to limit the subject-matter at the disposal of the artist? Some limitation might well, and will soon, I hope, be placed upon some of our newspapers and newspaper writers. For they give us the bald, sordid, disgusting facts of life. They chronicle, with degrading avidity, the sins of the second-rate, and with the conscientiousness of the illiterate give us accurate and prosaic details of the doings of people of absolutely no interest whatsoever. But the artist, who accepts the facts of life, and yet transforms them into shapes of beauty, and makes them vehicles of pity or of awe, and shows their colour-element, and their wonder, and their true ethical import also, and builds out of them a world more real than reality itself, and of loftier and more noble import—who shall set limits to him? Not the apostles of that new Journalism which is

but the old vulgarity 'writ large'.° Not the apostles of that new Puritanism, which is but the whine of the hypocrite, and is both writ and spoken
badly. The mere suggestion is ridiculous. Let us leave these wicked
people, and proceed to the discussion of the artistic qualifications
necessary for the true critic.

Ernest. And what are they? Tell me yourself.

Gilbert. Temperament° is the primary requisite for the critic—a
temperament exquisitely susceptible to beauty, and to the various
impressions that beauty gives us. Under what conditions, and by what
means, this temperament is engendered in race or individual, we will not
discuss at present. It is sufficient to note that it exists, and that there is in
us a beauty-sense, separate from the other senses and above them,
separate from the reason and of nobler import, separate from the soul
and of equal value—a sense that leads some to create, and others, the
finer spirits as I think, to contemplate merely. But to be purified and
made perfect, this sense requires some form of exquisite environment.
Without this it starves, or is dulled. You remember that lovely passage° in
which Plato describes how a young Greek should be educated, and with
what insistence he dwells upon the importance of surroundings, telling
us how the lad is to be brought up in the midst of fair sights and sounds,
so that the beauty of material things may prepare his soul for the
reception of the beauty that is spiritual. Insensibly, and without knowing
the reason why, he is to develop that real love of beauty which, as Plato is
never weary of reminding us, is the true aim of education. By slow
degrees there is to be engendered in him such a temperament as will lead
him naturally and simply to choose the good in preference to the bad,
and, rejecting what is vulgar and discordant, to follow by fine instinctive
taste all that possesses grace and charm and loveliness. Ultimately, in its
due course, this taste is to become critical and self-conscious, but at first
it is to exist purely as a cultivated instinct, and 'he who has received this
true culture of the inner man will with clear and certain vision perceive
the omissions and faults in art or nature,° and with a taste that cannot err,
while he praises, and finds his pleasure in what is good, and receives it
into his soul, and so becomes good and noble, he will rightly blame and
hate the bad, now in the days of his youth, even before he is able to know
the reason why': and so, when, later on, the critical and self-conscious
spirit develops in him, he 'will recognize and salute it as a friend with
whom his education has made him long familiar'. I need hardly say,
Ernest, how far we in England have fallen short of this ideal, and I can
imagine the smile that would illuminate the glossy face of the Philistine if
one ventured to suggest to him that the true aim of education was the love

of beauty, and that the methods by which education should work were the development of temperament, the cultivation of taste, and the creation of the critical spirit.

Yet, even for us, there is left some loveliness of environment, and the dulness of tutors and professors matters very little when one can loiter in the grey cloisters at Magdalen, and listen to some flute-like voice singing in Waynfleete's chapel, or lie in the green meadow, among the strange snake-spotted fritillaries, and watch the sunburnt noon smite to a finer gold the tower's gilded vanes, or wander up the Christ Church staircase beneath the vaulted ceiling's shadowy fans, or pass through the sculptured gateway of Laud's building in the College of St John.° Nor is it merely at Oxford, or Cambridge, that the sense of beauty can be formed and trained and perfected. All over England there is a Renaissance of the decorative Arts. Ugliness has had its day. Even in the houses of the rich there is taste, and the houses of those who are not rich have been made gracious and comely and sweet to live in. Caliban,° poor noisy Caliban, thinks that when he has ceased to make mows at a thing, the thing ceases to exist. But if he mocks no longer, it is because he has been met with mockery, swifter and keener than his own, and for a moment has been bitterly schooled into that silence which should seal for ever his uncouth distorted lips. What has been done up to now, has been chiefly in the clearing of the way. It is always more difficult to destroy than it is to create, and when what one has to destroy is vulgarity and stupidity, the task of destruction needs not merely courage but also contempt. Yet it seems to me to have been, in a measure, done. We have got rid of what was bad. We have now to make what is beautiful. And though the mission of the æsthetic movement is to lure people to contemplate, not to lead them to create, yet, as the creative instinct is strong in the Celt,° and it is the Celt who leads in art, there is no reason why in future years this strange Renaissance should not become almost as mighty in its way as was that new birth of Art that woke many centuries ago in the cities of Italy.

Certainly, for the cultivation of temperament, we must turn to the decorative arts: to the arts that touch us, not to the arts that teach us. Modern pictures are, no doubt, delightful to look at. At least, some of them are. But they are quite impossible to live with; they are too clever, too assertive, too intellectual. Their meaning is too obvious, and their method too clearly defined. One exhausts what they have to say in a very short time, and then they become as tedious as one's relations. I am very fond of the work of many of the Impressionist painters° of Paris and London. Subtlety and distinction have not yet left the school. Some of their arrangements and harmonies serve to remind one of the unapproachable beauty of Gautier's immortal *Symphonie en Blanc Majeur*,° that flawless masterpiece of colour and music which may have suggested the type as well as the titles of many of their best pictures. For a class that welcomes the incompetent with sympathetic eagerness, and that confuses the bizarre with the beautiful, and vulgarity with truth, they are extremely accomplished. They can do etchings that have the brilliancy of epigrams, pastels that are as fascinating as paradoxes, and as for their portraits, whatever the commonplace may say against them, no one can deny that they possess that unique and wonderful charm which belongs to works of pure fiction. But even the Impressionists, earnest and industrious as they are, will not do. I like them. Their white keynote, with its variations in lilac, was an era in colour. Though the moment does not make the man, the moment certainly makes the Impressionist, and for the moment in art, and the 'moment's monument' as Rossetti phrased it,° what may not be said? They are suggestive also. If they have not opened the eyes of the blind, they have at least given great encouragement to the short-sighted, and while their leaders may have all the inexperience of old age, their young men are far too wise to be ever sensible. Yet they will insist on treating painting as if it were a mode of autobiography invented for the use of the illiterate, and are always prating to us on their coarse gritty canvases of their unnecessary selves and their unnecessary opinions, and spoiling by a vulgar over-emphasis that fine contempt of nature which is the best and only modest thing about them. One tires, at the end, of the work of individuals whose individuality is always noisy, and generally uninteresting. There is far more to be said in favour of that newer school at Paris, the *Archaicistes*,° as they call themselves, who, refusing to leave the artist entirely at the mercy of the weather, do not find the ideal of art in mere atmospheric effect, but seek rather for the imaginative beauty of design and the loveliness of fair colour, and rejecting the tedious realism of those who merely paint what they see, try to see something worth seeing, and to see it not merely with actual and physical vision, but with that nobler vision of the soul which is as far wider in spiritual scope as it is far more splendid in artistic purpose. They, at any rate, work under those decorative conditions that each art requires for its perfection, and have sufficient æsthetic instinct to regret those sordid and stupid limitations of absolute modernity of form which have proved the ruin of so many of the Impressionists. Still, the art that is frankly decorative is the art to live with. It is, of all our visible arts, the one art that creates in us both mood and temperament. Mere colour, unspoiled by meaning, and unallied with definite form, can speak to the soul in a thousand different ways. The harmony that resides in the delicate proportions of lines and masses becomes mirrored in the mind. The repetitions of pattern give us rest. The marvels of design stir the imagination. In the mere loveliness of the materials employed there are latent elements of culture. Nor is this all. By its deliberate rejection of Nature as the ideal of beauty, as well as of the imitative method of the ordinary painter, decorative art not merely prepares the soul for the reception of true imaginative work, but develops in it that sense of form which is the basis of creative no less than of critical achievement. For the real artist is he who proceeds, not from feeling to form, but from form to thought and passion.° He does not first conceive an idea, and then say to himself, 'I will put my idea into a complex metre of fourteen lines', but, realizing the beauty of the sonnet-scheme, he conceives certain modes of music and methods of rhyme, and the mere form suggests what is to fill it and make it intellectually and emotionally complete. From time to time the world cries out against some charming artistic poet, because, to use its hackneyed and silly phrase, he has 'nothing to say'. But if he had something to say, he would probably say it, and the result would be tedious. It is just because he has no new message, that he can do beautiful work. He gains his inspiration from form, and from form purely, as an artist should. A real passion would ruin him. Whatever actually occurs is spoiled for art. All bad poetry springs from genuine feeling. To be natural is to be obvious, and to be obvious is to be inartistic.

Ernest. I wonder do you really believe what you say.

Gilbert. Why should you wonder? It is not merely in art that the body is the soul. In every sphere of life Form is the beginning of things. The rhythmic harmonious gestures of dancing convey, Plato tells us, both rhythm and harmony into the mind.° Forms are the food of faith, cried Newman in one of those great moments of sincerity that made us admire and know the man. He was right, though he may not have known how terribly right he was. The Creeds are believed, not because they are rational, but because they are repeated. Yes: Form is everything. It is the secret of life. Find expression for a sorrow, and it will become dear to you. Find expression for a joy, and you intensify its ecstasy. Do you wish to love? Use Love's Litany, and the words will create the yearning from which the world fancies that they spring. Have you a grief that corrodes your heart? Steep yourself in the language of grief, learn its utterance from Prince Hamlet and Queen Constance,° and you will find that mere expression is a mode of consolation, and that Form, which is the birth of passion, is also the death of pain. And so, to return to the sphere of Art, it is Form that creates not merely the critical temperament, but also the æsthetic instinct, that unerring instinct that reveals to one all things under their conditions of beauty. Start with the worship of form, and there is no secret in art that will not be revealed to you,° and remember that in criticism, as in creation, temperament is everything, and that it is, not by the time of their production, but by the temperaments to which they appeal, that the schools of art should be historically grouped.

Ernest. Your theory of education is delightful. But what influence will your critic, brought up in these exquisite surroundings, possess? Do you really think that any artist is ever affected by criticism?

Gilbert. The influence of the critic will be the mere fact of his own existence. He will represent the flawless type. In him the culture of the century will see itself realized. You must not ask of him to have any aim other than the perfecting of himself. The demand of the intellect, as has been well said, is simply to feel itself alive. The critic may, indeed, desire to exercise influence; but, if so, he will concern himself not with the individual, but with the age, which he will seek to wake into consciousness, and to make responsive, creating in it new desires and appetites, and lending it his larger vision and his nobler moods. The actual art of today will occupy him less than the art of tomorrow, far less than the art of yesterday, and as for this or that person at present toiling away, what do the industrious matter? They do their best, no doubt, and consequently we get the worst from them. It is always with the best intentions that the worst work is done. And besides, my dear Ernest, when a man reaches the age of forty, or becomes a Royal Academician,° or is elected a member of the Athenæum Club, or is recognized as a popular novelist, whose books are in great demand at suburban railway stations, one may have the amusement of exposing him, but one cannot have the pleasure of reforming him. And this is, I dare say, very fortunate for him; for I have no doubt that reformation is a much more painful process than punishment, is indeed punishment in its most aggravated and moral form—a fact which accounts for our entire failure as a community to reclaim that interesting phenomenon who is called the confirmed criminal.

Ernest. But may it not be that the poet is the best judge of poetry, and the painter of painting? Each art must appeal primarily to the artist who works in it. His judgment will surely be the most valuable?

Gilbert. The appeal of all art is simply to the artistic temperament.° Art does not address herself to the specialist. Her claim is that she is universal, and that in all her manifestations she is one. Indeed, so far from its being true that the artist is the best judge of art, a really great artist can never judge of other people's work at all, and can hardly, in fact, judge of his own. That very concentration of vision that makes a man an artist, limits by its sheer intensity his faculty of fine appreciation. The energy of creation hurries him blindly on to his own goal. The wheels of his chariot raise the dust as a cloud around him. The gods are hidden from each other. They can recognize their worshippers. That is all.

Ernest. You say that a great artist cannot recognize the beauty of work different from his own.

Gilbert. It is impossible for him to do so. Wordsworth saw in *Endymion* merely a pretty piece of Paganism, and Shelley, with his dislike of actuality, was deaf to Wordsworth's message, being repelled by its form, and Byron, that great passionate human incomplete creature, could appreciate neither the poet of the cloud nor the poet of the lake,° and the wonder of Keats was hidden from him. The realism of Euripides was hateful to Sophokles.° Those droppings of warm tears had no music for him. Milton, with his sense of the grand style, could not understand the method of Shakespeare, any more than could Sir Joshua° the method of Gainsborough. Bad artists always admire each other's work. They call it being large-minded and free from prejudice. But a truly great artist cannot conceive of life being shown, or beauty fashioned, under any conditions other than those that he has selected. Creation employs all its critical faculty within its own sphere. It may not use it in the sphere that belongs to others. It is exactly because a man cannot do a thing that he is the proper judge of it.°

Ernest. Do you really mean that?

Gilbert. Yes, for creation limits, while contemplation widens, the vision.

Ernest. But what about technique? Surely each art has its separate technique?

Gilbert. Certainly: each art has its grammar and its materials. There is no mystery about either, and the incompetent can always be correct. But, while the laws upon which Art rests may be fixed and certain, to find their true realization they must be touched by the imagination into such beauty that they will seem an exception, each one of them. Technique is really personality. That is the reason why the artist cannot teach it, why the pupil cannot learn it, and why the æsthetic critic can understand it.° To the great poet, there is only one method of music—his own. To the great painter, there is only one manner of painting—that which he himself employs. The æsthetic critic, and the æsthetic critic alone, can appreciate all forms and modes. It is to him that Art makes her appeal.

Ernest. Well, I think I have put all my questions to you. And now I must admit—

Gilbert. Ah! don't say that you agree with me. When people agree with me I always feel that I must be wrong.

Ernest. In that case I certainly won't tell you whether I agree with you or not. But I will put another question. You have explained to me that criticism is a creative art. What future has it?

Gilbert. It is to criticism that the future belongs. The subject-matter at the disposal of creation becomes every day more limited in extent and variety. Providence and Mr Walter Besant° have exhausted the obvious. If creation is to last at all, it can only do so on the condition of becoming far more critical than it is at present. The old roads and dusty highways have been traversed too often. Their charm has been worn away by plodding feet, and they have lost that element of novelty or surprise which is so essential for romance. He who would stir us now by fiction must either give us an entirely new background, or reveal to us the soul of man in its innermost workings. The first is for the moment being done for us by Mr Rudyard Kipling. As one turns over the pages of his *Plain Tales from the Hills*, one feels as if one were seated under a palm-tree reading life by superb flashes of vulgarity.° The bright colours of the bazaars dazzle one's eyes. The jaded, second-rate Anglo-Indians are in exquisite incongruity with their surroundings. The mere lack of style in the story-teller gives an odd journalistic realism to what he tells us. From the point of view of literature Mr Kipling is a genius who drops his aspirates. From the point of view of life, he is a reporter who knows vulgarity better than any one has ever known it. Dickens knew its clothes and its comedy. Mr Kipling knows its essence and its seriousness. He is our first authority on the second-rate, and has seen marvellous things through keyholes, and his backgrounds are real works of art. As for the second condition, we have had Browning, and Meredith is with us. But there is still much to be done in the sphere of introspection. People sometimes say that fiction is getting too morbid. As far as psychology is concerned, it has never been morbid enough. We have merely touched the surface of the soul, that is all. In one single ivory cell of the brain there are stored away things more marvellous and more terrible than even they have dreamed of, who, like the author of *Le Rouge et le Noir*,° have sought to track the soul into its most secret places, and to make life confess its dearest sins. Still, there is a limit even to the number of untried backgrounds, and it is possible that a further development of the habit of introspection may prove fatal to that creative faculty to which it seeks to supply fresh material. I myself am inclined to think that creation is doomed. It springs from too primitive, too natural an impulse.° However this may be, it is certain that the subject-matter at the disposal of creation is always diminishing, while the subject-matter of criticism increases daily. There are always new attitudes for the mind, and new points of view. The duty of imposing form upon chaos does not grow less as the world advances. There was never a time when Criticism was more needed than it is now. It is only by its means that Humanity can become conscious of the point at which it has arrived.

Hours ago, Ernest, you asked me the use of Criticism. You might just as well have asked me the use of thought. It is Criticism, as Arnold points out, that creates the intellectual atmosphere of the age.° It is Criticism, as I hope to point out myself some day, that makes the mind a fine instrument. We, in our educational system, have burdened the memory with a load of unconnected facts, and laboriously striven to impart our laboriously-acquired knowledge. We teach people how to remember, we never teach them how to grow. It has never occurred to us to try and develop in the mind a more subtle quality of apprehension and discernment. The Greeks did this, and when we come in contact with the Greek critical intellect, we cannot but be conscious that, while our subject-matter is in every respect larger and more varied than theirs, theirs is the only method by which this subject-matter can be interpreted. England has done one thing; it has invented and established Public Opinion, which is an attempt to organize the ignorance of the community, and to elevate it to the dignity of physical force. But Wisdom has always been hidden from it. Considered as an instrument of thought, the English mind is coarse and undeveloped. The only thing that can purify it is the growth of the critical instinct.

It is Criticism, again, that, by concentration, makes culture possible. It takes the cumbersome mass of creative work, and distils it into a finer essence. Who that desires to retain any sense of form could struggle through the monstrous multitudinous books that the world has produced, books in which thought stammers or ignorance brawls? The thread that is to guide us across the wearisome labyrinth is in the hands of Criticism. Nay more, where there is no record, and history is either lost or was never written, Criticism can recreate the past for us from the very smallest fragment of language or art, just as surely as the man of science can from some tiny bone, or the mere impress of a foot upon a rock, recreate for us the winged dragon or Titan lizard that once made the earth shake beneath its tread, can call Behemoth out of his cave, and make Leviathan° swim once more across the startled sea. Prehistoric history belongs to the philological and archæological critic. It is to him that the origins of things are revealed. The self-conscious deposits of an age are nearly always misleading. Through philological criticism alone we know more of the centuries of which no actual record has been preserved, than we do of the centuries that have left us their scrolls. It can do for us what can be done neither by physics nor metaphysics. It can give us the exact science of mind in the process of becoming. It can do for us what History cannot do. It can tell us what man thought before he learned how to write. You have asked me about the influence of Criticism. I think I have answered that question already; but there is this also to be said. It is Criticism that makes us cosmopolitan. The Manchester school° tried to make men realize the brotherhood of humanity, by pointing out the commercial advantages of peace. It sought to degrade the wonderful world into a common market-place for the buyer and the seller. It addressed itself to the lowest instincts, and it failed. War followed upon war, and the tradesman's creed did not prevent France and Germany from clashing together in blood-stained battle.° There are others of our own day who seek to appeal to mere emotional sympathies, or to the shallow dogmas of some vague system of abstract ethics. They have their Peace Societies, so dear to the senti-mentalists, and their proposals for unarmed International Arbitration, so popular among those who have never read history. But mere emotional sympathy will not do. It is too variable, and too closely connected with the passions; and a board of arbitrators who, for the general welfare of the race, are to be deprived of the power of putting their decisions into execution, will not be of much avail. There is only one thing worse than Injustice, and that is Justice without her sword in her hand. When Right is not Might, it is Evil.

No: the emotions will not make us cosmopolitan, any more than the greed for gain could do so. It is only by the cultivation of the habit of intellectual criticism that we shall be able to rise superior to race prejudices. Goethe—you will not misunderstand what I say—was a German of the Germans. He loved his country—no man more so. Its people were dear to him; and he led them. Yet, when the iron hoof of Napoleon trampled upon vineyard and cornfield, his lips were silent. 'How can one write songs of hatred without hating?' he said to Ecker-mann,° 'and how could I, to whom culture and barbarism are alone of importance, hate a nation which is among the most cultivated of the earth, and to which I owe so great a part of my own cultivation?' This note, sounded in the modern world by Goethe first, will become, I think, the starting point for the cosmopolitanism of the future. Criticism will annihilate race-prejudices, by insisting upon the unity of the human mind in the variety of its forms. If we are tempted to make war upon another nation, we shall remember that we are seeking to destroy an element of our own culture, and possibly its most important element. As long as war is regarded as wicked, it will always have its fascination. When it is looked upon as vulgar, it will cease to be popular. The change will, of course, be slow, and people will not be conscious of it. They will not say 'We will not war against France because her prose is perfect', but because the prose of France is perfect, they will not hate the land. Intellectual criticism will bind Europe together in bonds far closer than those that can be forged by shopman or sentimentalist. It will give us the peace that springs from understanding.°

Nor is this all. It is Criticism that, recognizing no position as final, and refusing to bind itself by the shallow shibboleths of any sect or school, creates that serene philosophic temper which loves truth for its own sake,° and loves it not the less because it knows it to be unattainable. How little we have of this temper in England, and how much we need it! The English mind is always in a rage. The intellect of the race is wasted in the sordid and stupid quarrels of second-rate politicians or third-rate theologians. It was reserved for a man of science to show us the supreme example of that 'sweet reasonableness'° of which Arnold spoke so wisely, and, alas! to so little effect. The author of the *Origin of Species*° had, at any rate, the philosophic temper. If one contemplates the ordinary pulpits and platforms of England, one can but feel the contempt of Julian,° or the indifference of Montaigne.° We are dominated by the fanatic, whose worst vice is his sincerity. Anything approaching to the free play of the mind is practically unknown amongst us. People cry out against the sinner, yet it is not the sinful, but the stupid, who are our shame. There is no sin except stupidity.

Ernest. Ah! what an antinomian° you are!

Gilbert. The artistic critic, like the mystic, is an antinomian always. To be good, according to the vulgar standard of goodness, is obviously quite easy. It merely requires a certain amount of sordid terror, a certain lack of imaginative thought, and a certain low passion for middle-class respectability. Æsthetics are higher than ethics. They belong to a more spiritual sphere. To discern the beauty of a thing is the finest point to which we can arrive.° Even a colour-sense is more important, in the development of the individual, than a sense of right and wrong. Æsthetics, in fact, are to Ethics in the sphere of conscious civilization, what, in the sphere of the external world, sexual is to natural selection. Ethics, like natural selection,° make existence possible. Æsthetics, like sexual selection, make life lovely and wonderful, fill it with new forms, and give it progress, and variety and change. And when we reach the true culture that is our aim, we attain to that perfection of which the saints have dreamed, the perfection of those to whom sin is impossible, not because they make the renunciations of the ascetic, but because they can do everything they wish without hurt to the soul, and can wish for nothing that can do the soul harm, the soul being an entity so divine that it is able to transform into elements of a richer experience, or a finer susceptibility, or a newer mode of thought, acts or passions that with the common would be commonplace, or with the uneducated ignoble, or with the shameful vile. Is this dangerous? Yes; it is dangerous—all ideas, as I told you, are so. But the night wearies, and the light flickers in the lamp. One more thing I cannot help saying to you. You have spoken against Criticism as being a sterile thing. The nineteenth century is a turning point in history simply on account of the work of two men, Darwin and Renan,° the one the critic of the Book of Nature, the other the critic of the books of God. Not to recognize this is to miss the meaning of one of the most important eras in the progress of the world.° Creation is always behind the age. It is Criticism that leads us. The Critical Spirit and the World-Spirit are one.°

Ernest. And he who is in possession of this spirit or whom this spirit possesses, will, I suppose, do nothing?

Gilbert. Like the Persephone of whom Landor tells us, the sweet pensive Persephone around whose white feet the asphodel and amaranth are blooming, he will sit contented 'in that deep, motionless, quiet which mortals pity, and which the gods enjoy'. He will look out upon the world and know its secret. By contact with divine things, he will become divine. His will be the perfect life, and his only.

Ernest. You have told me many strange things tonight, Gilbert. You have told me that it is more difficult to talk about a thing than to do it, and that to do nothing at all is the most difficult thing in the world; you have told me that all Art is immoral, and all thought dangerous; that criticism is more creative than creation, and that the highest criticism is that which reveals in the work of Art what the artist had not put there; that it is exactly because a man cannot do a thing that he is the proper judge of it; and that the true critic is unfair, insincere, and not rational. My friend, you are a dreamer.

Gilbert. Yes: I am a dreamer. For a dreamer is one who can only find his way by moonlight, and his punishment is that he sees the dawn before the rest of the world.

Ernest. His punishment?

Gilbert. And his reward. But see, it is dawn already. Draw back the curtains and open the windows wide. How cool the morning air is! Piccadilly lies at our feet like a long riband of silver. A faint purple mist hangs over the Park, and the shadows of the white houses are purple. It is too late to sleep. Let us go down to Covent Garden and look at the roses. Come! I am tired of thought.

SALOME

THE PERSONS OF THE PLAY

HEROD° ANTIPAS, TETRARCH° OF JUDÆA

IOKANAAN,° THE PROPHET

THE YOUNG SYRIAN, CAPTAIN OF THE GUARD

TIGELLINUS, A YOUNG ROMAN

A CAPPADOCIAN

A NUBIAN

FIRST SOLDIER

SECOND SOLDIER

THE PAGE OF HERODIAS

JEWS, NAZARENES, ETC.

A SLAVE

NAAMAN, THE EXECUTIONER

HERODIAS, WIFE OF THE TETRARCH

SALOME, DAUGHTER OF HERODIAS

THE SLAVES OF SALOME

SALOME

SCENE—*A great terrace in the Palace of Herod, set above the banqueting-hall. Some soldiers are leaning over the balcony. To the right there is a gigantic staircase, to the left, at the back, an old cistern° surrounded by a wall of green bronze. The moon is shining very brightly.*

THE YOUNG SYRIAN. How beautiful is the Princess Salome tonight!

THE PAGE OF HERODIAS. Look at the moon. How strange the moon seems! She is like a woman rising from a tomb. She is like a dead woman. One might fancy she was looking for dead things.

THE YOUNG SYRIAN. She has a strange look. She is like a little princess who wears a yellow veil, and whose feet are of silver. She is like a princess who has little white doves for feet. One might fancy she was dancing.

THE PAGE OF HERODIAS. She is like a woman who is dead. She moves very slowly.

[*Noise in the banqueting-hall.*]

FIRST SOLDIER. What an uproar! Who are those wild beasts howling?

SECOND SOLDIER. The Jews. They are always like that. They are disputing about their religion.

FIRST SOLDIER. Why do they dispute about their religion?

SECOND SOLDIER. I cannot tell. They are always doing it. The Pharisees, for instance, say that there are angels, and the Sadducees° declare that angels do not exist.

FIRST SOLDIER. I think it is ridiculous to dispute about such things.

THE YOUNG SYRIAN. How beautiful is the Princess Salome tonight!

THE PAGE OF HERODIAS. You are always looking at her. You look at her too much. It is dangerous to look at people in such fashion. Something terrible may happen.

THE YOUNG SYRIAN. She is very beautiful tonight.

FIRST SOLDIER. The Tetrarch has a sombre aspect.

SECOND SOLDIER. Yes; he has a sombre aspect.

FIRST SOLDIER. He is looking at something.

SECOND SOLDIER. He is looking at some one.

FIRST SOLDIER. At whom is he looking?

SECOND SOLDIER. I cannot tell.

THE YOUNG SYRIAN. How pale the Princess is! Never have I seen her so pale. She is like the shadow of a white rose in a mirror of silver.°

THE PAGE OF HERODIAS. You must not look at her. You look too much at her.

FIRST SOLDIER. Herodias has filled the cup of the Tetrarch.

THE CAPPADOCIAN. Is that the Queen Herodias, she who wears a black mitre sewed with pearls, and whose hair is powdered with blue dust?

FIRST SOLDIER. Yes; that is Herodias, the Tetrarch's wife.

SECOND SOLDIER. The Tetrarch is very fond of wine. He has wine of three sorts. One which is brought from the Island of Samothrace, and is purple like the cloak of Cæsar.

THE CAPPADOCIAN. I have never seen Cæsar.

SECOND SOLDIER. Another that comes from a town called Cyprus, and is as yellow as gold.

THE CAPPADOCIAN. I love gold.

SECOND SOLDIER. And the third is a wine of Sicily. That wine is as red as blood.

THE NUBIAN. The gods of my country are very fond of blood. Twice in the year we sacrifice to them young men and maidens: fifty young men and a hundred maidens. But I am afraid that we never give them quite enough, for they are very harsh to us.

THE CAPPADOCIAN. In my country there are no gods left. The Romans have driven them out. There are some who say that they have hidden themselves in the mountains, but I do not believe it. Three nights I have been on the mountains seeking them everywhere. I did not find them, and at last I called them by their names, and they did not come. I think they are dead.

FIRST SOLDIER. The Jews worship a God that one cannot see.

THE CAPPADOCIAN. I cannot understand that.

FIRST SOLDIER. In fact, they only believe in things that one cannot see.

THE CAPPADOCIAN. That seems to me altogether ridiculous.

THE VOICE OF IOKANAAN. After me shall come another mightier than I. I am not worthy so much as to unloose the latchet of his shoes.° When he cometh the solitary places shall be glad. They shall blossom like the rose.° The eyes of the blind shall see the day, and the ears of the deaf shall be opened.° The sucking child shall put his hand upon the dragon's lair, he shall lead the lions by their manes.°

SECOND SOLDIER. Make him be silent. He is always saying ridiculous things.

FIRST SOLDIER. No, no. He is a holy man. He is very gentle, too. Every day when I give him to eat he thanks me.

THE CAPPADOCIAN. Who is he?

FIRST SOLDIER. A prophet.

THE CAPPADOCIAN. What is his name?

FIRST SOLDIER. Iokanaan.

THE CAPPADOCIAN. Whence comes he?

FIRST SOLDIER. From the desert, where he fed on locusts and wild honey. He was clothed in camel's hair, and round his loins he had a leathern belt.° He was very terrible to look upon. A great multitude used to follow him. He even had disciples.

THE CAPPADOCIAN. What is he talking of?

FIRST SOLDIER. We can never tell. Sometimes he says things that affright one, but it is impossible to understand what he says.

THE CAPPADOCIAN. May one see him?

FIRST SOLDIER. No. The Tetrarch has forbidden it.

THE YOUNG SYRIAN. The Princess has hidden her face behind her fan! Her little white hands are fluttering like doves that fly to their dovecots. They are like white butterflies. They are just like white butterflies.

THE PAGE OF HERODIAS. What is that to you? Why do you look at her? You must not look at her. . . . Something terrible may happen.

THE CAPPADOCIAN [*Pointing to the cistern.*] What a strange prison!

SECOND SOLDIER. It is an old cistern.

THE CAPPADOCIAN. An old cistern! That must be a poisonous place in which to dwell!

SECOND SOLDIER. Oh, no! For instance, the Tetrarch's brother, his elder brother, the first husband of Herodias the Queen, was imprisoned there for twelve years. It did not kill him. At the end of the twelve years he had to be strangled.

THE CAPPADOCIAN. Strangled? Who dared to do that?

SECOND SOLDIER [*Pointing to the Executioner, a huge negro.*] That man yonder, Naaman.

THE CAPPADOCIAN. He was not afraid?

SECOND SOLDIER. Oh no! The Tetrarch sent him the ring.

THE CAPPADOCIAN. What ring?

SECOND SOLDIER. The death ring. So he was not afraid.

THE CAPPADOCIAN. Yet it is a terrible thing to strangle a king.

FIRST SOLDIER. Why? Kings have but one neck, like other folk.

THE CAPPADOCIAN. I think it terrible.

THE YOUNG SYRIAN. The Princess is getting up! She is leaving the table! She looks very troubled. Ah, she is coming this way. Yes, she is coming towards us. How pale she is! Never have I seen her so pale.

THE PAGE OF HERODIAS. Do not look at her. I pray you not to look at her.

THE YOUNG SYRIAN. She is like a dove that has strayed. . . . She is like a narcissus trembling in the wind. . . . She is like a silver flower.

[*Enter Salome.*]

SALOME. I will not stay. I cannot stay. Why does the Tetrarch look at me all the while with his mole's eyes under his shaking eyelids? It is strange that the husband of my mother looks at me like that. I know not what it means. Of a truth I know it too well.

THE YOUNG SYRIAN. You have left the feast, Princess?

SALOME. How sweet is the air here! I can breathe here! Within there are Jews from Jerusalem who are tearing each other in pieces over their foolish ceremonies, and barbarians who drink and drink and spill their wine on the pavement, and Greeks from Smyrna with painted eyes and painted cheeks, and frizzed hair curled in columns, and Egyptians silent and subtle, with long nails of jade and russet cloaks, and Romans brutal and coarse, with their uncouth jargon. Ah! how I loathe the Romans! They are rough and common, and they give themselves the airs of noble lords.

THE YOUNG SYRIAN. Will you be seated, Princess.

THE PAGE OF HERODIAS. Why do you speak to her? Oh! something terrible will happen. Why do you look at her?

SALOME. How good to see the moon! She is like a little piece of money, a little silver flower. She is cold and chaste. I am sure she is a virgin. She has the beauty of a virgin. Yes, she is a virgin. She has never defiled herself. She has never abandoned herself to men, like the other goddesses.

THE VOICE OF IOKANAAN. Behold! the Lord hath come. The Son of Man is at hand.° The centaurs have hidden themselves in the rivers, and the nymphs have left the rivers, and are lying beneath the leaves in the forests.

SALOME. Who was that who cried out?

SECOND SOLDIER. The prophet, Princess.

SALOME. Ah, the prophet! He of whom the Tetrarch is afraid?

SECOND SOLDIER. We know nothing of that, Princess. It was the prophet Iokanaan who cried out.

THE YOUNG SYRIAN. Is it your pleasure that I bid them bring your litter,° Princess? The night is fair in the garden.

SALOME. He says terrible things about my mother, does he not?

SECOND SOLDIER. We never understand what he says, Princess.

SALOME. Yes; he says terrible things about her.

[Enter a Slave.]

THE SLAVE. Princess, the Tetrarch prays you to return to the feast.

SALOME. I will not return.

THE YOUNG SYRIAN. Pardon me, princess, but if you return not some misfortune may happen.

SALOME. Is he an old man, this prophet?

THE YOUNG SYRIAN. Princess, it were better to return. Suffer me to lead you in.

SALOME. This prophet . . . is he an old man?

FIRST SOLDIER. No, Princess, he is quite young.

SECOND SOLDIER. One cannot be sure. There are those who say that he is Elias.°

SALOME. Who is Elias?

SECOND SOLDIER. A prophet of this country in bygone days, Princess.

THE SLAVE. What answer may I give the Tetrarch from the Princess?

THE VOICE OF IOKANAAN. Rejoice not, O land of Palestine, because the rod of him who smote thee is broken. For from the seed of the serpent shall come a basilisk, and that which is born of it shall devour the birds.°

SALOME. What a strange voice! I would speak with him.

FIRST SOLDIER. I fear it may not be, Princess. The Tetrarch does not suffer any one to speak with him. He has even forbidden the high priest to speak with him.

SALOME. I desire to speak with him.

FIRST SOLDIER. It is impossible, Princess.

SALOME. I will speak with him.

THE YOUNG SYRIAN. Would it not be better to return to the banquet?

SALOME. Bring forth this prophet.

[*Exit the Slave.*]

FIRST SOLDIER. We dare not, Princess.

SALOME [*Approaching the cistern and looking down into it.*] How black it is, down there! It must be terrible to be in so black a hole! It is like a tomb. . . . [*To the soldiers.*] Did you not hear me? Bring out the prophet. I would look on him.

SECOND SOLDIER. Princess, I beg you, do not require this of us.

SALOME. You are making me wait upon your pleasure.

FIRST SOLDIER. Princess, our lives belong to you, but we cannot do what you have asked of us. And indeed, it is not of us that you should ask this thing.

SALOME [*Looking at the young Syrian.*] Ah!

THE PAGE OF HERODIAS. Oh! what is going to happen? I am sure that something terrible will happen.

SALOME [*Going up to the young Syrian.*] Thou wilt do this thing for me, wilt thou not, Narraboth? Thou wilt do this thing for me. I have ever been kind towards thee. Thou wilt do it for me. I would but look at him, this strange prophet. Men have talked so much of him. Often I have heard the Tetrarch talk of him. I think he is afraid of him, the Tetrarch. Art thou, even thou, also afraid of him, Narraboth?

THE YOUNG SYRIAN. I fear him not, Princess; there is no man I fear. But the Tetrarch has formally forbidden that any man should raise the cover of this well.

SALOME. Thou wilt do this thing for me, Narraboth, and tomorrow when I pass in my litter beneath the gateway of the idol-sellers I will let fall for thee a little flower, a little green flower.°

THE YOUNG SYRIAN. Princess, I cannot, I cannot.

SALOME [*Smiling.*] Thou wilt do this thing for me, Narraboth. Thou knowest that thou wilt do this thing for me. And on the morrow when I shall pass in my litter by the bridge of the idol-buyers, I will look at thee through the muslin veils, I will look at thee, Narraboth, it may be I will smile at thee. Look at me, Narraboth, look at me. Ah! thou knowest that thou wilt do what I ask of thee. Thou knowest it. . . . I know that thou wilt do this thing.

THE YOUNG SYRIAN [*Signing to the third Soldier.*] Let the prophet come forth. . . . The Princess Salome desires to see him.

SALOME. Ah!

THE PAGE OF HERODIAS. Oh! How strange the moon looks! Like the hand of a dead woman who is seeking to cover herself with a shroud.

THE YOUNG SYRIAN. She has a strange aspect! She is like a little princess, whose eyes are eyes of amber. Through the clouds of muslin she is smiling like a little princess. [*The prophet comes out of the cistern. Salome looks at him and steps slowly back.*]

IOKANAAN. Where is he whose cup of abominations° is now full? Where is he, who in a robe of silver shall one day die in the face of all the people? Bid him come forth, that he may hear the voice of him who hath cried in the waste places° and in the houses of kings.

SALOME. Of whom is he speaking?

THE YOUNG SYRIAN. No one can tell, Princess.

IOKANAAN. Where is she who saw the images of men painted on the walls, even the images of the Chaldæans painted with colours, and gave herself up unto the lust of her eyes, and sent ambassadors into the land of Chaldæa?°

SALOME. It is of my mother that he is speaking.

THE YOUNG SYRIAN. Oh no, Princess.

SALOME. Yes: it is of my mother that he is speaking.

IOKANAAN. Where is she who gave herself unto the Captains of Assyria, who have baldricks° on their loins, and crowns of many colours on their heads? Where is she who hath given herself to the young men of the Egyptians, who are clothed in fine linen and hyacinth, whose shields are of gold, whose helmets are of silver, whose bodies are mighty? Go, bid her rise up from the bed of her abominations, from the bed of her incestuousness, that she may hear the words of him who prepareth the way of the Lord,° that she may repent her of her iniquities. Though she will not repent, but will stick fast in her abominations, go bid her come, for the fan of the Lord is in His hand.°

SALOME. Ah, but he is terrible, he is terrible!

THE YOUNG SYRIAN. Do not stay here, Princess, I beseech you.

SALOME. It is his eyes above all that are terrible. They are like black holes burned by torches in a tapestry of Tyre.° They are like the black caverns where the dragons live, the black caverns of Egypt in which the dragons make their lairs. They are like black lakes troubled by fantastic moons. . . .° Do you think he will speak again?

THE YOUNG SYRIAN. Do not stay here, Princess. I pray you do not stay here.

SALOME. How wasted he is! He is like a thin ivory statue. He is like an image of silver. I am sure he is chaste, as the moon is. He is like a moonbeam, like a shaft of silver. His flesh must be very cold, cold as ivory. . . . I would look closer at him.

THE YOUNG SYRIAN. No, no, Princess!

SALOME. I must look at him closer.

THE YOUNG SYRIAN. Princess! Princess!

IOKANAAN. Who is this woman who is looking at me? I will not have her look at me. Wherefore doth she look at me, with her golden eyes, under her gilded eyelids? I know not who she is. I do not desire to know who she is. Bid her begone. It is not to her that I would speak.

SALOME. I am Salome, daughter of Herodias, Princess of Judæa.

IOKANAAN. Back! daughter of Babylon!° Come not near the chosen of the Lord. Thy mother hath filled the earth with the wine of her iniquities, and the cry of her sinning hath come up even to the ears of God.

SALOME. Speak again, Iokanaan. Thy voice is as music to mine ear.

THE YOUNG SYRIAN. Princess! Princess! Princess!

SALOME. Speak again! Speak again, Iokanaan, and tell me what I must do.

IOKANAAN. Daughter of Sodom,° come not near me! But cover thy face with a veil, and scatter ashes upon thine head, and get thee to the desert, and seek out the Son of Man.

SALOME. Who is he, the Son of Man? Is he as beautiful as thou art, Iokanaan?

IOKANAAN. Get thee behind me! I hear in the palace the beating of the wings of the angel of death.°

THE YOUNG SYRIAN. Princess, I beseech thee to go within.

IOKANAAN. Angel of the Lord God, what dost thou here with thy sword? Whom seekest thou in this palace? The day of him who shall die in a robe of silver has not yet come.°

SALOME. Iokanaan!

IOKANAAN. Who speaketh?

SALOME. I am amorous of thy body, Iokanaan! Thy body is white, like the lilies of a field that the mower hath never mowed. Thy body is white like the snows that lie on the mountains of Judæa, and come down into the valleys. The roses in the garden of the Queen of Arabia are not so white as thy body. Neither the roses of the garden of the Queen of Arabia, the garden of spices of the Queen of Arabia, nor the feet of the dawn when they light on the leaves, nor the breast of the moon when she lies on the breast of the sea. . . . There is nothing in the world so white as thy body. Suffer me to touch thy body.

IOKANAAN. Back! daughter of Babylon! By woman came evil into the world. Speak not to me. I will not listen to thee. I listen but to the voice of the Lord God.

SALOME. Thy body is hideous. It is like the body of a leper. It is like a plastered wall, where vipers have crawled; like a plastered wall where the scorpions have made their nest. It is like a whited sepulchre, full of loathsome things.° It is horrible, thy body is horrible. It is of thy hair that I am enamoured, Iokanaan. Thy hair is like clusters of grapes, like the clusters of black grapes that hang from the vine-trees of Edom in the land of the Edomites. Thy hair is like the cedars of Lebanon, like the great cedars of Lebanon that gave their shade to the lions and to the robbers who would hide them by day. The long black nights, when the moon hides her face, when the stars are afraid, are not so black as thy hair. The silence that dwells in the forest is not so black. There is nothing in the world that is so black as thy hair. . . . Suffer me to touch thy hair.

IOKANAAN. Back, daughter of Sodom! Touch me not. Profane not the temple of the Lord God.

SALOME. Thy hair is horrible. It is covered with mire and dust. It is like a crown of thorns° placed on thy head. It is like a knot of serpents coiled round thy neck. I love not thy hair. . . . It is thy mouth that I desire,

IOKANAAN. Thy mouth is like a band of scarlet° on a tower of ivory.° It is like a pomegranate cut in twain with a knife of ivory. The pomegranate flowers that blossom in the gardens of Tyre, and are redder than roses, are not so red. The red blasts of trumpets that herald the approach of kings, and make afraid the enemy, are not so red. Thy mouth is redder than the feet of those who tread the wine in the wine-press. It is redder than the feet of the doves who inhabit the temples and are fed by the priests. It is redder than the feet of him who cometh from a forest where he hath slain a lion, and seen gilded tigers. Thy mouth is like a branch of coral that fishers have found in the twilight of the sea, the coral that they keep for the kings! . . . It is like the vermilion that the Moabites find in the mines of Moab, the vermilion that the kings take from them. It is like the bow of the King of the Persians, that is painted with vermilion, and is tipped with coral. There is nothing in the world so red as thy mouth. . . . Suffer me to kiss thy mouth.

IOKANAAN. Never! daughter of Babylon! Daughter of Sodom! never!

SALOME. I will kiss thy mouth, Iokanaan. I will kiss thy mouth.

THE YOUNG SYRIAN. Princess, Princess, thou who art like a garden of myrrh, thou who art the dove of all doves, look not at this man, look not at him! Do not speak such words to him. I cannot endure it. . . . Princess, do not speak these things.

SALOME. I will kiss thy mouth, Iokanaan.

THE YOUNG SYRIAN. Ah! [*He kills himself, and falls between Salome and Iokanaan.*]

THE PAGE OF HERODIAS. The young Syrian has slain himself! The young captain has slain himself! He has slain himself who was my friend! I gave him a little box of perfumes and ear-rings wrought in silver, and now he has killed himself! Ah, did he not say that some misfortune would happen? I, too, said it, and it has come to pass. Well I knew that the moon was seeking a dead thing, but I knew not that it was he whom she sought. Ah! why did I not hide him from the moon? If I had hidden him in a cavern she would not have seen him.

FIRST SOLDIER. Princess, the young captain has just slain himself.

SALOME. Suffer me to kiss thy mouth, Iokanaan.

IOKANAAN. Art thou not afraid, daughter of Herodias? Did I not tell thee that I had heard in the palace the beating of the wings of the angel of death, and hath he not come, the angel of death?

SALOME. Suffer me to kiss thy mouth.

IOKANAAN. Daughter of adultery, there is but one who can save thee. It is He of whom I spake. Go seek Him. He is in a boat on the sea of Galilee, and He talketh with His disciples. Kneel down on the shore of the sea, and call unto Him by His name. When He cometh to thee, and to all who call on Him He cometh, bow thyself at His feet and ask of Him the remission of thy sins.

SALOME. Suffer me to kiss thy mouth.

IOKANAAN. Cursed be thou! daughter of an incestuous mother, be thou accursed!

SALOME. I will kiss thy mouth, Iokanaan.

IOKANAAN. I will not look at thee. Thou art accursed, Salome, thou art accursed. [*He goes down into the cistern.*]

SALOME. I will kiss thy mouth, Iokanaan; I will kiss thy mouth.

FIRST SOLDIER. We must bear away the body to another place. The Tetrarch does not care to see dead bodies, save the bodies of those whom he himself has slain.

THE PAGE OF HERODIAS. He was my brother, and nearer to me than a brother. I gave him a little box full of perfumes, and a ring of agate that he wore always on his hand. In the evening we were wont to walk by the river, and among the almond-trees, and he used to tell me of the things of his country. He spake ever very low. The sound of his voice was like the sound of the flute, of one who playeth upon the flute. Also, he had much joy to gaze at himself in the river.° I used to reproach him for that.

SECOND SOLDIER. You are right; we must hide the body. The Tetrarch must not see it.

FIRST SOLDIER. The Tetrarch will not come to this place. He never comes on the terrace. He is too much afraid of the prophet.

[*Enter Herod, Herodias, and all the Court.*]

HEROD. Where is Salome? Where is the Princess? Why did she not return to the banquet as I commanded her? Ah! there she is!

HERODIAS. You must not look at her! You are always looking at her!

HEROD. The moon has a strange look tonight. Has she not a strange look? She is like a mad woman, a mad woman who is seeking everywhere for lovers. She is naked too. She is quite naked. The clouds are seeking to clothe her nakedness, but she will not let them. She shows herself naked in the sky. She reels through the clouds like a drunken woman. . . . I am sure she is looking for lovers. Does she not reel like a drunken woman? She is like a mad woman, is she not?

HERODIAS. No; the moon is like the moon, that is all. Let us go within. . . . We have nothing to do here.

HEROD. I will stay here! Manasseh, lay carpets there. Light torches. Bring forth the ivory tables, and the tables of jasper. The air here is sweet. I will drink more wine with my guests. We must show all honours to the ambassadors of Cæsar.

HERODIAS. It is not because of them that you remain.

HEROD. Yes; the air is very sweet. Come, Herodias, our guests await us. Ah! I have slipped! I have slipped in blood! It is an ill omen. It is a very ill omen. Wherefore is there blood here? . . . and this body, what does this body here? Think you I am like the King of Egypt, who gives no feast to his guests but that he shows them a corpse? Whose is it? I will not look on it.

FIRST SOLDIER. It is our captain, sire. It is the young Syrian whom you made captain of the guard but three days gone.

HEROD. I issued no order that he should be slain.

SECOND SOLDIER. He slew himself, sire.

HEROD. For what reason? I had made him captain of my guard!

SECOND SOLDIER. We do not know, sire. But with his own hand he slew himself.

HEROD. That seems strange to me. I had thought it was but the Roman philosophers who slew themselves. Is it not true, Tigellinus, that the philosophers at Rome slay themselves?

TIGELLINUS. There be some who slay themselves, sire. They are the Stoics.° The Stoics are people of no cultivation. They are ridiculous people. I myself regard them as being perfectly ridiculous.

HEROD. I also. It is ridiculous to kill one's-self.

TIGELLINUS. Everybody at Rome laughs at them. The Emperor has written a satire against them. It is recited everywhere.

HEROD. Ah! he has written a satire against them? Cæsar is wonderful. He can do everything. . . . It is strange that the young Syrian has slain himself. I am sorry he has slain himself. I am very sorry. For he was fair to look upon. He was even very fair. He had very languorous eyes. I remember that I saw that he looked languorously at Salome. Truly, I thought he looked too much at her.

HERODIAS. There are others who look too much at her.

HEROD. His father was a king. I drave him from his kingdom. And of his mother, who was a queen, you made a slave, Herodias. So he was here as my guest, as it were, and for that reason I made him my captain. I am sorry he is dead. Ho! why have you left the body here? It must be taken to some other place. I will not look at it,—away with it! [*They take away the body.*] It is cold here. There is a wind blowing. Is there not a wind blowing?

HERODIAS. No; there is no wind.

HEROD. I tell you there is a wind that blows. . . . And I hear in the air something that is like the beating of wings, like the beating of vast wings.° Do you not hear it?

HERODIAS. I hear nothing.

HEROD. I hear it no longer. But I heard it. It was the blowing of the wind. It has passed away. But no, I hear it again. Do you not hear it? It is just like a beating of wings.

HERODIAS. I tell you there is nothing. You are ill. Let us go within.

HEROD. I am not ill. It is your daughter who is sick to death. Never have I seen her so pale.

HERODIAS. I have told you not to look at her.

HEROD. Pour me forth wine. [*Wine is brought.*] Salome, come drink a little wine with me. I have here a wine that is exquisite. Cæsar himself sent it me. Dip into it thy little red lips, that I may drain the cup.

SALOME. I am not thirsty, Tetrarch.

HEROD. You hear how she answers me, this daughter of yours?

HERODIAS. She does right. Why are you always gazing at her?

HEROD. Bring me ripe fruits. [*Fruits are brought.*] Salome, come and eat fruits with me. I love to see in a fruit the mark of thy little teeth. Bite but a little of this fruit, that I may eat what is left.

SALOME. I am not hungry, Tetrarch.

HEROD [*To Herodias.*] You see how you have brought up this daughter of yours.

HERODIAS. My daughter and I come of a royal race. As for thee, thy father was a camel driver! He was a thief and a robber to boot!

HEROD. Thou liest!

HERODIAS. Thou knowest well that it is true.

HEROD. Salome, come and sit next to me. I will give thee the throne of thy mother.

SALOME. I am not tired, Tetrarch.

HERODIAS. You see in what regard she holds you.

HEROD. Bring me—What is it that I desire? I forget. Ah! ah! I remember.

THE VOICE OF IOKANAAN. Behold the time is come! That which I foretold has come to pass. The day that I spake of is at hand.

HERODIAS. Bid him be silent. I will not listen to his voice. This man is for ever hurling insults against me.

HEROD. He has said nothing against you. Besides, he is a very great prophet.

HERODIAS. I do not believe in prophets. Can a man tell what will come to pass? No man knows it. Also he is for ever insulting me. But I think you are afraid of him. . . . I know well that you are afraid of him.

HEROD. I am not afraid of him. I am afraid of no man.

HERODIAS. I tell you you are afraid of him. If you are not afraid of him why do you not deliver him to the Jews who for these six months past have been clamouring for him?

A JEW. Truly, my lord, it were better to deliver him into our hands.

HEROD. Enough on this subject. I have already given you my answer. I will not deliver him into your hands. He is a holy man. He is a man who has seen God.

A JEW. That cannot be. There is no man who hath seen God since the prophet Elias. He is the last man who saw God face to face. In these days God doth not show Himself. God hideth Himself. Therefore great evils have come upon the land.

ANOTHER JEW. Verily, no man knoweth if Elias the prophet did indeed see God. Peradventure it was but the shadow of God that he saw.

A THIRD JEW. God is at no time hidden. He showeth Himself at all times and in all places. God is in what is evil even as He is in what is good.

A FOURTH JEW. Thou shouldst not say that. It is a very dangerous doctrine. It is a doctrine that cometh from Alexandria, where men teach the philosophy of the Greeks. And the Greeks are Gentiles. They are not even circumcised.

A FIFTH JEW. No man can tell how God worketh. His ways are very dark. It may be that the things which we call evil are good, and that the things which we call good are evil. There is no knowledge of anything. We can but bow our heads to His will, for God is very strong. He breaketh in pieces the strong together with the weak, for He regardeth not any man.

FIRST JEW. Thou speakest truly. Verily, God is terrible. He breaketh in pieces the strong and the weak as men break corn in a mortar. But as for this man, he hath never seen God. No man hath seen God since the prophet Elias.

HERODIAS. Make them be silent. They weary me.

HEROD. But I have heard it said that Iokanaan is in very truth your prophet Elias.

THE JEW. That cannot be. It is more than three hundred years since the days of the prophet Elias.

HEROD. There be some who say that this man is Elias the prophet.

A NAZARENE. I am sure that he is Elias the prophet.

THE JEW. Nay, but he is not Elias the prophet.

THE VOICE OF IOKANAAN. Behold the day is at hand, the day of the Lord, and I hear upon the mountains the feet of Him who shall be the Saviour of the world.°

HEROD. What does that mean? The Saviour of the world?

TIGELLINUS. It is a title that Cæsar adopts.

HEROD. But Cæsar is not coming into Judæa. Only yesterday I received letters from Rome. They contained nothing concerning this matter. And you, Tigellinus, who were at Rome during the winter, you heard nothing concerning this matter, did you?

TIGELLINUS. Sire, I heard nothing concerning the matter. I was but explaining the title. It is one of Cæsar's titles.

HEROD. But Cæsar cannot come. He is too gouty. They say that his feet are like the feet of an elephant. Also there are reasons of state. He who leaves Rome loses Rome. He will not come. Howbeit, Cæsar is lord, he will come if such be his pleasure. Nevertheless, I think he will not come.

FIRST NAZARENE. It was not concerning Cæsar that the prophet spake these words, sire.

HEROD. How?—it was not concerning Cæsar?

FIRST NAZARENE. No, my lord.

HEROD. Concerning whom then did he speak?

FIRST NAZARENE. Concerning Messias,° who hath come.

A JEW. Messias hath not come.

FIRST NAZARENE. He hath come, and everywhere He worketh miracles!

HERODIAS. Ho! ho! miracles! I do not believe in miracles. I have seen too many. [To the Page.] My fan.

FIRST NAZARENE. This Man worketh true miracles. Thus, at a marriage which took place in a little town of Galilee, a town of some importance, He changed water into wine.° Certain persons who were present related it to me. Also He healed two lepers that were seated before the Gate of Capernaum simply by touching them.°

SECOND NAZARENE. Nay; it was two blind men that He healed at Capernaum.

FIRST NAZARENE. Nay; they were lepers. But He hath healed blind people also, and He was seen on a mountain talking with angels.

A SADDUCEE. Angels do not exist.

A PHARISEE. Angels exist, but I do not believe that this Man has talked with them.

FIRST NAZARENE. He was seen by a great multitude of people talking with angels.

HERODIAS. How these men weary me! They are ridiculous! They are altogether ridiculous! [To the Page.] Well! my fan? [The Page gives her the fan.] You have a dreamer's look. You must not dream. It is only sick people who dream. [She strikes the Page with her fan.]

SECOND NAZARENE. There is also the miracle of the daughter of Jairus.°

FIRST NAZARENE. Yea, that is sure. No man can gainsay it.

HERODIAS. Those men are mad. They have looked too long on the moon. Command them to be silent.

HEROD. What is this miracle of the daughter of Jairus?

FIRST NAZARENE. The daughter of Jairus was dead. This Man raised her from the dead.

HEROD. How! He raises people from the dead?

FIRST NAZARENE. Yea, sire; He raiseth the dead.

HEROD. I do not wish Him to do that. I forbid Him to do that. I suffer no man to raise the dead. This Man must be found and told that I forbid Him to raise the dead. Where is this Man at present?

SECOND NAZARENE. He is in every place, my lord, but it is hard to find Him.

FIRST NAZARENE. It is said that He is now in Samaria.

A JEW. It is easy to see that this is not Messias, if He is in Samaria. It is not to the Samaritans that Messias shall come. The Samaritans are accursed. They bring no offerings to the Temple.

SECOND NAZARENE. He left Samaria a few days since. I think that at the present moment He is in the neighbourhood of Jerusalem.

FIRST NAZARENE. No; He is not there. I have just come from Jerusalem. For two months they have had no tidings of Him.

HEROD. No matter! But let them find Him, and tell Him, thus saith Herod the King, 'I will not suffer Thee to raise the dead.' To change water into wine, to heal the lepers and the blind. . . . He may do these things if He will. I say nothing against these things. In truth I hold it a kindly deed to heal a leper. But no man shall raise the dead. . . . It would be terrible if the dead came back.

THE VOICE OF IOKANAAN. Ah! The wanton one! The harlot! Ah! the daughter of Babylon with her golden eyes and her gilded eyelids! Thus saith the Lord God, Let there come up against her a multitude of men. Let the people take stones and stone her.° . . .

HERODIAS. Command him to be silent!

THE VOICE OF IOKANAAN. Let the captains of the hosts pierce her with their swords, let them crush her beneath their shields.°

HERODIAS. Nay, but it is infamous.

THE VOICE OF IOKANAAN. It is thus that I will wipe out all wickedness from the earth, and that all women shall learn not to imitate her abominations.

HERODIAS. You hear what he says against me? You suffer him to revile her who is your wife!

HEROD. He did not speak your name.

HERODIAS. What does that matter? You know well that it is I whom he seeks to revile. And I am your wife, am I not?

HEROD. Of a truth, dear and noble Herodias, you are my wife, and before that you were the wife of my brother.

HERODIAS. It was thou didst snatch me from his arms.

HEROD. Of a truth I was stronger than he was. . . . But let us not talk of that matter. I do not desire to talk of it. It is the cause of the terrible words that the prophet has spoken. Peradventure on account of it a misfortune will come. Let us not speak of this matter. Noble Herodias, we are not mindful of our guests. Fill thou my cup, my well-beloved. Ho! fill with wine the great goblets of silver, and the great goblets of glass. I will drink to Cæsar. There are Romans here, we must drink to Cæsar.

ALL. Cæsar! Cæsar!

HEROD. Do you not see your daughter, how pale she is?

HERODIAS. What is it to you if she be pale or not?

HEROD. Never have I seen her so pale.

HERODIAS. You must not look at her.

THE VOICE OF IOKANAAN. In that day the sun shall become black like sackcloth of hair, and the moon shall become like blood, and the stars of the heaven shall fall upon the earth like unripe figs that fall from the fig-tree, and the kings of the earth shall be afraid.°

HERODIAS. Ah! ah! I should like to see that day of which he speaks, when the moon shall become like blood, and when the stars shall fall upon the earth like unripe figs. This prophet talks like a drunken man, . . . but I cannot suffer the sound of his voice. I hate his voice. Command him to be silent.

HEROD. I will not. I cannot understand what it is that he saith, but it may be an omen.

HERODIAS. I do not believe in omens. He speaks like a drunken man.

HEROD. It may be he is drunk with the wine of God.

HERODIAS. What wine is that, the wine of God? From what vineyards is it gathered? In what wine-press may one find it?

HEROD [*From this point he looks all the while at Salome.*] Tigellinus, when you were at Rome of late, did the Emperor speak with you on the subject of . . . ?

TIGELLINUS. On what subject, my lord?

HEROD. On what subject? Ah! I asked you a question, did I not? I have forgotten what I would have asked you.

HERODIAS. You are looking again at my daughter. You must not look at her. I have already said so.

HEROD. You say nothing else.

HERODIAS. I say it again.

HEROD. And that restoration of the Temple about which they have talked so much, will anything be done? They say that the veil of the Sanctuary has disappeared, do they not?°

HERODIAS. It was thyself didst steal it. Thou speakest at random and without wit. I will not stay here. Let us go within.

HEROD. Dance for me, Salome.

HERODIAS. I will not have her dance.

SALOME. I have no desire to dance, Tetrarch.

HEROD. Salome, daughter of Herodias, dance for me.

HERODIAS. Peace. Let her alone.

HEROD. I command thee to dance, Salome.

SALOME. I will not dance, Tetrarch.

HERODIAS [*Laughing*.] You see how she obeys you.

HEROD. What is it to me whether she dance or not? It is nought to me. Tonight I am happy. I am exceeding happy. Never have I been so happy.

FIRST SOLDIER. The Tetrarch has a sombre look. Has he not a sombre look?

SECOND SOLDIER. Yes, he has a sombre look.

HEROD. Wherefore should I not be happy? Cæsar, who is lord of the world, Cæsar, who is lord of all things, loves me well. He has just sent me most precious gifts. Also he has promised me to summon to Rome the King of Cappadocia, who is mine enemy. It may be that at Rome he will crucify him, for he is able to do all things that he has a mind to do. Verily, Cæsar is lord. Therefore I do well to be happy. I am very happy, never have I been so happy. There is nothing in the world that can mar my happiness.

THE VOICE OF IOKANAAN. He shall be seated on his throne. He shall be clothed in scarlet and purple. In his hand he shall bear a golden cup full of his blasphemies.° And the angel of the Lord shall smite him. He shall be eaten of worms.°

HERODIAS. You hear what he says about you. He says that you shall be eaten of worms.

HEROD. It is not of me that he speaks. He speaks never against me. It is of the King of Cappadocia that he speaks; the King of Cappadocia who is mine enemy. It is he who shall be eaten of worms. It is not I. Never has he spoken word against me, this prophet, save that I sinned in taking to wife the wife of my brother. It may be he is right. For, of a truth, you are sterile.

HERODIAS. I am sterile, I? You say that, you that are ever looking at my daughter, you that would have her dance for your pleasure? You speak as a fool. I have borne a child. You have gotten no child, no, not on one of your slaves. It is you who are sterile, not I.

HEROD. Peace, woman! I say that you are sterile. You have borne me no child, and the prophet says that our marriage is not a true marriage. He says that it is a marriage of incest, a marriage that will bring evils. . . . I fear he is right; I am sure that he is right. But it is not the hour to speak of these things. I would be happy at this moment. Of a truth, I am happy. There is nothing I lack.

HERODIAS. I am glad you are of so fair a humour tonight. It is not your custom. But it is late. Let us go within. Do not forget that we hunt at sunrise. All honours must be shown to Cæsar's ambassadors, must they not?

SECOND SOLDIER. The Tetrarch has a sombre look.

FIRST SOLDIER. Yes, he has a sombre look.

HEROD. Salome, Salome, dance for me. I pray thee dance for me. I am sad tonight. Yes, I am passing sad tonight. When I came hither I slipped in blood, which is an ill omen; also I heard in the air a beating of wings, a beating of giant wings. I cannot tell what that may mean. . . . I am sad tonight. Therefore dance for me. Dance for me, Salome, I beseech thee. If thou dancest for me thou mayest ask of me what thou wilt, and I will give it thee. Yes, dance for me, Salome, and whatsoever thou shalt ask of me I will give it thee, even unto the half of my kingdom.

SALOME [*Rising.*] Will you indeed give me whatsoever I shall ask of you, Tetrarch?

HERODIAS. Do not dance, my daughter.

HEROD. Whatsoever thou shalt ask of me, even unto the half of my kingdom.

SALOME. You swear it, Tetrarch?

HEROD. I swear it, Salome.

HERODIAS. Do not dance, my daughter.

SALOME. By what will you swear this thing, Tetrarch?

HEROD. By my life, by my crown, by my gods. Whatsoever thou shalt desire I will give it thee, even to the half of my kingdom, if thou wilt but dance for me. O Salome, Salome, dance for me!

SALOME. You have sworn an oath, Tetrarch.

HEROD. I have sworn an oath.

HERODIAS. My daughter, do not dance.

HEROD. Even to the half of my kingdom. Thou wilt be passing fair as a queen, Salome, if it please thee to ask for the half of my kingdom. Will she not be fair as a queen? Ah! it is cold here! There is an icy wind, and I hear . . . wherefore do I hear in the air this beating of wings? Ah! One might fancy a huge black bird that hovers over the terrace. Why can I not see it, this bird? The beat of its wings is terrible. The breath of the wind of its wings is terrible. It is a chill wind. Nay, but it is not cold, it is hot. I am choking. Pour water on my hands. Give me snow to eat. Loosen my mantle. Quick! quick! loosen my mantle. Nay, but leave it. It is my garland that hurts me, my garland of roses. The flowers are like fire. They have burned my forehead. [*He tears the wreath from his head, and throws it on the table.*] Ah! I can breathe now. How red those petals are! They are like stains of blood on the cloth. That does not matter. It is not wise to find symbols in everything that one sees. It makes life too full of terrors. It were better to say that stains of blood are as lovely as rose-petals. It were better far to say that. . . . But we will not speak of this. Now I am happy. I am passing happy. Have I not the right to be happy? Your daughter is going to dance for me. Wilt thou not dance for me, Salome? Thou hast promised to dance for me.

HERODIAS. I will not have her dance.

SALOME. I will dance for you, Tetrarch.

HEROD. You hear what your daughter says. She is going to dance for me. Thou doest well to dance for me, Salome. And when thou hast danced for me, forget not to ask of me whatsoever thou hast a mind to ask. Whatsoever thou shalt desire I will give it thee, even to the half of my kingdom. I have sworn it, have I not?

SALOME. Thou hast sworn it, Tetrarch.

HEROD. And I have never failed of my word. I am not of those who break their oaths. I know not how to lie. I am the slave of my word, and my word is the word of a king. The King of Cappadocia had ever a lying tongue, but he is no true king. He is a coward. Also he owes me money that he will not repay. He has even insulted my ambassadors. He has spoken words that were wounding. But Cæsar will crucify him when he comes to Rome. I know that Cæsar will crucify him. And if he crucify him not, yet will he die, being eaten of worms. The prophet has prophesied it. Well! Wherefore dost thou tarry, Salome?

SALOME. I am waiting until my slaves bring perfumes to me and the seven veils, and take from off my feet my sandals.

[*Slaves bring perfumes and the seven veils, and take off the sandals of Salome.*]

HEROD. Ah, thou art to dance with naked feet! 'Tis well! 'Tis well! Thy little feet will be like white doves. They will be like little white flowers that dance upon the trees. . . . No, no, she is going to dance on blood! There is blood spilt on the ground. She must not dance on blood. It were an evil omen.

HERODIAS. What is it to thee if she dance on blood? Thou hast waded deep enough in it. . . .

HEROD. What is it to me? Ah! look at the moon! She has become red. She has become red as blood. Ah! the prophet prophesied truly. He prophesied that the moon would become as blood. Did he not prophesy it? All of ye heard him prophesying it. And now the moon has become as blood. Do ye not see it?

HERODIAS. Oh yes, I see it well, and the stars are falling like unripe figs, are they not? and the sun is becoming black like sackcloth of hair, and the kings of the earth are afraid. That at least one can see. The prophet is justified of his words in that at least, for truly the kings of the earth are afraid. . . . Let us go within. You are sick. They will say at Rome that you are mad. Let us go within, I tell you.

THE VOICE OF IOKANAAN. Who is this who cometh from Edom, who is this who cometh from Bozra, whose raiment is dyed with purple, who shineth in the beauty of his garments, who walketh mighty in his greatness? Wherefore is thy raiment stained with scarlet?°

HERODIAS. Let us go within. The voice of that man maddens me. I will not have my daughter dance while he is continually crying out. I will not have her dance while you look at her in this fashion. In a word, I will not have her dance.

HEROD. Do not rise, my wife, my queen, it will avail thee nothing. I will not go within till she hath danced. Dance, Salome, dance for me.

HERODIAS. Do not dance, my daughter.

SALOME. I am ready, Tetrarch.

[*Salome dances the dance of the seven veils.*]°

HEROD. Ah! wonderful! wonderful! You see that she has danced for me, your daughter. Come near, Salome, come near, that I may give thee thy fee. Ah! I pay a royal price to those who dance for my pleasure. I will pay thee royally. I will give thee whatsoever thy soul desireth. What wouldst thou have? Speak.

SALOME [*Kneeling.*] I would that they presently bring me in a silver charger° . . .

HEROD [*Laughing.*] In a silver charger? Surely yes, in a silver charger. She is charming, is she not? What is it that thou wouldst have in a silver charger, O sweet and fair Salome, thou that art fairer than all the daughters of Judæa? What wouldst thou have them bring thee in a silver charger? Tell me. Whatsoever it may be, thou shalt receive it. My treasures belong to thee. What is it that thou wouldst have, Salome?

SALOME [*Rising.*] The head of Iokanaan.

HERODIAS. Ah! that is well said, my daughter.

HEROD. No, no!

HERODIAS. That is well said, my daughter.

HEROD. No, no, Salome. It is not that thou desirest. Do not listen to thy mother's voice. She is ever giving thee evil counsel. Do not heed her.

SALOME. It is not my mother's voice that I heed. It is for mine own pleasure that I ask the head of Iokanaan in a silver charger. You have sworn an oath, Herod. Forget not that you have sworn an oath.

HEROD. I know it. I have sworn an oath by my gods. I know it well. But I pray thee, Salome, ask of me something else. Ask of me the half of my kingdom, and I will give it thee. But ask not of me what thy lips have asked.

SALOME. I ask of you the head of Iokanaan.

HEROD. No, no, I will not give it thee.

SALOME. You have sworn an oath, Herod.

HERODIAS. Yes, you have sworn an oath. Everybody heard you. You swore it before everybody.

HEROD. Peace, woman! It is not to you I speak.

HERODIAS. My daughter has done well to ask the head of Iokanaan. He has covered me with insults. He has said unspeakable things against me. One can see that she loves her mother well. Do not yield, my daughter. He has sworn an oath, he has sworn an oath.

HEROD. Peace! Speak not to me! ... Salome, I pray thee be not stubborn. I have ever been kind toward thee. I have ever loved thee. ... It may be that I have loved thee too much. Therefore ask not this thing of me. This is a terrible thing, an awful thing to ask of me. Surely, I think thou art jesting. The head of a man that is cut from his body is ill to look upon, is it not? It is not meet that the eyes of a virgin should look upon such a thing. What pleasure couldst thou have in it. There is no pleasure that thou couldst have in it. No, no, it is not that thou desirest. Hearken to me. I have an emerald, a great emerald and round, that the minion of Cæsar has sent unto me. When thou lookest through this emerald thou canst see that which passeth afar off. Cæsar himself carries such an emerald when he goes to the circus. But my emerald is the larger. I know well that it is the larger. It is the largest emerald in the whole world. Thou wilt take that, wilt thou not? Ask it of me and I will give it thee.

SALOME. I demand the head of Iokanaan.

HEROD. Thou art not listening. Thou art not listening. Suffer me to speak, Salome.

SALOME. The head of Iokanaan!

HEROD. No, no, thou wouldst not have that. Thou sayest that but to trouble me, because that I have looked at thee and ceased not this night. It is true, I have looked at thee and ceased not this night. Thy beauty has troubled me. Thy beauty has grievously troubled me, and I have looked at thee overmuch. Nay, but I will look at thee no more. One should not look at anything. Neither at things, nor at people should one look. Only in mirrors is it well to look, for mirrors do but show us masks. Oh! oh! bring wine! I thirst. ... Salome, Salome, let us be as friends. Bethink thee. ... Ah! what would I say? What was 't? Ah! I remember it! ... Salome,—nay but come nearer to me; I fear thou wilt not hear my words,—Salome, thou knowest my white peacocks, my beautiful white peacocks,° that walk in the garden between the myrtles and the tall cypress-trees. Their beaks are gilded with gold and the grains that they eat are smeared with gold, and their feet are stained with purple. When they cry out the rain comes, and the moon shows herself in the heavens when they spread their tails. Two by two they walk between the cypress-trees and the black myrtles, and each has a slave to tend it. Sometimes they fly across the trees, and anon they couch in the grass, and round the pools of the water. There are not in all the world birds so wonderful. I know that Cæsar himself has no birds so fair as my birds. I will give thee fifty of my peacocks. They will follow thee whithersoever thou goest, and in the midst of them thou wilt be like unto the moon in the midst of a great white cloud. . . . I will give them to thee, all. I have but a hundred, and in the whole world there is no king who has peacocks like unto my peacocks. But I will give them all to thee. Only thou must loose me from my oath, and must not ask of me that which thy lips have asked of me.

[*He empties the cup of wine.*]

SALOME. Give me the head of Iokanaan!

HERODIAS. Well said, my daughter! As for you, you are ridiculous with your peacocks.

HEROD. Peace! you are always crying out. You cry out like a beast of prey. You must not cry in such fashion. Your voice wearies me. Peace, I tell you! . . . Salome, think on what thou art doing. It may be that this man comes from God. He is a holy man. The finger of God has touched him. God has put terrible words into his mouth. In the palace, as in the desert, God is ever with him. . . . It may be that He is, at least. One cannot tell, but it is possible that God is with him and for him. If he die also, peradventure some evil may befall me. Verily, he has said that evil will befall some one on the day whereon he dies. On whom should it fall if it fall not on me? Remember, I slipped in blood when I came hither. Also did I not hear a beating of wings in the air, a beating of vast wings? These are ill omens. And there were other things. I am sure that there were other things, though I saw them not. Thou wouldst not that some evil should befall me, Salome? Listen to me again.

SALOME. Give me the head of Iokanaan!

HEROD. Ah! thou art not listening to me. Be calm. As for me, am I not calm? I am altogether calm. Listen. I have jewels hidden in this place—jewels that thy mother even has never seen; jewels that are marvellous to look at. I have a collar of pearls, set in four rows. They are like unto moons chained with rays of silver. They are even as half a hundred moons caught in a golden net. On the ivory breast of a queen they have rested. Thou shalt be as fair as a queen when thou wearest them. I have amethysts of two kinds; one that is black like wine, and one that is red like wine that one has coloured with water. I have topazes yellow as are the eyes of tigers, and topazes that are pink as the eyes of a wood-pigeon, and green topazes that are as the eyes of cats. I have opals that burn always, with a flame that is cold as ice, opals that make sad men's minds, and are afraid of the shadows. I have onyxes like the eyeballs of a dead woman. I have moonstones that change when the moon changes, and are wan when they see the sun. I have sapphires big like eggs, and as blue as blue flowers. The sea wanders within them, and the moon comes never to trouble the blue of their waves. I have chrysolites and beryls, and chrysoprases and rubies; I have sardonyx and hyacinth stones, and stones of chalcedony, and I will give them all unto thee, all, and other things will I add to them. The King of the Indies has but even now sent me four fans fashioned from the feathers of parrots, and the King of Numidia a garment of ostrich feathers. I have a crystal, into which it is not lawful for a woman to look, nor may young men behold it until they have been beaten with rods. In a coffer of nacre I have three wondrous turquoises. He who wears them on his forehead can imagine things which are not, and he who carries them in his hand can turn the fruitful woman into a woman that is barren. These are great treasures. They are treasures above all price. But this is not all. In an ebony coffer I have two cups of amber that are like apples of pure gold. If an enemy pour poison into these cups they become like apples of silver. In a coffer incrusted with amber I have sandals incrusted with glass. I have mantles that have been brought from the land of the Seres,° and bracelets decked about with carbuncles and with jade that come from the city of Euphrates. . . . What desirest thou more than this, Salome? Tell me the thing that thou desirest, and I will give it thee. All that thou askest I will give thee, save one thing only. I will give thee all that is mine, save only the life of one man. I will give thee the mantle of the high priest. I will give thee the veil of the sanctuary.

THE JEWS. Oh! oh!

SALOME. Give me the head of Iokanaan!

HEROD [*Sinking back in his seat.*] Let her be given what she asks! Of a truth she is her mother's child! [*The first Soldier approaches. Herodias draws from the hand of the Tetrarch the ring of death, and gives it to the Soldier, who straightway bears it to the Executioner. The Executioner looks scared.*] Who has taken my ring? There was a ring on my right hand. Who has drunk my wine? There was wine in my cup. It was full of wine. Some one has drunk it! Oh! surely some evil will befall some one. [*The Executioner goes down into the cistern.*] Ah! wherefore did I give my oath? Hereafter let no king swear an oath. If he keep it not, it is terrible, and if he keep it, it is terrible also.

HERODIAS. My daughter has done well.

HEROD. I am sure that some misfortune will happen.

SALOME [*She leans over the cistern and listens.*] There is no sound. I hear nothing. Why does he not cry out, this man? Ah! if any man sought to kill me, I would cry out, I would struggle, I would not suffer. . . . Strike, strike, Naaman, strike, I tell you. . . . No, I hear nothing. There is a silence, a terrible silence. Ah! something has fallen upon the ground. I heard something fall. It was the sword of the executioner. He is afraid, this slave. He has dropped his sword. He dares not kill him. He is a coward, this slave! Let soldiers be sent. [*She sees the Page of Herodias and addresses him.*] Come hither. Thou wert the friend of him who is dead, wert thou not? Well, I tell thee, there are not dead men enough. Go to the soldiers and bid them go down and bring me the thing I ask, the thing the Tetrarch has promised me, the thing that is mine. [*The Page recoils. She turns to the soldiers.*] Hither, ye soldiers. Get ye down into this cistern and bring me the head of this man. Tetrarch, Tetrarch, command your soldiers that they bring me the head of Iokanaan.

[*A huge black arm, the arm of the Executioner, comes forth from the cistern, bearing on a silver shield the head of Iokanaan. Salome seizes it. Herod hides his face with his cloak. Herodias smiles and fans herself. The Nazarenes fall on their knees and begin to pray.*]

Ah! thou wouldst not suffer me to kiss thy mouth, Iokanaan. Well! I will kiss it now. I will bite it with my teeth as one bites a ripe fruit. Yes, I will kiss thy mouth, Iokanaan. I said it; did I not say it? I said it. Ah! I will kiss it now. . . . But wherefore dost thou not look at me, Iokanaan? Thine eyes that were so terrible, so full of rage and scorn, are shut now. Wherefore are they shut? Open thine eyes! Lift up thine eyelids, Iokanaan! Wherefore dost thou not look at me? Art thou afraid of me, Iokanaan, that thou wilt not look at me? . . . And thy tongue, that was like a red snake darting poison, it moves no more, it speaks no words, Iokanaan, that scarlet viper that spat its venom upon me. It is strange, is it not? How is it that the red viper stirs no longer? . . . Thou wouldst have none of me, Iokanaan. Thou rejectedst me. Thou didst speak evil words against me. Thou didst bear thyself toward me as to a harlot, as to a woman that is a wanton, to me, Salome, daughter of Herodias, Princess of Judæa! Well, I still live, but thou art dead, and thy head

belongs to me. I can do with it what I will. I can throw it to the dogs°
and to the birds of the air. That which the dogs leave, the birds of the
air shall devour. . . . Ah, Iokanaan, Iokanaan, thou wert the man that I
loved alone among men! All other men were hateful to me. But thou
wert beautiful! Thy body was a column of ivory° set upon feet of silver.
It was a garden full of doves and lilies of silver. It was a tower of silver
decked with shields of ivory. There was nothing in the world so white
as thy body. There was nothing in the world so black as thy hair. In the
whole world there was nothing so red as thy mouth. Thy voice was a
censer that scattered strange perfumes, and when I looked on thee I
heard a strange music. Ah! wherefore didst thou not look at me,
Iokanaan? With the cloak of thine hands, and with the cloak of thy
blasphemies thou didst hide thy face. Thou didst put upon thine eyes
the covering of him who would see his God. Well, thou hast seen thy
God, Iokanaan, but me, me, thou didst never see. If thou hadst seen
me thou hadst loved me. I saw thee, and I loved thee. Oh, how I loved
thee! I love thee yet, Iokanaan. I love only thee. . . . I am athirst for thy
beauty; I am hungry for thy body; and neither wine nor apples can
appease my desire. What shall I do now, Iokanaan? Neither the floods
nor the great waters can quench my passion.° I was a princess, and
thou didst scorn me. I was a virgin, and thou didst take my virginity
from me. I was chaste, and thou didst fill my veins with fire. . . . Ah!
ah! wherefore didst thou not look at me? If thou hadst looked at me
thou hadst loved me. Well I know that thou wouldst have loved me,
and the mystery of Love is greater than the mystery of Death.°

HEROD. She is monstrous, thy daughter; I tell thee she is monstrous. In
truth, what she has done is a great crime. I am sure that it is a crime
against some unknown God.

HERODIAS. I am well pleased with my daughter.° She has done well. And
I would stay here now.

HEROD [*Rising.*] Ah! There speaks my brother's wife! Come! I will not
stay in this place. Come, I tell thee. Surely some terrible thing will
befall. Manasseh, Issachar, Ozias, put out the torches. I will not look at
things, I will not suffer things to look at me. Put out the torches! Hide
the moon! Hide the stars! Let us hide ourselves in our palace,
Herodias. I begin to be afraid.

[*The slaves put out the torches. The stars disappear. A great cloud crosses the
moon and conceals it completely. The stage becomes quite dark. The
Tetrarch begins to climb the staircase.*]

THE VOICE OF SALOME. Ah! I have kissed thy mouth, Iokanaan, I have kissed thy mouth. There was a bitter taste on thy lips. Was it the taste of blood? . . . Nay; but perchance it was the taste of love. . . . They say that love hath a bitter taste. . . . But what matter? what matter? I have kissed thy mouth, Iokanaan, I have kissed thy mouth.

[*A ray of moonlight falls on Salome and illumines her.*]

HEROD [*Turning round and seeing Salome.*] Kill that woman!°
[*The soldiers rush forward and crush beneath their shields Salome, daughter of Herodias, Princess of Judæa.*]

CURTAIN.

LADY WINDERMERE'S FAN

A Play about a Good Woman

THE PERSONS OF THE PLAY°

LORD WINDERMERE

LORD DARLINGTON

LORD AUGUSTUS LORTON

MR DUMBY

MR CECIL GRAHAM

MR HOPPER

PARKER, Butler

LADY WINDERMERE

THE DUCHESS OF BERWICK

LADY AGATHA CARLISLE

LADY PLYMDALE

LADY STUTFIELD

LADY JEDBURGH

MRS COWPER-COWPER

MRS ERLYNNE

ROSALIE, Maid

THE SCENES OF THE PLAY

ACT I *Morning-room in Lord Windermere's house.*

ACT II *Drawing-room in Lord Windermere's house.*

ACT III *Lord Darlington's rooms.*

ACT IV *Same as Act I.*

Time . . . . *The Present.*
Place . . . . *London.*

The action of the play takes place within twenty-four hours,° beginning on a Tuesday afternoon at five o'clock, and ending the next day at 1.30 p.m.

LONDON: ST JAMES'S THEATRE

Lessee and Manager: Mr George Alexander
February 22nd, 1892

LORD WINDERMERE	*Mr George Alexander*
LORD DARLINGTON	*Mr Nutcombe Gould*
LORD AUGUSTUS LORTON	*Mr H. H. Vincent*
MR CECIL GRAHAM	*Mr Ben. Webster*
MR DUMBY	*Mr Vane-Tempest*
MR HOPPER	*Mr Alfred Holles*
PARKER (*Butler*)	*Mr V. Sansbury*
LADY WINDERMERE	*Miss Lily Hanbury*
THE DUCHESS OF BERWICK	*Miss Fanny Coleman*
LADY AGATHA CARLISLE	*Miss Laura Graves*
LADY PLYMDALE	*Miss Granville*
LADY JEDBURGH	*Miss B. Page*
LADY STUTFIELD	*Miss Madge Girdlestone*
MRS COWPER-COWPER	*Miss A. De Winton*
MRS ERLYNNE	*Miss Marion Terry*
ROSALIE (*Maid*)	*Miss Winifred Dolan*

LADY WINDERMERE'S FAN°

FIRST ACT

SCENE—*Morning-room of Lord Windermere's house in Carlton House Terrace.° Doors C. and R. Bureau with books and papers R. Sofa with small tea-table L. Window opening on to terrace L. Table R.*

[*Lady Windermere is at table R., arranging roses in a blue bowl.*]
[*Enter Parker.*]

PARKER. Is your ladyship at home this afternoon?

LADY WINDERMERE. Yes—who has called?

PARKER. Lord Darlington, my lady.

LADY WINDERMERE [*Hesitates for a moment.*] Show him up—and I'm at home to any one who calls.

PARKER. Yes, my lady.

[*Exit C.*]

LADY WINDERMERE. It's best for me to see him before tonight. I'm glad he's come.

[*Enter Parker C.*]

PARKER. Lord Darlington.

[*Enter Lord Darlington C.*]

[*Exit Parker.*]

LORD DARLINGTON. How do you do, Lady Windermere?

LADY WINDERMERE. How do you do, Lord Darlington? No, I can't shake hands with you. My hands are all wet with these roses. Aren't they lovely? They came up from Selby this morning.

LORD DARLINGTON. They are quite perfect. [*Sees a fan lying on the table.*] And what a wonderful fan! May I look at it?

LADY WINDERMERE. Do. Pretty, isn't it! It's got my name on it, and everything. I have only just seen it myself. It's my husband's birthday present to me. You know today is my birthday?

LORD DARLINGTON. No? Is it really?

LADY WINDERMERE. Yes, I'm of age today. Quite an important day in my life, isn't it? That is why I am giving this party tonight. Do sit down. [*Still arranging flowers.*]

LORD DARLINGTON [*Sitting down.*] I wish I had known it was your birthday, Lady Windermere. I would have covered the whole street in front of your house with flowers for you to walk on. They are made for you.

[*A short pause.*]

LADY WINDERMERE. Lord Darlington, you annoyed me last night at the Foreign Office. I am afraid you are going to annoy me again.

LORD DARLINGTON. I, Lady Windermere?

[*Enter Parker and Footman C., with tray and tea things.*]

LADY WINDERMERE. Put it there, Parker. That will do. [*Wipes her hands with her pocket-handkerchief, goes to tea-table L., and sits down.*] Won't you come over, Lord Darlington?

[*Exit Parker C.*]

LORD DARLINGTON [*Takes chair and goes across L.C.*] I am quite miserable, Lady Windermere. You must tell me what I did. [*Sits down at table L.*]

LADY WINDERMERE. Well, you kept paying me elaborate compliments the whole evening.

LORD DARLINGTON [*Smiling.*] Ah, nowadays we are all of us so hard up, that the only pleasant things to pay *are* compliments. They're the only things we *can* pay.

LADY WINDERMERE [*Shaking her head.*] No, I am talking very seriously. You mustn't laugh, I am quite serious. I don't like compliments, and I don't see why a man should think he is pleasing a woman enormously when he says to her a whole heap of things that he doesn't mean.

LORD DARLINGTON. Ah, but I did mean them. [*Takes tea which she offers him.*]

LADY WINDERMERE [*Gravely.*] I hope not. I should be sorry to have to quarrel with you, Lord Darlington. I like you very much, you know that. But I shouldn't like you at all if I thought you were what most other men are. Believe me, you are better than most other men, and I sometimes think you pretend to be worse.

LORD DARLINGTON. We all have our little vanities, Lady Windermere.

LADY WINDERMERE. Why do you make that your special one? [*Still seated at table L.*]

LORD DARLINGTON [*Still seated L.C.*] Oh, nowadays so many conceited people go about Society pretending to be good, that I think it shows rather a sweet and modest disposition to pretend to be bad. Besides, there is this to be said. If you pretend to be good, the world takes you very seriously. If you pretend to be bad, it doesn't. Such is the astounding stupidity of optimism.

LADY WINDERMERE. Don't you *want* the world to take you seriously then, Lord Darlington?

LORD DARLINGTON. No, not the world. Who are the people the world takes seriously? All the dull people one can think of, from the Bishops down to the bores. I should like *you* to take me very seriously, Lady Windermere, *you* more than any one else in life.

LADY WINDERMERE. Why—why me?

LORD DARLINGTON [*After a slight hesitation.*] Because I think we might be great friends. Let us be great friends. You may want a friend some day.

LADY WINDERMERE. Why do you say that?

LORD DARLINGTON. Oh—we all want friends at times.

LADY WINDERMERE. I think we're very good friends already, Lord Darlington. We can always remain so as long as you don't—

LORD DARLINGTON. Don't what?

LADY WINDERMERE. Don't spoil it by saying extravagant silly things to me. You think I am a Puritan, I suppose? Well, I have something of the Puritan in me. I was brought up like that. I am glad of it. My mother died when I was a mere child. I lived always with Lady Julia, my father's elder sister you know. She was stern to me, but she taught me, what the world is forgetting, the difference that there is between what is right and what is wrong. *She* allowed of no compromise. *I* allow of none.

LORD DARLINGTON. My dear Lady Windermere!

LADY WINDERMERE [*Leaning back on the sofa.*] You look on me as being behind the age.—Well, I am! I should be sorry to be on the same level as an age like this.

LORD DARLINGTON. You think the age very bad?

LADY WINDERMERE. Yes. Nowadays people seem to look on life as a speculation. It is not a speculation. It is a sacrament. Its ideal is Love. Its purification is sacrifice.

LORD DARLINGTON [*Smiling.*] Oh, anything is better than being sacrificed!

LADY WINDERMERE [*Leaning forward.*] Don't say that.

LORD DARLINGTON. I do say it. I feel it—I know it.

[*Enter Parker C.*]

PARKER. The men want to know if they are to put the carpets on the terrace for tonight, my lady?

LADY WINDERMERE. You don't think it will rain, Lord Darlington, do you?

LORD DARLINGTON. I won't hear of its raining on your birthday!

LADY WINDERMERE. Tell them to do it at once, Parker.

[*Exit Parker C.*]

LORD DARLINGTON [*Still seated.*] Do you think then—of course I am only putting an imaginary instance—do you think that in the case of a young married couple, say about two years married, if the husband suddenly becomes the intimate friend of a woman of—well, more than doubtful character, is always calling upon her, lunching with her, and probably paying her bills—do you think that the wife should not console herself?

LADY WINDERMERE [*Frowning.*] Console herself?

LORD DARLINGTON. Yes, I think she should—I think she has the right.

LADY WINDERMERE. Because the husband is vile—should the wife be vile also?

LORD DARLINGTON. Vileness is a terrible word, Lady Windermere.

LADY WINDERMERE. It is a terrible thing, Lord Darlington.

LORD DARLINGTON. Do you know I am afraid that good people do a great deal of harm in this world. Certainly the greatest harm they do is that they make badness of such extraordinary importance. It is absurd to divide people into good and bad. People are either charming or tedious. I take the side of the charming, and you, Lady Windermere, can't help belonging to them.

LADY WINDERMERE. Now, Lord Darlington. [*Rising and crossing R., front of him.*] Don't stir, I am merely going to finish my flowers. [*Goes to table R.C.*]

LORD DARLINGTON [*Rising and moving chair.*] And I must say I think you are very hard on modern life, Lady Windermere. Of course there is much against it, I admit. Most women, for instance, nowadays, are rather mercenary.

LADY WINDERMERE. Don't talk about such people.

LORD DARLINGTON. Well then, setting mercenary people aside, who, of course, are dreadful, do you think seriously that women who have committed what the world calls a fault should never be forgiven?

LADY WINDERMERE [*Standing at table.*] I think they should never be forgiven.

LORD DARLINGTON. And men? Do you think that there should be the same laws for men as there are for women?

LADY WINDERMERE. Certainly!

LORD DARLINGTON. I think life too complex a thing to be settled by these hard and fast rules.

LADY WINDERMERE. If we had 'these hard and fast rules', we should find life much more simple.

LORD DARLINGTON. You allow of no exceptions?

LADY WINDERMERE. None!

LORD DARLINGTON. Ah, what a fascinating Puritan you are, Lady Windermere!

LADY WINDERMERE. The adjective was unnecessary, Lord Darlington.

LORD DARLINGTON. I couldn't help it. I can resist everything except temptation.

LADY WINDERMERE. You have the modern affectation of weakness.

LORD DARLINGTON [*Looking at her.*] It's only an affectation, Lady Windermere.

[*Enter Parker C.*]

PARKER. The Duchess of Berwick and Lady Agatha Carlisle.

[*Enter the Duchess of Berwick and Lady Agatha Carlisle C.*]

[*Exit Parker C.*]

DUCHESS OF BERWICK [*Coming down C., and shaking hands.*] Dear Margaret, I am so pleased to see you. You remember Agatha, don't you? [*Crossing L.C.*] How do you do, Lord Darlington? I won't let you know my daughter, you are far too wicked.

LORD DARLINGTON. Don't say that, Duchess. As a wicked man I am a complete failure. Why, there are lots of people who say I have never really done anything wrong in the whole course of my life. Of course they only say it behind my back.°

DUCHESS OF BERWICK. Isn't he dreadful? Agatha, this is Lord Darlington. Mind you don't believe a word he says. [*Lord Darlington crosses*

R.C.] No, no tea, thank you, dear. [*Crosses and sits on sofa.*] We have just had tea at Lady Markby's. Such bad tea, too. It was quite undrinkable. I wasn't at all surprised. Her own son-in-law supplies it. Agatha is looking forward so much to your ball tonight, dear Margaret.

LADY WINDERMERE [*Seated L.C.*] Oh, you mustn't think it is going to be a ball, Duchess. It is only a dance in honour of my birthday. A small and early.

LORD DARLINGTON [*Standing L.C.*] Very small, very early, and very select, Duchess.

DUCHESS OF BERWICK [*On sofa L.*] Of course it's going to be select. But we know *that*, dear Margaret, about *your* house. It is really one of the few houses in London where I can take Agatha, and where I feel perfectly secure about dear Berwick. I don't know what society is coming to. The most dreadful people seem to go everywhere. They certainly come to my parties—the men get quite furious if one doesn't ask them. Really, some one should make a stand against it.

LADY WINDERMERE. *I* will, Duchess. I will have no one in my house about whom there is any scandal.

LORD DARLINGTON [*R.C.*] Oh, don't say that, Lady Windermere. I should never be admitted! [*Sitting.*]

DUCHESS OF BERWICK. Oh, men don't matter. With women it is different. We're good. Some of us are, at least. But we are positively getting elbowed into the corner. Our husbands would really forget our existence if we didn't nag at them from time to time, just to remind them that we have a perfect legal right to do so.

LORD DARLINGTON. It's a curious thing, Duchess, about the game of marriage—a game, by the way, that is going out of fashion—the wives hold all the honours, and invariably lose the odd trick.°

DUCHESS OF BERWICK. The odd trick? Is that the husband, Lord Darlington?

LORD DARLINGTON. It would be rather a good name for the modern husband.

DUCHESS OF BERWICK. Dear Lord Darlington, how thoroughly depraved you are!

LADY WINDERMERE. Lord Darlington is trivial.

LORD DARLINGTON. Ah, don't say that, Lady Windermere.

LADY WINDERMERE. Why do you *talk* so trivially about life, then?

LORD DARLINGTON. Because I think that life is far too important a thing ever to talk seriously about it.° [*Moves up C.*]

DUCHESS OF BERWICK. What does he mean? Do, as a concession to my poor wits, Lord Darlington, just explain to me what you really mean.

LORD DARLINGTON [*Coming down back of table.*] I think I had better not, Duchess. Nowadays to be intelligible is to be found out. Goodbye! [*Shakes hands with Duchess.*] And now—[*goes up stage*] Lady Windermere, goodbye. I may come tonight, mayn't I? Do let me come.

LADY WINDERMERE [*Standing up stage with Lord Darlington.*] Yes, certainly. But you are not to say foolish, insincere things to people.

LORD DARLINGTON [*Smiling.*] Ah! you are beginning to reform me. It is a dangerous thing to reform any one, Lady Windermere.

[*Bows, and exit C.*]

DUCHESS OF BERWICK [*Who has risen, goes C.*] What a charming, wicked creature! I like him so much. I'm quite delighted he's gone! How sweet you're looking! Where *do* you get your gowns? And now I must tell you how sorry I am for you, dear Margaret. [*Crosses to sofa and sits with Lady Windermere.*] Agatha darling!

LADY AGATHA. Yes, mamma. [*Rises.*]

DUCHESS OF BERWICK. Will you go and look over the photograph album that I see there?

LADY AGATHA. Yes, mamma. [*Goes to table up L.*]

DUCHESS OF BERWICK. Dear girl! She is so fond of photographs of Switzerland. Such a pure taste, I think. But I really am so sorry for you, Margaret.

LADY WINDERMERE [*Smiling.*] Why, Duchess?

DUCHESS OF BERWICK. Oh, on account of that horrid woman. She dresses so well, too, which makes it much worse, sets such a dreadful example. Augustus—you know my disreputable brother—such a trial to us all—well, Augustus is completely infatuated about her. It is quite scandalous, for she is absolutely inadmissible into society. Many a woman has a past, but I am told that she has at least a dozen, and that they all fit.

LADY WINDERMERE. Whom are you talking about, Duchess?

DUCHESS OF BERWICK. About Mrs Erlynne.

LADY WINDERMERE. Mrs Erlynne? I never heard of her, Duchess. And what *has* she to do with me?

DUCHESS OF BERWICK. My poor child! Agatha, darling!

LADY AGATHA. Yes, mamma.

DUCHESS OF BERWICK. Will you go out on the terrace and look at the sunset?

LADY AGATHA. Yes, mamma.

[Exit through window L.]

DUCHESS OF BERWICK. Sweet girl! So devoted to sunsets! Shows such refinement of feeling, does it not? After all, there is nothing like Nature, is there?

LADY WINDERMERE. But what is it, Duchess? Why do you talk to me about this person?

DUCHESS OF BERWICK. Don't you really know? I assure you we're all so distressed about it. Only last night at dear Lady Jansen's every one was saying how extraordinary it was that, of all men in London, Windermere should behave in such a way.

LADY WINDERMERE. My husband—what has *he* got to do with any woman of that kind?

DUCHESS OF BERWICK. Ah, what indeed, dear? That is the point. He goes to see her continually, and stops for hours at a time, and while he is there she is not at home to any one. Not that many ladies call on her, dear, but she has a great many disreputable men friends—my own brother particularly, as I told you—and that is what makes it so dreadful about Windermere. We looked upon *him* as being such a model husband, but I am afraid there is no doubt about it. My dear nieces—you know the Saville girls, don't you?—such nice domestic creatures—plain, dreadfully plain, but so good—well, they're always at the window doing fancy work, and making ugly things for the poor, which I think so useful of them in these dreadful socialistic days, and this terrible woman has taken a house in Curzon Street, right opposite them—such a respectable street, too. I don't know what we're coming to! And they tell me that Windermere goes there four and five times a week—they *see* him. They can't help it—and although they never talk scandal, they—well, of course—they remark on it to every one. And the worst of it all is that I have been told that this woman has got a great deal of money out of somebody, for it seems that she came to London six months ago without anything at all to speak of, and now she has this charming house in Mayfair, drives her ponies in the Park° every afternoon and all—well, all—since she has known poor dear Windermere.

LADY WINDERMERE. Oh, I can't believe it!

DUCHESS OF BERWICK. But it's quite true, my dear. The whole of London knows it. That is why I felt it was better to come and talk to you, and advise you to take Windermere away at once to Homburg or to Aix,° where he'll have something to amuse him, and where you can watch him all day long. I assure you, my dear, that on several occasions after I was first married, I had to pretend to be very ill, and was obliged to drink the most unpleasant mineral waters, merely to get Berwick out of town. He was so extremely susceptible. Though I am bound to say he never gave away any large sums of money to anybody. He is far too high-principled for that!

LADY WINDERMERE [Interrupting.] Duchess, Duchess, it's impossible! [Rising and crossing stage to C.] We are only married two years. Our child is but six months old. [Sits in chair R. of L. table.]

DUCHESS OF BERWICK. Ah, the dear pretty baby! How is the little darling? Is it a boy or a girl? I hope a girl—Ah, no, I remember it's a boy! I'm so sorry. Boys are so wicked. My boy is excessively immoral. You wouldn't believe at what hours he comes home. And he's only left Oxford a few months—I really don't know what they teach them there.

LADY WINDERMERE. Are all men bad?

DUCHESS OF BERWICK. Oh, all of them, my dear, all of them, without any exception. And they never grow any better. Men become old, but they never become good.

LADY WINDERMERE. Windermere and I married for love.

DUCHESS OF BERWICK. Yes, we begin like that. It was only Berwick's brutal and incessant threats of suicide that made me accept him at all, and before the year was out, he was running after all kinds of petticoats, every colour, every shape, every material. In fact before the honeymoon was over, I caught him winking at my maid, a most pretty, respectable girl. I dismissed her at once without a character°—No, I remember I passed her on to my sister; poor dear Sir George is so short-sighted, I thought it wouldn't matter. But it did, though—it was most unfortunate. [Rises.] And now, my dear child, I must go, as we are dining out. And mind you don't take this little aberration of Windermere's too much to heart. Just take him abroad, and he'll come back to you all right.

LADY WINDERMERE. Come back to me? [C.]

DUCHESS OF BERWICK [L.C.] Yes, dear, these wicked women get our husbands away from us, but they always come back, slightly damaged, of course. And don't make scenes, men hate them!

LADY WINDERMERE. It is very kind of you, Duchess, to come and tell me all this. But I can't believe that my husband is untrue to me.

DUCHESS OF BERWICK. Pretty child! I was like that once. Now I know that all men are monsters. [*Lady Windermere rings bell.*] The only thing to do is to feed the wretches well. A good cook does wonders, and that I know you have. My dear Margaret, you are not going to cry?

LADY WINDERMERE. You needn't be afraid, Duchess, I never cry.

DUCHESS OF BERWICK. That's quite right, dear. Crying is the refuge of plain women but the ruin of pretty ones. Agatha, darling!

LADY AGATHA [*Entering L.*] Yes, mamma. [*Stands back of table L.C.*]

DUCHESS OF BERWICK. Come and bid goodbye to Lady Windermere, and thank her for your charming visit. [*Coming down again.*] And by the way, I must thank you for sending a card to Mr Hopper—he's that rich young Australian people are taking such notice of just at present. His father made a great fortune by selling some kind of food in circular tins—most palatable, I believe—I fancy it is the thing the servants always refuse to eat. But the son is quite interesting. I think he's attracted by dear Agatha's clever talk. Of course, we should be very sorry to lose her, but I think that a mother who doesn't part with a daughter every season has no real affection. We're coming tonight, dear. [*Parker opens C. doors.*] And remember my advice, take the poor fellow out of town at once, it is the only thing to do. Goodbye, once more; come, Agatha.

[*Exeunt Duchess and Lady Agatha C.*]

LADY WINDERMERE. How horrible! I understand now what Lord Darlington meant by the imaginary instance of the couple not two years married. Oh! it can't be true—she spoke of enormous sums of money paid to this woman. I know where Arthur keeps his bank book—in one of the drawers of that desk. I might find out by that. I *will* find out. [*Opens drawer.*] No, it is some hideous mistake. [*Rises and goes C.*] Some silly scandal! He loves *me*! He loves *me*! But why should I not look? I am his wife, I have a right to look! [*Returns to bureau, takes out book and examines it, page by page, smiles and gives a sigh of relief.*] I knew it! there is not a word of truth in this stupid story. [*Puts book back in drawer. As she does so, starts and takes out another book.*] A second book—private—locked!° [*Tries to open it, but fails. Sees paper knife on bureau, and with it cuts cover from book. Begins to start at the first page.*]

'Mrs Erlynne—£600—Mrs Erlynne—£700—Mrs Erlynne—£400.' Oh! it is true! it is true! How horrible! [*Throws book on floor.*]

[*Enter Lord Windermere C.*]

LORD WINDERMERE. Well, dear, has the fan been sent home yet? [*Goes R.C. Sees book.*] Margaret, you have cut open my bank book. You have no right to do such a thing!

LADY WINDERMERE. You think it wrong that you are found out, don't you?

LORD WINDERMERE. I think it wrong that a wife should spy on her husband.

LADY WINDERMERE. I did not spy on you. I never knew of this woman's existence till half an hour ago. Some one who pitied me was kind enough to tell me what every one in London knows already—your daily visits to Curzon Street, your mad infatuation, the monstrous sums of money you squander on this infamous woman! [*Crossing L.*]

LORD WINDERMERE. Margaret! don't talk like that of Mrs Erlynne, you don't know how unjust it is!

LADY WINDERMERE [*Turning to him.*] You are very jealous of Mrs Erlynne's honour. I wish you had been as jealous of mine.

LORD WINDERMERE. Your honour is untouched, Margaret. You don't think for a moment that——[*Puts book back into desk.*]

LADY WINDERMERE. I think that you spend your money strangely. That is all. Oh, don't imagine I mind about the money. As far as I am concerned, you may squander everything we have. But what I *do* mind is that you who have loved me, you who have taught me to love you, should pass from the love that is given to the love that is bought. Oh, it's horrible! [*Sits on sofa.*] And it is I who feel degraded! *you* don't feel anything. I feel stained, utterly stained. You can't realize how hideous the last six months seem to me now—every kiss you have given me is tainted in my memory.

LORD WINDERMERE [*Crossing to her.*] Don't say that, Margaret. I never loved any one in the whole world but you.

LADY WINDERMERE [*Rises.*] Who is this woman, then? Why do you take a house for her?

LORD WINDERMERE. I did not take a house for her.

LADY WINDERMERE. You gave her the money to do it, which is the same thing.

LORD WINDERMERE. Margaret, as far as I have known Mrs Erlynne——

LADY WINDERMERE. Is there a Mr Erlynne—or is he a myth?

LORD WINDERMERE. Her husband died many years ago. She is alone in the world.

LADY WINDERMERE. No relations? [*A pause.*]

LORD WINDERMERE. None.

LADY WINDERMERE. Rather curious, isn't it? [*L.*]

LORD WINDERMERE [*L.C.*] Margaret, I was saying to you—and I beg you to listen to me—that as far as I have known Mrs Erlynne, she has conducted herself well. If years ago——

LADY WINDERMERE. Oh! [*Crossing R.C.*] I don't want details about her life!

LORD WINDERMERE [*C.*] I am not going to give you any details about her life. I tell you simply this—Mrs Erlynne was once honoured, loved, respected. She was well born, she had position—she lost everything—threw it away, if you like. That makes it all the more bitter. Misfortunes one can endure—they come from outside, they are accidents. But to suffer for one's own faults—ah!—there is the sting of life. It was twenty years ago, too. She was little more than a girl then. She had been a wife for even less time than you have.

LADY WINDERMERE. I am not interested in her—and—you should not mention this woman and me in the same breath. It is an error of taste. [*Sitting R. at desk.*]

LORD WINDERMERE. Margaret, you could save this woman. She wants to get back into society, and she wants you to help her. [*Crossing to her.*]

LADY WINDERMERE. Me!

LORD WINDERMERE. Yes, you.

LADY WINDERMERE. How impertinent of her! [*A pause.*]

LORD WINDERMERE. Margaret, I came to ask you a great favour, and I still ask it of you, though you have discovered what I had intended you should never have known, that I have given Mrs Erlynne a large sum of money. I want you to send her an invitation for our party tonight. [*Standing L. of her.*]

LADY WINDERMERE. You are mad! [*Rises.*]

LORD WINDERMERE. I entreat you. People may chatter about her, do chatter about her, of course, but they don't know anything definite against her. She has been to several houses—not to houses where you would go, I admit, but still to houses where women who are in what is called Society nowadays do go. That does not content her. She wants you to receive her once.

LADY WINDERMERE. As a triumph for her, I suppose?

LORD WINDERMERE. No; but because she knows that you are a good woman—and that if she comes here once she will have a chance of a happier, a surer life than she has had. She will make no further effort to know you. Won't you help a woman who is trying to get back?

LADY WINDERMERE. No! If a woman really repents, she never wishes to return to the society that has made or seen her ruin.

LORD WINDERMERE. I beg of you.

LADY WINDERMERE [*Crossing to door R.*] I am going to dress for dinner, and don't mention the subject again this evening. Arthur [*Going to him C.*], you fancy because I have no father or mother that I am alone in the world, and that you can treat me as you choose. You are wrong, I have friends, many friends.

LORD WINDERMERE [*L.C.*] Margaret, you are talking foolishly, recklessly. I won't argue with you, but I insist upon your asking Mrs Erlynne tonight.

LADY WINDERMERE [*R.C.*] I shall do nothing of the kind. [*Crossing L.C.*]

LORD WINDERMERE. You refuse? [*C.*]

LADY WINDERMERE. Absolutely!

LORD WINDERMERE. Ah, Margaret, do this for my sake; it is her last chance.

LADY WINDERMERE. What has that to do with me?

LORD WINDERMERE. How hard good women are!

LADY WINDERMERE. How weak bad men are!

LORD WINDERMERE. Margaret, none of us men may be good enough for the women we marry—that is quite true—but you don't imagine I would ever—oh, the suggestion is monstrous!

LADY WINDERMERE. Why should *you* be different from other men? I am told that there is hardly a husband in London who does not waste his life over *some* shameful passion.

LORD WINDERMERE. I am not one of them.

LADY WINDERMERE. I am not sure of that!

LORD WINDERMERE. You are sure in your heart. But don't make chasm after chasm between us. God knows the last few minutes have thrust us wide enough apart. Sit down and write the card.

LADY WINDERMERE. Nothing in the whole world would induce me.

LORD WINDERMERE [*Crossing to bureau.*] Then I will! [*Rings electric bell, sits and writes card.*]

LADY WINDERMERE. You are going to invite this woman? [*Crossing to him.*]

LORD WINDERMERE. Yes.

[*Pause. Enter Parker.*]

Parker!

PARKER. Yes, my lord. [*Comes down L.C.*]

LORD WINDERMERE. Have this note sent to Mrs Erlynne at No. 84A Curzon Street. [*Crossing to L.C. and giving note to Parker.*] There is no answer!

[*Exit Parker C.*]

LADY WINDERMERE. Arthur, if that woman comes here, I shall insult her.

LORD WINDERMERE. Margaret, don't say that.

LADY WINDERMERE. I mean it.

LORD WINDERMERE. Child, if you did such a thing, there's not a woman in London who wouldn't pity you.

LADY WINDERMERE. There is not a *good* woman in London who would not applaud me. We have been too lax. We must make an example. I propose to begin tonight. [*Picking up fan.*] Yes, you gave me this fan today; it was your birthday present. If that woman crosses my threshold, I shall strike her across the face with it.

LORD WINDERMERE. Margaret, you couldn't do such a thing.

LADY WINDERMERE. You don't know me! [*Moves R.*]

[*Enter Parker.*]

Parker!

PARKER. Yes, my lady.

LADY WINDERMERE. I shall dine in my own room. I don't want dinner, in fact. See that everything is ready by half-past ten. And, Parker, be sure you pronounce the names of the guests very distinctly tonight. Sometimes you speak so fast that I miss them. I am particularly anxious to hear the names quite clearly, so as to make no mistake. You understand, Parker?

PARKER. Yes, my lady.

LADY WINDERMERE. That will do!

[*Exit Parker C.*]

[*Speaking to Lord Windermere.*] Arthur, if that woman comes here—I warn you——

LORD WINDERMERE. Margaret, you'll ruin us!

LADY WINDERMERE. Us! From this moment my life is separate from yours. But if you wish to avoid a public scandal, write at once to this woman, and tell her that I forbid her to come here!

LORD WINDERMERE. I will not—I cannot—she must come!

LADY WINDERMERE. Then I shall do exactly as I have said. [*Goes R.*] You leave me no choice.

[*Exit R.*]

LORD WINDERMERE [*Calling after her.*] Margaret! Margaret! [*A pause.*] My God! What shall I do? I dare not tell her who this woman really is. The shame would kill her. [*Sinks down into a chair and buries his face in his hands.*]

ACT DROP

SECOND ACT

SCENE—*Drawing-room in Lord Windermere's house. Door R.U. opening into ball-room, where band is playing. Door L. through which guests are entering. Door L.U. opens on to illuminated terrace. Palms, flowers, and brilliant lights. Room crowded with guests. Lady Windermere is receiving them.*

DUCHESS OF BERWICK [*Up C.*] So strange Lord Windermere isn't here. Mr Hopper is very late, too. You have kept those five dances for him, Agatha? [*Comes down.*]

LADY AGATHA. Yes, mamma.

DUCHESS OF BERWICK [*Sitting on sofa.*] Just let me see your card.° I'm so glad Lady Windermere has revived cards.—They're a mother's only safeguard. You dear simple little thing! [*Scratches out two names.*] No nice girl should ever waltz with such particularly younger sons!° It looks so fast! The last two dances you might pass on the terrace with Mr Hopper.

[*Enter Mr Dumby and Lady Plymdale from the ball-room.*]

LADY AGATHA. Yes, mamma.

DUCHESS OF BERWICK [*Fanning herself.*] The air is so pleasant there.

PARKER. Mrs Cowper-Cowper. Lady Stutfield. Sir James Royston. Mr Guy Berkeley.

[*These people enter as announced.*]

DUMBY. Good evening, Lady Stutfield. I suppose this will be the last ball of the season?

LADY STUTFIELD. I suppose so, Mr Dumby. It's been a delightful season, hasn't it?

DUMBY. Quite delightful! Good evening, Duchess. I suppose this will be the last ball of the season?

DUCHESS OF BERWICK. I suppose so, Mr Dumby. It has been a very dull season, hasn't it?

DUMBY. Dreadfully dull! Dreadfully dull!

MRS COWPER-COWPER. Good evening, Mr Dumby. I suppose this will be the last ball of the season?

DUMBY. Oh, I think not. There'll probably be two more. [*Wanders back to Lady Plymdale.*]

PARKER. Mr Rufford. Lady Jedburgh and Miss Graham. Mr Hopper.

[*These people enter as announced.*]

HOPPER. How do you do, Lady Windermere? How do you do, Duchess? [*Bows to Lady Agatha.*]

DUCHESS OF BERWICK. Dear Mr Hopper, how nice of you to come so early. We all know how you are run after in London.

HOPPER. Capital place, London! They are not nearly so exclusive in London as they are in Sydney.

DUCHESS OF BERWICK. Ah! we know your value, Mr Hopper. We wish there were more like you. It would make life so much easier. Do you know, Mr Hopper, dear Agatha and I are so much interested in Australia. It must be so pretty with all the dear little kangaroos flying about. Agatha has found it on the map. What a curious shape it is! Just like a large packing case. However, it is a very young country, isn't it?

HOPPER. Wasn't it made at the same time as the others, Duchess?

DUCHESS OF BERWICK. How clever you are, Mr Hopper. You have a cleverness quite of your own. Now I mustn't keep you.

HOPPER. But I should like to dance with Lady Agatha, Duchess.

DUCHESS OF BERWICK. Well, I *hope* she has a dance left. Have you a dance left, Agatha?

LADY AGATHA. Yes, mamma.

DUCHESS OF BERWICK. The next one?

LADY AGATHA. Yes, mamma.

HOPPER. May I have the pleasure? [*Lady Agatha bows.*]

DUCHESS OF BERWICK. Mind you take great care of my little chatterbox, Mr Hopper.

[*Lady Agatha and Mr Hopper pass into ball-room.*]
[*Enter Lord Windermere L.*]

LORD WINDERMERE. Margaret, I want to speak to you.

LADY WINDERMERE. In a moment.

[*The music stops.*]

PARKER. Lord Augustus Lorton.

[*Enter Lord Augustus.*]

LORD AUGUSTUS. Good evening, Lady Windermere.

DUCHESS OF BERWICK. Sir James, will you take me into the ball-room? Augustus has been dining with us tonight. I really have had quite enough of dear Augustus for the moment.

[*Sir James Royston gives the Duchess his arm and escorts her into the ball-room.*]

PARKER. Mr and Mrs Arthur Bowden. Lord and Lady Paisley. Lord Darlington.

[*These people enter as announced.*]

LORD AUGUSTUS [*Coming up to Lord Windermere.*] Want to speak to you particularly, dear boy. I'm worn to a shadow. Know I don't look it. None of us men do look what we really are. Demmed good thing, too. What I want to know is this. Who is she? Where does she come from? Why hasn't she got any demmed relations? Demmed nuisance, relations! But they make one so demmed respectable.

LORD WINDERMERE. You are talking of Mrs Erlynne, I suppose? I only met her six months ago. Till then, I never knew of her existence.

LORD AUGUSTUS. You have seen a good deal of her since then.

LORD WINDERMERE [*Coldly.*] Yes, I have seen a good deal of her since then. I have just seen her.

LORD AUGUSTUS. Egad! the women are very down on her. I have been dining with Arabella this evening! By Jove! you should have heard what she said about Mrs Erlynne. She didn't leave a rag on her. . . . [*Aside.*] Berwick and I told her that didn't matter much, as the lady in question must have an extremely fine figure. You should have seen Arabella's expression! . . . But, look here, dear boy. I don't know what to do about Mrs Erlynne. Egad! I might be married to her; she treats me with such demmed indifference. She's deuced clever, too! She explains everything. Egad! she explains you. She has got any amount of explanations for you—and all of them different.

LORD WINDERMERE. No explanations are necessary about my friendship with Mrs Erlynne.

LORD AUGUSTUS. Hem! Well, look here, dear old fellow. Do you think she will ever get into this demmed thing called Society? Would you introduce her to your wife? No use beating about the confounded bush. Would you do that?

LORD WINDERMERE. Mrs Erlynne is coming here tonight.

LORD AUGUSTUS. Your wife has sent her a card?

LORD WINDERMERE. Mrs Erlynne has received a card.

LORD AUGUSTUS. Then she's all right, dear boy. But why didn't you tell me that before. It would have saved me a heap of worry and demmed misunderstandings!

[*Lady Agatha and Mr Hopper cross and exit on terrace L.U.E.*]

PARKER. Mr Cecil Graham!

[*Enter Mr Cecil Graham.*]

CECIL GRAHAM [*Bows to Lady Windermere, passes over and shakes hands with Lord Windermere.*] Good evening, Arthur. Why don't you ask me how I am? I like people to ask me how I am. It shows a wide-spread interest in my health. Now, tonight I am not at all well. Been dining with my people. Wonder why it is one's people are always so tedious? My father would talk morality after dinner. I told him he was old enough to know better. But my experience is that as soon as people are old enough to know better, they don't know anything at all. Hullo, Tuppy! Hear you're going to be married again; thought you were tired of that game.

LORD AUGUSTUS. You're excessively trivial, my dear boy, excessively trivial!

CECIL GRAHAM. By the way, Tuppy, which is it? Have you been twice married and once divorced, or twice divorced and once married? I say you've been twice divorced and once married. It seems so much more probable.

LORD AUGUSTUS. I have a very bad memory. I really don't remember which. [*Moves away R.*]

LADY PLYMDALE. Lord Windermere, I've something most particular to ask you.

LORD WINDERMERE. I am afraid—if you will excuse me—I must join my wife.

LADY PLYMDALE. Oh, you mustn't dream of such a thing. It's most dangerous nowadays for a husband to pay any attention to his wife in public. It always makes people think that he beats her when they're alone. The world has grown so suspicious of anything that looks like a happy married life. But I'll tell you what it is at supper. [*Moves towards door of ball-room.*]

LORD WINDERMERE [*C.*] Margaret! I *must* speak to you.

LADY WINDERMERE. Will you hold my fan for me, Lord Darlington? Thanks. [*Comes down to him.*]

LORD WINDERMERE [*Crossing to her.*] Margaret, what you said before dinner was, of course, impossible?

LADY WINDERMERE. That woman is not coming here tonight!

LORD WINDERMERE [*R. C.*] Mrs Erlynne is coming here, and if you in any way annoy or wound her, you will bring shame and sorrow on us both. Remember that! Ah, Margaret! only trust me! A wife should trust her husband!

LADY WINDERMERE [*C.*] London is full of women who trust their husbands. One can always recognize them. They look so thoroughly unhappy. I am not going to be one of them. [*Moves up.*] Lord Darlington, will you give me back my fan, please? Thanks. . . . A useful thing a fan, isn't it? . . . I want a friend tonight, Lord Darlington: I didn't know I would want one so soon.

LORD DARLINGTON. Lady Windermere! I knew the time would come some day; but why tonight?

LORD WINDERMERE. I *will* tell her. I must. It would be terrible if there were any scene. Margaret . . .

PARKER. Mrs Erlynne!

[*Lord Windermere starts. Mrs Erlynne enters, very beautifully dressed and very dignified. Lady Windermere clutches at her fan, then lets it drop on the floor. She bows coldly to Mrs Erlynne, who bows to her sweetly in turn, and sails into the room.*]

LORD DARLINGTON. You have dropped your fan, Lady Windermere. [*Picks it up and hands it to her.*]

MRS ERLYNNE [*C.*] How do you do, again, Lord Windermere? How charming your sweet wife looks! Quite a picture!

LORD WINDERMERE [*In a low voice.*] It was terribly rash of you to come!

MRS ERLYNNE [*Smiling.*] The wisest thing I ever did in my life. And, by the way, you must pay me a good deal of attention this evening. I am afraid of the women. You must introduce me to some of them. The men I can always manage. How do you do, Lord Augustus? You have quite neglected me lately. I have not seen you since yesterday. I am afraid you're faithless. Every one told me so.

LORD AUGUSTUS [*R.*] Now really, Mrs Erlynne, allow me to explain.

MRS ERLYNNE [*R.C.*] No, dear Lord Augustus, you can't explain anything. It is your chief charm.

LORD AUGUSTUS. Ah! if you find charms in me, Mrs Erlynne——

[*They converse together. Lord Windermere moves uneasily about the room watching Mrs Erlynne.*]

LORD DARLINGTON [*To Lady Windermere.*] How pale you are!

LADY WINDERMERE. Cowards are always pale!

LORD DARLINGTON. You look faint. Come out on the terrace.

LADY WINDERMERE. Yes. [*To Parker.*] Parker, send my cloak out.

MRS ERLYNNE [*Crossing to her.*] Lady Windermere, how beautifully your terrace is illuminated. Reminds me of Prince Doria's at Rome.°

[*Lady Windermere bows coldly, and goes off with Lord Darlington.*]

Oh, how do you do, Mr Graham? Isn't that your aunt, Lady Jedburgh? I should so much like to know her.

CECIL GRAHAM [*After a moment's hesitation and embarrassment.*] Oh, certainly, if you wish it. Aunt Caroline, allow me to introduce Mrs Erlynne.

MRS ERLYNNE. So pleased to meet you, Lady Jedburgh. [*Sits beside her on the sofa.*] Your nephew and I are great friends. I am so much interested in his political career. I think he's sure to be a wonderful success. He thinks like a Tory and talks like a Radical,° and that's so important nowadays. He's such a brilliant talker, too. But we all know from whom he inherits that. Lord Allandale was saying to me only yesterday, in the Park, that Mr Graham talks almost as well as his aunt.

LADY JEDBURGH [*R.*] Most kind of you to say these charming things to me!

[*Mrs Erlynne smiles, and continues conversation.*]

DUMBY [*To Cecil Graham.*] Did you introduce Mrs Erlynne to Lady Jedburgh?

CECIL GRAHAM. Had to, my dear fellow. Couldn't help it! That woman can make one do anything she wants. How, I don't know.

DUMBY. Hope to goodness she won't speak to me! [*Saunters towards Lady Plymdale.*]

MRS ERLYNNE [*C. To Lady Jedburgh.*] On Thursday? With great pleasure. [*Rises, and speaks to Lord Windermere, laughing.*] What a bore it is to have to be civil to these old dowagers! But they always insist on it!

LADY PLYMDALE [*To Mr Dumby.*] Who is that well-dressed woman talking to Windermere?

DUMBY. Haven't got the slightest idea! Looks like an *édition de luxe* of a wicked French novel, meant specially for the English market.

MRS ERLYNNE. So that is poor Dumby with Lady Plymdale? I hear she is frightfully jealous of him. He doesn't seem anxious to speak to me tonight. I suppose he is afraid of her. Those straw-coloured women have dreadful tempers. Do you know, I think I'll dance with you first, Windermere. [*Lord Windermere bites his lip and frowns.*] It will make Lord Augustus so jealous! Lord Augustus! [*Lord Augustus comes down.*] Lord Windermere insists on my dancing with him first, and, as it's his own house, I can't well refuse. You know I would much sooner dance with you.

LORD AUGUSTUS [*With a low bow.*] I wish I could think so, Mrs Erlynne.

MRS ERLYNNE. You know it far too well. I can fancy a person dancing through life with you and finding it charming.

LORD AUGUSTUS [*Placing his hand on his white waistcoat.*] Oh, thank you, thank you. You are the most adorable of all ladies!

MRS ERLYNNE. What a nice speech! So simple and so sincere! Just the sort of speech I like. Well, you shall hold my bouquet. [*Goes towards ball-room on Lord Windermere's arm.*] Ah, Mr Dumby, how are you? I am so sorry I have been out the last three times you have called. Come and lunch on Friday.

DUMBY [*With perfect nonchalance.*] Delighted!

[*Lady Plymdale glares with indignation at Mr Dumby. Lord Augustus follows Mrs Erlynne and Lord Windermere into the ball-room holding bouquet.*]

LADY PLYMDALE [*To Mr Dumby.*] What an absolute brute you are! I never can believe a word you say! Why did you tell me you didn't know her? What do you mean by calling on her three times running? You are not to lunch there; of course you understand that?

DUMBY. My dear Laura, I wouldn't dream of going!

LADY PLYMDALE. You haven't told me her name yet! Who is she?

DUMBY [*Coughs slightly and smooths his hair.*] She's a Mrs Erlynne.

LADY PLYMDALE. *That* woman!

DUMBY. Yes; that is what every one calls her.

LADY PLYMDALE. How very interesting! How intensely interesting! I really must have a good stare at her. [*Goes to door of ball-room and looks in.*] I have heard the most shocking things about her. They say she is ruining poor Windermere. And Lady Windermere, who goes in for being so proper, invites her! How extremely amusing! It takes a thoroughly good woman to do a thoroughly stupid thing. You are to lunch there on Friday!

DUMBY. Why?

LADY PLYMDALE. Because I want you to take my husband with you. He has been so attentive lately, that he has become a perfect nuisance. Now, this woman is just the thing for him. He'll dance attendance upon her as long as she lets him, and won't bother me. I assure you, women of that kind are most useful. They form the basis of other people's marriages.

DUMBY. What a mystery you are!

LADY PLYMDALE [*Looking at him.*] I wish *you* were!

DUMBY. I am—to myself. I am the only person in the world I should like to know thoroughly; but I don't see any chance of it just at present.

[*They pass into the ball-room, and Lady Windermere and Lord Darlington enter from the terrace.*]

LADY WINDERMERE. Yes. Her coming here is monstrous, unbearable. I know now what you meant today at tea time. Why didn't you tell me right out? You should have!

LORD DARLINGTON. I couldn't! A man can't tell these things about another man! But if I had known he was going to make you ask her here tonight, I think I would have told you. That insult, at any rate, you would have been spared.

LADY WINDERMERE. I did not ask her. He insisted on her coming—against my entreaties—against my commands. Oh! the house is tainted for me! I feel that every woman here sneers at me as she dances by with my husband. What have I done to deserve this? I gave him all my life. He took it—used it—spoiled it! I am degraded in my own eyes; and I lack courage—I am a coward! [*Sits down on sofa.*]

LORD DARLINGTON. If I know you at all, I know that you can't live with a man who treats you like this! What sort of life would you have with him? You would feel that he was lying to you every moment of the day. You would feel that the look in his eyes was false, his voice false, his touch false, his passion false. He would come to you when he was weary of others; you would have to comfort him. He would come to you when he was devoted to others; you would have to charm him. You would have to be to him the mask of his real life, the cloak to hide his secret.

LADY WINDERMERE. You are right—you are terribly right. But where am I to turn? You said you would be my friend, Lord Darlington.—Tell me, what am I to do? Be my friend now.

LORD DARLINGTON. Between men and women there is no friendship possible. There is passion, enmity, worship, love, but no friendship. I love you——

LADY WINDERMERE. No, no! [*Rises.*]

LORD DARLINGTON. Yes, I love you! You are more to me than anything in the whole world. What does your husband give you? Nothing. Whatever is in him he gives to this wretched woman, whom he has thrust into your society, into your home, to shame you before every one. I offer you my life——

LADY WINDERMERE. Lord Darlington!

LORD DARLINGTON. My life—my whole life. Take it, and do with it what you will. . . . I love you—love you as I have never loved any living thing. From the moment I met you I loved you, loved you blindly, adoringly, madly!° You did not know it then—you know it now! Leave this house tonight. I won't tell you that the world matters nothing, or the world's voice, or the voice of society. They matter a great deal. They matter far too much. But there are moments when one has to choose between living one's own life, fully, entirely, completely—or dragging out some false, shallow, degrading existence that the world in its hypocrisy demands. You have that moment now. Choose! Oh, my love, choose!

LADY WINDERMERE [*Moving slowly away from him, and looking at him with startled eyes.*] I have not the courage.

LORD DARLINGTON [*Following her.*] Yes; you have the courage. There may be six months of pain, of disgrace even, but when you no longer bear his name, when you bear mine, all will be well. Margaret, my love, my wife that shall be some day—yes, my wife! You know it! What are you now? This woman has the place that belongs by right to you. Oh! go—go out of this house, with head erect, with a smile upon your lips, with courage in your eyes. All London will know why you did it; and who will blame you? No one. If they do, what matter? Wrong? What is wrong? It's wrong for a man to abandon his wife for a shameless woman. It is wrong for a wife to remain with a man who so dishonours her. You said once you would make no compromise with things. Make none now. Be brave! Be yourself!

LADY WINDERMERE. I am afraid of being myself. Let me think! Let me wait! My husband may return to me. [*Sits down on sofa.*]

LORD DARLINGTON. And you would take him back! You are not what I thought you were. You are just the same as every other woman. You would stand anything rather than face the censure of a world, whose praise you would despise. In a week you will be driving with this woman in the Park. She will be your constant guest—your dearest friend. You would endure anything rather than break with one blow this monstrous tie. You are right. You have no courage; none!

LADY WINDERMERE. Ah, give me time to think. I cannot answer you now. [*Passes her hand nervously over her brow.*]

LORD DARLINGTON. It must be now or not at all.

LADY WINDERMERE [*Rising from the sofa.*] Then, not at all!

[*A pause.*]

LORD DARLINGTON. You break my heart!

LADY WINDERMERE. Mine is already broken.

[*A pause.*]

LORD DARLINGTON. Tomorrow I leave England. This is the last time I

shall ever look on you. You will never see me again. For one moment
our lives met—our souls touched. They must never meet or touch
again. Goodbye, Margaret.

[*Exit.*]

LADY WINDERMERE. How alone I am in life! How terribly alone!

[*The music stops. Enter the Duchess of Berwick and Lord Paisley laughing
and talking. Other guests come on from ball-room.*]

DUCHESS OF BERWICK. Dear Margaret, I've just been having such a
delightful chat with Mrs Erlynne. I am so sorry for what I said to you
this afternoon about her. Of course, she must be all right if *you* invite
her. A most attractive woman, and has such sensible views on life.
Told me she entirely disapproved of people marrying more than once,
so I feel quite safe about poor Augustus. Can't imagine why people
speak against her. It's those horrid nieces of mine—the Saville girls—
they're always talking scandal. Still, I should go to Homburg, dear, I
really should. She is just a little too attractive. But where is Agatha?
Oh, there she is! [*Lady Agatha and Mr Hopper enter from terrace L.U.E.*]
Mr Hopper, I am very, very angry with you. You have taken Agatha out
on the terrace, and she is so delicate.

HOPPER [*L.C.*] Awfully sorry, Duchess. We went out for a moment and
then got chatting together.

DUCHESS OF BERWICK [*C.*] Ah, about dear Australia, I suppose?

HOPPER. Yes!

DUCHESS OF BERWICK. Agatha, darling! [*Beckons her over.*]

LADY AGATHA. Yes, mamma!

DUCHESS OF BERWICK [*Aside.*] Did Mr Hopper definitely——

LADY AGATHA. Yes, mamma.

DUCHESS OF BERWICK. And what answer did you give him, dear child?

LADY AGATHA. Yes, mamma.

DUCHESS OF BERWICK [*Affectionately.*] My dear one! You always say the
right thing. Mr Hopper! James! Agatha has told me everything. How
cleverly you have both kept your secret.

HOPPER. You don't mind my taking Agatha off to Australia, then,
Duchess?

DUCHESS OF BERWICK [*Indignantly.*] To Australia? Oh, don't mention
that dreadful vulgar place.

HOPPER. But she said she'd like to come with me.

DUCHESS OF BERWICK [*Severely.*] Did you say that, Agatha?

LADY AGATHA. Yes, mamma.

DUCHESS OF BERWICK. Agatha, you say the most silly things possible. I think on the whole that Grosvenor Square would be a more healthy place to reside in. There are lots of vulgar people live in Grosvenor Square, but at any rate there are no horrid kangaroos crawling about. But we'll talk about that tomorrow. James, you can take Agatha down. You'll come to lunch, of course, James. At half-past one, instead of two. The Duke will wish to say a few words to you, I am sure.

HOPPER. I should like to have a chat with the Duke, Duchess. He has not said a single word to me yet.

DUCHESS OF BERWICK. I think you'll find he will have a great deal to say to you tomorrow.

[*Exit Lady Agatha with Mr Hopper.*]

And now goodnight, Margaret. I'm afraid it's the old, old story, dear. Love—well, not love at first sight, but love at the end of the season, which is so much more satisfactory.

LADY WINDERMERE. Good-night, Duchess.

[*Exit the Duchess of Berwick on Lord Paisley's arm.*]

LADY PLYMDALE. My dear Margaret, what a handsome woman your husband has been dancing with! I should be quite jealous if I were you! Is she a great friend of yours?

LADY WINDERMERE. No!

LADY PLYMDALE. Really? Goodnight, dear.

[*Looks at Mr Dumby and exit.*]

DUMBY. Awful manners young Hopper has!

CECIL GRAHAM. Ah! Hopper is one of Nature's gentlemen, the worst type of gentleman I know.

DUMBY. Sensible woman, Lady Windermere. Lots of wives would have objected to Mrs Erlynne coming. But Lady Windermere has that uncommon thing called common sense.

CECIL GRAHAM. And Windermere knows that nothing looks so like innocence as an indiscretion.

DUMBY. Yes; dear Windermere is becoming almost modern. Never thought he would.

[*Bows to Lady Windermere and exit.*]

LADY JEDBURGH. Goodnight, Lady Windermere. What a fascinating woman Mrs Erlynne is! She is coming to lunch on Thursday, won't you come too? I expect the Bishop and dear Lady Merton.

LADY WINDERMERE. I am afraid I am engaged, Lady Jedburgh.

LADY JEDBURGH. So sorry. Come, dear.

> [*Exeunt Lady Jedburgh and Miss Graham.*]

[*Enter Mrs Erlynne and Lord Windermere.*]

MRS ERLYNNE. Charming ball it has been! Quite reminds me of old days. [*Sits on sofa.*] And I see that there are just as many fools in society as there used to be. So pleased to find that nothing has altered! Except Margaret. She's grown quite pretty. The last time I saw her—twenty years ago, she was a fright in flannel. Positive fright, I assure you. The dear Duchess! and that sweet Lady Agatha! Just the type of girl I like! Well, really, Windermere, if I am to be the Duchess's sister-in-law—

LORD WINDERMERE [*Sitting L. of her.*] But are you——?

> [*Exit Mr Cecil Graham with rest of guests. Lady Windermere watches, with a look of scorn and pain, Mrs Erlynne and her husband. They are unconscious of her presence.*]

MRS ERLYNNE. Oh, yes! He's to call tomorrow at twelve o'clock! He wanted to propose tonight. In fact he did. He kept on proposing. Poor Augustus, you know how he repeats himself. Such a bad habit! But I told him I wouldn't give him an answer till tomorrow. Of course I am going to take him. And I daresay I'll make him an admirable wife, as wives go. And there is a great deal of good in Lord Augustus. Fortunately it is all on the surface. Just where good qualities should be. Of course you must help me in this matter.

LORD WINDERMERE. I am not called on to encourage Lord Augustus, I suppose?

MRS ERLYNNE. Oh, no! I do the encouraging. But you will make me a handsome settlement, Windermere, won't you?

LORD WINDERMERE [*Frowning.*] Is that what you want to talk to me about tonight?

MRS ERLYNNE. Yes.

LORD WINDERMERE [*With a gesture of impatience.*] I will not talk of it here.

MRS ERLYNNE [*Laughing.*] Then we will talk of it on the terrace. Even business should have a picturesque background. Should it not, Windermere? With a proper background women can do anything.

LORD WINDERMERE. Won't tomorrow do as well?

MRS ERLYNNE. No; you see, tomorrow I am going to accept him. And I think it would be a good thing if I was able to tell him that I had—well, what shall I say?—£2000 a year left to me by a third cousin—or a second husband—or some distant relative of that kind. It would be an additional attraction, wouldn't it? You have a delightful opportunity now of paying me a compliment, Windermere. But you are not very clever at paying compliments. I am afraid Margaret doesn't encourage you in that excellent habit. It's a great mistake on her part. When men give up saying what is charming, they give up thinking what is charming. But seriously, what do you say to £2000? £2500, I think. In modern life margin is everything. Windermere, don't you think the world an intensely amusing place? I do!

[*Exit on terrace with Lord Windermere. Music strikes up in ball-room.*]

LADY WINDERMERE. To stay in this house any longer is impossible. Tonight a man who loves me offered me his whole life. I refused it. It was foolish of me. I will offer him mine now. I will give him mine. I will go to him! [*Puts on cloak and goes to the door, then turns back. Sits down at table and writes a letter, puts it into an envelope, and leaves it on table.*] Arthur has never understood me. When he reads this, he will. He may do as he chooses now with his life. I have done with mine as I think best, as I think right. It is he who has broken the bond of marriage— not I. I only break its bondage.

[*Exit.*]

[*Parker enters L. and crosses towards the ball-room R. Enter Mrs Erlynne.*]

MRS ERLYNNE. Is Lady Windermere in the ball-room?

PARKER. Her ladyship has just gone out.

MRS ERLYNNE. Gone out? She's not on the terrace?

PARKER. No, madam. Her ladyship has just gone out of the house.

MRS ERLYNNE [*Starts, and looks at the servant with puzzled expression in her face.*] Out of the house?

PARKER. Yes, madam—her ladyship told me she had left a letter for his lordship on the table.

MRS ERLYNNE. A letter for Lord Windermere?

PARKER. Yes, madam.

MRS ERLYNNE. Thank you.

[Exit Parker. The music in the ball-room stops.]

Gone out of her house! A letter addressed to her husband! *[Goes over to bureau and looks at letter. Takes it up and lays it down again with a shudder of fear.]* No, no! It would be impossible! Life doesn't repeat its tragedies like that! Oh, why does this horrible fancy come across me? Why do I remember now the one moment of my life I most wish to forget? Does life repeat its tragedies? *[Tears letter open and reads it, then sinks down into a chair with a gesture of anguish.]* Oh, how terrible! The same words that twenty years ago I wrote to her father! and how bitterly I have been punished for it! No; my punishment, my real punishment is tonight, is now! *[Still seated R.]*

[Enter Lord Windermere L.U.E.]

LORD WINDERMERE. Have you said goodnight to my wife? *[Comes C.]*

MRS ERLYNNE *[Crushing letter in her hand.]* Yes.

LORD WINDERMERE. Where is she?

MRS ERLYNNE. She is very tired. She has gone to bed. She said she had a headache.

LORD WINDERMERE. I must go to her. You'll excuse me?

MRS ERLYNNE *[Rising hurriedly.]* Oh, no! It's nothing serious. She's only very tired, that is all. Besides, there are people still in the supper room. She wants you to make her apologies to them. She said she didn't wish to be disturbed. *[Drops letter.]* She asked me to tell you!

LORD WINDERMERE *[Picks up letter.]* You have dropped something.

MRS ERLYNNE. Oh yes, thank you, that is mine. *[Puts out her hand to take it.]*

LORD WINDERMERE *[Still looking at letter.]* But it's my wife's handwriting, isn't it?

MRS ERLYNNE *[Takes the letter quickly.]* Yes, it's—an address. Will you ask them to call my carriage, please?

LORD WINDERMERE. Certainly.

[Goes L. and Exit.]

MRS ERLYNNE. Thanks! What can I do? What can I do? I feel a passion awakening within me that I never felt before. What can it mean? The daughter must not be like the mother—that would be terrible. How can I save her? How can I save my child? A moment may ruin a life.

Who knows that better than I? Windermere must be got out of the house; that is absolutely necessary. [*Goes L.*] But how shall I do it? It must be done somehow. Ah!

[*Enter Lord Augustus R.U.E. carrying bouquet.*]

LORD AUGUSTUS. Dear lady, I am in such suspense! May I not have an answer to my request?

MRS ERLYNNE. Lord Augustus, listen to me. You are to take Lord Windermere down to your club at once, and keep him there as long as possible. You understand?

LORD AUGUSTUS. But you said you wished me to keep early hours!

MRS ERLYNNE [*Nervously.*] Do what I tell you. Do what I tell you.

LORD AUGUSTUS. And my reward?

MRS ERLYNNE. Your reward? Your reward? Oh! ask me that tomorrow. But don't let Windermere out of your sight tonight. If you do I will never forgive you. I will never speak to you again. I'll have nothing to do with you. Remember you are to keep Windermere at your club, and don't let him come back tonight.

[*Exit L.*]

LORD AUGUSTUS. Well, really, I might be her husband already. Positively I might. [*Follows her in a bewildered manner.*]

ACT DROP

THIRD ACT

SCENE—*Lord Darlington's Rooms. A large sofa is in front of fireplace R. At the back of the stage a curtain is drawn across the window. Doors L. and R. Table R. with writing materials. Table C. with syphons, glasses, and Tantalus frame.° Table L. with cigar and cigarette box. Lamps lit.*

LADY WINDERMERE [*Standing by the fireplace.*] Why doesn't he come? This waiting is horrible. He should be here. Why is he not here, to wake by passionate words some fire within me? I am cold—cold as a loveless thing. Arthur must have read my letter by this time. If he cared for me, he would have come after me, would have taken me back by force. But he doesn't care. He's entrammelled by this woman— fascinated by her—dominated by her. If a woman wants to hold a man, she has merely to appeal to what is worst in him. We make gods of men and they leave us. Others make brutes of them and they fawn and are faithful. How hideous life is! . . . Oh! it was mad of me to come here, horribly mad. And yet, which is the worst, I wonder, to be at the mercy of a man who loves one, or the wife of a man who in one's own house dishonours one? What woman knows? What woman in the whole world? But will he love me always, this man to whom I am giving my life? What do I bring him? Lips that have lost the note of joy, eyes that are blinded by tears, chill hands and icy heart. I bring him nothing. I must go back—no; I can't go back, my letter has put me in their power—Arthur would not take me back! That fatal letter! No! Lord Darlington leaves England tomorrow. I will go with him—I have no choice. [*Sits down for a few moments. Then starts up and puts on her cloak.*] No, no! I will go back, let Arthur do with me what he pleases. I can't wait here. It has been madness my coming. I must go at once. As for Lord Darlington—Oh! here he is! What shall I do? What can I say to him? Will he let me go away at all? I have heard that men are brutal, horrible . . . Oh! [*Hides her face in her hands.*]

[*Enter Mrs Erlynne L.*]

MRS ERLYNNE. Lady Windermere! [*Lady Windermere starts and looks up. Then recoils in contempt.*] Thank Heaven I am in time. You must go back to your husband's house immediately.

LADY WINDERMERE. Must?

MRS ERLYNNE [*Authoritatively.*] Yes, you must! There is not a second to be lost. Lord Darlington may return at any moment.

LADY WINDERMERE. Don't come near me!

MRS ERLYNNE. Oh! You are on the brink of ruin, you are on the brink of a hideous precipice. You must leave this place at once, my carriage is waiting at the corner of the street. You must come with me and drive straight home.

[*Lady Windermere throws off her cloak and flings it on the sofa.*]

What are you doing?

LADY WINDERMERE. Mrs Erlynne—if you had not come here, I would have gone back. But now that I see you, I feel that nothing in the whole world would induce me to live under the same roof as Lord Windermere. You fill me with horror. There is something about you that stirs the wildest—rage within me. And I know why you are here. My husband sent you to lure me back that I might serve as as blind to whatever relations exist between you and him.

MRS ERLYNNE. Oh! You don't think that—you can't.

LADY WINDERMERE. Go back to my husband, Mrs Erlynne. He belongs to you and not to me. I suppose he is afraid of a scandal. Men are such cowards. They outrage every law of the world, and are afraid of the world's tongue. But he had better prepare himself. He shall have a scandal. He shall have the worst scandal there has been in London for years. He shall see his name in every vile paper, mine on every hideous placard.

MRS ERLYNNE. No—no——

LADY WINDERMERE. Yes! he shall. Had he come himself, I admit I would have gone back to the life of degradation you and he had prepared for me—I was going back—but to stay himself at home, and to send you as his messenger—oh! it was infamous—infamous.

MRS ERLYNNE [C.] Lady Windermere, you wrong me horribly—you wrong your husband horribly. He doesn't know you are here—he thinks you are safe in your own house. He thinks you are asleep in your own room. He never read the mad letter you wrote to him!

LADY WINDERMERE [R.] Never read it!

MRS ERLYNNE. No—he knows nothing about it.

LADY WINDERMERE. How simple you think me! [Going to her.] You are lying to me!

MRS ERLYNNE [Restraining herself.] I am not. I am telling you the truth.

LADY WINDERMERE. If my husband didn't read my letter, how is it that you are here? Who told you I had left the house you were shameless enough to enter? Who told you where I had gone to? My husband told you, and sent you to decoy me back. [Crosses L.]

MRS ERLYNNE [R.C.] Your husband has never seen the letter. I—saw it, I opened it. I—read it.

LADY WINDERMERE [Turning to her.] You opened a letter of mine to my husband? You wouldn't dare!

MRS ERLYNNE. Dare! Oh! to save you from the abyss into which you are falling, there is nothing in the world I would not dare, nothing in the whole world. Here is the letter. Your husband has never read it. He never shall read it. [Going to fireplace.] It should never have been written. [Tears it and throws it into the fire.]

LADY WINDERMERE [With infinite contempt in her voice and look.] How do I know that that was my letter after all? You seem to think the commonest device can take me in!

MRS ERLYNNE. Oh! why do you disbelieve everything I tell you? What object do you think I have in coming here, except to save you from utter ruin, to save you from the consequence of a hideous mistake? That letter that is burnt now *was* your letter. I swear it to you!

LADY WINDERMERE [*Slowly.*] You took good care to burn it before I had examined it. I cannot trust you. You, whose whole life is a lie, how could you speak the truth about anything? [*Sits down.*]

MRS ERLYNNE [*Hurriedly.*] Think as you like about me—say what you choose against me, but go back, go back to the husband you love.

LADY WINDERMERE [*Sullenly.*] I do *not* love him!

MRS ERLYNNE. You do, and you know that he loves you.

LADY WINDERMERE. He does not understand what love is. He understands it as little as you do—but I see what you want. It would be a great advantage for you to get me back. Dear Heaven! what a life I would have then! Living at the mercy of a woman who has neither mercy nor pity in her, a woman whom it is an infamy to meet, a degradation to know, a vile woman, a woman who comes between husband and wife!

MRS ERLYNNE [*With a gesture of despair.*] Lady Windermere, Lady Windermere, don't say such terrible things. You don't know how terrible they are, how terrible and how unjust. Listen, you must listen! Only go back to your husband, and I promise you never to communicate with him again on any pretext—never to see him—never to have anything to do with his life or yours. The money that he gave me, he gave me not through love, but through hatred, not in worship, but in contempt. The hold I have over him——

LADY WINDERMERE [*Rising.*] Ah! you admit you have a hold!

MRS ERLYNNE. Yes, and I will tell you what it is. It is his love for you, Lady Windermere.

LADY WINDERMERE. You expect me to believe that?

MRS ERLYNNE. You must believe it! It is true. It is his love for you that has made him submit to—oh! call it what you like, tyranny, threats, anything you choose. But it is his love for you. His desire to spare you—shame, yes, shame and disgrace.

LADY WINDERMERE. What do you mean? You are insolent! What have I to do with you?

MRS ERLYNNE [*Humbly.*] Nothing. I know it—but I tell you that your husband loves you—that you may never meet with such love again in your whole life—that such love you will never meet—and that if you throw it away, the day may come when you will starve for love and it will not be given to you, beg for love and it will be denied you—Oh! Arthur loves you!

LADY WINDERMERE. Arthur? And you tell me there is nothing between you?

MRS ERLYNNE. Lady Windermere, before Heaven your husband is guiltless of all offence towards you! And I—I tell you that had it ever occurred to me that such a monstrous suspicion would have entered your mind, I would have died rather than have crossed your life or his—oh! died, gladly died! [*Moves away to sofa R.*]

LADY WINDERMERE. You talk as if you had a heart. Women like you have no hearts. Heart is not in you. You are bought and sold. [*Sits L.C.*]

MRS ERLYNNE [*Starts, with a gesture of pain. Then restrains herself, and comes over to where Lady Windermere is sitting. As she speaks, she stretches out her hands towards her, but does not dare to touch her.*] Believe what you choose about me. I am not worth a moment's sorrow. But don't spoil your beautiful young life on my account! You don't know what may be in store for you, unless you leave this house at once. You don't know what it is to fall into the pit, to be despised, mocked, abandoned, sneered at—to be an outcast! to find the door shut against one, to have to creep in by hideous byways, afraid every moment lest the mask should be stripped from one's face, and all the while to hear the laughter, the horrible laughter of the world, a thing more tragic than all the tears the world has ever shed. You don't know what it is. One pays for one's sin, and then one pays again, and all one's life one pays. You must never know that.—As for me, if suffering be an expiation, then at this moment I have expiated all my faults, whatever they have been; for tonight you have made a heart in one who had it not, made it and broken it.—But let that pass. I may have wrecked my own life, but I will not let you wreck yours. You—why, you are a mere girl, you would be lost. You haven't got the kind of brains that enables a woman to get back. You have neither the wit nor the courage. You couldn't stand dishonour. No! Go back, Lady Windermere, to the husband who loves you, whom you love. You have a child, Lady Windermere. Go back to that child who even now, in pain or in joy, may be calling to you. [*Lady Windermere rises.*] God gave you that child. He will require from you that you make his life fine, that you watch over him. What answer will you make to God if his life is ruined through you? Back to your house, Lady Windermere—your husband loves you! He has never swerved for a moment from the love he bears you. But even if he had a thousand loves, you must stay with your child. If he was harsh to you, you must stay with your child. If he ill-treated you, you must stay with your child. If he abandoned you, your place is with your child.

[*Lady Windermere bursts into tears and buries her face in her hands.*]

[*Rushing to her.*] Lady Windermere!

LADY WINDERMERE [*Holding out her hands to her, helplessly, as a child might do.*] Take me home. Take me home.

MRS ERLYNNE [*Is about to embrace her. Then restrains herself. There is a look of wonderful joy in her face.*] Come! Where is your cloak? [*Getting it from sofa.*] Here. Put it on. Come at once!

[*They go to the door.*]

LADY WINDERMERE. Stop! Don't you hear voices?

MRS ERLYNNE. No, no! There is no one!

LADY WINDERMERE. Yes, there is! Listen! Oh! that is my husband's voice! He is coming in! Save me! Oh, it's some plot! You have sent for him.

[*Voices outside.*]

MRS ERLYNNE. Silence! I'm here to save you, if I can. But I fear it is too late! There! [*Points to the curtain across the window.*] The first chance you have, slip out, if you ever get a chance!

LADY WINDERMERE. But you?

MRS ERLYNNE. Oh! never mind me. I'll face them.

[*Lady Windermere hides herself behind the curtain.*]

LORD AUGUSTUS [*Outside.*] Nonsense, dear Windermere, you must not leave me!

MRS ERLYNNE. Lord Augustus! Then it is I who am lost!

[*Hesitates for a moment, then looks round and sees door R., and exits through it.*]

[*Enter Lord Darlington, Mr Dumby, Lord Windermere, Lord Augustus Lorton, and Mr Cecil Graham.*]

DUMBY. What a nuisance their turning us out of the club at this hour! It's only two o'clock. [*Sinks into a chair.*] The lively part of the evening is only just beginning. [*Yawns and closes his eyes.*]

LORD WINDERMERE. It is very good of you, Lord Darlington, allowing Augustus to force our company on you, but I'm afraid I can't stay long.

LORD DARLINGTON. Really! I am so sorry! You'll take a cigar, won't you?

LORD WINDERMERE. Thanks! [*Sits down.*]

LORD AUGUSTUS [*To Lord Windermere.*] My dear boy, you must not dream of going. I have a great deal to talk to you about, of demmed importance, too. [*Sits down with him at L. table.*]

CECIL GRAHAM. Oh! We all know what that is! Tuppy can't talk about anything but Mrs Erlynne!

LORD WINDERMERE. Well, that is no business of yours, is it, Cecil?

CECIL GRAHAM. None! That is why it interests me. My own business always bores me to death. I prefer other people's.

LORD DARLINGTON. Have something to drink, you fellows. Cecil, you'll have a whisky and soda?

CECIL GRAHAM. Thanks. [*Goes to table with Lord Darlington.*] Mrs Erlynne looked very handsome tonight, didn't she?

LORD DARLINGTON. I am not one of her admirers.

CECIL GRAHAM. I usen't to be, but I am now. Why! she actually made me introduce her to poor dear Aunt Caroline. I believe she is going to lunch there.

LORD DARLINGTON [*In surprise.*] No?

CECIL GRAHAM. She is, really.

LORD DARLINGTON. Excuse me, you fellows. I'm going away tomorrow. And I have to write a few letters. [*Goes to writing table and sits down.*]

DUMBY. Clever woman, Mrs Erlynne.

CECIL GRAHAM. Hallo, Dumby! I thought you were asleep.

DUMBY. I am, I usually am!

LORD AUGUSTUS. A very clever woman. Knows perfectly well what a demmed fool I am—knows it as well as I do myself.

[*Cecil Graham comes towards him laughing.*]

Ah! you may laugh, my boy, but it is a great thing to come across a woman who thoroughly understands one.

DUMBY. It is an awfully dangerous thing. They always end by marrying one.

CECIL GRAHAM. But I thought, Tuppy, you were never going to see her again. Yes! you told me so yesterday evening at the club. You said you'd heard——[*Whispering to him.*]

LORD AUGUSTUS. Oh, she's explained that.

CECIL GRAHAM. And the Wiesbaden affair?°

LORD AUGUSTUS. She's explained that too.

DUMBY. And her income, Tuppy? Has she explained that?

LORD AUGUSTUS [*In a very serious voice.*] She's going to explain that tomorrow.

[*Cecil Graham goes back to C. table.*]

DUMBY. Awfully commercial, women nowadays. Our grandmothers threw their caps over the mills, of course, but, by Jove, their grand-daughters only throw their caps over mills that can raise the wind for them.

LORD AUGUSTUS. You want to make her out a wicked woman. She is not!

CECIL GRAHAM. Oh! Wicked women bother one. Good women bore one. That is the only difference between them.

LORD AUGUSTUS [*Puffing a cigar.*] Mrs Erlynne has a future before her.

DUMBY. Mrs Erlynne has a past before her.

LORD AUGUSTUS. I prefer women with a past. They're always so demmed amusing to talk to.

CECIL GRAHAM. Well, you'll have lots of topics of conversation with *her*, Tuppy. [*Rising and going to him.*]

LORD AUGUSTUS. You're getting annoying, dear boy; you're getting demmed annoying.

CECIL GRAHAM [*Puts his hands on his shoulders.*] Now, Tuppy, you've lost your figure and you've lost your character. Don't lose your temper; you have only got one.

LORD AUGUSTUS. My dear boy, if I wasn't the most good-natured man in London——

CECIL GRAHAM. We'd treat you with more respect, wouldn't we, Tuppy? [*Strolls away.*]

DUMBY. The youth of the present day are quite monstrous. They have absolutely no respect for dyed hair. [*Lord Augustus looks round angrily.*]

CECIL GRAHAM. Mrs Erlynne has a very great respect for dear Tuppy.

DUMBY. Then Mrs Erlynne sets an admirable example to the rest of her sex. It is perfectly brutal the way most women nowadays behave to men who are not their husbands.

LORD WINDERMERE. Dumby, you are ridiculous, and Cecil, you let your tongue run away with you. You must leave Mrs Erlynne alone. You don't really know anything about her, and you're always talking scandal against her.

CECIL GRAHAM [*Coming towards him L.C.*] My dear Arthur, I never talk scandal. *I* only talk gossip.

LORD WINDERMERE. What is the difference between scandal and gossip?

CECIL GRAHAM. Oh! gossip is charming! History is merely gossip. But scandal is gossip made tedious by morality. Now, I never moralize. A man who moralizes is usually a hypocrite, and a woman who moralizes is invariably plain. There is nothing in the whole world so unbecoming to a woman as a Nonconformist conscience. And most women know it, I'm glad to say.

LORD AUGUSTUS. Just my sentiments, dear boy, just my sentiments.

CECIL GRAHAM. Sorry to hear it, Tuppy; whenever people agree with me, I always feel I must be wrong.°

LORD AUGUSTUS. My dear boy, when I was your age——

CECIL GRAHAM. But you never were, Tuppy, and you never will be. [*Goes up C.*] I say, Darlington, let us have some cards. You'll play, Arthur, won't you.

LORD WINDERMERE. No, thanks, Cecil.

DUMBY [*With a sigh.*] Good heavens! how marriage ruins a man! It's as demoralizing as cigarettes, and far more expensive.

CECIL GRAHAM. You'll play, of course, Tuppy?

LORD AUGUSTUS [*Pouring himself out a brandy and soda at table.*] Can't, dear boy. Promised Mrs Erlynne never to play or drink again.

CECIL GRAHAM. Now, my dear Tuppy, don't be led astray into the paths of virtue. Reformed, you would be perfectly tedious. That is the worst of women. They always want one to be good. And if we are good, when they meet us, they don't love us at all. They like to find us quite irretrievably bad, and to leave us quite unattractively good.

LORD DARLINGTON [*Rising from R. table, where he has been writing letters.*] They always do find us bad!

DUMBY. I don't think we are bad. I think we are all good, except Tuppy.

LORD DARLINGTON. No, we are all in the gutter, but some of us are looking at the stars. [*Sits down at C. table.*]

DUMBY. We are all in the gutter, but some of us are looking at the stars? Upon my word, you are very romantic tonight, Darlington.

CECIL GRAHAM. Too romantic! You must be in love. Who is the girl?

LORD DARLINGTON. The woman I love is not free, or thinks she isn't. [*Glances instinctively at Lord Windermere while he speaks.*]

CECIL GRAHAM. A married woman, then! Well, there's nothing in the world like the devotion of a married woman. It's a thing no married man knows anything about.

LORD DARLINGTON. Oh! she doesn't love me. She is a good woman. She is the only good woman I have ever met in my life.

CECIL GRAHAM. The only good woman you have ever met in your life?

LORD DARLINGTON. Yes!

CECIL GRAHAM [*Lighting a cigarette.*] Well, you are a lucky fellow! Why, I have met hundreds of good women. I never seem to meet any but good women. The world is perfectly packed with good women. To know them is a middle-class education.°

LORD DARLINGTON. This woman has purity and innocence. She has everything we men have lost.

CECIL GRAHAM. My dear fellow, what on earth should we men do going about with purity and innocence? A carefully thought-out buttonhole is much more effective.

DUMBY. She doesn't really love you then?

LORD DARLINGTON. No, she does not!

DUMBY. I congratulate you, my dear fellow. In this world there are only two tragedies. One is not getting what one wants, and the other is getting it. The last is much the worst, the last is a real tragedy! But I am interested to hear she does not love you. How long could you love a woman who didn't love you, Cecil?

CECIL GRAHAM. A woman who didn't love me? Oh, all my life!

DUMBY. So could I. But it's so difficult to meet one.

LORD DARLINGTON. How can you be so conceited, Dumby?

DUMBY. I didn't say it as a matter of conceit. I said it as a matter of regret. I have been wildly, madly adored. I am sorry I have. It has been an immense nuisance. I should like to be allowed a little time to myself now and then.

LORD AUGUSTUS [*Looking round.*] Time to educate yourself, I suppose.

DUMBY. No, time to forget all I have learned. That is much more important, dear Tuppy. [*Lord Augustus moves uneasily in his chair.*]

LORD DARLINGTON. What cynics you fellows are!

CECIL GRAHAM. What is a cynic? [*Sitting on the back of the sofa.*]

LORD DARLINGTON. A man who knows the price of everything and the value of nothing.

CECIL GRAHAM. And a sentimentalist, my dear Darlington, is a man who sees an absurd value in everything, and doesn't know the market price of any single thing.°

LORD DARLINGTON. You always amuse me, Cecil. You talk as if you were a man of experience.

CECIL GRAHAM. I am. [*Moves up to front of fireplace.*]

LORD DARLINGTON. You are far too young!

CECIL GRAHAM. That is a great error. Experience is a question of instinct about life. I have got it. Tuppy hasn't. Experience is the name Tuppy gives to his mistakes. That is all. [*Lord Augustus looks round indignantly.*]

DUMBY. Experience is the name every one gives to their mistakes.°

CECIL GRAHAM [*Standing with his back to the fireplace.*] One shouldn't commit any. [*Sees Lady Windermere's fan on sofa.*]

DUMBY. Life would be very dull without them.

CECIL GRAHAM. Of course you are quite faithful to this woman you are in love with, Darlington, to this good woman?

LORD DARLINGTON. Cecil, if one really loves a woman, all other women in the world become absolutely meaningless to one. Love changes one—*I* am changed.

CECIL GRAHAM. Dear me! How very interesting! Tuppy, I want to talk to you. [*Lord Augustus takes no notice.*]

DUMBY. It's no use talking to Tuppy. You might just as well talk to a brick wall.

CECIL GRAHAM. But I like talking to a brick wall—it's the only thing in the world that never contradicts me! Tuppy!

LORD AUGUSTUS. Well, what is it? What is it? [*Rising and going over to Cecil Graham.*]

CECIL GRAHAM. Come over here. I want you particularly. [*Aside.*] Darlington has been moralizing and talking about the purity of love, and that sort of thing, and he has got some woman in his rooms all the time.

LORD AUGUSTUS. No, really! really!

CECIL GRAHAM [*In a low voice.*] Yes, here is her fan. [*Points to the fan.*]

LORD AUGUSTUS [*Chuckling.*] By Jove! By Jove!

LORD WINDERMERE [*Up by door.*] I am really off now, Lord Darlington. I am sorry you are leaving England so soon. Pray call on us when you come back! My wife and I will be charmed to see you!

LORD DARLINGTON [*Up stage with Lord Windermere.*] I am afraid I shall be away for many years. Goodnight!

CECIL GRAHAM. Arthur!

LORD WINDERMERE. What?

CECIL GRAHAM. I want to speak to you for a moment. No, do come!

LORD WINDERMERE [*Putting on his coat.*] I can't—I'm off!

CECIL GRAHAM. It is something very particular. It will interest you enormously.

LORD WINDERMERE [*Smiling.*] It is some of your nonsense, Cecil.

CECIL GRAHAM. It isn't! It isn't really.

LORD AUGUSTUS [*Going to him.*] My dear fellow, you mustn't go yet. I have a lot to talk to you about. And Cecil has something to show you.

LORD WINDERMERE [*Walking over.*] Well, what is it?

CECIL GRAHAM. Darlington has got a woman here in his rooms. Here is her fan. Amusing, isn't it? [*A pause.*]

LORD WINDERMERE. Good God! [*Seizes the fan—Dumby rises.*]

CECIL GRAHAM. What is the matter?

LORD WINDERMERE. Lord Darlington!

LORD DARLINGTON [*Turning round.*] Yes!

LORD WINDERMERE. What is my wife's fan doing here in your rooms? Hands off, Cecil. Don't touch me.

LORD DARLINGTON. Your wife's fan?

LORD WINDERMERE. Yes, here it is!

LORD DARLINGTON [*Walking towards him.*] I don't know!

LORD WINDERMERE. You must know. I demand an explanation. Don't hold me, you fool. [*To Cecil Graham.*]

LORD DARLINGTON [*Aside.*] She is here after all!

LORD WINDERMERE. Speak, sir! Why is my wife's fan here? Answer me! By God! I'll search your rooms, and if my wife's here, I'll——[*Moves.*]

LORD DARLINGTON. You shall not search my rooms. You have no right to do so. I forbid you!

LORD WINDERMERE. You scoundrel! I'll not leave your room till I have searched every corner of it! What moves behind that curtain? [*Rushes towards the curtain C.*]

MRS ERLYNNE [*Enters behind R.*] Lord Windermere!

LORD WINDERMERE. Mrs Erlynne!

[*Every one starts and turns round. Lady Windermere slips out from behind the curtain and glides from the room L.*]

MRS ERLYNNE. I am afraid I took your wife's fan in mistake for my own, when I was leaving your house tonight. I am so sorry. [*Takes fan from him. Lord Windermere looks at her in contempt. Lord Darlington in mingled astonishment and anger. Lord Augustus turns away. The other men smile at each other.*]

ACT DROP

FOURTH ACT

SCENE—*Same as in Act I.*

LADY WINDERMERE [*Lying on sofa.*] How can I tell him? I can't tell him. It would kill me. I wonder what happened after I escaped from that horrible room. Perhaps she told them the true reason of her being there, and the real meaning of that—fatal fan of mine. Oh, if he knows—how can I look him in the face again? He would never forgive me. [*Touches bell.*] How securely one thinks one lives—out of reach of temptation, sin, folly. And then suddenly—Oh! Life is terrible. It rules us, we do not rule it.

[*Enter Rosalie R.*]

ROSALIE. Did your ladyship ring for me?

LADY WINDERMERE. Yes. Have you found out at what time Lord Windermere came in last night?

ROSALIE. His lordship did not come in till five o'clock.

LADY WINDERMERE. Five o'clock? He knocked at my door this morning, didn't he?

ROSALIE. Yes, my lady—at half-past nine. I told him your ladyship was not awake yet.

LADY WINDERMERE. Did he say anything?

ROSALIE. Something about your ladyship's fan. I didn't quite catch what his lordship said. Has the fan been lost, my lady? I can't find it, and Parker says it was not left in any of the rooms. He has looked in all of them and on the terrace as well.

LADY WINDERMERE. It doesn't matter. Tell Parker not to trouble. That will do.

[*Exit Rosalie.*]

LADY WINDERMERE [*Rising.*] She is sure to tell him. I can fancy a person doing a wonderful act of self-sacrifice, doing it spontaneously, recklessly, nobly—and afterwards finding out that it costs too much. Why should she hesitate between her ruin and mine? . . . How strange! I would have publicly disgraced her in my own house. She accepts public disgrace in the house of another to save me. . . . There is a bitter irony in things, a bitter irony in the way we talk of good and bad women. . . . Oh, what a lesson! and what a pity that in life we only get our lessons when they are of no use to us! For even if she doesn't tell, I must. Oh! the shame of it, the shame of it. To tell it is to live through it all again. Actions are the first tragedy in life, words are the second. Words are perhaps the worst. Words are merciless. . . . Oh! [*Starts as Lord Windermere enters.*]

LORD WINDERMERE [*Kisses her.*] Margaret—how pale you look!

LADY WINDERMERE. I slept very badly.

LORD WINDERMERE [*Sitting on sofa with her.*] I am so sorry. I came in dreadfully late, and didn't like to wake you. You are crying, dear.

LADY WINDERMERE. Yes, I am crying, for I have something to tell you, Arthur.

LORD WINDERMERE. My dear child, you are not well. You've been doing too much. Let us go away to the country. You'll be all right at Selby. The season is almost over. There is no use staying on. Poor darling!

We'll go away today, if you like. [*Rises.*] We can easily catch the 3.40. I'll send a wire to Fannen. [*Crosses and sits down at table to write a telegram.*]

LADY WINDERMERE. Yes; let us go away today. No; I can't go today, Arthur. There is some one I must see before I leave town—some one who has been kind to me.

LORD WINDERMERE [*Rising and leaning over sofa.*] Kind to you?

LADY WINDERMERE. Far more than that. [*Rises and goes to him.*] I will tell you, Arthur, but only love me, love me as you used to love me.

LORD WINDERMERE. Used to? You are not thinking of that wretched woman who came here last night? [*Coming round and sitting R. of her.*] You don't still imagine—no, you couldn't.

LADY WINDERMERE. I don't. I know now I was wrong and foolish.

LORD WINDERMERE. It was very good of you to receive her last night— but you are never to see her again.

LADY WINDERMERE. Why do you say that? [*A pause.*]

LORD WINDERMERE [*Holding her hand.*] Margaret, I thought Mrs Erlynne was a woman more sinned against than sinning, as the phrase goes. I thought she wanted to be good, to get back into a place that she had lost by a moment's folly, to lead again a decent life. I believed what she told me—I was mistaken in her. She is bad—as bad as a woman can be.

LADY WINDERMERE. Arthur, Arthur, don't talk so bitterly about any woman. I don't think now that people can be divided into the good and the bad, as though they were two separate races or creations. What are called good women may have terrible things in them, mad moods of recklessness, assertion, jealousy, sin. Bad women, as they are termed, may have in them sorrow, repentance, pity, sacrifice. And I don't think Mrs Erlynne a bad woman—I know she's not.

LORD WINDERMERE. My dear child, the woman's impossible. No matter what harm she tries to do us, you must never see her again. She is inadmissible anywhere.

LADY WINDERMERE. But I want to see her. I want her to come here.

LORD WINDERMERE. Never!

LADY WINDERMERE. She came here once as *your* guest. She must come now as *mine*. That is but fair.

LORD WINDERMERE. She should never have come here.

LADY WINDERMERE [*Rising.*] It is too late, Arthur, to say that now. [*Moves away.*]

LORD WINDERMERE [*Rising.*] Margaret, if you knew where Mrs Erlynne went last night, after she left this house, you would not sit in the same room with her. It was absolutely shameless, the whole thing.

LADY WINDERMERE. Arthur, I can't bear it any longer. I must tell you. Last night——

[*Enter Parker with a tray on which lie Lady Windermere's fan and a card.*]

PARKER. Mrs Erlynne has called to return your ladyship's fan which she took away by mistake last night. Mrs Erlynne has written a message on the card.

LADY WINDERMERE. Oh, ask Mrs Erlynne to be kind enough to come up. [*Reads card.*] Say I shall be very glad to see her.

[*Exit Parker.*]

She wants to see me, Arthur.

LORD WINDERMERE [*Takes card and looks at it.*] Margaret, I *beg* you not to. Let me see her first, at any rate. She's a very dangerous woman. She is the most dangerous woman I know. You don't realize what you're doing.

LADY WINDERMERE. It is right that I should see her.

LORD WINDERMERE. My child, you may be on the brink of a great sorrow. Don't go to meet it. It is absolutely necessary that I should see her before you do.

LADY WINDERMERE. Why should it be necessary?

[*Enter Parker.*]

PARKER. Mrs Erlynne

[*Enter Mrs Erlynne.*]

[*Exit Parker.*]

MRS ERLYNNE. How do you do, Lady Windermere? [*To Lord Windermere.*] How do you do? Do you know, Lady Windermere, I am so sorry about your fan. I can't imagine how I made such a silly mistake. Most stupid of me. And as I was driving in your direction, I thought I would take the opportunity of returning your property in person with many apologies for my carelessness, and of bidding you goodbye.

LADY WINDERMERE. Goodbye? [*Moves towards sofa with Mrs Erlynne and sits down beside her.*] Are you going away, then, Mrs Erlynne?

MRS ERLYNNE. Yes; I am going to live abroad again. The English climate doesn't suit me. My—heart is affected here, and that I don't like. I prefer living in the south. London is too full of fogs and—and serious people, Lord Windermere. Whether the fogs produce the serious people or whether the serious people produce the fogs, I don't know, but the whole thing rather gets on my nerves, and so I'm leaving this afternoon by the Club Train.°

LADY WINDERMERE. This afternoon? But I wanted so much to come and see you.

MRS ERLYNNE. How kind of you! But I am afraid I have to go.

LADY WINDERMERE. Shall I never see you again, Mrs Erlynne?

MRS ERLYNNE. I am afraid not. Our lives lie too far apart. But there is a little thing I would like you to do for me. I want a photograph of you, Lady Windermere—would you give me one? You don't know how gratified I should be.

LADY WINDERMERE. Oh, with pleasure. There is one on that table. I'll show it to you. [*Goes across to the table.*]

LORD WINDERMERE [*Coming up to Mrs Erlynne and speaking in a low voice.*] It is monstrous your intruding yourself here after your conduct last night.

MRS ERLYNNE [*With an amused smile.*] My dear Windermere, manners before morals!°

LADY WINDERMERE [*Returning.*] I'm afraid it is very flattering—I am not so pretty as that. [*Showing photograph.*]

MRS ERLYNNE. You are much prettier. But haven't you got one of yourself with your little boy?

LADY WINDERMERE. I have. Would you prefer one of those?

MRS ERLYNNE. Yes.

LADY WINDERMERE. I'll go and get it for you, if you'll excuse me for a moment. I have one upstairs.

MRS ERLYNNE. So sorry, Lady Windermere, to give you so much trouble.

LADY WINDERMERE [*Moves to door R.*] No trouble at all, Mrs Erlynne.

MRS ERLYNNE. Thanks so much.

[*Exit Lady Windermere R.*]

You seem rather out of temper this morning, Windermere. Why should you be? Margaret and I get on charmingly together.

LORD WINDERMERE. I can't bear to see you with her. Besides, you have not told me the truth, Mrs Erlynne.

MRS ERLYNNE. I have not told *her* the truth, you mean.

LORD WINDERMERE [*Standing C.*] I sometimes wish you had. I should have been spared then the misery, the anxiety, the annoyance of the last six months. But rather than my wife should know—that the mother whom she was taught to consider as dead, the mother whom she has mourned as dead, is living—a divorced woman, going about under an assumed name, a bad woman preying upon life, as I know you now to be—rather than that, I was ready to supply you with money to pay bill after bill, extravagance after extravagance, to risk what occurred yesterday, the first quarrel I have ever had with my wife. You don't understand what that means to me. How could you? But I tell you that the only bitter words that ever came from those sweet lips of hers were on your account, and I hate to see you next her. You sully the innocence that is in her. [*Moves L.C.*] And then I used to think that with all your faults you were frank and honest. You are not.

MRS ERLYNNE. Why do you say that?

LORD WINDERMERE. You made me get you an invitation to my wife's ball.

MRS ERLYNNE. For my daughter's ball—yes.

LORD WINDERMERE. You came, and within an hour of your leaving the house you are found in a man's rooms—you are disgraced before every one. [*Goes up stage C.*]

MRS ERLYNNE. Yes.

LORD WINDERMERE [*Turning round on her.*] Therefore I have a right to look upon you as what you are—a worthless, vicious woman. I have the right to tell you never to enter this house, never to attempt to come near my wife——

MRS ERLYNNE [*Coldly.*] My daughter, you mean.

LORD WINDERMERE. You have no right to claim her as your daughter. You left her, abandoned her when she was but a child in the cradle, abandoned her for your lover, who abandoned you in turn.

MRS ERLYNNE [*Rising.*] Do you count that to his credit, Lord Windermere—or to mine?

LORD WINDERMERE. To his, now that I know you.

MRS ERLYNNE. Take care—you had better be careful.

LORD WINDERMERE. Oh, I am not going to mince words for you. I know you thoroughly.

MRS ERLYNNE [*Looking steadily at him.*] I question that.

LORD WINDERMERE. I *do* know you. For twenty years of your life you lived without your child, without a thought of your child. One day you read in the papers that she had married a rich man. You saw your hideous chance. You knew that to spare her the ignominy of learning that a woman like you was her mother, I would endure anything. You began your blackmailing.

MRS ERLYNNE [*Shrugging her shoulders.*] Don't use ugly words, Windermere. They are vulgar. I saw my chance, it is true, and took it.

LORD WINDERMERE. Yes, you took it—and spoiled it all last night by being found out.

MRS ERLYNNE [*With a strange smile.*] You are quite right, I spoiled it all last night.

LORD WINDERMERE. And as for your blunder in taking my wife's fan from here and then leaving it about in Darlington's rooms, it is unpardonable. I can't bear the sight of it now. I shall never let my wife use it again. The thing is soiled for me. You should have kept it and not brought it back.

MRS ERLYNNE. I think I *shall* keep it. [*Goes up.*] It's extremely pretty. [*Takes up fan.*] I shall ask Margaret to give it to me.

LORD WINDERMERE. I hope my wife will give it you.

MRS ERLYNNE. Oh, I'm sure she will have no objection.

LORD WINDERMERE. I wish that at the same time she would give you a miniature she kisses every night before she prays—It's the miniature of a young innocent-looking girl with beautiful dark hair.

MRS ERLYNNE. Ah, yes, I remember. How long ago that seems! [*Goes to sofa and sits down.*] It was done before I was married. Dark hair and an innocent expression were the fashion then, Windermere! [*A pause.*]

LORD WINDERMERE. What do you mean by coming here this morning? What is your object? [*Crossing L.C. and sitting.*]

MRS ERLYNNE [*With a note of irony in her voice.*] To bid goodbye to my dear daughter, of course. [*Lord Windermere bites his under lip in anger. Mrs Erlynne looks at him, and her voice and manner become serious. In her accents as she talks there is a note of deep tragedy. For a moment she reveals herself.*] Oh, don't imagine I am going to have a pathetic scene with her, weep on her neck and tell her who I am, and all that kind of thing. I have no ambition to play the part of a mother. Only once in my life have I known a mother's feelings. That was last night. They were terrible—they made me suffer—they made me suffer too much. For twenty years, as you say, I have lived childless,—I want to live childless still. [*Hiding her feelings with a trivial laugh.*] Besides, my dear Windermere, how on earth could I pose as a mother with a grown-up daughter? Margaret is twenty-one, and I have never admitted that I am more than twenty-nine, or thirty at the most. Twenty-nine when there are pink shades, thirty when there are not. So you see what difficulties it would involve. No, as far as I am concerned, let your wife cherish the memory of this dead, stainless mother. Why should I interfere with her illusions? I find it hard enough to keep my own. I lost one illusion last night. I thought I had no heart. I find I have, and a heart doesn't suit me, Windermere. Somehow it doesn't go with modern dress. It makes one look old. [*Takes up hand-mirror from table and looks into it.*] And it spoils one's career at critical moments.

LORD WINDERMERE. You fill me with horror—with absolute horror.

MRS ERLYNNE [*Rising.*] I suppose, Windermere, you would like me to retire into a convent or become a hospital nurse, or something of that kind, as people do in silly modern novels. That is stupid of you, Arthur; in real life we don't do such things—not as long as we have any good looks left, at any rate. No—what consoles one nowadays is not repentance, but pleasure. Repentance is quite out of date. And besides, if a woman really repents, she has to go to a bad dressmaker, otherwise no one believes in her. And nothing in the world would induce me to do that. No; I am going to pass entirely out of your two lives. My coming into them has been a mistake—I discovered that last night.

LORD WINDERMERE. A fatal mistake.

MRS ERLYNNE [*Smiling.*] Almost fatal.

LORD WINDERMERE. I am sorry now I did not tell my wife the whole thing at once.

MRS ERLYNNE. I regret my bad actions. You regret your good ones—that is the difference between us.

LORD WINDERMERE. I don't trust you. I *will* tell my wife. It's better for her to know, and from me. It will cause her infinite pain—it will humiliate her terribly, but it's right that she should know.

MRS ERLYNNE. You propose to tell her?

LORD WINDERMERE. I am going to tell her.

MRS ERLYNNE [*Going up to him.*] If you do, I will make my name so infamous that it will mar every moment of her life. It will ruin her, and make her wretched. If you dare to tell her, there is no depth of degradation I will not sink to, no pit of shame I will not enter. You shall not tell her—I forbid you.

LORD WINDERMERE. Why?

MRS ERLYNNE [*After a pause.*] If I said to you that I cared for her, perhaps loved her even—you would sneer at me, wouldn't you?

LORD WINDERMERE. I should feel it was not true. A mother's love means devotion, unselfishness, sacrifice. What could you know of such things?

MRS ERLYNNE. You are right. What could I know of such things? Don't let us talk any more about it—as for telling my daughter who I am, that I do not allow. It is my secret, it is not yours. If I make up my mind to tell her, and I think I will, I shall tell her before I leave the house—if not, I shall never tell her.

LORD WINDERMERE [*Angrily.*] Then let me beg of you to leave our house at once. I will make your excuses to Margaret.

[*Enter Lady Windermere R. She goes over to Mrs Erlynne with the photograph in her hand. Lord Windermere moves to back of sofa, and anxiously watches Mrs Erlynne as the scene progresses.*]

LADY WINDERMERE. I am so sorry, Mrs Erlynne, to have kept you waiting. I couldn't find the photograph anywhere. At last I discovered it in my husband's dressing-room—he had stolen it.

MRS ERLYNNE [*Takes the photograph from her and looks at it.*] I am not surprised—it is charming. [*Goes over to sofa with Lady Windermere, and sits down beside her. Looks again at the photograph.*] And so that is your little boy! What is he called?

LADY WINDERMERE. Gerard, after my dear father.

MRS ERLYNNE [*Laying the photograph down.*] Really?

LADY WINDERMERE. Yes. If it had been a girl, I would have called it after my mother. My mother had the same name as myself, Margaret.

MRS ERLYNNE. My name is Margaret too.

LADY WINDERMERE. Indeed!

MRS ERLYNNE. Yes. [*Pause.*] You are devoted to your mother's memory, Lady Windermere, your husband tells me.

LADY WINDERMERE. We all have ideals in life. At least we all should have. Mine is my mother.

MRS ERLYNNE. Ideals are dangerous things. Realities are better. They wound, but they're better.

LADY WINDERMERE [*Shaking her head.*] If I lost my ideals, I should lose everything.

MRS ERLYNNE. Everything?

LADY WINDERMERE. Yes. [*Pause.*]

MRS ERLYNNE. Did your father often speak to you of your mother?

LADY WINDERMERE. No, it gave him too much pain. He told me how my mother had died a few months after I was born. His eyes filled with tears as he spoke. Then he begged me never to mention her name to him again. It made him suffer even to hear it. My father—my father really died of a broken heart. His was the most ruined life I know.

MRS ERLYNNE [*Rising.*] I am afraid I must go now, Lady Windermere.

LADY WINDERMERE [*Rising.*] Oh no, don't.

MRS ERLYNNE. I think I had better. My carriage must have come back by this time. I sent it to Lady Jedburgh's with a note.

LADY WINDERMERE. Arthur, would you mind seeing if Mrs Erlynne's carriage has come back?

MRS ERLYNNE. Pray don't trouble, Lord Windermere.

LADY WINDERMERE. Yes, Arthur, do go, please.

[*Lord Windermere hesitates for a moment and looks at Mrs Erlynne. She remains quite impassive. He leaves the room.*]

[*To Mrs Erlynne.*] Oh! What am I to say to you? You saved me last night. [*Goes towards her.*]

MRS ERLYNNE. Hush—don't speak of it.

LADY WINDERMERE. I must speak of it. I can't let you think that I am going to accept this sacrifice. I am not. It is too great. I am going to tell my husband everything. It is my duty.

MRS ERLYNNE. It is not your duty—at least you have duties to others besides him. You say you owe me something?

LADY WINDERMERE. I owe you everything.

MRS ERLYNNE. Then pay your debt by silence. That is the only way in which it can be paid. Don't spoil the one good thing I have done in my life by telling it to any one. Promise me that what passed last night will remain a secret between us. You must not bring misery into your husband's life. Why spoil his love? You must not spoil it. Love is easily killed. Oh! how easily love is killed! Pledge me your word, Lady Windermere, that you will *never* tell him. I insist upon it.

LADY WINDERMERE [*With bowed head.*] It is your will, not mine.

MRS ERLYNNE. Yes, it is my will. And never forget your child—I like to think of you as a mother. I like you to think of yourself as one.

LADY WINDERMERE [*Looking up.*] I always will now. Only once in my life I have forgotten my own mother—that was last night. Oh, if I had remembered her I should not have been so foolish, so wicked.

MRS ERLYNNE [*With a slight shudder.*] Hush, last night is quite over.

[*Enter Lord Windermere.*]

LORD WINDERMERE. Your carriage has not come back yet, Mrs Erlynne.

MRS ERLYNNE. It makes no matter. I'll take a hansom. There is nothing in the world so respectable as a good Shrewsbury and Talbot.° And now, dear Lady Windermere, I am afraid it is really goodbye. [*Moves up C.*] Oh, I remember. You'll think me absurd, but do you know I've taken a great fancy to this fan that I was silly enough to run away with last night from your ball. Now, I wonder would you give it to me? Lord Windermere says you may. I know it is his present.

LADY WINDERMERE. Oh, certainly, if it will give you any pleasure. But it has my name on it. It has 'Margaret' on it.

MRS ERLYNNE. But we have the same Christian name.

LADY WINDERMERE. Oh, I forgot. Of course, do have it. What a wonderful chance our names being the same!

MRS ERLYNNE. Quite wonderful. Thanks—it will always remind me of you. [*Shakes hands with her.*]

[*Enter Parker.*]

PARKER. Lord Augustus Lorton. Mrs Erlynne's carriage has come.

[*Enter Lord Augustus.*]

LORD AUGUSTUS. Good morning, dear boy. Good morning, Lady Windermere. [*Sees Mrs Erlynne.*] Mrs Erlynne!

MRS ERLYNNE. How do you do, Lord Augustus? Are you quite well this morning?

LORD AUGUSTUS [*Coldly.*] Quite well, thank you, Mrs Erlynne.

MRS ERLYNNE. You don't look at all well, Lord Augustus. You stop up too late—it is so bad for you. You really should take more care of yourself. Goodbye, Lord Windermere. [*Goes towards door with a bow to Lord Augustus. Suddenly smiles and looks back at him.*] Lord Augustus! Won't you see me to my carriage? You might carry the fan.

LORD WINDERMERE. Allow me!

MRS ERLYNNE. No; I want Lord Augustus. I have a special message for the dear Duchess. Won't you carry the fan, Lord Augustus?

LORD AUGUSTUS. If you really desire it, Mrs Erlynne.

MRS ERLYNNE [*Laughing.*] Of course I do. You'll carry it so gracefully. You would carry off anything gracefully, dear Lord Augustus.

[*When she reaches the door she looks back for a moment at Lady Windermere. Their eyes meet. Then she turns, and exit C. followed by Lord Augustus.*]

LADY WINDERMERE. You will never speak against Mrs Erlynne again, Arthur, will you?

LORD WINDERMERE [*Gravely.*] She is better than one thought her.

LADY WINDERMERE. She is better than I am.

LORD WINDERMERE [*Smiling as he strokes her hair.*] Child, you and she belong to different worlds. Into your world evil has never entered.

LADY WINDERMERE. Don't say that, Arthur. There is the same world for all of us, and good and evil, sin and innocence, go through it hand in hand. To shut one's eyes to half of life that one may live securely is as though one blinded oneself that one might walk with more safety in a land of pit and precipice.

LORD WINDERMERE [*Moves down with her.*] Darling, why do you say that?

LADY WINDERMERE [*Sits on sofa.*] Because I, who had shut my eyes to life, came to the brink. And one who had separated us——

LORD WINDERMERE. We were never separated.

LADY WINDERMERE. We never must be again. Oh Arthur, don't love me less, and I will trust you more. I will trust you absolutely. Let us go to Selby. In the Rose Garden at Selby the roses are white and red.

[*Enter Lord Augustus C.*]

LORD AUGUSTUS. Arthur, she has explained everything!

[*Lady Windermere looks horribly frightened at this. Lord Windermere starts. Lord Augustus takes Windermere by the arm and brings him to front of stage. He talks rapidly and in a low voice. Lady Windermere stands watching them in terror.*]

My dear fellow, she has explained every demmed thing. We all wronged her immensely. It was entirely for my sake she went to Darlington's rooms. Called first at the Club—fact is, wanted to put me out of suspense—and being told I had gone on—followed—naturally frightened when she heard a lot of us coming in—retired to another room—I assure you, most gratifying to me, the whole thing. We all behaved brutally to her. She is just the woman for me. Suits me down to the ground. All the conditions she makes are that we live entirely out of England. A very good thing, too. Demmed clubs, demmed climate, demmed cooks, demmed everything. Sick of it all!

LADY WINDERMERE [*Frightened.*] Has Mrs Erlynne——?

LORD AUGUSTUS [*Advancing towards her with a low bow.*] Yes, Lady Windermere—Mrs Erlynne has done me the honour of accepting my hand.

LORD WINDERMERE. Well, you are certainly marrying a very clever woman!

LADY WINDERMERE [*Taking her husband's hand.*] Ah, you're marrying a very good woman!°

CURTAIN

AN IDEAL HUSBAND

THE PERSONS OF THE PLAY°

THE EARL OF CAVERSHAM, K.G.

VISCOUNT GORING, his Son

SIR ROBERT CHILTERN, Bart., Under-Secretary for Foreign Affairs

VICOMTE DE NANJAC, Attaché at the French Embassy in London

MR MONTFORD

MASON, Butler to Sir Robert Chiltern

PHIPPS, Lord Goring's Servant

JAMES
HAROLD } Footmen

LADY CHILTERN

LADY MARKBY

THE COUNTESS OF BASILDON

MRS MARCHMONT

MISS MABEL CHILTERN, SIR ROBERT CHILTERN'S SISTER

MRS CHEVELEY

THE SCENES OF THE PLAY

ACT I   *The Octagon Room in Sir Robert Chiltern's House in Grosvenor Square.*

ACT II   *Morning-room in Sir Robert Chiltern's House.*

ACT III   *The Library of Lord Goring's House in Curzon Street.*

ACT IV   *Same as Act II.*

Time . . . . The Present.
Place . . . . London.

The Action of the Play is completed within twenty-four hours.°

THEATRE ROYAL, HAYMARKET

Sole Lessee: Mr Herbert Beerbohm Tree
Managers: Mr Lewis Waller and Mr H. H. Morell
January 3rd, 1895

THE EARL OF CAVERSHAM	*Mr Alfred Bishop*
VISCOUNT GORING	*Mr Charles H. Hawtrey*
SIR ROBERT CHILTERN	*Mr Lewis Waller*
VICOMTE DE NANJAC	*Mr Cosmo Stuart*
MR MONTFORD	*Mr Harry Stanford*
PHIPPS	*Mr C. H. Brookfield*
MASON	*Mr H. Deane*
JAMES (Footman)	*Mr Charles Meyrick*
HAROLD (Footman)	*Mr Goodhart*
LADY CHILTERN	*Miss Julia Neilson*
LADY MARKBY	*Miss Fanny Brough*
COUNTESS OF BASILDON	*Miss Vane Featherston*
MRS MARCHMONT	*Miss Helen Forsyth*
MISS MABEL CHILTERN	*Miss Maude Millett*
MRS CHEVELEY	*Miss Florence West*

AN IDEAL HUSBAND

FIRST ACT

SCENE—*The octagon room at Sir Robert Chiltern's house in Grosvenor Square.*°

[*The room is brilliantly lighted and full of guests. At the top of the staircase stands Lady Chiltern, a woman of grave Greek beauty, about twenty-seven years of age. She receives the guests as they come up. Over the well of the staircase hangs a great chandelier with wax lights, which illumine a large eighteenth-century French tapestry—representing the Triumph of Love, from a design by Boucher*°—*that is stretched on the staircase wall. On the right is the entrance to the music-room. The sound of a string quartette is faintly heard. The entrance on the left leads to other reception-rooms. Mrs Marchmont and Lady Basildon,*° *two very pretty women, are seated together on a Louis Seize sofa. They are types of exquisite fragility. Their affectation of manner has a delicate charm. Watteau would have loved to paint them.*]

MRS MARCHMONT. Going on to the Hartlocks' tonight, Margaret?

LADY BASILDON. I suppose so. Are you?

MRS MARCHMONT. Yes. Horribly tedious parties they give, don't they?

LADY BASILDON. Horribly tedious! Never know why I go. Never know why I go anywhere.

MRS MARCHMONT. I come here to be educated.

LADY BASILDON. Ah! I hate being educated!

MRS MARCHMONT. So do I. It puts one almost on a level with the commercial classes, doesn't it? But dear Gertrude Chiltern is always telling me that I should have some serious purpose in life. So I come here to try to find one.

LADY BASILDON [*Looking round through her lorgnette.*] I don't see anybody here tonight whom one could possibly call a serious purpose. The man who took me in to dinner talked to me about his wife the whole time.

MRS MARCHMONT. How very trivial of him!

LADY BASILDON. Terribly trivial! What did your man talk about?

MRS MARCHMONT. About myself.

LADY BASILDON [*Languidly.*] And were you interested?

MRS MARCHMONT [*Shaking her head.*] Not in the smallest degree.

LADY BASILDON. What martyrs we are, dear Margaret!

MRS MARCHMONT [*Rising.*] And how well it becomes us, Olivia!

[*They rise and go towards the music-room. The Vicomte de Nanjac, a young attaché known for his neckties and his Anglomania, approaches with a low bow, and enters into conversation.*]

MASON [*Announcing guests from the top of the staircase.*] Mr and Lady Jane Barford. Lord Caversham.

[*Enter Lord Caversham, an old gentleman of seventy, wearing the riband and star of the Garter.° A fine Whig type. Rather like a portrait by Lawrence.*]°

LORD CAVERSHAM. Good evening, Lady Chiltern! Has my good-for-nothing young son been here?

LADY CHILTERN [*Smiling.*] I don't think Lord Goring has arrived yet.

MABEL CHILTERN [*Coming up to Lord Caversham.*] Why do you call Lord Goring good-for-nothing?

[*Mabel Chiltern is a perfect example of the English type of prettiness, the apple-blossom type. She has all the fragrance and freedom of a flower. There is ripple after ripple of sunlight in her hair, and the little mouth, with its parted lips, is expectant, like the mouth of a child. She has the fascinating tyranny of youth, and the astonishing courage of innocence. To sane people she is not reminiscent of any work of art. But she is really like a Tanagra statuette,° and would be rather annoyed if she were told so.*]

LORD CAVERSHAM. Because he leads such an idle life.

MABEL CHILTREN. How can you say such a thing? Why, he rides in the Row° at ten o'clock in the morning, goes to the Opera three times a week, changes his clothes at least five times a day, and dines out every night of the season. You don't call that leading an idle life, do you?

LORD CAVERSHAM [*Looking at her with a kindly twinkle in his eyes.*] You are a very charming young lady!

MABEL CHILTERN. How sweet of you to say that, Lord Caversham! Do come to us more often. You know we are always at home on Wednesdays, and you look so well with your star!

LORD CAVERSHAM. Never go anywhere now. Sick of London Society. Shouldn't mind being introduced to my own tailor; he always votes on the right side. But object strongly to being sent down to dinner with my wife's milliner. Never could stand Lady Caversham's bonnets.

MABEL CHILTERN. Oh, I love London Society! I think it has immensely improved. It is entirely composed now of beautiful idiots and brilliant lunatics. Just what Society should be.

LORD CAVERSHAM. Hum! Which is Goring? Beautiful idiot, or the other thing?

MABEL CHILTERN [*Gravely.*] I have been obliged for the present to put Lord Goring into a class quite by himself. But he is developing charmingly!

LORD CAVERSHAM. Into what?

MABEL CHILTERN [*With a little curtsey.*] I hope to let you know very soon, Lord Caversham!

MASON [*Announcing guests.*] Lady Markby. Mrs Cheveley.

[*Enter Lady Markby and Mrs Cheveley. Lady Markby is a pleasant, kindly, popular woman, with gray hair à la marquise° and good lace. Mrs Cheveley, who accompanies her, is tall and rather slight. Lips very thin and highly-coloured, a line of scarlet on a pallid face. Venetian red hair, aquiline nose, and long throat. Rouge accentuates the natural paleness of her complexion. Gray-green eyes that move restlessly. She is in heliotrope, with diamonds. She looks rather like an orchid, and makes great demands on one's curiosity. In all her movements she is extremely graceful. A work of art, on the whole, but showing the influence of too many schools.*]

LADY MARKBY. Good evening, dear Gertrude! So kind of you to let me bring my friend, Mrs Cheveley. Two such charming women should know each other!

LADY CHILTERN [*Advances towards Mrs Cheveley with a sweet smile. Then suddenly stops, and bows rather distantly.*] I think Mrs Cheveley and I have met before. I did not know she had married a second time.

LADY MARKBY [*Genially.*] Ah, nowadays people marry as often as they can, don't they? It is most fashionable. [*To Duchess of Maryborough.*] Dear Duchess, and how is the Duke? Brain still weak, I suppose? Well, that is only to be expected, is it not? His good father was just the same. There is nothing like race, is there?

MRS CHEVELEY [*Playing with her fan.*] But have we really met before, Lady Chiltern? I can't remember where. I have been out of England for so long.

LADY CHILTERN. We were at school together, Mrs Cheveley.

MRS CHEVELEY [*Superciliously.*] Indeed? I have forgotten all about my schooldays. I have a vague impression that they were detestable.

LADY CHILTERN [*Coldly.*] I am not surprised!

MRS CHEVELEY [*In her sweetest manner.*] Do you know, I am quite looking forward to meeting your clever husband, Lady Chiltern. Since he has been at the Foreign Office, he has been so much talked of in Vienna. They actually succeed in spelling his name right in the newspapers. That in itself is fame, on the continent.

LADY CHILTERN. I hardly think there will be much in common between you and my husband, Mrs Cheveley! [*Moves away.*]

VICOMTE DE NANJAC. Ah! chère Madame, quelle surprise! I have not seen you since Berlin!

MRS CHEVELEY. Not since Berlin, Vicomte. Five years ago!

VICOMTE DE NANJAC. And you are younger and more beautiful than ever. How do you manage it?

MRS CHEVELEY. By making it a rule only to talk to perfectly charming people like yourself.

VICOMTE DE NANJAC. Ah! you flatter me. You butter me, as they say here.

MRS CHEVELEY. Do they say that here? How dreadful of them!

VICOMTE DE NANJAC. Yes, they have a wonderful language. It should be more widely known.

[*Sir Robert Chiltern enters. A man of forty, but looking somewhat younger. Clean-shaven, with finely-cut features, dark-haired and dark-eyed. A personality of mark. Not popular—few personalities are. But intensely admired by the few, and deeply respected by the many. The note of his manner is that of perfect distinction, with a slight touch of pride. One feels that he is conscious of the success he has made in life. A nervous temperament, with a tired look. The firmly-chiselled mouth and chin contrast strikingly with the romantic expression in the deep-set eyes. The variance is suggestive of an almost complete separation of passion and intellect, as though thought and emotion were each isolated in its own sphere through some violence of will-power. There is nervousness in the nostrils, and in the pale, thin, pointed hands. It would be inaccurate to call him picturesque. Picturesqueness cannot survive the House of Commons. But Vandyck° would have liked to have painted his head.*]

SIR ROBERT CHILTERN. Good evening, Lady Markby! I hope you have brought Sir John with you?

LADY MARKBY. Oh! I have brought a much more charming person than

Sir John. Sir John's temper since he has taken seriously to politics has become quite unbearable. Really, now that the House of Commons is trying to become useful, it does a great deal of harm.

SIR ROBERT CHILTERN. I hope not, Lady Markby. At any rate we do our best to waste the public time, don't we? But who is this charming person you have been kind enough to bring to us?

LADY MARKBY. Her name is Mrs Cheveley! One of the Dorsetshire Cheveleys, I suppose. But I really don't know. Families are so mixed nowadays. Indeed, as a rule, everybody turns out to be somebody else.

SIR ROBERT CHILTERN. Mrs Cheveley? I seem to know the name.

LADY MARKBY. She has just arrived from Vienna.

SIR ROBERT CHILTERN. Ah! yes. I think I know whom you mean.

LADY MARKBY. Oh! she goes everywhere there, and has such pleasant scandals about all her friends. I really must go to Vienna next winter. I hope there is a good chef at the Embassy.

SIR ROBERT CHILTERN. If there is not, the Ambassador will certainly have to be recalled. Pray point out Mrs Cheveley to me. I should like to see her.

LADY MARKBY. Let me introduce you. [*To Mrs Cheveley.*] My dear, Sir Robert Chiltern is dying to know you!

SIR ROBERT CHILTERN [*Bowing.*] Everyone is dying to know the brilliant Mrs Cheveley. Our attachés at Vienna write to us about nothing else.

MRS CHEVELEY. Thank you, Sir Robert. An acquaintance that begins with a compliment is sure to develop into a real friendship. It starts in the right manner. And I find that I know Lady Chiltern already.

SIR ROBERT CHILTERN. Really?

MRS CHEVELEY. Yes. She has just reminded me that we were at school together. I remember it perfectly now. She always got the good conduct prize. I have a distinct recollection of Lady Chiltern always getting the good conduct prize!

SIR ROBERT CHILTERN [*Smiling.*] And what prizes did you get, Mrs Cheveley?

MRS CHEVELEY. My prizes came a little later on in life. I don't think any of them were for good conduct. I forget!

SIR ROBERT CHILTERN. I am sure they were for something charming!

MRS CHEVELEY. I don't know that women are always rewarded for being charming. I think they are usually punished for it! Certainly, more women grow old nowadays through the faithfulness of their admirers than through anything else! At least that is the only way I can account for the terribly haggard look of most of your pretty women in London!

SIR ROBERT CHILTERN. What an appalling philosophy that sounds! To attempt to classify you, Mrs Cheveley, would be an impertinence. But may I ask, at heart, are you an optimist or a pessimist? Those seem to be the only two fashionable religions left to us nowadays.

MRS CHEVELEY. Oh, I'm neither. Optimism begins in a broad grin, and Pessimism ends with blue spectacles.° Besides, they are both of them merely poses.

SIR ROBERT CHILTERN. You prefer to be natural?

MRS CHEVELEY. Sometimes. But it is such a very difficult pose to keep up.

SIR ROBERT CHILTERN. What would those modern psychological novelists, of whom we hear so much, say to such a theory as that?

MRS CHEVELEY. Ah! the strength of women comes from the fact that psychology cannot explain us. Men can be analysed, women . . . merely adored.

SIR ROBERT CHILTERN. You think science cannot grapple with the problem of women?

MRS CHEVELEY. Science can never grapple with the irrational. That is why it has no future before it, in this world.

SIR ROBERT CHILTERN. And women represent the irrational.

MRS CHEVELEY. Well-dressed women do.

SIR ROBERT CHILTERN [*With a polite bow.*] I fear I could hardly agree with you there. But do sit down. And now tell me, what makes you leave your brilliant Vienna for our gloomy London—or perhaps the question is indiscreet?

MRS CHEVELEY. Questions are never indiscreet. Answers sometimes are.

SIR ROBERT CHILTERN. Well, at any rate, may I know if it is politics or pleasure?

MRS CHEVELEY. Politics are my only pleasure. You see nowadays it is not fashionable to flirt till one is forty, or to be romantic till one is forty-five, so we poor women who are under thirty, or say we are, have nothing open to us but politics or philanthropy. And philanthropy seems to me to have become simply the refuge of people who wish to annoy their fellow-creatures. I prefer politics. I think they are more . . . becoming!

SIR ROBERT CHILTERN. A political life is a noble career!

MRS CHEVELEY. Sometimes. And sometimes it is a clever game, Sir Robert. And sometimes it is a great nuisance.

SIR ROBERT CHILTERN. Which do you find it?

MRS CHEVELEY. I? A combination of all three. [*Drops her fan.*]

SIR ROBERT CHILTERN [*Picks up fan.*] Allow me!

MRS CHEVELEY. Thanks.

SIR ROBERT CHILTERN. But you have not told me yet what makes you honour London so suddenly. Our season is almost over.

MRS CHEVELEY. Oh! I don't care about the London season! It is too matrimonial. People are either hunting for husbands, or hiding from them. I wanted to meet you. It is quite true. You know what a woman's curiosity is. Almost as great as a man's! I wanted immensely to meet you, and . . . to ask you to do something for me.

SIR ROBERT CHILTERN. I hope it is not a little thing, Mrs Cheveley. I find that little things are so very difficult to do.

MRS CHEVELEY [*After a moment's reflection.*] No, I don't think it is quite a little thing.

SIR ROBERT CHILTERN. I am so glad. Do tell me what it is.

MRS CHEVELEY. Later on. [*Rises.*] And now may I walk through your beautiful house? I hear your pictures are charming. Poor Baron Arnheim—you remember the Baron?—used to tell me you had some wonderful Corots.°

SIR ROBERT CHILTERN [*With an almost imperceptible start.*] Did you know Baron Arnheim well?

MRS CHEVELEY [*Smiling.*] Intimately. Did you?

SIR ROBERT CHILTERN. At one time.

MRS CHEVELEY. Wonderful man, wasn't he?

SIR ROBERT CHILTERN [*After a pause.*] He was very remarkable, in many ways.

MRS CHEVELEY. I often think it such a pity he never wrote his memoirs. They would have been most interesting.

SIR ROBERT CHILTERN. Yes: he knew men and cities well, like the old Greek.°

MRS CHEVELEY. Without the dreadful disadvantage of having a Penelope° waiting at home for him.

MASON. Lord Goring.

[*Enter Lord Goring. Thirty-four, but always says he is younger. A well-bred, expressionless face. He is clever, but would not like to be thought so. A flawless dandy, he would be annoyed if he were considered romantic. He plays with life, and is on perfectly good terms with the world. He is fond of being misunderstood. It gives him a post of vantage.*]

SIR ROBERT CHILTERN. Good evening, my dear Arthur! Mrs Cheveley, allow me to introduce to you Lord Goring, the idlest man in London.

MRS CHEVELEY. I have met Lord Goring before.

LORD GORING [*Bowing.*] I did not think you would remember me, Mrs Cheveley.

MRS CHEVELEY. My memory is under admirable control. And are you still a bachelor?

LORD GORING. I . . . believe so.

MRS CHEVELEY. How very romantic!

LORD GORING. Oh! I am not at all romantic. I am not old enough. I leave romance to my seniors.

SIR ROBERT CHILTERN. Lord Goring is the result of Boodle's Club,° Mrs Cheveley.

MRS CHEVELEY. He reflects every credit on the institution.

LORD GORING. May I ask are you staying in London long?

MRS CHEVELEY. That depends partly on the weather, partly on the cooking, and partly on Sir Robert.

SIR ROBERT CHILTERN. You are not going to plunge us into a European war, I hope?

MRS CHEVELEY. There is no danger, at present!

[*She nods to Lord Goring, with a look of amusement in her eyes, and goes out with Sir Robert Chiltern. Lord Goring saunters over to Mabel Chiltern.*]

MABEL CHILTERN. You are very late!

LORD GORING. Have you missed me?

MABEL CHILTERN. Awfully!

LORD GORING. Then I am sorry I did not stay away longer. I like being missed.

MABEL CHILTERN. How very selfish of you!

LORD GORING. I am very selfish.

MABEL CHILTERN. You are always telling me of your bad qualities, Lord Goring.

LORD GORING. I have only told you half of them as yet, Miss Mabel!

MABEL CHILTERN. Are the others very bad?

LORD GORING. Quite dreadful! When I think of them at night I go to sleep at once.

MABEL CHILTERN. Well, I delight in your bad qualities. I wouldn't have you part with one of them.

LORD GORING. How very nice of you! But then you are always nice. By the way, I want to ask you a question, Miss Mabel. Who brought Mrs Cheveley here? That woman in heliotrope, who has just gone out of the room with your brother?

MABEL CHILTERN. Oh, I think Lady Markby brought her. Why do you ask?

LORD GORING. I hadn't seen her for years, that is all.

MABEL CHILTERN. What an absurd reason!

LORD GORING. All reasons are absurd.

MABEL CHILTERN. What sort of woman is she?

LORD GORING. Oh! a genius in the daytime and a beauty at night!

MABEL CHILTERN. I dislike her already.

LORD GORING. That shows your admirable good taste.

VICOMTE DE NANJAC [*Approaching.*] Ah, the English young lady is the dragon of good taste, is she not? Quite the dragon of good taste.

LORD GORING. So the newspapers are always telling us.

VICOMTE DE NANJAC. I read all your English newspapers. I find them so amusing.

LORD GORING. Then, my dear Nanjac, you must certainly read between the lines.

VICOMTE DE NANJAC. I should like to, but my professor objects. [*To Mabel Chiltern.*] May I have the pleasure of escorting you to the music-room, Mademoiselle?

MABEL CHILTERN [*Looking very disappointed.*] Delighted, Vicomte, quite delighted! [*Turning to Lord Goring.*] Aren't you coming to the music-room?

LORD GORING. Not if there is any music going on, Miss Mabel.

MABEL CHILTERN [*Severely.*] The music is in German. You would not understand it.

[*Goes out with the Vicomte de Nanjac. Lord Caversham comes up to his son.*]

LORD CAVERSHAM. Well, sir! what are you doing here? Wasting your life as usual! You should be in bed, sir. You keep too late hours! I heard of you the other night at Lady Rufford's dancing till four o'clock in the morning!

LORD GORING. Only a quarter to four, father.

LORD CAVERSHAM. Can't make out how you stand London Society. The thing has gone to the dogs, a lot of damned nobodies talking about nothing.

LORD GORING. I love talking about nothing, father. It is the only thing I know anything about.

LORD CAVERSHAM. You seem to me to be living entirely for pleasure.

LORD GORING. What else is there to live for, father? Nothing ages like happiness.

LORD CAVERSHAM. You are heartless, sir, very heartless!

LORD GORING. I hope not, father. Good evening, Lady Basildon!

LADY BASILDON [*Arching two pretty eyebrows.*] Are you here? I had no idea you ever came to political parties!

LORD GORING. I adore political parties. They are the only place left to us where people don't talk politics.

LADY BASILDON. I delight in talking politics. I talk them all day long. But I can't bear listening to them. I don't know how the unfortunate men in the House stand these long debates.

LORD GORING. By never listening.

LADY BASILDON. Really?

LORD GORING [*In his most serious manner.*] Of course. You see, it is a very dangerous thing to listen. If one listens one may be convinced; and a man who allows himself to be convinced by an argument is a thoroughly unreasonable person.

LADY BASILDON. Ah! that accounts for so much in men that I have never understood, and so much in women that their husbands never appreciate in them!

MRS MARCHMONT [*With a sigh.*] Our husbands never appreciate anything in us. We have to go to others for that!

LADY BASILDON [*Emphatically.*] Yes, always to others, have we not?

LORD GORING [*Smiling.*] And those are the views of the two ladies who are known to have the most admirable husbands in London.

MRS MARCHMONT. That is exactly what we can't stand. My Reginald is quite hopelessly faultless. He is really unendurably so, at times! There is not the smallest element of excitement in knowing him.

LORD GORING. How terrible! Really, the thing should be more widely known!

LADY BASILDON. Basildon is quite as bad; he is as domestic as if he was a bachelor.

MRS MARCHMONT [*Pressing Lady Basildon's hand.*] My poor Olivia! We have married perfect husbands, and we are well punished for it.

LORD GORING. I should have thought it was the husbands who were punished.

MRS MARCHMONT [*Drawing herself up.*] Oh, dear no! They are as happy as possible! And as for trusting us, it is tragic how much they trust us.

LADY BASILDON. Perfectly tragic!

LORD GORING. Or comic, Lady Basildon?

LADY BASILDON. Certainly not comic, Lord Goring. How unkind of you to suggest such a thing!

MRS MARCHMONT. I am afraid Lord Goring is in the camp of the enemy, as usual. I saw him talking to that Mrs Cheveley when he came in.

LORD GORING. Handsome woman, Mrs Cheveley!

LADY BASILDON [*Stiffly.*] Please don't praise other women in our presence. You might wait for us to do that!

LORD GORING. I did wait.

MRS MARCHMONT. Well, we are not going to praise her. I hear she went to the Opera on Monday night, and told Tommy Rufford at supper that, as far as she could see, London Society was entirely made up of dowdies and dandies.

LORD GORING. She is quite right, too. The men are all dowdies and the women are all dandies, aren't they?

MRS MARCHMONT [*After a pause.*] Oh! do you really think that is what Mrs Cheveley meant?

LORD GORING. Of course. And a very sensible remark for Mrs Cheveley to make, too.

[*Enter Mabel Chiltern. She joins the group.*]

MABEL CHILTERN. Why are you talking about Mrs Cheveley? Everybody is talking about Mrs Cheveley! Lord Goring says—what did you say, Lord Goring, about Mrs Cheveley? Oh! I remember, that she was a genius in the daytime and a beauty at night.

LADY BASILDON. What a horrid combination! So very unnatural!

MRS MARCHMONT [*In her most dreamy manner.*] I like looking at geniuses, and listening to beautiful people.

LORD GORING. Ah! that is morbid of you, Mrs Marchmont!

MRS MARCHMONT [*Brightening to a look of real pleasure.*] I am so glad to hear you say that. Marchmont and I have been married for seven years, and he has never once told me that I was morbid. Men are so painfully unobservant!

LADY BASILDON [*Turning to her.*] I have always said, dear Margaret, that you were the most morbid person in London.

MRS MARCHMONT. Ah! but you are always sympathetic, Olivia!

MABEL CHILTERN. Is it morbid to have a desire for food? I have a great desire for food. Lord Goring, will you give me some supper?

LORD GORING. With pleasure, Miss Mabel. [*Moves away with her.*]

MABEL CHILTERN. How horrid you have been! You have never talked to me the whole evening!

LORD GORING. How could I? You went away with the child-diplomatist.

MABEL CHILTERN. You might have followed us. Pursuit would have been only polite. I don't think I like you at all this evening!

LORD GORING. I like you immensely.

MABEL CHILTERN. Well, I wish you'd show it in a more marked way!

[*They go downstairs.*]

MRS MARCHMONT. Olivia, I have a curious feeling of absolute faintness. I think I should like some supper very much. I know I should like some supper.

LADY BASILDON. I am positively dying for supper, Margaret!

MRS MARCHMONT. Men are so horribly selfish, they never think of these things.

LADY BASILDON. Men are grossly material, grossly material!

[*The Vicomte de Nanjac enters from the music-room with some other guests. After having carefully examined all the people present, he approaches Lady Basildon.*]

VICOMTE DE NANJAC. May I have the honour of taking you down to supper, Comtesse?

LADY BASILDON [*Coldly.*] I never take supper, thank you, Vicomte. [*The Vicomte is about to retire. Lady Basildon, seeing this, rises at once and takes his arm.*] But I will come down with you with pleasure.

VICOMTE DE NANJAC. I am so fond of eating! I am very English in all my tastes.

LADY BASILDON. You look quite English, Vicomte, quite English.

[*They pass out. Mr Montford, a perfectly groomed young dandy, approaches Mrs Marchmont.*]

MR MONTFORD. Like some supper, Mrs Marchmont?

MRS MARCHMONT [*Languidly.*] Thank you, Mr Montford, I never touch supper. [*Rises hastily and takes his arm.*] But I will sit beside you, and watch you.

MR MONTFORD. I don't know that I like being watched when I am eating!

MRS MARCHMONT. Then I will watch some one else.

MR MONTFORD. I don't know that I should like that either.

MRS MARCHMONT [*Severely.*] Pray, Mr Montford, do not make these painful scenes of jealousy in public!

[*They go downstairs with the other guests, passing Sir Robert Chiltern and Mrs Cheveley, who now enter.*]

SIR ROBERT CHILTERN. And are you going to any of our country houses before you leave England, Mrs Cheveley?

MRS CHEVELEY. Oh, no! I can't stand your English house-parties. In England people actually try to be brilliant at breakfast. That is so dreadful of them! Only dull people are brilliant at breakfast. And then the family skeleton is always reading family prayers. My stay in England really depends on you, Sir Robert. [*Sits down on the sofa.*]

SIR ROBERT CHILTERN [*Taking a seat beside her.*] Seriously?

MRS CHEVELEY. Quite seriously. I want to talk to you about a great political and financial scheme, about this Argentine Canal Company, in fact.

SIR ROBERT CHILTERN. What a tedious, practical subject for you to talk about, Mrs Cheveley!

MRS CHEVELEY. Oh, I like tedious, practical subjects. What I don't like are tedious, practical people. There is a wide difference. Besides, you are interested, I know, in International Canal schemes. You were Lord Radley's secretary, weren't you, when the Government bought the Suez Canal shares?°

SIR ROBERT CHILTERN. Yes. But the Suez Canal was a very great and splendid undertaking. It gave us our direct route to India. It had imperial value. It was necessary that we should have control. This Argentine scheme is a commonplace Stock Exchange swindle.

MRS CHEVELEY. A speculation, Sir Robert! A brilliant, daring speculation.

SIR ROBERT CHILTERN. Believe me, Mrs Cheveley, it is a swindle. Let us call things by their proper names. It makes matters simpler. We have all the information about it at the Foreign Office. In fact, I sent out a special Commission to inquire into the matter privately, and they report that the works are hardly begun, and as for the money already subscribed, no one seems to know what has become of it. The whole thing is a second Panama,° and with not a quarter of the chance of success that miserable affair ever had. I hope you have not invested in it. I am sure you are far too clever to have done that.

MRS CHEVELEY. I have invested very largely in it.

SIR ROBERT CHILTERN. Who could have advised you to do such a foolish thing?

MRS CHEVELEY. Your old friend—and mine.

SIR ROBERT CHILTERN. Who?

MRS CHEVELEY. Baron Arnheim.

SIR ROBERT CHILTERN [*Frowning.*] Ah! yes. I remember hearing, at the time of his death, that he had been mixed up in the whole affair.

MRS CHEVELEY. It was his last romance. His last but one, to do him justice.

SIR ROBERT CHILTERN [*Rising.*] But you have not seen my Corots yet. They are in the music-room. Corots seem to go with music, don't they? May I show them to you?

MRS CHEVELEY [*Shaking her head.*] I am not in a mood tonight for silver twilights, or rose-pink dawns. I want to talk business. [*Motions to him with her fan to sit down again beside her.*]

SIR ROBERT CHILTERN. I fear I have no advice to give you, Mrs Cheveley, except to interest yourself in something less dangerous. The success of the Canal depends, of course, on the attitude of England, and I am going to lay the report of the Commissioners before the House tomorrow night.

MRS CHEVELEY. That you must not do. In your own interests, Sir Robert, to say nothing of mine, you must not do that.

SIR ROBERT CHILTERN [*Looking at her in wonder.*] In my own interests? My dear Mrs Cheveley, what do you mean? [*Sits down beside her.*]

MRS CHEVELEY. Sir Robert, I will be quite frank with you. I want you to withdraw the report that you had intended to lay before the House, on the ground that you have reasons to believe that the Commissioners have been prejudiced or misinformed, or something. Then I want you to say a few words to the effect that the Government is going to reconsider the question, and that you have reason to believe that the Canal, if completed, will be of great international value. You know the sort of things ministers say in cases of this kind. A few ordinary platitudes will do. In modern life nothing produces such an effect as a good platitude. It makes the whole world kin.° Will you do that for me?

SIR ROBERT CHILTERN. Mrs Cheveley, you cannot be serious in making me such a proposition!

MRS CHEVELEY. I am quite serious.

SIR ROBERT CHILTERN [*Coldly.*] Pray allow me to believe that you are not!

MRS CHEVELEY [*Speaking with great deliberation and emphasis.*] Ah! but I am. And, if you do what I ask you, I . . . will pay you very handsomely!

SIR ROBERT CHILTERN. Pay me!

MRS CHEVELEY. Yes.

SIR ROBERT CHILTERN. I am afraid I don't quite understand what you mean.

MRS CHEVELEY [*Leaning back on the sofa and looking at him.*] How very disappointing! And I have come all the way from Vienna in order that you should thoroughly understand me.

SIR ROBERT CHILTERN. I fear I don't.

MRS CHEVELEY [*In her most nonchalant manner.*] My dear Sir Robert, you are a man of the world, and you have your price, I suppose. Everybody has nowadays. The drawback is that most people are so dreadfully expensive. I know I am. I hope you will be more reasonable in your terms.

SIR ROBERT CHILTERN [*Rises indignantly.*] If you will allow me, I will call your carriage for you. You have lived so long abroad, Mrs Cheveley, that you seem to be unable to realize that you are talking to an English gentleman.

MRS CHEVELEY [*Detains him by touching his arm with her fan, and keeping it there while she is talking.*] I realize that I am talking to a man who laid the foundation of his fortune by selling to a Stock Exchange speculator a Cabinet secret.

SIR ROBERT CHILTERN [*Biting his lip.*] What do you mean?

MRS CHEVELEY [*Rising and facing him.*] I mean that I know the real origin of your wealth and your career, and I have got your letter, too.

SIR ROBERT CHILTERN. What letter?

MRS CHEVELEY [*Contemptuously.*] The letter you wrote to Baron Arnheim, when you were Lord Radley's secretary, telling the Baron to buy Suez Canal shares—a letter written three days before the Government announced its own purchase.

SIR ROBERT CHILTERN [*Hoarsely.*] It is not true.

MRS CHEVELEY. You thought that letter had been destroyed. How foolish of you! It is in my possession.

SIR ROBERT CHILTERN. The affair to which you allude was no more than a speculation. The House of Commons had not yet passed the bill; it might have been rejected.

MRS CHEVELEY. It was a swindle, Sir Robert. Let us call things by their proper names. It makes everything simpler. And now I am going to sell you that letter, and the price I ask for it is your public support of the Argentine scheme. You made your own fortune out of one canal. You must help me and my friends to make our fortunes out of another!

SIR ROBERT CHILTERN. It is infamous, what you propose—infamous!

MRS CHEVELEY. Oh, no! This is the game of life as we all have to play it, Sir Robert, sooner or later!

SIR ROBERT CHILTERN. I cannot do what you ask me.

MRS CHEVELEY. You mean you cannot help doing it. You know you are standing on the edge of a precipice. And it is not for you to make terms. It is for you to accept them. Supposing you refuse——

SIR ROBERT CHILTERN. What then?

MRS CHEVELEY. My dear Sir Robert, what then? You are ruined, that is all! Remember to what a point your Puritanism in England has brought you. In old days nobody pretended to be a bit better than his neighbours. In fact, to be a bit better than one's neighbour was considered excessively vulgar and middle-class. Nowadays, with our modern mania for morality, everyone has to pose as a paragon of purity, incorruptibility, and all the other seven deadly virtues—and what is the result? You all go over like ninepins—one after the other. Not a year passes in England without somebody disappearing. Scandals used to lend charm, or at least interest, to a man—now they crush him. And yours is a very nasty scandal. You couldn't survive it. If it were known that as a young man, secretary to a great and important minister, you sold a Cabinet secret for a large sum of money, and that that was the origin of your wealth and career, you would be hounded out of public life, you would disappear completely. And after all, Sir Robert, why should you sacrifice your entire future rather than deal diplomatically with your enemy? For the moment I am your enemy. I admit it! And I am much stronger than you are. The big battalions are on my side. You have a splendid position, but it is your splendid position that makes you so vulnerable. You can't defend it! And I am in attack. Of course I have not talked morality to you. You must admit in fairness that I have spared you that. Years ago you did a clever, unscrupulous thing; it turned out a great success. You owe to it your fortune and position. And now you have got to pay for it. Sooner or later we all have to pay for what we do. You have to pay now. Before I leave you tonight, you have got to promise me to suppress your report, and to speak in the House in favour of this scheme.

SIR ROBERT CHILTERN. What you ask is impossible.

MRS CHEVELEY. You must make it possible. You are going to make it possible. Sir Robert, you know what your English newspapers are like. Suppose that when I leave this house I drive down to some newspaper office, and give them this scandal and the proofs of it! Think of their loathsome joy, of the delight they would have in dragging you down, of the mud and mire they would plunge you in. Think of the hypocrite with his greasy smile penning his leading article, and arranging the foulness of the public placard.°

SIR ROBERT CHILTERN. Stop! You want me to withdraw the report and to make a short speech stating that I believe there are possibilities in the scheme?

MRS CHEVELEY [*Sitting down on the sofa.*] Those are my terms.

SIR ROBERT CHILTERN [*In a low voice.*] I will give you any sum of money you want.

MRS CHEVELEY. Even you are not rich enough, Sir Robert, to buy back your past. No man is.

SIR ROBERT CHILTERN. I will not do what you ask me. I will not.

MRS CHEVELEY. You have to. If you don't . . . [*Rises from the sofa.*]

SIR ROBERT CHILTERN [*Bewildered and unnerved.*] Wait a moment! What did you propose? You said that you would give me back my letter, didn't you?

MRS CHEVELEY. Yes. That is agreed. I will be in the Ladies' Gallery° tomorrow night at half-past eleven. If by that time—and you will have had heaps of opportunity—you have made an announcement to the House in the terms I wish, I shall hand you back your letter with the prettiest thanks, and the best, or at any rate the most suitable, compliment I can think of. I intend to play quite fairly with you. One should always play fairly . . . when one has the winning cards. The Baron taught me that . . . amongst other things.

SIR ROBERT CHILTERN. You must let me have time to consider your proposal.

MRS CHEVELEY. No; you must settle now!

SIR ROBERT CHILTERN. Give me a week—three days!

MRS CHEVELEY. Impossible! I have got to telegraph to Vienna tonight.

SIR ROBERT CHILTERN. My God! what brought you into my life?

MRS CHEVELEY. Circumstances. [*Moves towards the door.*]

SIR ROBERT CHILTERN. Don't go. I consent. The report shall be withdrawn. I will arrange for a question to be put to me on the subject.

MRS CHEVELEY. Thank you. I knew we should come to an amicable agreement. I understood your nature from the first. I analysed you, though you did not adore me. And now you can get my carriage for me, Sir Robert. I see the people coming up from supper, and Englishmen always get romantic after a meal, and that bores me dreadfully.

[*Exit Sir Robert Chiltern.*]

[*Enter Guests, Lady Chiltern, Lady Markby, Lord Caversham, Lady Basildon, Mrs Marchmont, Vicomte de Nanjac, Mr Montford.*]

LADY MARKBY. Well, dear Mrs Cheveley, I hope you have enjoyed yourself. Sir Robert is very entertaining, is he not?

MRS CHEVELEY. Most entertaining! I have enjoyed my talk with him immensely.

LADY MARKBY. He has had a very interesting and brilliant career. And he has married a most admirable wife. Lady Chiltern is a woman of the very highest principles, I am glad to say. I am a little too old now, myself, to trouble about setting a good example, but I always admire people who do. And Lady Chiltern has a very ennobling effect on life, though her dinner-parties are rather dull sometimes. But one can't have everything, can one? And now I must go, dear. Shall I call for you tomorrow?

MRS CHEVELEY. Thanks.

LADY MARKBY. We might drive in the Park° at five. Everything looks so fresh in the Park now!

MRS CHEVELEY. Except the people!

LADY MARKBY. Perhaps the people are a little jaded. I have often observed that the Season as it goes on produces a kind of softening of the brain. However, I think anything is better than high intellectual pressure. That is the most unbecoming thing there is. It makes the noses of the young girls so particularly large. And there is nothing so difficult to marry as a large nose, men don't like them. Goodnight, dear! [*To Lady Chiltern.*] Goodnight, Gertrude!

[*Goes out on Lord Caversham's arm.*]

MRS CHEVELEY. What a charming house you have, Lady Chiltern! I have spent a delightful evening. It has been so interesting getting to know your husband.

LADY CHILTERN. Why did you wish to meet my husband, Mrs Cheveley?

MRS CHEVELEY. Oh, I will tell you. I wanted to interest him in this Argentine Canal scheme, of which I dare say you have heard. And I found him most susceptible—susceptible to reason, I mean. A rare thing in a man. I converted him in ten minutes. He is going to make a speech in the House tomorrow night in favour of the idea. We must go to the Ladies' Gallery and hear him! It will be a great occasion!

LADY CHILTERN. There must be some mistake. That scheme could never have my husband's support.

MRS CHEVELEY. Oh, I assure you it's all settled. I don't regret my tedious journey from Vienna now. It has been a great success. But, of course, for the next twenty-four hours the whole thing is a dead secret.

LADY CHILTERN [*Gently.*] A secret? Between whom?

MRS CHEVELEY [*With a flash of amusement in her eyes.*] Between your husband and myself.

SIR ROBERT CHILTERN [*Entering.*] Your carriage is here, Mrs Cheveley!

MRS CHEVELEY. Thanks! Good evening, Lady Chiltern! Goodnight, Lord Goring! I am at Claridge's.° Don't you think you might leave a card?

LORD GORING. If you wish it, Mrs Cheveley!

MRS CHEVELEY. Oh, don't be so solemn about it, or I shall be obliged to leave a card on you. In England I suppose that would be hardly considered *en règle.*° Abroad, we are more civilized. Will you see me down, Sir Robert? Now that we have both the same interests at heart we shall be great friends, I hope!

[*Sails out on Sir Robert Chiltern's arm. Lady Chiltern goes to the top of the staircase and looks down at them as they descend. Her expression is troubled. After a little time she is joined by some of the guests, and passes with them into another reception-room.*]

MABEL CHILTERN. What a horrid woman!

LORD GORING. You should go to bed, Miss Mabel.

MABEL CHILTERN. Lord Goring!

LORD GORING. My father told me to go to bed an hour ago. I don't see why I shouldn't give you the same advice. I always pass on good advice. It is the only thing to do with it. It is never of any use to oneself.

MABEL CHILTERN. Lord Goring, you are always ordering me out of the room. I think it most courageous of you. Especially as I am not going to bed for hours. [*Goes over to the sofa.*] You can come and sit down if you like, and talk about anything in the world, except the Royal Academy,° Mrs Cheveley, or novels in Scotch dialect.° They are not improving subjects. [*Catches sight of something that is lying on the sofa half-hidden by the cushion.*] What is this? Some one has dropped a diamond brooch! Quite beautiful, isn't it? [*Shows it to him.*] I wish it was mine, but Gertrude won't let me wear anything but pearls, and I am thoroughly sick of pearls. They make one look so plain, so good and so intellectual. I wonder whom the brooch belongs to.

LORD GORING. I wonder who dropped it.

MABEL CHILTERN. It is a beautiful brooch.

LORD GORING. It is a handsome bracelet.

MABEL CHILTERN. It isn't a bracelet. It's a brooch.

LORD GORING. It can be used as a bracelet. [*Takes it from her, and, pulling out a green letter-case, puts the ornament carefully in it, and replaces the whole thing in his breast-pocket with the most perfect sang-froid.*]

MABEL CHILTERN. What are you doing?

LORD GORING. Miss Mabel, I am going to make a rather strange request to you.

MABEL CHILTERN [*Eagerly.*] Oh, pray do! I have been waiting for it all the evening.

LORD GORING [*Is a little taken aback, but recovers himself.*] Don't mention to anybody that I have taken charge of this brooch. Should anyone write and claim it, let me know at once.

MABEL CHILTERN. That is a strange request.

LORD GORING. Well, you see I gave this brooch to somebody once, years ago.

MABEL CHILTERN. You did?

LORD GORING. Yes.

[*Lady Chiltern enters alone. The other guests have gone.*]

MABEL CHILTERN. Then I shall certainly bid you goodnight. Goodnight, Gertrude!
[*Exit.*]

LADY CHILTERN. Goodnight, dear! [*To Lord Goring.*] You saw whom Lady Markby brought here tonight.

LORD GORING. Yes. It was an unpleasant surprise. What did she come here for?

LADY CHILTERN. Apparently to try and lure Robert to uphold some fraudulent scheme in which she is interested. The Argentine Canal, in fact.

LORD GORING. She has mistaken her man, hasn't she?

LADY CHILTERN. She is incapable of understanding an upright nature like my husband's!

LORD GORING. Yes. I should fancy she came to grief if she tried to get Robert into her toils. It is extraordinary what astounding mistakes clever women make.

LADY CHILTERN. I don't call women of that kind clever. I call them stupid!

LORD GORING. Same thing often. Goodnight, Lady Chiltern!

LADY CHILTERN. Goodnight!

[*Enter Sir Robert Chiltern.*]

SIR ROBERT CHILTERN. My dear Arthur, you are not going? Do stop a little!

LORD GORING. Afraid I can't, thanks. I have promised to look in at the Hartlocks'. I believe they have got a mauve Hungarian band that plays mauve Hungarian music. See you soon. Goodbye!

[*Exit.*]

SIR ROBERT CHILTERN. How beautiful you look tonight, Gertrude!

LADY CHILTERN. Robert, it is not true, is it? You are not going to lend your support to this Argentine speculation? You couldn't!

SIR ROBERT CHILTERN [*Starting.*] Who told you I intended to do so?

LADY CHILTERN. That woman who has just gone out, Mrs Cheveley, as she calls herself now. She seemed to taunt me with it. Robert, I know this woman. You don't. We were at school together. She was untruthful, dishonest, an evil influence on everyone whose trust or friendship she could win. I hated, I despised her. She stole things, she was a thief. She was sent away for being a thief. Why do you let her influence you?

SIR ROBERT CHILTERN. Gertrude, what you tell me may be true, but it happened many years ago. It is best forgotten! Mrs Cheveley may have changed since then. No one should be entirely judged by their past.

LADY CHILTERN [*Sadly.*] One's past is what one is. It is the only way by which people should be judged.

SIR ROBERT CHILTERN. That is a hard saying, Gertrude!

LADY CHILTERN. It is a true saying, Robert. And what did she mean by boasting that she had got you to lend your support, your name to a thing I have heard you describe as the most dishonest and fraudulent scheme there has ever been in political life?

SIR ROBERT CHILTERN [*Biting his lip.*] I was mistaken in the view I took. We all may make mistakes.

LADY CHILTERN. But you told me yesterday that you had received the report from the Commission, and that it entirely condemned the whole thing.

SIR ROBERT CHILTERN [*Walking up and down.*] I have reasons now to believe that the Commission was prejudiced, or, at any rate, misinformed. Besides, Gertrude, public and private life are different things. They have different laws, and move on different lines.

LADY CHILTERN. They should both represent man at his highest. I see no difference between them.

SIR ROBERT CHILTERN [*Stopping.*] In the present case, on a matter of practical politics, I have changed my mind. That is all.

LADY CHILTERN. All!

SIR ROBERT CHILTERN [*Sternly.*] Yes!

LADY CHILTERN. Robert! Oh! it is horrible that I should have to ask you such a question—Robert, are you telling me the whole truth?

SIR ROBERT CHILTERN. Why do you ask me such a question?

LADY CHILTERN [*After a pause.*] Why do you not answer it?

SIR ROBERT CHILTERN [*Sitting down.*] Gertrude, truth is a very complex thing, and politics is a very complex business. There are wheels within wheels. One may be under certain obligations to people that one must pay. Sooner or later in political life one has to compromise. Everyone does.

LADY CHILTERN. Compromise? Robert, why do you talk so differently tonight from the way I have always heard you talk? Why are you changed?

SIR ROBERT CHILTERN. I am not changed. But circumstances alter things.

LADY CHILTERN. Circumstances should never alter principles!

SIR ROBERT CHILTERN. But if I told you——

LADY CHILTERN. What?

SIR ROBERT CHILTERN. That it was necessary, vitally necessary.

LADY CHILTERN. It can never be necessary to do what is not honourable. Or if it be necessary, then what is it that I have loved!° But it is not, Robert; tell me it is not. Why should it be? What gain would you get? Money? We have no need of that! And money that comes from a tainted source is a degradation. Power? But power is nothing in itself. It is power to do good that is fine—that, and that only. What is it, then? Robert, tell me why you are going to do this dishonourable thing!

SIR ROBERT CHILTERN. Gertrude, you have no right to use that word.

I told you it was a question of rational compromise. It is no more than that.

LADY CHILTERN. Robert, that is all very well for other men, for men who treat life simply as a sordid speculation; but not for you, Robert, not for you. You are different. All your life you have stood apart from others. You have never let the world soil you. To the world, as to myself, you have been an ideal always. Oh! be that ideal still. That great inheritance throw not away—that tower of ivory do not destroy. Robert, men can love what is beneath them—things unworthy, stained, dishonoured. We women worship when we love; and when we lose our worship, we lose everything. Oh! don't kill my love for you, don't kill that!

SIR ROBERT CHILTERN. Gertrude!

LADY CHILTERN. I know that there are men with horrible secrets in their lives—men who have done some shameful thing, and who in some critical moment have to pay for it, by doing some other act of shame— oh! don't tell me you are such as they are! Robert, is there in your life any secret dishonour or disgrace? Tell me, tell me at once, that——

SIR ROBERT CHILTERN. That what?

LADY CHILTERN [*Speaking very slowly.*] That our lives may drift apart.

SIR ROBERT CHILTERN. Drift apart?

LADY CHILTERN. That they may be entirely separate. It would be better for us both.

SIR ROBERT CHILTERN. Gertrude, there is nothing in my past life that you might not know.

LADY CHILTERN. I was sure of it, Robert, I was sure of it. But why did you say those dreadful things, things so unlike your real self? Don't let us ever talk about the subject again. You will write, won't you, to Mrs Cheveley, and tell her that you cannot support this scandalous scheme of hers? If you have given her any promise you must take it back, that is all!

SIR ROBERT CHILTERN. Must I write and tell her that?

LADY CHILTERN. Surely, Robert! What else is there to do?

SIR ROBERT CHILTERN. I might see her personally. It would be better.

LADY CHILTERN. You must never see her again, Robert. She is not a woman you should ever speak to. She is not worthy to talk to a man like you. No; you must write to her at once, now, this moment, and let your letter show her that your decision is quite irrevocable!

SIR ROBERT CHILTERN. Write this moment!

LADY CHILTERN. Yes.

SIR ROBERT CHILTERN. But it is so late. It is close on twelve.

LADY CHILTERN. That makes no matter. She must know at once that she has been mistaken in you—and that you are not a man to do anything base or underhand or dishonourable. Write here, Robert. Write that you decline to support this scheme of hers, as you hold it to be a dishonest scheme. Yes—write the word dishonest. She knows what that word means. [*Sir Robert Chiltern sits down and writes a letter. His wife takes it up and reads it.*] Yes; that will do. [*Rings bell.*] And now the envelope. [*He writes the envelope slowly. Enter Mason.*] Have this letter sent at once to Claridge's Hotel. There is no answer. [*Exit Mason. Lady Chiltern kneels down beside her husband and puts her arms round him.*] Robert, love gives one a sort of instinct to things. I feel tonight that I have saved you from something that might have been a danger to you, from something that might have made men honour you less than they do. I don't think you realize sufficiently, Robert, that you have brought into the political life of our time a nobler atmosphere, a finer attitude towards life, a freer air of purer aims and higher ideals—I know it, and for that I love you, Robert.

SIR ROBERT CHILTERN. Oh, love me always, Gertrude, love me always!

LADY CHILTERN. I will love you always, because you will always be worthy of love. We needs must love the highest when we see it!° [*Kisses him and rises and goes out.*]

[*Sir Robert Chiltern walks up and down for a moment; then sits down and buries his face in his hands. The Servant enters and begins putting out the lights. Sir Robert Chiltern looks up.*]

SIR ROBERT CHILTERN. Put out the lights, Mason, put out the lights!°

[*The Servant puts out the lights. The room becomes almost dark. The only light there is comes from the great chandelier that hangs over the staircase and illumines the tapestry of the Triumph of Love.*]

ACT DROP.

SECOND ACT

SCENE—*Morning-room at Sir Robert Chiltern's house.*

[*Lord Goring, dressed in the height of fashion, is lounging in an armchair. Sir Robert Chiltern is standing in front of the fireplace. He is evidently in a state of great mental excitement and distress. As the scene progresses he paces nervously up and down the room.*]

LORD GORING. My dear Robert, it's a very awkward business, very awkward indeed. You should have told your wife the whole thing. Secrets from other people's wives are a necessary luxury in modern life. So, at least, I am always told at the club by people who are bald enough to know better. But no man should have a secret from his own wife. She invariably finds it out. Women have a wonderful instinct about things. They can discover everything except the obvious.

SIR ROBERT CHILTERN. Arthur, I couldn't tell my wife. When could I have told her? Not last night. It would have made a life-long separation between us, and I would have lost the love of the one woman in the world I worship, of the only woman who has ever stirred love within me. Last night it would have been quite impossible. She would have turned from me in horror . . . in horror and in contempt.

LORD GORING. Is Lady Chiltern as perfect as all that?

SIR ROBERT CHILTERN. Yes; my wife is as perfect as all that.

LORD GORING [*Taking off his left-hand glove.*] What a pity! I beg your pardon, my dear fellow, I didn't quite mean that. But if what you tell me is true, I should like to have a serious talk about life with Lady Chiltern.

SIR ROBERT CHILTERN. It would be quite useless.

LORD GORING. May I try?

SIR ROBERT CHILTERN. Yes; but nothing could make her alter her views.

LORD GORING. Well, at the worst it would simply be a psychological experiment.

SIR ROBERT CHILTERN. All such experiments are terribly dangerous.

LORD GORING. Everything is dangerous, my dear fellow. If it wasn't so, life wouldn't be worth living. . . . Well, I am bound to say that I think you should have told her years ago.

SIR ROBERT CHILTERN.   When? When we were engaged? Do you think she would have married me if she had known that the origin of my fortune is such as it is, the basis of my career such as it is, and that I had done a thing that I suppose most men would call shameful and dishonourable?

LORD GORING [*Slowly.*]   Yes; most men would call it ugly names. There is no doubt of that.

SIR ROBERT CHILTERN [*Bitterly.*]   Men who every day do something of the same kind themselves. Men who, each one of them, have worse secrets in their own lives.

LORD GORING.   That is the reason they are so pleased to find out other people's secrets. It distracts public attention from their own.

SIR ROBERT CHILTERN.   And, after all, whom did I wrong by what I did? No one.

LORD GORING [*Looking at him steadily.*]   Except yourself, Robert.

SIR ROBERT CHILTERN [*After a pause.*]   Of course I had private information about a certain transaction contemplated by the Government of the day, and I acted on it. Private information is practically the source of every large modern fortune.

LORD GORING [*Tapping his boot with his cane.*]   And public scandal invariably the result.

SIR ROBERT CHILTERN [*Pacing up and down the room.*]   Arthur, do you think that what I did nearly eighteen years ago should be brought up against me now? Do you think it fair that a man's whole career should be ruined for a fault done in one's boyhood almost. I was twenty-two at the time, and I had the double misfortune of being well-born and poor, two unforgivable things nowadays. Is it fair that the folly, the sin of one's youth, if men choose to call it a sin, should wreck a life like mine, should place me in the pillory, should shatter all that I have worked for, all that I have built up? Is it fair, Arthur?

LORD GORING.   Life is never fair, Robert. And perhaps it is a good thing for most of us that it is not.

SIR ROBERT CHILTERN.   Every man of ambition has to fight his century with its own weapons. What this century worships is wealth. The God of this century is wealth. To succeed one must have wealth. At all costs one must have wealth.

LORD GORING.   You underrate yourself, Robert. Believe me, without wealth you could have succeeded just as well.

SIR ROBERT CHILTERN. When I was old, perhaps. When I had lost my passion for power, or could not use it. When I was tired, worn out, disappointed. I wanted my success when I was young. Youth is the time for success. I couldn't wait.

LORD GORING. Well, you certainly have had your success while you are still young. No one in our day has had such a brilliant success. Under-Secretary for Foreign Affairs at the age of forty—that's good enough for anyone, I should think.

SIR ROBERT CHILTERN. And if it is all taken away from me now? If I lose everything over a horrible scandal? If I am hounded from public life?

LORD GORING. Robert, how could you have sold yourself for money?

SIR ROBERT CHILTERN [Excitedly.] I did not sell myself for money. I bought success at a great price. That is all.

LORD GORING [Gravely.] Yes; you certainly paid a great price for it. But what first made you think of doing such a thing?

SIR ROBERT CHILTERN. Baron Arnheim.

LORD GORING. Damned scoundrel!

SIR ROBERT CHILTERN. No; he was a man of a most subtle and refined intellect. A man of culture, charm, and distinction. One of the most intellectual men I ever met.

LORD GORING. Ah! I prefer a gentlemanly fool any day. There is more to be said for stupidity than people imagine. Personally I have a great admiration for stupidity. It is a sort of fellow-feeling, I suppose. But how did he do it? Tell me the whole thing.

SIR ROBERT CHILTERN [Throws himself into an armchair by the writing-table.] One night after dinner at Lord Radley's the Baron began talking about success in modern life as something that one could reduce to an absolutely definite science. With that wonderfully fascinating quiet voice of his he expounded to us the most terrible of all philosophies, the philosophy of power, preached to us the most marvellous of all gospels, the gospel of gold. I think he saw the effect he had produced on me, for some days afterwards he wrote and asked me to come and see him. He was living then in Park Lane, in the house Lord Woolcomb has now. I remember so well how, with a strange smile on his pale curved lips, he led me through his wonderful picture gallery, showed me his tapestries, his enamels, his jewels, his carved ivories, made me wonder at the strange loveliness of the luxury in which he lived; and then told me that luxury was nothing but a background, a painted scene in a play, and that power, power over other men, power over the world was the one thing worth having, the one supreme pleasure worth knowing, the one joy one never tired of, and that in our century only the rich possessed it.°

LORD GORING [*With great deliberation.*] A thoroughly shallow creed.

SIR ROBERT CHILTERN [*Rising.*] I didn't think so then. I don't think so now. Wealth has given me enormous power. It gave me at the very outset of my life freedom, and freedom is everything. You have never been poor, and never known what ambition is. You cannot understand what a wonderful chance the Baron gave me. Such a chance as few men get.

LORD GORING. Fortunately for them, if one is to judge by results. But tell me definitely, how did the Baron finally persuade you to—well, to do what you did?

SIR ROBERT CHILTERN. When I was going away he said to me that if I ever could give him any private information of real value he would make me a very rich man. I was dazed at the prospect he held out to me, and my ambition and my desire for power were at that time boundless. Six weeks later certain private documents passed through my hands.

LORD GORING [*Keeping his eyes steadily fixed on the carpet.*] State documents?

SIR ROBERT CHILTERN. Yes.

[*Lord Goring sighs, then passes his hand across his forehead and looks up.*]

LORD GORING. I had no idea that you, of all men in the world, could have been so weak, Robert, as to yield to such a temptation as Baron Arnheim held out to you.

SIR ROBERT CHILTERN. Weak? Oh, I am sick of hearing that phrase. Sick of using it about others. Weak? Do you really think, Arthur, that it is weakness that yields to temptation? I tell you that there are terrible temptations that it requires strength, strength and courage, to yield to. To stake all one's life on a single moment, to risk everything on one throw, whether the stake be power or pleasure, I care not—there is no weakness in that. There is a horrible, a terrible courage. I had that courage. I sat down the same afternoon and wrote Baron Arnheim the letter this woman now holds. He made three-quarters of a million over the transaction.

LORD GORING. And you?

SIR ROBERT CHILTERN. I received from the Baron £110,000.

LORD GORING. You were worth more, Robert.

SIR ROBERT CHILTERN. No; that money gave me exactly what I wanted, power over others. I went into the House immediately. The Baron advised me in finance from time to time. Before five years I had almost trebled my fortune. Since then everything that I have touched has turned out a success. In all things connected with money I have had a luck so extraordinary that sometimes it has made me almost afraid. I remember having read somewhere, in some strange book, that when the gods wish to punish us they answer our prayers.

LORD GORING. But tell me, Robert, did you never suffer any regret for what you had done?

SIR ROBERT CHILTERN. No. I felt that I had fought the century with its own weapons, and won.

LORD GORING [*Sadly.*] You thought you had won?

SIR ROBERT CHILTERN. I thought so. [*After a long pause.*] Arthur, do you despise me for what I have told you?

LORD GORING. [*With deep feeling in his voice.*] I am very sorry for you, Robert, very sorry indeed.

SIR ROBERT CHILTERN. I don't say that I suffered any remorse. I didn't. Not remorse in the ordinary, rather silly sense of the word. But I have paid conscience money many times. I had a wild hope that I might disarm destiny. The sum Baron Arnheim gave me I have distributed twice over in public charities since then.

LORD GORING [*Looking up.*] In public charities? Dear me! what a lot of harm you must have done, Robert!°

SIR ROBERT CHILTERN. Oh, don't say that, Arthur; don't talk like that.

LORD GORING. Never mind what I say, Robert. I am always saying what I shouldn't say. In fact, I usually say what I really think. A great mistake nowadays. It makes one so liable to be misunderstood. As regards this dreadful business, I will help you in whatever way I can. Of course you know that.

SIR ROBERT CHILTERN. Thank you, Arthur, thank you. But what is to be done? What can be done?

LORD GORING [*Leaning back with his hands in his pockets.*] Well, the English can't stand a man who is always saying he is in the right, but they are very fond of a man who admits that he has been in the wrong. It is one of the best things in them. However, in your case, Robert, a

confession would not do. The money, if you will allow me to say so, is
. . . awkward. Besides, if you did make a clean breast of the whole
affair, you would never be able to talk morality again. And in England a
man who can't talk morality twice a week to a large, popular, immoral
audience is quite over as a serious politician. There would be nothing
left for him as a profession except Botany or the Church. A confession
would be of no use. It would ruin you.

SIR ROBERT CHILTERN. It would ruin me. Arthur, the only thing for me to
do now is to fight the thing out.

LORD GORING [*Rising from his chair.*] I was waiting for you to say that,
Robert. It is the only thing to do now. And you must begin by telling
your wife the whole story.

SIR ROBERT CHILTERN. That I will not do.

LORD GORING. Robert, believe me, you are wrong.

SIR ROBERT CHILTERN. I couldn't do it. It would kill her love for me. And
now about this woman, this Mrs Cheveley. How can I defend myself
against her? You knew her before, Arthur, apparently.

LORD GORING. Yes.

SIR ROBERT CHILTERN. Did you know her well?

LORD GORING [*Arranging his necktie.*] So little that I got engaged to be
married to her once, when I was staying at the Tenbys'. The affair
lasted for three days . . . nearly.

SIR ROBERT CHILTERN. Why was it broken off?

LORD GORING [*Airily.*] Oh, I forget. At least, it makes no matter. By the
way, have you tried her with money? She used to be confoundedly
fond of money.

SIR ROBERT CHILTERN. I offered her any sum she wanted. She refused.

LORD GORING. Then the marvellous gospel of gold breaks down
sometimes. The rich can't do everything, after all.

SIR ROBERT CHILTERN. Not everything. I suppose you are right. Arthur, I
feel that public disgrace is in store for me. I feel certain of it. I never
knew what terror was before. I know it now. It is as if a hand of ice were
laid upon one's heart. It is as if one's heart were beating itself to death
in some empty hollow.

LORD GORING [*Striking the table.*] Robert, you must fight her. You must
fight her.

SIR ROBERT CHILTERN. But how?

LORD GORING. I can't tell you how, at present. I have not the smallest idea. But everyone has some weak point. There is some flaw in each one of us. [*Strolls over to the fireplace and looks at himself in the glass.*] My father tells me that even I have faults. Perhaps I have. I don't know.

SIR ROBERT CHILTERN. In defending myself against Mrs Cheveley, I have a right to use any weapon I can find, have I not?

LORD GORING [*Still looking in the glass.*] In your place I don't think I should have the smallest scruple in doing so. She is thoroughly well able to take care of herself.

SIR ROBERT CHILTERN [*Sits down at the table and takes a pen in his hand.*] Well, I shall send a cipher telegram to the Embassy at Vienna, to inquire if there is anything known against her. There may be some secret scandal she might be afraid of.

LORD GORING [*Settling his buttonhole.*] Oh, I should fancy Mrs Cheveley is one of those very modern women of our time who find a new scandal as becoming as a new bonnet, and air them both in the Park every afternoon at five-thirty. I am sure she adores scandals, and that the sorrow of her life at present is that she can't manage to have enough of them.

SIR ROBERT CHILTERN [*Writing.*] Why do you say that?

LORD GORING [*Turning round.*] Well, she wore far too much rouge last night, and not quite enough clothes. That is always a sign of despair in a woman.

SIR ROBERT CHILTERN [*Striking a bell.*] But it is worth my wiring to Vienna, is it not?

LORD GORING. It is always worth while asking a question, though it is not always worth while answering one.

[*Enter Mason.*]

SIR ROBERT CHILTERN. Is Mr Trafford in his room?

MASON. Yes, Sir Robert.

SIR ROBERT CHILTERN [*Puts what he has written into an envelope, which he then carefully closes.*] Tell him to have this sent off in cipher at once. There must not be a moment's delay.

MASON. Yes, Sir Robert.

SIR ROBERT CHILTERN. Oh! just give that back to me again.

[*Writes something on the envelope. Mason then goes out with the letter.*]

SIR ROBERT CHILTERN. She must have had some curious hold over Baron Arnheim. I wonder what it was.

LORD GORING [*Smiling.*] I wonder.

SIR ROBERT CHILTERN. I will fight her to the death, as long as my wife knows nothing.

LORD GORING [*Strongly.*] Oh, fight in any case—in any case.

SIR ROBERT CHILTERN [*With a gesture of despair.*] If my wife found out, there would be little left to fight for. Well, as soon as I hear from Vienna, I shall let you know the result. It is a chance, just a chance, but I believe in it. And as I fought the age with its own weapons, I will fight her with her weapons. It is only fair, and she looks like a woman with a past, doesn't she?

LORD GORING. Most pretty women do. But there is a fashion in pasts just as there is a fashion in frocks. Perhaps Mrs Cheveley's past is merely a slightly *décolleté*° one, and they are excessively popular nowadays. Besides, my dear Robert, I should not build too high hopes on frightening Mrs Cheveley. I should not fancy Mrs Cheveley is a woman who would be easily frightened. She has survived all her creditors, and she shows wonderful presence of mind.

SIR ROBERT CHILTERN. Oh! I live on hopes now. I clutch at every chance. I feel like a man on a ship that is sinking. The water is round my feet, and the very air is bitter with storm. Hush! I hear my wife's voice.

[*Enter Lady Chiltern in walking dress.*]

LADY CHILTERN. Good afternoon, Lord Goring!

LORD GORING. Good afternoon, Lady Chiltern! Have you been in the Park?

LADY CHILTERN. No: I have just come from the Woman's Liberal Association,° where, by the way, Robert, your name was received with loud applause, and now I have come in to have my tea. [*To Lord Goring.*] You will wait and have some tea, won't you?

LORD GORING. I'll wait for a short time, thanks.

LADY CHILTERN. I will be back in a moment. I am only going to take my hat off.

LORD GORING [*In his most earnest manner.*] Oh! please don't. It is so pretty. One of the prettiest hats I ever saw. I hope the Woman's Liberal Association received it with loud applause.

LADY CHILTERN [*With a smile.*] We have much more important work to do than to look at each other's bonnets, Lord Goring.

LORD GORING. Really? What sort of work?

LADY CHILTERN. Oh! dull, useful, delightful things, Factory Acts, Female Inspectors, the Eight Hours' Bill, the Parliamentary Franchise. . . .° Everything, in fact, that you would find thoroughly uninteresting.

LORD GORING. And never bonnets?

LADY CHILTERN [*With mock indignation.*] Never bonnets, never!

[*Lady Chiltern goes out through the door leading to her boudoir.*]

SIR ROBERT CHILTERN [*Takes Lord Goring's hand.*] You have been a good friend to me, Arthur, a thoroughly good friend.

LORD GORING. I don't know that I have been able to do much for you, Robert, as yet. In fact, I have not been able to do anything for you, as far as I can see. I am thoroughly disappointed with myself.

SIR ROBERT CHILTERN. You have enabled me to tell you the truth. That is something. The truth has always stifled me.

LORD GORING. Ah! the truth is a thing I get rid of as soon as possible! Bad habit, by the way. Makes one very unpopular at the club . . . with the older members. They call it being conceited. Perhaps it is.

SIR ROBERT CHILTERN. I would to God that I had been able to tell the truth . . . to live the truth. Ah! that is the great thing in life, to live the truth. [*Sighs, and goes towards the door.*] I'll see you soon again, Arthur, shan't I?

LORD GORING. Certainly. Whenever you like. I'm going to look in at the Bachelors' Ball° tonight, unless I find something better to do. But I'll come round tomorrow morning. If you should want me tonight by any chance, send round a note to Curzon Street.

SIR ROBERT CHILTERN. Thank you.

[*As he reaches the door, Lady Chiltern enters from her boudoir.*]

LADY CHILTERN. You are not going, Robert?

SIR ROBERT CHILTERN. I have some letters to write, dear.

LADY CHILTERN [*Going to him.*] You work too hard, Robert. You seem never to think of yourself, and you are looking so tired.

SIR ROBERT CHILTERN. It is nothing, dear, nothing.

[*He kisses her and goes out.*]

LADY CHILTERN [*To Lord Goring.*] Do sit down. I am so glad you have called. I want to talk to you about . . . well, not about bonnets, or the Woman's Liberal Association. You take far too much interest in the first subject, and not nearly enough in the second.

LORD GORING. You want to talk to me about Mrs Cheveley?

LADY CHILTERN. Yes. You have guessed it. After you left last night I found out that what she had said was really true. Of course I made Robert write her a letter at once, withdrawing his promise.

LORD GORING. So he gave me to understand.

LADY CHILTERN. To have kept it would have been the first stain on a career that has been stainless always. Robert must be above reproach. He is not like other men. He cannot afford to do what other men do. [*She looks at Lord Goring, who remains silent.*] Don't you agree with me? You are Robert's greatest friend. You are our greatest friend, Lord Goring. No one, except myself, knows Robert better than you do. He has no secrets from me, and I don't think he has any from you.

LORD GORING. He certainly has no secrets from me. At least I don't think so.

LADY CHILTERN. Then am I not right in my estimate of him? I know I am right. But speak to me frankly.

LORD GORING [*Looking straight at her.*] Quite frankly?

LADY CHILTERN. Surely. You have nothing to conceal, have you?

LORD GORING. Nothing. But, my dear Lady Chiltern, I think, if you will allow me to say so, that in practical life——

LADY CHILTERN [*Smiling.*] Of which you know so little, Lord Goring——

LORD GORING. Of which I know nothing by experience, though I know something by observation. I think that in practical life there is something about success, actual success, that is a little unscrupulous, something about ambition that is unscrupulous always. Once a man has set his heart and soul on getting to a certain point, if he has to climb the crag, he climbs the crag; if he has to walk in the mire——

LADY CHILTERN. Well?

LORD GORING. He walks in the mire. Of course I am only talking generally about life.

LADY CHILTERN [*Gravely.*] I hope so. Why do you look at me so strangely, Lord Goring?

LORD GORING. Lady Chiltern, I have sometimes thought that ... perhaps you are a little hard in some of your views on life. I think that ... often you don't make sufficient allowances. In every nature there are elements of weakness, or worse than weakness. Supposing, for instance, that—that any public man, my father, or Lord Merton, or Robert, say, had, years ago, written some foolish letter to some one ...

LADY CHILTERN. What do you mean by a foolish letter?

LORD GORING. A letter gravely compromising one's position. I am only putting an imaginary case.

LADY CHILTERN. Robert is as incapable of doing a foolish thing as he is of doing a wrong thing.

LORD GORING [*After a long pause.*] Nobody is incapable of doing a foolish thing. Nobody is incapable of doing a wrong thing.

LADY CHILTERN. Are you a Pessimist? What will the other dandies say? They will all have to go into mourning.

LORD GORING [*Rising.*] No, Lady Chiltern, I am not a Pessimist. Indeed I am not sure that I quite know what Pessimism really means. All I do know is that life cannot be understood without much charity, cannot be lived without much charity. It is love, and not German philosophy, that is the true explanation of this world, whatever may be the explanation of the next. And if you are ever in trouble, Lady Chiltern, trust me absolutely, and I will help you in every way I can. If you ever want me, come to me for my assistance, and you shall have it. Come at once to me.

LADY CHILTERN [*Looking at him in surprise.*] Lord Goring, you are talking quite seriously. I don't think I ever heard you talk seriously before.

LORD GORING [*Laughing.*] You must excuse me, Lady Chiltern. It won't occur again, if I can help it.

LADY CHILTERN. But I like you to be serious.

[*Enter Mabel Chiltern, in the most ravishing frock.*]

MABEL CHILTERN. Dear Gertrude, don't say such a dreadful thing to Lord Goring. Seriousness would be very unbecoming to him. Good afternoon, Lord Goring! Pray be as trivial as you can.

LORD GORING. I should like to, Miss Mabel, but I am afraid I am ... a little out of practice this morning; and besides, I have to be going now.

MABEL CHILTERN. Just when I have come in! What dreadful manners you have! I am sure you were very badly brought up.

LORD GORING. I was.

MABEL CHILTERN. I wish I had brought you up!

LORD GORING. I am so sorry you didn't.

MABEL CHILTERN. It is too late now, I suppose?

LORD GORING [*Smiling.*] I am not so sure.

MABEL CHILTERN. Will you ride tomorrow morning?

LORD GORING. Yes, at ten.

MABEL CHILTERN. Don't forget.

LORD GORING. Of course I shan't. By the way, Lady Chiltern, there is no list of your guests in 'The Morning Post'° of today. It has apparently been crowded out by the County Council,° or the Lambeth Conference,° or something equally boring. Could you let me have a list? I have a particular reason for asking you.

LADY CHILTERN. I am sure Mr Trafford will be able to give you one.

LORD GORING. Thanks, so much.

MABEL CHILTERN. Tommy is the most useful person in London.

LORD GORING [*Turning to her.*] And who is the most ornamental?

MABEL CHILTERN [*Triumphantly.*] I am.

LORD GORING. How clever of you to guess it! [*Takes up his hat and cane.*] Goodbye, Lady Chiltern! You will remember what I said to you, won't you?

LADY CHILTERN. Yes; but I don't know why you said it to me.

LORD GORING. I hardly know myself. Goodbye, Miss Mabel!

MABEL CHILTERN [*With a little moue° of disappointment.*] I wish you were not going. I have had four wonderful adventures this morning; four and a half, in fact. You might stop and listen to some of them.

LORD GORING. How very selfish of you to have four and a half! There won't be any left for me.

MABEL CHILTERN. I don't want you to have any. They would not be good for you.

LORD GORING. That is the first unkind thing you have ever said to me. How charmingly you said it! Ten tomorrow.

MABEL CHILTERN. Sharp.

LORD GORING. Quite sharp. But don't bring Mr Trafford.

MABEL CHILTERN [*With a little toss of the head.*] Of course I shan't bring Tommy Trafford. Tommy Trafford is in great disgrace.

LORD GORING. I am delighted to hear it.

[*Bows and goes out.*]

MABEL CHILTERN. Gertrude, I wish you would speak to Tommy Trafford.

LADY CHILTERN. What has poor Mr Trafford done this time? Robert says he is the best secretary he has ever had.

MABEL CHILTERN. Well, Tommy has proposed to me again. Tommy really does nothing but propose to me. He proposed to me last night in the music-room, when I was quite unprotected, as there was an elaborate trio going on. I didn't dare to make the smallest repartee, I need hardly tell you. If I had, it would have stopped the music at once. Musical people are so absurdly unreasonable. They always want one to be perfectly dumb at the very moment when one is longing to be absolutely deaf. Then he proposed to me in broad daylight this morning, in front of that dreadful statue of Achilles.° Really, the things that go on in front of that work of art are quite appalling. The police should interfere. At luncheon I saw by the glare in his eye that he was going to propose again, and I just managed to check him in time by assuring him that I was a bimetallist. Fortunately I don't know what bimetallism means.° And I don't believe anybody else does either. But the observation crushed Tommy for ten minutes. He looked quite shocked. And then Tommy is so annoying in the way he proposes. If he proposed at the top of his voice, I should not mind so much. That might produce some effect on the public. But he does it in a horrid confidential way. When Tommy wants to be romantic he talks to one just like a doctor. I am very fond of Tommy, but his methods of proposing are quite out of date. I wish, Gertrude, you would speak to him, and tell him that once a week is quite often enough to propose to anyone, and that it should always be done in a manner that attracts some attention.

LADY CHILTERN. Dear Mabel, don't talk like that. Besides, Robert thinks very highly of Mr Trafford. He believes he has a brilliant future before him.

MABEL CHILTERN. Oh! I wouldn't marry a man with a future before him for anything under the sun.

LADY CHILTERN. Mabel!

MABEL CHILTERN. I know, dear. You married a man with a future, didn't you? But then Robert was a genius, and you have a noble, self-sacrificing character. You can stand geniuses. I have no character at all, and Robert is the only genius I could ever bear. As a rule, I think they are quite impossible. Geniuses talk so much, don't they? Such a bad habit! And they are always thinking about themselves, when I want them to be thinking about me. I must go round now and rehearse at Lady Basildon's. You remember we are having tableaux,° don't you? The Triumph of something, I don't know what! I hope it will be triumph of me. Only triumph I am really interested in at present. [*Kisses Lady Chiltern and goes out; then comes running back.*] Oh, Gertrude, do you know who is coming to see you? That dreadful Mrs Cheveley, in a most lovely gown. Did you ask her?

LADY CHILTERN [*Rising.*] Mrs Cheveley! Coming to see me? Impossible!

MABEL CHILTERN. I assure you she is coming upstairs, as large as life and not nearly so natural.

LADY CHILTERN. You need not wait, Mabel. Remember, Lady Basildon is expecting you.

MABEL CHILTERN. Oh! I must shake hands with Lady Markby. She is delightful. I love being scolded by her.

[*Enter Mason.*]

MASON. Lady Markby. Mrs Cheveley.

[*Enter Lady Markby and Mrs Cheveley.*]

LADY CHILTERN [*Advancing to meet them.*] Dear Lady Markby, how nice of you to come and see me! [*Shakes hands with her, and bows somewhat distantly to Mrs Cheveley.*] Won't you sit down, Mrs Cheveley?

MRS CHEVELEY. Thanks. Isn't that Miss Chiltern? I should like so much to know her.

LADY CHILTERN. Mabel, Mrs Cheveley wishes to know you. [*Mabel Chiltern gives a little nod.*]

MRS CHEVELEY [*Sitting down.*] I thought your frock so charming last night, Miss Chiltern. So simple and . . . suitable.

MABEL CHILTERN. Really? I must tell my dressmaker. It will be such a surprise to her. Goodbye, Lady Markby!

LADY MARKBY. Going already?

MABEL CHILTERN. I am so sorry but I am obliged to. I am just off to rehearsal. I have got to stand on my head in some tableaux.

LADY MARKBY. On your head, child? Oh! I hope not. I believe it is most unhealthy. [*Takes a seat on the sofa next Lady Chiltern.*]

MABEL CHILTERN. But it is for an excellent charity: in aid of the Undeserving,° the only people I am really interested in. I am the secretary, and Tommy Trafford is treasurer.

MRS CHEVELEY. And what is Lord Goring?

MABEL CHILTERN. Oh! Lord Goring is president.

MRS CHEVELEY. The post should suit him admirably, unless he has deteriorated since I knew him first.

LADY MARKBY [*Reflecting.*] You are remarkably modern, Mabel. A little too modern, perhaps. Nothing is so dangerous as being too modern. One is apt to grow old-fashioned quite suddenly. I have known many instances of it.

MABEL CHILTERN. What a dreadful prospect!

LADY MARKBY. Ah! my dear, you need not be nervous. You will always be as pretty as possible. That is the best fashion there is, and the only fashion that England succeeds in setting.

MABEL CHILTERN [*With a curtsey.*] Thank you so much, Lady Markby, for England . . . and myself.

[*Goes out.*]

LADY MARKBY [*Turning to Lady Chiltern.*] Dear Gertrude, we just called to know if Mrs Cheveley's diamond brooch has been found.

LADY CHILTERN. Here?

MRS CHEVELEY. Yes. I missed it when I got back to Claridge's, and I thought I might possibly have dropped it here.

LADY CHILTERN. I have heard nothing about it. But I will send for the butler and ask. [*Touches the bell.*]

MRS CHEVELEY. Oh, pray don't trouble, Lady Chiltern. I daresay I lost it at the Opera, before we came on here.

LADY MARKBY. Ah yes, I suppose it must have been at the Opera. The fact is, we all scramble and jostle so much nowadays that I wonder we have anything at all left on us at the end of an evening. I know myself that when I am coming back from the Drawing Room,° I always feel as if I hadn't a shred on me, except a small shred of decent reputation, just enough to prevent the lower classes making painful observations through the windows of the carriage. The fact is that our Society is terribly overpopulated. Really, some one should arrange a proper scheme of assisted emigration.° It would do a great deal of good.

MRS CHEVELEY. I quite agree with you, Lady Markby. It is nearly six years since I have been in London for the season, and I must say Society has become dreadfully mixed. One sees the oddest people everywhere.

LADY MARKBY. That is quite true, dear. But one needn't know them. I'm sure I don't know half the people who come to my house. Indeed, from all I hear, I shouldn't like to.

[Enter Mason.]

LADY CHILTERN. What sort of a brooch was it that you lost, Mrs Cheveley?

MRS CHEVELEY. A diamond snake-brooch with a ruby, a rather large ruby.

LADY MARKBY. I thought you said there was a sapphire on the head, dear?

MRS CHEVELEY [Smiling.] No, Lady Markby—a ruby.

LADY MARKBY [Nodding her head.] And very becoming, I am quite sure.

LADY CHILTERN. Has a ruby and diamond brooch been found in any of the rooms this morning, Mason?

MASON. No, my lady.

MRS CHEVELEY. It really is of no consequence, Lady Chiltern. I am so sorry to have put you to any inconvenience.

LADY CHILTERN [Coldly.] Oh, it has been no inconvenience. That will do, Mason. You can bring tea.

[Exit Mason.]

LADY MARKBY. Well, I must say it is most annoying to lose anything. I remember once at Bath, years ago, losing in the Pump Room° an exceedingly handsome cameo bracelet that Sir John had given me. I don't think he has ever given me anything since, I am sorry to say. He has sadly degenerated. Really, this horrid House of Commons quite ruins our husbands for us. I think the Lower House by far the greatest blow to a happy married life that there has been since that terrible thing called the Higher Education of Women° was invented.

LADY CHILTERN. Ah! it is heresy to say that in this house, Lady Markby. Robert is a great champion of the Higher Education of Women, and so, I am afraid, am I.

MRS CHEVELEY. The higher education of men is what I should like to see. Men need it so sadly.

LADY MARKBY. They do, dear. But I am afraid such a scheme would be quite unpractical. I don't think man has much capacity for development. He has got as far as he can, and that is not far, is it? With regard to women, well, dear Gertrude, you belong to the younger generation, and I am sure it is all right if you approve of it. In my time, of course, we were taught not to understand anything. That was the old system, and wonderfully interesting it was. I assure you that the amount of things I and my poor dear sister were taught not to understand was quite extraordinary. But modern women understand everything, I am told.

MRS CHEVELEY. Except their husbands. That is the one thing the modern woman never understands.

LADY MARKBY. And a very good thing too, dear, I daresay. It might break up many a happy home if they did. Not yours, I need hardly say, Gertrude. You have married a pattern husband. I wish I could say as much for myself. But since Sir John has taken to attending the debates regularly, which he never used to do in the good old days, his language has become quite impossible. He always seems to think that he is addressing the House, and consequently whenever he discusses the state of the agricultural labourer, or the Welsh Church, or something quite improper of that kind, I am obliged to send all the servants out of the room. It is not pleasant to see one's own butler, who has been with one for twenty-three years, actually blushing at the sideboard, and the footmen making contortions in corners like persons in circuses. I assure you my life will be quite ruined unless they send John at once to the Upper House. He won't take any interest in politics then, will he? The House of Lords is so sensible. An assembly of gentlemen. But in his present state, Sir John is really a great trial. Why, this morning before breakfast was half over, he stood up on the hearthrug, put his hands in his pockets, and appealed to the country at the top of his voice. I left the table as soon as I had my second cup of tea, I need hardly say. But his violent language could be heard all over the house! I trust, Gertrude, that Sir Robert is not like that?

LADY CHILTERN. But I am very much interested in politics, Lady Markby. I love to hear Robert talk about them.

LADY MARKBY. Well, I hope he is not as devoted to Blue Books° as Sir John is. I don't think they can be quite improving reading for anyone.

MRS CHEVELEY [*Languidly.*] I have never read a Blue Book. I prefer books . . . in yellow covers.°

LADY MARKBY [*Genially unconscious.*] Yellow is a gayer colour, is it not? I used to wear yellow a good deal in my early days, and would do so now if Sir John was not so painfully personal in his observations, and a man on the question of dress is always ridiculous, is he not?

MRS CHEVELEY. Oh, no! I think men are the only authorities on dress.

LADY MARKBY. Really? One wouldn't say so from the sort of hats they wear, would one?

[*The butler enters, followed by the footman. Tea is set on a small table close to Lady Chiltern.*]

LADY CHILTERN. May I give you some tea, Mrs Cheveley?

MRS CHEVELEY. Thanks. [*The butler hands Mrs Cheveley a cup of tea on a salver.*]

LADY CHILTERN. Some tea, Lady Markby?

LADY MARKBY. No thanks, dear. [*The servants go out.*] The fact is, I have promised to go round for ten minutes to see poor Lady Brancaster, who is in very great trouble. Her daughter, quite a well-brought-up girl, too, has actually become engaged to be married to a curate in Shropshire. It is very sad, very sad indeed. I can't understand this modern mania for curates. In my time we girls saw them, of course, running about the place like rabbits. But we never took any notice of them, I need hardly say. But I am told that nowadays country society is quite honeycombed with them. I think it most irreligious. And then the eldest son has quarrelled with his father, and it is said that when they meet at the club Lord Brancaster always hides himself behind the money article in 'The Times'. However, I believe that is quite a common occurrence nowadays and that they have to take in extra copies of 'The Times' at all the clubs in St James's Street; there are so many sons who won't have anything to do with their fathers, and so many fathers who won't speak to their sons. I think, myself, it is very much to be regretted.

MRS CHEVELEY. So do I. Fathers have so much to learn from their sons nowadays.

LADY MARKBY. Really, dear? What?

MRS CHEVELEY. The art of living. The only really Fine Art we have produced in modern times.

LADY MARKBY [*Shaking her head.*] Ah! I am afraid Lord Brancaster knew a good deal about that. More than his poor wife ever did. [*Turning to Lady Chiltern.*] You know Lady Brancaster, don't you, dear?

LADY CHILTERN. Just slightly. She was staying at Langton last autumn, when we were there.

LADY MARKBY. Well, like all stout women, she looks the very picture of happiness, as no doubt you noticed. But there are many tragedies in her family, besides this affair of the curate. Her own sister, Mrs Jekyll, had a most unhappy life; through no fault of her own, I am sorry to say. She ultimately was so broken-hearted that she went into a convent, or on to the operatic stage, I forget which. No; I think it was decorative art-needlework she took up. I know she had lost all sense of pleasure in life. [*Rising.*] And now, Gertrude, if you will allow me, I shall leave Mrs Cheveley in your charge and call back for her in a quarter of an hour. Or perhaps, dear Mrs Cheveley, you wouldn't mind waiting in the carriage while I am with Lady Brancaster. As I intend it to be a visit of condolence, I shan't stay long.

MRS CHEVELEY [*Rising.*] I don't mind waiting in the carriage at all, provided there is somebody to look at one.

LADY MARKBY. Well, I hear the curate is always prowling about the house.

MRS CHEVELEY. I am afraid I am not fond of girl friends.

LADY CHILTERN [*Rising.*] Oh, I hope Mrs Cheveley will stay here a little. I should like to have a few minutes' conversation with her.

MRS CHEVELEY. How very kind of you, Lady Chiltern! Believe me, nothing would give me greater pleasure.

LADY MARKBY. Ah! no doubt you both have many pleasant reminiscences of your schooldays to talk over together. Goodbye, dear Gertrude! Shall I see you at Lady Bonar's tonight? She has discovered a wonderful new genius. He does . . . nothing at all, I believe. That is a great comfort, is it not?

LADY CHILTERN. Robert and I are dining at home by ourselves tonight, and I don't think I shall go anywhere afterwards. Robert, of course, will have to be in the House. But there is nothing interesting on.

LADY MARKBY. Dining at home by yourselves? Is that quite prudent? Ah,

I forgot, your husband is an exception. Mine is the general rule, and nothing ages a woman so rapidly as having married the general rule.

[*Exit Lady Markby.*]

MRS CHEVELEY. Wonderful woman, Lady Markby, isn't she? Talks more and says less than anybody I ever met. She is made to be a public speaker. Much more so than her husband, though he is a typical Englishman, always dull and usually violent.

LADY CHILTERN [*Makes no answer, but remains standing. There is a pause. Then the eyes of the two women meet. Lady Chiltern looks stern and pale. Mrs Cheveley seems rather amused.*] Mrs Cheveley, I think it is right to tell you quite frankly that, had I known who you really were, I should not have invited you to my house last night.

MRS CHEVELEY [*With an impertinent smile.*] Really?

LADY CHILTERN. I could not have done so.

MRS CHEVELEY. I see that after all these years you have not changed a bit, Gertrude.

LADY CHILTERN. I never change.

MRS CHEVELEY [*Elevating her eyebrows.*] Then life has taught you nothing?

LADY CHILTERN. It has taught me that a person who has once been guilty of a dishonest and dishonourable action may be guilty of it a second time, and should be shunned.

MRS CHEVELEY. Would you apply that rule to everyone?

LADY CHILTERN. Yes, to everyone, without exception.

MRS CHEVELEY. Then I am sorry for you, Gertrude, very sorry for you.

LADY CHILTERN. You see now, I am sure, that for many reasons any further acquaintance between us during your stay in London is quite impossible?

MRS CHEVELEY [*Leaning back in her chair.*] Do you know, Gertrude, I don't mind your talking morality a bit. Morality is simply the attitude we adopt towards people whom we personally dislike. You dislike me. I am quite aware of that. And I have always detested you. And yet I have come here to do you a service.

LADY CHILTERN [*Contemptuously.*] Like the service you wished to render my husband last night, I suppose. Thank heaven, I saved him from that.

MRS CHEVELEY [*Starting to her feet.*] It was you who made him write that insolent letter to me? It was you who made him break his promise?

LADY CHILTERN. Yes.

MRS CHEVELEY. Then you must make him keep it. I give you till tomorrow morning—no more. If by that time your husband does not solemnly bind himself to help me in this great scheme in which I am interested——

LADY CHILTERN. This fraudulent speculation——

MRS CHEVELEY. Call it what you choose. I hold your husband in the hollow of my hand, and if you are wise you will make him do what I tell him.

LADY CHILTERN [*Rising and going towards her.*] You are impertinent. What has my husband to do with you? With a woman like you?

MRS CHEVELEY [*With a bitter laugh.*] In this world like meets with like. It is because your husband is himself fraudulent and dishonest that we pair so well together. Between you and him there are chasms. He and I are closer than friends. We are enemies linked together. The same sin binds us.

LADY CHILTERN. How dare you class my husband with yourself? How dare you threaten him or me? Leave my house. You are unfit to enter it.

[*Sir Robert Chiltern enters from behind. He hears his wife's last words, and sees to whom they are addressed. He grows deadly pale.*]

MRS CHEVELEY. Your house! A house bought with the price of dishonour. A house, everything in which has been paid for by fraud. [*Turns round and sees Sir Robert Chiltern.*] Ask him what the origin of his fortune is! Get him to tell you how he sold to a stockbroker a Cabinet secret. Learn from him to what you owe your position.

LADY CHILTERN. It is not true! Robert! It is not true!

MRS CHEVELEY [*Pointing at him with outstretched finger.*] Look at him! Can he deny it? Does he dare to?

SIR ROBERT CHILTERN. Go! Go at once. You have done your worst now.

MRS CHEVELEY. My worst? I have not yet finished with you, with either of you. I give you both till tomorrow at noon. If by then you don't do what I bid you to do, the whole world shall know the origin of Robert Chiltern.

[*Sir Robert Chiltern strikes the bell. Enter Mason.*]

SIR ROBERT CHILTERN. Show Mrs Cheveley out.

[*Mrs Cheveley starts; then bows with somewhat exaggerated politeness to Lady Chiltern, who makes no sign of response. As she passes by Sir Robert Chiltern, who is standing close to the door, she pauses for a moment and looks him straight in the face. She then goes out, followed by the servant, who closes the door after him. The husband and wife are left alone. Lady Chiltern stands like some one in a dreadful dream. Then she turns round and looks at her husband. She looks at him with strange eyes, as though she was seeing him for the first time.*]

LADY CHILTERN. You sold a Cabinet secret for money! You began your life with fraud! You built up your career on dishonour! Oh, tell me it is not true! Lie to me! Lie to me! Tell me it is not true!

SIR ROBERT CHILTERN. What this woman said is quite true. But, Gertrude, listen to me. You don't realize how I was tempted. Let me tell you the whole thing. [*Goes towards her.*]

LADY CHILTERN. Don't come near me. Don't touch me. I feel as if you had soiled me for ever. Oh! what a mask you have been wearing all these years! A horrible painted mask! You sold yourself for money. Oh! a common thief were better. You put yourself up to sale to the highest bidder! You were bought in the market. You lied to the whole world. And yet you will not lie to me.

SIR ROBERT CHILTERN [*Rushing towards her.*] Gertrude! Gertrude!

LADY CHILTERN [*Thrusting him back with outstretched hands.*] No, don't speak! Say nothing! Your voice wakes terrible memories—memories of things that made me love you—memories of words that made me love you—memories that now are horrible to me. And how I worshipped you! You were to me something apart from common life, a thing pure, noble, honest, without stain. The world seemed to me finer because you were in it, and goodness more real because you lived. And now—oh, when I think that I made of a man like you my ideal! the ideal of my life!

SIR ROBERT CHILTERN. There was your mistake. There was your error. The error all women commit. Why can't you women love us, faults and all? Why do you place us on monstrous pedestals? We have all feet of clay, women as well as men; but when we men love women, we love them knowing their weaknesses, their follies, their imperfections, love them all the more, it may be, for that reason. It is not the perfect, but the imperfect, who have need of love. It is when we are wounded by our own hands, or by the hands of others, that love should come to cure us—else what use is love at all? All sins, except a sin against itself, Love should forgive. All lives, save loveless lives, true Love should pardon. A man's love is like that. It is wider, larger, more human than a woman's. Women think that they are making ideals of men. What they are making of us are false idols merely. You made your false idol of me, and I had not the courage to come down, show you my wounds, tell you my weaknesses. I was afraid that I might lose your love, as I have lost it now. And so, last night you ruined my life for me—yes, ruined it! What this woman asked of me was nothing compared to what she offered to me. She offered security, peace, stability. The sin of my youth, that I had thought was buried, rose up in front of me, hideous, horrible, with its hands at my throat. I could have killed it for ever, sent it back into its tomb, destroyed its record, burned the one witness against me. You prevented me. No one but you, you know it. And now what is there before me but public disgrace, ruin, terrible shame, the mockery of the world, a lonely dishonoured life, a lonely dishonoured death, it may be, some day? Let women make no more ideals of men! let them not put them on altars and bow before them, or they may ruin other lives as completely as you—you whom I have so wildly loved— have ruined mine!

[*He passes from the room. Lady Chiltern rushes towards him, but the door is closed when she reaches it. Pale with anguish, bewildered, helpless, she sways like a plant in the water. Her hands, outstretched, seem to tremble in the air like blossoms in the wind. Then she flings herself down beside a sofa and buries her face. Her sobs are like the sobs of a child.*]

ACT DROP.

THIRD ACT

SCENE—*The Library in Lord Goring's house. An Adam° room. On the right is the door leading into the hall. On the left, the door of the smoking-room. A pair of folding doors at the back open into the drawing-room. The fire is lit. Phipps, the butler, is arranging some newspapers on the writing-table. The distinction of Phipps is his impassivity. He has been termed by enthusiasts the Ideal Butler. The Sphinx is not so incommunicable. He is a mask with a manner. Of his intellectual or emotional life history knows nothing. He represents the dominance of form.*

[*Enter Lord Goring in evening dress with a buttonhole. He is wearing a silk hat and Inverness cape.° White-gloved, he carries a Louis Seize cane. His are all the delicate fopperies of Fashion. One sees that he stands in immediate relation to modern life, makes it indeed, and so masters it. He is the first well-dressed philosopher in the history of thought.*]

LORD GORING. Got my second buttonhole° for me, Phipps?

PHIPPS. Yes, my lord. [*Takes his hat, cane and cape, and presents new buttonhole on salver.*]

LORD GORING. Rather distinguished thing, Phipps. I am the only person of the smallest importance in London at present who wears a buttonhole.

PHIPPS. Yes, my lord. I have observed that.

LORD GORING [*Taking out old buttonhole.*] You see, Phipps, Fashion is what one wears oneself. What is unfashionable is what other people wear.

PHIPPS. Yes, my lord.

LORD GORING. Just as vulgarity is simply the conduct of other people.

PHIPPS. Yes, my lord.

LORD GORING [*Putting in new buttonhole.*] And falsehoods the truths of other people.

PHIPPS. Yes, my lord.

LORD GORING. Other people are quite dreadful. The only possible society is oneself.

PHIPPS. Yes, my lord.

LORD GORING. To love oneself is the beginning of a life-long romance, Phipps.

PHIPPS. Yes, my lord.

LORD GORING [*Looking at himself in the glass.*] Don't think I quite like this buttonhole, Phipps. Makes me look a little too old. Makes me almost in the prime of life, eh, Phipps?

PHIPPS. I don't observe any alteration in your lordship's appearance.

LORD GORING. You don't, Phipps?

PHIPPS. No, my lord.

LORD GORING. I am not quite sure. For the future a more trivial buttonhole, Phipps, on Thursday evenings.

PHIPPS. I will speak to the florist, my lord. She has had a loss in her family lately, which perhaps accounts for the lack of triviality your lordship complains of in the buttonhole.

LORD GORING. Extraordinary thing about the lower classes in England—they are always losing their relations.

PHIPPS. Yes, my lord! They are extremely fortunate in that respect.

LORD GORING [*Turns round and looks at him. Phipps remains impassive.*] Hum! Any letters, Phipps?

PHIPPS. Three, my lord. [*Hands letters on a salver.*]

LORD GORING [*Takes letters.*] Want my cab round in twenty minutes.

PHIPPS. Yes, my lord. [*Goes towards door.*]

LORD GORING [*Holds up letter in pink envelope.*] Ahem! Phipps, when did this letter arrive?

PHIPPS. It was brought by hand just after your lordship went to the Club.

LORD GORING. That will do. [*Exit Phipps.*] Lady Chiltern's handwriting on Lady Chiltern's pink notepaper. That is rather curious. I thought Robert was to write. Wonder what Lady Chiltern has got to say to me? [*Sits at bureau and opens letter, and reads it.*] 'I want you. I trust you. I am coming to you. Gertrude.' [*Puts down the letter with a puzzled look. Then takes it up, and reads it again slowly.*] 'I want you. I trust you. I am coming to you.' So she has found out everything! Poor woman! Poor woman! [*Pulls out watch and looks at it.*] But what an hour to call! Ten o'clock! I shall have to give up going to the Berkshires'. However, it is always nice to be expected, and not to arrive. I am not expected at the Bachelors', so I shall certainly go there. Well, I will make her stand by her husband. That is the only thing for her to do. That is the only thing for any woman to do. It is the growth of the moral sense in women that makes marriage such a hopeless, one-sided institution. Ten o'clock. She should be here soon. I must tell Phipps I am not in to anyone else. [*Goes towards bell.*]

[*Enter Phipps.*]

PHIPPS. Lord Caversham.

LORD GORING. Oh, why will parents always appear at the wrong time? Some extraordinary mistake in nature, I suppose. [*Enter Lord Caversham.*] Delighted to see you, my dear father. [*Goes to meet him.*]

LORD CAVERSHAM. Take my cloak off.

LORD GORING. Is it worth while, father?

LORD CAVERSHAM. Of course it is worth while, sir. Which is the most comfortable chair?

LORD GORING. This one, father. It is the chair I use myself, when I have visitors.

LORD CAVERSHAM. Thank ye. No draught, I hope, in this room?

LORD GORING. No, father.

LORD CAVERSHAM [*Sitting down.*] Glad to hear it. Can't stand draughts. No draughts at home.

LORD GORING. Good many breezes, father.

LORD CAVERSHAM. Eh? Eh? Don't understand what you mean. Want to have a serious conversation with you, sir.

LORD GORING. My dear father! At this hour?

LORD CAVERSHAM. Well, sir, it is only ten o'clock. What is your objection to the hour? I think the hour is an admirable hour!

LORD GORING. Well, the fact is, father, this is not my day for talking seriously. I am very sorry, but it is not my day.

LORD CAVERSHAM. What do you mean, sir?

LORD GORING. During the season, father, I only talk seriously on the first Tuesday in every month, from four to seven.

LORD CAVERSHAM. Well, make it Tuesday, sir, make it Tuesday.

LORD GORING. But it is after seven, father, and my doctor says I must not have any serious conversation after seven. It makes me talk in my sleep.

LORD CAVERSHAM. Talk in your sleep, sir? What does that matter? You are not married.

LORD GORING. No, father, I am not married.

LORD CAVERSHAM. Hum! That is what I have come to talk to you about, sir. You have got to get married, and at once. Why, when I was your age, sir, I had been an inconsolable widower for three months, and was already paying my addresses to your admirable mother. Damme, sir, it is your duty to get married. You can't be always living for pleasure. Every man of position is married nowadays. Bachelors are not fashionable any more. They are a damaged lot. Too much is known about them. You must get a wife, sir. Look where your friend Robert Chiltern has got to by probity, hard work, and a sensible marriage with a good woman. Why don't you imitate him, sir? Why don't you take him for your model?

LORD GORING. I think I shall, father.

LORD CAVERSHAM. I wish you would, sir. Then I should be happy. At present I make your mother's life miserable on your account. You are heartless, sir, quite heartless.

LORD GORING. I hope not, father.

LORD CAVERSHAM. And it is high time for you to get married. You are thirty-four years of age, sir.

LORD GORING. Yes, father, but I only admit to thirty-two—thirty-one and a half when I have a really good buttonhole. This buttonhole is not ... trivial enough.

LORD CAVERSHAM. I tell you you are thirty-four, sir. And there is a draught in your room, besides, which makes your conduct worse. Why did you tell me there was no draught, sir? I feel a draught, sir, I feel it distinctly.

LORD GORING. So do I, father. It is a dreadful draught. I will come and see you tomorrow, father. We can talk over anything you like. Let me help you on with your cloak, father.

LORD CAVERSHAM. No, sir; I have called this evening for a definite purpose, and I am going to see it through at all costs to my health or yours. Put down my cloak, sir.

LORD GORING. Certainly, father. But let us go into another room. [*Rings bell.*] There is a dreadful draught here. [*Enter Phipps.*] Phipps, is there a good fire in the smoking-room?

PHIPPS. Yes, my lord.

LORD GORING. Come in there, father. Your sneezes are quite heart-rending.

LORD CAVERSHAM. Well, sir, I suppose I have a right to sneeze when I choose?

LORD GORING [*Apologetically.*] Quite so, father. I was merely expressing sympathy.

LORD CAVERSHAM. Oh, damn sympathy. There is a great deal too much of that sort of thing going on nowadays.

LORD GORING. I quite agree with you, father. If there was less sympathy in the world there would be less trouble in the world.

LORD CAVERSHAM [*Going towards the smoking-room.*] That is a paradox, sir. I hate paradoxes.

LORD GORING. So do I, father. Everybody one meets is a paradox nowadays. It is a great bore. It makes society so obvious.

LORD CAVERSHAM [*Turning round, and looking at his son beneath his bushy eyebrows.*] Do you always really understand what you say, sir?

LORD GORING [*After some hesitation.*] Yes, father, if I listen attentively.

LORD CAVERSHAM [*Indignantly.*] If you listen attentively! . . . Conceited young puppy!

[*Goes off grumbling into the smoking-room. Phipps enters.*]

LORD GORING. Phipps, there is a lady coming to see me this evening on particular business. Show her into the drawing-room when she arrives. You understand?

PHIPPS. Yes, my lord.

LORD GORING. It is a matter of the gravest importance, Phipps.

PHIPPS. I understand, my lord.

LORD GORING. No one else is to be admitted, under any circumstances.

PHIPPS. I understand, my lord. [*Bell rings.*]

LORD GORING. Ah! that is probably the lady. I shall see her myself.

[*Just as he is going towards the door Lord Caversham enters from the smoking-room.*]

LORD CAVERSHAM. Well, sir? am I to wait attendance on you?

LORD GORING [*Considerably perplexed.*] In a moment, father. Do excuse me. [*Lord Caversham goes back.*] Well, remember my instructions, Phipps—into that room.

PHIPPS. Yes, my lord.

[*Lord Goring goes into the smoking-room. Harold, the footman, shows Mrs Cheveley in. Lamia-like,° she is in green and silver. She has a cloak of black satin, lined with dead rose-leaf silk.*]

HAROLD. What name, madam?

MRS CHEVELEY [*To Phipps, who advances towards her.*] Is Lord Goring not here? I was told he was at home?

PHIPPS. His lordship is engaged at present with Lord Caversham, madam.

[*Turns a cold, glassy eye on Harold, who at once retires.*]

MRS CHEVELEY [*To herself.*] How very filial!

PHIPPS. His lordship told me to ask you, madam, to be kind enough to wait in the drawing-room for him. His lordship will come to you there.

MRS CHEVELEY [*With a look of surprise.*] Lord Goring expects me?

PHIPPS. Yes, madam.

MRS CHEVELEY. Are you quite sure?

PHIPPS. His lordship told me that if a lady called I was to ask her to wait in the drawing-room. [*Goes to the door of the drawing-room and opens it.*] His lordship's directions on the subject were very precise.

MRS CHEVELEY [*To herself.*] How thoughtful of him! To expect the unexpected shows a thoroughly modern intellect. [*Goes towards the drawing-room and looks in.*] Ugh! How dreary a bachelor's drawing-room always looks. I shall have to alter all this. [*Phipps brings the lamp from the writing-table.*] No, I don't care for that lamp. It is far too glaring. Light some candles.

PHIPPS [*Replaces lamp.*] Certainly, madam.

MRS CHEVELEY. I hope the candles have very becoming shades.

PHIPPS. We have had no complaints about them, madam, as yet.

[*Passes into the drawing-room and begins to light the candles.*]

MRS CHEVELEY [*To herself.*] I wonder what woman he is waiting for tonight. It will be delightful to catch him. Men always look so silly when they are caught. And they are always being caught. [*Looks about room and approaches the writing-table.*] What a very interesting room! What a very interesting picture! Wonder what his correspondence is like. [*Takes up letters.*] Oh, what a very uninteresting correspondence! Bills and cards, debts and dowagers! Who on earth writes to him on pink paper? How silly to write on pink paper! It looks like the beginning of a middle-class romance. Romance should never begin with sentiment. It should begin with science and end with a settlement. [*Puts letter down, then takes it up again.*] I know that handwriting. That is Gertrude Chiltern's. I remember it perfectly. The ten commandments in every stroke of the pen, and the moral law all over the page. Wonder what Gertrude is writing to him about? Something horrid about me, I suppose. How I detest that woman! [*Reads it.*] 'I trust you. I want you. I am coming to you. Gertrude.' 'I trust you. I want you. I am coming to you.'

[*A look of triumph comes over her face. She is just about to steal the letter, when Phipps comes in.*]

PHIPPS. The candles in the drawing-room are lit, madam, as you directed.

MRS CHEVELEY. Thank you. [*Rises hastily, and slips the letter under a large silver-cased blotting-book that is lying on the table.*]

PHIPPS. I trust the shades will be to your liking, madam. They are the most becoming we have. They are the same as his lordship uses himself when he is dressing for dinner.

MRS CHEVELEY [*With a smile.*] Then I am sure they will be perfectly right.

PHIPPS [*Gravely.*] Thank you, madam.

[*Mrs Cheveley goes into the drawing-room. Phipps closes the door and retires. The door is then slowly opened, and Mrs Cheveley comes out and creeps stealthily towards the writing-table. Suddenly voices are heard from the smoking-room. Mrs Cheveley grows pale, and stops. The voices grow louder, and she goes back into the drawing-room, biting her lip.*]

[*Enter Lord Goring and Lord Caversham.*]

LORD GORING [*Expostulating.*] My dear father, if I am to get married, surely you will allow me to choose the time, place, and person? Particularly the person.

LORD CAVERSHAM [*Testily.*] That is a matter for me, sir. You would probably make a very poor choice. It is I who should be consulted, not you. There is property at stake. It is not a matter for affection. Affection comes later on in married life.

LORD GORING. Yes. In married life affection comes when people thoroughly dislike each other, father, doesn't it? [*Puts on Lord Caversham's cloak for him.*]

LORD CAVERSHAM. Certainly, sir. I mean certainly not, sir. You are talking very foolishly tonight. What I say is that marriage is a matter for common sense.

LORD GORING. But women who have common sense are so curiously plain, father, aren't they? Of course I only speak from hearsay.

LORD CAVERSHAM. No woman, plain or pretty, has any common sense at all, sir. Common sense is the privilege of our sex.

LORD GORING. Quite so. And we men are so self-sacrificing that we never use it, do we, father?

LORD CAVERSHAM. I use it, sir. I use nothing else.

LORD GORING. So my mother tells me.

LORD CAVERSHAM. It is the secret of your mother's happiness. You are very heartless, sir, very heartless.

LORD GORING. I hope not, father.

[*Goes out for a moment. Then returns, looking rather put out, with Sir Robert Chiltern.*]

SIR ROBERT CHILTERN. My dear Arthur, what a piece of good luck meeting you on the doorstep. Your servant had just told me you were not at home. How extraordinary!

LORD GORING. The fact is, I am horribly busy tonight, Robert, and I gave orders I was not at home to anyone. Even my father had a comparatively cold reception. He complained of a draught the whole time.

SIR ROBERT CHILTERN. Ah! you must be at home to me, Arthur. You are my best friend. Perhaps by tomorrow you will be my only friend. My wife has discovered everything.

LORD GORING. Ah! I guessed as much!

SIR ROBERT CHILTERN [*Looking at him.*] Really! How?

LORD GORING [*After some hesitation.*] Oh, merely by something in the expression of your face as you came in. Who told her?

SIR ROBERT CHILTERN. Mrs Cheveley herself. And the woman I love knows that I began my career with an act of low dishonesty, that I built up my life upon sands of shame—that I sold, like a common huckster, the secret that had been intrusted to me as a man of honour. I thank heaven poor Lord Radley died without knowing that I betrayed him. I would to God I had died before I had been so horribly tempted, or had fallen so low. [*Burying his face in his hands.*]

LORD GORING [*After a pause.*] You have heard nothing from Vienna yet, in answer to your wire?

SIR ROBERT CHILTERN [*Looking up.*] Yes; I got a telegram from the first secretary at eight o'clock tonight.

LORD GORING. Well?

SIR ROBERT CHILTERN. Nothing is absolutely known against her. On the contrary, she occupies a rather high position in society. It is a sort of open secret that Baron Arnheim left her the greater portion of his immense fortune. Beyond that I can learn nothing.

LORD GORING. She doesn't turn out to be a spy, then?

SIR ROBERT CHILTERN. Oh! spies are of no use nowadays. Their profession is over. The newspapers do their work instead.

LORD GORING. And thunderingly well they do it.

SIR ROBERT CHILTERN. Arthur, I am parched with thirst. May I ring for something? Some hock and seltzer?

LORD GORING. Certainly. Let me. [*Rings the bell.*]

SIR ROBERT CHILTERN. Thanks! I don't know what to do, Arthur, I don't know what to do, and you are my only friend. But what a friend you are—the one friend I can trust. I can trust you absolutely, can't I?

[*Enter Phipps.*]

LORD GORING. My dear Robert, of course. Oh! [*To Phipps.*] Bring some hock and seltzer.°

PHIPPS. Yes, my lord.

LORD GORING. And Phipps!

PHIPPS. Yes, my lord.

LORD GORING. Will you excuse me for a moment, Robert? I want to give some directions to my servant.

SIR ROBERT CHILTERN. Certainly.

LORD GORING. When that lady calls, tell her that I am not expected home this evening. Tell her that I have been suddenly called out of town. You understand?

PHIPPS. The lady is in that room, my lord. You told me to show her into that room, my lord.

LORD GORING. You did perfectly right. [*Exit Phipps.*] What a mess I am in. No; I think I shall get through it. I'll give her a lecture through the door. Awkward thing to manage, though.

SIR ROBERT CHILTERN. Arthur, tell me what I should do. My life seems to have crumbled about me. I am a ship without a rudder in a night without a star.

LORD GORING. Robert, you love your wife, don't you?

SIR ROBERT CHILTERN. I love her more than anything in the world. I used to think ambition the great thing. It is not. Love is the great thing in the world. There is nothing but love, and I love her. But I am defamed in her eyes. I am ignoble in her eyes. There is a wide gulf between us now. She has found me out, Arthur, she has found me out.

LORD GORING. Has she never in her life done some folly—some indiscretion—that she should not forgive your sin?

SIR ROBERT CHILTERN. My wife! Never! She does not know what weakness or temptation is. I am of clay like other men. She stands apart as good women do—pitiless in her perfection—cold and stern and without mercy. But I love her, Arthur. We are childless, and I have no one else to love, no one else to love me. Perhaps if God had sent us children she might have been kinder to me. But God has given us a lonely house. And she has cut my heart in two. Don't let us talk of it. I was brutal to her this evening. But I suppose when sinners talk to saints they are brutal always. I said to her things that were hideously true, on my side, from my standpoint, from the standpoint of men. But don't let us talk of that.

LORD GORING. Your wife will forgive you. Perhaps at this moment she is forgiving you. She loves you, Robert. Why should she not forgive?

SIR ROBERT CHILTERN. God grant it! God grant it! [*Buries his face in his hands.*] But there is something more I have to tell you, Arthur.

[*Enter Phipps with drinks.*]

PHIPPS [*Hands hock and seltzer to Sir Robert Chiltern.*] Hock and seltzer, sir.

SIR ROBERT CHILTERN. Thank you.

LORD GORING. Is your carriage here, Robert?

SIR ROBERT CHILTERN. No; I walked from the club.

LORD GORING. Sir Robert will take my cab, Phipps.

PHIPPS. Yes, my lord.

[*Exit.*]

LORD GORING. Robert, you don't mind my sending you away?

SIR ROBERT CHILTERN. Arthur, you must let me stay for five minutes. I have made up my mind what I am going to do tonight in the House. The debate on the Argentine Canal is to begin at eleven. [*A chair falls in the drawing-room.*] What is that?

LORD GORING. Nothing.

SIR ROBERT CHILTERN. I heard a chair fall in the next room. Some one has been listening.

LORD GORING. No, no; there is no one there.

SIR ROBERT CHILTERN. There is some one. There are lights in the room, and the door is ajar. Some one has been listening to every secret of my life. Arthur, what does this mean?

LORD GORING. Robert, you are excited, unnerved. I tell you there is no one in that room. Sit down, Robert.

SIR ROBERT CHILTERN. Do you give me your word that there is no one there?

LORD GORING. Yes.

SIR ROBERT CHILTERN. Your word of honour? [*Sits down.*]

LORD GORING. Yes.

SIR ROBERT CHILTERN [*Rises.*] Arthur, let me see for myself.

LORD GORING. No, no.

SIR ROBERT CHILTERN. If there is no one there why should I not look in that room? Arthur, you must let me go into that room and satisfy myself. Let me know that no eavesdropper has heard my life's secret. Arthur, you don't realize what I am going through.

LORD GORING. Robert, this must stop. I have told you that there is no one in that room—that is enough.

SIR ROBERT CHILTERN [*Rushes to the door of the room.*] It is not enough. I insist on going into this room. You have told me there is no one there, so what reason can you have for refusing me?

LORD GORING. For God's sake, don't! There is some one there. Some one whom you must not see.

SIR ROBERT CHILTERN. Ah, I thought so!

LORD GORING. I forbid you to enter that room.

SIR ROBERT CHILTERN. Stand back. My life is at stake. And I don't care who is there. I will know who it is to whom I have told my secret and my shame. [*Enters room.*]

LORD GORING. Great Heavens! his own wife!

[*Sir Robert Chiltern comes back, with a look of scorn and anger on his face.*]

SIR ROBERT CHILTERN. What explanation have you to give me for the presence of that woman here?

LORD GORING. Robert, I swear to you on my honour that that lady is stainless and guiltless of all offence towards you.

SIR ROBERT CHILTERN. She is a vile, an infamous thing!

LORD GORING. Don't say that, Robert! It was for your sake she came here. It was to try and save you she came here. She loves you and no one else.

SIR ROBERT CHILTERN. You are mad. What have I to do with her intrigues with you? Let her remain your mistress! You are well suited to each other. She, corrupt and shameful—you, false as a friend, treacherous as an enemy even——

LORD GORING. It is not true, Robert. Before heaven, it is not true. In her presence and in yours I will explain all.

SIR ROBERT CHILTERN. Let me pass, sir. You have lied enough upon your word of honour.

[*Sir Robert Chiltern goes out. Lord Goring rushes to the door of the drawing-room, when Mrs Cheveley comes out, looking radiant and much amused.*]

MRS CHEVELEY [*With a mock curtsey.*] Good evening, Lord Goring!

LORD GORING. Mrs Cheveley! Great Heavens! . . . May I ask what you were doing in my drawing-room?

MRS CHEVELEY. Merely listening. I have a perfect passion for listening through keyholes. One always hears such wonderful things through them.

LORD GORING. Doesn't that sound rather like tempting Providence?

MRS CHEVELEY. Oh! surely Providence can resist temptation by this time. [*Makes a sign to him to take her cloak off, which he does.*]

LORD GORING. I am glad you have called. I am going to give you some good advice.

MRS CHEVELEY. Oh! pray don't. One should never give a woman anything that she can't wear in the evening.

LORD GORING. I see you are quite as wilful as you used to be.

MRS CHEVELEY. Far more! I have greatly improved. I have had more experience.

LORD GORING. Too much experience is a dangerous thing. Pray have a cigarette. Half the pretty women in London smoke cigarettes. Personally I prefer the other half.

MRS CHEVELEY. Thanks. I never smoke. My dressmaker wouldn't like it, and a woman's first duty in life is to her dressmaker, isn't it? What the second duty is, no one has as yet discovered.

LORD GORING. You have come here to sell me Robert Chiltern's letter, haven't you?

MRS CHEVELEY. To offer it to you on conditions. How did you guess that?

LORD GORING. Because you haven't mentioned the subject. Have you got it with you?

MRS CHEVELEY [*Sitting down.*] Oh, no! A well-made dress has no pockets.

LORD GORING. What is your price for it?

MRS CHEVELEY. How absurdly English you are! The English think that a cheque-book can solve every problem in life. Why, my dear Arthur, I have very much more money than you have, and quite as much as Robert Chiltern has got hold of. Money is not what I want.

LORD GORING. What do you want then, Mrs Cheveley?

MRS CHEVELEY. Why don't you call me Laura?

LORD GORING. I don't like the name.

MRS CHEVELEY. You used to adore it.

LORD GORING. Yes: that's why. [*Mrs Cheveley motions to him to sit down beside her. He smiles, and does so.*]

MRS CHEVELEY. Arthur, you loved me once.

LORD GORING. Yes.

MRS CHEVELEY. And you asked me to be your wife.

LORD GORING. That was the natural result of my loving you.

MRS CHEVELEY. And you threw me over because you saw, or said you saw, poor old Lord Mortlake trying to have a violent flirtation with me in the conservatory at Tenby.

LORD GORING. I am under the impression that my lawyer settled that matter with you on certain terms . . . dictated by yourself.

MRS CHEVELEY. At that time I was poor; you were rich.

LORD GORING. Quite so. That is why you pretended to love me.

MRS CHEVELEY [*Shrugging her shoulders.*] Poor old Lord Mortlake, who had only two topics of conversation, his gout and his wife! I never could quite make out which of the two he was talking about. He used the most horrible language about them both. Well, you were silly, Arthur. Why, Lord Mortlake was never anything more to me than an amusement. One of those utterly tedious amusements one only finds at an English country house on an English country Sunday. I don't think anyone at all morally responsible for what he or she does at an English country house.

LORD GORING. Yes. I know lots of people think that.

MRS CHEVELEY. I loved you, Arthur.

LORD GORING. My dear Mrs Cheveley, you have always been far too clever to know anything about love.

MRS CHEVELEY. I did love you. And you loved me. You know you loved me; and love is a very wonderful thing. I suppose that when a man has once loved a woman, he will do anything for her, except continue to love her? [*Puts her hand on his.*]

LORD GORING [*Taking his hand away quietly.*] Yes: except that.

MRS CHEVELEY [*After a pause.*] I am tired of living abroad. I want to come back to London. I want to have a charming house here. I want to have a salon. If one could only teach the English how to talk, and the Irish how to listen, society here would be quite civilized. Besides, I have arrived at the romantic stage. When I saw you last night at the Chilterns', I knew you were the only person I had ever cared for, if I ever have cared for anybody, Arthur. And so, on the morning of the day you marry me, I will give you Robert Chiltern's letter. That is my offer. I will give it to you now, if you promise to marry me.

LORD GORING. Now?

MRS CHEVELEY [*Smiling.*] Tomorrow.

LORD GORING. Are you really serious?

MRS CHEVELEY. Yes, quite serious.

LORD GORING. I should make you a very bad husband.

MRS CHEVELEY. I don't mind bad husbands. I have had two. They amused me immensely.

LORD GORING. You mean that you amused yourself immensely, don't you?

MRS CHEVELEY. What do you know about my married life?

LORD GORING. Nothing: but I can read it like a book.

MRS CHEVELEY. What book?

LORD GORING [*Rising.*] The Book of Numbers.°

MRS CHEVELEY. Do you think it quite charming of you to be so rude to a woman in your own house?

LORD GORING. In the case of very fascinating women, sex is a challenge, not a defence.

MRS CHEVELEY. I suppose that is meant for a compliment. My dear Arthur, women are never disarmed by compliments. Men always are. That is the difference between the two sexes.

LORD GORING. Women are never disarmed by anything, as far as I know them.

MRS CHEVELEY [*After a pause.*] Then you are going to allow your greatest friend, Robert Chiltern, to be ruined, rather than marry some one who really has considerable attractions left. I thought you would have risen to some great height of self-sacrifice, Arthur. I think you should. And the rest of your life you could spend in contemplating your own perfections.

LORD GORING. Oh! I do that as it is. And self-sacrifice is a thing that should be put down by law. It is so demoralizing to the people for whom one sacrifices oneself. They always go to the bad.

MRS CHEVELEY. As if anything could demoralize Robert Chiltern! You seem to forget that I know his real character.

LORD GORING. What you know about him is not his real character. It was an act of folly done in his youth, dishonourable, I admit, shameful, I admit, unworthy of him, I admit, and therefore ... not his true character.

MRS CHEVELEY. How you men stand up for each other!

LORD GORING. How you women war against each other!

MRS CHEVELEY [*Bitterly.*] I only war against one woman, against Gertrude Chiltern. I hate her. I hate her now more than ever.

LORD GORING. Because you have brought a real tragedy into her life, I suppose.

MRS CHEVELEY [*With a sneer.*] Oh, there is only one real tragedy in a woman's life. The fact that her past is always her lover, and her future invariably her husband.

LORD GORING. Lady Chiltern knows nothing of the kind of life to which you are alluding.

MRS CHEVELEY. A woman whose size in gloves is seven and three-quarters never knows much about anything. You know Gertrude has always worn seven and three-quarters? That is one of the reasons why there was never any moral sympathy between us. . . . Well, Arthur, I suppose this romantic interview may be regarded as at an end. You admit it was romantic, don't you? For the privilege of being your wife I was ready to surrender a great prize, the climax of my diplomatic career. You decline. Very well. If Sir Robert doesn't uphold my Argentine scheme, I expose him. *Voilà tout.*°

LORD GORING. You mustn't do that. It would be vile, horrible, infamous.

MRS CHEVELEY [*Shrugging her shoulders.*] Oh! don't use big words. They mean so little. It is a commercial transaction. That is all. There is no good mixing up sentimentality in it. I offered to sell Robert Chiltern a certain thing. If he won't pay me my price, he will have to pay the world a greater price. There is no more to be said. I must go. Goodbye. Won't you shake hands?

LORD GORING. With you? No. Your transaction with Robert Chiltern may pass as a loathsome commercial transaction of a loathsome commercial age; but you seem to have forgotten that you who came here tonight to talk of love, you whose lips desecrated the word love, you to whom the thing is a book closely sealed, went this afternoon to the house of one of the most noble and gentle women in the world to degrade her husband in her eyes, to try and kill her love for him, to put poison in her heart, and bitterness in her life, to break her idol and, it may be, spoil her soul. That I cannot forgive you. That was horrible. For that there can be no forgiveness.

MRS CHEVELEY. Arthur, you are unjust to me. Believe me, you are quite unjust to me. I didn't go to taunt Gertrude at all. I had no idea of doing anything of the kind when I entered. I called with Lady Markby simply to ask whether an ornament, a jewel, that I lost somewhere last night, had been found at the Chilterns'. If you don't believe me, you can ask Lady Markby. She will tell you it is true. The scene that occurred happened after Lady Markby had left, and was really forced on me by Gertrude's rudeness and sneers. I called, oh!—a little out of malice if you like—but really to ask if a diamond brooch of mine had been found. That was the origin of the whole thing.

LORD GORING. A diamond snake-brooch with a ruby?

MRS CHEVELEY. Yes. How do you know?

LORD GORING. Because it is found. In point of fact, I found it myself, and stupidly forgot to tell the butler anything about it as I was leaving. [*Goes over to the writing-table and pulls out the drawers.*] It is in this drawer. No, that one. This is the brooch, isn't it? [*Holds up the brooch.*]

MRS CHEVELEY. Yes. I am so glad to get it back. It was . . . a present.

LORD GORING. Won't you wear it?

MRS CHEVELEY. Certainly, if you pin it in. [*Lord Goring suddenly clasps it on her arm.*] Why do you put it on as a bracelet? I never knew it could be worn as a bracelet.

LORD GORING. Really?

MRS CHEVELEY [*Holding out her handsome arm.*] No; but it looks very well on me as a bracelet, doesn't it?

LORD GORING. Yes; much better than when I saw it last.

MRS CHEVELEY. When did you see it last?

LORD GORING [*Calmly.*] Oh, ten years ago, on Lady Berkshire, from whom you stole it.

MRS CHEVELEY [*Starting.*] What do you mean?

LORD GORING. I mean that you stole that ornament from my cousin, Mary Berkshire, to whom I gave it when she was married. Suspicion fell on a wretched servant, who was sent away in disgrace. I recognized it last night. I determined to say nothing about it till I had found the thief. I have found the thief now, and I have heard her own confession.

MRS CHEVELEY [*Tossing her head.*] It is not true.

LORD GORING. You know it is true. Why, thief is written across your face at this moment.

MRS CHEVELEY. I will deny the whole affair from beginning to end. I will say that I have never seen this wretched thing, that it was never in my possession.

[*Mrs Cheveley tries to get the bracelet off her arm, but fails. Lord Goring looks on amused. Her thin fingers tear at the jewel to no purpose. A curse breaks from her.*]

LORD GORING. The drawback of stealing a thing, Mrs Cheveley, is that one never knows how wonderful the thing that one steals is. You can't get that bracelet off, unless you know where the spring is. And I see you don't know where the spring is. It is rather difficult to find.

MRS CHEVELEY. You brute! You coward! [*She tries again to unclasp the bracelet, but fails.*]

LORD GORING. Oh! don't use big words. They mean so little.

MRS CHEVELEY [*Again tears at the bracelet in a paroxysm of rage, with inarticulate sounds. Then stops, and looks at Lord Goring.*] What are you going to do?

LORD GORING. I am going to ring for my servant. He is an admirable servant. Always comes in the moment one rings for him. When he comes I will tell him to fetch the police.

MRS CHEVELEY [*Trembling.*] The police? What for?

LORD GORING. Tomorrow the Berkshires will prosecute you. That is what the police are for.

MRS CHEVELEY [*Is now in an agony of physical terror. Her face is distorted. Her mouth awry. A mask has fallen from her. She is, for the moment, dreadful to look at.*] Don't do that. I will do anything you want. Anything in the world you want.

LORD GORING. Give me Robert Chiltern's letter.

MRS CHEVELEY. Stop! Stop! Let me have time to think.

LORD GORING. Give me Robert Chiltern's letter.

MRS CHEVELEY. I have not got it with me. I will give it to you tomorrow.

LORD GORING. You know you are lying. Give it to me at once. [*Mrs Cheveley pulls the letter out, and hands it to him. She is horribly pale.*] This is it?

MRS CHEVELEY [*In a hoarse voice.*] Yes.

LORD GORING [*Takes the letter, examines it, sighs, and burns it over the lamp.*] For so well dressed a woman, Mrs Cheveley, you have moments of admirable common sense. I congratulate you.

MRS CHEVELEY [*Catches sight of Lady Chiltern's letter, the cover of which is just showing from under the blotting-book.*] Please get me a glass of water.

LORD GORING. Certainly.

[*Goes to the corner of the room and pours out a glass of water. While his back is turned Mrs Cheveley steals Lady Chiltern's letter. When Lord Goring returns with the glass she refuses it with a gesture.*]

MRS CHEVELEY. Thank you. Will you help me on with my cloak?

LORD GORING. With pleasure. [*Puts her cloak on.*]

MRS CHEVELEY. Thanks. I am never going to try to harm Robert Chiltern again.

LORD GORING. Fortunately you have not got the chance, Mrs Cheveley.

MRS CHEVELEY. Well, if even I had the chance, I wouldn't. On the contrary, I am going to render him a great service.

LORD GORING. I am charmed to hear it. It is a reformation.

MRS CHEVELEY. Yes. I can't bear so upright a gentleman, so honourable an English gentleman, being so shamefully deceived, and so——

LORD GORING. Well?

MRS CHEVELEY. I find that somehow Gertrude Chiltern's dying speech and confession has strayed into my pocket.

LORD GORING. What do you mean?

MRS CHEVELEY [*With a bitter note of triumph in her voice.*] I mean that I am going to send Robert Chiltern the love letter his wife wrote to you tonight.

LORD GORING. Love letter?

MRS CHEVELEY [*Laughing.*] 'I want you. I trust you. I am coming to you. Gertrude.'

[*Lord Goring rushes to the bureau and takes up the envelope, finds it empty, and turns round.*]

LORD GORING. You wretched woman, must you always be thieving? Give me back that letter. I'll take it from you by force. You shall not leave my room till I have got it.

[*He rushes towards her, but Mrs Cheveley at once puts her hand on the electric bell that is on the table. The bell sounds with shrill reverberations, and Phipps enters.*]

MRS CHEVELEY [*After a pause.*] Lord Goring merely rang that you should show me out. Goodnight, Lord Goring!

[*Goes out, followed by Phipps. Her face is illumined with evil triumph. There is joy in her eyes. Youth seems to have come back to her. Her last glance is like a swift arrow. Lord Goring bites his lip, and lights a cigarette.*]

ACT DROP.

FOURTH ACT

SCENE—*Same as Act II.*

[*Lord Goring is standing by the fireplace with his hands in his pockets. He is looking rather bored.*]

LORD GORING [*Pulls out his watch, inspects it, and rings the bell.*] It is a great nuisance. I can't find anyone in this house to talk to. And I am full of interesting information. I feel like the latest edition of something or other.

[*Enter Servant.*]

JAMES. Sir Robert is still at the Foreign Office, my lord.

LORD GORING. Lady Chiltern not down yet?

JAMES. Her ladyship has not yet left her room. Miss Chiltern has just come in from riding.

LORD GORING [*To himself.*] Ah! that is something.

JAMES. Lord Caversham has been waiting some time in the library for Sir Robert. I told him your lordship was here.

LORD GORING. Thank you. Would you kindly tell him I've gone?

JAMES [*Bowing.*] I shall do so, my lord.

[*Exit Servant.*]

LORD GORING. Really, I don't want to meet my father three days running. It is a great deal too much excitement for any son. I hope to goodness he won't come up. Fathers should be neither seen nor heard. That is the only proper basis for family life. Mothers are different. Mothers are darlings. [*Throws himself down into a chair, picks up a paper and begins to read it.*]

[*Enter Lord Caversham.*]

LORD CAVERSHAM. Well, sir, what are you doing here? Wasting your time as usual, I suppose?

LORD GORING [*Throws down paper and rises.*] My dear father, when one pays a visit it is for the purpose of wasting other people's time, not one's own.

LORD CAVERSHAM. Have you been thinking over what I spoke to you about last night?

LORD GORING. I have been thinking about nothing else.

LORD CAVERSHAM. Engaged to be married yet?

LORD GORING [*Genially.*] Not yet: but I hope to be before lunch-time.

LORD CAVERSHAM [*Caustically.*] You can have till dinner-time if it would be of any convenience to you.

LORD GORING. Thanks awfully, but I think I'd sooner be engaged before lunch.

LORD CAVERSHAM. Humph! Never know when you are serious or not.

LORD GORING. Neither do I, father.

[*A pause.*]

LORD CAVERSHAM. I suppose you have read 'The Times' this morning?

LORD GORING [*Airily.*] 'The Times'? Certainly not. I only read 'The Morning Post'. All that one should know about modern life is where the Duchesses are; anything else is quite demoralizing.

LORD CAVERSHAM. Do you mean to say you have not read 'The Times'' leading article on Robert Chiltern's career?

LORD GORING. Good heavens! No. What does it say?

LORD CAVERSHAM. What should it say, sir? Everything complimentary, of course. Chiltern's speech last night on this Argentine Canal Scheme was one of the finest pieces of oratory ever delivered in the House since Canning.°

LORD GORING. Ah! Never heard of Canning. Never wanted to. And did . . . did Chiltern uphold the scheme?

LORD CAVERSHAM. Uphold it, sir? How little you know him! Why, he denounced it roundly, and the whole system of modern political finance. This speech is the turning-point in his career, as 'The Times' points out. You should read this article, sir. [*Opens 'The Times'.*] 'Sir Robert Chiltern . . . most rising of all our young statesmen . . . Brilliant orator . . . Unblemished career . . . Well-known integrity of character . . . Represents what is best in English public life . . . Noble contrast to the lax morality so common among foreign politicians.' They will never say that of you, sir.

LORD GORING. I sincerely hope not, father. However, I am delighted at what you tell me about Robert, thoroughly delighted. It shows he has got pluck.

LORD CAVERSHAM. He has got more than pluck, sir, he has got genius.

LORD GORING. Ah! I prefer pluck. It is not so common, nowadays, as genius is.

LORD CAVERSHAM. I wish you would go into Parliament.

LORD GORING. My dear father, only people who look dull ever get into the House of Commons, and only people who are dull ever succeed there.

LORD CAVERSHAM. Why don't you try to do something useful in life?

LORD GORING. I am far too young.

LORD CAVERSHAM [*Testily.*] I hate this affectation of youth, sir. It is a great deal too prevalent nowadays.

LORD GORING. Youth isn't an affectation. Youth is an art.

LORD CAVERSHAM. Why don't you propose to that pretty Miss Chiltern?

LORD GORING. I am of a very nervous disposition, especially in the morning.

LORD CAVERSHAM. I don't suppose there is the smallest chance of her accepting you.

LORD GORING. I don't know how the betting stands today.

LORD CAVERSHAM. If she did accept you she would be the prettiest fool in England.

LORD GORING. That is just what I should like to marry. A thoroughly sensible wife would reduce me to a condition of absolute idiocy in less than six months.

LORD CAVERSHAM. You don't deserve her, sir.

LORD GORING. My dear father, if we men married the women we deserved, we should have a very bad time of it.

[*Enter Mabel Chiltern.*]

MABEL CHILTERN. Oh! . . . How do you do, Lord Caversham? I hope Lady Caversham is quite well?

LORD CAVERSHAM. Lady Caversham is as usual, as usual.

LORD GORING. Good morning, Miss Mabel!

MABEL CHILTERN [*Taking no notice at all of Lord Goring, and addressing herself exclusively to Lord Caversham.*] And Lady Caversham's bonnets . . . are they at all better?

LORD CAVERSHAM. They have had a serious relapse, I am sorry to say.

LORD GORING. Good morning, Miss Mabel!

MABEL CHILTERN [*To Lord Caversham.*] I hope an operation will not be necessary.

LORD CAVERSHAM [*Smiling at her pertness.*] If it is we shall have to give Lady Caversham a narcotic. Otherwise she would never consent to have a feather touched.

LORD GORING [*With increased emphasis.*] Good morning, Miss Mabel!

MABEL CHILTERN [*Turning round with feigned surprise.*] Oh, are you here? Of course you understand that after your breaking your appointment I am never going to speak to you again.

LORD GORING. Oh, please don't say such a thing. You are the one person in London I really like to have to listen to me.

MABEL CHILTERN. Lord Goring, I never believe a single word that either you or I say to each other.

LORD CAVERSHAM. You are quite right, my dear, quite right . . . as far as he is concerned, I mean.

MABEL CHILTERN. Do you think you could possibly make your son behave a little better occasionally? Just as a change.

LORD CAVERSHAM. I regret to say, Miss Chiltern, that I have no influence at all over my son. I wish I had. If I had, I know what I would make him do.

MABEL CHILTERN. I am afraid that he has one of those terribly weak natures that are not susceptible to influence.

LORD CAVERSHAM. He is very heartless, very heartless.

LORD GORING. It seems to me that I am a little in the way here.

MABEL CHILTERN. It is very good for you to be in the way, and to know what people say of you behind your back.

LORD GORING. I don't at all like knowing what people say of me behind my back. It makes me far too conceited.

LORD CAVERSHAM. After that, my dear, I really must bid you good morning.

MABEL CHILTERN. Oh! I hope you are not going to leave me all alone with Lord Goring? Especially at such an early hour in the day.

LORD CAVERSHAM. I am afraid I can't take him with me to Downing Street. It is not the Prime Minister's day for seeing the unemployed.°

[Shakes hands with Mabel Chiltern, takes up his hat and stick, and goes out, with a parting glare of indignation at Lord Goring.]

MABEL CHILTERN [Takes up roses and begins to arrange them in a bowl on the table.] People who don't keep their appointments in the Park° are horrid.

LORD GORING. Detestable.

MABEL CHILTERN. I am glad you admit it. But I wish you wouldn't look so pleased about it.

LORD GORING. I can't help it. I always look pleased when I am with you.

MABEL CHILTERN [Sadly.] Then I suppose it is my duty to remain with you?

LORD GORING. Of course it is.

MABEL CHILTERN. Well, my duty is a thing I never do, on principle. It always depresses me. So I am afraid I must leave you.

LORD GORING. Please don't, Miss Mabel. I have something very particular to say to you.

MABEL CHILTERN [Rapturously.] Oh! is it a proposal?

LORD GORING [Somewhat taken aback.] Well, yes, it is—I am bound to say it is.

MABEL CHILTERN [*With a sigh of pleasure.*] I am so glad. That makes the second today.

LORD GORING [*Indignantly.*] The second today? What conceited ass has been impertinent enough to dare to propose to you before I had proposed to you?

MABEL CHILTERN. Tommy Trafford, of course. It is one of Tommy's days for proposing. He always proposes on Tuesdays and Thursdays, during the season.

LORD GORING. You didn't accept him, I hope?

MABEL CHILTERN. I make it a rule never to accept Tommy. That is why he goes on proposing. Of course, as you didn't turn up this morning, I very nearly said yes. It would have been an excellent lesson both for him and for you if I had. It would have taught you both better manners.

LORD GORING. Oh! bother Tommy Trafford. Tommy is a silly little ass. I love you.

MABEL CHILTERN. I know. And I think you might have mentioned it before. I am sure I have given you heaps of opportunities.

LORD GORING. Mabel, do be serious. Please be serious.

MABEL CHILTERN. Ah! that is the sort of thing a man always says to a girl before he has been married to her. He never says it afterwards.

LORD GORING [*Taking hold of her hand.*] Mabel, I have told you that I love you. Can't you love me a little in return?

MABEL CHILTERN. You silly Arthur! If you knew anything about . . . anything, which you don't, you would know that I adore you. Everyone in London knows it except you. It is a public scandal the way I adore you. I have been going about for the last six months telling the whole of society that I adore you. I wonder you consent to have anything to say to me. I have no character left at all. At least, I feel so happy that I am quite sure I have no character left at all.

LORD GORING [*Catches her in his arms and kisses her. Then there is a pause of bliss.*] Dear! Do you know I was awfully afraid of being refused!

MABEL CHILTERN [*Looking up at him.*] But you never have been refused yet by anybody, have you, Arthur? I can't imagine anyone refusing you.

LORD GORING [*After kissing her again.*] Of course I'm not nearly good enough for you, Mabel.

MABEL CHILTERN [*Nestling close to him.*] I am so glad, darling. I was afraid you were.

LORD GORING [*After some hesitation.*] And I'm . . . I'm a little over thirty.

MABEL CHILTERN. Dear, you look weeks younger than that.

LORD GORING [*Enthusiastically.*] How sweet of you to say so! . . . And it is only fair to tell you frankly that I am fearfully extravagant.

MABEL CHILTERN. But so am I, Arthur. So we're sure to agree. And now I must go and see Gertrude.

LORD GORING. Must you really? [*Kisses her.*]

MABEL CHILTERN. Yes.

LORD GORING. Then do tell her I want to talk to her particularly. I have been waiting here all the morning to see either her or Robert.

MABEL CHILTERN. Do you mean to say you didn't come here expressly to propose to me?

LORD GORING [*Triumphantly.*] No; that was a flash of genius.

MABEL CHILTERN. Your first.

LORD GORING [*With determination.*] My last.

MABEL CHILTERN. I am delighted to hear it. Now don't stir. I'll be back in five minutes. And don't fall into any temptations while I am away.

LORD GORING. Dear Mabel, while you are away, there are none. It makes me horribly dependent on you.

[*Enter Lady Chiltern.*]

LADY CHILTERN. Good morning, dear! How pretty you are looking!

MABEL CHILTERN. How pale you are looking, Gertrude! It is most becoming!

LADY CHILTERN. Good morning, Lord Goring!

LORD GORING [*Bowing.*] Good morning, Lady Chiltern!

MABEL CHILTERN [*Aside to Lord Goring.*] I shall be in the conservatory, under the second palm tree on the left.

LORD GORING. Second on the left?

MABEL CHILTERN [*With a look of mock surprise.*] Yes; the usual palm tree.

[*Blows a kiss to him, unobserved by Lady Chiltern, and goes out.*]

LORD GORING. Lady Chiltern, I have a certain amount of very good news to tell you. Mrs Cheveley gave me up Robert's letter last night, and I burned it. Robert is safe.

LADY CHILTERN [*Sinking on the sofa.*] Safe! Oh! I am so glad of that. What a good friend you are to him—to us!

LORD GORING. There is only one person now that could be said to be in any danger.

LADY CHILTERN. Who is that?

LORD GORING [*Sitting down beside her.*] Yourself.

LADY CHILTERN. I! In danger? What do you mean?

LORD GORING. Danger is too great a word. It is a word I should not have used. But I admit I have something to tell you that may distress you, that terribly distresses me. Yesterday evening you wrote me a very beautiful, womanly letter, asking me for my help. You wrote to me as one of your oldest friends, one of your husband's oldest friends. Mrs Cheveley stole that letter from my rooms.

LADY CHILTERN. Well, what use is it to her? Why should she not have it?

LORD GORING [*Rising.*] Lady Chiltern, I will be quite frank with you. Mrs Cheveley puts a certain construction on that letter and proposes to send it to your husband.

LADY CHILTERN. But what construction could she put on it? . . . Oh! not that! not that! If I in—in trouble, and wanting your help, trusting you, propose to come to you . . . that you may advise me . . . assist me . . . Oh! are there women so horrible as that. . . ? And she proposes to send it to my husband? Tell me what happened. Tell me all that happened.

LORD GORING. Mrs Cheveley was concealed in a room adjoining my library, without my knowledge. I thought that the person who was waiting in that room to see me was yourself. Robert came in unexpectedly. A chair or something fell in the room. He forced his way in, and he discovered her. We had a terrible scene. I still thought it was you. He left me in anger. At the end of everything Mrs Cheveley got possession of your letter—she stole it, when or how, I don't know.

LADY CHILTERN. At what hour did this happen?

LORD GORING. At half-past ten. And now I propose that we tell Robert the whole thing at once.

LADY CHILTERN [*Looking at him with amazement that is almost terror.*] You want me to tell Robert that the woman you expected was not Mrs Cheveley, but myself? That it was I whom you thought was concealed in a room in your house, at half-past ten o'clock at night? You want me to tell him that?

LORD GORING. I think it is better that he should know the exact truth.

LADY CHILTERN [*Rising.*] Oh, I couldn't, I couldn't!

LORD GORING. May I do it?

LADY CHILTERN. No.

LORD GORING [*Gravely.*] You are wrong, Lady Chiltern.

LADY CHILTERN. No. The letter must be intercepted. That is all. But how can I do it? Letters arrive for him every moment of the day. His secretaries open them and hand them to him. I dare not ask the servants to bring me his letters. It would be impossible. Oh! why don't you tell me what to do?

LORD GORING. Pray be calm, Lady Chiltern, and answer the questions I am going to put to you. You said his secretaries open his letters.

LADY CHILTERN. Yes.

LORD GORING. Who is with him today? Mr Trafford, isn't it?

LADY CHILTERN. No. Mr Montfort, I think.

LORD GORING. You can trust him?

LADY CHILTERN [*With a gesture of despair.*] Oh! how do I know?

LORD GORING. He would do what you asked him, wouldn't he?

LADY CHILTERN. I think so.

LORD GORING. Your letter was on pink paper. He could recognize it without reading it, couldn't he? By the colour?

LADY CHILTERN. I suppose so.

LORD GORING. Is he in the house now?

LADY CHILTERN. Yes.

LORD GORING. Then I will go and see him myself, and tell him that a certain letter, written on pink paper, is to be forwarded to Robert today, and that all costs it must not reach him. [*Goes to the door, and opens it.*] Oh! Robert is coming upstairs with the letter in his hand. It has reached him already.

LADY CHILTERN [*With a cry of pain.*] Oh! you have saved his life; what have you done with mine?

[*Enter Sir Robert Chiltern. He has the letter in his hand, and is reading it. He comes towards his wife, not noticing Lord Goring's presence.*]

SIR ROBERT CHILTERN. 'I want you. I trust you. I am coming to you. Gertrude.' Oh, my love! Is this true? Do you indeed trust me, and want me? If so, it was for me to come to you, not for you to write of coming to me. This letter of yours, Gertrude, makes me feel that nothing that the world may do can hurt me now. You want me, Gertrude?

[*Lord Goring, unseen by Sir Robert Chiltern, makes an imploring sign to Lady Chiltern to accept the situation and Sir Robert's error.*]

LADY CHILTERN. Yes.

SIR ROBERT CHILTERN. You trust me, Gertrude?

LADY CHILTERN. Yes.

SIR ROBERT CHILTERN. Ah! why did you not add you loved me?

LADY CHILTERN [*Taking his hand.*] Because I loved you.

[*Lord Goring passes into the conservatory.*]

SIR ROBERT CHILTERN [*Kisses her.*] Gertrude, you don't know what I feel. When Montfort passed me your letter across the table—he had opened it by mistake, I suppose, without looking at the handwriting on the envelope—and I read it—oh! I did not care what disgrace or punishment was in store for me, I only thought you loved me still.

LADY CHILTERN. There is no disgrace in store for you, nor any public shame. Mrs Cheveley has handed over to Lord Goring the document that was in her possession, and he has destroyed it.

SIR ROBERT CHILTERN. Are you sure of this, Gertrude?

LADY CHILTERN. Yes; Lord Goring has just told me.

SIR ROBERT CHILTERN. Then I am safe! Oh! what a wonderful thing to be safe! For two days I have been in terror. I am safe now. How did Arthur destroy my letter? Tell me.

LADY CHILTERN. He burned it.

SIR ROBERT CHILTERN. I wish I had seen that one sin of my youth burning to ashes. How many men there are in modern life who would like to see their past burning to white ashes before them! Is Arthur still here?

LADY CHILTERN. Yes; he is in the conservatory.

SIR ROBERT CHILTERN. I am so glad now I made that speech last night in the House, so glad. I made it thinking that public disgrace might be the result. But it has not been so.

LADY CHILTERN. Public honour has been the result.

SIR ROBERT CHILTERN. I think so. I fear so, almost. For although I am safe from detection, although every proof against me is destroyed, I suppose, Gertrude . . . I suppose I should retire from public life? [*He looks anxiously at his wife.*]

LADY CHILTERN [*Eagerly.*] Oh yes, Robert, you should do that. It is your duty to do that.

SIR ROBERT CHILTERN. It is much to surrender.

LADY CHILTERN. No; it will be much to gain.

[*Sir Robert Chiltern walks up and down the room with a troubled expression. Then comes over to his wife, and puts his hand on her shoulder.*]

SIR ROBERT CHILTERN. And you would be happy living somewhere alone with me, abroad perhaps, or in the country away from London, away from public life? You would have no regrets?

LADY CHILTERN. Oh! none, Robert.

SIR ROBERT CHILTERN [*Sadly.*] And your ambition for me? You used to be ambitious for me.

LADY CHILTERN. Oh, my ambition! I have none now, but that we two may love each other. It was your ambition that led you astray. Let us not talk about ambition.

[*Lord Goring returns from the conservatory, looking very pleased with himself, and with an entirely new buttonhole that some one has made for him.*]

SIR ROBERT CHILTERN [*Going towards him.*] Arthur, I have to thank you for what you have done for me. I don't know how I can repay you. [*Shakes hands with him.*]

LORD GORING. My dear fellow, I'll tell you at once. At the present moment, under the usual palm tree . . . I mean in the conservatory . . .

[*Enter Mason.*]

MASON. Lord Caversham.

LORD GORING. That admirable father of mine really makes a habit of turning up at the wrong moment. It is very heartless of him, very heartless indeed.

[*Enter Lord Caversham. Mason goes out.*]

LORD CAVERSHAM. Good morning, Lady Chiltern! Warmest congratulations to you, Chiltern, on your brilliant speech last night. I have just left the Prime Minister, and you are to have the vacant seat in the Cabinet.

SIR ROBERT CHILTERN [*With a look of joy and triumph.*] A seat in the Cabinet?

LORD CAVERSHAM. Yes; here is the Prime Minister's letter. [*Hands letter.*]

SIR ROBERT CHILTERN [*Takes letter and reads it.*] A seat in the Cabinet!

LORD CAVERSHAM. Certainly, and you well deserve it too. You have got what we want so much in political life nowadays—high character, high moral tone, high principles. [*To Lord Goring.*] Everything that you have not got, sir, and never will have.

LORD GORING. I don't like principles, father. I prefer prejudices.

[*Sir Robert Chiltern is on the brink of accepting the Prime Minister's offer, when he sees his wife looking at him with her clear, candid eyes. He then realizes that it is impossible.*]

SIR ROBERT CHILTERN. I cannot accept this offer, Lord Caversham. I have made up my mind to decline it.

LORD CAVERSHAM. Decline it, sir!

SIR ROBERT CHILTERN. My intention is to retire at once from public life.

LORD CAVERSHAM [*Angrily.*] Decline a seat in the Cabinet, and retire from public life? Never heard such damned nonsense in the whole course of my existence. I beg your pardon, Lady Chiltern. Chiltern, I beg your pardon. [*To Lord Goring.*] Don't grin like that, sir.

LORD GORING. No, father.

LORD CAVERSHAM. Lady Chiltern, you are a sensible woman, the most sensible woman in London, the most sensible woman I know. Will you kindly prevent your husband from making such a . . . from talking such . . . Will you kindly do that, Lady Chiltern?

LADY CHILTERN. I think my husband is right in his determination, Lord Caversham. I approve of it.

LORD CAVERSHAM. You approve of it? Good Heavens!

LADY CHILTERN [*Taking her husband's hand.*] I admire him for it. I admire him immensely for it. I have never admired him so much before. He is finer than even I thought him. [*To Sir Robert Chiltern.*] You will go and write your letter to the Prime Minister now, won't you? Don't hesitate about it, Robert.

SIR ROBERT CHILTERN [*With a touch of bitterness.*] I suppose I had better write it at once. Such offers are not repeated. I will ask you to excuse me for a moment, Lord Caversham.

LADY CHILTERN. I may come with you, Robert, may I not?

SIR ROBERT CHILTERN. Yes, Gertrude.

[*Lady Chiltern goes out with him.*]

LORD CAVERSHAM. What is the matter with this family? Something wrong here, eh? [*Tapping his forehead.*] Idiocy? Hereditary, I suppose. Both of them, too. Wife as well as husband. Very sad. Very sad indeed! And they are not an old family. Can't understand it.

LORD GORING. It is not idiocy, father, I assure you.

LORD CAVERSHAM. What is it then, sir?

LORD GORING [*After some hesitation.*] Well, it is what is called nowadays a high moral tone, father. That is all.

LORD CAVERSHAM. Hate these new-fangled names. Same thing as we used to call idiocy fifty years ago. Shan't stay in this house any longer.

LORD GORING [*Taking his arm.*] Oh! just go in here for a moment, father. Third palm tree to the left, the usual palm tree.

LORD CAVERSHAM. What, sir?

LORD GORING. I beg your pardon, father, I forgot. The conservatory, father, the conservatory—there is some one there I want you to talk to.

LORD CAVERSHAM. What about, sir?

LORD GORING. About me, father.

LORD CAVERSHAM [*Grimly.*] Not a subject on which much eloquence is possible.

LORD GORING. No, father; but the lady is like me. She doesn't care much for eloquence in others. She thinks it a little loud.

[*Lord Caversham goes into the conservatory. Lady Chiltern enters.*]

LORD GORING. Lady Chiltern, why are you playing Mrs Cheveley's cards?

LADY CHILTERN [*Startled.*] I don't understand you.

LORD GORING. Mrs Cheveley made an attempt to ruin your husband. Either to drive him from public life, or to make him adopt a dishonourable position. From the latter tragedy you saved him. The former you are now thrusting on him. Why should you do him the wrong Mrs Cheveley tried to do and failed?

LADY CHILTERN. Lord Goring?

LORD GORING [*Pulling himself together for a great effort, and showing the philosopher that underlies the dandy.*] Lady Chiltern, allow me. You wrote me a letter last night in which you said you trusted me and wanted my help. Now is the moment when you really want my help, now is the time when you have got to trust me, to trust in my counsel and judgment. You love Robert. Do you want to kill his love for you? What sort of existence will he have if you rob him of the fruits of his ambition, if you take him from the splendour of a great political career, if you close the doors of public life against him, if you condemn him to sterile failure, he who was made for triumph and success? Women are not meant to judge us, but to forgive us when we need forgiveness. Pardon, not punishment, is their mission. Why should you scourge him with rods for a sin done in his youth, before he knew you, before he knew himself? A man's life is of more value than a woman's. It has larger issues, wider scope, greater ambitions. A woman's life revolves in curves of emotions. It is upon lines of intellect that a man's life progresses. Don't make any terrible mistake, Lady Chiltern. A woman who can keep a man's love, and love him in return, has done all the world wants of women, or should want of them.

LADY CHILTERN [*Troubled and hesitating.*] But it is my husband himself who wishes to retire from public life. He feels it is his duty. It was he who first said so.

LORD GORING. Rather than lose your love, Robert would do anything, wreck his whole career, as he is on the brink of doing now. He is making for you a terrible sacrifice. Take my advice, Lady Chiltern, and do not accept a sacrifice so great. If you do, you will live to repent it bitterly. We men and women are not made to accept such sacrifices from each other. We are not worthy of them. Besides, Robert has been punished enough.

LADY CHILTERN. We have both been punished. I set him up too high.

LORD GORING [*With deep feeling in his voice.*] Do not for that reason set him down now too low. If he has fallen from his altar, do not thrust him into the mire. Failure to Robert would be the very mire of shame. Power is his passion. He would lose everything, even his power to feel love. Your husband's life is at this moment in your hands, your husband's love is in your hands. Don't mar both for him.

[*Enter Sir Robert Chiltern.*]

SIR ROBERT CHILTERN. Gertrude, here is the draft of my letter. Shall I read it to you?

LADY CHILTERN. Let me see it.

[*Sir Robert hands her the letter. She reads it, and then, with a gesture of passion, tears it up.*]

SIR ROBERT CHILTERN. What are you doing?

LADY CHILTERN. A man's life is of more value than a woman's. It has larger issues, wider scope, greater ambitions. Our lives revolve in curves of emotions. It is upon lines of intellect that a man's life progresses. I have just learnt this, and much else with it, from Lord Goring. And I will not spoil your life for you, nor see you spoil it as a sacrifice to me, a useless sacrifice!

SIR ROBERT CHILTERN. Gertrude! Gertrude!

LADY CHILTERN. You can forget. Men easily forget. And I forgive. That is how women help the world. I see that now.

SIR ROBERT CHILTERN [*Deeply overcome by emotion, embraces her.*] My wife! my wife! [*To Lord Goring.*] Arthur, it seems that I am always to be in your debt.

LORD GORING. Oh dear no, Robert. Your debt is to Lady Chiltern, not to me!

SIR ROBERT CHILTERN. I owe you much. And now tell me what you were going to ask me just now as Lord Caversham came in.

LORD GORING. Robert, you are your sister's guardian, and I want your consent to my marriage with her. That is all.

LADY CHILTERN. Oh, I am so glad! I am so glad! [*Shakes hands with Lord Goring.*]

LORD GORING. Thank you, Lady Chiltern.

SIR ROBERT CHILTERN [*With a troubled look.*] My sister to be your wife?

LORD GORING. Yes.

SIR ROBERT CHILTERN [*Speaking with great firmness.*] Arthur, I am very sorry, but the thing is quite out of the question. I have to think of Mabel's future happiness. And I don't think her happiness would be safe in your hands. And I cannot have her sacrificed!

LORD GORING. Sacrificed!

SIR ROBERT CHILTERN. Yes, utterly sacrificed. Loveless marriages are horrible. But there is one thing worse than an absolutely loveless marriage. A marriage in which there is love, but on one side only; faith, but on one side only; devotion, but on one side only, and in which of the two hearts one is sure to be broken.

LORD GORING. But I love Mabel. No other woman has any place in my life.

LADY CHILTERN. Robert, if they love each other, why should they not be married?

SIR ROBERT CHILTERN. Arthur cannot bring Mabel the love that she deserves.

LORD GORING. What reason have you for saying that?

SIR ROBERT CHILTERN [*After a pause.*] Do you really require me to tell you?

LORD GORING. Certainly I do.

SIR ROBERT CHILTERN. As you choose. When I called on you yesterday evening I found Mrs Cheveley concealed in your rooms. It was between ten and eleven o'clock at night. I do not wish to say anything more. Your relations with Mrs Cheveley have, as I said to you last night, nothing whatsoever to do with me. I know you were engaged to be married to her once. The fascination she exercised over you then seems to have returned. You spoke to me last night of her as of a woman pure and stainless, a woman whom you respected and honoured. That may be so. But I cannot give my sister's life into your hands. It would be wrong of me. It would be unjust, infamously unjust to her.

LORD GORING. I have nothing more to say.

LADY CHILTERN. Robert, it was not Mrs Cheveley whom Lord Goring expected last night.

SIR ROBERT CHILTERN. Not Mrs Cheveley! Who was it then?

LORD GORING. Lady Chiltern!

LADY CHILTERN. It was your own wife. Robert, yesterday afternoon Lord Goring told me that if ever I was in trouble I could come to him for help, as he was our oldest and best friend. Later on, after that terrible scene in this room, I wrote to him telling him that I trusted him, that I had need of him, that I was coming to him for help and advice. [*Sir Robert Chiltern takes the letter out of his pocket.*] Yes, that letter. I didn't go to Lord Goring's, after all. I felt that it is from ourselves alone that help can come. Pride made me think that. Mrs Cheveley went. She stole my letter and sent it anonymously to you this morning, that you should think . . . Oh! Robert, I cannot tell you what she wished you to think. . . .

SIR ROBERT CHILTERN. What! Had I fallen so low in your eyes that you thought that even for a moment I could have doubted your goodness? Gertrude, Gertrude, you are to me the white image of all good things, and sin can never touch you. Arthur, you can go to Mabel, and you have my best wishes! Oh! stop a moment. There is no name at the beginning of this letter. The brilliant Mrs Cheveley does not seem to have noticed that. There should be a name.

LADY CHILTERN. Let me write yours. It is you I trust and need. You and none else.

LORD GORING. Well, really, Lady Chiltern, I think I should have back my own letter.

LADY CHILTERN [*Smiling.*] No; you shall have Mabel. [*Takes the letter and writes her husband's name on it.*]

LORD GORING. Well, I hope she hasn't changed her mind. It's nearly twenty minutes since I saw her last.

[*Enter Mabel Chiltern and Lord Caversham.*]

MABEL CHILTERN. Lord Goring, I think your father's conversation much more improving than yours. I am only going to talk to Lord Caversham in the future, and always under the usual palm tree.

LORD GORING. Darling! [*Kisses her.*]

LORD CAVERSHAM [*Considerably taken aback.*] What does this mean, sir? You don't mean to say that this charming, clever young lady, has been so foolish as to accept you?

LORD GORING. Certainly, father! And Chiltern's been wise enough to accept the seat in the Cabinet.

LORD CAVERSHAM. I am very glad to hear that, Chiltern . . . I congratulate you, sir. If the country doesn't go to the dogs or the Radicals, we shall have you Prime Minister, some day.

[*Enter Mason.*]

MASON. Luncheon is on the table, my Lady!

[*Mason goes out.*]

LADY CHILTERN. You'll stop to luncheon, Lord Caversham, won't you?

LORD CAVERSHAM. With pleasure, and I'll drive you down to Downing Street afterwards, Chiltern. You have a great future before you, a great future. Wish I could say the same for you, sir. [*To Lord Goring.*] But your career will have to be entirely domestic.

LORD GORING. Yes, father, I prefer it domestic.

LORD CAVERSHAM. And if you don't make this young lady an ideal husband, I'll cut you off with a shilling.

MABEL CHILTERN. An ideal husband! Oh, I don't think I should like that. It sounds like something in the next world.

LORD CAVERSHAM. What do you want him to be then, dear?

MABEL CHILTERN. He can be what he chooses. All I want is to be . . . to be . . . oh! a real wife to him.

LORD CAVERSHAM. Upon my word, there is a good deal of common sense in that, Lady Chiltern.

[*They all go out except Sir Robert Chiltern. He sinks into a chair, wrapt in thought. After a little time Lady Chiltern returns to look for him.*]

LADY CHILTERN [*Leaning over the back of the chair.*] Aren't you coming in, Robert?

SIR ROBERT CHILTERN [*Taking her hand.*] Gertrude, is it love you feel for me, or is it pity merely?

LADY CHILTERN [*Kisses him.*] It is love, Robert. Love, and only love. For both of us a new life is beginning.

CURTAIN.

THE IMPORTANCE
OF BEING EARNEST
A Trivial Comedy for Serious People

THE PERSONS OF THE PLAY

JOHN WORTHING, J.P.

ALGERNON MONCRIEFF

REV. CANON CHASUBLE, D.D.

MERRIMAN, Butler

LANE,° Manservant

LADY BRACKNELL

HON. GWENDOLEN FAIRFAX°

CECILY CARDEW

MISS PRISM, Governess

THE SCENES OF THE PLAY

ACT I *Algernon Moncrieff's Flat in Half Moon Street, W.*
ACT II *The Garden at the Manor House, Woolton.*
ACT III *Drawing-Room at the Manor House, Woolton.*

Time
The Present.

LONDON: ST JAMES'S THEATRE

Lessee and Manager: Mr George Alexander
February 14th, 1895

JOHN WORTHING, J.P.	*Mr George Alexander*
ALGERNON MONCRIEFF	*Mr Allen Aynesworth*
REV. CANON CHASUBLE, D.D.	*Mr H. H. Vincent*
MERRIMAN (*Butler*)	*Mr Frank Dyall*
LANE (*Manservant*)	*Mr F. Kinsey Peile*
LADY BRACKNELL	*Miss Rose Leclercq*
HON. GWENDOLEN FAIRFAX	*Miss Irene Vanbrugh*
CECILY CARDEW	*Miss Evelyn Millard*
MISS PRISM (*Governess*)	*Mrs George Canninge*

THE IMPORTANCE OF BEING EARNEST

FIRST ACT

SCENE—*Morning-room in Algernon's flat in Half Moon Street. The room is luxuriously and artistically furnished. The sound of a piano is heard in the adjoining room.*

[*Lane is arranging afternoon tea on the table, and after the music has ceased, Algernon enters.*]

ALGERNON. Did you hear what I was playing, Lane?

LANE. I didn't think it polite to listen, sir.

ALGERNON. I'm sorry for that, for your sake. I don't play accurately—anyone can play accurately—but I play with wonderful expression. As far as the piano is concerned, sentiment is my forte. I keep science for Life.

LANE. Yes, sir.

ALGERNON. And, speaking of the science of Life, have you got the cucumber sandwiches cut for Lady Bracknell?

LANE. Yes, sir. [*Hands them on a salver.*]

ALGERNON [*Inspects them, takes two, and sits down on the sofa.*] Oh! . . . by the way, Lane, I see from your book that on Thursday night, when Lord Shoreham and Mr Worthing were dining with me, eight bottles of champagne are entered as having been consumed.

LANE. Yes, sir; eight bottles and a pint.

ALGERNON. Why is it that at a bachelor's establishment the servants invariably drink the champagne? I ask merely for information.

LANE. I attribute it to the superior quality of the wine, sir. I have often observed that in married households the champagne is rarely of a first-rate brand.

ALGERNON. Good Heavens! Is marriage so demoralizing as that?

LANE. I believe it *is* a very pleasant state, sir. I have had very little experience of it myself up to the present. I have only been married once. That was in consequence of a misunderstanding between myself and a young person.

ALGERNON [*Languidly.*] I don't know that I am much interested in your family life, Lane.

LANE. No, sir; it is not a very interesting subject. I never think of it myself.

ALGERNON. Very natural, I am sure. That will do, Lane, thank you.

LANE. Thank you, sir.

[*Lane goes out.*]

ALGERNON. Lane's views on marriage seem somewhat lax. Really, if the lower orders don't set us a good example, what on earth is the use of them? They seem, as a class, to have absolutely no sense of moral responsibility.

[*Enter Lane.*]

LANE. Mr Ernest Worthing.

[*Enter Jack.*]

[*Lane goes out.*]

ALGERNON. How are you, my dear Ernest? What brings you up to town?

JACK. Oh, pleasure, pleasure! What else should bring one anywhere? Eating as usual, I see, Algy!

ALGERNON [*Stiffly.*] I believe it is customary in good society to take some slight refreshment at five o'clock. Where have you been since last Thursday?

JACK [*Sitting down on the sofa.*] In the country.

ALGERNON. What on earth do you do there?

JACK [*Pulling off his gloves.*] When one is in town one amuses oneself. When one is in the country one amuses other people. It is excessively boring.

ALGERNON. And who are the people you amuse?

JACK [*Airily.*] Oh, neighbours, neighbours.

ALGERNON. Got nice neighbours in your part of Shropshire?

JACK. Perfectly horrid! Never speak to one of them.

ALGERNON. How immensely you must amuse them! [*Goes over and takes sandwich.*] By the way, Shropshire is your county, is it not?

JACK. Eh? Shropshire? Yes, of course. Hallo! Why all these cups? Why cucumber sandwiches? Why such reckless extravagance in one so young? Who is coming to tea?

ALGERNON. Oh! merely Aunt Augusta and Gwendolen.

JACK. How perfectly delightful!

ALGERNON. Yes, that is all very well; but I am afraid Aunt Augusta won't quite approve of your being here.

JACK. May I ask why?

ALGERNON. My dear fellow, the way you flirt with Gwendolen is perfectly disgraceful. It is almost as bad as the way Gwendolen flirts with you.

JACK. I am in love with Gwendolen. I have come up to town expressly to propose to her.

ALGERNON. I thought you had come up for pleasure? . . . I call that business.

JACK. How utterly unromantic you are!

ALGERNON. I really don't see anything romantic in proposing. It is very romantic to be in love. But there is nothing romantic about a definite proposal. Why, one may be accepted. One usually is, I believe. Then the excitement is all over. The very essence of romance is uncertainty. If ever I get married, I'll certainly try to forget the fact.

JACK. I have no doubt about that, dear Algy. The Divorce Court° was specially invented for people whose memories are so curiously constituted.

ALGERNON. Oh! there is no use speculating on that subject. Divorces are made in Heaven——[*Jack puts out his hand to take a sandwich. Algernon at once interferes.*] Please don't touch the cucumber sandwiches. They are ordered specially for Aunt Augusta. [*Takes one and eats it.*]

JACK. Well, you have been eating them all the time.

ALGERNON. That is quite a different matter. She is my aunt. [*Takes plate from below.*] Have some bread and butter. The bread and butter is for Gwendolen. Gwendolen is devoted to bread and butter.

JACK [*Advancing to table and helping himself.*] And very good bread and butter it is too.

ALGERNON. Well, my dear fellow, you need not eat as if you were going to eat it all. You behave as if you were married to her already. You are not married to her already, and I don't think you ever will be.

JACK. Why on earth do you say that?

ALGERNON. Well, in the first place girls never marry the men they flirt with. Girls don't think it right.

JACK. Oh, that is nonsense!

ALGERNON. It isn't. It is a great truth. It accounts for the extraordinary number of bachelors that one sees all over the place. In the second place, I don't give my consent.

JACK. Your consent!

ALGERNON. My dear fellow, Gwendolen is my first cousin. And before I allow you to marry her, you will have to clear up the whole question of Cecily. [*Rings bell*.]

JACK. Cecily! What on earth do you mean? What do you mean, Algy, by Cecily? I don't know anyone of the name of Cecily.

[*Enter Lane*.]

ALGERNON. Bring me that cigarette case Mr Worthing left in the smoking-room the last time he dined here.

LANE. Yes, sir.

[*Lane goes out.*]

JACK. Do you mean to say you have had my cigarette case all this time? I wish to goodness you had let me know. I have been writing frantic letters to Scotland Yard° about it. I was very nearly offering a large reward.

ALGERNON. Well, I wish you would offer one. I happen to be more than usually hard up.

JACK. There is no good offering a large reward now that the thing is found.

[*Enter Lane with the cigarette case on a salver. Algernon takes it at once. Lane goes out.*]

ALGERNON. I think that is rather mean of you, Ernest, I must say. [*Opens case and examines it.*] However, it makes no matter, for, now that I look at the inscription inside, I find that the thing isn't yours after all.

JACK. Of course it's mine. [*Moving to him.*] You have seen me with it a hundred times, and you have no right whatsoever to read what is written inside. It is a very ungentlemanly thing to read a private cigarette case.

ALGERNON. Oh! it is absurd to have a hard-and-fast rule about what one should read and what one shouldn't. More than half of modern culture depends on what one shouldn't read.

JACK. I am quite aware of the fact, and I don't propose to discuss modern culture. It isn't the sort of thing one should talk of in private. I simply want my cigarette case back.

ALGERNON. Yes; but this isn't your cigarette case. This cigarette case is a present from someone of the name of Cecily, and you said you didn't know anyone of that name.

JACK. Well, if you want to know, Cecily happens to be my aunt.

ALGERNON. Your aunt!

JACK. Yes. Charming old lady she is, too. Lives at Tunbridge Wells.° Just give it back to me, Algy.

ALGERNON [*Retreating to back of sofa.*] But why does she call herself little Cecily if she is your aunt and lives at Tunbridge Wells? [*Reading.*] 'From little Cecily with her fondest love'.

JACK [*Moving to sofa and kneeling upon it.*] My dear fellow, what on earth is there in that? Some aunts are tall, some aunts are not tall. That is a matter that surely an aunt may be allowed to decide for herself. You seem to think that every aunt should be exactly like your aunt! That is absurd! For Heaven's sake give me back my cigarette case. [*Follows Algernon round the room.*]

ALGERNON. Yes. But why does your aunt call you her uncle? 'From little Cecily, with her fondest love to her dear Uncle Jack.' There is no objection, I admit, to an aunt being a small aunt, but why an aunt, no matter what her size may be, should call her own nephew her uncle, I can't quite make out. Besides, your name isn't Jack at all; it is Ernest.

JACK. It isn't Ernest; it's Jack.

ALGERNON. You have always told me it was Ernest. I have introduced you to everyone as Ernest. You answer to the name of Ernest. You look as if your name was Ernest. You are the most earnest looking person I ever saw in my life. It is perfectly absurd your saying that your name isn't Ernest. It's on your cards. Here is one of them. [*Taking it from case.*] 'Mr Ernest Worthing, B. 4, The Albany.'° I'll keep this as a proof that your name is Ernest if ever you attempt to deny it to me, or to Gwendolen, or to anyone else. [*Puts the card in his pocket.*]

JACK. Well, my name is Ernest in town and Jack in the country, and the cigarette case was given to me in the country.

ALGERNON. Yes, but that does not account for the fact that your small Aunt Cecily, who lives at Tunbridge Wells, calls you her dear uncle. Come, old boy, you had much better have the thing out at once.

JACK. My dear Algy, you talk exactly as if you were a dentist. It is very vulgar to talk like a dentist when one isn't a dentist. It produces a false impression.

ALGERNON. Well, that is exactly what dentists always do. Now, go on! Tell me the whole thing. I may mention that I have always suspected you of being a confirmed and secret Bunburyist,° and I am quite sure of it now.

JACK. Bunburyist? What on earth do you mean by a Bunburyist?

ALGERNON. I'll reveal to you the meaning of that incomparable expression as soon as you are kind enough to inform me why you are Ernest in town and Jack in the country.

JACK. Well, produce my cigarette case first.

ALGERNON. Here it is. [*Hands cigarette case.*] Now produce your explanation, and pray make it improbable. [*Sits on sofa.*]

JACK. My dear fellow, there is nothing improbable about my explanation at all. In fact it's perfectly ordinary. Old Mr Thomas Cardew, who adopted me when I was a little boy, made me in his will guardian to his grand-daughter, Miss Cecily Cardew. Cecily who addresses me as her uncle from motives of respect that you could not possibly appreciate, lives at my place in the country under the charge of her admirable governess, Miss Prism.

ALGERNON. Where is that place in the country, by the way?

JACK. That is nothing to you, dear boy. You are not going to be invited. . . . I may tell you candidly that the place is not in Shropshire.

ALGERNON. I suspected that, my dear fellow! I have Bunburyed all over Shropshire on two separate occasions. Now, go on. Why are you Ernest in town and Jack in the country?

JACK. My dear Algy, I don't know whether you will be able to understand my real motives. You are hardly serious enough. When one is placed in the position of guardian, one has to adopt a very high moral tone on all subjects. It's one's duty to do so. And as a high moral tone can hardly be said to conduce very much to either one's health or one's happiness, in order to get up to town I have always pretended to have a younger brother of the name of Ernest, who lives in the Albany, and gets into the most dreadful scrapes. That, my dear Algy, is the whole truth pure and simple.

ALGERNON. The truth is rarely pure and never simple. Modern life would be very tedious if it were either, and modern literature a complete impossibility!

JACK. That wouldn't be at all a bad thing.

ALGERNON. Literary criticism is not your forte, my dear fellow. Don't try it. You should leave that to people who haven't been at a University. They do it so well in the daily papers. What you really are is a Bunburyist. I was quite right in saying you were a Bunburyist. You are one of the most advanced Bunburyists I know.

JACK. What on earth do you mean?

ALGERNON. You have invented a very useful younger brother called Ernest, in order that you may be able to come up to town as often as you like. I have invented an invaluable permanent invalid called Bunbury, in order that I may be able to go down into the country whenever I choose. Bunbury is perfectly invaluable. If it wasn't for Bunbury's extraordinary bad health, for instance, I wouldn't be able to dine with you at Willis's° tonight, for I have been really engaged to Aunt Augusta for more than a week.

JACK. I haven't asked you to dine with me anywhere tonight.

ALGERNON. I know. You are absurdly careless about sending out invitations. It is very foolish of you. Nothing annoys people so much as not receiving invitations.

JACK. You had much better dine with your Aunt Augusta.

ALGERNON. I haven't the smallest intention of doing anything of the kind. To begin with, I dined there on Monday, and once a week is quite enough to dine with one's own relations. In the second place, whenever I do dine there I am always treated as a member of the family, and sent down° with either no woman at all, or two. In the third place, I know perfectly well whom she will place me next to, tonight. She will place me next Mary Farquhar, who always flirts with her own husband across the dinner-table. That is not very pleasant. Indeed, it is not even decent . . . and that sort of thing is enormously on the increase. The amount of women in London who flirt with their own husbands is perfectly scandalous. It looks so bad. It is simply washing one's clean linen in public. Besides, now that I know you to be a confirmed Bunburyist I naturally want to talk to you about Bunburying. I want to tell you the rules.

JACK. I'm not a Bunburyist at all. If Gwendolen accepts me, I am going to kill my brother, indeed I think I'll kill him in any case. Cecily is a little too much interested in him. It is rather a bore. So I am going to get rid of Ernest. And I strongly advise you to do the same with Mr . . . with your invalid friend who has the absurd name.

ALGERNON. Nothing will induce me to part with Bunbury, and if you ever get married, which seems to me extremely problematic, you will be very glad to know Bunbury. A man who marries without knowing Bunbury has a very tedious time of it.

JACK. That is nonsense. If I marry a charming girl like Gwendolen, and she is the only girl I ever saw in my life that I would marry, I certainly won't want to know Bunbury.

ALGERNON. Then your wife will. You don't seem to realize, that in married life three is company and two is none.

JACK [*Sententiously.*] That, my dear young friend, is the theory that the corrupt French Drama° has been propounding for the last fifty years.

ALGERNON. Yes; and that the happy English home has proved in half the time.

JACK. For heaven's sake, don't try to be cynical. It's perfectly easy to be cynical.

ALGERNON. My dear fellow, it isn't easy to be anything nowadays. There's such a lot of beastly competition about. [*The sound of an electric bell is heard.*] Ah! that must be Aunt Augusta. Only relatives, or creditors, ever ring in that Wagnerian manner.° Now, if I get her out of the way for ten minutes, so that you can have an opportunity for proposing to Gwendolen, may I dine with you tonight at Willis's?

JACK. I suppose so, if you want to.

ALGERNON. Yes, but you must be serious about it. I hate people who are not serious about meals. It is so shallow of them.

[*Enter Lane.*]

LANE. Lady Bracknell and Miss Fairfax.

[*Algernon goes forward to meet them. Enter Lady Bracknell and Gwendolen.*]

LADY BRACKNELL. Good afternoon, dear Algernon, I hope you are behaving very well.

ALGERNON. I'm feeling very well, Aunt Augusta.

LADY BRACKNELL. That's not quite the same thing. In fact the two things rarely go together. [*Sees Jack and bows to him with icy coldness.*]

ALGERNON [*To Gwendolen.*] Dear me, you are smart!

GWENDOLEN. I am always smart! Aren't I, Mr Worthing?

JACK. You're quite perfect, Miss Fairfax.

GWENDOLEN. Oh! I hope I am not that. It would leave no room for developments, and I intend to develop in many directions. [*Gwendolen and Jack sit down together in the corner.*]

LADY BRACKNELL. I'm sorry if we are a little late, Algernon, but I was obliged to call on dear Lady Harbury. I hadn't been there since her poor husband's death. I never saw a woman so altered; she looks quite twenty years younger. And now I'll have a cup of tea, and one of those nice cucumber sandwiches you promised me.

ALGERNON. Certainly, Aunt Augusta. [*Goes over to tea-table.*]

LADY BRACKNELL. Won't you come and sit here, Gwendolen?

GWENDOLEN. Thanks, mamma, I'm quite comfortable where I am.

ALGERNON [*Picking up empty plate in horror.*] Good heavens! Lane! Why are there no cucumber sandwiches? I ordered them specially.

LANE [*Gravely.*] There were no cucumbers in the market this morning, sir. I went down twice.

ALGERNON. No cucumbers!

LANE. No, sir. Not even for ready money.

ALGERNON. That will do, Lane, thank you.

LANE. Thank you, sir.

[*Goes out.*]

ALGERNON. I am greatly distressed, Aunt Augusta, about there being no cucumbers, not even for ready money.

LADY BRACKNELL. It really makes no matter, Algernon. I had some crumpets with Lady Harbury, who seems to me to be living entirely for pleasure now.

ALGERNON. I hear her hair has turned quite gold from grief.°

LADY BRACKNELL. It certainly has changed its colour. From what cause I, of course, cannot say. [*Algernon crosses and hands tea.*] Thank you. I've quite a treat for you tonight, Algernon. I am going to send you down with Mary Farquhar. She is such a nice woman, and so attentive to her husband. It's delightful to watch them.

ALGERNON. I am afraid, Aunt Augusta, I shall have to give up the pleasure of dining with you tonight after all.

LADY BRACKNELL [*Frowning.*] I hope not, Algernon. It would put my table completely out. Your uncle would have to dine upstairs. Fortunately he is accustomed to that.

ALGERNON. It is a great bore, and, I need hardly say, a terrible disappointment to me, but the fact is I have just had a telegram to say that my poor friend Bunbury is very ill again. [*Exchanges glances with Jack.*] They seem to think I should be with him.

LADY BRACKNELL. It is very strange. This Mr Bunbury seems to suffer from curiously bad health.

ALGERNON. Yes; poor Bunbury is a dreadful invalid.

LADY BRACKNELL. Well, I must say, Algernon, that I think it is high time that Mr Bunbury made up his mind whether he was going to live or to die. This shilly-shallying with the question is absurd. Nor do I in any way approve of the modern sympathy with invalids. I consider it morbid. Illness of any kind is hardly a thing to be encouraged in others. Health is the primary duty of life. I am always telling that to your poor uncle, but he never seems to take much notice . . . as far as any improvement in his ailments goes. I should be much obliged if you would ask Mr Bunbury, from me, to be kind enough not to have a relapse on Saturday, for I rely on you to arrange my music for me. It is my last reception, and one wants something that will encourage conversation, particularly at the end of the season when everyone has practically said whatever they had to say, which, in most cases, was probably not much.

ALGERNON. I'll speak to Bunbury, Aunt Augusta, if he is still conscious, and I think I can promise you he'll be all right by Saturday. Of course the music is a great difficulty. You see, if one plays good music, people don't listen, and if one plays bad music people don't talk. But I'll run over the programme I've drawn out, if you will kindly come into the next room for a moment.

LADY BRACKNELL. Thank you, Algernon. It is very thoughtful of you. [*Rising, and following Algernon.*] I'm sure the programme will be delightful, after a few expurgations. French songs I cannot possibly allow. People always seem to think that they are improper, and either look shocked, which is vulgar, or laugh, which is worse. But German sounds a thoroughly respectable language,° and indeed, I believe is so. Gwendolen, you will accompany me.

GWENDOLEN. Certainly, mamma.

[*Lady Bracknell and Algernon go into the music-room, Gwendolen remains behind.*]

JACK. Charming day it has been, Miss Fairfax.

GWENDOLEN. Pray don't talk to me about the weather, Mr Worthing.

Whenever people talk to me about the weather, I always feel quite certain that they mean something else. And that makes me so nervous.

JACK. I do mean something else.

GWENDOLEN. I thought so. In fact, I am never wrong.

JACK. And I would like to be allowed to take advantage of Lady Bracknell's temporary absence . . .

GWENDOLEN. I would certainly advise you to do so. Mamma has a way of coming back suddenly into a room that I have often had to speak to her about.

JACK [*Nervously*.] Miss Fairfax, ever since I met you I have admired you more than any girl . . . I have ever met since . . . I met you.

GWENDOLEN. Yes, I am quite aware of the fact. And I often wish that in public, at any rate, you had been more demonstrative. For me you have always had an irresistible fascination. Even before I met you I was far from indifferent to you. [*Jack looks at her in amazement.*] We live, as I hope you know, Mr Worthing, in an age of ideals. The fact is constantly mentioned in the more expensive monthly magazines, and has reached the provincial pulpits I am told: and my ideal has always been to love some one of the name of Ernest. There is something in that name that inspires absolute confidence. The moment Algernon first mentioned to me that he had a friend called Ernest, I knew I was destined to love you.

JACK. You really love me, Gwendolen?°

GWENDOLEN. Passionately!

JACK. Darling! You don't know how happy you've made me.

GWENDOLEN. My own Ernest!

JACK. But you don't really mean to say that you couldn't love me if my name wasn't Ernest?

GWENDOLEN. But your name is Ernest.

JACK. Yes, I know it is. But supposing it was something else? Do you mean to say you couldn't love me then?

GWENDOLEN [*Glibly*.] Ah! that is clearly a metaphysical speculation, and like most metaphysical speculations has very little reference at all to the actual facts of real life, as we know them.

JACK. Personally, darling, to speak quite candidly, I don't much care about the name of Ernest . . . I don't think the name suits me at all.

GWENDOLEN. It suits you perfectly. It is a divine name. It has a music of its own. It produces vibrations.

JACK. Well, really, Gwendolen, I must say that I think there are lots of other much nicer names. I think Jack, for instance, a charming name.

GWENDOLEN. Jack? . . . No, there is very little music in the name Jack, if any at all, indeed. It does not thrill. It produces absolutely no vibrations. . . . I have known several Jacks, and they all, without exception, were more than usually plain. Besides, Jack is a notorious domesticity for John! And I pity any woman who is married to a man called John. She would probably never be allowed to know the entrancing pleasure of a single moment's solitude. The only really safe name is Ernest.

JACK. Gwendolen, I must get christened at once—I mean we must get married at once. There is no time to be lost.

GWENDOLEN. Married, Mr Worthing?

JACK [*Astounded.*] Well . . . surely. You know that I love you, and you led me to believe, Miss Fairfax, that you were not absolutely indifferent to me.

GWENDOLEN. I adore you. But you haven't proposed to me yet. Nothing has been said at all about marriage. The subject has not even been touched on.

JACK. Well . . . may I propose to you now?

GWENDOLEN. I think it would be an admirable opportunity. And to spare you any possible disappointment, Mr Worthing, I think it only fair to tell you quite frankly beforehand that I am fully determined to accept you.

JACK. Gwendolen!

GWENDOLEN. Yes, Mr Worthing, what have you got to say to me?

JACK. You know what I have got to say to you.

GWENDOLEN. Yes, but you don't say it.

JACK. Gwendolen, will you marry me? [*Goes on his knees.*]

GWENDOLEN. Of course I will, darling. How long you have been about it! I am afraid you have had very little experience in how to propose.

JACK. My own one, I have never loved anyone in the world but you.

GWENDOLEN. Yes, but men often propose for practice. I know my brother Gerald does. All my girl-friends tell me so. What wonderfully blue eyes you have, Ernest! They are quite, quite, blue. I hope you will always look at me just like that, especially when there are other people present.

[*Enter Lady Bracknell.*]

LADY BRACKNELL. Mr Worthing! Rise, sir, from this semi-recumbent posture. It is most indecorous.

GWENDOLEN. Mamma! [*He tries to rise; she restrains him.*] I must beg you to retire. This is no place for you. Besides, Mr Worthing has not quite finished yet.

LADY BRACKNELL. Finished what, may I ask?

GWENDOLEN. I am engaged to Mr Worthing, mamma. [*They rise together.*]

LADY BRACKNELL. Pardon me, you are not engaged to anyone. When you do become engaged to some one, I, or your father, should his health permit him, will inform you of the fact. An engagement should come on a young girl as a surprise, pleasant or unpleasant, as the case may be. It is hardly a matter that she could be allowed to arrange for herself. . . . And now I have a few questions to put to you, Mr Worthing. While I am making these inquiries, you, Gwendolen, will wait for me below in the carriage.

GWENDOLEN [*Reproachfully.*] Mamma!

GWENDOLEN. In the carriage, Gwendolen! [*Gwendolen goes to the door. She and Jack blow kisses to each other behind Lady Bracknell's back. Lady Bracknell looks vaguely about as if she could not understand what the noise was. Finally turns round.*] Gwendolen, the carriage!

GWENDOLEN. Yes, mamma.

[*Goes out, looking back at Jack.*]

LADY BRACKNELL [*Sitting down.*] You can take a seat, Mr Worthing.

[*Looks in her pocket for note-book and pencil.*]

JACK. Thank you, Lady Bracknell, I prefer standing.

LADY BRACKNELL [*Pencil and note-book in hand.*] I feel bound to tell you that you are not down on my list of eligible young men, although I have the same list as the dear Duchess of Bolton has. We work together, in fact. However, I am quite ready to enter your name, should your answers be what a really affectionate mother requires. Do you smoke?

JACK. Well, yes, I must admit I smoke.

LADY BRACKNELL. I am glad to hear it. A man should always have an occupation of some kind.° There are far too many idle men in London as it is. How old are you?

JACK. Twenty-nine.

LADY BRACKNELL. A very good age to be married at. I have always been of opinion that a man who desires to get married should know either everything or nothing.° Which do you know?

JACK [*After some hesitation.*] I know nothing, Lady Bracknell.

LADY BRACKNELL. I am pleased to hear it. I do not approve of anything that tampers with natural ignorance. Ignorance is like a delicate exotic fruit; touch it and the bloom is gone. The whole theory of modern education is radically unsound. Fortunately in England, at any rate, education produces no effect whatsoever. If it did, it would prove a serious danger to the upper classes, and probably lead to acts of violence in Grosvenor Square. What is your income?

JACK. Between seven and eight thousand a year.

LADY BRACKNELL [*Makes a note in her book.*] In land, or in investments?

JACK. In investments, chiefly.

LADY BRACKNELL. That is satisfactory. What between the duties expected of one during one's lifetime, and the duties exacted from one after one's death, land has ceased to be either a profit or a pleasure. It gives one position, and prevents one from keeping it up. That's all that can be said about land.

JACK. I have a country house with some land, of course, attached to it, about fifteen hundred acres, I believe; but I don't depend on that for my real income. In fact, as far as I can make out, the poachers are the only people who make anything out of it.

LADY BRACKNELL. A country house! How many bedrooms? Well, that point can be cleared up afterwards. You have a town house, I hope? A girl with a simple, unspoiled nature, like Gwendolen, could hardly be expected to reside in the country.

JACK. Well, I own a house in Belgrave Square, but it is let by the year to Lady Bloxham. Of course, I can get it back whenever I like, at six months' notice.

LADY BRACKNELL. Lady Bloxham? I don't know her.

JACK. Oh, she goes about very little. She is a lady considerably advanced in years.

LADY BRACKNELL. Ah, nowadays that is no guarantee of respectability of character. What number in Belgrave Square?

JACK. 149.

LADY BRACKNELL [*Shaking her head.*] The unfashionable side. I thought there was something. However, that could easily be altered.

JACK. Do you mean the fashion, or the side?

LADY BRACKNELL [*Sternly.*] Both, if necessary, I presume. What are your politics?

JACK. Well, I am afraid I really have none. I am a Liberal Unionist.°

LADY BRACKNELL. Oh, they count as Tories. They dine with us. Or come in the evening, at any rate. Now to minor matters. Are your parents living?

JACK. I have lost both my parents.

LADY BRACKNELL. Both? To lose one parent may be regarded as a misfortune—to lose *both* seems like carelessness. Who was your father? He was evidently a man of some wealth. Was he born in what the Radical papers call the purple of commerce, or did he rise from the ranks of the aristocracy?

JACK. I am afraid I really don't know. The fact is, Lady Bracknell, I said I had lost my parents. It would be nearer the truth to say that my parents seem to have lost me . . . I don't actually know who I am by birth. I was . . . well, I was found.

LADY BRACKNELL. Found!

JACK. The late Mr Thomas Cardew, an old gentleman of a very charitable and kindly disposition, found me, and gave me the name of Worthing, because he happened to have a first-class ticket for Worthing in his pocket at the time. Worthing is a place in Sussex. It is a seaside resort.

LADY BRACKNELL. Where did the charitable gentleman who had a first-class ticket for this seaside resort find you?

JACK [*Gravely.*] In a hand-bag.°

LADY BRACKNELL. A hand-bag?

JACK [*Very seriously.*] Yes, Lady Bracknell. I was in a hand-bag—a somewhat large, black leather hand-bag, with handles to it—an ordinary hand-bag in fact.

LADY BRACKNELL. In what locality did this Mr James, or Thomas, Cardew come across this ordinary hand-bag?

JACK. In the cloak-room° at Victoria Station. It was given to him in mistake for his own.

LADY BRACKNELL. The cloak-room at Victoria Station?

JACK. Yes. The Brighton line.

LADY BRACKNELL. The line is immaterial. Mr Worthing, I confess I feel somewhat bewildered by what you have just told me. To be born, or at any rate bred, in a hand-bag, whether it had handles or not, seems to me to display a contempt for the ordinary decencies of family life that reminds one of the worst excesses of the French Revolution. And I presume you know what that unfortunate movement led to? As for the particular locality in which the hand-bag was found, a cloak-room at a railway station might serve to conceal a social indiscretion—has probably, indeed, been used for that purpose before now—but it could hardly be regarded as an assured basis for a recognized position in good society.

JACK. May I ask you then what you would advise me to do? I need hardly say I would do anything in the world to ensure Gwendolen's happiness.

LADY BRACKNELL. I would strongly advise you, Mr Worthing, to try and acquire some relations as soon as possible, and to make a definite effort to produce at any rate one parent, of either sex, before the season is quite over.

JACK. Well, I don't see how I could possibly manage to do that. I can produce the hand-bag at any moment. It is in my dressing-room at home. I really think that should satisfy you, Lady Bracknell.

LADY BRACKNELL. Me, sir! What has it to do with me? You can hardly imagine that I and Lord Bracknell would dream of allowing our only daughter—a girl brought up with the utmost care—to marry into a cloak-room, and form an alliance with a parcel? Good morning, Mr Worthing!

[*Lady Bracknell sweeps out in majestic indignation.*]

JACK. Good morning! [*Algernon, from the other room, strikes up the Wedding March. Jack looks perfectly furious, and goes to the door.*] For goodness' sake don't play that ghastly tune, Algy! How idiotic you are!

[*The music stops, and Algernon enters cheerily.*]

ALGERNON. Didn't it go off all right, old boy? You don't mean to say Gwendolen refused you? I know it is a way she has. She is always refusing people. I think it is most ill-natured of her.

JACK. Oh, Gwendolen is as right as a trivet.° As far as she is concerned, we are engaged. Her mother is perfectly unbearable. Never met such a Gorgon°. . . I don't really know what a Gorgon is like, but I am quite sure that Lady Bracknell is one. In any case, she is a monster, without being a myth, which is rather unfair . . . I beg your pardon, Algy, I suppose I shouldn't talk about your own aunt in that way before you.

ALGERNON. My dear boy, I love hearing my relations abused. It is the only thing that makes me put up with them at all. Relations are simply a tedious pack of people, who haven't got the remotest knowledge of how to live, nor the smallest instinct about when to die.

JACK. Oh, that is nonsense!

ALGERNON. It isn't!

JACK. Well, I won't argue about the matter. You always want to argue about things.

ALGERNON. That is exactly what things were originally made for.

JACK. Upon my word, if I thought that, I'd shoot myself . . . [*A pause.*] You don't think there is any chance of Gwendolen becoming like her mother in about a hundred and fifty years, do you Algy?

ALGERNON. All women become like their mothers. That is their tragedy. No man does. That's his.

JACK. Is that clever?

ALGERNON. It is perfectly phrased! and quite as true as any observation in civilized life should be.

JACK. I am sick to death of cleverness. Everybody is clever nowadays. You can't go anywhere without meeting clever people. The thing has become an absolute public nuisance. I wish to goodness we had a few fools left.

ALGERNON. We have.

JACK. I should extremely like to meet them. What do they talk about?

ALGERNON. The fools? Oh! about the clever people, of course.

JACK. What fools!

ALGERNON. By the way, did you tell Gwendolen the truth about your being Ernest in town, and Jack in the country?

JACK [*In a very patronizing manner.*] My dear fellow, the truth isn't quite the sort of thing one tells to a nice sweet refined girl. What extraordinary ideas you have about the way to behave to a woman!

ALGERNON. The only way to behave to a woman is to make love to her,° if she is pretty, and to someone else if she is plain.

JACK. Oh, that is nonsense.

ALGERNON. What about your brother? What about the profligate Ernest?

JACK. Oh, before the end of the week I shall have got rid of him. I'll say he died in Paris of apoplexy. Lots of people die of apoplexy, quite suddenly, don't they?

ALGERNON. Yes, but it's hereditary, my dear fellow. It's a sort of thing that runs in families. You had much better say a severe chill.

JACK. You are sure a severe chill isn't hereditary, or anything of that kind?

ALGERNON. Of course it isn't!

JACK. Very well, then. My poor brother Ernest is carried off suddenly in Paris, by a severe chill. That gets rid of him.

ALGERNON. But I thought you said that . . . Miss Cardew was a little too much interested in your poor brother Ernest? Won't she feel his loss a good deal?

JACK. Oh, that is all right. Cecily is not a silly romantic girl, I am glad to say. She has got a capital appetite, goes long walks, and pays no attention at all to her lessons.

ALGERNON. I would rather like to see Cecily.

JACK. I will take very good care you never do. She is excessively pretty, and she is only just eighteen.°

ALGERNON. Have you told Gwendolen yet that you have an excessively pretty ward who is only just eighteen?

JACK. Oh! one doesn't blurt these things out to people. Cecily and Gwendolen are perfectly certain to be extremely great friends. I'll bet you anything you like that half an hour after they have met, they will be calling each other sister.

ALGERNON. Women only do that when they have called each other a lot of other things first. Now, my dear boy, if we want to get a good table at Willis's, we really must go and dress. Do you know it is nearly seven?

JACK [Irritably.] Oh! it always is nearly seven.

ALGERNON. Well, I'm hungry.

JACK. I never knew you when you weren't. . . .

ALGERNON. What shall we do after dinner? Go to a theatre?

JACK. Oh no! I loathe listening.

ALGERNON. Well, let us go to the Club?°

JACK. Oh, no! I hate talking.

ALGERNON. Well, we might trot round to the Empire° at ten?

JACK. Oh no! I can't bear looking at things. It is so silly.

ALGERNON. Well, what shall we do?

JACK. Nothing!

ALGERNON. It is awfully hard work doing nothing.° However, I don't
mind hard work where there is no definite object of any kind.

[*Enter Lane.*]

LANE. Miss Fairfax.

[*Enter Gwendolen. Lane goes out.*]

ALGERNON. Gwendolen, upon my word!

GWENDOLEN. Algy, kindly turn your back. I have something very
particular to say to Mr Worthing.

ALGERNON. Really, Gwendolen, I don't think I can allow this at all.

GWENDOLEN. Algy, you always adopt a strictly immoral attitude towards
life. You are not quite old enough to do that.

[*Algernon retires to the fireplace.*]

JACK. My own darling!

GWENDOLEN. Ernest, we may never be married. From the expression on
mamma's face I fear we never shall. Few parents nowadays pay any
regard to what their children say to them. The old-fashioned respect
for the young is fast dying out. Whatever influence I ever had over
mamma, I lost at the age of three. But although she may prevent us
from becoming man and wife, and I may marry someone else, and
marry often,° nothing that she can possibly do can alter my eternal
devotion to you.

JACK. Dear Gwendolen!

GWENDOLEN. The story of your romantic origin, as related to me by
mamma, with unpleasing comments, has naturally stirred the deeper
fibres of my nature. Your Christian name has an irresistible fascination. The simplicity of your character makes you exquisitely incomprehensible to me. Your town address at the Albany I have. What is
your address in the country?

JACK. The Manor House, Woolton, Hertfordshire.

[*Algernon, who has been carefully listening, smiles to himself, and writes the address on his shirt-cuff. Then picks up the Railway Guide.*]

GWENDOLEN. There is a good postal service, I suppose? It may be necessary to do something desperate. That of course will require serious consideration. I will communicate with you daily.

JACK. My own one!

GWENDOLEN. How long do you remain in town?

JACK. Till Monday.

GWENDOLEN. Good! Algy, you may turn round now.

ALGERNON. Thanks, I've turned round already.

GWENDOLEN. You may also ring the bell.

JACK. You will let me see you to your carriage, my own darling?

GWENDOLEN. Certainly.

JACK [*To Lane, who now enters.*] I will see Miss Fairfax out.

LANE. Yes, sir.

[*Jack and Gwendolen go off.*]

[*Lane presents several letters on a salver to Algernon. It is to be surmised that they are bills, as Algernon, after looking at the envelopes, tears them up.*]

ALGERNON. A glass of sherry, Lane.

LANE. Yes, sir.

ALGERNON. Tomorrow, Lane, I'm going Bunburying.

LANE. Yes, sir.

ALGERNON. I shall probably not be back till Monday. You can put up my dress clothes, my smoking jacket, and all the Bunbury suits . . .

LANE. Yes, sir. [*Handing sherry.*]

ALGERNON. I hope tomorrow will be a fine day, Lane.

LANE. It never is, sir.

ALGERNON. Lane, you're a perfect pessimist.

LANE. I do my best to give satisfaction, sir.

[*Enter Jack. Lane goes off.*]

JACK. There's a sensible, intellectual girl! the only girl I ever cared for in my life. [*Algernon is laughing immoderately.*] What on earth are you so amused at?

ALGERNON. Oh, I'm a little anxious about poor Bunbury, that is all.

JACK. If you don't take care, your friend Bunbury will get you into a serious scrape some day.

ALGERNON. I love scrapes. They are the only things that are never serious.

JACK. Oh, that's nonsense, Algy. You never talk anything but nonsense.

ALGERNON. Nobody ever does.

[*Jack looks indignantly at him, and leaves the room. Algernon lights a cigarette, reads his shirt-cuff, and smiles.*]

ACT DROP.

SECOND ACT

SCENE—*Garden at the Manor House. A flight of gray stone steps leads up to the house. The garden, an old-fashioned one, full of roses. Time of year, July. Basket chairs,° and a table covered with books, are set under a large yew tree.*

[*Miss Prism discovered seated at the table. Cecily is at the back watering flowers.*]

MISS PRISM [*Calling.*] Cecily, Cecily! Surely such a utilitarian occupation as the watering of flowers is rather Moulton's duty than yours? Especially at a moment when intellectual pleasures await you. Your German grammar is on the table. Pray open it at page fifteen. We will repeat yesterday's lesson.

CECILY [*Coming over very slowly.*] But I don't like German. It isn't at all a becoming language. I know perfectly well that I look quite plain after my German lesson.

MISS PRISM. Child, you know how anxious your guardian is that you should improve yourself in every way. He laid particular stress on your German, as he was leaving for town yesterday. Indeed, he always lays stress on your German° when he is leaving for town.

CECILY. Dear Uncle Jack is so very serious! Sometimes he is so serious that I think he cannot be quite well.

MISS PRISM [*Drawing herself up.*] Your guardian enjoys the best of health, and his gravity of demeanour is especially to be commended in one so comparatively young as he is. I know no one who has a higher sense of duty and responsibility.

CECILY. I suppose that is why he often looks a little bored when we three are together.

MISS PRISM. Cecily! I am surprised at you. Mr Worthing has many troubles in his life. Idle merriment and triviality would be out of place in his conversation. You must remember his constant anxiety about that unfortunate young man his brother.

CECILY. I wish Uncle Jack would allow that unfortunate young man, his brother, to come down here sometimes. We might have a good influence over him, Miss Prism. I am sure you certainly would. You know German, and geology, and things of that kind influence a man very much. [*Cecily begins to write in her diary.*]

MISS PRISM [*Shaking her head.*] I do not think that even I could produce any effect on a character that according to his own brother's admission is irretrievably weak and vacillating. Indeed I am not sure that I would desire to reclaim him. I am not in favour of this modern mania for turning bad people into good people at a moment's notice. As a man sows so let him reap.° You must put away your diary, Cecily. I really don't see why you should keep a diary at all.

CECILY. I keep a diary in order to enter the wonderful secrets of my life. If I didn't write them down I should probably forget all about them.

MISS PRISM. Memory, my dear Cecily, is the diary that we all carry about with us.

CECILY. Yes, but it usually chronicles the things that have never happened, and couldn't possibly have happened. I believe that Memory is responsible for nearly all the three-volume novels that Mudie sends us.°

MISS PRISM. Do not speak slightingly of the three-volume novel, Cecily. I wrote one myself in earlier days.

CECILY. Did you really, Miss Prism? How wonderfully clever you are! I hope it did not end happily? I don't like novels that end happily. They depress me so much.

MISS PRISM. The good ended happily, and the bad unhappily. That is what Fiction means.

CECILY. I suppose so. But it seems very unfair. And was your novel ever published?

MISS PRISM. Alas! no. The manuscript unfortunately was abandoned. I use the word in the sense of lost or mislaid. To your work, child, these speculations are profitless.

CECILY [*Smiling.*] But I see dear Dr Chasuble coming up through the garden.

MISS PRISM [*Rising and advancing.*] Dr Chasuble! This is indeed a pleasure.

[*Enter Canon Chasuble.*]

CHASUBLE. And how are we this morning? Miss Prism, you are, I trust, well?

CECILY. Miss Prism has just been complaining of a slight headache. I think it would do her so much good to have a short stroll with you in the Park, Dr Chasuble.

MISS PRISM. Cecily, I have not mentioned anything about a headache.

CECILY. No, dear Miss Prism, I know that, but I felt instinctively that you had a headache. Indeed I was thinking about that, and not about my German lesson, when the Rector came in.

CHASUBLE. I hope Cecily, you are not inattentive.

CECILY. Oh, I am afraid I am.

CHASUBLE. That is strange. Were I fortunate enough to be Miss Prism's pupil, I would hang upon her lips. [*Miss Prism glares.*] I spoke metaphorically.—My metaphor was drawn from bees. Ahem! Mr Worthing I suppose, has not returned from town yet?

MISS PRISM. We do not expect him till Monday afternoon.

CHASUBLE. Ah yes, he usually likes to spend his Sunday in London. He is not one of those whose sole aim is enjoyment, as, by all accounts, that unfortunate young man his brother seems to be. But I must not disturb Egeria and her pupil any longer.

MISS PRISM. Egeria? My name is Lætitia,° Doctor.

CHASUBLE [*Bowing.*] A classical allusion merely, drawn from the Pagan authors. I shall see you both no doubt at Evensong?

MISS PRISM. I think, dear Doctor, I will have a stroll with you. I find I have a headache after all, and a walk might do it good.

CHASUBLE. With pleasure, Miss Prism, with pleasure. We might go as far as the schools and back.

MISS PRISM. That would be delightful. Cecily, you will read your Political Economy in my absence. The chapter on the Fall of the Rupee° you may omit. It is somewhat too sensational. Even these metallic problems have their melodramatic side.

[*Goes down the garden with Dr Chasuble.*]

CECILY [*Picks up books and throws them back on table.*] Horrid Political Economy! Horrid Geography! Horrid, horrid German!

[*Enter Merriman with a card on a salver.*]

MERRIMAN. Mr Ernest Worthing has just driven over from the station. He has brought his luggage with him.

CECILY [*Takes the card and reads it.*] 'Mr Ernest Worthing, B. 4 The Albany, W.' Uncle Jack's brother! Did you tell him Mr Worthing was in town?

MERRIMAN. Yes, Miss. He seemed very much disappointed. I mentioned that you and Miss Prism were in the garden. He said he was anxious to speak to you privately for a moment.

CECILY. Ask Mr Ernest Worthing to come here. I suppose you had better talk to the housekeeper about a room for him.

MERRIMAN. Yes, Miss.

[*Merriman goes off.*]

CECILY. I have never met any really wicked person before. I feel rather frightened. I am so afraid he will look just like everyone else.

[*Enter Algernon, very gay and debonnair.*]

He does!

ALGERNON [*Raising his hat.*] You are my little cousin Cecily, I'm sure.

CECILY. You are under some strange mistake. I am not little. In fact, I believe I am more than usually tall for my age. [*Algernon is rather taken aback.*] But I am your cousin Cecily. You, I see from your card, are Uncle Jack's brother, my cousin Ernest, my wicked cousin Ernest.

ALGERNON. Oh! I am not really wicked at all, cousin Cecily. You mustn't think that I am wicked.

CECILY. If you are not, then you have certainly been deceiving us all in a very inexcusable manner. I hope you have not been leading a double life, pretending to be wicked and being really good all the time. That would be hypocrisy.

ALGERNON [*Looks at her in amazement.*] Oh! Of course I have been rather reckless.

CECILY. I am glad to hear it.

ALGERNON. In fact, now you mention the subject, I have been very bad in my own small way.

CECILY.　I don't think you should be so proud of that, although I am sure it must have been very pleasant.

ALGERNON.　It is much pleasanter being here with you.

CECILY.　I can't understand how you are here at all. Uncle Jack won't be back till Monday afternoon.

ALGERNON.　That is a great disappointment. I am obliged to go up by the first train on Monday morning. I have a business appointment that I am anxious . . . to miss.

CECILY.　Couldn't you miss it anywhere but in London?

ALGERNON.　No: the appointment is in London.

CECILY.　Well, I know, of course, how important it is not to keep a business engagement, if one wants to retain any sense of the beauty of life, but still I think you had better wait till Uncle Jack arrives. I know he wants to speak to you about your emigrating.

ALGERNON.　About my what?

CECILY.　Your emigrating. He has gone up to buy your outfit.

ALGERNON.　I certainly wouldn't let Jack buy my outfit. He has no taste in neckties at all.

CECILY.　I don't think you will require neckties. Uncle Jack is sending you to Australia.°

ALGERNON.　Australia! I'd sooner die.

CECILY.　Well, he said at dinner on Wednesday night, that you would have to choose between this world, the next world, and Australia.

ALGERNON.　Oh, well! The accounts I have received of Australia and the next world, are not particularly encouraging. This world is good enough for me, cousin Cecily.

CECILY.　Yes, but are you good enough for it?

ALGERNON.　I'm afraid I'm not that. That is why I want you to reform me. You might make that your mission, if you don't mind, cousin Cecily.

CECILY.　I'm afraid I've no time, this afternoon.

ALGERNON.　Well, would you mind my reforming myself this afternoon?

CECILY.　It is rather Quixotic of you. But I think you should try.

ALGERNON.　I will. I feel better already.

CECILY.　You are looking a little worse.

ALGERNON.　That is because I am hungry.

CECILY. How thoughtless of me. I should have remembered that when one is going to lead an entirely new life, one requires regular and wholesome meals. Won't you come in?

ALGERNON. Thank you. Might I have a buttonhole first? I never have any appetite unless I have a buttonhole first.

CECILY. A Maréchal Niel?° [Picks up scissors.]

ALGERNON. No, I'd sooner have a pink rose.

CECILY. Why? [Cuts a flower.]

ALGERNON. Because you are like a pink rose, Cousin Cecily.

CECILY. I don't think it can be right for you to talk to me like that. Miss Prism never says such things to me.

ALGERNON. Then Miss Prism is a short-sighted old lady. [Cecily puts the rose in his buttonhole.] You are the prettiest girl I ever saw.

CECILY. Miss Prism says that all good looks are a snare.

ALGERNON. They are a snare that every sensible man would like to be caught in.

CECILY. Oh! I don't think I would care to catch a sensible man. I shouldn't know what to talk to him about.

[They pass into the house. Miss Prism and Dr Chasuble return.]

MISS PRISM. You are too much alone, dear Dr Chasuble. You should get married. A misanthrope I can understand—a womanthrope,° never!

CHASUBLE [With a scholar's shudder.] Believe me, I do not deserve so neologistic a phrase. The precept as well as the practice of the Primitive Church° was distinctly against matrimony.

MISS PRISM [Sententiously.] That is obviously the reason why the Primitive Church has not lasted up to the present day. And you do not seem to realize, dear Doctor, that by persistently remaining single, a man converts himself into a permanent public temptation. Men should be more careful; this very celibacy leads weaker vessels astray.

CHASUBLE. But is a man not equally attractive when married?

MISS PRISM. No married man is ever attractive except to his wife.

CHASUBLE. And often, I've been told, not even to her.

MISS PRISM. That depends on the intellectual sympathies of the woman. Maturity can always be depended on. Ripeness can be trusted. Young women are green. [Dr Chasuble starts.] I spoke horticulturally. My metaphor was drawn from fruits. But where is Cecily?

CHASUBLE. Perhaps she followed us to the schools.

[*Enter Jack slowly from the back of the garden. He is dressed in the deepest mourning,° with crape hat-band and black gloves.*]

MISS PRISM. Mr Worthing!

CHASUBLE. Mr Worthing?

MISS PRISM. This is indeed a surprise. We did not look for you till Monday afternoon.

JACK [*Shakes Miss Prism's hand in a tragic manner.*] I have returned sooner than I expected. Dr Chasuble, I hope you are well?

CHASUBLE. Dear Mr Worthing, I trust this garb of woe does not betoken some terrible calamity?

JACK. My brother.

MISS PRISM. More shameful debts and extravagance?

CHASUBLE. Still leading his life of pleasure?

JACK [*Shaking his head.*] Dead!

CHASUBLE. Your brother Ernest dead?

JACK. Quite dead.

MISS PRISM. What a lesson for him! I trust he will profit by it.

CHASUBLE. Mr Worthing, I offer you my sincere condolence. You have at least the consolation of knowing that you were always the most generous and forgiving of brothers.

JACK. Poor Ernest! He had many faults, but it is a sad, sad blow.

CHASUBLE. Very sad indeed. Were you with him at the end?

JACK. No. He died abroad; in Paris, in fact. I had a telegram last night from the manager of the Grand Hotel.°

CHASUBLE. Was the cause of death mentioned?

JACK. A severe chill, it seems.

MISS PRISM. As a man sows, so shall he reap.

CHASUBLE [*Raising his hand.*] Charity, dear Miss Prism, charity! None of us are perfect. I myself am peculiarly susceptible to draughts. Will the interment take place here?

JACK. No. He seemed to have expressed a desire to be buried in Paris.

CHASUBLE. In Paris! [*Shakes his head.*] I fear that hardly points to any very serious state of mind at the last. You would no doubt wish me to make some slight allusion to this tragic domestic affliction next

Sunday. [*Jack presses his hand convulsively.*] My sermon on the meaning of the manna in the wilderness can be adapted to almost any occasion, joyful, or, as in the present case, distressing. [*All sigh.*] I have preached it at harvest celebrations, christenings, confirmations, on days of humiliation and festal days. The last time I delivered it was in the Cathedral, as a charity sermon on behalf of the Society for the Prevention of Discontent among the Upper Orders. The Bishop, who was present, was much struck by some of the analogies I drew.

JACK. Ah! that reminds me, you mentioned christenings I think, Dr Chasuble? I suppose you know how to christen all right? [*Dr Chasuble looks astounded.*] I mean, of course, you are continually christening, aren't you?

MISS PRISM. It is, I regret to say, one of the Rector's most constant duties in this parish. I have often spoken to the poorer classes on the subject. But they don't seem to know what thrift is.

CHASUBLE. But is there any particular infant in whom you are interested, Mr Worthing? Your brother was, I believe, unmarried, was he not?

JACK. Oh, yes.

MISS PRISM [*Bitterly.*] People who live entirely for pleasure usually are.

JACK. But it is not for any child, dear Doctor. I am very fond of children. No! the fact is, I would like to be christened myself, this afternoon, if you have nothing better to do.

CHASUBLE. But surely, Mr Worthing, you have been christened already?

JACK. I don't remember anything about it.

CHASUBLE. But have you any grave doubts on the subject?

JACK. I certainly intend to have. Of course I don't know if the thing would bother you in any way, or if you think I am a little too old now.

CHASUBLE. Not at all. The sprinkling, and, indeed, the immersion of adults is a perfectly canonical practice.°

JACK. Immersion!

CHASUBLE. You need have no apprehensions. Sprinkling is all that is necessary, or indeed I think advisable. Our weather is so changeable. At what hour would you wish the ceremony performed?

JACK. Oh, I might trot round about five if that would suit you.

CHASUBLE. Perfectly, perfectly! In fact I have two similar ceremonies to perform at that time. A case of twins that occurred recently in one of the outlying cottages on your own estate. Poor Jenkins the carter, a most hard-working man.

JACK. Oh! I don't see much fun in being christened along with other babies. It would be childish. Would half-past five do?

CHASUBLE. Admirably! Admirably! [*Takes out watch.*] And now, dear Mr Worthing, I will not intrude any longer into a house of sorrow. I would merely beg you not to be too much bowed down by grief. What seem to us bitter trials are often blessings in disguise.

MISS PRISM. This seems to me a blessing of an extremely obvious kind.

[*Enter Cecily from the house.*]

CECILY. Uncle Jack! Oh, I am pleased to see you back. But what horrid clothes you have got on! Do go and change them.

MISS PRISM. Cecily!

CHASUBLE. My child! my child!

[*Cecily goes towards Jack; he kisses her brow in a melancholy manner.*]

CECILY. What is the matter, Uncle Jack? Do look happy! You look as if you had toothache, and I have got such a surprise for you. Who do you think is in the dining-room? Your brother!

JACK. Who?

CECILY. Your brother Ernest. He arrived about half an hour ago.

JACK. What nonsense! I haven't got a brother.

CECILY. Oh, don't say that. However badly he may have behaved to you in the past he is still your brother. You couldn't be so heartless as to disown him. I'll tell him to come out. And you will shake hands with him, won't you, Uncle Jack?

[*Runs back into the house.*]

CHASUBLE. These are very joyful tidings.

MISS PRISM. After we had all been resigned to his loss, his sudden return seems to me peculiarly distressing.

JACK. My brother is in the dining-room? I don't know what it all means. I think it is perfectly absurd.

[*Enter Algernon and Cecily hand in hand. They come slowly up to Jack.*]

JACK. Good heavens! [*Motions Algernon away.*]

ALGERNON. Brother John, I have come down from town to tell you that I am very sorry for all the trouble I have given you, and that I intend to lead a better life in the future.

[*Jack glares at him and does not take his hand.*]

CECILY. Uncle Jack, you are not going to refuse your own brother's hand?

JACK. Nothing will induce me to take his hand. I think his coming down here disgraceful. He knows perfectly well why.

CECILY. Uncle Jack, do be nice. There is some good in everyone. Ernest has just been telling me about his poor invalid friend Mr Bunbury whom he goes to visit so often. And surely there must be much good in one who is kind to an invalid, and leaves the pleasures of London to sit by a bed of pain.

JACK. Oh! he has been talking about Bunbury has he?

CECILY. Yes, he has told me all about poor Mr Bunbury, and his terrible state of health.

JACK. Bunbury! Well, I won't have him talk to you about Bunbury or about anything else. It is enough to drive one perfectly frantic.

ALGERNON. Of course I admit that the faults were all on my side. But I must say that I think that Brother John's coldness to me is peculiarly painful. I expected a more enthusiastic welcome, especially considering it is the first time I have come here.

CECILY. Uncle Jack, if you don't shake hands with Ernest I will never forgive you.

JACK. Never forgive me?

CECILY. Never, never, never!

JACK. Well, this is the last time I shall ever do it. [*Shakes hands with Algernon and glares.*]

CHASUBLE. It's pleasant, is it not, to see so perfect a reconciliation? I think we might leave the two brothers together.

MISS PRISM. Cecily, you will come with us.

CECILY. Certainly, Miss Prism. My little task of reconciliation is over.

CHASUBLE. You have done a beautiful action today, dear child.

MISS PRISM. We must not be premature in our judgments.

CECILY. I feel very happy.

[*They all go off.*]

JACK. You young scoundrel, Algy, you must get out of this place as soon as possible. I don't allow any Bunburying here.

[*Enter Merriman.*]

MERRIMAN. I have put Mr Ernest's things in the room next to yours, sir. I suppose that is all right?

JACK. What?

MERRIMAN. Mr Ernest's luggage, sir. I have unpacked it and put it in the room next to your own.

JACK. His luggage?

MERRIMAN. Yes, sir. Three portmanteaus, a dressing-case, two hat-boxes, and a large luncheon-basket.

ALGERNON. I am afraid I can't stay more than a week this time.

JACK. Merriman, order the dog-cart° at once. Mr Ernest has been suddenly called back to town.

MERRIMAN. Yes, sir.

[*Goes back into the house.*]

ALGERNON. What a fearful liar you are, Jack. I have not been called back to town at all.

JACK. Yes, you have.

ALGERNON. I haven't heard anyone call me.

JACK. Your duty as a gentleman calls you back.

ALGERNON. My duty as a gentleman has never interfered with my pleasures in the smallest degree.

JACK. I can quite understand that.

ALGERNON. Well, Cecily is a darling.

JACK. You are not to talk of Miss Cardew like that. I don't like it.

ALGERNON. Well, I don't like your clothes. You look perfectly ridiculous in them. Why on earth don't you go up and change? It is perfectly childish to be in deep mourning for a man who is actually staying for a whole week with you in your house as a guest. I call it grotesque.

JACK. You are certainly not staying with me for a whole week as a guest or anything else. You have got to leave . . . by the four-five train.

ALGERNON. I certainly won't leave you so long as you are in mourning. It would be most unfriendly. If I were in mourning you would stay with me, I suppose. I should think it very unkind if you didn't.

JACK. Well, will you go if I change my clothes?

ALGERNON. Yes, if you are not too long. I never saw anybody take so long to dress, and with such little result.

JACK. Well, at any rate, that is better than being always over-dressed as you are.

ALGERNON. If I am occasionally a little over-dressed, I make up for it by being always immensely over-educated.°

JACK. Your vanity is ridiculous, your conduct an outrage, and your presence in my garden utterly absurd. However, you have got to catch the four-five, and I hope you will have a pleasant journey back to town. This Bunburying, as you call it, has not been a great success for you.

[*Goes into the house.*]

ALGERNON. I think it has been a great success. I'm in love with Cecily, and .hat is everything.

[*Enter Cecily at the back of the garden. She picks up the can and begins to water the flowers.*]

But I must see her before I go, and make arrangements for another Bunbury. Ah, there she is.

CECILY. Oh, I merely came back to water the roses. I thought you were with Uncle Jack.

ALGERNON. He's gone to order the dog-cart for me.

CECILY. Oh, is he going to take you for a nice drive?

ALGERNON. He's going to send me away.

CECILY. Then have we got to part?

ALGERNON. I am afraid so. It's a painful parting.

CECILY. It is always painful to part from people whom one has known for a very brief space of time. The absence of old friends one can endure with equanimity. But even a momentary separation from anyone to whom one has just been introduced is almost unbearable.

ALGERNON. Thank you.

[*Enter Merriman.*]

MERRIMAN. The dog-cart is at the door, sir.

[*Algernon looks appealingly at Cecily.*]

CECILY. It can wait, Merriman . . . for . . . five minutes.

MERRIMAN. Yes, Miss.

[*Exit Merriman.*]

ALGERNON. I hope, Cecily, I shall not offend you if I state quite frankly and openly that you seem to me to be in every way the visible personification of absolute perfection.

CECILY. I think your frankness does you great credit, Ernest. If you will allow me I will copy your remarks into my diary. [*Goes over to table and begins writing in diary.*]

ALGERNON. Do you really keep a diary? I'd give anything to look at it. May I?

CECILY. Oh no. [*Puts her hand over it.*] You see, it is simply a very young girl's record of her own thoughts and impressions, and consequently meant for publication. When it appears in volume form I hope you will order a copy. But pray, Ernest, don't stop. I delight in taking down from dictation. I have reached 'absolute perfection'. You can go on. I am quite ready for more.

ALGERNON [*Somewhat taken aback.*] Ahem! Ahem!

CECILY. Oh, don't cough, Ernest. When one is dictating one should speak fluently and not cough. Besides, I don't know how to spell a cough. [*Writes as Algernon speaks.*]

ALGERNON [*Speaking very rapidly.*] Cecily, ever since I first looked upon your wonderful and incomparable beauty, I have dared to love you wildly, passionately, devotedly, hopelessly.°

CECILY. I don't think that you should tell me that you love me wildly, passionately, devotedly, hopelessly. Hopelessly doesn't seem to make much sense, does it?

ALGERNON. Cecily!

[*Enter Merriman.*]

MERRIMAN. The dog-cart is waiting, sir.

ALGERNON. Tell it to come round next week, at the same hour.

MERRIMAN [*Looks at Cecily, who makes no sign.*] Yes, sir.

[*Merriman retires.*]

CECILY. Uncle Jack would be very much annoyed if he knew you were staying on till next week, at the same hour.

ALGERNON. Oh, I don't care about Jack. I don't care for anybody in the whole world but you. I love you, Cecily. You will marry me, won't you?

CECILY. You silly boy! Of course. Why, we have been engaged for the last three months.

ALGERNON. For the last three months?

CECILY. Yes, it will be exactly three months on Thursday.

ALGERNON. But how did we become engaged?

CECILY. Well, ever since dear Uncle Jack first confessed to us that he had a younger brother who was very wicked and bad, you of course have formed the chief topic of conversation between myself and Miss Prism. And of course a man who is much talked about is always very attractive. One feels there must be something in him after all. I daresay it was foolish of me, but I fell in love with you, Ernest.

ALGERNON. Darling! And when was the engagement actually settled?

CECILY. On the 14th of February last. Worn out by your entire ignorance of my existence, I determined to end the matter one way or the other, and after a long struggle with myself I accepted you under this dear old tree here. The next day I bought this little ring in your name, and this is the little bangle with the true lovers' knot I promised you always to wear.

ALGERNON. Did I give you this? It's very pretty, isn't it?

CECILY. Yes, you've wonderfully good taste, Ernest. It's the excuse I've always given for your leading such a bad life. And this is the box in which I keep all your dear letters. [*Kneels at table, opens box, and produces letters tied up with blue ribbon.*]

ALGERNON. My letters! But my own sweet Cecily, I have never written you any letters.

CECILY. You need hardly remind me of that, Ernest. I remember only too well that I was forced to write your letters for you. I wrote always three times a week, and sometimes oftener.

ALGERNON. Oh, do let me read them, Cecily?

CECILY. Oh, I couldn't possibly. They would make you far too conceited. [*Replaces box.*] The three you wrote me after I had broken off the engagement are so beautiful, and so badly spelled, that even now I can hardly read them without crying a little.

ALGERNON. But was our engagement ever broken off?

CECILY. Of course it was. On the 22nd of last March. You can see the entry if you like. [*Shows diary.*] 'Today I broke off my engagement with Ernest. I feel it is better to do so. The weather still continues charming.'

ALGERNON. But why on earth did you break it off? What had I done? I had done nothing at all. Cecily, I am very much hurt indeed to hear you broke it off. Particularly when the weather was so charming.

CECILY. It would hardly have been a really serious engagement if it hadn't been broken off at least once. But I forgave you before the week was out.

ALGERNON [*Crossing to her, and kneeling.*] What a perfect angel you are, Cecily.

CECILY. You dear romantic boy. [*He kisses her, she puts her fingers through his hair.*] I hope your hair curls naturally, does it?

ALGERNON. Yes, darling, with a little help from others.

CECILY. I am so glad.

ALGERNON. You'll never break off our engagement again, Cecily?

CECILY. I don't think I could break it off now that I have actually met you. Besides, of course, there is the question of your name.

ALGERNON. Yes, of course. [*Nervously.*]

CECILY. You must not laugh at me, darling, but it had always been a girlish dream of mine to love some one whose name was Ernest. [*Algernon rises, Cecily also.*] There is something in that name that seems to inspire absolute confidence. I pity any poor married woman whose husband is not called Ernest.

ALGERNON. But, my dear child, do you mean to say you could not love me if I had some other name?

CECILY. But what name?

ALGERNON. Oh, any name you like—Algernon—for instance . . .

CECILY. But I don't like the name of Algernon.

ALGERNON. Well, my own dear, sweet, loving little darling, I really can't see why you should object to the name of Algernon. It is not at all a bad name. In fact, it is rather an aristocratic name. Half of the chaps who get into the Bankruptcy Court are called Algernon. But seriously, Cecily . . . [*Moving to her*] . . . if my name was Algy, couldn't you love me?

CECILY [*Rising.*] I might respect you, Ernest, I might admire your character, but I fear that I should not be able to give you my undivided attention.

ALGERNON. Ahem! Cecily! [*Picking up hat.*] Your Rector here is, I suppose, thoroughly experienced in the practice of all the rites and ceremonials of the Church?

CECILY. Oh yes. Dr Chasuble is a most learned man. He has never written a single book, so you can imagine how much he knows.

ALGERNON. I must see him at once on a most important christening—I mean on most important business.

CECILY. Oh!

ALGERNON. I shan't be away more than half an hour.

CECILY. Considering that we have been engaged since February the 14th, and that I only met you today for the first time, I think it is rather hard that you should leave me for so long a period as half an hour. Couldn't you make it twenty minutes?

ALGERNON. I'll be back in no time.

[*Kisses her and rushes down the garden.*]

CECILY. What an impetuous boy he is! I like his hair so much. I must enter his proposal in my diary.

[*Enter Merriman.*]

MERRIMAN. A Miss Fairfax has just called to see Mr Worthing. On very important business Miss Fairfax states.

CECILY. Isn't Mr Worthing in his library?

MERRIMAN. Mr Worthing went over in the direction of the Rectory some time ago.

CECILY. Pray ask the lady to come out here; Mr Worthing is sure to be back soon. And you can bring tea.

MERRIMAN. Yes, Miss.

[*Goes out.*]

CECILY. Miss Fairfax! I suppose one of the many good elderly women who are associated with Uncle Jack in some of his philanthropic work in London. I don't quite like women who are interested in philanthropic work. I think it is so forward of them.

[*Enter Merriman.*]

MERRIMAN. Miss Fairfax.

[*Enter Gwendolen.*]

[*Exit Merriman.*]

CECILY [*Advancing to meet her.*] Pray let me introduce myself to you. My name is Cecily Cardew.

GWENDOLEN. Cecily Cardew? [*Moving to her and shaking hands.*] What a very sweet name! Something tells me that we are going to be great friends. I like you already more than I can say. My first impressions of people are never wrong.

CECILY. How nice of you to like me so much after we have known each other such a comparatively short time. Pray sit down.

GWENDOLEN [*Still standing up.*] I may call you Cecily, may I not?

CECILY. With pleasure!

GWENDOLEN. And you will always call me Gwendolen, won't you.

CECILY. If you wish.

GWENDOLEN. Then that is all quite settled, is it not?

CECILY. I hope so.

[*A pause. They both sit down together.*]

GWENDOLEN. Perhaps this might be a favourable opportunity for my mentioning who I am. My father is Lord Bracknell. You have never heard of papa, I suppose?

CECILY. I don't think so.

GWENDOLEN. Outside the family circle, papa, I am glad to say, is entirely unknown. I think that is quite as it should be. The home seems to me to be the proper sphere for the man. And certainly once a man begins to neglect his domestic duties he becomes painfully effeminate, does he not? And I don't like that. It makes men so very attractive. Cecily, mamma, whose views on education are remarkably strict, has brought me up to be extremely short-sighted; it is part of her system; so do you mind my looking at you through my glasses?

CECILY. Oh! not at all, Gwendolen. I am very fond of being looked at.

GWENDOLEN [*After examining Cecily carefully through a lorgnette.*] You are here on a short visit I suppose.

CECILY. Oh no! I live here.

GWENDOLEN [*Severely.*] Really? Your mother, no doubt, or some female relative of advanced years, resides here also?

CECILY. Oh no! I have no mother, nor, in fact, any relations.

GWENDOLEN. Indeed?

CECILY. My dear guardian, with the assistance of Miss Prism, has the arduous task of looking after me.

GWENDOLEN. Your guardian?

CECILY. Yes, I am Mr Worthing's ward.

GWENDOLEN. Oh! It is strange he never mentioned to me that he had a ward. How secretive of him! He grows more interesting hourly. I am not sure, however, that the news inspires me with feelings of unmixed delight. [*Rising and going to her.*] I am very fond of you, Cecily; I have liked you ever since I met you! But I am bound to state that now that I know that you are Mr Worthing's ward, I cannot help expressing a wish you were—well just a little older than you seem to be—and not quite so very alluring in appearance. In fact, if I may speak candidly——

CECILY. Pray do! I think that whenever one has anything unpleasant to say, one should always be quite candid.

GWENDOLEN. Well, to speak with perfect candour, Cecily, I wish that you were fully forty-two, and more than usually plain for your age. Ernest has a strong upright nature. He is the very soul of truth and honour. Disloyalty would be as impossible to him as deception. But even men of the noblest possible moral character are extremely susceptible to the influence of the physical charms of others. Modern, no less than Ancient History, supplies us with many most painful examples of what I refer to. If it were not so, indeed, History would be quite unreadable.

CECILY. I beg your pardon, Gwendolen, did you say Ernest?

GWENDOLEN. Yes.

CECILY. Oh, but it is not Mr Ernest Worthing who is my guardian. It is his brother—his elder brother.

GWENDOLEN [*Sitting down again.*] Ernest never mentioned to me that he had a brother.

CECILY. I am sorry to say they have not been on good terms for a long time.

GWENDOLEN. Ah! that accounts for it. And now that I think of it I have never heard any man mention his brother. The subject seems distasteful to most men. Cecily, you have lifted a load from my mind. I was growing almost anxious. It would have been terrible if any cloud had come across a friendship like ours, would it not? Of course you are quite, quite sure that it is not Mr Ernest Worthing who is your guardian?

CECILY. Quite sure. [*A pause.*] In fact, I am going to be his.

GWENDOLEN [*Enquiringly.*] I beg your pardon?

CECILY [*Rather shy and confidingly.*] Dearest Gwendolen, there is no reason why I should make a secret of it to you. Our little county newspaper is sure to chronicle the fact next week. Mr Ernest Worthing and I are engaged to be married.

GWENDOLEN [*Quite politely, rising.*] My darling Cecily, I think there must be some slight error. Mr Ernest Worthing is engaged to me. The announcement will appear in the 'Morning Post'° on Saturday at the latest.

CECILY [*Very politely, rising.*] I am afraid you must be under some misconception. Ernest proposed to me exactly ten minutes ago. [*Shows diary.*]

GWENDOLEN [*Examines diary through her lorgnette carefully.*] It is certainly very curious, for he asked me to be his wife yesterday afternoon at 5.30. If you would care to verify the incident, pray do so. [*Produces diary of her own.*] I never travel without my diary. One should always have something sensational to read in the train. I am so sorry, dear Cecily, if it is any disappointment to you, but I am afraid *I* have the prior claim.

CECILY. It would distress me more than I can tell you, dear Gwendolen, if it caused you any mental or physical anguish, but I feel bound to point out that since Ernest proposed to you he clearly has changed his mind.

GWENDOLEN [*Meditatively.*] If the poor fellow has been entrapped into any foolish promise I shall consider it my duty to rescue him at once, and with a firm hand.

CECILY [*Thoughtfully and sadly.*] Whatever unfortunate entanglement my dear boy may have got into, I will never reproach him with it after we are married.

GWENDOLEN. Do you allude to me, Miss Cardew, as an entanglement? You are presumptuous. On an occasion of this kind it becomes more than a moral duty to speak one's mind. It becomes a pleasure.

CECILY. Do you suggest, Miss Fairfax, that I entrapped Ernest into an engagement? How dare you? This is no time for wearing the shallow mask of manners. When I see a spade I call it a spade.

GWENDOLEN [*Satirically.*] I am glad to say that I have never seen a spade. It is obvious that our social spheres have been widely different.

[*Enter Merriman, followed by the footman. He carries a salver, table cloth, and plate stand. Cecily is about to retort. The presence of the servants exercises a restraining influence, under which both girls chafe.*]

MERRIMAN. Shall I lay tea here as usual, Miss?

CECILY [*Sternly, in a calm voice.*] Yes, as usual.

[*Merriman begins to clear table and lay cloth. A long pause. Cecily and Gwendolen glare at each other.*]

GWENDOLEN. Are there many interesting walks in the vicinity, Miss Cardew?

CECILY. Oh! yes! a great many. From the top of one of the hills quite close one can see five counties.

GWENDOLEN. Five counties! I don't think I should like that. I hate crowds.

CECILY [*Sweetly.*] I suppose that is why you live in town?

[*Gwendolen bites her lip, and beats her foot nervously with her parasol.*]

GWENDOLEN [*Looking round.*] Quite a well-kept garden this is, Miss Cardew,

CECILY. So glad you like it, Miss Fairfax.

GWENDOLEN. I had no idea there were any flowers in the country.

CECILY. Oh, flowers are as common here, Miss Fairfax, as people are in London.

GWENDOLEN. Personally, I cannot understand how anybody manages to exist in the country, if anybody who is anybody does. The country always bores me to death.

CECILY. Ah! This is what the newspapers call agricultural depression,° is it not? I believe the aristocracy are suffering very much from it just at present. It is almost an epidemic amongst them, I have been told. May I offer you some tea, Miss Fairfax?

GWENDOLEN [*With elaborate politeness.*] Thank you. [*Aside.*] Detestable girl! But I require tea!

CECILY [*Sweetly.*] Sugar?

GWENDOLEN [*Superciliously.*] No, thank you. Sugar is not fashionable any more.

[*Cecily looks angrily at her, takes up the tongs and puts four lumps of sugar into the cup.*]

CECILY [*Severely.*] Cake or bread and butter?

GWENDOLEN [*In a bored manner.*] Bread and butter, please. Cake is rarely seen at the best houses nowadays.

CECILY [*Cuts a very large slice of cake, and puts it on the tray.*] Hand that to Miss Fairfax.

[*Merriman does so, and goes out with footman. Gwendolen drinks the tea and makes a grimace. Puts down cup at once, reaches out her hand to the bread and butter, looks at it, and finds it is cake. Rises in indignation.*]

GWENDOLEN. You have filled my tea with lumps of sugar, and though I asked most distinctly for bread and butter, you have given me cake. I am known for the gentleness of my disposition, and the extraordinary sweetness of my nature, but I warn you, Miss Cardew, you may go too far.

CECILY [*Rising.*] To save my poor, innocent, trusting boy from the machinations of any other girl there are no lengths to which I would not go.

GWENDOLEN. From the moment I saw you I distrusted you. I felt that you were false and deceitful. I am never deceived in such matters. My first impressions of people are invariably right.

CECILY. It seems to me, Miss Fairfax, that I am trespassing on your valuable time. No doubt you have many other calls of a similar character to make in the neighbourhood.

[*Enter Jack.*]

GWENDOLEN [*Catching sight of him.*] Ernest! My own Ernest!

JACK. Gwendolen! Darling! [*Offers to kiss her.*]

GWENDOLEN [*Drawing back.*] A moment! May I ask if you are engaged to be married to this young lady? [*Points to Cecily.*]

JACK [*Laughing.*] To dear little Cecily! Of course not! What could have put such an idea into your pretty little head?

GWENDOLEN. Thank you. You may! [*Offers her cheek.*]

CECILY [*Very sweetly.*] I knew there must be some misunderstanding, Miss Fairfax. The gentleman whose arm is at present round your waist is my dear guardian, Mr John Worthing.

GWENDOLEN. I beg your pardon?

CECILY. This is Uncle Jack.

GWENDOLEN [*Receding.*] Jack! Oh!

[*Enter Algernon.*]

CECILY. Here is Ernest.

ALGERNON [*Goes straight over to Cecily without noticing anyone else.*] My own love! [*Offers to kiss her.*]

CECILY [*Drawing back.*] A moment, Ernest! May I ask you—are you engaged to be married to this young lady?

ALGERNON [*Looking round.*] To what young lady? Good heavens! Gwendolen!

CECILY. Yes, to good heavens, Gwendolen, I mean to Gwendolen.

ALGERNON [*Laughing.*] Of course not! What could have put such an idea into your pretty little head?

CECILY. Thank you. [*Presenting her cheek to be kissed.*] You may.

[*Algernon kisses her.*]

GWENDOLEN. I felt there was some slight error, Miss Cardew. The gentleman who is now embracing you is my cousin, Mr Algernon Moncrieff.

CECILY [*Breaking away from Algernon.*] Algernon Moncrieff! Oh!

[*The two girls move towards each other and put their arms round each other's waists as if for protection.*]

CECILY. Are you called Algernon?

ALGERNON. I cannot deny it.

CECILY. Oh!

GWENDOLEN. Is your name really John?

JACK [*Standing rather proudly.*] I could deny it if I liked. I could deny anything if I liked. But my name certainly is John. It has been John for years.

CECILY [*To Gwendolen.*] A gross deception has been practised on both of us.

GWENDOLEN. My poor wounded Cecily!

CECILY. My sweet wronged Gwendolen!

GWENDOLEN [*Slowly and seriously.*] You will call me sister, will you not?

[*They embrace. Jack and Algernon groan and walk up and down.*]

CECILY [*Rather brightly.*] There is just one question I would like to be allowed to ask my guardian.

GWENDOLEN. An admirable idea! Mr Worthing, there is just one question I would like to be permitted to put to you. Where is your brother Ernest? We are both engaged to be married to your brother

Ernest, so it is a matter of some importance to us to know where your brother Ernest is at present.

JACK [*Slowly and hesitatingly.*] Gwendolen—Cecily—it is very painful for me to be forced to speak the truth. It is the first time in my life that I have ever been reduced to such a painful position, and I am really quite inexperienced in doing anything of the kind. However I will tell you quite frankly that I have no brother Ernest. I have no brother at all. I never had a brother in my life, and I certainly have not the smallest intention of ever having one in the future.

CECILY [*Surprised.*] No brother at all?

JACK [*Cheerily.*] None!

GWENDOLEN [*Severely.*] Had you never a brother of any kind?

JACK [*Pleasantly.*] Never. Not even of any kind.

GWENDOLEN. I am afraid it is quite clear, Cecily, that neither of us is engaged to be married to anyone.

CECILY. It is not a very pleasant position for a young girl suddenly to find herself in. Is it?

GWENDOLEN. Let us go into the house. They will hardly venture to come after us there.

CECILY. No, men are so cowardly, aren't they?

[*They retire into the house with scornful looks.*]

JACK. This ghastly state of things is what you call Bunburying, I suppose?

ALGERNON. Yes, and a perfectly wonderful Bunbury it is. The most wonderful Bunbury I have ever had in my life.

JACK. Well, you've no right whatsoever to Bunbury here.

ALGERNON. That is absurd. One has a right to Bunbury anywhere one chooses. Every serious Bunburyist knows that.

JACK. Serious Bunburyist! Good heavens!

ALGERNON. Well, one must be serious about something, if one wants to have any amusement in life. I happen to be serious about Bunburying. What on earth you are serious about I haven't got the remotest idea. About everything, I should fancy. You have such an absolutely trivial nature.

JACK. Well, the only small satisfaction I have in the whole of this wretched business is that your friend Bunbury is quite exploded. You won't be able to run down to the country quite so often as you used to do, dear Algy. And a very good thing too.

ALGERNON. Your brother is a little off colour, isn't he, dear Jack? You won't be able to disappear to London quite so frequently as your wicked custom was. And not a bad thing either.

JACK. As for your conduct towards Miss Cardew, I must say that your taking in a sweet, simple, innocent girl like that is quite inexcusable. To say nothing of the fact that she is my ward.

ALGERNON. I can see no possible defence at all for your deceiving a brilliant, clever, thoroughly experienced young lady like Miss Fairfax. To say nothing of the fact that she is my cousin.

JACK. I wanted to be engaged to Gwendolen, that is all. I love her.

ALGERNON. Well, I simply wanted to be engaged to Cecily. I adore her.

JACK. There is certainly no chance of your marrying Miss Cardew.

ALGERNON. I don't think there is much likelihood, Jack, of you and Miss Fairfax being united.

JACK. Well, that is no business of yours.

ALGERNON. If it was my business, I wouldn't talk about it. [*Begins to eat muffins.*] It is very vulgar to talk about one's business. Only people like stockbrokers do that, and then merely at dinner parties.

JACK. How you can sit there, calmly eating muffins when we are in this horrible trouble, I can't make out. You seem to me to be perfectly heartless.

ALGERNON. Well, I can't eat muffins in an agitated manner. The butter would probably get on my cuffs. One should always eat muffins quite calmly. It is the only way to eat them.

JACK. I say it's perfectly heartless your eating muffins at all, under the circumstances.

ALGERNON. When I am in trouble, eating is the only thing that consoles me. Indeed, when I am in really great trouble, as anyone who knows me intimately will tell you, I refuse everything except food and drink. At the present moment I am eating muffins because I am unhappy. Besides, I am particularly fond of muffins. [*Rising.*]

JACK [*Rising.*] Well, that is no reason why you should eat them all in that greedy way. [*Takes muffins from Algernon.*]

ALGERNON [*Offering tea-cake.*] I wish you would have tea-cake instead. I don't like tea-cake.

JACK. Good heavens! I suppose a man may eat his own muffins in his own garden.

ALGERNON. But you have just said it was perfectly heartless to eat muffins.

JACK. I said it was perfectly heartless of you, under the circumstances. That is a very different thing.

ALGERNON. That may be. But the muffins are the same. [*He seizes the muffin-dish from Jack.*]

JACK. Algy, I wish to goodness you would go.

ALGERNON. You can't possibly ask me to go without having some dinner. It's absurd. I never go without my dinner. No one ever does, except vegetarians and people like that. Besides I have just made arrangements with Dr Chasuble to be christened at a quarter to six under the name of Ernest.

JACK. My dear fellow, the sooner you give up that nonsense the better. I made arrangements this morning with Dr Chasuble to be christened myself at 5.30, and I naturally will take the name of Ernest. Gwendolen would wish it. We can't both be christened Ernest. It's absurd. Besides, I have a perfect right to be christened if I like. There is no evidence at all that I ever have been christened by anybody. I should think it extremely probable I never was, and so does Dr Chasuble. It is entirely different in your case. You have been christened already.

ALGERNON. Yes, but I have not been christened for years.

JACK. Yes, but you have been christened. That is the important thing.

ALGERNON. Quite so. So I know my constitution can stand it. If you are not quite sure about your ever having been christened, I must say I think it rather dangerous your venturing on it now. It might make you very unwell. You can hardly have forgotten that someone very closely connected with you was very nearly carried off this week in Paris by a severe chill.

JACK. Yes, but you said yourself that a severe chill was not hereditary.

ALGERNON. It usen't to be, I know—but I daresay it is now. Science is always making wonderful improvements in things.

JACK [*Picking up the muffin-dish.*] Oh, that is nonsense; you are always talking nonsense.

ALGERNON. Jack, you are at the muffins again! I wish you wouldn't.

There are only two left. [*Takes them.*] I told you I was particularly fond of muffins.

JACK. But I hate tea-cake.

ALGERNON. Why on earth then do you allow tea-cake to be served up for your guests? What ideas you have of hospitality!

JACK. Algernon! I have already told you to go. I don't want you here. Why don't you go!

ALGERNON. I haven't quite finished my tea yet! and there is still one muffin left.

[*Jack groans, and sinks into a chair. Algernon still continues eating.*]

ACT DROP.

THIRD ACT

SCENE—*Morning-room at the Manor House.*

[*Gwendolen and Cecily are at the window, looking out into the garden.*]

GWENDOLEN. The fact that they did not follow us at once into the house, as anyone else would have done, seems to me to show that they have some sense of shame left.

CECILY. They have been eating muffins. That looks like repentance.

GWENDOLEN [*After a pause.*] They don't seem to notice us at all. Couldn't you cough?

CECILY. But I haven't got a cough.

GWENDOLEN. They're looking at us. What effrontery!

CECILY. They're approaching. That's very forward of them.

GWENDOLEN. Let us preserve a dignified silence.

CECILY. Certainly. It's the only thing to do now.

[*Enter Jack followed by Algernon. They whistle some dreadful popular air from a British Opera.*]

GWENDOLEN. This dignified silence seems to produce an unpleasant effect.

CECILY. A most distasteful one.

GWENDOLEN. But we will not be the first to speak.

CECILY. Certainly not.

GWENDOLEN. Mr Worthing, I have something very particular to ask you. Much depends on your reply.

CECILY. Gwendolen, your common sense is invaluable. Mr Moncrieff, kindly answer me the following question. Why did you pretend to be my guardian's brother?

ALGERNON. In order that I might have an opportunity of meeting you.

CECILY [To Gwendolen.] That certainly seems a satisfactory explanation, does it not?

GWENDOLEN. Yes, dear, if you can believe him.

CECILY. I don't. But that does not affect the wonderful beauty of his answer.

GWENDOLEN. True. In matters of grave importance, style, not sincerity° is the vital thing. Mr Worthing, what explanation can you offer to me for pretending to have a brother? Was it in order that you might have an opportunity of coming up to town to see me as often as possible?

JACK. Can you doubt it, Miss Fairfax?

GWENDOLEN. I have the gravest doubts upon the subject. But I intend to crush them. This is not the moment for German scepticism.° [Moving to Cecily.] Their explanations appear to be quite satisfactory, especially Mr Worthing's. That seems to me to have the stamp of truth upon it.

CECILY. I am more than content with what Mr Moncrieff said. His voice alone inspires one with absolute credulity.

GWENDOLEN. Then you think we should forgive them?

CECILY. Yes. I mean no.

GWENDOLEN. True! I had forgotten. There are principles at stake that one cannot surrender. Which of us should tell them? The task is not a pleasant one.

CECILY. Could we not both speak at the same time?

GWENDOLEN. An excellent idea! I nearly always speak at the same time as other people. Will you take the time from me?

CECILY. Certainly.

[Gwendolen beats time with uplifted finger.]

GWENDOLEN and CECILY [Speaking together.] Your Christian names are still an insuperable barrier. That is all!

JACK and ALGERNON [*Speaking together.*] Our Christian names! Is that all? But we are going to be christened this afternoon.

GWENDOLEN [*To Jack.*] For my sake you are prepared to do this terrible thing?

JACK. I am.

CECILY [*To Algernon.*] To please me you are ready to face this fearful ordeal?

ALGERNON. I am!

GWENDOLEN. How absurd to talk of the equality of the sexes! Where questions of self-sacrifice are concerned, men are infinitely beyond us.

JACK. We are. [*Clasps hands with Algernon.*]

CECILY. They have moments of physical courage of which we women know absolutely nothing.

GWENDOLEN [*To Jack.*] Darling!

ALGERNON [*To Cecily.*] Darling! [*They fall into each other's arms.*]

[*Enter Merriman. When he enters he coughs loudly, seeing the situation.*]

MERRIMAN. Ahem! Ahem! Lady Bracknell!

JACK. Good heavens!

[*Enter Lady Bracknell. The couples separate in alarm.*]   [*Exit Merriman.*]

LADY BRACKNELL. Gwendolen! What does this mean?

GWENDOLEN. Merely that I am engaged to be married to Mr Worthing, mamma.

LADY BRACKNELL. Come here. Sit down. Sit down immediately. Hesitation of any kind is a sign of mental decay in the young, of physical weakness in the old. [*Turns to Jack.*] Apprised, sir, of my daughter's sudden flight by her trusty maid, whose confidence I purchased by means of a small coin, I followed her at once by a luggage train.° Her unhappy father is, I am glad to say, under the impression that she is attending a more than usually lengthy lecture by the University Extension Scheme° on the Influence of a permanent income on Thought. I do not propose to undeceive him. Indeed I have never undeceived him on any question. I would consider it wrong. But of course, you will clearly understand that all communication between yourself and my daughter must cease immediately from this moment. On this point, as indeed on all points, I am firm.

JACK. I am engaged to be married to Gwendolen, Lady Bracknell!

528 THE IMPORTANCE OF BEING EARNEST

LADY BRACKNELL. You are nothing of the kind, sir. And now, as regards Algernon! . . . Algernon!

ALGERNON. Yes, Aunt Augusta.

LADY BRACKNELL. May I ask if it is in this house that your invalid friend Mr Bunbury resides?

ALGERNON [*Stammering.*] Oh! No! Bunbury doesn't live here. Bunbury is somewhere else at present. In fact, Bunbury is dead.

LADY BRACKNELL. Dead! When did Mr Bunbury die? His death must have been extremely sudden.

ALGERNON [*Airily.*] Oh! I killed Bunbury this afternoon. I mean poor Bunbury died this afternoon.

LADY BRACKNELL. What did he die of?

ALGERNON. Bunbury? Oh, he was quite exploded.

LADY BRACKNELL. Exploded! Was he the victim of a revolutionary outrage?° I was not aware that Mr Bunbury was interested in social legislation. If so, he is well punished for his morbidity.

ALGERNON. My dear Aunt Augusta, I mean he was found out! The doctors found out that Bunbury could not live, that is what I mean—so Bunbury died.

LADY BRACKNELL. He seems to have had great confidence in the opinion of his physicians. I am glad, however, that he made up his mind at the last to some definite course of action, and acted under proper medical advice. And now that we have finally got rid of this Mr Bunbury, may I ask, Mr Worthing, who is that young person whose hand my nephew Algernon is now holding in what seems to me a peculiarly unnecessary manner?

JACK. That lady is Miss Cecily Cardew, my ward.

[*Lady Bracknell bows coldly to Cecily.*]

ALGERNON. I am engaged to be married to Cecily, Aunt Augusta.

LADY BRACKNELL. I beg your pardon?

CECILY. Mr Moncrieff and I are engaged to be married, Lady Bracknell.

LADY BRACKNELL [*With a shiver, crossing to the sofa and sitting down.*] I do not know whether there is anything peculiarly exciting in the air of this particular part of Hertfordshire, but the number of engagements that go on seems to me considerably above the proper average that statistics have laid down for our guidance. I think some preliminary enquiry on my part would not be out of place. Mr Worthing, is Miss Cardew at all connected with any of the larger railway stations in London? I merely desire information. Until yesterday I had no idea that there were any families or persons whose origin was a Terminus.

[*Jack looks perfectly furious, but restrains himself.*]

JACK [*In a clear, cold voice.*] Miss Cardew is the granddaughter of the late Mr Thomas Cardew of 149, Belgrave Square, S.W.; Gervase Park, Dorking, Surrey; and the Sporran, Fifeshire, N.B.°

LADY BRACKNELL. That sounds not unsatisfactory. Three addresses always inspire confidence, even in tradesmen. But what proof have I of their authenticity?

JACK. I have carefully preserved the Court Guides° of the period. They are open to your inspection, Lady Bracknell.

LADY BRACKNELL [*Grimly.*] I have known strange errors in that publication.

JACK. Miss Cardew's family solicitors are Messrs Markby, Markby, and Markby.

LADY BRACKNELL. Markby, Markby, and Markby? A firm of the very highest position in their profession. Indeed I am told that one of the Mr Markbys is occasionally to be seen at dinner parties. So far I am satisfied.

JACK [*Very irritably.*] How extremely kind of you, Lady Bracknell! I have also in my possession, you will be pleased to hear, certificates of Miss Cardew's birth, baptism, whooping cough, registration, vaccination, confirmation, and the measles; both the German and the English variety.

LADY BRACKNELL. Ah! A life crowded with incident, I see; though perhaps somewhat too exciting for a young girl. I am not myself in favour of premature experiences. [*Rises, looks at her watch.*] Gwendolen! the time approaches for our departure. We have not a moment to lose. As a matter of form, Mr Worthing, I had better ask you if Miss Cardew has any little fortune?

JACK. Oh! about a hundred and thirty thousand pounds in the Funds.° That is all. Goodbye, Lady Bracknell. So pleased to have seen you.

LADY BRACKNELL [*Sitting down again.*] A moment, Mr Worthing. A hundred and thirty thousand pounds! And in the Funds! Miss Cardew seems to me a most attractive young lady, now that I look at her. Few girls of the present day have any really solid qualities, any of the qualities that last, and improve with time. We live, I regret to say, in an age of surfaces. [*To Cecily.*] Come over here, dear. [*Cecily goes across.*] Pretty child! your dress is sadly simple, and your hair seems almost as Nature might have left it. But we can soon alter all that. A thoroughly experienced French maid produces a really marvellous result in a very brief space of time. I remember recommending one to young Lady Lancing, and after three months her own husband did not know her.

JACK [*Aside.*] And after six months nobody knew her.

LADY BRACKNELL [*Glares at Jack for a few moments. Then bends, with a practised smile, to Cecily.*] Kindly turn round, sweet child. [*Cecily turns completely round.*] No, the side view is what I want. [*Cecily presents her profile.*] Yes, quite as I expected. There are distinct social possibilities in your profile. The two weak points in our age are its want of principle and its want of profile. The chin a little higher, dear. Style largely depends on the way the chin is worn. They are worn very high, just at present. Algernon!

ALGERNON. Yes, Aunt Augusta!

LADY BRACKNELL. There are distinct social possibilities in Miss Cardew's profile.

ALGERNON. Cecily is the sweetest, dearest, prettiest girl in the whole world. And I don't care twopence about social possibilities.

LADY BRACKNELL. Never speak disrespectfully of Society, Algernon. Only people who can't get into it do that. [*To Cecily.*] Dear child, of course you know that Algernon has nothing but his debts to depend upon. But I do not approve of mercenary marriages. When I married Lord Bracknell I had no fortune of any kind. But I never dreamed for a moment of allowing that to stand in my way. Well, I suppose I must give my consent.

ALGERNON. Thank you, Aunt Augusta.

LADY BRACKNELL. Cecily, you may kiss me!

CECILY [*Kisses her.*] Thank you, Lady Bracknell.

LADY BRACKNELL. You may also address me as Aunt Augusta for the future.

CECILY. Thank you, Aunt Augusta.

LADY BRACKNELL. The marriage, I think, had better take place quite soon.

ALGERNON. Thank you, Aunt Augusta.

CECILY. Thank you, Aunt Augusta.

LADY BRACKNELL. To speak frankly, I am not in favour of long engagements. They give people the opportunity of finding out each other's character before marriage, which I think is never advisable.

JACK. I beg your pardon for interrupting you, Lady Bracknell, but this engagement is quite out of the question. I am Miss Cardew's guardian, and she cannot marry without my consent until she comes of age. That consent I absolutely decline to give.

LADY BRACKNELL. Upon what grounds may I ask? Algernon is an extremely, I may almost say an ostentatiously, eligible young man. He has nothing, but he looks everything. What more can one desire?

JACK. It pains me very much to have to speak frankly to you, Lady Bracknell, about your nephew, but the fact is that I do not approve at all of his moral character. I suspect him of being untruthful.

[*Algernon and Cecily look at him in indignant amazement.*]

LADY BRACKNELL. Untruthful! My nephew Algernon? Impossible! He is an Oxonian.°

JACK. I fear there can be no possible doubt about the matter. This afternoon, during my temporary absence in London on an important question of romance, he obtained admission to my house by means of the false pretence of being my brother. Under an assumed name he drank, I've just been informed by my butler, an entire pint bottle of my Perrier-Jouet, Brut, '89;° a wine I was specially reserving for myself. Continuing his disgraceful deception, he succeeded in the course of the afternoon in alienating the affections of my only ward. He subsequently stayed to tea, and devoured every single muffin. And what makes his conduct all the more heartless is, that he was perfectly well aware from the first that I have no brother, that I never had a brother, and that I don't intend to have a brother, not even of any kind. I distinctly told him so myself yesterday afternoon.

LADY BRACKNELL. Ahem! Mr Worthing, after careful consideration I have decided entirely to overlook my nephew's conduct to you.

JACK. That is very generous of you, Lady Bracknell. My own decision, however, is unalterable. I decline to give my consent.

LADY BRACKNELL [*To Cecily.*] Come here, sweet child. [*Cecily goes over.*] How old are you, dear?

CECILY. Well, I am really only eighteen, but I always admit to twenty when I go to evening parties.

LADY BRACKNELL. You are perfectly right in making some slight alteration. Indeed, no woman should ever be quite accurate about her age. It looks so calculating. . . . [*In a meditative manner.*] Eighteen, but admitting to twenty at evening parties. Well, it will not be very long before you are of age and free from the restraints of tutelage. So I don't think your guardian's consent is, after all, a matter of any importance.

JACK. Pray excuse me, Lady Bracknell, for interrupting you again, but it is only fair to tell you that according to the terms of her grandfather's will Miss Cardew does not come legally of age till she is thirty-five.

LADY BRACKNELL. That does not seem to me to be a grave objection. Thirty-five is a very attractive age. London society is full of women of the very highest birth who have, of their own free choice, remained thirty-five for years. Lady Dumbleton is an instance in point. To my own knowledge she has been thirty-five ever since she arrived at the age of forty, which was many years ago now. I see no reason why our dear Cecily should not be even still more attractive at the age you mention than she is at present. There will be a large accumulation of property.

CECILY. Algy, could you wait for me till I was thirty-five?

ALGERNON. Of course I could, Cecily. You know I could.

CECILY. Yes, I felt it instinctively, but I couldn't wait all that time. I hate waiting even five minutes for anybody. It always makes me rather cross. I am not punctual myself, I know, but I do like punctuality in others, and waiting, even to be married, is quite out of the question.

ALGERNON. Then what is to be done, Cecily?

CECILY. I don't know, Mr Moncrieff.

LADY BRACKNELL. My dear Mr Worthing, as Miss Cardew states positively that she cannot wait till she is thirty-five—a remark which I am bound to say seems to me to show a somewhat impatient nature—I would beg of you to reconsider your decision.

JACK. But my dear Lady Bracknell, the matter is entirely in your own hands. The moment you consent to my marriage with Gwendolen, I will most gladly allow your nephew to form an alliance with my ward.

LADY BRACKNELL [*Rising and drawing herself up.*] You must be quite aware that what you propose is out of the question.

JACK. Then a passionate celibacy is all that any of us can look forward to.

LADY BRACKNELL. That is not the destiny I propose for Gwendolen. Algernon, of course, can choose for himself. [*Pulls out her watch.*] Come, dear; [*Gwendolen rises*] we have already missed five, if not six, trains. To miss any more might expose us to comment on the platform.

[*Enter Dr Chasuble.*]

CHASUBLE. Everything is quite ready for the christenings.

LADY BRACKNELL. The christenings, sir! Is not that somewhat premature?

CHASUBLE [*Looking rather puzzled, and pointing to Jack and Algernon.*] Both these gentlemen have expressed a desire for immediate baptism.

LADY BRACKNELL. At their age? The idea is grotesque and irreligious! Algernon, I forbid you to be baptized. I will not hear of such excesses. Lord Bracknell would be highly displeased if he learned that that was the way in which you wasted your time and money.

CHASUBLE. Am I to understand then that there are to be no christenings at all this afternoon?

JACK. I don't think that, as things are now, it would be of much practical value to either of us, Dr Chasuble.

CHASUBLE. I am grieved to hear such sentiments from you, Mr Worthing. They savour of the heretical views of the Anabaptists,° views that I have completely refuted in four of my unpublished sermons. However, as your present mood seems to be one peculiarly secular, I will return to the church at once. Indeed, I have just been informed by the pew-opener° that for the last hour and a half Miss Prism has been waiting for me in the vestry.

LADY BRACKNELL [*Starting.*] Miss Prism! Did I hear you mention a Miss Prism?

CHASUBLE. Yes, Lady Bracknell. I am on my way to join her.

LADY BRACKNELL. Pray allow me to detain you for a moment. This matter may prove to be one of vital importance to Lord Bracknell and myself. Is this Miss Prism a female of repellent aspect, remotely connected with education?

CHASUBLE [*Somewhat indignantly.*] She is the most cultivated of ladies, and the very picture of respectability.

LADY BRACKNELL. It is obviously the same person. May I ask what position she holds in your household?

CHASUBLE [*Severely.*] I am a celibate, madam.

JACK [*Interposing.*] Miss Prism, Lady Bracknell, has been for the last three years Miss Cardew's esteemed governess and valued companion.

LADY BRACKNELL. In spite of what I hear of her, I must see her at once. Let her be sent for.

CHASUBLE [*Looking off.*] She approaches; she is nigh.

[*Enter Miss Prism hurriedly.*]

MISS PRISM. I was told you expected me in the vestry, dear Canon. I have been waiting for you there for an hour and three quarters. [*Catches sight of Lady Bracknell who has fixed her with a stony glare. Miss Prism grows pale and quails. She looks anxiously round as if desirous to escape.*]

LADY BRACKNELL [*In a severe, judicial voice.*] Prism! [*Miss Prism bows her head in shame.*] Come here, Prism! [*Miss Prism approaches in a humble manner.*] Prism! Where is that baby? [*General consternation. The Canon starts back in horror. Algernon and Jack pretend to be anxious to shield Cecily and Gwendolen from hearing the details of a terrible public scandal.*] Twenty-eight years ago, Prism, you left Lord Bracknell's house, Number 104, Upper Grosvenor Street, in charge of a perambulator that contained a baby, of the male sex. You never returned. A few weeks later, through the elaborate investigations of the Metropolitan police, the perambulator was discovered at midnight, standing by itself in a remote corner of Bayswater. It contained the manuscript of a three-volume novel of more than usually revolting sentimentality. [*Miss Prism starts in involuntary indignation.*] But the baby was not there! [*Everyone looks at Miss Prism.*] Prism! Where is that baby? [*A pause.*]

MISS PRISM. Lady Bracknell, I admit with shame that I do not know. I only wish I did. The plain facts of the case are these. On the morning of the day you mention, a day that is for ever branded on my memory, I prepared as usual to take the baby out in its perambulator. I had also with me a somewhat old, but capacious hand-bag in which I had intended to place the manuscript of a work of fiction that I had written during my few unoccupied hours. In a moment of mental abstraction, for which I never can forgive myself, I deposited the manuscript in the bassinette,° and placed the baby in the hand-bag.

JACK [*Who has been listening attentively.*] But where did you deposit the hand-bag?

MISS PRISM. Do not ask me, Mr Worthing.

JACK. Miss Prism, this is a matter of no small importance to me. I insist on knowing where you deposited the hand-bag that contained that infant.

MISS PRISM. I left it in the cloak-room of one of the larger railway stations in London.

JACK. What railway station?

MISS PRISM [*Quite crushed.*] Victoria. The Brighton line. [*Sinks into a chair.*]

JACK. I must retire to my room for a moment. Gwendolen, wait here for me.

GWENDOLEN. If you are not too long, I will wait here for you all my life.

[*Exit Jack in great excitement.*]

CHASUBLE. What do you think this means, Lady Bracknell?

LADY BRACKNELL. I dare not even suspect, Dr Chasuble. I need hardly tell you that in families of high position strange coincidences are not supposed to occur. They are hardly considered the thing.

[*Noises heard overhead as if someone was throwing trunks about. Everyone looks up.*]

CECILY. Uncle Jack seems strangely agitated.

CHASUBLE. Your guardian has a very emotional nature.

LADY BRACKNELL. This noise is extremely unpleasant. It sounds as if he was having an argument. I dislike arguments of any kind. They are always vulgar, and often convincing.

CHASUBLE [*Looking up.*] It has stopped now. [*The noise is redoubled.*]

LADY BRACKNELL. I wish he would arrive at some conclusion.

GWENDOLEN. This suspense is terrible. I hope it will last.

[*Enter Jack with a hand-bag of black leather in his hand.*]

JACK [*Rushing over to Miss Prism.*] Is this the hand-bag, Miss Prism? Examine it carefully before you speak. The happiness of more than one life depends on your answer.

MISS PRISM [*Calmly.*] It seems to be mine. Yes, here is the injury it received through the upsetting of a Gower Street omnibus in younger and happier days. Here is the stain on the lining caused by the explosion of a temperance beverage, an incident that occurred at Leamington. And here, on the lock, are my initials. I had forgotten that in an extravagant mood I had had them placed there. The bag is undoubtedly mine. I am delighted to have it so unexpectedly restored to me. It has been a great inconvenience being without it all these years.

JACK [*In a pathetic voice.*] Miss Prism, more is restored to you than this hand-bag. I was the baby you placed in it.

MISS PRISM [*Amazed.*] You?

JACK [*Embracing her.*] Yes . . . mother!

MISS PRISM [*Recoiling in indignant astonishment.*] Mr Worthing! I am unmarried!

JACK. Unmarried! I do not deny that is a serious blow. But after all, who has the right to cast a stone° against one who has suffered? Cannot repentance wipe out an act of folly? Why should there be one law for men, and another for women?° Mother, I forgive you. [*Tries to embrace her again.*]

MISS PRISM [*Still more indignant.*] Mr Worthing, there is some error. [*Pointing to Lady Bracknell.*] There is the lady who can tell you who you really are.

JACK [*After a pause.*] Lady Bracknell, I hate to seem inquisitive, but would you kindly inform me who I am?

LADY BRACKNELL. I am afraid that the news I have to give you will not altogether please you. You are the son of my poor sister, Mrs Moncrieff, and consequently Algernon's elder brother.

JACK. Algy's elder brother! Then I have a brother after all. I knew I had a brother! I always said I had a brother! Cecily—how could you have ever doubted that I had a brother. [*Seizes hold of Algernon.*] Dr Chasuble, my unfortunate brother. Miss Prism, my unfortunate brother. Gwendolen, my unfortunate brother. Algy, you young scoundrel, you will have to treat me with more respect in the future. You have never behaved to me like a brother in all your life.

ALGERNON. Well, not till today, old boy, I admit. I did my best, however, though I was out of practice. [*Shakes hands.*]

GWENDOLEN [*To Jack.*] My own! But what own are you? What is your Christian name, now that you have become someone else?

JACK. Good heavens! . . . I had quite forgotten that point. Your decision on the subject of my name is irrevocable, I suppose?

GWENDOLEN. I never change, except in my affections.

CECILY. What a noble nature you have, Gwendolen!

JACK. Then the question had better be cleared up at once. Aunt Augusta, a moment. At the time when Miss Prism left me in the hand-bag, had I been christened already?

LADY BRACKNELL. Every luxury that money could buy, including christening, had been lavished on you by your fond and doting parents.

JACK. Then I was christened! That is settled. Now, what name was I given? Let me know the worst.

LADY BRACKNELL. Being the eldest son you were naturally christened after your father.

JACK [*Irritably.*] Yes, but what was my father's Christian name?

LADY BRACKNELL [*Meditatively.*] I cannot at the present moment recall what the General's Christian name was. But I have no doubt he had one. He was eccentric, I admit. But only in later years. And that was the result of the Indian climate, and marriage, and indigestion, and other things of that kind.

JACK. Algy! Can't you recollect what our father's Christian name was?

ALGERNON. My dear boy, we were never even on speaking terms. He died before I was a year old.

JACK. His name would appear in the Army Lists° of the period, I suppose, Aunt Augusta?

LADY BRACKNELL. The General was essentially a man of peace, except in his domestic life. But I have no doubt his name would appear in any military directory.

JACK. The Army Lists of the last forty years are here. These delightful records should have been my constant study. [*Rushes to bookcase and tears the books out.*] M. Generals ... Mallam, Maxbohm,° Magley, what ghastly names they have—Markby, Migsby, Mobbs, Moncrieff! Lieutenant 1840, Captain, Lieutenant-Colonel, Colonel, General 1869, Christian names, Ernest John. [*Puts book very quietly down and speaks quite calmly.*] I always told you, Gwendolen, my name was Ernest, didn't I? Well, it is Ernest after all. I mean it naturally is Ernest.

LADY BRACKNELL. Yes, I remember now that the General was called Ernest. I knew I had some particular reason for disliking the name.

GWENDOLEN. Ernest! My own Ernest! I felt from the first that you could have no other name!

JACK. Gwendolen, it is a terrible thing for a man to find out suddenly that all his life he has been speaking nothing but the truth. Can you forgive me?

GWENDOLEN. I can. For I feel that you are sure to change.

JACK. My own one!

CHASUBLE [*To Miss Prism.*] Lætitia! [*Embraces her.*]

MISS PRISM [*Enthusiastically.*] Frederick! At last!

ALGERNON. Cecily! [*Embraces her.*] At last!

JACK. Gwendolen! [*Embraces her.*] At last!

LADY BRACKNELL. My nephew, you seem to be displaying signs of triviality.

JACK. On the contrary, Aunt Augusta, I've now realized for the first time in my life the vital Importance of Being Earnest.

TABLEAU.

CURTAIN.

THE HARLOT'S HOUSE

We caught the tread of dancing feet,
We loitered down the moonlit street,
And stopped beneath the Harlot's house.

Inside, above the din and fray,
We heard the loud musicians play
The 'Treues Liebes Herz', of Strauss.°

Like strange mechanical grotesques,
Making fantastic arabesques,
The shadows raced across the blind.

We watched the ghostly dancers spin   10
To sound of horn and violin,
Like black leaves wheeling in the wind.

Like wire-pulled automatons,
Slim silhouetted skeletons
Went sidling through the slow quadrille,

Then took each other by the hand,°
And danced a stately saraband;
Their laughter echoed thin and shrill.

Sometimes a clock-work puppet pressed
A phantom lover to her breast,   20
Sometimes they seemed to try and sing,

Sometimes a horrible Marionette°
Came out, and smoked its cigarette
Upon the steps like a live thing.

Then turning to my love I said,
'The dead are dancing with the dead,
The dust is whirling with the dust.'

But she, she heard the violin,
And left my side, and entered in;
Love passed into the house of Lust.   30

Then suddenly the tune went false,
The dancers wearied of the waltz,
The shadows ceased to wheel and whirl,

And down the long and silent street,
The dawn with silver-sandalled feet,
Crept like a frightened girl.

THE SPHINX

In a dim corner of my room for longer than my fancy thinks
A beautiful and silent Sphinx has watched me through the shifting
   gloom.

Inviolate and immobile she does not rise she does not stir
For silver moons are naught to her and naught to her the suns that reel.

Red follows grey across the air the waves of moonlight ebb and flow
But with the dawn she does not go and in the night-time she is there.

Dawn follows dawn and nights grow old and all the while this curious cat
Lies couching on the Chinese mat with eyes of satin rimmed with gold.

Upon the mat she lies and leers and on the tawny throat of her
Flutters the soft and silky fur or ripples to her pointed ears.   10

Come forth my lovely seneschal!° so somnolent, so statuesque!
Come forth you exquisite grotesque! half woman and half animal!°

Come forth my lovely languorous Sphinx! and put your head upon my
   knee!
And let me stroke your throat and see your body spotted like the lynx!

And let me touch those curving claws of yellow ivory and grasp
The tail that like a monstrous asp coils round your heavy velvet paws!

A thousand weary centuries are thine while I have hardly seen
Some twenty summers° cast their green for autumn's gaudy liveries.

But you can read the hieroglyphs on the great sandstone obelisks,°
And you have talked with Basilisks,° and you have looked on Hippogriffs. 20

O tell me, were you standing by when Isis to Osiris° knelt?
And did you watch the Egyptian melt her union for Antony°

And drink the jewel-drunken wine and bend her head in mimic awe
To see the huge Pro-Consul draw the salted tunny from the brine?

And did you mark the Cyprian kiss white Adon° on his catafalque?
And did you follow Amenalk, the god of Heliopolis?°

And did you talk with Thoth, and did you hear the moon-horned Io
   weep?°
And know the painted kings who sleep beneath the wedge-shaped
   pyramid?

Lift up your large black satin eyes which are like cushions where one
    sinks!

Fawn at my feet fantastic Sphinx! and sing me all your memories!   30

Sing to me of the Jewish maid who wandered with the Holy Child,°
And how you led them through the wild, and how they slept beneath your
    shade.

Sing to me of that odorous green eve when couching by the marge
You heard from Adrian's gilded barge the laughter of Antinous°

And lapped the stream and fed your drouth and watched with hot and
    hungry stare
The ivory body of that rare young slave with his pomegranate mouth!

Sing to me of the labyrinth in which the twy-formed Bull° was stalled!
Sing to me of the night you crawled across the temple's granite plinth

When through the purple corridors the screaming scarlet Ibis° flew
In terror, and a horrid dew dripped from the moaning mandragores,°   40

And the great torpid Crocodile° within the tank shed slimy tears,
And tare the jewels from his ears and staggered back into the Nile,

And the priests cursed you with shrill psalms as in your claws you seized
    their snake
And crept away with it to slake your passion by the shuddering palms.

Who were your lovers? who were they who wrestled for you in the dust?
Which was the vessel of your lust? what leman had you, every day?

Did giant Lizards come and crouch before you on the reedy banks?
Did Gryphons° with great metal flanks leap on you in your trampled
    couch?

Did monstrous Hippopotami come sidling toward you in the mist?
Did gilt-scaled Dragons writhe and twist with passion as you passed
    them by?   50

And from the brick-built Lycian tomb what horrible Chimæra° came
With fearful heads and fearful flame to breed new wonders from your
    womb?

Or had you shameful secret quests and did you harry to your home
Some Nereid° coiled in amber foam with curious rock crystal breasts?

Or did you treading through the froth call to the brown Sidonian
For tidings of Leviathan, Leviathan or Behemoth?°

Or did you when the sun was set climb up the cactus-covered slope
To meet your swarthy Ethiop whose body was of polished jet?

Or did you while the earthen skiffs dropped down the grey Nilotic flats
At twilight and the flickering bats flew round the temple's triple glyphs° 60

Steal to the border of the bar° and swim across the silent lake
And slink ino the vault and make the pyramid your lúpanar°

Till from each black sarcophagus rose up the painted swathèd dead?
Or did you lure unto your bed the ivory-horned Tragelaphos?°

Or did you love the God of Flies who plagued the Hebrews° and was
    splashed
With wine unto the waist? or Pasht, who had green beryls for her eyes?

Or that young God, the Tyrian,° who was more amorous than the dove
Of Ashtaroth?° or did you love the God of the Assyrian

Whose wings, like strange transparent talc,° rose high above his hawk-
    faced head,
Painted with silver and with red and ribbed with rods of oreichalch?° 70

Or did huge Apis° from his car leap down and lay before your feet
Big blossoms of the honey-sweet and honey-coloured nenuphar?°

How subtle-secret is your smile! Did you love none then? Nay, I know
Great Ammon° was your bedfellow! He lay with you beside the Nile!

The river-horses° in the slime trumpeted when they saw him come
Odorous with Syrian galbanum and smeared with spikenard and with
    thyme.

He came along the river-bank like some tall galley argent-sailed,
He strode across the waters,° mailed in beauty, and the waters sank.

He strode across the desert sand: he reached the valley where you lay:
He waited till the dawn of day: then touched your black breasts with his
    hand.
                                                                        80

You kissed his mouth with mouths of flame: you made the hornèd god
    your own
You stood behind him on his throne: you called him by his secret name.°

You whispered monstrous oracles into the caverns of his ears:
With blood of goats and blood of steers you taught him monstrous
    miracles.

White Ammon was your bedfellow! Your chamber was the steaming
    Nile!
And with your curved archaic smile you watched his passion come and
    go.

With Syrian oils his brows were bright: and widespread as a tent at noon
His marble limbs made pale the moon and lent the day a larger light.

His long hair was nine cubits'° span and coloured like that yellow gem
Which hidden in their garment's hem the merchants bring from
    Kurdistan.

His face was as the must° that lies upon a vat of new-made wine:
The seas could not insapphirine° the perfect azure of his eyes.

His thick soft throat was white as milk and threaded with thin veins of
    blue:
And curious pearls like frozen dew were broidered on his flowing silk.

On pearl and porphyry° pedestalled he was too bright to look upon:
For on his ivory breast there shone the wondrous ocean-emerald,

That mystic moonlit jewel which some diver of the Colchian caves
Had found beneath the blackening waves and carried to the Colchian
    witch.°

Before his gilded galiot ran naked vine-wreathed Corybants,°
And lines of swaying elephants knelt down to draw his chariot,

And lines of swarthy Nubians bare up his litter as he rode
Down the great granite-paven road between the nodding peacock-fans.

The merchants brought him steatite from Sidon in their painted ships:
The meanest cup that touched his lips was fashioned from a chrysolite.

The merchants brought him cedar-chests of rich apparel bound with
    cords:
His train was borne by Memphian° Lords: young Kings were glad to be
    his guests.

Ten hundred shaven priests did bow to Ammon's altar day and night,
Ten hundred lamps did wave their light through Ammon's carven
    house—and now

Foul snake and speckled adder with their young ones crawl from stone to
    stone
For ruined is the house and prone the great rose-marble monolith!°

Wild ass or trotting jackal comes and couches in the mouldering gates:
Wild satyrs call unto their mates across the fallen fluted drums.

And on the summit of the pile the blue-faced ape of Horus sits
And gibbers while the figtree splits the pillars of the peristyle.°

The god is scattered here and there: deep hidden in the windy sand
I saw his giant granite hand still clenched in impotent despair.°

And many a wandering caravan of stately negroes silken-shawled,
Crossing the desert, halts appalled before the neck that none can span.

And many a bearded Bedouin draws back his yellow-striped burnous°
To gaze upon the Titan thews° of him who was thy paladin.°   120

Go, seek his fragments on the moor and wash them in the evening dew,
And from their pieces make anew thy mutilated paramour!

Go, seek them where they lie alone and from their broken pieces make
Thy bruisèd bedfellow! and wake mad passions in the senseless stone!

Charm his dull ear with Syrian hymns! He loved your body! Oh, be kind,
Pour spikenard on his hair, and wind soft rolls of linen round his limbs!

Wind round his head the figured coins! Stain with red fruits those pallid
        lips!
Weave purple for his shrunken hips! and purple for his barren loins!

Away to Egypt! Have no fear. Only one God has ever died.
Only one God has let his side be wounded by a soldier's spear.   130

But these, thy lovers, are not dead. Still by the hundred-cubit gate°
Dog-faced Anubis° sits in state with lotus-lilies for thy head.

Still from his chair of porphyry gaunt Memnon° strains his lidless eyes
Across the empty land, and cries each yellow morning unto thee.

And Nilus with his broken horn lies in his black and oozy bed
And till thy coming will not spread his waters on the withering corn.

Your lovers are not dead, I know. They will rise up and hear your voice
And clash their cymbals and rejoice and run to kiss your mouth! And so,

Set wings upon your argosies!° Set horses to your ebon car!
Back to your Nile! Or if you are grown sick of dead divinities   140

Follow some roving lion's spoor across the copper-coloured plain,
Reach out and hale him by the mane and bid him be your paramour!

Couch by his side upon the grass and set your white teeth in his throat
And when you hear his dying note lash your long flanks of polished brass

And take a tiger for your mate, whose amber sides are flecked with black,
And ride upon his gilded back in triumph through the Theban gate,

And toy with him in amorous jests, and when he turns, and snarls, and
     gnaws,
O smite him with your jasper claws! and bruise him with your agate
     breasts!

Why are you tarrying? Get hence! I weary of your sullen ways,
I weary of your steadfast gaze, your somnolent magnificence.   150

Your horrible and heavy breath makes the light flicker in the lamp,
And on my brow I feel the damp and dreadful dews of night and death.

Your eyes are like fantastic moons that shiver in some stagnant lake,°
Your tongue is like a scarlet snake that dances to fantastic tunes,

Your pulse makes poisonous melodies, and your black throat is like the
     hole
Left by some torch or burning coal on Saracenic tapestries.

Away! the sulphur-coloured stars are hurrying through the Western
     Gate!
Away! or it may be too late to climb their silent silver cars!

See, the dawn shivers round the grey gilt-dialled towers,° and the rain
Streams down each diamonded pane and blurs with tears the wannish
     day.   160

What snake-tressed Fury° fresh from Hell, with uncouth gestures
     and unclean,
Stole from the poppy-drowsy Queen° and led you to a student's cell?

What songless tongueless ghost of Sin crept through the curtains of the
     night,
And saw my taper burning bright, and knocked, and bade you enter in.

Are there not others more accursed, whiter with leprosies than I?
Are Abana and Pharphar° dry that you come here to slake your thirst?

Get hence, you loathsome Mystery! Hideous animal, get hence!
You wake in me each bestial sense, you make me what I would not be.

You make my creed a barren sham, you wake foul dreams of sensual life,
And Atys° with his blood-stained knife were better than the thing I am. 170

False Sphinx! False Sphinx! By reedy Styx old Charon, leaning on
    his oar,°

Waits for my coin. Go thou before, and leave me to my Crucifix,

Whose pallid burden, sick with pain, watches the world with wearied
    eyes,

And weeps for every soul that dies, and weeps for every soul in vain.°

THE BALLAD OF READING GAOL

In Memoriam
C. T. W.
Sometime Trooper of the Royal Horse Guards.
Obiit H.M. Prison, Reading, Berkshire,
July 7th, 1896.°

THE BALLAD OF READING GAOL

I

HE did not wear his scarlet coat,°
  For blood and wine are red,
And blood and wine were on his hands
  When they found him with the dead,
The poor dead woman whom he loved,
  And murdered in her bed.

He walked amongst the Trial men
  In a suit of shabby gray;
A cricket cap was on his head,
  And his step seemed light and gay;   10
But I never saw a man who looked
  So wistfully at the day.

I never saw a man who looked
  With such a wistful eye
Upon that little tent of blue
  Which prisoners call the sky,
And at every drifting cloud that went
  With sails of silver by.

I walked, with other souls in pain,
  Within another ring,   20
And was wondering if the man had done
  A great or little thing,
When a voice behind me whispered low,
  'That fellow's got to swing.'

Dear Christ! the very prison walls
 Suddenly seemed to reel,
And the sky above my head became
 Like a casque of scorching steel;
And, though I was a soul in pain,
 My pain I could not feel.   30

I only knew what hunted thought
 Quickened his step, and why
He looked upon the garish day
 With such a wistful eye;
The man had killed the thing he loved,
 And so he had to die.

      *

Yet each man kills the thing he loves,°
 By each let this be heard,
Some do it with a bitter look,
 Some with a flattering word,   40
The coward does it with a kiss,°
 The brave man with a sword!

Some kill their love when they are young,
 And some when they are old;
Some strangle with the hands of Lust,
 Some with the hands of Gold:
The kindest use a knife, because
 The dead so soon grow cold.

Some love too little, some too long,
 Some sell, and others buy;   50
Some do the deed with many tears,
 And some without a sigh:
For each man kills the thing he loves,
 Yet each man does not die.

      *

He does not die a death of shame
 On a day of dark disgrace,
Nor have a noose about his neck,
 Nor a cloth upon his face,
Nor drop feet foremost through the floor
 Into an empty space.   60

He does not sit with silent men°
    Who watch him night and day;
Who watch him when he tries to weep,
    And when he tries to pray;
Who watch him lest himself should rob
    The prison of its prey.

He does not wake at dawn to see
    Dread figures throng his room,
The shivering Chaplain robed in white,
    The Sheriff stern with gloom,   70
And the Governor all in shiny black,
    With the yellow face of Doom.

He does not rise in piteous haste
    To put on convict-clothes,
While some coarse-mouthed Doctor gloats, and notes
    Each new and nerve-twitched pose,
Fingering a watch whose little ticks
    Are like horrible hammer-blows.

He does not know that sickening thirst
    That sands one's throat, before   80
The hangman with his gardener's gloves
    Slips through the padded door,
And binds one with three leathern thongs,°
    That the throat may thirst no more.

He does not bend his head to hear
    The Burial Office read,
Nor, while the terror of his soul
    Tells him he is not dead,
Cross his own coffin, as he moves
    Into the hideous shed.°   90

He does not stare upon the air
    Through a little roof of glass:
He does not pray with lips of clay
    For his agony to pass;
Nor feel upon his shuddering cheek
    The kiss of Caiaphas.°

II

Six weeks our guardsman walked the yard,
  In the suit of shabby gray:
His cricket cap was on his head,
  And his step seemed light and gay,   100
But I never saw a man who looked
  So wistfully at the day.

I never saw a man who looked
  With such a wistful eye
Upon that little tent of blue
  Which prisoners call the sky,
And at every wandering cloud that trailed
  Its ravelled fleeces by.

He did not wring his hands, as do
  Those witless men who dare   110
To try to rear the changeling Hope
  In the cave of black Despair:
He only looked upon the sun,
  And drank the morning air.

He did not wring his hands nor weep,
  Nor did he peek° or pine,
But he drank the air as though it held
  Some healthful anodyne;
With open mouth he drank the sun
  As though it had been wine!°   120

And I and all the souls in pain,
  Who tramped the other ring,
Forgot if we ourselves had done
  A great or little thing,
And watched with gaze of dull amaze
  The man who had to swing.

And strange it was to see him pass
  With a step so light and gay,
And strange it was to see him look
  So wistfully at the day,   130
And strange it was to think that he
  Had such a debt to pay.

*

For oak and elm have pleasant leaves
   That in the spring-time shoot:
But grim to see is the gallows-tree,
   With its adder-bitten root,
And, green or dry, a man must die
   Before it bears its fruit!°

The loftiest place is that seat of grace
   For which all worldlings try: 140
But who would stand in hempen band
   Upon a scaffold high,
And through a murderer's collar take
   His last look at the sky?

It is sweet to dance to violins
   When Love and Life are fair:
To dance to flutes, to dance to lutes
   Is delicate and rare:
But it is not sweet with nimble feet
   To dance upon the air!   150

So with curious eyes and sick surmise
   We watched him day by day,
And wondered if each one of us
   Would end the self-same way,
For none can tell to what red Hell
   His sightless soul may stray.

*

At last the dead man walked no more
   Amongst the Trial Men,
And I knew that he was standing up
   In the black dock's dreadful pen,   160
And that never would I see his face
   In God's sweet world again.

Like two doomed ships that pass in storm
   We had crossed each other's way:
But we made no sign, we said no word,
   We had no word to say;
For we did not meet in the holy night,°
   But in the shameful day.

A prison wall was round us both,
  Two outcast men we were: 170
The world had thrust us from its heart,
  And God from out His care:
And the iron gin° that waits for Sin
  Had caught us in its snare.

III

IN Debtors' Yard the stones are hard,
  And the dripping wall is high,
So it was there he took the air
  Beneath the leaden sky,
And by each side a Warder walked,
  For fear the man might die.   180

Or else he sat with those who watched
  His anguish night and day;
Who watched him when he rose to weep,
  And when he crouched to pray;
Who watched him lest himself should rob
  Their scaffold of its prey.

The Governor was strong upon
  The Regulations Act:
The Doctor said that Death was but
  A scientific fact: 190
And twice a day the Chaplain called,
  And left a little tract.

And twice a day he smoked his pipe,
  And drank his quart of beer:
His soul was resolute, and held
  No hiding-place for fear;
He often said that he was glad
  The hangman's hands were near.

But why he said so strange a thing
  No Warder dared to ask: 200
For he to whom a watcher's doom
  Is given as his task,
Must set a lock upon his lips,
  And make his face a mask.

Or else he might be moved, and try
   To comfort or console:
And what should Human Pity do
   Pent up in Murderers' Hole?
What word of grace in such a place
   Could help a brother's soul?   210

*

With slouch and swing around the ring
   We trod the Fools' Parade!
We did not care: we knew we were
   The Devil's Own Brigade:
And shaven head and feet of lead
   Make a merry masquerade.

We tore the tarry rope° to shreds
   With blunt and bleeding nails;
We rubbed the doors, and scrubbed the floors,
   And cleaned the shining rails: 220
And, rank by rank, we soaped the plank,
   And clattered with the pails.

We sewed the sacks, we broke the stones,°
   We turned the dusty drill:°
We banged the tins, and bawled the hymns,
   And sweated on the mill:°
But in the heart of every man
   Terror was lying still.

So still it lay that every day
   Crawled like a weed-clogged wave: 230
And we forgot the bitter lot
   That waits for fool and knave,
Till once, as we tramped in from work,
   We passed an open grave.

With yawning mouth the yellow hole
   Gaped for a living thing;
The very mud cried out for blood°
   To the thirsty asphalte ring:
And we knew that ere one dawn grew fair
   Some prisoner had to swing.   240

Right in we went, with soul intent
  On Death and Dread and Doom:
The hangman, with his little bag,
  Went shuffling through the gloom:
And each man trembled as he crept
  Into his numbered tomb.°

*

That night the empty corridors
  Were full of forms of Fear,
And up and down the iron town
  Stole feet we could not hear,   250
And through the bars that hide the stars
  White faces seemed to peer.

He lay as one who lies and dreams
  In a pleasant meadow-land,
The watchers watched him as he slept,
  And could not understand
How one could sleep so sweet a sleep
  With a hangman close at hand.

But there is no sleep when men must weep
  Who never yet have wept:
So we—the fool, the fraud, the knave—   260
  That endless vigil kept,
And through each brain on hands of pain
  Another's terror crept.

*

Alas! it is a fearful thing
  To feel another's guilt!
For, right within, the sword of Sin
  Pierced to its poisoned hilt,
And as molten lead were the tears we shed
  For the blood we had not spilt.   270

The Warders with their shoes of felt
  Crept by each padlocked door,
And peeped and saw, with eyes of awe,
  Gray figures on the floor,
And wondered why men knelt to pray
  Who never prayed before.

All through the night we knelt and prayed,
    Mad mourners of a corse!
The troubled plumes of midnight were
    The plumes upon a hearse:°   280
And bitter wine upon a sponge°
    Was the savour of Remorse.

*

The gray cock crew, the red cock crew,°
    But never came the day:
And crooked shapes of Terror crouched,
    In the corners where we lay:
And each evil sprite that walks by night
    Before us seemed to play.

They glided past, they glided fast,°
    Like travellers through a mist: 290
They mocked the moon in a rigadoon°
    Of delicate turn and twist,
And with formal pace and loathsome grace
    The phantoms kept their tryst.

With mop and mow° we saw them go,
    Slim shadows hand in hand:
About, about, in ghostly rout
    They trod a saraband:
And the damned grotesques made arabesques,°
    Like the wind upon the sand!   300

With the pirouettes of marionettes,
    They tripped on pointed tread:
But with flutes of Fear they filled the ear,
    As their grisly masque they led,
And loud they sang, and long they sang,
    For they sang to wake the dead.

'*Oho!*' they cried, '*The world is wide,*
    But fettered limbs go lame!
And once, or twice, to throw the dice
    Is a gentlemanly game,   310
But he does not win who plays with Sin
    In the secret House of Shame.'

*

No things of air these antics were,°
   That frolicked with such glee:
To men whose lives were held in gyves,°
   And whose feet might not go free,
Ah! wounds of Christ! they were living things,
   Most terrible to see.

Around, around, they waltzed and wound;
   Some wheeled in smirking pairs;   320
With the mincing step of a demirep°
   Some sidled up the stairs:
And with subtle sneer, and fawning leer,
   Each helped us at our prayers.

*

The morning wind began to moan,
   But still the night went on:
Through its giant loom the web of gloom
   Crept till each thread was spun:
And, as we prayed, we grew afraid
   Of the Justice of the Sun.   330

The moaning wind went wandering round
   The weeping prison-wall:
Till like a wheel of turning steel
   We felt the minutes crawl:
O moaning wind! what had we done
   To have such a seneschal?°

At last I saw the shadowed bars,
   Like a lattice wrought in lead,
Move right across the whitewashed wall
   That faced my three-plank bed,   340
And I knew that somewhere in the world
   God's dreadful dawn was red.

*

At six o'clock we cleaned our cells,
   At seven all was still,
But the sough and swing of a mighty wing°
   The prison seemed to fill,
For the Lord of Death with icy breath
   Had entered in to kill.

He did not pass in purple pomp,
　　Nor ride a moon-white steed.　　　　　　　350
Three yards of cord and a sliding board
　　Are all the gallows' need:
So with rope of shame the Herald came
　　To do the secret deed.

*

We were as men who through a fen
　　Of filthy darkness grope:
We did not dare to breathe a prayer,
　　Or to give our anguish scope:
Something was dead in each of us,
　　And what was dead was Hope.　　　　　　　360

For Man's grim Justice goes its way,
　　And will not swerve aside:
It slays the weak, it slays the strong,
　　It has a deadly stride:
With iron heel it slays the strong,
　　The monstrous parricide!

*

We waited for the stroke of eight:°
　　Each tongue was thick with thirst:
For the stroke of eight is the stroke of Fate
　　That makes a man accursed,　　　　　　　370
And Fate will use a running noose°
　　For the best man and the worst.

We had no other thing to do,
　　Save to wait for the sign° to come:
So, like things of stone in a valley lone,
　　Quiet we sat and dumb:
But each man's heart beat thick and quick,
　　Like a madman on a drum!

*

With sudden shock the prison-clock
　　Smote on the shivering air,　　　　　　　380
And from all the gaol rose up a wail
　　Of impotent despair,
Like the sound that frightened marshes hear
　　From some leper in his lair.

And as one sees most fearful things
   In the crystal of a dream,
We saw the greasy hempen rope
   Hooked to the blackened beam,
And heard the prayer the hangman's snare
   Strangled into a scream.   390

And all the woe that moved him so
   That he gave that bitter cry,°
And the wild regrets, and the bloody sweats,°
   None knew so well as I:
For he who lives more lives than one
   More deaths than one must die.

IV

THERE is no chapel on the day
   On which they hang a man:
The Chaplain's heart is far too sick,
   Or his face is far too wan,   400
Or there is that written in his eyes
   Which none should look upon.

So they kept us close till nigh on noon,
   And then they rang the bell,
And the Warders with their jingling keys
   Opened each listening cell,
And down the iron stair we tramped,
   Each from his separate Hell.

Out into God's sweet air we went,
   But not in wonted way,   410
For this man's face was white with fear,
   And that man's face was gray,
And I never saw sad men who looked
   So wistfully at the day.

I never saw sad men who looked
   With such a wistful eye
Upon that little tent of blue
   We prisoners called the sky,
And at every careless cloud that passed
   In happy freedom by.   420

But there were those amongst us all
    Who walked with downcast head,
And knew that, had each got his due,
    They should have died instead:
He had but killed a thing that lived,
    Whilst they had killed the dead.

For he who sins a second time
    Wakes a dead soul to pain,
And draws it from its spotted shroud,
    And makes it bleed again,   430
And makes it bleed great gouts of blood,
    And makes it bleed in vain!°

                    *

Like ape or clown, in monstrous garb
    With crooked arrows starred,
Silently we went round and round
    The slippery asphalte yard;
Silently we went round and round,
    And no man spoke a word.

Silently we went round and round,
    And through each hollow mind   440
The Memory of dreadful things
    Rushed like a dreadful wind,
And Horror stalked before each man,
    And Terror crept behind.

                    *

The Warders strutted up and down,
    And kept their herd of brutes,
Their uniforms were spick and span,
    And they wore their Sunday suits,
But we knew the work they had been at,
    By the quicklime° on their boots.   450

For where a grave had opened wide,
    There was no grave at all:
Only a stretch of mud and sand
    By the hideous prison-wall,
And a little heap of burning lime,
    That the man should have his pall.

For he has a pall, this wretched man,
   Such as few men can claim:
Deep down below a prison-yard,
   Naked for greater shame,   460
He lies, with fetters on each foot,
   Wrapt in a sheet of flame!

And all the while the burning lime
   Eats flesh and bone away,
It eats the brittle bone by night,
   And the soft flesh by day,
It eats the flesh and bone by turns,
   But it eats the heart alway.

*

For three long years they will not sow
   Or root or seedling there: 470
For three long years the unblessed spot
   Will sterile be and bare,
And look upon the wondering sky
   With unreproachful stare.°

They think a murderer's heart would taint
   Each simple seed they sow.
It is not true! God's kindly earth
   Is kindlier than men know,
And the red rose would but blow more red,
   The white rose whiter blow.   480

Out of his mouth a red, red rose!
   Out of his heart a white!
For who can say by what strange way,
   Christ brings His will to light,
Since the barren staff the pilgrim bore
   Bloomed in the great Pope's sight?°

*

But neither milk-white rose nor red
   May bloom in prison air;
The shard, the pebble, and the flint,
   Are what they give us there: 490
For flowers have been known to heal
   A common man's despair.

So never will wine-red rose or white,
  Petal by petal, fall
On that stretch of mud and sand that lies
  By the hideous prison-wall,
To tell the men who tramp the yard
  That God's Son died for all.

*

Yet though the hideous prison-wall
  Still hems him round and round,   500
And a spirit may not walk by night
  That is with fetters bound,
And a spirit may but weep that lies
  In such unholy ground,

He is at peace—this wretched man—
  At peace, or will be soon:
There is no thing to make him mad,
  Nor does Terror walk at noon,
For the lampless Earth in which he lies
  Has neither Sun nor Moon.   510

*

They hanged him as a beast is hanged:
  They did not even toll
A requiem that might have brought
  Rest to his startled soul,
But hurriedly they took him out,
  And hid him in a hole.

They stripped him of his canvas clothes,
  And gave him to the flies:
They mocked the swollen purple throat,
  And the stark and staring eyes: 520
And with laughter loud they heaped the shroud
  In which their convict lies.

The Chaplain would not kneel to pray
  By his dishonoured grave:
Nor mark it with that blessed Cross
  That Christ for sinners gave,

Because the man was one of those
   Whom Christ came down to save.

Yet all is well; he has but passed
   To Life's appointed bourne:°   530
And alien tears will fill for him
   Pity's long-broken urn,
For his mourners will be outcast men,
   And outcasts always mourn.

               v

I KNOW not whether Laws be right,
   Or whether Laws be wrong;
All that we know who lie in gaol
   Is that the wall is strong;
And that each day is like a year,
   A year whose days are long.   540

But this I know, that every Law
   That men have made for Man,
Since first Man took his brother's life,
   And the sad world began,
But straws the wheat and saves the chaff
   With a most evil fan.°

This too I know—and wise it were
   If each could know the same—
That every prison that men build
   Is built with bricks of shame,   550
And bound with bars lest Christ should see
   How men their brothers maim.

With bars they blur the gracious moon,
   And blind the goodly sun:
And they do well to hide their Hell,
   For in it things are done
That Son of God nor son of Man
   Ever should look upon!

             *

The vilest deeds like poison weeds
  Bloom well in prison-air: 560
It is only what is good in Man
  That wastes and withers there:
Pale Anguish keeps the heavy gate,
  And the Warder is Despair.

For they starve the little frightened child°
  Till it weeps both night and day:
And they scourge the weak, and flog the fool,
  And gibe the old and gray,
And some grow mad, and all grow bad,
  And none a word may say.   570

Each narrow cell in which we dwell
  Is a foul and dark latrine,
And the fetid breath of living Death
  Chokes up each grated screen,
And all, but Lust, is turned to dust
  In Humanity's machine.

The brackish water that we drink
  Creeps with a loathsome slime,
And the bitter bread they weigh in scales
  Is full of chalk and lime,°   580
And Sleep will not lie down, but walks
  Wild-eyed, and cries to Time.

                    *

But though lean Hunger and green Thirst
  Like asp with adder fight,
We have little care of prison fare,
  For what chills and kills outright
Is that every stone one lifts by day
  Becomes one's heart by night.

With midnight always in one's heart,
  And twilight in one's cell,   590
We turn the crank, or tear the rope,
  Each in his separate Hell,
And the silence is more awful far
  Than the sound of a brazen bell.

And never a human voice comes near
   To speak a gentle word:
And the eye that watches through the door
   Is pitiless and hard:
And by all forgot, we rot and rot,
   With soul and body marred.   600

And thus we rust Life's iron chain
   Degraded and alone:
And some men curse, and some men weep,
   And some men make no moan:
But God's eternal Laws are kind
   And break the heart of stone.

               *

And every human heart that breaks,
   In prison-cell or yard,
Is as that broken box that gave
   Its treasure to the Lord,   610
And filled the unclean leper's house
   With the scent of costliest nard.°

Ah! happy they whose hearts can break
   And peace of pardon win!
How else may man make straight his plan
   And cleanse his soul from Sin?
How else but through a broken heart°
   May Lord Christ enter in?

               *

And he of the swollen purple throat,
   And the stark and staring eyes,   620
Waits for the holy hands that took
   The Thief to Paradise;°
And a broken and a contrite heart
   The Lord will not despise.°

The man in red who reads the Law°
   Gave him three weeks of life,
Three little weeks in which to heal
   His soul of his soul's strife,
And cleanse from every blot of blood
   The hand that held the knife.   630

And with tears of blood he cleansed the hand,
   The hand that held the steel:
For only blood can wipe out blood,
   And only tears can heal:
And the crimson stain that was of Cain°
   Became Christ's snow-white seal.°

VI

IN Reading gaol by Reading town
   There is a pit of shame,
And in it lies a wretched man
   Eaten by teeth of flame,   640
In a burning winding-sheet he lies,
   And his grave has got no name.

And there, till Christ call forth the dead,
   In silence let him lie:
No need to waste the foolish tear,
   Or heave the windy sigh:
The man had killed the thing he loved,
   And so he had to die.

And all men kill the thing they love,
   By all let this be heard,   650
Some do it with a bitter look,
   Some with a flattering word,
The coward does it with a kiss,
   The brave man with a sword!

POEMS IN PROSE

THE ARTIST

ONE evening there came into his soul the desire to fashion an image of *The Pleasure that abideth for a Moment*. And he went forth into the world to look for bronze. For he could only think in bronze.

But all the bronze of the whole world had disappeared, nor anywhere in the whole world was there any bronze to be found, save only the bronze of the image of *The Sorrow that endureth for Ever*.

Now this image he had himself, and with his own hands, fashioned, and had set it on the tomb of the one thing he had loved in life. On the tomb of the dead thing he had most loved had he set this image of his own fashioning, that it might serve as a sign of the love of man that dieth not, and a symbol of the sorrow of man that endureth for ever. And in the whole world there was no other bronze save the bronze of this image.

And he took the image he had fashioned, and set it in a great furnace, and gave it to the fire.

And out of the bronze of the image of *The Sorrow that endureth for Ever* he fashioned an image of *The Pleasure that abideth for a Moment*.

THE DISCIPLE

When Narcissus died the pool of his pleasure changed from a cup of sweet waters into a cup of salt tears, and the Oreads came weeping through the woodland that they might sing to the pool and give it comfort.

And when they saw that the pool had changed from a cup of sweet waters into a cup of salt tears, they loosened the green tresses of their hair and cried to the pool and said, 'We do not wonder that you should mourn in this manner for Narcissus, so beautiful was he.'

'But was Narcissus beautiful?' said the pool.

'Who should know that better than you?' answered the Oreads. 'Us did he ever pass by, but you he sought for, and would lie on your banks and look down at you, and in the mirror of your waters he would mirror his own beauty.'

And the pool answered, 'But I loved Narcissus because, as he lay on my banks and looked down at me, in the mirror of his eyes I saw ever my own beauty mirrored.'

THE HOUSE OF JUDGMENT

And there was silence in the House of Judgment, and the Man came naked before God.

And God opened the Book of the Life of the Man.

And God said to the Man, 'Thy life hath been evil, and thou hast shown cruelty to those who were in need of succour, and to those who lacked help thou hast been bitter and hard of heart. The poor called to thee and thou did'st not hearken, and thine ears were closed to the cry of My afflicted. The inheritance of the fatherless thou did'st take unto thyself, and thou did'st send the foxes into the vineyard of thy neighbour's field. Thou did'st take the bread of the children and give it to the dogs to eat, and my lepers who lived in the marshes, and were at peace and praised Me, thou did'st drive forth on to the highways, and on Mine earth out of which I made thee thou did'st spill innocent blood.'

And the Man made answer and said, 'Even so did I.'

And again God opened the Book of the Life of the Man.

And God said to the Man, 'Thy life hath been evil, and the Beauty I have shown thou hast sought for, and the Good I have hidden thou did'st pass by. The walls of thy chamber were painted with images, and from the bed of thine abominations thou did'st rise up to the sound of flutes. Thou did'st build seven altars to the sins I have suffered, and did'st eat of the thing that may not be eaten, and the purple of thy raiment was broidered with the three signs of shame. Thine idols were neither of gold nor of silver that endure, but of flesh that dieth. Thou did'st stain their hair with perfumes and put pomegranates in their hands. Thou did'st stain their feet with saffron and spread carpets before them. With antimony thou did'st stain their eyelids and their bodies thou did'st smear with myrrh. Thou did'st bow thyself to the ground before them, and the thrones of thine idols were set in the sun. Thou did'st show to the sun thy shame and to the moon thy madness.'

And the Man made answer and said, 'Even so did I.'

And a third time God opened the Book of the Life of the Man.

And God said to the Man, 'Evil hath been thy life, and with evil did'st thou requite good, and with wrongdoing kindness. The hands that fed thee thou did'st wound, and the breasts that gave thee suck thou did'st despise. He who came to thee with water went away thirsting, and the outlawed men who hid thee in their tents at night thou did'st betray before dawn. Thine enemy who spared thee thou did'st snare in an ambush, and the friend who walked with thee thou did'st sell for a price, and to those who brought thee Love thou did'st ever give Lust in thy turn.'

And the Man made answer and said, 'Even so did I.'

And God closed the Book of the Life of the Man, and said, 'Surely I will send thee into Hell. Even into Hell will I send thee.'

And the Man cried out, 'Thou canst not.'

And God said to the Man, 'Wherefore can I not send thee to Hell, and for what reason?'

'Because in Hell have I always lived,' answered the Man.

And there was silence in the House of Judgment.

And after a space God spake, and said to the Man, 'Seeing that I may not send thee into Hell, surely I will send thee unto Heaven. Even unto Heaven will I send thee.'

And the Man cried out, 'Thou canst not.'

And God said to the Man, 'Wherefore can I not send thee unto Heaven, and for what reason?'

'Because never, and in no place, have I been able to imagine it,' answered the Man.

And there was silence in the House of Judgment.

A FEW MAXIMS FOR THE INSTRUCTION OF THE OVER-EDUCATED

Education is an admirable thing. But it is well to remember from time to time that nothing that is worth knowing can be taught.

Public opinion exists only where there are no ideas.

The English are always degrading truths into facts. When a truth becomes a fact it loses all its intellectual value.

It is a very sad thing that nowadays there is so little useless information.

The only link between Literature and the Drama left to us in England at the present moment is the bill of the play.

In old days books were written by men of letters and read by the public. Nowadays books are written by the public and read by nobody.

Most women are so artificial that they have no sense of Art. Most men are so natural that they have no sense of Beauty.

Friendship is far more tragic than love. It lasts longer.

What is abnormal in Life stands in normal relations to Art. It is the only thing in Life that stands in normal relations to Art.

A subject that is beautiful in itself gives no suggestion to the artist. It lacks imperfection.

The only thing that the artist cannot see is the obvious. The only thing that the public can see is the obvious. The result is the Criticism of the Journalist.

Art is the only serious thing in the world. And the artist is the only person who is never serious.

To be really mediæval one should have no body. To be really modern one should have no soul. To be really Greek one should have no clothes.

Dandyism is the assertion of the absolute modernity of Beauty.

The only thing that can console one for being poor is extravagance. The only thing that can console one for being rich is economy.

One should never listen. To listen is a sign of indifference to one's hearers.

Even the disciple has his uses. He stands behind one's throne, and at the moment of one's triumph whispers in one's ear that, after all, one is immortal.

The criminal classes are so close to us that even the policeman can see them. They are so far away from us that only the poet can understand them.

Those whom the gods love grow young.

PHRASES AND PHILOSOPHIES FOR THE USE OF THE YOUNG

The first duty in life is to be as artificial as possible. What the second duty is no one has as yet discovered.

Wickedness is a myth invented by good people to account for the curious attractiveness of others.

If the poor only had profiles there would be no difficulty in solving the problem of poverty.

Those who see any difference between soul and body have neither.

A really well-made buttonhole is the only link between Art and Nature.

Religions die when they are proved to be true. Science is the record of dead religions.

The well-bred contradict other people. The wise contradict themselves.

Nothing that actually occurs is of the smallest importance.

Dullness is the coming of age of seriousness.

In all unimportant matters, style, not sincerity, is the essential. In all important matters, style, not sincerity, is the essential.

If one tells the truth, one is sure, sooner or later, to be found out.

Pleasure is the only thing one should live for. Nothing ages like happiness.

It is only by not paying one's bills that one can hope to live in the memory of the commercial classes.

No crime is vulgar, but all vulgarity is crime. Vulgarity is the conduct of others.

Only the shallow know themselves.

Time is waste of money.

One should always be a little improbable.

There is a fatality about all good resolutions. They are invariably made too soon.

The only way to atone for being occasionally a little over-dressed is by being always absolutely over-educated.

To be premature is to be perfect.

Any preoccupation with ideas of what is right or wrong in conduct shows an arrested intellectual development.

Ambition is the last refuge of the failure.

A truth ceases to be true when more than one person believes in it.

In examinations the foolish ask questions that the wise cannot answer.

Greek dress was in its essence inartistic. Nothing should reveal the body but the body.

One should either be a work of art, or wear a work of art.

It is only the superficial qualities that last. Man's deeper nature is soon found out.

Industry is the root of all ugliness.

The ages live in history through their anachronisms.

It is only the gods who taste of death. Apollo has passed away, but Hyacinth, whom men say he slew, lives on. Nero and Narcissus are always with us.

The old believe everything: the middle-aged suspect everything: the young know everything.

The condition of perfection is idleness: the aim of perfection is youth.

Only the great masters of style ever succeed in being obscure.

There is something tragic about the enormous number of young men there are in England at the present moment who start life with perfect profiles, and end by adopting some useful profession.

To love oneself is the beginning of a life-long romance.

NOTES

IN the explanatory notes that follow I have used the following abbreviations for works by Wilde:

LASC	Lord Arthur Savile's Crime
DG	*The Picture of Dorian Gray*
DL	*The Decay of Lying*
CA I and *CA II*	*The Critic as Artist*, Parts I and II
LWF	*Lady Windermere's Fan*
IH	*An Ideal Husband*
IBE	*The Importance of Being Earnest*
BRG	*The Ballad of Reading Gaol*
PPUY	Phrases and Philosophies for the Use of the Young
'The Soul of Man'	'The Soul of Man under Socialism', in *Fortnightly Review* XLIX, 290 (February 1891), 292–319
CSF	*Complete Shorter Fiction*, ed. I. Murray (1979)
Rev	*Reviews* (1908)
Misc	*Miscellanies* (1908)
L and *SL*	*The Letters of Oscar Wilde* (1962) and *Selected Letters of Oscar Wilde* (1979), both ed. Rupert Hart-Davis. As *SL* is available and *L* long out of print, references are made wherever possible to *SL*, and only where necessary to *L*.
ML	*More Letters of Oscar Wilde* ed. Rupert Hart-Davis (1985)

I have used the following abbreviations for other works:

Super III	Matthew Arnold, *Lectures and Essays in Criticism*, ed. R. H. Super (Michigan, 1962; vol. iii of *The Complete Prose Works of Matthew Arnold*)
Mason	*Bibliography of Oscar Wilde* by Stuart Mason [Christopher Millard] (1914)
Hill	Walter Pater, *The Renaissance: Studies in Art and Poetry. The 1893 Text*, ed. with textual and explanatory notes by Donald L. Hill (1980)
GAME	James McNeill Whistler, *The Gentle Art of Making Enemies* (1890)
Ellmann	Richard Ellmann, *Oscar Wilde* (1987)

All biblical quotations are from the Authorized Version.

LORD ARTHUR SAVILE'S CRIME

This story was serialized in *Court and Society Review* in 1887 and, slightly revised, appeared in volume form in *Lord Arthur Savile's Crime and Other Stories* (1891).

1 *A Study of Duty*. In the first version of the story, the sub-title was 'A Study of Cheiromancy', drawing attention to the fashionable pursuit of palmistry.

Speaker's Levée. The Speaker of the House of Commons traditionally entertains members: he is the only subject who holds levées which are attended in court dress.

disguised as artists. See *DG* p. 50n.

Debrett. Debrett's Peerage, Baronetage, Knightage and Companionage, in many editions, gives the names, positions, and marriages of men of rank, and details their children.

3 *on a fait . . . ainsi.* It is the way of the world.

rascette. 'The Rascettes are the lines at the junction of the wrist and hand.' From 'The Cheiromancy of Today' by Wilde's friend Edward Heron-Allen, published in *Lippincott's Monthly Magazine* for July 1890, immediately following the first version of *The Picture of Dorian Gray.* Heron-Allen interested Wilde in cheiromancy, and indirectly inspired this story. His rather slight novel, *Ashes of the Future (A Study of Mere Human Nature): The Suicide of Sylvester Gray* (1888) is an important and long-overlooked source for *Dorian Gray*: see my 1974 OEN edition of the novel, pp. xxi–xxiv.

5 *misunderstanding.* Typically, Wilde borrowed and polished this epigram from Henry James's *The Portrait of a Lady* (1881): 'There's no more usual basis of union than a mutual misunderstanding.'

6 *Boulanger.* Through Radical influence, French Minister of War at the time Wilde was writing; for Parisians, a hero and reformer, who stirred up 'Boulanger fever'.

7 *Gorgon's head.* In Greek legend, the sight of the Gorgon's head turned anyone to stone. When Perseus slew her, her head was fixed on the shield of Pallas, goddess of wisdom. *Nemesis.* Goddess of retribution.

8 *your club.* A gentleman's club betrayed something of his lifestyle and status: Mr Podgers' lack of a club underlines his social inferiority.

portière. Door-curtain.

11 *Arcady.* The ideal region of rural contentment.

12 *Tanagra.* Terracotta statuettes found in tombs in this ancient city of Boeotia.

14 *Bailey's Magazine.* Correctly, two sporting journals, *Ruff's Guide to the Turf* and *Baily's Magazine of Sports and Pastimes*—an indication of the most necessary works of reference in the library of a gentlemen's club.

Buckingham. A gentlemen's club. Existing members could veto any new candidates for membership by 'black-balling' them, with a secret veto.

monsieur le mauvais sujet. You rascal.

15 *On a fait . . . pour moi.* Men lost their heads for me.

16 *Venice.* The Lido is an island of pleasure-resorts where Venetians came for sea-bathing. Florian's is a café on the Piazza of San Marco.

17 *Pinetum.* The Pine Forest of Ravenna. The Hotel Royal Danieli is the first Venetian hotel in a contemporary Baedeker.

19 *revolutionary tendencies.* Wilde enjoys making fun of the Russian Nihilists and

Anarchists supposedly busy in London preparing to dynamite the rulers of Russia. Cf. *DL* p. 230n., and a more serious treatment in Conrad's *The Secret Agent* (1907). Wilde's most immediate source would appear to be the character and situation of Zero, the ineffective maker of explosions in R. L. Stevenson's *New Arabian Nights: The Dynamiter* (1885).

23 *Mudie.* See below, p. 501n.

Dorcas Society. A ladies' association in a church for the purpose of making and providing clothes for the poor.

cap of Liberty. The conical cap given in Roman times to slaves on emancipation, and often used as a republican symbol.

25 *dusky air.* Cf. the poem 'Impression du Matin' (1881), 'St Paul's/Loomed like a bubble o'er the town'.

THE HAPPY PRINCE

This story was first published in 1888 in *The Happy Prince and Other Tales*. On the surface it is entirely in the tradition of the very popular Hans Andersen (see p. 37n.), but it owes a lot to Wilde's reading in his French masters.

28 *Charity Children.* Pupils of a school, supported by charitable bequests, for the education of the poor.

29 *Sans-Souci.* Without care or concern. This was the name of the Prussian King Frederick the Great's palace in Potsdam.

30 *Egypt.* Wilde's swallow has been influenced by Gautier. His yearning for Egypt is based on a poem from Gautier's *Emaux et Camées*, 'Ce Que Disent les Hirondelles'. See *DG* p. 170, and *The Sphinx*, headnote.

31 *Ghetto.* The quarter in a city to which Jews were restricted.

Memnon. See *The Sphinx*, ll. 133–4n.

33 *red ibises.* See *The Sphinx*, l. 39n.

35 *Angels.* Cf. Andersen's tale 'The Angel'.

THE DEVOTED FRIEND

First published in *The Happy Prince and Other Tales* (1888).

36 *a Green Linnet.* It is no accident that it is the linnet who tells this essentially moral story: Wilde was well acquainted with Wordsworth's famous little poem 'The Tables Turned' (cf. *DL* p. 223), and this stanza, which generally expresses the opposite to his own ideas:

> Books! 'tis a dull and endless strife:
> Come, hear the woodland linnet,
> How sweet his music! on my life,
> There's more of wisdom in it.

37 *named Hans.* Wilde's fairy tales are generally indebted to Hans Andersen (1805–75), Danish poet and fabulist, fêted in England in the 1840s. The framework of pondlife here is reminiscent of Andersen's 'In the Duck-

Yard', and Hugh the Miller's idea of friendship resembles the Hen's attitude in 'The Ugly Duckling', but Wilde's calling this excessively devoted hero Hans may signal a gentle mockery of Andersen's worst sentimental excesses.

38 *finer thing also.* An early statement of a central theme of *The Critic as Artist.*

   blue spectacles. See *IH* p. 397n.

39 *Burgomaster.* The chief magistrate of a Dutch or Flemish town: used loosely for any member of the governing body of a foreign municipality.

THE PICTURE OF DORIAN GRAY

The novel was first published in *Lippincott's Monthly Magazine* in July 1890. When Wilde republished it in book form in 1891 he added a Preface and substantially enlarged and altered the text. For further information on revisions and sources see my Oxford English Novels edition (1974). Much of the witty dialogue in the novel was re-used in later plays, especially *A Woman of No Importance.*

48 *The Preface.* First printed in *The Fortnightly Review*, 1 (March 1891) as 'A Preface to *Dorian Gray*'. Wilde's addition of the Preface is a self-conscious echoing of Gautier, who incorporated his most outspoken artistic manifesto in the Preface to his novel *Mademoiselle de Maupin* (1835). The last three sentences of this Preface are especially close to Gautier's.

   everything. At the last moment (*L* 289), Wilde added this aphorism from 'The Soul of Man', published in *The Fortnightly Review* (February 1891).

50 *only place.* Cf. LASC p. 1. The Royal Academy was founded by George III in 1768. The annual exhibition was large and 'Establishment'-dominated by Hallward's day. In July 1877 Wilde recognized the merits of the newly opened Grosvenor Gallery, and he twice reviewed exhibitions there (*Misc*, 5–23, 24–9). The Grosvenor's championship of the Pre-Raphaelites helped to make famous the 'greenery-yallery, Grosvenor Gallery, / Foot-in-the-grave young man' of Gilbert and Sullivan's *Patience*, for many an image of Wilde himself.

   Narcissus. See the prose poem 'The Disciple', and cf. *Salome*, p. 311.

51 *wrong thing.* Echoes Rochester's epitaph for Charles II: 'Here lies a Great and Mighty King / Whose Promise none rely'd on; / He never said a Foolish Thing / Nor ever did a Wise One.'

53 *crush.* A crowded social gathering.

   of the firm. See Act 1 of *The Duchess of Padua* (1883): 'As for conscience, / Conscience is but the name which cowardice / Fleeing from battle scrawls upon its shield.'

   Stars and Garters. People wearing the insignia of various orders of knight-hood: 'The Star and Garter' is also a common name for a public house.

54 *restaurant.* Wilde is reputed to have said of Mark André Raffalovich, his successor in the friendship of the young poet John Gray, that he came to

London to found a *salon*, and only succeeded in founding a saloon (*L* 173 n.).

55 *Antinoüs*. Beautiful page to the Roman Emperor Hadrian, beloved by him. After his mysterious drowning in the Nile (AD 130), Hadrian ordered extravagant monuments to his memory.

56 *Agnew*. Picture dealer in Old Bond Street.

57 *in a phrase*. Wilde later used the same words to summarize his own achievement: see *SL* 194, quoted Introduction p. xii.

58 *model lodging-houses*. Originally, one of a number of lodging-houses, established *c.*1840–5 by various philanthropists to secure the comfort and orderly conduct of the inmates. The designation was later misapplied to any large lodging-house, often of a very low class.

East End. Cf. *DL* p. 219.

60 *the world*. James 1: 27.

62 *yield to it*. In Balzac's *Old Goriot*, Rastignac is influenced by Vautrin rather as Lord Henry influences Dorian here. This sentence comes from an exchange in that novel: '"Temptations can be got rid of." "How?" "By yielding to them."'

in the brain. An idea repeatedly stressed by Emerson. See e.g.: 'All the marked events of our day, all the cities, all the colonizations, may be traced back to their origin in a private brain' ('Considerations by the Way'). Cf. *Rev* 405, *SL* 211.

For nearly ten minutes. The next two paragraphs are heavily dependent, even to verbal echoes, on Pater's *Gaston de Latour*, the third chapter of which was published in *Macmillan's Magazine* in August 1888 (pp. 259–60). *Dorian Gray* often follows a pattern established by Pater's first novel, *Marius the Epicurean*, and this one.

into the air. See Longfellow, 'The Arrow and the Song': 'I shot an arrow into the air, / It fell to earth, I know not where.'

63 *been wine*. Cf. *BRG* l. 120.

but the senses. Cf. Pater, in *Marius the Epicurean* (1885) vol. i. 29: 'a valuable, because partly practicable, belief that all the maladies of the soul might be reached through the subtle gateways of the body'.

65 *new sensations*. Cf. Pater's Conclusion to *The Renaissance* (1873): 'What we have to do is to be for ever curiously testing new opinions and courting new impressions.'

new Hedonism. The theory of ethics in which pleasure is regarded as the chief good, the proper end of action. Pater objected strenuously to the term, because the 'pleasures' implied were so vague, and included coarse as well as refined experiences. Wilde, or at least Lord Henry, developed this 'new Hedonism' from their interpretations of the almost infamous Conclusion to the first edition of Pater's *Renaissance* (Hill 186–90, 271–4).

68 *painted of me.* Dorian's reactions are reminiscent of D'Albert's yearnings in Gautier's *Mademoiselle de Maupin*: see ch. v.

69 *as a rational animal.* Traditional in manuals of logic. Cf. *CA II* p. 280.

71 *Prim.* Juan Prim (1814–70), Spanish soldier and statesman; a distinguished general, with a chequered career, who opposed Queen Isabella's tyranny. He was assassinated just after heading a successful revolt which elected Amadeo I as king.

to his valet. Despite Madame Cornuel, 'no man is a hero to his valet'.

72 *English Blue-book.* General colloquial descriptive term for one of the Society directories of the period.

73 *good-looking chap.* The romantic background supplied here for the orphan Dorian is very similar to those of the Young King and the Infanta (*CSF* 171–2, 186–8).

jarvies. Hackney-coachmen.

Americans just now. Wilde frequently made fun of Americans: see below pp. 76–7, LASC p. 15, and e.g. 'The American Invasion' (*Misc* 77–82), 'The American Man' (Mason 22–7), and 'The Canterville Ghost' (*CSF* 59–87).

74 *meanest flower might blow.* Cf. the last lines of Wordsworth's 'Immortality Ode'.

75 *Buonarotti.* Michelangelo Buonarotti (1475–1564), Italian sculptor, painter, and poet. Cf. p. 136, where Wilde cites Michelangelo as a great lover of men, as he would do again in court. Pater has an essay on Michelangelo's poetry in *The Renaissance*.

77 *cast-off clothes.* The origin of the quip is in Oliver Wendell Holmes's *The Autocrat of the Breakfast Table*.

79 *Silenus.* In Greek mythology, a drunken attendant of Bacchus and closely allied to the satyrs, of whom he appears as the leader. Elderly satyrs were called Sileni.

wise Omar. See the *Rubaiyat of Omar Khayyam*, in popular translation by Edward Fitzgerald (1859): devoted to the theme of drinking and making merry.

pipe laughing. See Browning's *Pied Piper of Hamelin*.

80 *Academy of Letters.* The French Academy of Letters, founded informally in 1629, and established by parliament as a tribunal to preserve and purify the language. It contained forty members, who were meant to contain all the chief literary men of France. Arnold wanted a similar Academy in Britain.

81 *by Clodion.* Claude Michel Clodion (1738–1814), French sculptor inspired by the antique.

Les Cent Nouvelles. Collection of licentious French tales, Italian-influenced (1462).

Margaret of Valois. Also known as Margaret of Navarre (see p. 180).

Margaret (1553–1615) married Henri of Navarre, and was famous for beauty, learning, and loose conduct.

Clovis Eve. Nicolas Eve, official binder of the French court. Usually credited with introducing 'fanfare' binding, which included fragile branches bearing myriads of leaves, or other tiny motifs.

thief of time. The conventional proverb asserts the contrary, that procrastination is the thief of time.

Manon Lescaut. Novel by Abbé de Prévost (1731) in which the hero, de Grieux, is ready to sacrifice all for his love, but Manon, although fond of him, cannot overcome her passion for splendour, comfort, and luxury.

82 *Wardour Street.* Then known for antique dealers.

frangipanni. Red jasmine.

85 *The Idiot Boy, or Dumb but Innocent.* Lord Henry invented this one, but within a recognizable genre: plays that are recorded include *The Idiot of Heidelburg, The Idiot of the Mill, The Idiot of the Mountain,* and *Idiot Witness; Or, A Tale of Blood.*

les grandpères ont toujours tort. Older people are always wrong.

imagine a girl. Dorian's description of Sibyl is noticeably similar to Wilde's description of Constance Lloyd, his future wife, in 1883 (*L* 154).

hautbois. Oboe.

91 *as Giordano Bruno thought.* Lord Henry here topically reflects the ideas in Pater's 'Giordano Bruno', published in the *Fortnightly Review* in August 1889, and posthumously republished in revised form as the last chapter of Pater's unfinished novel *Gaston de Latour* (1896).

92 *bismuth-whitened hands.* White bismuth used in cosmetics, especially theatrical make-up.

93 *Prince Charming.* Not just Cinderella's prince; also a soubriquet often used for the eponymous Prince Otto in R. L. Stevenson's tale (1886).

97 *gold-fields.* Gold was discovered in New South Wales in 1851, and this occasioned a massive inrush of immigrants. The goldmines flourished until approximately 1891.

98 *through the window.* The proverb says: 'When poverty comes in at the door, love creeps out at the window.'

99 *orris-root.* Iris rhizome, which has a scent like violets: used powdered as perfume, and for medical purposes.

Achilles Statue. See *IH* p. 429n.

103 *Messalina.* The wife of the Emperor Claudius, a byword for her profligacy, who was put to death in AD 48.

104 *playing Rosalind.* Confusion here: Dorian himself said on pp. 88, 90 that she was to play Imogen. In Gautier's *Mademoiselle de Maupin* the ambiguous central figure's true sex is revealed to D'Albert in a performance of *As You*

Like It, described in ch. xi. Wilde refers respectfully to this description in a review of *As You Like It* in 1883 (*Rev* 32).

Tanagra figurine. See p. 12n.

105 *thing he loves.* Cf. *BRG* l. 37 and n.

107 *fine-champagne.* Liqueur brandy.

brougham. A one-horse closed carriage with two or four wheels, for two or four persons.

hansom. The forerunners of modern taxis; they held two passengers, the driver on an elevated seat behind.

109 *holy palmers' kiss. Romeo and Juliet*, I. v. 95–8. Apparently I. iii., where Juliet first appears, was cut in this production.

110 *speak tonight.* ibid. II. ii. 85–7.

next we meet. ibid. II. ii. 116–22.

111 *absolutely nothing.* Cf. Lady Bracknell in *IBE* p. 493.

112 *sick of shadows.* This seems a deliberate echo of Tennyson's 'The Lady of Shalott', where the lady turns from art to life: 'I am half sick of shadows.'

114 *Covent Garden.* Cf. the emergence of the hero from horror and night to beauty and morning at Covent Garden in LASC pp. 10–11.

116 *for impossible things.* A recurrent preoccupation for Wilde as for Gautier (see e.g. D'Albert, the young hero of *Mademoiselle de Maupin*). Cf. *CA I* p. 264 and *SL* 64.

121 *Patti night.* Adelina Patti (1843–1919), popular soprano opera singer, born in Madrid, appearing first in London in 1861.

122 *gold-latten.* Latten—a mixed metal of yellow colour, resembling brass.

123 *asphodel.* In Greek mythology, flower of the dead.

124 *of us all.* An inversion of *Hamlet*, III. i. 83, 'Thus conscience does make cowards of us all.'

126 *pity of it.* Cf. *Othello*, IV. i. 191–2.

129 *la consolation des arts.* See *Misc.* 271: 'that *consolation des arts* which is the keynote of Gautier's poetry, the secret of modern life foreshadowed', etc.

131 *Georges Petit.* The vast and fashionable Paris gallery of Georges Petit, established in 1882, welcomed the most varied trends and showed the works of the Impressionists during the period of their first success.

133 *Adrian's barge.* See above, p. 55.

136 *bore him.* This passage has marked similarities to the speech of Wilde on 'the Love that dare not speak its name' that produced public applause at Wilde's first trial (see Ellmann 435).

137 *Fonthill.* William Beckford, author of *Vathek*, collected at Fonthill, which he built in Gothic style, a wide range of works of art sold at auction in 1822.

138 *cassone.* Chest.

139 *nacre.* Mother-of-pearl.

141 *novel without a plot.* Identified by some with Huysmans's *A Rebours*; others have seen the central influence on Lord Henry and Dorian to be Pater. In the typescript Wilde sent to *Lippincott's Monthly Magazine*, the novel had a title, an author, and a hero, which he later deleted: '*Le Secret de Raoul* par Catulle Sarrazin'. At the end of ch. xi Wilde describes three chapters of the 'wonderful novel' which have no resemblance to *A Rebours*. Clearly Wilde originally intended to construct a quite fictional 'golden book' for Dorian, which could parallel the long accounts of 'golden books' in Pater's novels, the *Metamorphoses* of Apuleius for Marius, and the works of Ronsard for Gaston de Latour. The deleted title, *Le Secret de Raoul*, is the more interesting when we learn that the unpublished chapters of *Gaston* include one describing a peasant named Raoul, who kills and then dies for love of a handsome lord.

to sum up. Like Pater's Marius, who assimilated in turn several religious views of the ancient world.

argot. Jargon, slang.

Symbolistes. See 'The Decadent Movement in Literature', where Arthur Symons sees the brothers Goncourt as creators of a new prose style, and Verlaine of a verse style. Mallarmé, Maeterlinck, and Huysmans are also included.

142 *from the world.* James 1: 27.

143 *with gratification.* See *Antony and Cleopatra*, II. ii. 239–42.

144 *worship of beauty.* Also quoted by Pater in *Marius the Epicurean*, vol. i. 34: 'he [Marius] was of the number of those who, in the words of a poet who came long after, must be "made perfect by the love of visible beauty."' The quotation is not from Dante, and the nearest source seems to be *Mademoiselle de Maupin* once more. Gautier's D'Albert is described as 'an exclusive worshipper of form', and says in ch. v, 'I worship beauty of form above all things'.

visible world existed. Noted in the *Journal des Goncourt* (1 May 1857). Also see again *Mademoiselle de Maupin*, ch. viii, where D'Albert writes: 'You know the eagerness with which I have sought for physical beauty, and the importance that I attach to form, and the love of the visible world that possesses me.' Cf. *SL* 237.

'*Satyricon*'. Petronius, the 'leader of fashion': one of the Roman Emperor Nero's companions, and director of the pleasures of the imperial court. *The Satyricon*, a satirical prose romance with verse interspersed, survives fragmentarily. Huysmans dwells on it in some detail in *A Rebours*, ch. iii.

145 *a new Hedonism.* See p. 65n.

146 *dalmatic.* The dalmatic is not worn at Benediction, here implied. Robert Ross, a Roman Catholic, altered it to 'vestment' in the 1908 edition. The original *Lippincott* version has 'cope', more specifically and still correctly, as a cope is worn for Benediction.

antinomianism. Avowed rejection of the moral law. Pater's Conclusion to *The Renaissance* is echoed again in this paragraph.

Darwinismus movement. Chiefly represented by Ernst Heinrich Haeckel 1834–1919, who espoused Darwin's evolutionary theories in 1862.

147 *study perfumes.* As does Des Esseintes, the protagonist of Huysmans's *A Rebours*, at much greater length and with perverse ingenuity.

strangest instruments. It is typical of Wilde's method in this chapter that all the musical references here, from *juruparis* to the drums of Bernal Diaz, are copied, often word for word, from one short chapter on 'The American Indians' in the South Kensington Museum Art Handbook *Musical Instruments* by Carl Engel.

148 *of his own soul.* See *CA I*, p. 264n.

Anne de Joyeuse. Henri III, who had a 'more than feminine' weakness for jewels, had a weakness also for his favourites, or *mignons*, who like him were curled and powdered and groomed. He made the chief of these a duke, with the name of Joyeuse, and had him married to the queen's sister.

had collected. Every one of these stones, from chrysoberyl to turquoise, is described with identical adjectives in A. H. Church's *Precious Stones*, a South Kensington Museum Art Handbook first published in 1882 (ch. vii). Des Esseintes chooses stones from a similar collection to set in the shell of a live tortoise.

about jewels. Every detail cited in this long paragraph and the next two, and every authority named, is copied, often word for word, from William Jones, *History and Mystery of Precious Stones* (1880). Jones tirelessly consulted British and foreign experts and dedicated his compilation to Ruskin.

150 *to embroideries.* All the examples in these two paragraphs are drawn from *Embroidery and Lace: Their Manufacture and History from the Remotest Antiquity to the Present Day* by Ernest Lefébure, tr. Alan S. Cole. Wilde reviewed this book appreciatively and at length in *Woman's World*, of which he was editor, in November 1888. His review, as well as Lefébure's text, is extensively pillaged for this description (*Rev* 327–41).

151 *ecclesiastical vestments.* Dorian shares this taste with Huysmans's Des Esseintes.

153 *blackballed.* Refused membership.

than morals. See also Mrs Erlynne in *LWF* p. 379: 'My dear Windermere, manners before morals!'

154 *terrible thing.* Cf. *CA II* p. 284.

myriad sensations. Cf. Dr Jekyll in the last chapter of Stevenson's *Strange Case of Dr Jekyll and Mr Hyde*: 'I hazard a guess that man will be ultimately known for a mere polity of multifarious, incongruous and independent denizens.'

by the Court for his handsome face. In fact, 'caressed by KING JAMES for' etc., *The Miscellaneous Works of . . . Francis Osborn* (1722), ii. 133. Huysmans's

Des Esseintes also had an ancestor who was a court favourite, and whom he resembled.

155 *Carlton House.* In London, where the Prince Regent, the future George IV, entertained with magnificence.

as Tiberius. The stories of Roman Emperors from Tiberius to Nero are to be found in Suetonius's *Lives of the Caesars* and the *Annals* of Tacitus. Huysmans mentions the same incidents in the reign of Elagabalus as Wilde does.

156 *monstrous or mad.* Accounts of all the figures in this long paragraph are in John Addington Symonds's *Renaissance in Italy* (7 vols., 1875–86), especially I, chs. ii and vi: Wilde's borrowing retains clear verbal echoes.

The Renaissance . . . poisoned by a book. Possibly a guarded reference to the 'poisonous' quality of Pater's *Renaissance*.

157 *ulster.* A long loose overcoat of rough cloth: not obviously the garb of a gentleman.

159 *the Dudley.* In Egyptian Hall, Piccadilly. 'In 1850 Lord Dudley placed his fine collection of pictures for public inspection in what has since been known as the Dudley Gallery, in which are now held the well-established annual exhibitions of "Cabinet Paintings" and "Drawings in Black and White"' (H. B. Wheatley, *London Past and Present*, 1891, ii).

164 *awful lesson.* Cf. a crux in *Dr Jekyll and Mr Hyde* ('Incident of the Letter'): 'I have had a lesson—O God, Utterson, what a lesson I have had!'

165 *white as snow.* 'Though your sins be as scarlet, they shall be as white as snow', Isaiah I: 18. Cf. *BRG* l. 636.

167 *some red star.* In Pater's 'Denys L'Auxerrois', this indicates Nature's participation in a kind of wild, Dionysian revelry: 'The planet Mars drew nearer to the earth than usual, hanging in the low sky like a fiery red lamp' (*Imaginary Portraits*, 1887).

bull's eye. A lantern made of bull's eye, or hemispherical, glass.

the Blue Book. See above, p. 72n.

168 *woman's memory.* See above, p. 123: 'That awful memory of woman!'

169 *Basil Hallward.* In his memoir of the poisoner Wainewright, 'Pen, Pencil and Poison', the murderer's pictures reflect his own evil, and Wilde tells how: 'M. Zola, in one of his novels [*Thérèse Raquin*, 1867], tells us of a young man who, having committed a murder, takes to art, and paints greenish impressionist portraits of perfectly respectable people, all of which bear a strange resemblance to his victim' (*Intentions*, 1891).

Emaux et Camées. Charpentier's edition of 1881 has the Jacquemart etching. Lacenaire was a celebrated murderer who died by the guillotine. The poet touched the cold flesh 'scarcely rid of its torture stain', the mummified yellow hand with 'satyr's fingers'. This aristocratic soft hand, free of the 'honest calluses of work', makes Dorian more aware of what his own hand has done.

stanzas upon Venice. There are three 'Variations sur le Carneval de Venise'; this is from the second, 'Sur les lagunes'. The lines in which Dorian sees 'the whole of Venice' are inspired by the air of 'The Carnival of Venice'. Gautier says in the next stanza: 'Tout Venise vit dans cet air'.

170   *the swallows.* 'Ce Que Disent les Hirondelles: chanson d'automne' *(Emaux et Camées,* 159). At the onset of autumn, six swallows meet and tell their adventures: one has been, as here, to Smyrna. Cf. 'The Happy Prince' p. 30 and n., and *The Sphinx,* l. 39n.

   the Obelisk. Two poems form the 'Nostalgies d'Obélisques': this is a fairly accurate account of the first, 'L'Obélisque de Paris'.

   the Louvre. The 'monstre charmant' is of doubtful sex: 'Est-ce un jeune homme? est-ce une femme? / Une déesse, ou bien un dieu?' ('Contralto'). Gautier was particularly interested in the idea of the hermaphrodite, and bisexuality: see *Mademoiselle de Maupin, passim.*

171   *Rubinstein.* Anton Grigorowitz Rubinstein (1830–94), popular Russian pianist whose compositions are now forgotten, but whose reputation as a performer survives.

179   *chaudfroid.* Dish of meat, poultry, etc., in jelly.

180   *de Navarre.* See note on Margaret of Valois, p. 81 above.

181   *Debrett.* See above, p. 1n.

182   *doctrinaire.* Often applied as a term of reproach by 'practical' men to theorists, 'merely' theoretical.

   image precious. Wilde wrote to Lord Alfred Douglas in 1897: 'When I wrote, in my aphorisms, that it was simply the feet of clay that made the gold of the image precious, it was of you I was thinking' *(SL* 192). But see *SL* 89, where evidence shows he had met Douglas once, at most, when he wrote this sentence.

   over-educated. Cf. PPUY.

183   *started.* The closeness of this whole paragraph to a scene in William Sharp's novel, *Children of To-morrow* (London, 1889), and other points of similarity, have been pointed out by me in *DUJ* (December 1987).

185   *lamp-lit blind.* This description owes much to Wilde's poem 'The Harlot's House' (1885), especially l. 9 and ll. 22–4.

192   *Tartuffe.* An odious hypocrite, subject of Molière's comedy of that name (1664). Napoleon described England as 'a nation of shopkeepers'.

195   *Sphinxes without secrets.* Wilde wrote a short story called 'The Sphinx without a Secret' *(CSF* 52–8), and see also the account of Vivian's vague friend, *DL* p. 231. In an essay on Poe, Baudelaire called public opinion 'ce sphinx sans énigme'.

   Parthian manner. Parthian horsemen baffled their enemies by rapid manœuvres, and discharged their missiles backward while in real or pretended flight.

201 *strawberry leaves.* These figure on the coronet of a duke, marquis, or earl.

204 *Perdita . . . Florizel.* See Shakespeare's *Winter's Tale.*

205 *vinaigrette box.* Small ornamental box containing a sponge charged with some aromatic or pungent salts.

206 *Waterbury watch.* A very common pocket watch, too cheap to be worth a murderer's time. See *L* 623, where Wilde writes after prison to request one for himself.

207 *face without a heart. Hamlet*, IV. vii. 108–9.

own soul. Mark 8: 36: 'For what shall it profit a man, if he shall gain the whole world, and lose his own soul?'

209 *Marsyas.* A Phrygian flute-player, who challenged Apollo to a contest of skill, but being beaten by the god was flayed alive for his presumption. A frequent allusion in Wilde.

sound of music. Lord Henry's tribute to Dorian here appropriately echoes Pater's description of the *Mona Lisa* in the *Renaissance*, once more comparing him to a painting.

somewhere. In 'Bishop Blougram's Apology' ll. 183–6:
> Just when we are safest, there's a sunset-touch,
> A fancy from a flower-bell, some one's death,
> A chorus-ending from Euripides,
> And that's enough for fifty hopes and fears . . .

212 *mad letter.* Wilde was to write a very similar letter to Lord Alfred Douglas in January 1893 (*SL* 107 and n.).

THE DECAY OF LYING: AN OBSERVATION

In *De Profundis* Wilde describes the beginnings of this work, over a cheap dinner with Robert Ross (*SL* 157). It was first published in *The Nineteenth Century* in January 1889 (NC), and was revised and reprinted in the first edition of *Intentions* (1891) (FE). Only important changes will be signalled here: much of the revision is a matter of filling out arguments with further material, and small stylistic changes. Wilde was a great reader, and in the 1880s a busy reviewer, and the dialogue shows a catholic knowledge of the contemporary literary scene, especially in Britain and France. The dialogue defends and promotes romance, and attacks realism in this modern scene, but as the title indicates it also addresses itself to Plato, the first critic to describe fiction as lying, and to take moral exception to it, and Cyril quotes Aristotle on the first page. The notes give some indication of the compressed references here, showing briefly for example how Wilde pursued his baiting of the American painter James McNeill Whistler, both in NC and in additions for FE: after a close friendship, Whistler had famously accused Wilde of plagiarism of ideas, and Wilde clearly enjoyed provoking him further, and following his French masters Baudelaire and Gautier by writing at length in FE about painting, a province Whistler wished writers to keep clear of. Wilde appreciated the advantages of the dialogue form, as he indicates at *CA II*, pp. 282–3. Here, as in *Dorian Gray* and the comedies, conversational exchange is part of the pleasure the work has to offer, but it is also clear from the start that the participants include one who will win and one who will be persuaded, and which voice will predominate. The participants, Cyril and Vivian, are mischievously named after Wilde's two sons, who were respectively 3½ and 2 when the dialogue first appeared.

215 *Aristotle once said.* In the *Poetics* Aristotle suggested that through mimesis [i.e. capturing the essential quality] of action, character, and emotion, the artist completes nature.

Morris' poorest workman. William Morris (1834–96), poet, artist, craftsman, decorator, and social reformer, founded a shop to provide largely hand-made wallpaper, tapestry, furniture, etc., which genuinely revolutionized taste. Wilde has gone up market from NC, where he refers to the more commercial Maples in Tottenham Court Road.

phrased it. See Wordsworth, 'Power of Music', l. 4, which in fact reads: 'In the street that from Oxford hath borrowed its name.'

216 *the word 'Whim'.* In his essay 'Self-Reliance' of 1841 Emerson's main advice is 'Trust thyself', and his notion of self-reliance has much in common with the Individualism that Wilde preaches in his essay 'The Soul of Man'. Emerson says: 'I shun father and mother and wife and brother when my genius calls me. I would write on the lintels of the doorpost, *Whim.*'

the Sophist. Scholar-philosophers of the fifth century BC who travelled and taught the art of persuasion, for use in law courts and politics. More recently, captious or intentionally fallacious reasoner.

Leontine schools. Leontini was an ancient Greek settlement in Sicily. The most famous product of Leontine schools was Gorgias (c.483–375 BC), Greek sophist and rhetorician, who transplanted rhetoric to Greece.

217 *Retrospective Review.* A short-lived periodical (1820–8) intended to rouse interest in 'the old and venerable literature of the country': it was briefly revived once before Vivian's time (1853–4) but this revival by Vivian is fictitious.

The Tired Hedonists. Heavy (self-) mockery here: the young speaker is himself, he claims, a pleasure seeker already exhausted by his pleasures, looking to the past and posing as admiring one of the cruellest of Roman Emperors, Domitian. He became Emperor in AD 81, ruling well at first but then guilty of 'most atrocious cruelties'. Ellmann says Wilde called Lord Alfred Douglas 'the young Domitian' (363).

Blue-Book. A report or other paper printed by parliament.

document humain . . . coin de la création. Human document, and corner of the universe, both phrases associated with the Naturalist novelist Zola, who wrote in *Mes haines*: 'Une oeuvre d'art est un coin de la création vu à travers un tempérament'; the title of one of the articles in *Le Roman expérimental* is 'Les documents humains'.

ideas. Here Wilde mischievously uses a phrase his former friend Whistler had used of him, in angry accusations of plagiarism: 'Oscar . . . has the

588   NOTES

courage of the opinions . . . of others' (*GAME*, 164). Vivian's argument owes something also to J. P. Mahaffy's *The Principles of the Art of Conversation*, which Wilde reviewed in 1887, and which makes a less paradoxical case: 'Even a consummate liar, though generally vulgar, and therefore offensive, is a better ingredient in company than the scrupulously truthful man, who weighs every statement, questions every fact, and corrects every inaccuracy' (78).

218 *as Plato saw*. In bk. x of his *Republic*, Plato rejected poetry: it frustrated true wisdom by extolling the illusory phenomena of this world; by lying.

Robert Louis Stevenson. 1850–94, Scottish writer of the *New Arabian Nights* (1882), improbable contemporary adventure stories, and the romantic thrillers *Treasure Island* (1883) and *Kidnapped* (1886). *The Black Arrow: A Tale of the Two Roses* (1888) is a historical novel of the time of Henry VI; *Strange Case of Dr Jekyll and Mr Hyde* (1886), a contemporary story of divided personality, may have in small part inspired *Dorian Gray*.

Lancet. British medical periodical, founded 1823.

Rider Haggard. Henry Rider Haggard (1856–1925), another romance writer, who became known with *King Solomon's Mines* (1885) and *She* (1887). His other novels of many kinds, including the modern analytical kind, have sunk without trace.

219 *Henry James*. 1843–1916, American novelist and later a playwright whose failures coincided in London with Wilde's greatest comic successes. His 1880s novels were mainly concerned with the impact on American sensibilities of the older European civilization.

Hall Caine. 1853–1931, British novelist, biographer of Rossetti. Wilde deplored the haste with which his Rossetti biography appeared, and Richard Le Gallienne records him saying, 'Whenever a great man dies, Hall Caine and William Sharp go in with the undertakers.' A veiled reference persists in *CA I*, p. 243. Caine's astonishing popularity as novelist began with *The Deemster* (1887), set in the Isle of Man.

James Payn. 1830–98, editor of the *Cornhill* 1882–96, author of dozens of popular novels with a quick eye for the comic and love of harmless fun.

William Black. 1841–98, prolific London-based Scottish novelist. *The Strange Adventures of a Phaeton* (1872) characteristically blended travel book and fiction. *Phaeton*. Carriage, or chariot. The accounts of Caine, Payn, and Black were added for FE.

Mrs Oliphant. Margaret Oliphant (1828–97), outstandingly prolific Scottish novelist and non-fiction writer, who supported an extended family by her pen.

Marion Crawford. Francis Marion Crawford (1854–1909). American novelist and historian whose residence in Italy and conversion to Catholicism are reflected in his novels.

d'Italie. Apparently a misremembering of a story told by Italian actress Adelaide Ristori in her *Etudes et Souvenirs*, which Wilde reviewed in 1888

(*Rev* 251–7). Ristori tells of a censor from Verona so sensitive about politics that he insisted the phrase 'Beautiful sky of Italy' be rendered: 'Beautiful sky of Lombardy Venetia!'

Robert Elsmere. Novel by Mrs Humphry Ward (1851–1920), a niece of Matthew Arnold. It was published in 1888, and quickly went through many editions. It dealt with a young clergyman who lost his faith in the miraculous element of Christianity, under so much threat at the time, and took to social work. It reflected the anxieties of many troubled readers. Mrs Ward was brought in touch with many who worked among the poor of London's East End. Cf. *DG* p. 58.

lost ideas. Matthew Arnold had famously called Oxford the 'home of lost causes'.

Maupassant. Guy de Maupassant (1850–93), French novelist and short-story writer, who associated with Zola and other disciples of Naturalism. Wilde was to admire *Une Vie* (1883) in a post-prison letter (*L* 784).

Zola. Emile Zola (1840–1902), French novelist and short-story writer, co-founder of the 'Naturalist school': his central ideas were about heredity and a certain cerebral infirmity. *Germinal* deals with French miners; *L'Assommoir* with drunkenness; *Nana* with lewdness, and *Pot-Bouille* with the lower bourgeois and their servants. Wilde's opposition to Naturalism and realism is here plain. Cf. p. 217n.

pronunciamiento. More commonly pronunciamento, a proclamation or manifesto. Vivian pretends to misunderstand Zola here: 'esprit' has more than one sense. Zola says, 'The man of genius has no need of wit': Vivian takes him to mean, 'The man of genius is never witty.'

220 *Tartuffe.* Eponymous hero of Molière's masterpiece, a study of hypocrisy (1664). NC reads here: 'It is simply the rage of Caliban on seeing his own face in a glass', but Wilde had already re-used this aphorism before the appearance of this dialogue in FE, in 'A Preface to *Dorian Gray*', first published in *The Fortnightly Review* 1 (March 1891). See *DG* p. 48.

Pentonville omnibus. Writing about *The Mill on the Floss* in *Fiction Fair and Foul* (1880–1).

Daudet. Alphonse Daudet (1840–97), French writer associated with Naturalism. Delobelle is a broken-down actor who inhabits Risler's tenement in *Fromont jeune et Risler aîné* (1874); Valmajour is a ridiculous character in *Numa Roumestan* (1881), and the poet in *Jack* (1876) is Amaury d'Argenton, Daudet's most perfect picture of an artistic fraud. There is no such volume as *Vingt ans de ma Vie littéraire*: either a slip or a mischievous deliberate mistake for two titles published in 1888, *Trente ans de Paris* and *Souvenirs d'un homme de lettres*, both of which stress the foundation of fact in the fictional plots and characters.

Bourget. Paul Bourget (1852–1935), French novelist and critic much occupied with contemporary psychology. He made his name with *Cruelle Enigme* (1885) and *André Chenier* (1887). His *Le Disciple* (1889: see p. 221 below) is a long, heavy novel, seen as an indictment of positivist philosophy.

Faubourg St Germain. As implied, the home of really 'good' or aristocratic society in Paris. Wilde took this so much for granted that NC has simply 'the Faubourg'.

opinions. 'Religious opinions' is slyly added to the list of 'accidentals' in FE.

221 *The Deemster.* The Deemster (1887) by Hall Caine; *The Daughter of Heth*—in fact *A Daughter of Heth* (1871) by William Black; *Le Disciple* (1889) by Paul Bourget; *Mr Isaacs* (1882) by Marion Crawford: *Robert Elsmere*, see note to p. 219.

Literature and Dogma. Matthew Arnold (1822–88), poet and critic. His *Literature and Dogma* (1873) attempts to salvage religion for late nineteenth-century believers by re-establishing it on verifiable spiritual experience, and the unassailable facts of moral experience.

Evidences. William Paley (1743–1805), theologian and moralist. His *A View of the Evidences of Christianity* (1794) is of a traditional cast. Wilde listed it along with 'all argumentative books and all books that try to prove anything', in a list of 'Books not to read at all' in 1886 (*Rev* 43).

Colenso. John William Colenso (1814–83), Bishop of Natal, who caused great alarm and excitement by casting doubt on the traditional accounts of the Pentateuch (the first five books of the Old Testament). See Matthew Arnold's scathing account, in 'The Bishop and the Philosopher', in *Essays in Criticism: First Series* (1865).

Green. Thomas Hill Green (1836–82). Idealist philosopher with intense interest in social questions who figures in *Robert Elsmere* as 'Mr Gray'.

Meredith. George Meredith (1828–1909), English novelist and poet who has been accused of 'artificiality and forced wit'. Cf. *Rev* 261.

Touchstone. As You Like It, II. iv. 55.

Baal. Here, a false god.

Balzac. Honoré de Balzac, French novelist (1799–1850). His large series of novels called *La Comédie Humaine* attempts a complete picture of modern civilization, making particular note of attitudes to money. Wilde frequently alludes to Lucien de Rubempré, the impoverished young poet in *Les Illusions Perdues* and *Splendeurs et misères des courtisanes*, one clear model for Dorian Gray. Like Dorian, he is beautiful, and willing to sell his soul for brilliance: his relationship with the sinister older man, Vautrin, foreshadows Dorian's with Lord Henry, and he loves Coralie, a good-hearted actress who experiences the conflict between real and acted love in ch. 38 of *Les Illusions Perdues* as Sibyl Vane also does. See also *Rev* 77–9.

222 *genius.* A paraphrase of a passage in Baudelaire's essay on Théophile Gautier.

Holbein. Hans Holbein (1497–1543), German portrait painter, best known in England for his portrait of Henry VIII.

Salammbô . . . Vicomte de Bragelonne. Historical novels by Flaubert (1862), Thackeray (1852), Charles Reade (1861), and Alexandre Dumas *père* (1850).

once said. Gautier, in the 'Preface' to *Mademoiselle de Maupin* (1835). See *L* 181.

Hecuba. Wife of King Priam of Troy. See the scene of Hamlet and the players, *Hamlet*, IV. ii. 551–3.

Reade. Charles Reade (1814–84), novelist and poet. His historical novel *The Cloister and the Hearth* (1861) is set in the fifteenth century: the first of his novels designed to expose social abuse was *It Is Never Too Late To Mend* (1857).

Romola. George Eliot's historical novel *Romola* (1862–3), set in Savonarola's Italy, characteristically appeals to Vivian more than *Daniel Deronda* (1874–6), which deals with contemporary life.

Dickens. Charles Dickens (1812–70) set out to expose the poor-law and the workhouse system in *Oliver Twist* (1838).

223 *mess of facts.* A deliberate echo of the Bible story of Esau who 'sold his birthright for a mess of pottage', Genesis: 25.

work of Art. This sentence, which again mischievously echoes Whistler (*GAME* 151), was deliberately added to FE. Whistler had publicly accused Wilde of plagiarism (see p. 217n. above, and below p. 232, and *GAME* 236–8). The original assertion, that one touch of nature will make the whole world kin, is from Shakespeare's *Troilus and Cressida*, III. iii. 175. Cf. *IH* p. 406: 'In modern life nothing produces such an effect as a good platitude. It makes the whole world kin.'

the sermons. As You Like It, II. i. 17.

great Ode. NC has: 'the "Ode to Immortality"'.

vernal wood. See Wordsworth's 'The Tables Turned'. Cf. p. 36n.

224 *non-existent.* Vivian's argument here is very similar to Whistler's 'Ten O'Clock' lecture of 1885: see *GAME* 135–59.

true decadence. 'True' is inserted here in FE, for emphasis of the unexpected nature of the doctrine.

Titans. In ancient Greek mythology, giants, sons of Heaven and Earth, eventually overthrown by Zeus and the other Olympians.

the object . . . complex beauty. In NC, this passage and others noted below are italicized: mature reconsideration clearly found this way of indicating key passages unsatisfactorily crude.

225 *Art surrenders . . . everything.* Originally italicized.

Meister. In a short poem, 'Natur und Kunst' (Nature and Art).

palinode. The withdrawal in a piece of writing of ideas expressed elsewhere in other work(s) by the same author.

226 *Philistine.* Originally a race inhabiting Palestine in biblical times; since Matthew Arnold's *Culture and Anarchy* (1869), those who are indifferent or hostile to artistic and cultural values.

the second. i.e. more concerned to keep the Sabbath than to heed the prohibition of making and worshipping graven images of anything in the universe. The religion of Islam has conditioned Moslem art, which traditionally refrained from portraying living creatures and became largely an art of ornament. Cf. *Rev* 331.

The proper . . . but Art. Originally italicized.

Herodotus. Greek historian (*c.*485–425 BC), called by Cicero the father of history, not of lies.

sciolists. Pretenders to knowledge.

Cicero (106–43 BC), Roman orator, statesman, and man of letters, some of whose powerful speeches of legal pleading have survived. Four of the writers on this list, Cicero, Suetonius, Marco Polo, and Cellini, also appeared on Wilde's public list of 'Books to read' in 1886 (*Rev* 43).

Suetonius. Roman historian (AD 75–160) famous for his lives of the first twelve Caesars.

Tacitus. Roman historian (AD *c.*55–120) famous for his biography of his father-in-law Agricola and *Annals* of the Julian emperors.

Pliny. Pliny (AD 23–79), friend of Tacitus, wrote his *Historia Naturalis* in AD 77. It makes no distinction between the true and the false, but is the only source on many matters.

Hanno. Carthaginian navigator of 6th–5th centuries BC, whose *Periplus* records his exploration of the western coast of Africa.

Froissart. Jean Froissart (*c.*1333–*c.*1405), French historian and poet.

Sir Thomas Mallory. Malory (d. 1471), was English author of the prose romance the *Morte d'Arthur*.

Polo. Marco Polo (1254–1324), Venetian traveller to China and the court of Kublai Khan who left an account, often too marvellous, of his travels.

Olaus Magnus. 1490–1558, Swedish historian.

Aldrovandus. Ulisse Aldrovandi (1522–1605), Italian naturalist, author of a great work on birds, insects, and mollusca.

Conrad Lycosthenes. 1518–61, Swiss philologist and theologian.

Benvenuto Cellini. See *CA I* p. 241n.

Casanuova. Giovanni Jacopo Casanova (1725–98), Italian autobiographer and famed sexual adventurer who left twelve volumes of *Memoirs.*

Defoe. Daniel Defoe (1660–1731), English author, adventurer and spy, author of novels *Robinson Crusoe* and *Moll Flanders*, and *A Journal of the Plague Year* (1722), written as if an eye-witness account of the Great Plague of London in 1664, when he was only in fact a small child.

Boswell. James Boswell (1740–95), Scottish man of letters and biographer of his friend Dr Samuel Johnson.

Napoleon's despatches. Napoleon Bonaparte (1769–1821), French Emperor. In *Representative Men* Emerson describes Napoleon as 'a boundless liar', and goes on: 'All his bulletins are proverbs for saying what he wished to be believed.'

Carlyle. Thomas Carlyle (1795–1881), Scottish essayist and historian. His *French Revolution* (1837) established his reputation.

George Washington. 1732–99, first president of the USA. Traditionally he confessed to his father that he cut down a cherry tree with his hatchet: 'I cannot tell a lie.' Vivian is right to doubt the story, probably the invention of biographer Mason Weems.

227 *Philistine.* See above, note to p. 226.

Megatherium. A gigantic extinct South American monster resembling a ground-sloth.

Royal Society. Incorporated by Charles II in 1662 for the advancement of the physical sciences.

Incorporated Authors. A possible dig at the Society of Authors, founded in 1884 by Walter Besant to promote the business interests of authors and fight for their rights. Wilde was unhappy at a banquet in July 1888, because seated next to Lady Colin Campbell, with whom he was not on speaking terms since she had referred to him as 'The Great White Slug'.

Burnand. Francis Cowley Burnand (1836–1917), English novelist and burlesque writer, editor of *Punch.* Popular dramatist with hits like *Black-eyed Susan*, which ran for 400 nights. He had satirized Wilde in *The Colonel* in 1881.

Spencer. Herbert Spencer (1820–1903), English evolutionary philosopher whose philosophy was deeply enmeshed in the scientific outlook of his day.

Saturday Review. A reference to an anonymous notice of Wilde's own *The Happy Prince* in the *Saturday Review* (20 October 1888). Wilde blamed Walter Pollock, but the author was Robert Ross's brother Alexander, a founder and secretary of the Society of Authors (see above 227). Wilde's story 'The Nightingale and the Rose' was faulted for emotion and natural history, but the story of a bird's immolating herself on a thorn to stain a rose to red to help a student to win his love hardly aspires to natural history!

228 *Nature.* See *Hamlet*, III. ii. 17–20.

living man. See Shelley's *Prometheus Unbound*, I. 748.

Life . . . imitates life. Originally italicized.

229 *painters.* The reference is first to Dante Gabriel Rossetti (1828–82), one of the founder-members of the Pre-Raphaelite Brotherhood, whose paintings of Elizabeth Siddal and Janey Morris in particular gave a new notion of feminine beauty, and second to his disciple Edward Burne-Jones (1833–98), whose paintings of women, referred to here, were often medieval, ethereal and dreamlike. Wilde had lauded them in his 1877 review of the Grosvenor Gallery (*Misc* 6–7), and his editor Robert Ross makes Burne-Jones a major influence on Wilde in his Introduction to that volume (p. xx).

He indicates that Whistler was of less importance to Wilde's mature thought than 'Pater, Ruskin, Arnold and Burne-Jones'.

Pheidias, Praxiteles: regarded as the two greatest ancient Greek sculptors.

Jack Sheppard . . . Dick Turpin. Sheppard (1701–24) was immortalized for his burglaries and escapes from Newgate prison. Brewer calls him 'certainly the most popular criminal ever led to Tyburn for execution'. *Dick Turpin*: noted highwayman, executed at York in 1739. Both the heroes of popular romances.

230 *Schopenhauer.* Artur Schopenhauer (1788–1860), German pessimist philosopher.

Nihilist. In tsarist Russia Nihilism was a terrorist movement aiming at the overturn of all the existing institutions of society in order to build it up anew on different principles. *Ivan Turgenev* (1818–83), a Russian novelist, whose greatest work, *Fathers and Children* (1862), portrayed the Nihilists and coined the term (first English translation 1867). Wilde contributed an anonymous translation from Turgenev's French, 'A Fire at Sea', to *Macmillan's Magazine*, LIV. 319 (May 1886), 39–44. *Fyodor Dostoevsky* (1821–81), Russian novelist whose novels, very unsympathetic to the Nihilists, began to appear in English translations in the 1880s. Wilde praised *Crime and Punishment* highly in his review of *Insult and Injury* in 1887 (*Rev* 158). His hitherto unidentified anonymous review of *Crime and Punishment* is in *Pall Mall Gazette*, 28 May 1886. Wilde's own first play was *Vera: or, The Nihilists* (1880), privately printed in 1883. He wrote to Marie Prescott, who played Vera in New York: 'I have tried in it to express within the limits of art that Titan cry of the peoples for liberty, which in the Europe of our day is threatening thrones, and making governments unstable from Spain to Russia, and from north to southern seas. But it is a play not of politics but of passion. It deals with no theories of government, but with men and women simply; and modern Nihilistic Russia, with all the terror of its tyranny and the marvel of its masterpieces, is merely the fiery and fervent background in front of which the persons of my dream live and love.' (*L* 148–9)

Robespierre . . . Rousseau. Jean-Jacques Rousseau (1712–78), philosopher from Geneva. His works, especially *Emile* and *Du contrat sociale*, inspired Robespierre (1758–94), one of the leaders of the French Revolution, who continually made Rousseau's ideas the justification of his own ideas and actions. Far from fulfilling Rousseau's ideas, however, he was in fact betraying them.

People's Palace. Walter Besant's *All Sorts and Conditions of Men* (1882) tells how the wealthiest heiress in England builds a vast Palace of Delight for the poor and the slum-dwellers. P. J. Keating: 'if Besant's novel did not inspire the idea, the publicity arising from it brought the necessary money pouring in.' In May 1887 Queen Victoria opened the People's Palace in Mile End Road, and 'during its brief existence as a cultural catalyst the Palace did attempt to bring a whole new range of experiences . . . within the reach of the working man. . . . Besant was appointed editor of the Palace Journal' (*The*

Working Classes in Victorian Fiction, 1971). Wilde applied unsuccessfully in 1886 for the post of Secretary to the Beaumont Trust, which administered the People's Palace (*ML* 61–2).

Balzac. See note to p. 221 above. All three characters here are young men of ambition who confront (and sooner or later yield to) temptation, and are found in more than one volume of *La Comédie Humaine.*

Becky Sharp. Becky Sharp, later Mrs Rawdon Crawley, is the aspiring central character of Thackeray's *Vanity Fair* (1847–8), and the noble Colonel Newcome dies affectingly in *The Newcomes* (1853–5), as Vivian describes.

story of transformation. Strange Case of Dr Jekyll and Mr Hyde (1886).

231 *vagueness of character.* Cf. Wilde's short story of 1887, 'The Sphinx without a Secret' (*CSF* 53–8). See p. 195n.

Proteus . . . Odysseus. Proteus was an old man of the sea who tended the flocks of Poseidon and could change his form at will. But Vivian is misremembering the *Odyssey* here: it was not Odysseus but Menelaus who overcame Proteus, as he tells Telemachus in Book 4.

Bellini. Giovanni Bellini (*c.*1430–1516), greatest Venetian painter of his time.

Florio's. Properly Florian's, a café in the Piazza of San Marco, recommended by Baedeker in 1877 for good ices.

232 *Aristotle.* In *Physica*, for example, nature is seen as 'an innate impulse to movement', or energy.

Rolla. Title and eponymous hero of a long poem (1833) by French poet Alfred de Musset (1810–57). Debauched and godless, a great Byronic figure, Rolla is redeemed by a moment of love.

Werther. In Goethe's self-revelatory cautionary novel *Sorrows of Werther* (1774) the eponymous hero commits suicide because his beloved is betrothed and then married to his friend.

curious one. The following argument, that Nature also imitates Art, is the most significant portion of the dialogue that Wilde added to it for FE. It continues to page 234, line 7, 'which is better'. His addressing himself to painting here could be seen as deliberate baiting of Whistler. He had accused Wilde of plagiarism, and these pages seem deliberately provocative, the 'atmospheric' writing about evening river scenes deliberately echoing a part of Whistler's famous 'Ten O'Clock' lecture (*GAME* 144). In Wilde's original review of this lecture, he slyly suggests that Whistler's own prose, which he is happy to echo both there and here, is itself indebted to Corot (*Misc* 65). The Wilde/Whistler relationship has been clearly set out in Birgit Borelius, 'Oscar Wilde, Whistler and Colour', *Scripta Minora Regiae Societatis Humaniorum Litterarum Lundensis*, 1966–7, 3 (Lund: Gleerup, 1968), although I think she overestimates Whistler's centrality for Wilde's dialogues (p. 44). She has not compared NC and FE of *The Decay of Lying*, or pointed to this sizeable addition and the brief one at p. 223n above.

Impressionists. A loose association of French artists including at various times

Monet, Renoir, Sisley, Bazille, Manet, and Dégas, exhibiting 1874–86 and painting with great sensitivity to the effects of weather, season, and light.

233 *Corots and Daubignys.* Corot (1796–1875), greatest French landscape painter of the first half of the nineteenth century. *Daubigny* (1817–79), one of the earliest exponents of *plein-air* painting in France.

Monets and Pisaros. Monet (1840–1926), French Impressionist painter, especially of landscape. *Pisaro.* Actually Pissarro (1830–1903), French Impressionist landscape painter.

Turner. J. M. W. Turner (1775–1851), English painter: most original genius in landscape painting during the nineteenth century. A controversial painter, he was defended and elucidated by Ruskin in *Modern Painters.*

Renés. René is hero and title of a romance by Chateaubriand (1801). He is a man of social inaction, conscious of possessing a superior genius, but his pride produces in him a morbid bitterness of spirit.

Vautrins. Vautrin, also known as Trompe-la-Mort, Herrera, and Collin, is the master criminal in Balzac's *Père Goriot, Les Illusions Perdues,* and *Splendeurs et misères des courtisanes.*

Cuyp. Albert Cuyp (1620–91), Dutch painter who excelled in painting cattle, moonlight, wintry landscapes, etc.

Rousseau. Henri Rousseau, known as 'Le Douanier' (1844–1910), French primitive painter, sometimes seen as more surrealist than primitive.

234 *Henry Moore.* 1831–95, English painter especially of seascapes.

Art . . . itself. Originally italicized.

Mr Pater. See Walter Pater's essay 'The School of Giorgione' added to *The Renaissance* in 1888.

Apollo . . . Marsyas. See p. 209n.

shadows of the cave. In bk. vii of Plato's *Republic* occurs his famous apologue of the men who live bound in a cavern, so that they can see only the shadows of real objects projected by a bright fire on its inner wall.

many-petalled rose. A reference to the glowing, many-petalled rose in the climactic vision of Dante's *Paradiso.*

Tiberius. 44 BC–AD 37, Roman emperor in succession to Augustus. Tacitus's *Annals* (115–17) describe his lust, cruelty, and violence, and his move to Capri to indulge them more freely.

Antonines. Antoninus Pius (AD 86–161) diligent, tolerant, and frugal, succeeded to the Roman Empire AD 138–61. His daughter Faustina married his successor Marcus Aurelius, a philosopher and another ruler of good character who ruled AD 161–80. Arnold's essay 'Marcus Aurelius' memorably contrasts the two dynasties (*Essays in Criticism: First Series,* 1865).

Sistine. The Sistine Chapel in the Vatican, painted by Perugino, Botticelli, and others, with the famous painted ceiling by Michelangelo.

235 *MSS.* Manuscripts.

Hokusai. 1760–1849, one of the most renowned masters of the Japanese colour print; a prolific painter, print designer, and book illustrator. *Hokkei.* Pupil of Hokusai (1780–1850).

charming painters. Mortimer Menpes (1859–1938), Australian disciple of Whistler, self-described as 'Painter, Etcher, Raconteur and Rifle Shot'. Menpes was an indifferent painter, but had more one-man shows of his work than any other artist of his day. His Japanese exhibition in Dowdeswell's Gallery in April and May of 1888 brought him fame. FE has additionally: 'whose tiny full length portraits of children are so beautiful and so powerful that he should be named the Velasquez to the Court of Lilliput'. The cut may just be to clarify the argument, or to mollify Menpes (who was godfather to Wilde's son Vyvyan), or to delete an implicit reference to Whistler, often compared to Velázquez. Wilde added the passage 'And so . . . see it anywhere' to FE, strengthening Vivian's general argument.

236 *Aristophanes.* *c.*448–*c.*380 BC, Athenian comic poet whose comedies are full of caricatures of leading personages of the time.

They . . . anything. Originally italicized.

gates of ivory . . . gates of horn. Gates of Dreams: in Greek legend, the ivory gate and the gate of horn, through which fictitious and true dreams respectively issue.

Myers's two bulky volumes. F. W. H. Myers (1843–1901), poet and inspector of schools. A founder of the Society for Psychical Research, 1882, he helped to edit the *Proceedings* of the Society, and contributed the introduction to the chief concrete result, the two volumes of *Phantasms of the Living* (1886).

237 *St Thomas.* The original 'Doubting Thomas', the disciple who said he would not believe in the Resurrection without very tangible proof.

either University. i.e. Oxford or Cambridge.

sly devising. In *The Odyssey*, xiii, Odysseus lies to his protective goddess Athena in disguise, and she smiles at 'thy words of sly devising which thou lov'st from the root of thine heart' (Morris, l. 295).

tragedy. Ion, eponymous hero of Euripides' tragedy (*c.*417 BC). The blameless hero is persuaded to conceal what he believes to be the truth of his parentage. Ultimately he will become king and founder of the Ionian people.

odes. 'Of the Danaid Hypermnestra', *Odes* III. xi. 35: 'Splendide mendax et in omnia virgo / Nobilis aevum'—'With glorious falsehood . . . a maid famous to all time.'

Sanchez. Francisco Sanchez, who wrote *A Treatise on the Noble and High Science of Nescience* (1581).

Republic. In bks. ii and iii of the *Republic*, the education of the future Guardians involves censorship of stories they may be told against the dignity of the gods, and about the horrors of death and Hades, to safeguard their moral character and courage.

238 *Academe.* An olive grove on the Cephissus river near Athens, once owned by Academus: here Plato and his followers taught philosophy, and thus his school was called the Academy. See also the remark ascribed to Aristotle: 'Plato is dear to me, but dearer still is truth.'

marvellous tale. See part vii of *The Temptation of St Antony*, also an important source for *The Sphinx*.

Behemoth . . . Leviathan, etc. Behemoth and *Leviathan*: the hippopotamus and the crocodile or whale from the Book of Job; Wilde always mentions them together (cf. *CA II* p. 293, and *Sphinx*, l. 56). *Basilisk* and *Hippogriff*: fabulous reptile and griffin with the body of a horse, also occur together to produce an exotic effect in *The Sphinx*, l. 20.

Blue Bird. The song of Wilde's Blue Bird is reminiscent of the nightingale to D'Albert in Gautier's *Mademoiselle de Maupin*: 'It was the history of the loves which had not been mine that this nightingale sang. Never was a history more accurate and true . . . It told me what I had been unable to tell myself, and explained to me what I had been unable to understand; it gave a voice to my dreaming, and caused the phantom, mute until then, to reply.' (ch. iv). Cf. also Gilbert on the message of art, *CA I* pp. 243, 263–4, and the extended *Portrait of Mr W. H.* (NY, 1921), 112–15.

239 *Second Empire.* 1852–70.

like a ghost. From 'Now sleeps the crimson petal, now the white', one of the lyrics from *The Princess* by Tennyson (1847). Wilde also quotes the song in 'The Birthday of the Infanta', and weaves variations on it throughout 'The Nightingale and the Rose' (*CSF* 194, 104–9). Wilde got this quotation wrong in NC, but corrected it for FE. See below, p. 324n.

with silver. See ll. 9–10 of 'The Evening Star' in Blake's *Poetical Sketches*.

THE CRITIC AS ARTIST—PART I

The original title of this work was 'The True Function and Value of Criticism: with some Remarks on the Importance of Doing Nothing'. It was published in two parts in *The Nineteenth Century*, in July and September 1890 (NC), and was revised, renamed, and reprinted in the first edition of *Intentions* in 1891 (FE). There are only a few changes between NC and FE in Part I, mostly infelicities being ironed out. There are more in Part II, but only changes of some importance will be indicated. The first title is significant: it suggests that Wilde is setting out to answer Matthew Arnold's essay 'The Function of Criticism at the Present Time', in *Essays in Criticism: First Series*, 1865 (Super III, 256–85). Arnold redefines criticism as 'the endeavour . . . to see the object as in itself it really is' (258), agrees that 'the critical power is of lower rank than the creative' (260), but that this distance has been exaggerated, and asserts that before any great creative work can be accomplished, there must be 'a great critical effort' (261) on the part of the poet and in his culture, in politics and religion as well as native and foreign literature: '*a disinterested endeavour to learn and to propagate the best that is known and thought in the world*' (283). Wilde's characters deal with these subjects, but the concerns of the dialogue go beyond this: Wilde continues to be pervasively influenced by Pater, to engage with Whistler, and to admire Renan and Emerson, while he gives more attention to Plato and the ancient world generally, and less to contemporary literature than in *The Decay of Lying*.

241 *doing nothing.* Idleness is frequently affected by Wilde's dandies: cf. *IBE*, where Lady Bracknell is glad to hear that Jack smokes: 'A man should always have an occupation of some kind. There are far too many idle men in London as it is' (p. 493).

Gilbert and Ernest. 'Gilbert' immediately recalls Sir William Schwenk Gilbert, author of the *Bab Ballads* and librettist of the Gilbert and Sullivan operas, a master of extravaganza and satirical nonsense. 'Ernest' is doomed by his name to be the loser here: Wilde consistently preached the Importance of *not* being Earnest.

Cicero . . . Madame de Sévigné. Cicero, Roman orator, statesman, and letter-writer (106–43 BC); *Balzac*, French novelist (1799–1850), corresponded for more than 15 years with Polish Madame Hanska, whom he married shortly before his death; *Flaubert*, French novelist (1821–80), one of Wilde's masters, his letters to George Sand published 1884, others 1887–93; *Berlioz*, French composer and autobiographer (1803–69); *Byron*, Romantic poet (1788–1824) whose legend dominates the century and whose letters, often from foreign exile, are prolific and provocative; *Madame de Sévigné*, 1626–96, French writer whose 25 years of letters reveal both herself and the inner history of the time. The delightfulness of egotism in literature was briefly sketched by J. P. Mahaffy, Dublin professor of Classics who befriended the young Wilde, in *The Principles of the Art of Conversation* (1887), a book reviewed by Wilde (*Rev* 242–7).

Rousseau. Jean-Jacques Rousseau (1712–78), Genevan political philosopher and author of *Confessions* (1781), a work remarkable for a frankness unsurpassed at that time.

Cellini. Benvenuto Cellini (1500–71), Italian goldsmith, sculptor, engraver, adventurer, and autobiographer.

life to stone. Holding the Gorgon's head, his bronze Perseus with the head of Medusa.

Montaigne. Michel de Montaigne (1533–92), French essayist and author of an account of his tour in Germany, Switzerland, and Italy. In spite of the scepticism of his writings, he devoutly received the last rites of the Church.

Monica. Saint Augustine of Hippo (354–430), greatest of the Latin fathers of the Church, son of St Monica, spent many years as a Manichaean before returning to the Christian Church and writing his *Confessions*.

242 *Cardinal Newman.* John Henry Newman (1801–90), English theologian who after years of leading the High Church party at Oxford left the Anglican Church and retired to Littlemore, where he was received into the Roman Catholic faith in 1845. Gilbert is quoting from his *Apologia pro Vita Sua* (1864). Wilde was himself attracted to Catholicism at Oxford, and considered going to Newman to be received: *SL* 12.

Pepys. Samuel Pepys (1633–1703), England's most famous diarist. His *Diary* ran from 1 January 1660 to 31 May 1669.

valour. Characteristic reversal of proverbial cliché.

say. As You Like It, v. iv. 97.

Boswell. A reference not only to James Boswell's life of Samuel Johnson, but also to Oliver Wendell Holmes's *The Autocrat at the Breakfast Table* (1857), which is sub-titled 'Every Man his own Boswell'.

biography. Gilbert quotes the first sentence of Wilde's anonymous 1887 review of a biographical essay on Whistler by Walter Dowdeswell (Mason 28–31): the piece was not reprinted in *Reviews*, perhaps because much of its content, about the limitations of painting as compared to literature, was re-employed in this dialogue (p. 264–5n.). See *DL* p. 232n and Borelius, cited there.

vulgarize them. Material reused from another periodical review: see *Rev* 148–53, and *L.* 182 n.

243 *undertaker.* See *DL* p. 219n. on Hall Caine.

Academician. William Powell Frith (1819–1909), English painter noted for huge, densely populated canvases such as *Ramsgate Sands* (1854), *Derby Day* (1858), and *The Railway Station* (1862). Wilde featured among many others in his *Private View of the Royal Academy* (1883). He published *My Autobiography and Reminiscences* (1887) and *Further Reminiscences* (1888).

one's tears. See also below, p. 264, and *DL* p. 238.

244 *Browning Society.* The Browning Society was founded in London in 1881 and lasted until 1892, and other societies followed in the provinces and in America, with the purpose of elucidating obscurities and encouraging the study of Browning's poetry.

Broad Church Party. Popular term for those in the Church of England who sought to interpret the creeds in a broad and liberal manner.

Great Writers' Series. Walter Scott was a literary publisher of the time, and Wilde reviewed several of his 'Great Writers' series, including those on Longfellow by Eric S. Robertson, on Coleridge by Hall Caine, on Dickens by Frank T. Marzials, on Rossetti by Joseph Knight, on Keats by W. M. Rossetti: he generally praised the bibliographies by 'Mr Anderson of the British Museum' more highly than the lives.

Titan. See p. 224n.

hill. Pierus, a mountain of Thessaly sacred to the Muses, goddesses who presided over poetry, music, dancing, and all the liberal arts.

245 *Pegasus.* The winged horse of the Muses.

tettix. Cicada.

that live. As God is seen to do in Genesis: 2.

George Meredith. See *DL* p. 221n.

old friend. Whistler. See p. 247n. art-congresses.

246 *Hermes*. Messenger of the gods.

child of Leto. Leto a Titaness, mother by Zeus of Apollo (here indicated) and Artemis.

ἁβρῶς βαίνοντες διὰ λαμπροτάτου αἰθέρος, 'Treading delicately through the most brilliant air.'

Phaedrus. A dialogue by Plato. Socrates and Phaedrus sit under a plane tree by the Ilissus and discuss rhetoric, the divine madness of poetry and the god-given madness of love.

agnus castus. A species of Vitex, a tree of the verbena family, once believed to be a preservative of chastity.

Tanagra. See above, p. 12n.

asphodel. In Greek mythology, the flower of the dead.

Polyxena. Daughter of Priam, sometimes portrayed as the beloved of Achilles.

Marathon. The Athenians beat the Persians at Marathon in 490 BC, the first time that Greeks won a victory over Persians in a fixed battle.

Salaminian bay. The Greeks won a decisive sea victory over the Persians in 480 BC at Salamis.

247 *palmates*. A hand-shaped ornament.

Thetis. One of the sea deities, daughter of Nereus. *Nereids*. Sea Nymphs.

Phaedra. Daughter of Minos and Pasiphae, wife of Theseus, whom Venus inspired with an unconquerable passion for Hippolytus, Theseus' son by Hippolyta. See Euripides' *Hippolyta*, where Phaedra is a pure woman, betrayed to Hippolytus by her nurse.

Persephone. Also Proserpine, daughter of Ceres, goddess of corn, seized by Hades, god of the underworld. Spent six months in Hades and six months on earth alternately.

ΚΑΛΟΣ ΑΛΚΙΒΙΑΔΗΣ or ΚΑΛΟΣ ΧΑΡΜΙΔΗΣ. 'Beautiful Alcibiades' or 'Beautiful Charmides'.

Dionysus. Greek god of vegetation, wine, and uncontrolled emotions. *Maenads*: frenzied women who accompanied him.

must-stained. Stained with new wine, or wine in process of fermentation.

Silenus. See above, p. 79n.

Higginbotham. See 'The Function of Criticism at the Present Time' in Super III, 273. A misquotation, although retaining the sense: Arnold has: 'by the Ilissus there was no Wragg, poor thing!'

art-congresses. Alert contemporary readers would have seen Ernest as aping Whistler here: he had famously declared: 'The creature critic is of comparatively modern growth' (*GAME* 27): 'Let the work, then, be received in silence, as it was in the days to which the penmen still point as an era when art was at its apogee' (30), and see 'The Ten O'Clock', *passim*. But Ernest is not plagiarizing from Whistler: behind both stands the Preface to Gautier's *Mademoiselle de Maupin* (1835): 'There was no art criticism under Julius II, and I am not acquainted with any feuilleton on Daniel de Volterre, Sebastian del Piombo, Michael Angelo, or Raphael, nor on Ghiberti della Porte or Benvenuto Cellini; and yet I think that for people who had no newspapers, and who knew neither the word ART nor the word ARTISTIC, they had for all that a fair amount of talent, and did not acquit themselves badly in their calling.' Ellmann comments that Wilde 'knew, as Whistler had perhaps forgotten, that many of Whistler's attitudes had been formed by Gautier's Preface to *Mademoiselle de Maupin*' (Ellmann 225).

248 *Darwinian principle.* A slight modification by Gilbert of Darwin's evolutionary principle of the survival of the fittest.

misunderstood. Cf. Ralph Waldo Emerson (1803–82) in his essay 'Self-Reliance': 'Is it so bad then to be misunderstood? Pythagoras was misunderstood, and Socrates, and Jesus, and Luther, and Copernicus, and Galileo, and Newton, and every pure and wise spirit that ever took flesh. To be great is to be misunderstood.' Wilde quotes this line of Emerson in a public letter to Whistler in 1885 (*SL* 60), and ends a fiction review of 1887: 'it is only mediocrities and old maids who consider it a grievance to be misunderstood' (*Rev* 167). See also a speech of 1894 (Mason 53).

be taught. Cf. PPUY.

Prince Florizel. The lover of Perdita in Shakespeare's *A Winter's Tale*, but R. L. Stevenson used a modern version of this Prince in his *New Arabian Nights* (1882), to which Wilde refers here. Florizel used to go out in a 'search for extravagant adventures' and 'played the part of Providence' in many strange events. 'The fair Cuban' figures largely in *More New Arabian Nights* (1885), where she tells invented life-stories to three different young men, and with ironic truthfulness she prefaces the one entitled 'Story of the Fair Cuban', 'I am not what I seem.'

250 *Hegesias.* Hegesias of Magnesia (third century BC), historian and orator. All ancient judgements of his style are hostile: as the typical 'Asianist', he was the *bête noire* of classicizing writers from the time of Cicero.

of life. Matthew Arnold (1822–88) in *Literature and Dogma* (1872).

paeon. A foot of four syllables, any one long and three short.

251 κάθαρσις. Catharsis: purification [of the emotions].

produces. Wilde here credits Aristotle with Pater's central idea of the impression the work produces on the critic, thus giving Pater's view the authority of antiquity as opposed to Arnold's. Cf. lower down his description of Aristotle's *Poetics* as 'a perfect piece of aesthetic criticism'.

perilous stuff. Macbeth, v. iii. 44.

252 *Alexandria.* A city in Egypt, founded by Alexander the Great in 331 BC, famous as one of the chief intellectual centres of the Hellenistic world. By 200 BC it was the largest city in the world and its library was world-famous until destroyed by fire. Authors of the Alexandrian or Hellenistic age wrote

under the authoritative Museum of Alexandria, a literary academy, and for a more cosmopolitan audience. Great emphasis was put on rhetoric and history, but the speciality was philosophy, with particular stress on Epicurus and the Stoics.

Sicyon. Corinth's western neighbour: in the fourth century it possessed the leading school of painters.

plagiarism. Whistler's most famous gibes against Wilde were of plagiarism: see notes to *DL* pp. 217, 223, 232. Here Gilbert easily rebuts what Ernest had seemed to owe to Whistler at p. 247 above.

Greeks . . . mediævalism. Gilbert uses the same kind of distinction here that Matthew Arnold did in *Culture and Anarchy* (1869), making the famous division between Hellenism and Hebraism.

253 *μονόχρονος ἡδονή.* Momentary pleasure.

critical. Ernest is quoting Arnold's essay, 'The Function of Criticism at the Present Time': 'Everybody, too, would be willing to admit, as a general proposition, that the critical faculty is lower than the inventive' (Super III, 259).

of life. In his essay 'Joubert' in *Essays in Criticism, First Series* (Super III, 209).

wiser than they knew. Emerson, in two essays, 'The Over-Soul' and 'Compensation'.

254 *for ever.* A slight misquotation from Tennyson's *Idylls of the King*, where he describes Camelot: 'The city is built / To music, therefore never built at all, / And therefore built for ever.'

creates the age. Cf. *DL* p. 230, where Vivian argues that literature creates or anticipates the age. Gilbert follows Emerson in 'Self-Reliance': 'An institution is the lengthened shadow of one man . . . and all history resolves itself very easily into the biography of a few stout and earnest persons.'

Alexandria. See above, p. 252n.

255 *Anthology.* The *Greek Anthology*, a collection of poems begun by Meleager of Gadara about 60 BC and later (10th century AD) expanded to include selections from over 300 writers.

Scotch dialect. Cf. *IH* p. 411, and generally. The 'industrious writer' mentioned here is William Sharp, later 'Fiona Macleod'. Wilde reviewed his *Romantic Ballads and Poems of Phantasy*, with a manifesto-like preface advocating a Romantic Revival, in 1888, and he concluded: 'Dialect, archaisms and the like, will not do' (*Rev* 358).

three-volumed novel. See below, p. 501n.

256 *Newnham graduates.* Newnham College Cambridge, 1880, founded for the residence and instruction of ladies. Girton, the first such college, had opened in 1873. In the 1880s the favourite targets of the humour of 'Mr Punch' were lady doctors and 'sweet girl graduates'.

257 *the thistle.* Jesus warns that false prophets are known by their fruits: 'Do men gather grapes of thorns, or figs of thistles?' (Matthew 7: 16)

chastity. Arnold repeatedly quotes this in his essay 'Numbers: or The Majority and the Remnant'.

Magdalen. From Mary Magdalene, from whom Jesus cast out devils, a Magdalen became a name for a repentant prostitute.

Lucretias. A virtuous and beautiful Roman lady raped by Sextus, the son of Tarquin, king of Rome, who killed herself after making her father and husband swear vengeance: used as a type of conjugal fidelity.

of evils. See 'The Soul of Man' *passim*, and a similar statement 293: 'Charity creates a multitude of sins.'

258 *Ilion.* Troy.

Aulis. Agamemnon, king of Argos, commandant-in-chief of the allied Greeks who besieged Troy. The fleet being delayed by adverse winds at Aulis, Agamemnon sacrificed his daughter Iphigenia to Diana, and the winds became favourable. His wife Clytemnestra lived in adultery with Egistheus, and killed Agamemnon in his bath on his return from Troy.

Antigone. Daughter and companion of Oedipus, who was condemned by her uncle Creon, ruler of Thebes, to be buried alive for insisting on carrying out burial rites for her dead brother, although he had been a rebel.

is dead. A misquotation from *Love's Labours Lost*, v. ii. 652: 'The sweet warman is dead and rotten.'

skull of Helen. Lucian, Greek writer born *c.*AD 120, best known for his satirical dialogues. For Menippus and Helen see *Dialogues of the Dead*, xviii.

of Leda. Helen of Troy, the daughter of Leda and of Jupiter, who turned into the likeness of a swan to court her.

Lord of the Myrmidons. Achilles.

Dodona. Jupiter's oracle at Dodona was supposed to be the most ancient in Greece.

Euphorbus. A famous Trojan, the first to wound Achilles' constant companion Patroclus, after which Hector, son of Priam, killed him.

259 οἶνοψ πόντος. Wine-dark sea.

Danaoi. The Greeks.

Veronese. His *Vision of St Helen* (*c.*1572) is in the National Gallery, London: she was the finder of the True Cross.

chords. The painting is *The Concert*, or *Fête Champêtre*, from about 1510, in the Louvre, Paris. See below, p. 283 and n.

Corot. Dance of the Nymphs in the Louvre, Paris (1850–1).

Green-tressed Goddess. 'Green-haired goddess' in 'Hymn to the Earth', ll. 8–10.

261 *style.* i.e. *Madame Bovary* (1857).

Lewis Morris's poems. Mr (later Sir) Lewis Morris (1833–1907), Welsh poet, author of e.g. *Songs of Two Worlds*, 'sonorous verse and placid optimism', and very popular. His collected poems were published in one volume in 1890.

M. Ohnet's novels. Georges Ohnet (1848–1918), French novelist, published a series of novels, *Les Batailles de la Vie*, some of which went beyond a hundredth edition.

Henry Arthur Jones. This last example was added to FE. Henry Arthur Jones (1851–1929) English dramatist seen as co-founder with Pinero of the 'realist problem' drama in Britain.

Bestia Trionfans. Spaccio della bestia Trionfante (1584) was the best-known work of Giordano Bruno, published in England and dedicated to Sir Philip Sidney. The Triumphant Beast is not the Pope, as used sometimes to be thought (Bruno was burned to death for heresy in Rome in 1600): Bruno says in the dedication that it is 'the vices which predominate, and oppose the divine part [of the soul]'.

own soul. Anatole France defines criticism as 'the adventures of a soul among masterpieces' (*La Vie Littéraire*, 1888).

262 *impressions.* Gilbert adopts this doctrine from the Preface to Pater's famous *Renaissance* (1873). The 'other theory' that Ernest refers to is Arnold's dictum that the object of criticism is to see the object as in itself it really is' (Super III, 258). Pater quotes Arnold, suavely agrees, and continues: 'and in aesthetic criticism the first step towards seeing one's object as it really is, is to know one's own impression as it really is, to discriminate it, to realise it distinctly' (Hill xix). Thus he virtually reverses Arnold's doctrine.

Cumnor cowslips. In Arnold's 'Thyrsis', the poet laments that Proserpina, once lured from the underworld by the pipes of 'Dorian shepherds', does not know England: 'But ah, of our poor Thames she never heard! / Her foot the Cumnor cowslips never stirred, / And we should tease her with our plaint in vain!'

Turner. John Ruskin (1819–1900), writer on art and on its relationship with society. In *Modern Painters* (1843–60) he championed Turner, at the time one of England's most controversial painters.

dreamed of. In his essay 'Leonardo da Vinci' in *The Renaissance* Pater creates a famous prose-poem meditation on the painting known as *La Gioconda* or *Mona Lisa*, which Gilbert quotes at length here. It was an enormously influential piece of writing, and when in 1936 Yeats set out to edit *The Oxford Book of Modern Verse* he included part of this description, printed as verse, as the first modern 'poem'.

263 *come.* See 1 Corinthians 10: 11.

Tannhäuser. Richard Wagner (1813–83), German composer, wrote his opera *Tannhäuser* (1845) about a legendary German hero who loves Venus. This medieval version of Venus lived in the hollow world under the Horsel Mount in Germany. Her beauty tempted Christian knights and pilgrims to their damnation. When Tannhäuser asks the pope for absolution he refuses, until his dry staff buds: a few days later the staff does bud, but when the pope sends to look for him Tannhäuser has disappeared. See also *SL* 357, *BRG* l. 486, 'The Young King' (*CSF* 183), and Pater's account of the legend in Hill 5.

264 *different things.* For the effects of music, cf. p. 243 above, and *DL* p. 238, Blue Bird.

ΕΡΩΣ ΤΩΝ ΑΔΥΝΑΤΩΝ. Love of the impossible.

right things. Plato's ideal education in *The Republic* involves such music: see below, p. 286. The words in inverted commas are a slight misquotation of Wilde's own poem, 'Humanitad' (1881): 'To make the Body and the Spirit one / With all right things.'

265 *For the domain . . . madness of Lear.* This passage is derived, often word for word, from Wilde's anonymous review of an essay by Walter Dowdeswell on Whistler in 1887 (Mason 29–30). Cf. p. 242n.

266 *across it.* The peacocks are there all the same: see the footnote Wilde added to his first Grosvenor Gallery review: 'I was surprised lately at Ravenna to come across a mosaic ceiling done in the keynote of a peacock's tail—blue, green, purple, and gold—and with four peacocks in the four spandrils' (*Misc* 19 n).

ortolans. i.e. consumed a famous red Burgundy and some small birds, a great table delicacy. Cf. a bitter reference in *De Profundis*, *SL* 235.

THE CRITIC AS ARTIST—PART II

As in *DL*, passages originally italicized are noted. One such example survives, surely by accident, in FE at p. 269. There are more revisions than in Part I.

267 *discussing everything.* A new subtitle: in NC it was the same as Part I, 'With some remarks upon the importance of doing nothing'.

Thersites. A deformed, scurrilous officer in the Greek army that went to the siege at Troy: generally, a malevolent, impudent railer against the powers that be. Cf. Wilde's letter to the Editor of the *Scots Observer*, (9 July 1890) about a review of *Dorian Gray*: 'The editor of the *Scots Observer* should not have allowed Thersites to make mows in his review' (*L* 267).

ease in Zion. In *Culture and Anarchy* Arnold quotes a saying attributed to Carlyle, to show the difference between Hebraism and Hellenism: 'Socrates is terribly *at ease in Zion.*'

Lincoln. Mark Pattison (1813–84), English scholar and critic who was elected rector of Lincoln College, Oxford, in 1861. His book on Milton (1879) was in the 'Men of Letters' series.

268 *Agamemnon.* Aeschylus (525–456 BC) the father of Greek tragedy.

Pericles. Athenian statesman (*c.*490–429 BC) who presided over the 'Golden Age' of that city.

name. The Greek Sphinx was a legendary female monster who terrorized the city of Thebes with a riddle, which asked what animal walked on four legs in the morning, two at noon, and three in the evening. The answer—

man—was given by Oedipus. The oracle told Laius, Oedipus' father, that he must perish by the hands of his son, so the baby's feet were wounded and it was left to die. Adopted by a shepherd, he was raised in ignorance of his parentage.

it is . . . others. Originally italicized.

269 *Mantegna.* Early Renaissance painter in North Italy, with a passionate interest in ancient Roman monuments, often depicted in his paintings.

Rubinstein. See above, p. 171n.

Obiter Dicta. Augustine Birrell (1850–1933), British politician and author, entered Parliament in 1889. His essays include *Obiter Dicta* (1884–7). See *Rev* 251–3, where Wilde first takes issue with Birrell on this subject.

will seek . . . touched. This italicization uniquely survives, surely by accident, from NC.

270 *poet.* Virgil (70–19 BC) in Book I of his *Aeneid* talks of 'lacrimae rerum', 'the tears of things'.

Divine Comedy. Dante Alighieri (1265–1321), Italian poet whose major work, the *Divine Comedy*, is divided into three sections, *Hell*, *Purgatory*, and *Heaven*. Much of this extended setpiece, everything from 'Through the dim' p. 271 l. 2 to 'all the stars' l. 31, was excised from NC by the editor, James Knowles, and restored by Wilde to FE. For further information consult a modern edition of the *Divine Comedy*: Gilbert's references follow Dante's order throughout.

272 *Florentine.* Dante.

masterpiece. Charles Baudelaire (1821–67), French poet, author of *Les Fleurs du mal* (1857), dedicated to his friend Théophile Gautier (1811–72), French poet, novelist, and critic. Gautier's key essay on Baudelaire was first printed as 'Notice' to *Les Fleurs du mal* in 1868, and 'Madrigal Triste', the poem quoted, was added to the volume in the same edition.

273 *honey.* See 1 Samuel 14:43, where Jonathan says: 'I did but taste a little honey with the end of the rod that was in mine hand, and, lo, I must die.' Cf. Wilde's sonnet 'Hélàs', and Pater in 'Winckelmann' (Hill 177).

Perdita. See *A Winter's Tale*, IV. iv.

Meleager. Greek poet of the *Anthology*, in the reign of Seleucis of Syria about 150 BC. *Heliodore*: one of the favourites of King Seleucis Philopator.

Fantine. In Victor Hugo's *Les Misérables* (1862), Fantine is an unfortunate young mother who sacrifices for her child first her golden hair and then her front teeth: for her 'bloodstained smile' see ch. v, 'Degradation'.

Manon Lescaut. See above, p. 81n.

Tyrian. Adonis, mortal lover of Venus.

Orestes. Brother of Electra, he avenged the murder of his father Agamemnon by his mother Clytemnestra and her lover Egistheus, and was pursued by the Furies.

274 *Spinoza.* Dutch–Jewish philosopher and theologian (1632–77). The passage Gilbert quotes is from part iv of the *Ethics*, probably via Matthew Arnold, who quotes and translates it from the Latin in his 'Spinoza and the Bible' (Super III, 177).

Greeks. Aristotle's idea of catharsis, purification of the emotions, through tragedy.

Brabantio. i.e. Desdemona in Shakespeare's *Othello.*

For emotion . . . society. Originally italicized.

275 *Let me . . . intellectual.* Originally italicized.

energy also. Cf. Commonplace Book, 189, where Wilde approves Aristotle's case for contemplation for its own sake: 'its duty is to comprehend the world not to make it better'.

citta divina. Gilbert picks up this (wrong) reference from Pater's essay 'Sandro Botticelli' in *The Renaissance* (1873): it should read 'La citta di Vita', title of a long poem (1455–64) by Matteo Palmiri which was condemned for unorthodoxy. Cf. Wilde's previous reference in *Misc* 271 and *Rev* 514, and Hill 218, 336–7.

fruitio Dei. Enjoyment of God.

Academic philosopher. i.e. Platonic philosopher. Cf. Wilde's earlier lecture, 'The English Renaissance of Art' (1882) from which Gilbert is quoting: 'like the philosopher of the Platonic vision, the poet is the spectator of all time and of all existence' (*Misc* 256).

so high. In his essay 'Coleridge' in *Appreciations* (1889).

Philo. Philo (b. *c.*20 BC), most important representative of Hellenistic Judaism, whose doctrine of God starts from the idea that God is a Being absolutely bare of quality.

Eckhart. Johannes (Meister) Eckhart (*c.*1260–1327), German mystic; his teaching was a mystic pantheon influenced by religious mysticism and speculative philosophy.

Böhme. Jacob Boehme (1575–1624), German mystic, claimed he was often carried up to heaven, like the Apostle Paul. His followers were known as Behemists, or the Illuminati: Brewer describes Swedenborgians as Illuminati also.

Swedenborg. Emanuel Swedenborg (1688–1772), Swedish mystic and theologian who believed he had direct access to the spiritual world.

276 *read Kant.* In his essay 'Winckelmann' Pater says: 'Kant's influence over the culture of Goethe, which he tells us could not have been resisted by him without loss, consisted in a severe limitation to the concrete' (Hill 144).

absolutely . . . make alive. This passage is reproduced unaltered from Wilde's review of Pater's *Appreciations* (*Rev* 539–40).

our doom. See Micah 7: 2 and Daniel 5.

Nemesis. Goddess of vengeance.

Fates. The three fatal sisters drew out the threads of life: Clotho held the spindle, Lachesis drew out the thread, and Atropos cut it off.

of the dead. Gilbert here is clearly indebted to Pater's setpiece description of the *Mona Lisa*: see Hill 97–9.

277 *Leopardi.* Giacomo Leopardi (1798–1837), Italian poet, an invalid who lived latterly in constant bodily anguish and hopeless despondency.

*Theocritus. c.*310–250 BC, Greek pastoral poet.

Vidal. Pierre Vidal, Provençal troubadour who accompanied Richard Coeur de Lion to Cyprus, 1190.

Lancelot. Leaving the scene of his adulterous union with Arthur's queen, Guinevere.

Abelard. The priest (1079–1142) who loved Heloise and was castrated by order of her uncle. Pater retells the story in *The Renaissance* (Hill 3–6). *Villon*: b. 1431: great but highly criminal French poet.

Endymion. Old mythical story of a mortal youth beloved by the moon. Gilbert refers to Keats's poetic version of the story, published in 1818.

Atys. See *The Sphinx*, l. 170 n.

Dane. Hamlet.

thought in the world. See Arnold's 'The Function of Criticism' (Super III, 283).

being. See Introduction, pp. xviii–xix.

278 ΒΙΟΣ ΘΕΩΡΗΤΙΚΟΣ. The contemplative life.

self-centred. Cf. 'Soul of Man', 299 and *passim*, and Emerson in 'Self-Reliance', *passim*.

his harness. See 1 Kings 22: 34, where Ahab is killed.

For action . . . a mood. Originally italicized.

disinterested. 'Disinterestedness' is the key quality of general criticism for Arnold.

The sure . . . useful. Originally italicized.

failure. Thus overturning the Darwinian evolutionary law, the survival of the fittest.

279 *Fabianists.* The Fabian Society was founded in 1884 by socialistic intellectuals, closely bound up with the British Labour Party. It was named after the Roman general Fabius, 'the Delayer', who saved Rome from the Carthaginians in the third century BC by a war of attrition. Led by Sidney and Beatrice Webb and Bernard Shaw, the Fabians advocated socialism by piecemeal parliamentary reform instead of risking disaster by total revolution.

Utopia. An imaginary country, the Platonic ideal of a country, invented by Sir Thomas More in his *Utopia* (1516). Cf. 'The Soul of Man', 303–4.

wilderness. As John the Baptist prepared the way for Jesus: see e.g. Matthew 3: 3.

educate others. Cf. Wilde's review of *Chuang Tzŭ* (*Rev* 537). See also Emerson's 'Nominalist and Realist': 'Society gains nothing whilst a man, not himself renovated, attempts to renovate things around him.'

abroad. Lord Brougham in a speech to the London Mechanics Institute (1825): 'Look out, gentlemen, the schoolmaster is abroad!'

280 *saw it.* For Goethe and self-culture see Pater's essay 'Winckelmann' in Hill 182–4.

An idea . . . at all. Originally italicized.

animal. See *DG* p. 69n.

Chuang Tsŭ. See Introduction, pp. xviii–xix and 'Soul of Man', 301.

281 *The difference . . . merely.* Originally italicized.

own mind. Also quoted at *Rev* 404, and glossed at *DL* p. 232n.

282 *impressions.* Close echoes here of the 'Conclusion' to Pater's *Renaissance* (Hill, 186–90).

nouveau frisson. New thrill or sensation.

Luministe. Painters especially interested in effects of light: a term used in connection with Impressionism.

Symboliste in poetry. French poets deriving from Baudelaire; chiefly Verlaine, Rimbaud, and Mallarmé. See p. 141n.

Russia. See *L* 488, where Wilde admired Kropotkin, 'a man with the soul of that beautiful white Christ that seems coming out of Russia'. Kropotkin was an anarchist, imprisoned in Russia and France for his political views and escaped to England. He returned to Russia in 1917 at the time of the Revolution.

Penshurst oaks. Walter Savage Landor (1775–1864), English writer, best known for his several series of *Imaginary Conversations*, the bulk of which were written between 1824 and 1829. He has three dialogues between Milton and Marvel, number vi concerning comedy and tragedy, and one between Lord Brooke and Sir Philip Sidney at Penshurst, Sidney's home in Kent.

Imaginary Portraits. Wilde reviewed this 'singularly attractive' book in 1887 (*Rev* 172–5). The last portrait is of Duke Carl of Rosenmold, and illustrates 'the passion for the imaginative world of art': it may have helped to inspire Wilde's story 'The Young King' (*CSF*, 171–84). The passage on the Aufklärung here is a close echo of Pater, and also echoed in 'Mr W. H.' (*CSF* 163).

283 *Lucian.* See above, p. 258n.

Bruno. Giordano Bruno (1548–1600), restless, speculative Italian thinker. *Spaccio della bestia trionfante* (1584), his best known work, is in dialogue form. See n. to p. 261, above.

old Pagan. Landor: see above p. 282n.

painter and poet. See such dramatic monologues as 'Fra Lippo Lippi' and 'Andrea del Sarto' for painters, and for poets, 'Cleon'.

M. Renan. Ernest Renan (1823–92), French philologist and historian. Famous for his *Life of Jesus* (1863), expressing his loss of faith in traditional Christianity, and e.g. *Dialogues et Fragments philosophiques* (1876). In the latter he seems to anticipate Gilbert's prophecy that the future belongs to criticism, and the subject matter for creation diminishes daily: 'Le temps viendra où l'art sera une chose du passé, une création faite une fois pour toutes, création des âges non réfléchis, qu'on adorera, tout en reconnaissant qu'il n'y a plus à en faire.'

colour also. Dante Gabriel Rossetti (1828–82), English poet and painter. His sonnets include 'For a Venetian Pastoral, by Giorgione' and 'For Ruggiero and Angelica, by Ingres'. The picture attributed to Giorgione is clearly the same as *The Concert*, which Gilbert describes at p. 259 above. Different modern experts have attributed the picture to Giorgione or to Titian, and have called it *The Concert* or *Fête Champêtre*. Pater discusses the picture and refers to Rossetti's sonnet in 'The School of Giorgione', which appeared in the *Fortnightly Review* (October 1877), and in the 1888 edition of *The Renaissance* (Hill 384). Rossetti's *Collected Poems* include fourteen 'Sonnets and Verses for Rossetti's own Works of Art'.

284 *all schools of Art.* Cf. previous polishing of this paragraph and the epigram about the auctioneer at *Misc* 88, 123, and other uses in *Rev* 44, 110, 189.

as Plato saw. In *The Republic* Plato banishes the poets from his ideal city.

dangerous thing. Gilbert adapts Pope's famous line from the *Essay on Criticism*, 'A little learning is a dangerous thing.'

at things. Gilbert is here particularly indebted to the penultimate paragraph of the 'Conclusion' to Pater's *Renaissance* (Hill 189).

own opinions. In Emerson's 'Self-Reliance', he adamantly opposes conformity and consistency, and in 'Nominalist and Realist' he writes: 'I am always insincere, as always knowing there are other moods' (quoted by Wilde at *Misc* 39).

285 *actually moral.* This speech of Gilbert's on morals and journalism is added for FE.

come again. Cf. *Othello*, III. iii. 9–12: 'And when I love thee not, / Chaos is come again.'

Tartuffe. Cf. *DL* p. 220.

Chadband. In Charles Dickens's *Bleak House*, a hypocritical clergyman.

286 *writ large.* Cf. Milton, 'On the New Forcers of Conscience under the Long Parliament': 'New Presbyter is but old Priest writ large.'

Temperament. The keynote to Pater's 'Preface' to *The Renaissance*: 'what is important . . . is . . . a certain kind of temperament' (Hill xxi).

passage. Early in *The Republic*, bk. iii, ll. 401–2. Cf. above p. 264. Wilde's approval dates back at least to his Commonplace Book of (?) 1880, where he describes it as 'a scheme of the noblest education'. The quotation here is close to Jowett's translation.

will . . . nature. Originally italicized.

287 *St John.* Wilde was a student at Oxford 1874–8. He belonged to Magdalen College which was founded by William of Waynfleete in 1448. William Laud (1573–1645), later Archbishop of Canterbury, was made president of his old college, St John's, in 1611. Compare 'the tower's gilded vanes' with *The Sphinx*, 159, 'grey gilt-dialled towers'. Cf. also a similar tribute to Oxford in *Rev* 22–3.

Caliban. See Shakespeare's *The Tempest*, and the 'Preface' to *Dorian Gray*, p. 48.

Celt. This passage was added for FE. Renan and Matthew Arnold wrote at length, and controversially, about the Celts, but the immediate spur to this passage is surely Grant Allen's 'The Celt in English Art' which appeared in the *Fortnightly Review* (February 1891, 267–77) near Wilde's essay 'The Soul of Man under Socialism'. See *L* 286 and note. Wilde could hardly be unmoved by this sentence of Allen's: 'Mr Oscar Wilde, whom only fools ever mistook for a mere charlatan, and whom wise men know for a man of rare insight and strong common-sense, is an Irishman to the core.'

Impressionist painters. See notes to *DL* pp. 232–3. This passage, to p. 288, l. 38, was added to FE, in despite of Whistler.

288 *Majeur.* Théophile Gautier (1811–72), French poet, novelist, and critic, whose poem 'Symphonie en Blanc Majeur' appeared in his most famous collection, *Emaux et Camées*. It can be seen to have influenced both painters and poets, including Wilde himself in his *Poems* (1881); for example, 'Symphony in yellow'. Gilbert carefully avoids here mentioning Whistler's series of paintings, 'Symphonies in White'.

phrased it. 'A Sonnet is a moment's monument', Rossetti writes, in the introductory sonnet to his great sonnet-sequence *The House of Life*.

Archaicistes. See Introduction, p. xvii.

289 *For the . . . passion.* Originally italicized.

into the mind. See *Republic* iii. 412. For Newman, see above p. 242 and n.

Constance. The mother of Arthur in Shakespeare's *King John*.

290 *to you.* Cf. Matthew 6: 33.

Academician. The Royal Academy of Arts founded in 1768 to promote the arts. There were forty academicians only, so those elected tended to be well-established figures already. Cf. LASC 1 and *DG* p. 50n.

The appeal . . . temperament. Originally italicized.

291 *cloud . . . lake.* Shelley published 'The Cloud' in 1819. Wordsworth's poetry is much concerned with the English Lake District.

Sophokles. The Greek tragedian Sophocles was the rival of Euripides for public praise: they were jealous and antagonistic rivals: 'droppings of warm tears' is a quotation from a short poem by Elizabeth Barrett Browning, 'Wine of Cyprus', st. 7.

Joshua. Sir Joshua Reynolds (1723–92), English portrait painter and first president of the Royal Academy. He has a critical appreciation of his contemporary Thomas Gainsborough in his fourteenth *Discourse.*

It is exactly . . . judge of it. Originally italicized.

Technique . . . understand it. Originally italicized.

292 *Besant.* 1835–1901, English novelist, often in partnership with James Rice, until the latter's death in 1881. Thereafter novels concerned with social reform: see *DL* p. 230n.

vulgarity. Plain Tales from the Hills (1888), short stories. Cf. Coleridge's comment on the great actor Edmund Kean: 'To see him act, is like reading Shakespeare by flashes of lightning.'

le Noir. Marie Henri Beyle (1783–1842), French writer under the pseudonym of Stendhal. *Le Rouge et le Noir* (1831) and *La Chartreuse de Parme* (1839) were unappreciated in his own time, but had considerable vogue from 1880. Wilde says (*Rev* 379) that he is 'often tempted to think [him] the greatest of French novelists'.

293 *I myself . . . impulse.* Originally italicized.

atmosphere of the age. The underlying argument of 'The Function of Criticism at the Present Time', Super III, 258–85.

Behemoth . . . Leviathan. See above, *DL* p. 238n.

294 *Manchester school.* A mid-nineteenth-century party of English Radicals, including Cobden, Bright, and Milner Gibson, which identified itself with free-trade principles and resistance to government interference, supported a policy of *laissez-faire*, and in foreign affairs was a peace party, insisting strongly on non-intervention.

blood-stained battle. In the Franco-Prussian War, 1870–1.

Eckermann. Conversations of Goethe with Eckermann and Soret, tr. John Oxenford (2 vols., 1850): see ii. 259, a conversation from 1830.

295 *understanding.* Variant on 'the peace of God, which passeth all understanding': Philippians 4: 7.

truth for its own sake. Cf. Emerson's essay 'The Over-Soul': 'the best minds, who love truth for its own sake, think much less of property in truth.'

sweet reasonableness. 'The method and secret and sweet reasonableness of Jesus': *Literature and Dogma*, ch. xii.

Origin of Species. See below, p. 295, natural selection.

Julian. Julian 'the Apostate' (AD 331–63). Nephew of Constantine the Great, he secretly converted to paganism, and as sole emperor revoked the privileges of the Christians and sought to revive paganism.

Montaigne. See above, p. 241n.

antinomian. One who maintains that the moral law is not binding.

To discern . . . arrive. Originally italicized.

natural selection. Charles Darwin's discovery of natural selection is elaborated in *The Origin of Species by Means of Natural Selection* (1859). In *The Descent of Man* (1871) he developed his important supplementary theory of sexual selection.

296 *Renan.* See above, p. 283n.

of the world. This final argument is present in Wilde's mind at least as far back as the Commonplace Book of (?) 1880, where he notes (p. 163) that different cultures have appropriate arts: for the Egyptians it was architecture, for the Greeks sculpture, for the middle ages painting—and music and poetry; but for modern life it is 'the scientific spirit of criticism.'

Creation . . . are one. Originally italicized.

SALOME

Text. It is a measure of what has been judged the unsatisfactoriness of the following text, originally Lord Alfred Douglas's translation of *Salome* from Wilde's French, that Wilde's son, Vyvyan Holland, his biographer, Richard Ellmann, and critic Rodney Shewan have each found it necessary to re-translate the play. Robert Ross in his 1908 edition of the Works gave only Wilde's French version. Douglas defends his translation in his *Autobiography*, but more important is the evidence of a number of Wilde's letters that he found the translation unsatisfactory but accepted it with some (probably extensive) alterations. The principles of this edition indicate that we must use either the French original or this translation by Lord Alfred Douglas and amended by Wilde, and the latter is more generally accessible.

Salome is of course heavily indebted to the Bible, as the notes indicate, but only the most striking echoes are here drawn attention to: there are many more. Other literary sources include Flaubert's *Hérodias* (1871), Huysmans's *A Rebours* (1884), and Maeterlinck's *La Princesse Maleine* (1890) and *Les Sept Princesses* (1891). Wilde's Herod and Herodias occasionally also echo Shakespeare's guilty couples, Macbeth and Lady Macbeth, and Claudius and Gertrude. The text of the play was used as libretto for Richard Strauss's widely successful opera *Salome*.

300 *Herod.* As Ross early noted, Wilde's Tetrarch is based on Herod Antipas (Matthew 14: 1), but combines features of the other two New Testament Herods, Herod the Great (Matthew 2: 1), the father of Herod Antipas, who was responsible for the Massacre of the Innocents, and Herod Agrippa (Acts 12: 23), persecutor of the early Christian Church, who was 'eaten by worms'. Herod Antipas married his brother's wife, Herodias, and was denounced therefore by John the Baptist, here Iokanaan. He beheaded John (the fullest gospel account is at Matthew 6: 14–29), and later had Christ scourged and was reconciled to Pilate.

Tetrarch. Governor of a quarter of a country.

Iokanaan. Hebrew name for John the Baptist, used also by Flaubert in his *Hérodias.*

301 *cistern.* Artificial water-tank.

Pharisees . . . Sadducees. Two great Jewish sects, both fervent upholders of the Law, the first open to ideas of divine intervention, angels, and personal resurrection, the second more conservative.

302 *a mirror of silver.* An echo of 'The Nightingale and the Rose', *CSF* 108. See above *DG* 109.

of his shoes. Mark 1: 7.

303 *like the rose.* Isaiah 35: 1.

shall be opened. Isaiah 35: 5.

by their manes. Isaiah 11: 6–8.

a leathern belt. Matthew 3: 4.

305 *is at hand.* Matthew 3: 1.

your litter. Portable couch with curtains.

he is Elias. The New Testament form of Elijah the Old Testament prophet and precursor of John the Baptist: see John 1: 21–3.

devour the birds. Isaiah 14: 29.

306 *little green flower.* Possibly an allusion to the infamous artificially green carnation sported by Wilde and many of his friends. See *IH* p.440n.

307 *cup of abominations.* Revelations 17: 4. See below, note to p.309 'not yet come'.

in the waste places. John 1: 23.

land of Chaldæa. For this and Iokanaan's next speech see the prophet Ezekiel 23, especially verses 7–9, 12–16.

baldricks. Belts, for swords, bugles, etc.

way of the Lord. Matthew 3: 3, Isaiah 40: 3.

308 *in His hand.* Matthew 3: 12. A metaphor from the winnowing of grain. Cf. *BRG* l. 546.

a tapestry of Tyre. Cf. *The Sphinx*, ll. 155–6: 'Your black throat is like the hole / Left by some torch or burning coal on Saracenic tapestries.'

fantastic moons. Cf. *The Sphinx*, l. 153: 'Your eyes are like fantastic moons that shiver in some stagnant lake.'

daughter of Babylon. Execration used by Isaiah and other Old Testament prophets; cf. also Revelation 17.

Daughter of Sodom. A wicked city destroyed by God, along with Gomorrah, in Genesis 19.

309 *angel of death.* This pervasive and powerful metaphor has an immediately secular source: John Bright made a stirring speech in the House of Commons, 23 February 1855, denouncing the Crimean War: 'The angel of death has been abroad throughout the land; you may almost hear the beating of his wings.'

not yet come. Acts 12: 23, where the angel of God struck down Herod Agrippa 'arrayed in royal apparel'.

loathsome things. Matthew 23: 27: 'for ye are like unto whited sepulchres, which indeed appear beautiful outward, but are within full of dead men's bones, and of all uncleanness.'

crown of thorns. Such as Christ was crowned with; see Mark 15: 17.

310 *band of scarlet.* Song of Solomon 4: 3.

tower of ivory. Song of Solomon 7: 4.

311 *in the river.* Like Narcissus; cf. *DG* p. 50.

312 *the Stoics.* A school of Greek philosophers who held that virtue was the sole good and most objects of desire, such as health or happiness, at best morally indifferent. Their founder, Zeno of Citium (342–270 BC), committed suicide in extreme old age, and many Stoics encouraged suicide.

313 *vast wings.* See above, p. 309.

315 *of the world.* Isaiah 52: 7.

316 *Messias.* Messiah, the Anointed One, whose coming to rescue and redeem Israel was foretold by the prophets.

water into wine. The first miracle, at Cana: see John 2.

by touching them. For healing of a leper and a man sick of the palsy at Capernaum, see Matthew 8.

daughter of Jairus. Mark 5: 22–43.

317 *and stone her.* e.g. Leviticus 20: 2.

beneath their shields. This (non-biblical) prophecy of Iokanaan is fulfilled at the end of the play.

318 *shall be afraid.* Iokanaan quotes Revelation 6: 12–13, 15–16.

319 *do they not?* The veil of the Sanctuary, which separated off the 'most holy place' of the Temple, is said by Matthew, Mark, and Luke to have been 'rent in twain' at the moment of Christ's death. This passage seems derived from Flaubert's *Salammbô*, where Matho, who loves Salammbô, steals the veil of the goddess Tanith for her.

of his blasphemies. Revelation 17: 3–4.

eaten of worms. Acts 12: 23.

322 *stained with scarlet.* Iokanaan quotes Isaiah 63: 1–2, where Christ's coming is shown.

323 *dance of the seven veils.* Wilde seems to have invented the now legendary dance.

charger. A large flat dish: see Matthew 14: 8.

324 *my white peacocks.* See the lyric from Tennyson's *The Princess*, 'Now sleeps the crimson petal . . .', echoed here, especially the line 'Now droops the milk-white peacock like a ghost'. See above, p. 239n.

326 *land of the Seres.* China, the country of the silkworms.

328 *to the dogs.* In Matthew 7: 6, Jesus says: 'Give not that which is holy to the dogs.'

column of ivory. Salome again uses language reminiscent of the Song of Solomon generally.

quench my passion. See Song of Solomon 8 for the wine and apples, and especially 8: 7: 'Many waters cannot quench love, neither can the floods drown it.'

mystery of Death. Cf. Song of Solomon 8: 6, 'for love is as strong as death; jealousy is cruel as the grave'. See also 'The Nightingale and the Rose' (*CSF* 108), where the dying bird sings 'of the Love that is perfected by Death, of the Love that dies not in the tomb', and *DG* p. 75: 'There was something fascinating in this son of Love and Death.' Also the climactic message of the Canterville Ghost (*CSF* 78–9): 'You can open for me the portals of Death's house, for Love is always with you, and Love is stronger than Death.'

with my daughter. An ironic echo of the voice of God at the transfiguration of Christ: 'This is my beloved Son, in whom I am well pleased, hear ye him' (Matthew 17: 5).

329 *Kill that woman.* There is no precedent for this: it is not part of the gospel story.

LADY WINDERMERE'S FAN

The play was first published in 1893. Ellmann says Wilde based the plot on the situation of Lillie Langtry, fashionable beauty and friend of the Prince of Wales, whom Wilde had very publicly admired. When in 1881 she became pregnant, she returned to Jersey and quietly had her daughter (not by her husband), and the child was discreetly brought up in Jersey, while her mother continued as beauty, public figure, and actress. 'When he offered her the part [of Mrs Erlynne], Mrs Langtry scoffed at the idea that she could play a woman with a grown-up daughter. (She was then thirty-nine.)' (Ellmann 109)

The notes here give just a few examples of Wilde's habit of pruning and re-using epigrams in different works, sometimes over years. More detailed treatment of the play can be found in Ian Small's New Mermaid edition (1980), to which I am indebted for some notes.

332 *Persons of the Play.* It is typical of Wilde's Society comedies that there is a high percentage of titles, and names are taken from places, such as Darlington and Windermere. Wilde takes care not to use current titles.

twenty-four hours. Wilde draws attention to the fact that this play, like *An Ideal Husband*, is in accordance with the Aristotelian Unity of Time (within 24 hours) as well as of Place (central London).

334 *Carlton House Terrace.* Like addresses in the comedies generally, this address places the characters socially: it was an area of prestigious clubs, and the town houses of diplomats and statesmen. It is safe to assume given addresses point to expensive and fashionable parts of central London.

338 *behind my back.* See a similar use of this epigram by Lord Henry Wotton, *DG* p. 180: it was adapted again for Lord Illingworth in *A Woman of No Importance.*

339 *odd trick.* In whist or bridge, the honours are the four highest cards of each suit, ace, king, queen, and jack: their holder has a winning hand, but a player with clearly inferior cards may win an occasional trick of the thirteen.

340 *about it.* Epigram reused from the early play *Vera*: 'Ah! my dear Count, life is much too important a thing ever to talk seriously about it.' (*Salome, A Florentine Tragedy, Vera*, 1908, 180)

341 *the Park.* Hyde Park.

342 *or to Aix.* Continental spas or health resorts at Homburg near Frankfurt and Aix-les-Bains near Geneva. In 1892 Wilde himself 'took the waters' at Homburg, a favourite spa of the English aristocracy and royalty.

without a character. Without references to enable her to get another position.

343 *private—locked!* Not bank issue: a locked private notebook which Lord Windermere uses to record transactions.

348 *see your card.* The dance card had the numbers of the dances printed on it, and was filled up by partners in advance; this allowed chaperones to scrutinize, and, like the Duchess here, to interfere in advance also.

particularly younger sons! Young men of good family but no expectations of inherited rank or fortune.

353 *Prince Doria's at Rome.* Prince Alfonzo Doria-Pamphili had married into the English nobility. His Palazzo Doria is one of the finest palaces in Rome: Mrs Erlynne can boast very acceptable acquaintance.

354 *like a Radical.* He has traditional Conservative ideas, but argues as if strongly reformist.

356 *adoringly, madly!* Cf. Algernon's declaration to Cecily, at dictation speed, in *IBE*, directly parodying this avowal, p. 512.

363 *Tantalus frame.* A device in which decanters or bottles of wine could be on display yet locked up, so inaccessible.

370 *Wiesbaden.* One of the oldest and most famous (and fashionable) of German watering-places.

371 *must be wrong.* Cf. Gilbert in *CA II* p. 292.

372 *middle-class education.* The allusion here is to Sir Richard Steele's famous essay on the difference between love and lust in *The Tatler*, 49 (2 August 1709): 'To love her is a liberal education.'

373 *single thing.* Cf. *DG* p. 82 and *De Profundis* in *SL* 229.

their mistakes. This epigram is polished in two earlier contexts. In *Vera* (1880) the cynical Prince Paul remarks: 'Experience, the name men give to their mistakes. I never commit any' (*Salome, A Florentine Tragedy, Vera*, 173). In *DG* Lord Henry muses: 'Experience was of no ethical value. It was merely the name men gave to their mistakes' (p. 91).

379 *the Club Train.* 'Club trains' were luxurious expresses from London's Cannon Street to Dover, inaugurated to connect London with Paris for the 1889 Paris Exhibition. They ran between 1889 and 1893.

manners before morals. Cf. *DG* p. 153: 'Society . . . feels instinctively that manners are of more importance than morals.'

385 *Shrewsbury and Talbot.* Lord Shrewsbury and Talbot's rubber-tyred and luxuriously appointed cabs were introduced about 1880. They were the quietest and most comfortable cabs of the time, and very popular.

387 *good woman!* Cf. the last line of *Le Demi-Monde* (1855), by Dumas *fils*: 'You're marrying the honestest woman I know'.

AN IDEAL HUSBAND

The play was published by Leonard Smithers in 1899. While revising it, Wilde wrote to the publisher: 'I really think it reads the best of my plays' (*ML* 181). More detailed treatment is given to the play in Russell Jackson's New Mermaid edition, in *Two Society Comedies* (1983), to which I am indebted for some notes.

390 *persons of the play.* As in *LWF*, a high percentage of titles, and names are often place-names, like Goring, Chiltern. Chiltern has an extra nuance in a play which turns on whether a politician should resign, because acceptance of the 'Chiltern Hundreds' is the best-known way for an MP to vacate his seat between elections.

twenty-four hours. Wilde draws attention to the fact that this play, like *LWF*, is in accordance with the Aristotelian Unity of Time (within 24 hours) as of Place (central London).

392 *Grosvenor Square.* It is safe to assume from context that given addresses in the social comedies are always prestigious. In 1892 Grosvenor Square had twenty-two titled tenants out of fifty-one addresses, and residents in 1895 included Lord Randolph Churchill.

Boucher . . . Watteau. Jackson comments: 'The paintings by Boucher (1703–70) and Watteau (1684–1721) reflect fashionable interest in these French painters of pastoral, mythological, and delicately erotic subjects.' In an early manuscript of the play Mrs Cheveley tells Sir Robert that the Baron left her 'a little villa he had in Hungary—with some Boucher tapestries and nice Louis Seize furniture—the sort of background that just suits me' (Jackson, op. cit., 286). The stage directions were considerably elaborated for the publication of the play as a volume, and the descriptions of the principal characters, often in terms of paintings, were added then. *Louis Seize.* Louis XVI of France (1754–93), last French king before the Revolution, executed after the proclamation of the Republic.

Mrs Marchmont and Lady Basildon. They make a quite interchangeable pair, clearly types rather than individuals: no commentator seems yet to have noticed that in their first exchanges, Margaret Basildon and Olivia Marchmont become Olivia Basildon and Margaret Marchmont.

393 *Garter.* The highest order of knighthood in Great Britain.

portrait by Lawrence. Sir Thomas Lawrence (1769–1830) was the most notable British portraitist of his generation, though much of his work is now thought over-facile and blatant in colouring. In 'Pen, Pencil, and Poison', his essay on the painter and poisoner Thomas Griffiths Wainewright, Wilde compares Wainewright's style with that of Lawrence, 'a painter for whose work he had always entertained a great admiration' (*Intentions*, 1891, 81).

Tanagra statuette. See p. 12n.

the Row. Rotten Row in Hyde Park, where fashionable people rode.

394 *à la marquise.* In a popular style derived from the period of Louis XV.

395 *Vandyck.* Sir Anthony Vandyck, Flemish painter (1599–1641), worked in London from 1631 and painted many portraits of Charles I's court.

397 *blue spectacles.* Worn to protect the eyes from strong light: also the opposite of the rose-tinted spectacles the optimist proverbially looks through. Cf. 'The Devoted Friend', p. 38.

398 *wonderful Corots.* See above, pp. 233n. and 259n.

399 *like the old Greek.* Odysseus, described in bk. i of Homer's *Odyssey*: 'He saw the cities of many men, and knew their mind.'

Penelope. Odysseus' wife.

Boodle's Club. One of the oldest clubs in London, founded in 1762. It moved to its very elegant club house in St James's in 1783. Its members were mostly country gentlemen, but also included Edward Gibbon, William Wilberforce, and Beau Brummell. It acquired an early reputation for high gambling and good food.

405 *Suez Canal shares.* The purchase of Suez shares took place in 1875, on Disraeli's initiative.

second Panama. After the Panama Canal project foundered in 1889, with massive debts and unaccounted-for expenditures, a national scandal in France resulted in legal action against the speculators, who were revealed to have involved senators and deputies in the corruption. A series of trials took place in Paris in 1892–3 but one of the principal backers of the scheme, Baron Jaques Reinach, took his life on the day he was to face the court.

406 *the whole world kin.* Mrs Cheveley plays with a line from Shakespeare's Troilus and Cressida, III.iii.175: 'One touch of nature makes the whole world kin.' Cf. *DL* p. 223n.

408 *public placard.* Wilde had attended sessions of the Parnell Commission, which cleared the apologist of Irish Home Rule of inciting political murder, and soon after saw Parnell brought down by newspapers and public obloquy, because of his involvement in a divorce case.

409 *Ladies' Gallery.* A separate Ladies' Gallery, with a grille in front of it, was provided above the Press Gallery in the House of Commons.

410 *the Park.* Hyde Park.

411 *Claridge's.* A fashionable hotel in Brook Street, Mayfair.

en règle. Correct etiquette.

Royal Academy. See above, p. 50n.

novels in Scotch dialect. Cf. *CA I* p. 255 and n.

414 *what is it that I have loved!* Cf. *DG* p. 164, where Basil says: 'Christ! what a thing I must have worshipped!'

416 *when we see it.* A quotation from Tennyson's *Idylls of the King*, where Guinevere laments her mistaken choice of love: 'We needs must love the highest when we see it. / Not Lancelot nor another.' Cf. *Misc* 110: 'This is indeed something so rare that when we meet it we cannot fail to love it.'

put out the lights! Reminiscent of Othello about to kill Desdemona (v. ii. 7): 'Put out the light, and then put out the light.'

420 *possessed it.* This reads like a variation on Lord Henry Wotton's 'temptation' of Dorian Gray.

421 *must have done.* A recurrent theme: see e.g. Gilbert's denunciation of charity in *CA I* p. 257: 'Charity, as even those of whose religion it makes a formal part have been compelled to acknowledge, creates a multitude of evils', and *CA II* pp. 278–81.

424 *décolleté.* Low-cut, as in a very revealing evening dress.

Woman's Liberal Association. Founded 1886, it opposed Gladstone in 1892 by supporting the campaign for women's suffrage. Constance Wilde was a member, and an active campaigner and speaker.

425 *Parliamentary Franchise.* In its 1892 election manifesto the Liberal Party had pledged itself to introduce legislation on the limiting of working hours, the introduction of female inspectors to monitor the application of the Factory Acts, and the reform of the franchise.

Bachelors' Ball. The London season included 'private' dances, given by the parents of marriageable girls, and 'public' festivities, organized by associations of like-minded acquaintances: the Bachelors' Ball was among the latter.

428 *Morning Post.* See below, note to p. 518n.

County Council. The London County Council was formed in 1889 to gather together the functions of local government in the capital previously discharged by parish 'vestries'.

Lambeth Conference. The Lambeth Conference of Anglican bishops is held about every ten years at Lambeth Palace, London residence of the Archbishop of Canterbury.

moue. Pout.

429 *dreadful statue of Achilles.* The naked, heroic statue of Achilles in Hyde Park was erected in 1822, inscribed by 'the women of England' to the Duke of Wellington and his army. Cf. 'The English Renaissance of Art', where Wilde claims to have heard Swinburne insisting at dinner 'that Achilles is even now more actual and real than Wellington' (*Misc* 258).

what bimetallism means. The system of allowing the unrestricted currency of two metals (e.g. gold and silver) at a fixed ratio to each other, as coined money.

430 *tableaux. Tableaux vivants*, in which performers (usually amateur) gave a costumed representation of some familiar painting or historical scene, were a popular pastime and were often staged for charitable fund-raising events.

431 *Undeserving.* See above p. 421. The distinction between 'deserving' and 'undeserving' poor was important in Victorian philanthropy.

the Drawing Room. The formal presentation of ladies to the Queen and her court took place at a 'Drawing-Room'. Lady Markby would have been presenting *débutantes* to the court.

432 *assisted emigration.* Frequently advocated as a radical means of reforming the criminal classes, practised by a number of charitable organizations as an aid to the respectable as well as to the 'fallen'. Also of course the fate Jack Worthing devises for his scapegrace brother in *IBE* p. 504n.

Pump Room. Associated with the spa's social life as much as its medicinal purposes.

Higher Education of Women. The appropriateness of university studies for women was still a matter of dispute, although the establishment of women's colleges at Oxford and Cambridge and the more enlightened policy of London University had advanced the cause.

434 *Blue Books.* Reports or other papers printed by parliament.

yellow covers. These would be French novels, usually sold in yellow paper wrappers, and by popular belief immoral or improper.

439 *Adam Room.* i.e. designed and decorated by one or both of the brothers Adam, Scottish architects who transformed London architecture and interior decoration in the second half of the eighteenth century.

Inverness Cape. A cloak or overcoat with cape: stylish.

440 *buttonhole.* See PPUY: 'A really well-made buttonhole is the only link between Art and Nature', and *IBE*, II where Algernon tells Cecily: 'I never have any appetite unless I have a buttonhole first' (p. 505). Like Lord Goring, Wilde was a fashion leader with his introduction of the green carnation: 'I invented that magnificent flower . . . The flower is a work of art' (*Misc* 175). Like him, Wilde also carried a Louis Seize cane: Lord Goring certainly seems to be Wilde's Ideal Wilde, as the added stage-directions and descriptions make clear.

444 *Lamia-like.* In Keats's poem 'Lamia', a serpent assumes a woman's shape. She is described as: 'a gordian shape of dazzling hue / Vermilion-spotted, golden, green and blue', with 'silver mail, and golden brede'.

448 *hock and seltzer.* White wine and soda-water was a well-known restorative, used by Dorian Gray (*DG* p. 158) and by Wilde himself. Cf. Betjeman's poem on his arrest, which begins: 'He sipped at a weak hock and seltzer / As he gazed at the London skies.'

453 *The Book of Numbers.* A pun: the fourth book of the Old Testament, and what amounts to a charge of promiscuity. Lord Goring is as near here as he ever gets to losing his poise and his dandyism.

454 *Voilà tout.* That is all.

460 *since Canning.* George Canning (1770–1827), talented and versatile English statesman and orator.

462 *seeing the unemployed.* Jackson notes: 'Concern about the unemployed as a group, and as a political force, had come to a head in the Trafalgar Square riot in 1886. It was a commonplace of the conservative press that only workshy ne'er-do-wells took part, and *The Times* used inverted commas for the collective noun—"the unemployed"—in its report of the disturbance.'

the Park. Hyde Park.

THE IMPORTANCE OF BEING EARNEST

The play was published in 1899. More detailed treatment of the play and material cut before the first production can be found in Russell Jackson's New Mermaid edition (1980), to which I am indebted for some notes.

478 *Lane.* Named after the publisher John Lane, with whom Wilde's relations were not always easy.

Hon. Gwendolen Fairfax. 'Hon.' indicates that Gwendolen is the daughter of a viscount or baron, but the title is never used colloquially, so she is correctly addressed as 'Miss Fairfax'.

482 *Divorce Court.* In England the Divorce Court was established in 1857 by the Matrimonial Causes Act.

483 *Scotland Yard.* Headquarters of the London Metropolitan Police.

484 *Tunbridge Wells.* (Royal) Tunbridge Wells, Kent, had been fashionable as an inland watering place since the seventeenth century.

The Albany. Fashionable 'bachelor chambers' in central London, off Piccadilly.

485 *Bunburyist.* The name contains a private joke, like the butler Lane above, and Maxbohm, p. 537. Wilde had a friend, Henry S. Bunbury, who lived in Gloucestershire.

486 *at Willis's.* A fashionable restaurant in King Street, near the St James's Theatre, much frequented by Wilde.

sent down. Guests assembled upstairs in the drawing-room before dinner; each gentleman was appointed escort to a lady for the evening, and 'went down' to the dining-room with her.

487 *corrupt French Drama.* The plays of Dumas *fils*, Scribe, Augier, and others were popular and influential in England, but had to be censored for the taste of Victorian England, as their treatment of sexual matters was considered too liberal and frank.

Wagnerian manner. The operas of Richard Wagner were popular with the *avant-garde,* but Philistine humour labelled them as too loud and over-powering. Cf. *DG* p. 81, where Lady Henry Wotton appreciates its loudness: 'It is so loud that one can talk the whole time without other people hearing what one says.'

488 *gold from grief.* Cf. *DG* p. 179.

489 *French . . . German.* French is seen throughout as decadent, wicked, and fun; German as ponderous, dull, and respectable: cf. p. 500.

490 *Gwendolen.* Jack's use of her first name is appropriate only because an engagement is clearly imminent.

493 *of some kind.* See *CA I* p. 241n.

   everything or nothing. Cf. *DG* p. 111.

494 *Liberal Unionist.* Strictly speaking, Liberal Unionists were originally members of Gladstone's Liberal Party, who voted against his 1886 bill for Home Rule for Ireland, but as Jackson points out, Jack uses the term as the equivalent of today's 'Don't know'.

   in a hand-bag. In the 1890s, a small piece of luggage to be carried by either sex.

495 *cloak-room.* The left-luggage office.

496 *right as a trivet.* i.e. very dependable, like a three-legged stand for a pot or kettle.

   Gorgon. Mythological monster, with snakes for hair, the sight of which turned the beholder to stone.

497 *make love to her.* Pay court to her.

   only just eighteen. She has just reached what Society regards as marriageable age.

498 *the Club.* Gentlemen's clubs, used as meeting and eating places by their (usually select) membership.

   the Empire. The Empire Theatre of Varieties, a music hall in Leicester Square, famous for its 'promenade', which had been attacked only the year before by a Mrs Chant in her Purity Campaign: a very topical reference.

   hard work doing nothing. Cf. *CA passim,* especially p. 275, 'to do nothing at all is the most difficult thing in the world, the most difficult and the most intellectual'.

   marry often. Wilde reviewed a 'handbook to marriage' called *How to be Happy though Married,* in which a bachelor advised a young friend to 'marry early and marry often' (*Rev* 36).

500 *basket chairs.* Chairs made of wickerwork.

   German. See above, p. 489n.

501 *let him reap.* Galatians 6: 7: 'whatsoever a man soweth, that shall he also reap.'

   three-volume novels that Mudie sends us. Subscribers to Mudie's Circulating

Library could arrange to be sent a monthly box of the latest publications. It was such libraries that for many years sustained the three-volume novel, outmoded by new technology, and by the time of writing definitely old-fashioned. Cf. *CA I* p. 255.

502 *Egeria . . . Lætitia.* In Roman mythology, Egeria was a nymph who taught King Numa Pompilius the principles later enshrined in the city's laws, and she is associated with Diana and chastity. Letitia inappropriately means joy or happiness.

Fall of the Rupee. Political Economy was an unusual subject in the curriculum for a girl's private education. The Fall of the Rupee refers to the fluctuating value of the Indian rupee since 1873, the rupee at one point being worth only one shilling compared with two shillings before 1873.

504 *Australia.* Convicts ceased to be sent to Australia by the mid-nineteenth century, but in plays scapegoats of various kinds were often despatched there for reformation or punishment (e.g. *IH* p. 432). But see the worldly Duchess of Berwick's attitude in *LWF*, pp. 349, 358–9.

505 *Maréchal Niel.* A yellow noisette rose, first introduced into England in the 1860s.

womanthrope. Cf. *CA I* p. 256.

Primitive Church. Canon Chasuble is named after a church vestment affected by High Churchmen of his time, who stressed the historical continuity of the Anglican Church with Catholic Christianity: thus his interest in the early or Primitive Church.

506 *deepest mourning.* Completely black clothes were worn for some months after the death of a close relative. Crape, a thin fabric, usually of artificial silk, was particularly favoured.

Grand Hotel. The Grand Hotel in the Boulevard des Capucines was one of the most luxurious in Paris: Wilde stayed there in November–December 1891.

507 *canonical practice.* Two methods of baptism, by which a person might be received into the Church, sprinkling with a few drops of holy water, or total submersion in water, are both, says the canon, according to the law of the Church.

510 *dog-cart.* Light, horse-drawn two-wheeled vehicle, originally used as a sporting vehicle, with a box for carrying pointer dogs.

511 *over-educated.* Cf. *DG* p. 182 and PPUY.

512 *devotedly, hopelessly.* A parody of Lord Darlington's declaration at *LWF* p. 356.

518 *Morning Post.* For many years this, rather than the more expensive and austere *Times*, was the chief source of fashionable gossip, and the proper place to announce engagements and marriages.

519 *agricultural depression.* From the early 1870s British agriculture suffered a severe depression, because of increased importation of cheap foreign

produce and a succession of bad seasons. More and more workers were being attracted from the land to great industrial cities.

526 *style not sincerity.* Cf. this epigram, polished and extended, in PPUY and the treatment of sincerity at *CA II* pp. 284–5 and *DG* p. 55.

German scepticism. Wilde added 'German' here when revising the play for the first edition in 1899: see earlier gibes about German at p. 489, 500. He added to *IH* p. 427 at a similar stage: 'It is love, and not German philosophy, that is the true explanation of this world . . .'

527 *a luggage train.* A train for transporting goods, not passengers.

University Extension Scheme. The University of London's Extension Scheme was a pioneer among extramural teaching departments.

528 *outrage.* The trial of the Walsall anarchists in 1892 and a series of incidents involving explosives on the Continent and (in 1894) in London had established political assassination in the public consciousness. But Wilde referred to such incidents as early as 1887: see LASC *passim.*

529 *Sporran, Fifeshire, N.B.* A Scottish estate was appropriate, but the address shows disdain for Scottish niceties: Fife, not Fifeshire, is the proper form, and by 1870 at latest Scotland, rather than N.B. for North Britain. Irishmen like Wilde also objected to being considered 'West Britons'.

Court Guides. The Court Guide: an annual publication which, in addition to royalty, listed the names and London addresses of the British aristocracy and gentry. The presumption was that those so listed had been 'presented' at Court to the sovereign.

in the Funds. Government stocks, now called Consols (or Consolidated Funds), yielded an unspectacular but dependable income.

531 *Oxonian.* The fact that Algernon has been to an Oxford college is seen as guarantee of integrity.

Perrier-Jouet, Brut, '89. A dry champagne of the 1889 vintage. Cf. *De Profundis*, where Wilde remembers specially reserving this wine with Lord Alfred Douglas at Willis's (*SL* 235).

533 *Anabaptists.* The Anabaptists, who believed in adult baptism, flourished in Europe in the sixteenth century, but the name was applied by their enemies to contemporary Baptists.

pew-opener. A person employed to open the doors of private pews for their occupants.

534 *bassinette.* Perambulator.

536 *cast a stone.* Christ was asked for judgement on the woman taken in adultery and replied: 'He that is without sin among you, let him first cast a stone at her' (John 8: 7).

one law for men. Wilde here parodies the views of 'good' characters in previous plays: cf. *LWF* p. 338 and *A Woman of No Importance, passim.*

537 *Army Lists.* Official lists of all the commissioned officers in the army.

Maxbohm. A private joke: Max Beerbohm, writer and artist, was a friend of Wilde's.

THE HARLOT'S HOUSE

This poem was first published in *The Dramatic Review* (11 April 1885). It exemplifies his self-conscious participation in a tradition. Among its literary ancestors is a set of verses entitled 'The Haunted Palace' in Edgar Allan Poe's *The Fall of the House of Usher*. In ll. 7–18 of this poem Wilde uses the medieval tradition of the dance of death, or *danse macabre*, an ominous dance of the living with the dead, which had been notably used by Baudelaire in 'Danse Macabre' (*Les Fleurs du mal* cxxi) and by Gautier. He used this tradition again in ll. 289–324 of *The Ballad of Reading Gaol*, which have some verbal echoes of this poem.

539 l. 6. *'Treues Liebes Herz' of Strauss*. 'The Heart of True Love', a waltz by Viennese composer Johann Strauss (1825–99).

ll. 16–18 *by the hand*. Wilde is very close to Gautier here. In 'Bûchers et Tombeaux' in *Emaux et Camées* Gautier used similar theme, rhythm, and rhymes:

> Le jeune au vieux donne le main,
> L'irrésistible sarabande
> Met en branle le genre humain.

ll. 22–4. *a horrible Marionette*. Wilde reused this material in *Dorian Gray* when describing Dorian's desperate journey to the opium den, to find oblivion after Basil's murder (*DG* p. 185).

THE SPHINX

See Note on the Text, paragraph two. This poem was begun when Wilde was at Oxford (see ll. 17–18, 159, 162), and almost completed in Paris in 1883 (14 lines were added after the final draft in the year before publication in 1894). French literary influence predominates, including the 'cat' poems in Baudelaire's *Les Fleurs du mal* (xxiv, li, and lxvi). Flaubert's *Temptation of St Antony* underlies some exotic vocabulary and a delight in monsters, and Gautier had much to say about monsters, statues, and sexual ambiguity, especially in *Mademoiselle de Maupin*, 'One of Cleopatra's Nights', and 'The Mummy's Romance'. Gautier and Flaubert had established virtually a tradition of attraction to the monstrous, the ambiguously sexed, the statue, inside which Wilde is writing.

Wilde was not concerned to reflect the best Egyptian scholarship available, and often used ancient classics like Herodotus. He repeatedly sacrifices accuracy to unusual, trisyllabic rhyme: thus he writes Heliopolis instead of Thebes (l. 26), and makes no sense at l. 99. Some phrases defy explanation, because they evolved accidentally in composition: e.g. l. 68, 'the dove of Ashtaroth' (earlier 'the dove of Cythera'), l. 114, 'the blue-faced ape of Horus' (earlier 'the blue-faced ape of Nubia'), and ll. 65–6, 'God of Flies who plagued the Hebrews and was splashed / With wine . . .' (earlier 'that pale God with almond eyes and almond body'). For more detail on all these matters, see I. Murray, 'Some Problems of editing Wilde's poem *The Sphinx* ', in *Durham University Journal* (1989).

541 l. 11. *seneschal*. Steward in control of a household.

l. 12. *half woman and half animal.* The Egyptian sphinx was with very few exceptions shown as male, while the Greek sphinx was female. Wilde deliberately confuses the traditions: his sphinxes are always female, and apart from this poem usually derive from one witticism, the notion of women as 'sphinxes without secrets'. See above p. 195n.

l. 18. *twenty summers.* Wilde here echoes the poem with which he won the Newdigate Prize at Oxford, *Ravenna*, where he describes himself, even then inaccurately, as 'one who scarce has seen / Some twenty summers cast their doublets green, / For Autumn's livery.' Both poems also echo Gautier: 'Oh! I think that a hundred thousand centuries of nothingness will be needed to rest me after these twenty years of life' (*Mademoiselle de Maupin*, ch. v).

l. 19. *hieroglyphs . . . obelisks.* Pictorial characters before the development of writing, here inscribed on monuments in the form of tapering shafts.

l. 20. *Basilisk.* Also cockatrice; fabulous reptile with lethal breath and/or evil eye, hatched by a serpent from a cock's egg! *Hippogriff:* griffin with the body of a horse.

l. 21. *Isis . . . Osiris.* Egyptian goddess of divine motherhood with posthumous child Horus bred up to avenge his father, Osiris, both brother and husband of Isis, killed and dismembered by his brother Seth. Thereafter Osiris was symbol of life and rebirth and lord of the dead.

l. 22. *Egyptian . . . Antony.* A vignette of the love of Antony and Cleopatra. 'Melt her union' holds a deliberate ambiguity. The phrase has an obvious sexual connotation, and also uses 'union' in an archaic sense, as a large and very valuable pearl, such as tradition tells us Cleopatra melted in wine and drank, to demonstrate the extravagance of her love. Tradition says she caught Antony cheating at fishing, so had a salt fish attached to his line under water.

l. 25. *the Cyprian . . . Adon.* Venus, much worshipped in Cyprus, loved Adonis, a beautiful youth who was killed by a boar. *Catafalque:* coffin-stand.

l. 26. *Amenalk.* A form of Ammon or Amun. *Heliopolis:* a town situated near the head of the Delta, a highly important religious centre from very early times.

l. 27. *Thoth.* The Egyptian Hermes, represented with head of ibis on a human body: protector of Osiris. *Io:* A Greek mythological priestess, beloved of Zeus; changed into a heifer to avoid Hera's pursuing champions. Later identified with Egyptian Isis.

542   l. 31. *Jewish maid . . . Holy Child.* Reference to the flight of the Holy Family into Egypt under divine guidance to escape Herod's Massacre of the Innocents (Matthew 2:13).

l. 34. *Adrian . . . Antinous.* See above p. 55n.

l. 37. *labyrinth . . . twy-formed Bull.* The Cretan Labyrinth was said to have been designed by Dedalus for King Minos of Crete, to hide the Minotaur, a monster with the body of a man and the head of a bull. *Twy-formed:* having two forms.

l. 39. *scarlet Ibis*. Sacred bird of ancient Egypt, the manifestation of the god Thoth. For Egyptians its white plumage symbolized the sun, and its black plumage the moon. *Britannica* notes it is a popular error, especially among painters, that the scarlet ibis (found in tropical and subtropical America) was the sacred ibis of the Egyptians. Cp. *DG* 170 and above p. 30n.

l. 40. *moaning mandragores*. The plant mandrake, historically used for narcotic properties. *OED*: 'The forked root [of the mandrake] is thought to resemble the human form, and was fabled to utter a deadly shriek when plucked up from the ground.' This is one of many examples of exotic and unusual words Wilde found in Flaubert's *Temptation of Saint Antony*: others include tragelaphos and oreichalch.

l. 41. *Crocodile*. Most Egyptian gods took the shape of some animal, which was regarded as sacred. Egyptians bred and pampered one particular member of the sacred species.

l. 48. *Gryphon*. A fabulous animal usually represented as having the head and wings of an eagle and the body and hindquarters of a lion.

l. 51. *Lycian tomb . . . Chimæra*. In Greek myth, the Chimera was a fabulous monster, born in Lycia and killed by Bellerophon. Wilde writes admiringly of Flaubert's dialogue of Sphinx and Chimera in the *Temptation of St Antony* at *DL* p. 238 and *Rev* 536.

l. 54. *Nereid*. Sea-nymph.

l. 56. *Leviathan or Behemoth*. See *DL* p. 238n.

543   l. 60. *glyph*. Architectural term for an ornamental groove or channel, usually vertical.

l. 61. *bar*. A bank of sand, silt, etc. across the mouth of a river or harbour which obstructs navigation.

l. 62. *lúpanar*. Brothel.

l. 64. *Tragelaphos*. A fabulous beast, compounded of a goat and a stag.

ll. 65–6. *the God of Flies who plagued the Hebrews*. The God of Flies is Baal: it was the God of the Old Testament who sent plagues of flies, not on the Hebrews but their persecutors the Egyptians (Exodus 8: 21–31). Neither is 'splashed / With wine unto the waist': in an earlier version this is said of 'that pale God with almond eyes and almond body', and Wilde carelessly cobbles this line in a late change.

l. 67. *the Tyrian*. Adonis, see l. 25 above.

l. 68. *Ashtaroth*. A general name for all Syrian goddesses. The god of the Assyrian is the god Assur, represented with falcon head and wings.

l. 69. *talc*. A name formerly applied to various transparent, translucent, or shining minerals as talc proper, mica, selenite.

l. 70. oreichalch. A kind of yellow copper ore: another Flaubertian word, not in *OED*.

l. 71. *Apis*. Bullheaded god.

l. 72. *nenuphar.* Water-lily.

l. 74.*Ammon.* Ammon or Amun, king of the gods, also a god of fertility, said to be the procreator of the pharaohs.

l. 75. *river-horses.* Hippopotami.

l. 78. *strode across the waters.* This makes Ammon reminiscent of Christ, as does the description of funeral rites below, ll. 126–8.

l. 82. *secret name.* If the secret name of a god became known, his magic powers were lessened.

544   l. 89. *cubit.* An ancient measure of length derived from the length of the forearm; usually 18–22 inches.

l.91. *must.* New wine or juice of the grape either unfermented or before fermentation is complete. Figuratively, any thing fresh or new.

l.92. *insapphirine.* Apparently a Wilde coinage, on the model of Shakespeare's use of 'incarnadine' in *Macbeth* (II. ii. 62), meaning 'could [not] make more blue'.

l.95. *porphyry.* A very hard, durable stone of a deep purplish red used by ancient sculptors.

l.98. *Colchian witch.* Medea, a famous sorceress of Asiatic Scythia who married Jason the leader of the Argonauts and helped him to win the Golden Fleece.

l.99. *galiot . . . Corybants.* A small galley or boat; priests of the Phrygian worship of Cybele: with both words clearly chosen for sound rather than meaning, the line makes intriguing nonsense!

l.106.*Memphian.* Memphis was the old capital of Lower Egypt.

l.110. *rose-marble monolith.* As the immediate inspiration for Rossetti's 'The Burden of Nineveh' was his witnessing the arrival of a colossal human-headed winged bull from Nimrud at the British Museum, so Wilde's poem is influenced by the Museum's outstanding collection of Egyptian antiquities. In particular, a colossal head in red granite, along with its one attendant arm, now attributed to Amenophis III, seems to inspire this line, and l. 116.

545   l. 114. *peristyle.* A row of columns.

l. 116–28. *giant granite hand still clenched in impotent despair.* Forces a memory of Shelley's Ozymandias, before moving into an echo of Isis collecting the fourteen pieces of the murdered Osiris and putting them together, and into a subdued memory of the death and anointing of Christ. This is underlined by the repetition in ll. 129 and 130 that 'Only one God' has died.

l. 119. *burnous.* A mantle or cloak with a hood extensively worn by Arabs and Moors.

l. 120. *Titan thews . . . paladin.* Gigantic muscular development: *paladin*: knightly hero, renowned champion.

l. 131. *the hundred-cubit gate.* See also 'the Theban gate' (l. 146). The

Egyptian city of Thebes was called 'the Hundred-Gated': Homer says out of each gate the Thebans could send out 200 war-chariots.

l. 132. *Dog-faced Anubis.* God of the dead, with the head of a dog or jackal.

l. 133–4. *Memnon.* According to Tacitus' *Annals*, a black statue at Thebes which, being struck with the rays of the morning sun, gave out musical sounds. Wilde would also know striking pictures of the site at Thebes where the vast head and arm mentioned above (l. 110) were found, where only two huge colossi of Memnon remain upright.

l. 139. *argosies.* Merchant vessels of the largest size and capacity.

546 ll. 153–6. *stagnant lake.* Close echoes in these lines of *Salome* p. 308.

l. 159. *grey gilt-dialled towers.* Presumably intended to evoke Oxford with its 'dreaming spires' as site for the 'student's cell'. Cf. *CA II* p. 287, 'the tower's gilded vanes'.

l. 161. *snake-tressed Fury.* In Dante's journey through Hell the Furies threaten him with the snake-haired Gorgon Medusa, the sight of whom in the ancient world was said to turn the beholder to stone.

l. 162. *poppy-drowsy Queen.* Persephone: see above, p. 247n.

l. 166. *Abana and Pharphar.* See the story of Naaman the Syrian leper at 2 Kings 5: told to wash in the Jordan for a cure, he at first preferred these, his own sacred rivers running through Damascus.

l. 170. *Atys* (or Attis). Phrygian shepherd, beloved of Cybele, who promised her he would live in celibacy. After breaking his vow he castrated himself and died.

547 ll. 171–2. *on his oar.* The river Styx was one of the five rivers of Hell: the ferryman Charon ferried the spirits of the dead across, and received an obol coin as fee, which was placed in the mouth of the corpse.

l. 174. *in vain.* This phrase seems to contradict any conviction or hope otherwise found in this return to a Christian ambience at the end of the poem.

THE BALLAD OF READING GAOL

Wilde was moved from Wandsworth to Reading Gaol on 23 November 1895, and served the rest of his sentence there. He was released on 18 May 1897. While he was there, a judicial hanging was carried out, the first in the prison for eighteen years, and this inspired the poem. This is the only one of Wilde's works directly inspired by life, and the only work of art he created after his release from prison. But he wrote in *More Letters* (171): 'The idea for *The Ballad* came to me while I was in the dock, waiting for my sentence to be pronounced.' See also *De Profundis*, where he talks about his feelings in the dock (*SL* 230). The poem is divided into six 'cantos', but it is clear from Wilde's *Selected Letters* (311) that he wanted divisions indicated inside the numbered cantos: here they are marked by asterisks. There is much illuminating material about the poem and its composition in the *Selected Letters*, and in *More Letters*, *passim*. The author's name on early editions was omitted: Wilde used his prison cell number as a pen name: 'C. 3. 3.'. I am indebted for some of the notes here to H. Montgomery Hyde (ed.), *The Annotated Oscar Wilde* (1982).

548 *1896.* Charles Thomas Wooldridge, who had been a trooper in the Royal Horse Guards, was sentenced to death for the premeditated murder of his wife. She had aroused his jealousy, and he lay in wait for her on the road near her house and slit her throat there three times (not in bed, as the poem says). The sentence was carried out on 7 July 1896 at Reading Gaol.

l. 1. *scarlet coat.* Poetic licence: the Royal Horse Guards uniform was dark blue with red trimmings.

549 l. 37. *he loves.* See the trial scene in *The Merchant of Venice* (IV. i. 66–7):
> *Bassanio.* Do all men kill the things they do not love?
> *Shylock.* Hates any man the thing he would not kill?

l. 41. *with a kiss.* Judas.

550 l. 61. *silent men.* A prisoner in the condemned cell was kept under continuous observation.

l. 83. *leathern thongs.* The prisoner to be executed was bound at wrists, elbows, and knees.

l. 90. *hideous shed.* Wilde wrote to Ross: 'With regard to the adjectives, I admit there are far too many "dreadfuls" and "fearfuls". The difficulty is that the objects in prison have no shape or form. To take an example: the shed in which people are hanged is a little shed with a glass roof, like a photographer's studio on the sands at Margate. For eighteen months I thought it *was* the studio for photographing prisoners. There is no adjective to describe it. I call it "hideous" because it became so to me after I knew its use' (*SL* 311).

l. 96. *Caiaphas.* Caiaphas was high priest in the year Christ was crucified, and condemned him (Matthew 26: 65). The priests paid Judas to betray Christ with a kiss, and Caiaphas declared: 'it is expedient for us, that one man should die for the people' (John 11: 50). Wilde wrote: 'By "Caiaphas" I do not mean the present Chaplain of Reading: he is a good-natured fool, one of the silliest of God's silly sheep: a typical clergyman in fact. I mean any priest of God who assists at the unjust and cruel punishments of man' (*SL* 315: see also 318, and his letter of 23 March 1898 to the *Daily Chronicle*, 334–8).

551 l. 116. *peek.* Usually 'peak' or pine: droop in health or spirits.

l. 120. *been wine.* Cf. *DG* p. 63, where Dorian buries his face in lilac-blossoms, 'feverishly drinking in their perfume as if it had been wine'.

552 l. 138. *bears its fruit.* Before the modern gallows, criminals were hanged from trees, usually oak or elm, from which the leaves had been shorn. Wilde's image also incorporates the tradition that if a tree's roots were bitten by an adder, this would destroy its leaves and fruit for a season.

l. 167. *holy night.* Wilde here recalls and overturns a famous line from

Longfellow's *The Theologian's Tale* (1874): 'Ships that pass in the night, and speak with each other in passing', etc.

553   l. 173. *iron gin.* Trap or snare.

554   l. 216. *tarry rope.* 'Picking oakum' was a traditional pastime for prisoners, unpicking old rope for caulking ships' seams. It was boring and painful, breaking nails and tearing the flesh of the fingers. Wilde picked oakum at Pentonville Prison only.

l. 223. *sacks . . . stones.* Sewing mailbags and breaking stones, more accepted tasks for prisoners.

l. 224. *the dusty drill.* A narrow iron drum on legs with a long handle which scooped up and dropped cups of sand. Known as 'the crank', it was particularly pointless work.

l. 226. *the mill.* i.e. the treadmill, often used as a punishment. The crank and the treadmill were both abolished by the Prison Act of 1898, about which Wilde wrote to the *Daily Chronicle* when the measure was before Parliament (*SL* 334–8).

l. 237. *cried out for blood.* Cf. Genesis 4: 10.

555   l. 246. *numbered tomb.* Prisoners were kept in solitary confinement in numbered cells: Wilde's cell at Reading was C. 3. 3., the third cell on the third floor of Block C.

556   l. 280. *a hearse.* Ornaments of black feathers used at funerals.

l. 281. *upon a sponge.* Shortly before his death on the cross, Jesus was offered a sponge full of vinegar.

l. 283. *cock crew.* Reminiscent of Peter's denial of Christ: see Matthew 27.

ll. 289–324. *glided fast.* Wilde draws on the medieval tradition of the dance of death, or *danse macabre*, here, as it had been reshaped by Baudelaire and Gautier. See 'The Harlot's House'.

l. 291. *rigadoon.* Lively dance for two persons.

l. 295 *mop and mow.* Grimaces.

l. 299. *arabesques.* Cf. 'The Harlot's House', ll. 8–9.

557   l. 313. *antics.* Archaic: mountebanks or clowns.

l. 315. *gyves.* Shackles.

l. 321. *demirep.* A woman of doubtful reputation.

l. 336. *seneschal.* Steward.

l. 345. *mighty wing.* The same powerful metaphor from John Bright that Wilde had used in *Salome* p. 309 and *passim*.

558   l. 367. *of eight.* The hour for weekday hangings.

l. 371. *running noose.* To ensure a strong jolt and a quick death as the rope tightened, the rope ran through a metal eyelet to avoid any friction.

l. 374. *the sign.* The 'sign' was the tolling of the bell of St Lawrence's

Church, Reading, which began a quarter of an hour before the execution and continued for some time afterwards.

559   l. 392. *bitter cry*. See Genesis, 27: 34.

l. 393. *bloody sweats*. See Luke's account of Christ's agony in the garden, 22: 44: 'And being in an agony he prayed more earnestly: and his sweat was as it were great drops of blood falling down to the ground.'

560   l. 432. *in vain*. Cf. *The Sphinx*, l. 174.

l. 450. *quicklime*. Intended to decompose a dead body quickly.

561   l. 474. *unreproachful stare*. Cf. the end of 'The Fisherman and his Soul', *CSF* 235–6.

l. 486. *great Pope's sight*. See *CA I* p. 263n.

563   l. 530. *bourne*. Cf. *Hamlet*, III. i. 79–80.

l. 546. *evil fan*. Cf. Iokanaan at *Salome* p. 308. The metaphor is from the winnowing of grain: here Wilde contrasts the Divine and the human Law. See Matthew 3: 12: 'Whose fan is in his hand, and he will thoroughly purge his floor, and gather his wheat into the garner; but he will burn up the chaff with unquenchable fire.'

564   l. 565. *frightened child*. For an extended prose account of the material in this stanza see Wilde's letter to the *Daily Chronicle*, 27 May 1897 (SL 269–75).

l. 580. *chalk and lime*. Adulteration of bread with chalk and lime was still common. Tennyson had denounced it in *Maud* (1850): 'And chalk and alum and plaster are sold to the poor for bread' (l. 39).

565   l. 612. *costliest nard*. See Mark 14: 3, John 12: 3, where a woman breaks a box of precious ointment and anoints Jesus with it.

l. 617. *a broken heart*. A recurrent image: see the endings of 'The Happy Prince' (above) and 'The Fisherman and his Soul' (*CSF* 234).

l. 622. *to Paradise*. See Luke 23: 43, where Jesus makes his promise to the repentant thief crucified beside him.

l. 624. *not despise*. See Psalm 51: 17: 'The sacrifices of God are a broken spirit: a broken and a contrite heart, O God, thou wilt not despise.' This verse is quoted at the climactic end of Meinhold's *The Amber Witch*, which Wilde said was among his 'favourite romantic reading when a boy' (See *CSF* 2–3).

l. 625. *the Law*. The sentencing judge.

566   l. 635. *Cain*. With the death of his brother Abel, Cain became the first murderer. But God set a mark on Cain that forbade anyone to kill him (Genesis 4: 1–16).

l. 636. *snow-white seal*. See 2 Corinthians 1: 22; also Isaiah 1: 18: 'though your sins be as scarlet, they shall be as white as snow; though they be red like crimson, they shall be as wool.' Basil quotes this to Dorian just before his murder, *DG* p.165.

POEMS IN PROSE

Wilde had a store of resonant, thought-provoking stories of this kind, which he used and re-used in conversation, but he only ever published five of these, although records of many others exist. He published 'The House of Judgment' and 'The Disciple' in *The Spirit Lamp*, in February and June 1893, and revised and republished them in *The Fortnightly Review* in July 1894, along with 'The Artist', 'The Doer of Good', and 'The Master'.

567 *The Disciple.* Wilde's ironic version of the story of Narcissus, a story to which he often returns. Narcissus was an exceptionally beautiful youth who fell in love with his own reflection, leading to despair and death.

568 *The House of Judgment.* The source of this story is in Lady Wilde's *Ancient Legends of Ireland* (1888), but Wilde has taken part of a longer folk-tale and transformed it creatively.

APHORISMS

570 *A Few Maxims for the Instruction of the Over-Educated.* These aphorisms first appeared anonymously in the *Saturday Review* on 17 November 1894.

572 *Phrases and Philosophies for the Use of the Young.* In *De Profundis* we have Wilde's account of how at Lord Alfred Douglas's request he sent to an undergraduate magazine called *The Chameleon* 'a page of paradoxes destined originally for the *Saturday Review*', and how 'a few months later I find myself standing in the dock of the Old Bailey on account of the character of the magazine' (*SL* 170). The relevant (and only) number of *The Chameleon* appeared in December 1894. Many of these epigrams had figured in previous works. See Mason 14–20 for an account of Wilde's cross-examination in court about his contribution to *The Chameleon*.

FURTHER READING

MAJOR EDITIONS

[Works] First Collected Edition, ed. Robert Ross (1908).
The Letters of Oscar Wilde, ed. Rupert Hart-Davis (1962).
Selected Letters of Oscar Wilde, ed. Rupert Hart-Davis (1979).
More Letters of Oscar Wilde, ed. Rupert Hart-Davis (1985).
The Picture of Dorian Gray, ed. Isobel Murray (Oxford English Novels, 1974).
The Picture of Dorian Gray, ed. Donald L. Lawler (Norton Critical Edition, 1988).
The Complete Shorter Fiction of Oscar Wilde, ed. Isobel Murray (1979).
The Importance of Being Earnest, ed. Russell Jackson (New Mermaids, 1980).
Lady Windermere's Fan, ed. Ian Small (New Mermaids, 1980).
Two Society Comedies [*A Woman of No Importance*, ed. Ian Small, and *An Ideal Husband*, ed. Russell Jackson] (New Mermaids, 1983).

BIBLIOGRAPHY

Fletcher, Ian, and Stokes, John, 'Oscar Wilde', *Anglo-Irish Literature: A Review of Research*, ed. Richard J. Finneran (NY, 1976), 48–137.
—— 'Oscar Wilde', *Recent Research on Anglo-Irish Writers*, ed. Richard J. Finneran (NY, 1983), 21–47. [Together these descriptive and evaluative accounts of Wilde scholarship and criticism are by far the best guide to scholarship and criticism on Wilde.]
Mason, Stuart [Christopher Millard], *Bibliography of Oscar Wilde* (1914; reprinted 1967).
Mikhail, E. H., *Oscar Wilde: An Annotated Bibliography of Criticism* (1978).

BIOGRAPHY

Ellmann, Richard, *Oscar Wilde* (1987).
Hyde, H. Montgomery, *Oscar Wilde: A Biography* (1976).